Anatole France,
best novels

In this book:
The Seven Wives Of Bluebeard
Translator: D. B. Stewart

The White Stone
Translator: Charles E. Roche

The Revolt of the Angels
Translator: Mrs. Wilfrid Jackson

The Gods are Athirst
Translator: Mrs. Wilfrid Jackson

Anatole France (1844 –1924) was a French poet, journalist, and novelist. He was a successful novelist, with several best-sellers. Ironic and skeptical, he was considered in his day the ideal French man of letters. He was a member of the Académie française, and won the 1921 Nobel Prize for Literature "in recognition of his brilliant literary achievements, characterized as they are by a nobility of style, a profound human sympathy, grace, and a true Gallic temperament".

In this book:

The Seven Wives Of Bluebeard

CHAPTER I

THE strangest, the most varied, the most erroneous opinions have been expressed with regard to the famous individual commonly known as Bluebeard. None, perhaps, was less tenable than that which made of this gentleman a personification of the Sun. For this is what a certain school of comparative mythology set itself to do, some forty years ago. It informed the world that the seven wives of Bluebeard were the Dawns, and that his two brothers-in-law were the morning and the evening Twilight, identifying them with the Dioscuri, who delivered Helena when she was rapt away by Theseus. We must remind those readers who may feel tempted to believe this that in 1817 a learned librarian of Agen, Jean-Baptiste PÃ©rÃ©s, demonstrated, in a highly plausible manner, that Napoleon had never existed, and that the story of this supposed great captain was nothing but a solar myth. Despite the most ingenious diversions of the wits, we cannot possibly doubt that Bluebeard and Napoleon did both actually exist.

An hypothesis no better founded is that which Consists in identifying Bluebeard with the Marshal de Rais, who was strangled by the arm of the Law above the bridges of Nantes on 26th of October, 1440. Without inquiring, with M. Salomon Reinach, whether the Marshal committed the crimes for which he was condemned, or whether his wealth, coveted by a greedy prince, did not in some degree contribute to his undoing, there is nothing in his life that resembles what we find in Bluebeard's; this alone is enough to prevent our confusing them or merging the two individuals into one.

Charles Perrault, who, about 1660, had the merit of composing the first biography of this *seigneur*, justly remarkable for having married seven wives, made him an accomplished villain, and the most perfect model of cruelty that ever trod the earth. But it is permissible to doubt, if not his sincerity, at least the correctness of his information. He may, perhaps, have been prejudiced against his hero. He would not have been the first example of a poet or historian who liked to darken the colours of his pictures. If we have what seems a flattering portrait of Titus, it would seem, on the other hand, that Tacitus has painted Tiberius much blacker than the reality. Macbeth, whom legend and Shakespeare accuse of crimes, was in reality a just and a wise king. He never treacherously murdered the old king, Duncan. Duncan, while yet young, was defeated in a great battle, and was found dead on the morrow at a spot called the Armourer's Shop. He had slain several of the kinsfolk of Gruchno, the wife of Macbeth. The latter made Scotland prosperous; he encouraged trade, and was regarded as the defender of the middle classes, the true King of the townsmen. The nobles of the clans never forgave him for defeating Duncan, nor for protecting the artisans. They destroyed him, and dishonoured his memory. Once he was dead the good King Macbeth was known only by the statements of his enemies. The genius of Shakespeare imposed these lies upon the human consciousness. I had long suspected that Bluebeard was the victim of a similar fatality. All the circumstances of his life, as I found them related, were far from satisfying my mind, and from gratifying that craving for logic and lucidity by which I am incessantly consumed. On reflection, I perceived that they involved insurmountable difficulties. There was so great a desire to make me believe in the man's cruelty that it could not fail to make me doubt it.

These presentiments did not mislead me. My intuitions, which had their origin in a certain knowledge of human nature, were soon to be changed into certainty, based upon irrefutable proofs.

In the house of a stone-cutter in St. Jean-des-Bois, I found several papers relating to Bluebeard; amongst others his defence, and an anonymous complaint against his murderers, which was not proceeded with, for what reasons I know not. These papers confirmed me in the belief that he was good and unfortunate, and that his memory has been overwhelmed by unworthy slanders. From that time forth, I regarded it as my duty to write his true history, without permitting myself any illusion as to the success of such an undertaking. I am well aware that this attempt at rehabilitation is destined to fall into silence and oblivion. How can the cold, naked Truth fight against the glittering enchantments of Falsehood?

CHAPTER II

SOMEWHERE about 1650 there lived on his estate, between CompiÃ¨gne and Pierrefonds, a wealthy noble, by name Bernard de Montragoux, whose ancestors had held the most important posts in the kingdom. But he dwelt far from the Court, in that peaceful obscurity which then veiled all save that on which the king bestowed his glance. His castle of Guillettes abounded in valuable furniture, gold and silver ware, tapestry and embroideries, which he kept in coffers; not that he hid his treasures for fear of damaging them by use; he was, on the contrary, generous and magnificent. But in those days, in the country, the nobles willingly led a very simple life, feeding their people at their own table, and dancing on Sundays with the girls of the village.

On certain occasions, however, they gave splendid entertainments, which contrasted with the dullness of everyday life. So it was necessary that they should hold a good deal of handsome furniture and beautiful tapestries in reserve. This was the case with Monsieur de Montragoux.

His castle, built in the Gothic period, had all its rudeness. From without it looked wild and gloomy enough, with the stumps of its great towers, which had been thrown down at the time of the monarchy's troubles, in the reign of the late King Louis. Within it offered a much pleasanter prospect. The rooms were decorated in the Italian taste, as was the great gallery on the ground floor, loaded with embossed decorations in high relief, pictures and gilding.

At one end of this gallery there was a closet usually known as "the little cabinet." This is the only name by which Charles Perrault refers to it. It is as well to note that it was also called the "Cabinet of the Unfortunate Princesses," because a Florentine painter had portrayed on the walls the tragic stories of Dirce, daughter of the Sun, bound by the sons of Antiope to the horns of a bull, Niobe weeping on Mount Sipylus for her children, pierced by the divine arrows, and Procris inviting to her bosom the javelin of Cephalus. These figures had a look of life about them, and the porphyry tiles with which the floor was covered seemed dyed in the blood of these unhappy women. One of the doors of the Cabinet gave upon the moat, which had no water in it.

The stables formed a sumptuous building, situated at some distance from the castle. They contained stalls for sixty horses, and coach-houses for twelve gilded coaches. But what made Guillettes so bewitching a residence were the woods and canals surrounding it, in which one could devote oneself to the pleasures of angling and the chase.

Many of the dwellers in that country-side knew Monsieur de Montragoux only by the name of Bluebeard, for this was the only name that the common people gave him. And in truth his beard was blue, but it was blue only because it was black, and it was because it was so black that it was blue. Monsieur de Montragoux must not be imagined as having the monstrous aspect of the threefold Typhon whom one sees in Athens, laughing in his triple indigo-blue beard. We shall get much nearer the reality by comparing the *seigneur* of Guillettes to those actors or priests whose freshly shaven cheeks have a bluish gloss.

Monsieur de Montragouz did not wear a pointed beard like his grandfather at the Court of King Henry II; nor did he wear it like a fan, as did his great-grandfather who was killed at the battle of Marignan. Like Monsieur de Turenne, he had only a slight moustache, and a chin-tuft; his cheeks had a bluish look; but whatever may have been said of him, this good gentleman was by no means disfigured thereby, nor did he inspire any fear on that account. He only looked the more virile, and if it made him look a little fierce, it had not the effect of making the women dislike him. Bernard de Montragoux was a very fine man, tall, broad across the shoulders, moderately stout, and well favoured; albeit of a rustic habit, smacking of the woods rather than of drawing-rooms and assemblies. Still, it is true that he did not please the ladies as much as he should have pleased them, built as he was, and wealthy. Shyness was the reason; shyness, not his beard. Women exercised an invincible attraction for him, and at the same time inspired him with an insuperable fear. He feared them as much as he loved them. This was the origin and initial cause of all his misfortunes. Seeing a lady for the first time, he would have died rather than speak to her, and however much attracted he may have been, he stood before her in gloomy silence. His feelings revealed themselves only through his eyes, which he rolled in a terrible manner. This timidity exposed him to every kind of misfortune, and, above all, it prevented his forming a becoming connection with modest and reserved women; and betrayed him, defenceless, to the attempts of the most impudent and audacious. This was his life's misfortune.

Left an orphan from his early youth, and having rejected, owing to this sort of bashfulness and fear, which he was unable to overcome, the very advantageous and honourable alliances which had presented themselves, he married a Mademoiselle Colette Passage, who had recently settled down in that part of the country, after amassing a little money by making a bear dance through the towns and villages of the kingdom. He loved her with all his soul. And to do her justice, there was something pleasing about her, though she was what she was a fine woman with an ample bosom, and a complexion that was still sufficiently fresh, although a little sunburnt by the open air. Great were her joy and surprise on first becoming a lady of quality. Her heart, which was not bad, was touched by the kindness of a husband in such a high position, and with such a stout, powerful body, who was to her the most obedient of servants and devoted of lovers. But after a few months she grew weary because she could no longer go to and fro on the face of the earth. In the midst of wealth, overwhelmed with love and care, she could find no greater pleasure than that of going to see the companion of her wandering life, in the cellar where he languished with a chain round his neck and a ring through his nose, and kissing him on the eyes and weeping. Seeing her full of care, Monsieur de Montragouz himself became careworn, and this only added to his companion's melancholy. The consideration and forethought which he lavished on her turned the poor woman's head. One morning, when he awoke, Monsieur de Montragoux found Colette no longer at his side. In vain he searched for her throughout the castle.

The door of the Cabinet of the Unfortunate Princesses was open. It was through this door that she had gone to reach the open country with her bear. The sorrow of Bluebeard was painful to behold. In spite of the innumerable messengers sent forth in search of her, no news was ever received of Colette Passage.

Monsieur de Montragoux was still mourning her when he happened to dance, at the fair of Guillettes, with Jeanne de La Cloche, daughter of the Police Lieutenant of CompiÃ¨gne, who inspired him with love. He asked her in marriage, and obtained her forthwith. She loved wine, and drank it to excess. So much did this taste increase that after a few months she looked like a leather bottle with a round red face atop of it. The worst of it was that this leather bottle would run mad, incessantly rolling about the reception-rooms and the staircases, crying, swearing, and hiccoughing; vomiting wine and insults at everything that got in her way. Monsieur de Montragoux was dazed with disgust and horror. But he quite suddenly recovered his courage, and set himself, with as much firmness as patience, to cure his wife of so disgusting a vice, Prayers, remonstrances, supplications, and threats: he employed every possible means. All was useless. He forbade her wine from his cellar: she got it from outside, and was more abominably drunk than ever.

To deprive her of her taste for a beverage that she loved too well, he put valerian in the bottles. She thought he was trying to poison her, sprang upon him, and drove three inches of kitchen knife into his belly. He expected to die of it, but he did not abandon his habitual kindness.

"She is more to be pitied than blamed," he said.

One day, when he had forgotten to close the door of the Cabinet of the Unfortunate Princesses, Jeanne de La Cloche entered by it, quite out of her mind, as usual, and seeing the figures on the walls in postures of affliction, ready to give up the ghost, she mistook them for living women, and fled terror-stricken into the country, screaming murder. Hearing Bluebeard calling her and running after her, she threw herself, mad with terror, into a pond, and was there drowned. It is difficult to believe, yet certain, that her husband, so compassionate was his soul, was much afflicted by her death.

6

Six weeks after the accident he quietly married Gigonne, the daughter of his steward, Traignel. She wore wooden shoes, and smelt of onions. She was a fine-looking girl enough, except that she squinted with one eye, and limped with one foot. As soon as she was married, this goose-girl, bitten by foolish ambition, dreamed of nothing but further greatness and splendour. She was not satisfied that her brocade dresses were rich enough, her pearl necklaces beautiful enough, her rubies big enough, her coaches sufficiently gilded, her lakes, woods, and lands sufficiently vast. Bluebeard, who had never had any leaning toward ambition, trembled at the haughty humour of his spouse. Unaware, in his straightforward simplicity, whether the mistake lay in thinking magnificently like his wife, or modestly as he himself did, he accused himself of a mediocrity of mind which was thwarting the noble desires of his consort, and, full of uncertainty, he would sometimes exhort her to taste with moderation the good things of this world, while at others he roused himself to pursue fortune along the verge of precipitous heights. He was prudent, but conjugal affection bore him beyond the reach of prudence. Gigonne thought of nothing but cutting a figure in the world, being received at Court, and becoming the King's mistress. Unable to gain her point, she pined away with vexation, contracting a jaundice, of which she died. Bluebeard, full of lamentation, built her a magnificent tomb.

This worthy *seigneur* overwhelmed by constant domestic adversity, would not perhaps have chosen another wife: but he was himself chosen for a husband by Mademoiselle Blanche de Gibeaumex, the daughter of a cavalry officer, who had but one ear; he used to relate that he had lost the other in the King's service. She was full of intelligence, which she employed in deceiving her husband. She betrayed him with every man of quality in the neighbourhood. She was so dexterous that she deceived him in his own castle, almost under his very eyes, without his perceiving it. Poor Bluebeard assuredly suspected something, but he could not say what. Unfortunately for her, while she gave her whole mind to tricking her husband, she was not sufficiently careful in deceiving her lovers; by which I mean that she betrayed them, one for another. One day she was surprised in the Cabinet of the Unfortunate Princesses, in the company of a gentleman whom she loved, by a gentleman whom she had loved, and the latter, in a transport of jealousy, ran her through with his sword. A few hours later the unfortunate lady was there found dead by one of the castle servants, and the fear inspired by the room increased.

Poor Bluebeard, learning at one blow of his ample dishonour, and the tragic death of his wife, did not console himself for the latter misfortune by any consideration of the former. He had loved Blanche de Gibeaumez with a strange ardour, more dearly than he had loved Jeanne de La Cloche, Gigonne Traignel, or even Colette Passage. On learning that she had consistently betrayed him, and that now she would never betray him again, he experienced a grief and a mental perturbation which, far from being appeased, daily increased in violence. So intolerable were his sufferings that he contracted a malady which caused his life to be despaired of.

The physicians, having employed various medicines without effect, advised him that the only remedy proper to his complaint was to take a young wife. He then thought of his young cousin, AngÃ¨le de La

Garandine, whom he believed would be willingly bestowed upon him, as she had no property. What encouraged him to take her to wife was the fact that she was reputed to be simple and ignorant of the world. Having been deceived by a woman of intelligence, he felt more comfortable with a fool. He married Mademoiselle de La Garandine, and quickly perceived the falsity of his calculations. Angèle was kind, Angèle was good, and Angèle loved him; she had not, in herself, any leanings toward evil, but the least astute person could quickly lead her astray at any moment. It was enough to tell her: "Do this for fear of bogies; comes in here or the were-wolf will eat you;" or "Shut your eyes, and take this drop of medicine," and the innocent girl would straightway do so, at the will of the rascals who wanted of her that which it was very natural to want of her, for she was pretty. Monsieur de Montragouz, injured and betrayed by this innocent girl, as much as and more than he had been by Blanche de Gibeaumex, had the additional pain of knowing it, for Angèle was too candid to conceal anything from him. She used to tell him: "Sir, some one told me this; some one did that to me; some one took so and so away from me; I saw that; I felt so and so." And by her ingenuousness she caused her lord to suffer torments beyond imagination. He endured them like a Stoic. Still he finally had to tell the simple creature that she was a goose, and to box her ears. This, for him, was the beginning of a reputation for cruelty, which was not fated to be diminished. A mendicant monk, who was passing Gulllettes while Monsieur de Montragouz was out shooting woodcock, found Madame Angèle sewing a doll's petticoat. This worthy friar, discovering that she was as foolish as she was beautiful, took her away on his donkey, having persuaded her that the Angel Gabriel was waiting in a wood, to give her a pair of pearl garters. It is believed that she must have been eaten by a wolf, for she was never seen again.

After such a disastrous experience, how was it that Bluebeard could make up his mind to contract yet another union? It would be impossible to understand it, were we not well aware of the power which a fine pair of eyes exerts over a generous heart.

The honest gentleman met, at a neighbouring château which he was in the habit of frequenting, a young orphan of quality, by name Alix de Pontalcin, who, having been robbed of all her property by a greedy trustee, thought only of entering a convent. Officious friends intervened to alter her determination and persuade her to accept the hand of Monsieur de Montragoux. Her beauty was perfect. Bluebeard, who was promising himself the enjoyment of an infinite happiness in her arms, was once more deluded in his hopes, and this time experienced a disappointment, which, owing to his disposition, was bound to make an even greater impression upon him than all the afflictions which he had suffered in his previous marriages. Alix de Pontalcin obstinately refused to give actuality to the union to which she had nevertheless consented.

In vain did Monsieur de Montragoux press her to become his wife; she resisted prayers, tears, and objurgations, she refused her husband's lightest caresses, and rushed off to shut herself into the Cabinet of the Unfortunate Princesses, where she remained, alone and intractable, for whole nights at a time.

The cause of a resistance so contrary to laws both human and divine was never known; it was attributed to Monsieur de Montragoux's blue beard, but our previous remarks on the subject of his beard render such a supposition far from probable. In any case, it is a difficult subject to discuss. The unhappy husband underwent the cruellest sufferings. In order to forget them, he hunted with desperation, exhausting horses, hounds, and huntsmen. But when he returned home, foundered and overtired, the mere sight of Mademoiselle de Pontalcin was enough to revive his energies and his torments. Finally, unable to endure the situation any longer, he applied to Rome for the annulment of a marriage which was nothing better than a trap; and in consideration of a handsome present to the Holy Father he obtained it in accordance with canon law. If Monsieur de Montragoux discarded Mademoiselle de Pontalcin with all the marks of respect due to a woman, and without breaking his cane across her back, it was because he had a valiant soul, a great heart, and was master of himself as well as of Guillettes. But he swore that, for the future, no female should enter his apartments. Happy had he been if he had held to his oath to the end!

CHAPTER III

SOME years had elapsed since Monsieur de Montragoux had rid himself of his sixth wife, and only a confused recollection remained in the country-side of the domestic calamities which had fallen upon this worthy *seigneur's* house. Nobody knew what had become of his wives, and hair-raising tales were told in the village at night; some believed them, others did not. About this time, a widow, past the prime of life, Dame Sidonie de Lespoisse, came to settle with her children in the manor of La Motte-Giron, about two leagues, as the crow flies, from the castle of Guillettes. Whence she came, or who her husband had been, not a soul knew. Some believed, because they had heard it said, that he had held certain posts in Savoy or Spain; others said that he had died in the Indies; many had the idea that the widow was possessed of immense estates, while others doubted it strongly. However, she lived in a notable style, and invited all the nobility of the country-side to La Motte-Giron. She had two daughters, of whom the elder, Anne, on the verge of becoming an old maid, was a very astute person: Jeanne, the younger, ripe for marriage, concealed a precocious knowledge of the world under an appearance of simplicity. The Dame de Lespoisse had also two sons, of twenty and twenty-two years of age; very fine well-made young fellows, of whom one was a Dragoon, and the other a Musketeer. I may add, having seen his commission, that he was a Black Musketeer. When on foot, this was not apparent, for the Black Musketeers were distinguished from the Grey not by the colour of their uniform, but by the hides of their horses. All alike wore blue surcoats laced with gold. As for the Dragoons, they were to be recognized by a kind of fur bonnet, of which the tail fell gallantly over the ear. The Dragoons had the reputation of being scamps, a scapegrace crowd, witness the song:

> *"Mama, here the dragoons come,*
> *Let us haste away."*

But you might have searched in vain through His Majesty's two regiments of Dragoons for a bigger rake, a more accomplished sponger, or a viler rogue than Cosme de Lespoisset. Compared with him, his brother was an honest lad. Drunkard and gambler, Pierre de Lespoisse pleased the ladies, and won at cards; these were the only ways of gaining a living known to him.

Their mother, Dame de Lespoisse, was making a splash at Motte-Giron only in order to catch gulls. As a matter of fact, she had not a penny, and owed for everything, even to her false teeth. Her clothes and furniture, her coach, her horses, and her servants had all been lent by Parisian moneylenders, who threatened to withdraw them all if she did not presently marry one of her daughters to some rich nobleman, and the respectable Sidonie was expecting to find herself at any moment naked in an empty house. In a hurry to find a son-in-law, she had at once cast her eye upon Monsieur de Montragoux, whom she summed up as being simple-minded, easy to deceive, extremely mild, and quick to fall in love under his rude and bashful exterior. Her two daughters entered into her plans, and every time they met him, riddled poor Bluebeard with glances which pierced him to the depths of his heart. He soon fell a victim to the potent charms of the two Demoiselles de Lespoisse. Forgetting his oath, he thought of nothing but marrying one of them, finding them equally beautiful. After some delay, caused less by hesitation than timidity, he went to Motte-Giron in great state, and made his petition to the Dame de Lespoisse, leaving to her the choice of which daughter she would give him. Madame Sidonie obligingly replied that she held him in high esteem, and that she authorized him to pay his court to whichever of the ladies he should prefer.

"Learn to please, monsieur," she said. "I shall be the first to applaud your success."

In order to make their better acquaintance, Bluebeard invited Anne and Jeanne de Lespoisse, with their mother, brothers, and a multitude of ladies and gentlemen to pass a fortnight at the castle of Guillettes. There was a succession of walking, hunting, and fishing parties, dances and festivities, dinners and entertainments of every sort. A young *seigneur*, the Chevalier de Merlus, whom the ladies Lespoisse had brought with them, organized the beats. Bluebeard had the best packs of hounds and the largest turnout in the countryside. The ladies rivalled the ardour of the gentlemen in hunting the deer. They did not always hunt the animal down, but the hunters and their ladies wandered away in couples, found one another, and again wandered off into the woods. For choice, the Chevalier de la Merlus would lose himself with Jeanne de Lespoisse, and both would return to the castle at night, full of their adventures, and pleased with their day's sport.

After a few days' observation, the good *seigneur* of Montragoux felt a decided preference for Jeanne, the younger sister, rather than the elder, as she was fresher, which is not saying that she was less experienced. He allowed his preference to appear; there was no reason why he should conceal it, for it was a befitting preference; moreover, he was a plain dealer. He paid court to the young lady as best he could, speaking little, for want of practice; but he gazed at her, rolling his rolling eyes, and emitting from the depths of his bowels sighs which might have overthrown an oak tree. Sometimes he would burst out laughing, whereupon the crockery trembled, and the windows rattled. Alone of all the party, he failed to remark the assiduous attentions of the Chevalier de la Merlus to Madame de Lespoisse's younger daughter, or if he did remark them he saw no harm in them. His experience of women was not sufficient to make him suspicious, and he trusted when he loved. My grandmother used to say that in life experience is worthless, and that one remains the same as when one begins. I believe she was right, and the true story that I am now unfolding is not of a nature to prove her wrong.

Bluebeard displayed an unusual magnificence in these festivities. When night arrived the lawns before the castle were lit by a thousand torches, and tables served by men-servants and maids dressed as fauns and dryads groaned under all the tastiest things which the country-side and the forest produced. Musicians provided a continual succession of beautiful symphonies. Towards the end of the meal the schoolmaster and schoolmistress, followed by the boys and girls of the village, appeared before the guests, and read a complimentary address to the *seigneur* of Montragoux and his friends. An astrologer in a pointed cap approached the ladies, and foretold their future love-affairs from the lines of their hands, Bluebeard ordered drink to be given for all his vassals, and he himself distributed bread and meat to the poor families.

At ten o'clock, for fear of the evening dew, the company retired to the apartments, lit by a multitude of candles, and there tables were prepared for every sort of game: lansquenet, billiards, reversi, bagatelle, pigeon-holes, turnstile, porch, beast, hoca, brelan, draughts, backgammon, dice, basset, and calbas. Bluebeard was uniformly unfortunate in these various games, at which he lost large sums every night. He could console himself for his continuous run of bad luck by watching the three Lespoisse ladies win a great deal of money. Jeanne, the younger, who often backed the game of the Chevalier de la Merlus, heaped up mountains of gold. Madame de Lespoisse's two sons also did very well at reversi and basset; their luck was invariably best at the more hazardous games. The play went on until late into the night. No one slept during these marvellous festivities, and as the earliest biographer of Bluebeard has said: "They spent the whole night in playing tricks on one another." These hours were the most delightful of the whole twenty-four; for then, under cover of jesting, and taking advantage of the darkness, those who felt drawn toward one another would hide together in the depths of some alcove. The Chevelier de la Merlus would disguise himself at one time as a devil, at another as a ghost or a were-wolf in order to frighten the sleepers, but he always ended by slipping into the room of Mademoiselle Jeanne de Lespoisse. The good *seigneur* of Montragoux was not overlooked in these games. The two sons of Madame de Lespoisse put irritant powder in his bed, and burnt in his room substances which emitted a disgusting smell. Or they would arrange a jug of water over his door so that the worthy *seigneur* could not open the door without the whole of the water being upset upon his head. In short, they played on him all sorts of practical jokes, to the diversion of the whole company, and Bluebeard bore them with his natural good humour.

He made his request, to which Madame de Lespoisse acceded, although, as she said, it wrung her heart to think of giving her girls in marriage.

11

The marriage was celebrated at Motte-Giron with extraordinary magnificence. The Demoiselle Jeanne, amazingly beautiful, was dressed entirely in *point de France*, her head covered with a thousand ringlets. Her sister Anne wore a dress of green velvet, embroidered with gold. Their mother's dress was of golden tissue, trimmed with black chenille, with a *parure* of pearls and diamonds. Monsieur de Montragoux wore all his great diamonds on a suit of black velvet; he made a very fine appearance; his expression of timidity and innocence contrasting strongly with his blue chin and his massive build. The bride's brothers were of course handsomely arrayed, but the Chevalier de la Merlus, in a suit of rose velvet trimmed with pearls, shone with unparalleled splendour.

Immediately after the ceremony, the Jews who had hired out to the bride's family and her lover all these fine clothes and rich jewels resumed possession of them and posted back to Paris with them.

CHAPTER IV

FOR a month Monsieur de Montragoux was the happiest of men. He adored his wife, and regarded her as an angel of purity. She was something quite different, but far shrewder men than poor Bluebeard might have been deceived as he was, for she was a person of great cunning and astuteness, and allowed herself submissively to be ruled by her mother, who was the cleverest jade in the whole kingdom of France. She established herself at Guillettes with her eldest daughter Anne, her two sons, Pierre and Cosme, and the Chevalier de la Merlus, who kept as close to Madame de Montragoux as if he had been her shadow. Her good husband was a little annoyed at this; he would have liked to keep his wife always to himself, but he did not take exception to the affection which she felt for this young gentleman, as she had told him that he was her foster-brother.

Charles Perrault relates that a month after having contracted this union, Bluebeard was compelled to make a journey of six weeks' duration on some important business. He does not seem to be aware of the reasons for this journey, and it has been suspected that it was an artifice, which the jealous husband resorted to, according to custom, in order to surprise his wife. The truth is quite otherwise. Monsieur de Montragouz went to Le Perche to receive the heritage of his cousin of Outarde, who had been killed gloriously by a cannon-ball at the battle of the Dunes, while casting dice upon a drum.

Before leaving, Monsieur de Montragoux begged his wife to indulge in every possible distraction during his absence.

"Invite all your friends, madame," he said, "go riding with them, amuse yourselves, and have a pleasant time."

He handed over to her all the keys of the house, thus indicating that in his absence she was the sole and sovereign mistress of all the *seigneurie* of Guillettes.

"This," he said, "is the key of the two great wardrobes; this of the gold and silver not in daily use; this of the strong-boxes which contain my gold and silver; this of the caskets where my jewels are kept; and this is a pass-key into all the rooms. As for this little key, it is that of the Cabinet, at the end of the Gallery, on the ground floor; open everything, and go where you will."

Charles Perrault claims that Monsieur de Montragoux added:

"But as for the little Cabinet, I forbid you to enter that; and I forbid you so expressly that if you do enter it, I cannot say to what lengths my anger will not go."

The historian of Bluebeard in placing these words on record, has fallen into the error of adopting, without, verification, the version concocted after the event by the ladies Lespoisse. Monsieur de Montragoux expressed himself very differently. When he handed to his wife the key of the little Cabinet, which was none other than the Cabinet of the Unfortunate Princesses, to which we have already frequently alluded, he expressed the desire that his beloved Jeanne should not enter that part of the house which he regarded as fatal to his domestic happiness. It was through this room, indeed, that his first wife, and the best of all of them, had fled, when she ran away with her bear; here Blanche de Gibeaumex had repeatedly betrayed him with various gentlemen; and lastly, the porphyry pavement was stained by the blood of a beloved criminal. Was not this enough to make Monsieur de Montragoux connect the idea of this room with cruel memories and fateful forebodings?

The words which he addressed to Jeanne de Lespoisse convey the desires and impressions which were troubling his mind. They were actually as follows:

"For you, madame, nothing of mine is hidden, and I should feel that I was doing you an injury did I fail to hand over to you all the keys of a dwelling which belongs to you. You may therefore enter this little cabinet, as you may enter all the other rooms of the house; but if you will take my advice you will do nothing of the kind, to oblige me, and in consideration of the painful ideas which, for me, are connected with this room, and the forebodings of evil which these ideas, despite myself, call up into my mind. I should be inconsolable were any mischance to befall you, or were I to bring misfortune upon you. You will, madame, forgive these fears, which are happily unfounded, as being only the outcome of my anxious affection and my watchful love."

With these words the good *seigneur* embraced his wife and posted off to Le Perche.

"The friends and neighbours," says Charles Perrault, "did not wait to be asked to visit the young bride; so full were they of impatience to see all the wealth of her house. They proceeded at once to inspect all the rooms, cabinets, and wardrobes, each of which was richer and more beautiful than the last; and there was no end to their envy and their praises of their friend's good fortune."

All the historians who have dealt with this subject have added that Madame de Montsagoux took no pleasure in the sight of all these riches, by reason of her impatience to open the little Cabinet. This is perfectly correct, and as Perrault has said: "So urgent was her curiosity that, without considering that it was unmannerly to leave her guests, she went down to it by a little secret staircase, and in such a hurry that two or three times she thought she would break her neck." The fact is beyond question. But what no one has told us is that the reason why she was so anxious to reach this apartment was that the Chevalier de la Merlus was awaiting her there.

Since she had come to make her home in the castle of Guillettes she had met this young gentleman in the Cabinet every day, and oftener twice a day than once, without wearying of an intercourse so unseemly in a young married woman. It is Impossible to hesitate, as to the nature of the ties connecting Jeanne with the Chevalier: they were anything but respectable, anything but chaste, Alas, had Madame de Montragoux merely betrayed her husband's honour, she would no doubt have incurred the blame of posterity; but the most austere of moralists might have found excuses for her. He might allege, in favour of so young a woman, the laxity of the morals of the period; the examples of the city and the Court; the too certain effects of a bad training, and the advice of an immoral mother, for Madame Sidonie de Lespoisse countenanced her daughter's intrigues. The wise might have forgiven her a fault too amiable to merit their severity; her errors would have seemed too common to be crimes, and the world would simply have considered that she was behaving like other people. But Jeanne de Lespoisse, not content with betraying her husband's honour, did not hesitate to attempt his life.

It was in the little Cabinet, otherwise known as the Cabinet of the Unfortunate Princesses, that Jeanne de Lespoisse, Dame de Montragoux, in concert with the Chevalier de la Merlus, plotted the death of a kind and faithful husband. She declared later that, on entering the room, she saw hanging there the bodies of six murdered women, whose congealed blood covered the tiles, and that recognizing in these unhappy women the first six wives of Bluebeard, she foresaw the fate which awaited herself. She must, in this case, have mistaken the paintings on the walls for mutilated corpses, and her hallucinations must be compared with those of Lady Macbeth. But it is extremely probable that Jeanne imagined this horrible sight in order to relate it afterwards, justifying her husband's murderers by slandering their victim.

The death of Monsieur de Montragouz was determined upon. Certain letters which lie before me compel the belief that Madame Sidonie Lespoisse had her part in the plot. As for her elder daughter, she may be described as the soul of the conspiracy. Anne de Lespoisse was the wickedest of the whole family. She was a stranger to sensual weakness, remaining chaste in the midst of the profligacy of the house; it was not a case of refusing pleasures which she thought unworthy of her; the truth was that she took pleasure only in cruelty. She engaged her two brothers, Cosme and Pierre, in the enterprise by promising them the command of a regiment.

CHAPTER V

IT now rests with us to trace, with the aid of authentic documents, and reliable evidence, the most atrocious, treacherous, and cowardly domestic crime of which the record has come down to us. The murder whose circumstances we are about to relate can only be compared to that committed on the night of the 9th March, 1449, on the person of Guillaume de Flavy, by his wife Blanche d'Overbreuc, a young and slender woman, the bastard d'Orbandas, and the barber Jean Bocquillon.

They stifled Guillaume with a pillow, battered him pitilessly with a club, and bled him at the throat like a calf. Blanche d'Overbreuc proved that her husband had determined to have her drowned, while Jeanne de Lespoisse betrayed a loving husband to a gang of unspeakable scoundrels. We will record the facts with all possible restraint. Bluebeard returned rather earlier than expected. This it was gave rise to the quite mistaken idea that, a prey to the blackest jealousy, he was wishful to surprise his wife. Full of joy and confidence, if he thought of giving her a surprise it was an agreeable one. His kindness and tenderness, and his joyous, peaceable air would have softened the most savage hearts. The Chevalier de la Merlus, and the whole execrable brood of Lespoisse saw therein nothing but an additional facility for taking his life, and possessing themselves of his wealth, still further increased by his new inheritance.

His young wife met him with a smiling face, allowing herself to be embraced and led to the conjugal chamber, where she did everything to please the good man. The following morning she returned him the bunch of keys which had been confided to her care. But there was missing that of the Cabinet of the Unfortunate Princesses, commonly called the little Cabinet. Bluebeard gently demanded its delivery, and after putting him off for a time on various pretexts Jeanne returned it to him.

There now arises a question which cannot be solved without leaving the limited domain of history to enter the indeterminate regions of philosophy.

Charles Perrault specifically states that the key of the little Cabinet was a fairy key, that is to say, it was magical, enchanted, endowed with properties contrary to the laws of nature, at all events, as we conceive them. We have no proof to the contrary. This is a fitting moment to recall the precept of my illustrious master, Monsieur du Clos des Lunes, a member of the Institute: "When the supernatural makes its appearance, it must not be rejected by the historian." I shall therefore content myself with recalling as regards this key, the unanimous opinion of all the old biographers of Bluebeard; they all affirm that it was a fairy key. This is a point of great importance. Moreover, this key is not the only object created by human industry which has proved to be endowed with marvellous properties. Tradition abounds with examples of enchanted swords. Arthur's was a magic sword. And so was that of Joan of Arc, on the undeniable authority of Jean Chartier; and the proof afforded by that illustrious chronicler is that when the blade was broken the two pieces refused to be welded together again despite all the efforts of the most competent armourers. Victor Hugo speaks in one of his poems of those "magic stairways still obscured below." Many authors even admit that there are men-magicians who can turn themselves into wolves. We shall not undertake to combat such a firm and constant belief, and we shall not pretend to decide whether the key of the little Cabinet was or was not enchanted, for our reserve does not imply that we are in any uncertainty, and therein resides its merit. But where we find ourselves in our proper domain, or to be more precise within our own jurisdiction, where we once more become judges of facts, and writers of circumstances, is where we read that the key was flecked with blood. The authority of the texts does not so far impress us as to compel us to believe this. It was not flecked with blood. Blood had flowed in the little cabinet, but at a time already remote. Whether the key had been washed or whether it had dried, it was impossible that it should be so stained, and what, in her agitation, the criminal wife mistook for a blood-stain on the iron, was the reflection of the sky still empurpled by the roses of dawn.

Monsieur de Montragoux, on seeing the key, perceived none the less that his wife had entered the little cabinet. He noticed that it now appeared cleaner and brighter than when he had given it to her, and was of opinion that this polish could only come from use.

This produced a painful impression upon him, and he said to his wife, with a mournful smile:

"My darling, you have been into the little cabinet. May there result no grievous outcome for either of us! From that room emanates a malign influence from which I would have protected you. If you, in your turn should become subjected to it, I should never get over it. Forgive me; when we love we are superstitious."

On these words, although Bluebeard cannot have frightened her, for his words and demeanour expressed only love and melancholy, the young lady of Montragoux began shrieking at the top of her voice: "Help! Help! he's killing me!" This was the signal agreed upon. On hearing it, the Chevalier de la Merlus and the two sons of Madame de Lespoisse were to have thrown themselves upon Bluebeard and run him through with their swords.

But the Chevalier, whom Jeanne had hidden in a cupboard in the room, appeared alone. Monsieur de Montragoux, seeing him leap forth sword in hand, placed himself on guard. Jeanne fled terror-stricken, and met her sister Anne in the gallery. She was not, as has been related, on a tower; for all the towers had been thrown down by order of Cardinal Richelieu. Anne was striving to put heart into her two brothers, who, pale and quaking, dared not risk so great a stake. Jeanne hastily implored them: "Quick, quick, brothers, save my lover!" Pierre and Cosme then rushed at Bluebeard. They found him, having disarmed the Chevalier de la Merlus, holding him down with his knee; they treacherously ran their swords through his body from behind, and continued to strike at him long after he had breathed his last.

Bluebeard had no heirs. His wife remained mistress of his property. She used a part of it to provide a dowry for her sister Anne, another part to buy captains' commissions for her two brothers, and the rest to marry the Chevalier de la Merlus, who became a very respectable man as soon as he was wealthy.

The Revolt of the Angels

CHAPTER I

CONTAINING IN A FEW LINES THE HISTORY OF A FRENCH

FAMILY FROM 1789 TO THE PRESENT DAY

BENEATH the shadow of St. Sulpice the ancient mansion of the d'Esparvieu family rears its austere three stories between a moss-grown fore-court and a garden hemmed in, as the years have elapsed, by ever loftier and more intrusive buildings, wherein, nevertheless, two tall chestnut trees still lift their withered heads.

Here from 1825 to 1857 dwelt the great man of the family, Alexandre Bussart d'Esparvieu, Vice-President of the Council of State under the Government of July, Member of the Academy of Moral and Political Sciences, and author of an *Essay on the Civil and Religious Institutions of Nations*, in three octavo volumes, a work unfortunately left incomplete.

This eminent theorist of a Liberal monarchy left as heir to his name his fortune and his fame, Fulgence-Adolphe Bussart d'Esparvieu, senator under the Second Empire, who added largely to his patrimony by buying land over which the Avenue de l'Impératice was destined ultimately to pass, and who made a remarkable speech in favour of the temporal power of the popes.

Fulgence had three sons. The eldest, Marc-Alexandre, entering the army, made a splendid career for himself: he was a good speaker. The second, Gaétan, showing no particular aptitude for anything, lived mostly in the country, where he hunted, bred horses, and devoted himself to music and painting. The third son, René, destined from his childhood for the law, resigned his deputyship to avoid complicity in the Ferry decrees against the religious orders; and later, perceiving the revival under the presidency of Monsieur Fallières of the days of Decius and Diocletian, put his knowledge and zeal at the service of the persecuted Church.

From the Concordat of 1801 down to the closing years of the Second Empire all the d'Esparvieus attended mass for the sake of example. Though sceptics in their inmost hearts, they looked upon religion as an instrument of government.

Mark and René were the first of their race to show any sign of sincere devotion. The General, when still a colonel, had dedicated his regiment to the Sacred Heart, and he practised his faith with a fervour remarkable even in a soldier, though we all know that piety, daughter of Heaven, has marked out the hearts of the generals of the Third Republic as her chosen dwelling-place on earth.

Faith has its vicissitudes. Under the old order the masses were believers, not so the aristocracy or the educated middle class. Under the First Empire the army from top to bottom was entirely irreligious. To-day the masses believe nothing. The middle classes wish to believe, and succeed at times, as did Marc and René d'Esparvieu. Their brother Gaétan, on the contrary, the country gentleman, failed to attain to faith. He was an agnostic, a term commonly employed by the modish to avoid the odious one of freethinker. And he openly declared himself an agnostic, contrary to the admirable custom which deems it better to withhold the avowal.

In the century in which we live there are so many modes of belief and of unbelief that future historians will have difficulty in finding their way about. But are we any more successful in disentangling the condition of religious beliefs in the time of Symmachus or of Ambrose?

A fervent Christian, René d'Esparvieu was deeply attached to the liberal ideas his ancestors had transmitted to him as a sacred heritage. Compelled to oppose a Jacobin and atheistical Republic, he still called himself Republican. And it was in the name of liberty that he demanded the independence and sovereignty of the Church.

During the long debates on the Separation and the quarrels over the Inventories, the synods of the bishops and the assemblies of the faithful were held in his house. While the most authoritatively accredited leaders of the Catholic party: prelates, generals, senators, deputies, journalists, were met together in the big green drawing-room, and every soul present turned towards Rome with a tender submission or enforced obedience; while Monsieur d'Esparvieu, his elbow on the marble chimney-piece, opposed civil law to canon law, and protested eloquently against the spoliation of the Church of France, two faces of other days, immobile and speechless, looked down on the modern crowd; on the right of the fire-place, painted by David, was Romain Bussart, a working-farmer at Esparvieu in shirt-sleeves and drill trousers, with a rough-and-ready air not untouched with cunning. He had good reason to smile: the worthy man laid the foundation of the family fortunes when he bought Church lands. On the left, painted by Gérard in full-dress bedizened with orders, was the peasant's son, Baron Emile Bussart d'Esparvieu, prefect under the Empire, Keeper of the Great Seal under Charles X, who died in 1837, churchwarden of his parish, with couplets from *La Pucelle* on his lips.

René d'Esparvieu married in 1888 Marie-Antoinette Coupelle, daughter of Baron Coupelle, ironmaster at Blainville (Haute Loire). Madame René d'Esparvieu had been president since 1903 of the Society of Christian Mothers. These perfect spouses, having married off their eldest daughter in 1908, had three children still at home—a girl and two boys.

Léon, the younger, aged seven, had a room next to his mother and his sister Berthe. Maurice, the elder, lived in a little pavilion comprising two rooms at the bottom of the garden. The young man thus gained a freedom which enabled him to endure family life. He was rather good-looking, smart without too much pretence, and the faint smile which merely raised one corner of his mouth did not lack charm.

At twenty-five Maurice possessed the wisdom of Ecclesiastes. Doubting whether a man hath any profit of all his labour which he taketh under the sun he never put himself out about anything. From his earliest childhood this young hopeful's sole concern with work had been considering how he might best avoid it, and it was through his remaining ignorant of the teaching of the *École de Droit* that he became a doctor of law and a barrister at the Court of Appeal.

He neither pleaded nor practised. He had no knowledge and no desire to acquire any; wherein he conformed to his genius whose engaging fragility he forbore to overload; his instinct fortunately telling him that it was better to understand little than to misunderstand a lot.

As Monsieur l'Abbé Patouille expressed it, Maurice had received from Heaven the benefits of a Christian education. From his childhood piety was shown to him in the example of his home, and when on leaving college he was entered at the *École de Droit*, he found the lore of the doctors, the virtues of the confessors, and the constancy of the nursing mothers of the Church assembled around the paternal hearth. Admitted to social and political life at the time of the great persecution of the Church of France, Maurice did not fail to attend every manifestation of youthful Catholicism; he lent a hand with his parish barricades at the time of the Inventories, and with his companions he unharnessed the archbishop's horses when he was driven out from his palace. He showed on all these occasions a modified zeal; one never saw him in the front ranks of the heroic band exciting soldiers to a glorious disobedience or flinging mud and curses at the agents of the law.

He did his duty, nothing more; and if he distinguished himself on the occasion of the great pilgrimage of 1911 among the stretcher-bearers at Lourdes, we have reason to fear it was but to please Madame de la Verdelière, who admired men of muscle. Abbé Patouille, a friend of the family and deeply versed in the knowledge of souls, knew that Maurice had only moderate aspirations to martyrdom. He reproached him with his lukewarmness, and pulled his ear, calling him a bad lot. Anyway, Maurice remained a believer.

Amid the distractions of youth his faith remained intact, since he left it severely alone. He had never examined a single tenet. Nor had he enquired a whit more closely into the ideas of morality current in the grade of society to which he belonged. He took them just as they came. Thus in every situation that arose he cut an eminently respectable figure which he would have assuredly failed to do, had he been given to meditating on the foundations of morality. He was irritable and hot-tempered and possessed of a sense of honour which he was at great pains to cultivate. He was neither vain nor ambitious. Like the majority of Frenchmen, he disliked parting with his money. Women would never have obtained anything from him had they not known the way to make him give. He believed he despised them; the truth was he adored them. He indulged his appetites so naturally that he never suspected that he had any. What people did not know, himself least of all,—though the gleam that occasionally shone in his fine, light-brown eyes might have furnished the hint—was that he had a warm heart and was capable of friendship. For the rest, he was, in the ordinary intercourse of life, no very brilliant specimen.

CHAPTER II

WHEREIN USEFUL INFORMATION WILL BE FOUND CONCERNING A LIBRARY WHERE STRANGE THINGS WILL SHORTLY COME TO PASS

DESIROUS of embracing the whole circle of human knowledge, and anxious to bequeath to the world a concrete symbol of his encyclopædic genius and a display in keeping with his pecuniary resources, Baron Alexandre d'Esparvieu had formed a library of three hundred and sixty thousand volumes, both printed and in manuscript, whereof the greater part emanated from the Benedictines of Ligugé.

By a special clause in his will he enjoined his heirs to add to his library, after his death, whatever they might deem worthy of note in natural, moral, political, philosophical, and religious science.

He had indicated the sums which might be drawn from his estate for the fulfilment of this object, and charged his eldest son, Fulgence-Adolphe, to proceed with these additions. Fulgence-Adolphe accomplished with filial respect the wishes expressed by his illustrious father.

After him, this huge library, which represented more than one child's share of the estate, remained undivided between the Senator's three sons and two daughters; and René d'Esparvieu, on whom devolved the house in the Rue Garancière, became the guardian of the valuable collection. His two sisters, Madame Paulet de Saint-Fain and Madame Cuissart, repeatedly demanded that such a large but unremunerative piece of property should be turned into money. But René and Gaétan bought in the shares of their two co-legatees, and the library was saved. René d'Esparvieu even busied himself in adding to it, thus fulfilling the intentions of its founder. But from year to year he lessened the number and importance of the acquisitions, opining that the intellectual output in Europe was on the wane.

Nevertheless, Gaétan enriched it, out of his funds, with works published both in France and abroad which he thought good, and he was not lacking in judgment, though his brothers would never allow that he had a particle. Thanks to this man of leisurely and inquiring mind, Baron Alexandre's collection was kept practically up to date. Even at the present day the d'Esparvieu library, in the departments of theology, jurisprudence, and history is one of the finest private libraries in all Europe. Here you may study physical science, or to put it better, physical sciences in all their branches, and for that matter metaphysic or metaphysics, that is to say, all that is connected with physics and has no other name, so impossible is it to designate by a substantive that which has no substance, and is but a dream and an illusion. Here you may contemplate with admiration philosophers addressing themselves to the solution, dissolution, and resolution of the Absolute, to the determination of the Indeterminate and to the definition of the Infinite.

Amid this pile of books and booklets, both sacred and profane, you may find everything down to the latest and most fashionable pragmatism.

Other libraries there are, more richly abounding in bindings of venerable antiquity and illustrious origin, whose smooth and soft-hued texture render them delicious to the touch; bindings which the gilder's art has enriched with gossamer, lace-work, foliage, flowers, emblematic devices, and coats of arms; bindings that charm the studious eye with their tender radiance. Other libraries perhaps harbour a greater array of manuscripts illuminated with delicate and brilliant miniatures by artists of Venice, Flanders, or Touraine. But in handsome, sound editions of ancient and modern writers, both sacred and profane, the d'Esparvieu library is second to none. Here one finds all that has come down to us from antiquity; all the Fathers of the Church, the Apologists and the Decretalists, all the Humanists of the Renaissance, all the Encylopædists, the whole world of philosophy and science. Therefore it was that Cardinal Merlin, when he deigned to visit it, remarked:

"There is no man whose brain is equal to containing all the knowledge which is piled upon these shelves. Happily it doesn't matter."

Monseigneur Cachepot, who worked there often when a curate in Paris, was in the habit of saying:

"I see here the stuff to make many a Thomas Aquinas and many an Arius, if only the modern mind had not lost its ancient ardour for good and evil."

There was no gainsaying that the manuscripts formed the more valuable portion of this immense collection. Noteworthy indeed was the unpublished correspondence of Gassendi, of Father Mersenne, and of Pascal, which threw a new light on the spirit of the seventeenth century. Nor must we forget the Hebrew Bibles, the Talmuds, the Rabbinical treatises, printed and in manuscript, the Aramaic and Samaritan texts, on sheepskin and on tablets of sycamore; in fine, all these antique and valuable copies collected in Egypt and in Syria by the celebrated Moïse de Dina, and acquired at a small cost by Alexandre d'Esparvieu in 1836, when the learned Hebraist died of old age and poverty in Paris.

The Esparvienne library occupied the whole of the second floor of the old house. The works thought to be of but mediocre interest, such as books of Protestant exegesis of the nineteenth and twentieth centuries, the gift of Monsieur Gaétan, were relegated unbound to the limbo of the upper regions. The catalogue, with its various supplements, ran into no less than eighteen folio volumes. It was quite up to date, and the library was in perfect order. Monsieur Julien Sariette, archivist and palæographer, who, being poor and retiring, used to make his living by teaching, became, in 1895, tutor to young Maurice on the recommendation of the Bishop of Agra, and with scarcely an interval found himself curator of the Bibliothèque Esparvienne.

Endowed with business-like energy and dogged patience, Monsieur Sariette himself classified all the members of this vast body. The system he invented and put into practice was so complicated, the labels he put on the books were made up of so many capital letters and small letters, both Latin and Greek, so many Arabic and Roman numerals, asterisks, double asterisks, triple asterisks, and those signs which in arithmetic express powers and roots, that the mere study of it would have involved more time and labour than would have been required for the complete mastery of algebra, and as no one could be found who would give the hours, that might be more profitably employed in discovering the law of numbers, to the solving of these cryptic symbols, Monsieur Sariette remained the only one capable of finding his way among the intricacies of his system, and without his help it had become an utter impossibility to discover, among the three hundred and sixty thousand volumes confided to his care, the particular volume one happened to require. Such was the result of his labours. Far from complaining about it, he experienced on the contrary a lively satisfaction.

Monsieur Sariette loved his library. He loved it with a jealous love. He was there every day at seven o'clock in the morning busy cataloguing at a huge mahogany desk. The slips in his handwriting filled an enormous case standing by his side surmounted by a plaster bust of Alexandre d'Esparvieu. Alexandre wore his hair brushed straight back, and had a sublime look on his face. Like Chateaubriand, he affected little feathery side whiskers. His lips were pursed, his bosom bare. Punctually at midday Monsieur Sariette used to sally forth to lunch at a *crèmerie* in the narrow gloomy Rue des Canettes. It was known as the *Crèmerie des Quatre Évêques*, and had once been the haunt of Baudelaire, Theodore de Banville, Charles Asselineau, and a certain grandee of Spain who had translated the "Mysteries of Paris" into the language of the *conquistadores*. And the ducks that paddled so nicely on the old stone sign which gave its name to the street used to recognize Monsieur Sariette. At a quarter to one, to the very minute, he went back to his library, where he remained until seven o'clock. He then again betook himself to the *Quatre Évêques*, and sat down to his frugal dinner, with its crowning glory of stewed prunes. Every evening, after dinner, his crony, Monsieur Guinardon, universally known as Père Guinardon, a scene-painter and picture-restorer, who used to do work for churches, would come from his garret in the Rue Princesse to have his coffee and liqueur at the *Quatre Évêques*, and the two friends would play their game of dominoes.

Old Guinardon, who was like some rugged old tree still full of sap, was older than he could bring himself to believe. He had known Chenavard. His chastity was positively ferocious, and he was for ever denouncing the impurities of neo-paganism in language of alarming obscenity. He loved talking. Monsieur Sariette was a ready listener. Old Guinardon's favourite subject was the Chapelle des Anges in St. Sulpice, in which the paintings were peeling off the walls, and which he was one day to restore; when, that is, it should please God, for, since the Separation, the churches belonged solely to God, and no one would undertake the responsibility of even the most urgent repairs. But old Guinardon demanded no salary.

"Michael is my patron saint," he said. "And I have a special devotion for the Holy Angels."

After they had had their game of dominoes, Monsieur Sariette, very thin and small, and old Guinardon, sturdy as an oak, hirsute as a lion, and tall as a Saint Christopher, went off chatting away side by side across the Place Saint Sulpice, heedless of whether the night were fine or stormy. Monsieur Sariette always went straight home, much to the regret of the painter, who was a gossip and a nightbird.

The following day, as the clock struck seven, Monsieur Sariette would take up his place in the library, and resume his cataloguing. As he sat at his desk, however, he would dart a Medusa-like look at anyone who entered, fearing lest he should prove to be a book-borrower. It was not merely the magistrates, politicians, and prelates whom he would have liked to turn to stone when they came to ask for the loan of a book with an air of authority bred of their familiarity with the master of the house. He would have done as much to Monsieur Gaétan, the library's ·benefactor, when he wanted some gay or scandalous old volume wherewith to beguile a wet day in the country. He would have meted out similar treatment to Madame René d'Esparvieu, when she came to look for a book to read to her sick poor in hospital, and even to Monsieur René d'Esparvieu himself, who generally contented himself with the Civil Code and a volume of Dalloz. The borrowing of the smallest book seemed like dragging his heart out. To refuse a volume even to such as had the most incontestable right to it, Monsieur Sariette would invent countless far-fetched or clumsy fibs, and did not even shrink from slandering himself as curator or from casting doubts on his own vigilance by saying that such and such a book was mislaid or lost, when a moment ago he had been gloating over that very volume or pressing it to his bosom. And when ultimately forced to part with a volume he would take it back a score of times from the borrower before he finally relinquished it.

He was always in agony lest one of the objects confided to his care should escape him. As the guardian of three hundred and sixty thousand volumes, he had three hundred and sixty thousand reasons for alarm. Sometimes he woke at night bathed in sweat, and uttering a cry of fear, because he had dreamed he had seen a gap on one of the shelves of his bookcases. It seemed to him a monstrous, unheard-of, and most grievous thing that a volume should leave its habitat. This noble rapacity exasperated Monsieur René d'Esparvieu, who, failing to understand the good qualities of his paragon of a librarian, called him an old maniac. Monsieur Sariette knew nought of this injustice, but he would have braved the cruellest misfortune and endured opprobrium and insult to safeguard the integrity of his trust. Thanks to his assiduity, his vigilance and zeal, or, in a word, to his love, the Esparvienne library had not lost so much as a single leaflet under his supervision during the sixteen years which had now rolled by, this ninth of September, 1912.

CHAPTER III

WHEREIN THE MYSTERY BEGINS

AT seven o'clock on the evening of that day, having as usual replaced all the books which had been taken from their shelves, and having assured himself that he was leaving everything in good order, he quitted the library, double-locking the door after him. According to his usual habit, he dined at the *Crèmerie des Quatre Évêques*, read his newspaper, *La Croix*, and at ten o'clock went home to his little house in the Rue du Regard. The good man had no trouble and no presentiment of evil; his sleep was peaceful. The next morning at seven o'clock to the minute, he entered the little room leading to the library, and, according to his daily habit, doffed his grand frock-coat, and taking down an old one which hung in a cupboard over his washstand, put it on. Then he went in to his workroom, where for sixteen years he had been cataloguing six days out of the seven, under the lofty gaze of Alexandre d'Esparvieu. Preparing to make a round of the various rooms, he entered the first and largest, which contained works on theology and religion in huge cupboards whose cornices were adorned with bronze-coloured busts of poets and orators of ancient days.

Two enormous globes representing the earth and the heavens filled the window-embrasures. But at his first step Monsieur Sariette stopped dead, stupefied, powerless alike to doubt or to credit what his eyes beheld. On the blue cloth cover of the writing-table books lay scattered about pell-mell, some lying flat, some standing upright. A number of quartos were heaped up in a tottering pile. Two Greek lexicons, one inside the other, formed a single being more monstrous in shape than the human couples of the divine Plato. A gilt-edged folio was all a-gape, showing three of its leaves disgracefully dog's-eared.

Having, after an interval of some moments, recovered from his profound amazement, the librarian went up to the table and recognised in the confused mass his most valuable Hebrew, French, and Latin Bibles, a unique Talmud, Rabbinical treatises printed and in manuscript, Aramaic and Samaritan texts and scrolls from the synagogues—in fine, the most precious relics of Israel all lying in a disordered heap, gaping and crumpled.

Monsieur Sariette found himself confronted with an inexplicable phenomenon; nevertheless he sought to account for it. How eagerly he would have welcomed the idea that Monsieur Gaétan, who, being a thoroughly unprincipled man, presumed on the right gained him by his fatal liberality towards the library to rummage there unhindered during his sojourns in Paris, had been the author of this terrible disorder. But Monsieur Gaétan was away travelling in Italy. After pondering for some minutes Monsieur Sariette's next supposition was that Monsieur René d'Esparvieu had entered the library late in the evening with the keys of his manservant Hippolyte, who, for the past twenty-five years, had looked after the second floor and the attics. Monsieur René d'Esparvieu, however, never worked at night, and did not read Hebrew. Perhaps, thought Monsieur Sariette, perhaps he had brought or allowed to be brought to this room some priest, or Jerusalem monk, on his way through Paris; some Oriental *savant* given to scriptural exegesis. Monsieur Sariette next wondered whether the Abbé Patouille, who had an enquiring mind, and also a habit of dog's-earing his books, had, peradventure, flung himself on these talmudic and biblical texts, fired with sudden zeal to lay bare the soul of Shem. He even asked himself for a moment whether Hippolyte, the old manservant, who had swept and dusted the library for a quarter of a century, and had been slowly poisoned by the dust of accumulated knowledge, had allowed his curiosity to get the better of him, and had been there during the night, ruining his eyesight and his reason, and losing his soul poring by moonlight over these undecipherable symbols. Monsieur Sariette even went so far as to imagine that young Maurice, on leaving his club or some nationalist meeting, might have torn these Jewish volumes from their shelves, out of hatred for old Jacob and his modern posterity; for this young man of family was a declared anti-semite, and only consorted with those Jews who were as anti-semitic as himself. It was giving a very free rein to his imagination, but Monsieur Sariette's brain could not rest, and went wandering about among speculations of the wildest extravagance.

Impatient to know the truth, the zealous guardian of the library called the manservant.

Hippolyte knew nothing. The porter at the lodge could not furnish any clue. None of the domestics had heard a sound. Monsieur Sariette went down to the study of Monsieur René d'Esparvieu, who received him in nightcap and dressing-gown, listened to his story with the air of a serious man bored with idle chatter, and dismissed him with words which conveyed a cruel implication of pity.

"Do not worry, my good Monsieur Sariette; be sure that the books were lying where you left them last night."

Monsieur Sariette reiterated his enquiries a score of times, discovered nothing, and suffered such anxiety that sleep entirely forsook him. When, on the following day at seven o'clock he entered the room with the busts and globes, and saw that all was in order, he heaved a sigh of relief. Then suddenly his heart beat fit to burst. He had just seen lying flat on the mantelpiece a paper-bound volume, a modern work, the boxwood paper-knife which had served to cut its pages still thrust between the leaves. It was a dissertation on the two parallel versions of Genesis, a work which Monsieur Sariette had relegated to the attic, and which had never left it up to now, no one in Monsieur d'Esparvieu's circle having had the curiosity to differentiate between the parts for which the polytheistic and monotheistic contributors were respectively responsible in the formation of the first of the sacred books. This book bore the label R > $3214^{VIII}/_2$. And this painful truth was suddenly borne in upon the mind of Monsieur Sariette: to wit, that the most scientific system of numbering will not help to find a book if the book is no longer in its place. Every day of the ensuing month found the table littered with books. Greek and Latin lay cheek by jowl with Hebrew. Monsieur Sariette asked himself whether these nocturnal flittings were the work of evil-doers who entered by the skylights to steal valuable and precious volumes. But he found no traces of burglary, and, notwithstanding the most minute search, failed to discover that anything had disappeared. Terrible anxiety took possession of his mind, and he fell to wondering whether it was possible that some monkey in the neighbourhood came down the chimney and acted the part of a person engaged in study. Deriving his knowledge of the habits of these animals in the main from the paintings of Watteau and Chardin, he took it that, in the art of imitating gestures or assuming characters they resembled Harlequin, Scaramouch, Zerlin, and the Doctors of the Italian comedy; he imagined them handling a palette and brushes, pounding drugs in a mortar, or turning over the leaves of an old treatise on alchemy beside an athanor. And so it was that, when, on one unhappy morning, he saw a huge blot of ink on one of the leaves of the third volume of the polyglot Bible bound in blue morocco and adorned with the arms of the Comte de Mirabeau, he had no doubt that a monkey was the author of the evil deed. The monkey had been pretending to take notes and had upset the inkpot. It must be a monkey belonging to a learned professor.

Imbued with this idea, Monsieur Sariette carefully studied the topography of the district, so as to draw a cordon round the group of houses amid which the d'Esparvieu house stood. Then he visited the four surrounding streets, asking at every door if there was a monkey in the house. He interrogated porters and their wives, washer-women, servants, a cobbler, a greengrocer, a glazier, clerks in bookshops, a priest, a bookbinder, two guardians of the peace, children, thus testing the diversity of character and variety of temper in one and the same people; for the replies he received were quite dissimilar in nature; some were rough, some were gentle; there were the coarse and the polished, the simple and the ironical, the prolix and the abrupt, the brief and even the silent. But of the animal he sought he had had neither sight nor sound, when under the archway of an old house in the Rue Servandoni, a small freckled, red-haired girl who looked after the door, made reply:

"There is Monsieur Ordonneau's monkey; would you care to see it?"

And without another word she conducted the old man to a stable at the other end of the yard. There on some rank straw and old bits of cloth, a young macaco with a chain round his middle sat and shivered. He was no taller than a five-year-old child. His livid face, his wrinkled brow, his thin lips were all expressive of mortal sadness. He fixed on the visitor the still lively gaze of his yellow eyes. Then with his small dry hand he seized a carrot, put it to his mouth, and forthwith flung it away. Having looked at the newcomers for a moment, the exile turned away his head, as if he expected nothing further of mankind or of life. Sitting huddled up, one knee in his hand, he made no further movement, but at times a dry cough shook his breast.

"It's Edgar," said the small girl. "He is for sale, you know."

But the old book-lover, who had come armed with anger and resentment, thinking to find a cynical enemy, a monster of malice, an antibibliophile, stopped short, surprised, saddened, and overcome, before this little being devoid of strength and joy and hope.

Recognising his mistake, troubled by the almost human face which sorrow and suffering made more human still, he murmured "Forgive me" and bowed his head.

TWO months elapsed; the domestic upheaval did not subside, and Monsieur Sariette's thoughts turned to the Freemasons. The papers he read were full of their crimes. Abbé Patouille deemed them capable of the darkest deeds, and believed them to be in league with the Jews and meditating the total overthrow of Christendom.

Having now arrived at the acme of power, they wielded a dominating influence in all the principal departments of State, they ruled the Chambers, there were five of them in the Ministry, and they filled the Élysée. Having some time since assassinated a President of the Republic because he was a patriot, they were getting rid of the accomplices and witnesses of their execrable crime. Few days passed without Paris being terror-stricken at some mysterious murder hatched in their Lodges. These were facts concerning which no doubt was possible. By what means did they gain access to the library? Monsieur Sariette could not imagine. What task had they come to fulfil? Why did they attack sacred antiquity and the origins of the Church? What impious designs were they forming? A heavy shadow hung over these terrible undertakings. The Catholic archivist feeling himself under the eye of the sons of Hiram was terrified and fell ill.

Scarcely had he recovered, when he resolved to pass the night in the very spot where these terrible mysteries were enacted, and to take the subtle and dangerous visitors by surprise. It was an enterprise that demanded all his slender courage. Being a man of delicate physique and of nervous temperament, Monsieur Sariette was naturally inclined to be fearful. On the 8th of January at nine o'clock in the evening, while the city lay asleep under a whirling snowstorm, he built up a good fire in the room containing the busts of the ancient poets and philosophers, and ensconced himself in an arm-chair at the chimney corner, a rug over his knees. On a small stand within reach of his hand were a lamp, a bowl of black coffee, and a revolver borrowed from the youthful Maurice. He tried to read his paper, *La Croix*, but the letters danced beneath his eyes. So he stared hard in front of him, saw nothing but the shadows, heard nothing but the wind, and fell asleep.

When he awoke the fire was out, the lamp was extinguished, leaving an acrid smell behind. But all around, the darkness was filled with milky brightness and phosphorescent lights. He thought he saw something flutter on the table. Stricken to the marrow with cold and terror, but upheld by a resolve stronger than any fear, he rose, approached the table, and passed his hands over the cloth. He saw nothing; even the lights faded, but under his fingers he felt a folio wide open; he tried to close it, the book resisted, jumped up and hit the imprudent librarian three blows on the head.

Monsieur Sariette fell down unconscious....

Since then things had gone from bad to worse. Books left their allotted shelves in greater profusion than ever, and sometimes it was impossible to replace them; they disappeared. Monsieur Sariette discovered fresh losses daily. The Bollandists were now an imperfect set, thirty volumes of exegesis were missing. He himself had become unrecognisable. His face had shrunk to the size of one's fist and grown yellow as a lemon, his neck was elongated out of all proportion, his shoulders drooped, the clothes he wore hung on him as on a peg. He ate nothing, and at the *Crèmerie des Quatre Évêques* he would sit with dull eyes and bowed head, staring fixedly and vacantly at the saucer where, in a muddy juice, floated his stewed prunes. He did not hear old Guinardon relate how he had at last begun to restore the Delacroix paintings at St. Sulpice.

Monsieur René d'Esparvieu, when he heard the unhappy curator's alarming reports, used to answer drily:

"These books have been mislaid, they are not lost; look carefully, Monsieur Sariette, look carefully and you will find them."

And he murmured behind the old man's back:

"Poor old Sariette is in a bad way."

"I think," replied Abbé Patouille, "that his brain is going."

CHAPTER V

WHEREIN EVERYTHING SEEMS STRANGE BECAUSE EVERYTHING IS LOGICAL

THE Chapel of the Holy Angels, which lies on the right hand as you enter the Church of St. Sulpice, was hidden behind a scaffolding of planks. Abbé Patouille, Monsieur Gaétan, Monsieur Maurice, his nephew, and Monsieur Sariette, entered in single file through the low door cut in the wooden hoarding, and found old Guinardon on the top of his ladder standing in front of the Heliodorus. The old artist, surrounded by all sorts of tools and materials, was putting a white paste in the crack which cut in two the High Priest Onias. Zéphyrine, Paul Baudry's favourite model, Zéphyrine, who had lent her golden hair and polished shoulders to so many Magdalens, Marguerites, sylphs, and mermaids, and who, it is said, was beloved of the Emperor Napoleon III, was standing at the foot of the ladder with tangled locks, cadaverous cheeks, and dim eyes, older than old Guinardon, whose life she had shared for more than half a century. She had brought the painter's lunch in a basket.

Although the slanting rays fell grey and cold through the leaded and iron-barred window, Delacroix's colouring shone resplendent, and the roses on the cheeks of men and angels dimmed with their glorious beauty the rubicund countenance of old Guinardon, which stood out in relief against one of the temple's columns. These frescoes of the Chapel of the Holy Angels, though derided and insulted when they first appeared, have now become part of the classic tradition, and are united in immortality with the masterpieces of Rubens and Tintoretto.

Old Guinardon, bearded and long-haired, looked like Father Time effacing the works of man's genius. Gaétan, in alarm, called out to him:

"Carefully, Monsieur Guinardon, carefully. Do not scrape too much."

The painter reassured him.

"Fear nothing, Monsieur Gaétan. I do not paint in that style. My art is a higher one. I work after the manner of Cimabue, Giotto, and Beato Angelico, not in the style of Delacroix. This surface here is too heavily charged with contrast and opposition to give a really sacred effect. It is true that Chenavard said that Christianity loves the picturesque, but Chenavard was a rascal with neither faith nor principle—an infidel.... Look, Monsieur d'Esparvieu, I fill up the crevice, I relay the scales of paint which are peeling. That is all.... The damage, due to the sinking of the wall, or more probably to a seismic shock, is confined to a very small space. This painting of oil and wax applied on a very dry foundation is far more solid than one might think.

"I saw Delacroix engaged on this work. Impassioned but anxious, he modelled feverishly, scraped out, re-painted unceasingly; his mighty hand made childish blunders, but the thing is done with the mastery of a genius and the inexperience of a schoolboy. It is a marvel how it holds."

The good man was silent, and went on filling in the crevice.

"How classic and traditional the composition is," said Gaétan. "Time was when one could recognise nothing but its amazing novelty; now one can see in it a multitude of old Italian formulas."

"I may allow myself the luxury of being just, I possess the qualifications," said the old man from the top of his lofty ladder. "Delacroix lived in a blasphemous and godless age. A painter of the decadence, he was not without pride nor grandeur. He was greater than his times. But he lacked faith, single-heartedness, and purity. To be able to see and paint angels he needed that virtue of angels and primitives, that supreme virtue which, with God's help, I do my best to practise, chastity."

"Hold your tongue, Michel; you are as big a brute as any of them."

Thus Zéphyrine, devoured with jealousy because that very morning on the stairs she had seen her lover kiss the bread-woman's daughter, to wit the youthful Octavie, who was as squalid and radiant as one of Rembrandt's Brides. She had loved Michel madly in the happy days long since past, and love had never died out in Zéphyrine's heart.

Old Guinardon received the flattering insult with a smile that he dissembled, and raised his eyes to the ceiling, where the archangel Michael, terrible in azure cuirass and gilt helmet, was springing heavenwards in all the radiance of his glory.

Meanwhile Abbé Patouille, blinking, and shielding his eyes with his hat against the glaring light from the window, began to examine the pictures one after another: Heliodorus being scourged by the angels, St. Michael vanquishing the Demons, and the combat of Jacob and the Angel.

"All this is exceedingly fine," he murmured at last, "but why has the artist only represented wrathful angels on these walls? Look where I will in this chapel, I see but heralds of celestial anger, ministers of divine vengeance. God wishes to be feared; He wishes also to be loved. I would fain perceive on these walls messengers of peace and of clemency. I should like to see the Seraphim who purified the lips of the prophet, St. Raphael who gave back his sight to old Tobias, Gabriel who announced the Mystery of the Incarnation to Mary, the Angel who delivered St. Peter from his chains, the Cherubim who bore the dead St. Catherine to the top of Sinai. Above all, I should like to be able to contemplate those heavenly guardians which God gives to every man baptized in His name. We each have one who follows all our steps, who comforts us and upholds us. It would be pleasant indeed to admire these enchanting spirits, these beautiful faces."

"Ah, Abbé! it depends on the point of view," answered Gaétan. "Delacroix was no sentimentalist. Old Ingres was not very far wrong in saying that this great man's work reeks of fire and brimstone. Look at the sombre, splendid beauty of those angels, look at those androgynes so proud and fierce, at those pitiless youths who lift avenging rods against Heliodorus, note this mysterious wrestler touching the patriarch on the hip...."

"Hush," said Abbé Patouille. "According to the Bible he is no angel like the others; if he be an angel, he is the Angel of Creation, the Eternal Son of God. I am surprised that the Venerable

Curé of St. Sulpice, who entrusted the decoration of this chapel to Monsieur Eugène Delacroix, did not tell him that the patriarch's symbolic struggle with Him who was nameless took place in profound darkness, and that the subject is quite out of place here, since it prefigures the Incarnation of Jesus Christ. The best artists go astray when they fail to obtain their ideas of Christian iconography from a qualified ecclesiastic. The institutions of Christian art form the subject of numerous works with which you are doubtless acquainted, Monsieur Sariette."

Monsieur Sariette was gazing vacantly about him. It was the third morning after his adventurous night in the library. Being, however, thus called upon by the venerable ecclesiastic, he pulled himself together and replied:

"On this subject we may with advantage consult Molanus, *De Historia Sacrarum Imaginum et Picturarum*, in the edition given us by Noël Paquot, dated Louvain, 1771; Cardinal Frederico Borromeo, *De Pictura Sacra*, and the Iconography of Didron; but this last work must be read with caution."

Having thus spoken, Monsieur Sariette relapsed into silence. He was pondering on his devastated library.

"On the other hand," continued Abbé Patouille, "since an example of the holy anger of the angels was necessary in this chapel, the painter is to be commended for having depicted for us in imitation of Raphael the heavenly messengers who chastised Heliodorus. Ordered by Seleucus, King of Syria, to carry off the treasures contained in the Temple, Heliodorus was stricken by an angel in a cuirass of gold mounted on a magnificently caparisoned steed. Two other angels smote him with rods. He fell to earth, as Monsieur Delacroix shows us here, and was swallowed up in darkness. It is right and salutary that this adventure should be cited as an example to the Republican Commissioners of Police and to the sacrilegious agents of the law. There will always be Heliodoruses, but, let it be known, every time they lay their hands on the property of the Church, which is the property of the poor, they shall be chastised with rods and blinded by the angels."

"I should like this painting, or, better still, Raphael's sublimer conception of the same subject, to be engraved in little pictures fully coloured, and distributed as rewards in all the schools."

"Uncle," said young Maurice, with a yawn, "I think these things are simply ghastly. I prefer Matisse and Metzinger."

These words fell unheeded, and old Guinardon from his ladder held forth:

"Only the primitives caught a glimpse of Heaven. Beauty is only to be found between the thirteenth and fifteenth centuries. The antique, the impure antique, which regained its pernicious influence over the minds of the sixteenth century, inspired poets and painters with criminal notions and immodest conceptions, with horrid impurities, filth. All the artists of the Renaissance were swine, including Michael-Angelo."

Then, perceiving that Gaétan was on the point of departure, Père Guinardon assumed an air of bonhomie, and said to him in a confidential tone:

"Monsieur Gaétan, if you're not afraid of climbing up my five flights, come and have a look at my den. I've got two or three little canvases I wouldn't mind parting with, and they might interest you. All good, honest, straightforward stuff. I'll show you, among other things, a tasty, spicy little Baudouin that would make your mouth water."

At this speech Gaétan made off. As he descended the church steps and turned down the Rue Princesse, he found himself accompanied by old Sariette, and fell to unburdening himself to him, as he would have done to any human creature, or indeed to a tree, a lamp-post, a dog, or his own shadow, of the indignation with which the æsthetic theories of the old painter inspired him.

"Old Guinardon overdoes it with his Christian art and his Primitives! Whatever the artist conceives of Heaven is borrowed from earth; God, the Virgin, the Angels, men and women, saints, the light, the clouds. When he was designing figures for the chapel windows at Dreux, old Ingres drew from life a pure, fine study of a woman, which may be seen, among many others, in the Musée Bonnat at Bayonne. Old Ingres had written at the bottom of the page in case he should forget: 'Mademoiselle Cécile, admirable legs and thighs'—and so as to make Mademoiselle Cécile into a saint in Paradise, he gave her a robe, a cloak, a veil, inflicting thus a shameful decline in her estate, for the tissues of Lyons and Genoa are worthless compared with the youthful living tissue, rosy with pure blood; the most beautiful draperies are despicable compared with the lines of a beautiful body. In fact, clothing for flesh that is desirable and ripe for wedlock is an unmerited shame, and the worst of humiliations"; and Gaétan, walking carelessly in the gutter of the Rue Garancière, continued: "Old Guinardon is a pestilential idiot. He blasphemes Antiquity, sacred Antiquity, the age when the gods were kind. He exalts an epoch when the painter and the sculptor had all their lessons to learn over again. In point of fact, Christianity has run contrary to art in so much as it has not favoured the study of the nude. Art is the representation of nature, and nature is pre-eminently the human body; it is the nude."

"Pardon, pardon," purred old Sariette. "There is such a thing as spiritual, or, as one might term it, inward beauty, which, since the days of Fra Angelico down to those of Hippolyte Flandrin, Christian art has—"

But Gaétan, never hearing a word of all this, went on hurling his impetuous observations at the stones of the old street and the snow-laden clouds overhead:

"The Primitives cannot be judged as a whole, for they are utterly unlike each other. This old madman confounds them all together. Cimabue is a corrupt Byzantine, Giotto gives hints of powerful genius, but his modelling is bad, and, like children, he gives all his characters the same face. The early Italians have grace and joy, because they are Italians. The Venetians have an instinct for fine colour. But when all is said and done these exquisite craftsmen enamel and gild rather than paint. There is far too much softness about the heart and the colouring of your saintly Angelico for me. As for the Flemish school, that's quite another pair of shoes. They can use their hands, and in glory of workmanship they are on a level with the Chinese lacquer-workers. The technique of the brothers Van Eyck is a marvel, but I cannot discover in their Adoration of the Lamb the charm and mystery that some have vaunted. Everything in it is treated with a pitiless perfection; it is vulgar in feeling and cruelly ugly. Memling may touch one perhaps; but he creates nothing but sick wretches and cripples; under the heavy, rich, and ungraceful robing of his virgins and saints one divines some very lamentable anatomy. I did not wait for Rogier van der Wyden to call himself Roger de la Pasture and turn Frenchman in order to prefer him to Memling. This Rogier or Roger is less of a ninny; but then he is more lugubrious, and the rigidity of his lines bears eloquent testimony to his poverty-stricken figures. It is a strange perversion to take pleasure in these carnivalesque figures when one can have the paintings of Leonardo, Titian, Correggio, Velasquez, Rubens, Rembrandt, Poussin, or Prud'hon. Really it is a perverted instinct."

Meanwhile the Abbé Patouille and Maurice d'Esparvieu were strolling leisurely along in the wake of the esthete and the librarian. As a general rule the Abbé Patouille was little inclined to talk theology with laymen, or, for that matter, with clerics either. Carried away, however, by the attractiveness of the subject, he was telling the youthful Maurice all about the sacred mission of those guardian angels which Monsieur Delacroix had so inopportunely excluded from his picture. And in order to give more adequate expression to his thoughts on such lofty themes, the Abbé Patouille borrowed whole phrases and sentences from Bossuet. He had got them up by heart to put in his sermons, for he adhered strongly to tradition.

"Yes, my son," he was saying, "God has appointed tutelary spirits to be near us. They come to us laden with His gifts. They return laden with our prayers. Such is their task. Not an hour, not a moment passes but they are at our side, ready to help us, ever fervent and unwearying guardians, watchmen that never slumber."

"Quite so, Abbé," murmured Maurice, who was wondering by what cunning artifice he could get on the soft side of his mother and persuade her to give him some money of which he was urgently in need.

CHAPTER VI

WHEREIN PÈRE SARIETTE DISCOVERS HIS MISSING TREASURES

NEXT morning Monsieur Sariette entered Monsieur René d'Esparvieu's study without knocking. He raised his arms to the heavens, his few hairs were standing straight up on his head. His eyes were big with terror. In husky tones he stammered out the dreadful news. A very old manuscript of Flavius Josephus; sixty volumes of all sizes; a priceless jewel, namely, a *Lucretius* adorned with the arms of Philippe de Vendôme, Grand Prior of France, with notes in Voltaire's own hand; a manuscript of Richard Simon, and a set of Gassendi's correspondence with Gabriel Naudé, comprising two hundred and thirty-eight unpublished letters, had disappeared. This time the owner of the library was alarmed.

He mounted in haste to the abode of the philosophers and the globes, and there with his own eyes confirmed the magnitude of the disaster.

There were yawning gaps on many a shelf. He searched here and there, opened cupboards, dragged out brooms, dusters, and fire-extinguishers, rattled the shovel in the coke fire, shook out Monsieur Sariette's best frock-coat that was hanging in the cloak-room, and then stood and gazed disconsolately at the empty places left by the Gassendi portfolios.

For the past half-century the whole learned world had been loudly clamouring for the publication of this correspondence. Monsieur René d'Esparvieu had not responded to the universal desire, unwilling either to assume so heavy a task, or to resign it to others. Having found much boldness of thought in these letters, and many passages of more libertine tendency than the piety of the twentieth century could endure, he preferred that they should remain unpublished; but he felt himself responsible for their safe-keeping, not only to his country but to the whole civilized world.

"How can you have allowed yourself to be robbed of such a treasure?" he asked severely of Monsieur Sariette.

"How can I have allowed myself to be robbed of such a treasure?" repeated the unhappy librarian. "Monsieur, if you opened my breast, you would find that question engraved upon my heart."

Unmoved by this powerful utterance, Monsieur d'Esparvieu continued with pent-up fury:

"And you have discovered no single sign that would put you on the track of the thief, Monsieur Sariette? You have no suspicion, not the faintest idea, of the way these things have come to pass? You have seen nothing, heard nothing, noticed nothing, learnt nothing? You must grant this is unbelievable. Think, Monsieur Sariette, think of the possible consequences of this unheard-of theft, committed under your eyes. A document of inestimable value in the history of the human mind disappears. Who has stolen it? Why has it been stolen? Who will gain by it? Those who have got possession of it doubtless know that they will be unable to dispose of it in France. They will go and sell it in America or Germany. Germany is greedy for such literary monuments. Should the correspondence of Gassendi with Gabriel Naudé go over to Berlin, if it is published there by German savants, what a disaster, nay, what a scandal! Monsieur Sariette, have you not thought of that?..."

Beneath the stroke of an accusation all the more cruel in that he brought it against himself, Monsieur Sariette stood stupefied, and was silent. And Monsieur d'Esparvieu continued to overwhelm him with bitter reproaches.

"And you make no effort. You devise nothing to find these inestimable treasures. Make enquiries, bestir yourself, Monsieur Sariette; use your wits. It is well worth while."

And Monsieur d'Esparvieu went out, throwing an icy glance at his librarian.

Monsieur Sariette sought the lost books and manuscripts in every spot where he had already sought them a hundred times, and where they could not possibly be. He even looked in the coke-box and under the leather seat of his arm-chair. When midday struck he mechanically went downstairs. At the foot of the stairs he met his old pupil Maurice, with whom he exchanged a bow. But he only saw men and things as through a mist.

The broken-hearted curator had already reached the hall when Maurice called him back.

"Monsieur Sariette, while I think of it, do have the books removed that are choking up my garden-house."

"What books, Maurice?"

"I could not tell you, Monsieur Sariette, but there are some in Hebrew, all worm-eaten, with a whole heap of old papers. They are in my way. You can't turn round in the passage."

"Who took them there?"

"I'm bothered if I know."

And the young man rushed off to the dining-room, the luncheon gong having sounded quite a minute ago.

Monsieur Sariette tore away to the summer-house. Maurice had spoken the truth. About a hundred volumes were there, on tables, on chairs, even on the floor. When he saw them he was divided betwixt joy and fear, filled with amazement and anxiety. Happy in the finding of his lost treasure, dreading to lose it again, and completely overwhelmed with astonishment, the man of books alternately babbled like an infant and uttered the hoarse cries of a maniac. He recognised his Hebrew Bibles, his ancient Talmuds, his very old manuscript of Flavius Josephus, his portfolios of Gassendi's letters to Gabriel Naudé, and his richest jewel of all, to wit, *Lucretius* adorned with the arms of the Grand Prior of France, and with notes in Voltaire's own hand. He laughed, he cried, he kissed the morocco, the calf, the parchment, and vellum, even the wooden boards studded with nails.

As fast as Hippolyte, the manservant, returned with an armful to the library, Monsieur Sariette, with a trembling hand, restored them piously to their places.

CHAPTER VII

OF A SOMEWHAT LIVELY INTEREST, WHEREOF THE MORAL WILL, I HOPE, APPEAL GREATLY TO MY READERS, SINCE IT CAN BE EXPRESSED BY THIS SORROWFUL QUERY: "THOUGHT, WHITHER DOST THOU LEAD ME?" FOR IT IS A UNIVERSALLY ADMITTED TRUTH THAT IT IS UNHEALTHY TO THINK AND THAT TRUE WISDOM LIES IN NOT THINKING AT ALL

ALL the books were now once more assembled in the pious keeping of Monsieur Sariette. But this happy reunion was not destined to last. The following night twenty volumes left their places, among them the *Lucretius* of Prior de Vendôme. Within a week the old Hebrew and Greek texts had all returned to the summer-house, and every night during the ensuing month they left their shelves and secretly went on the same path. Others betook themselves no one knew whither.

On hearing of these mysterious occurrences, Monsieur René d'Esparvieu merely remarked with frigidity to his librarian:

"My poor Sariette, all this is very queer, very queer indeed."

And when Monsieur Sariette tentatively advised him to lodge a formal complaint or to inform the Commissaire de Police, Monsieur d'Esparvieu cried out upon him:

"What are you suggesting, Monsieur Sariette? Divulge domestic secrets, make a scandal! You cannot mean it. I have enemies, and I am proud of it. I think I have deserved them. What I might complain about is that I am wounded in the house of my friend, attacked with unheard-of violence, by fervent loyalists, who, I grant you, are good Catholics, but exceedingly bad Christians.... In a word, I am watched, spied upon, shadowed, and you suggest, Monsieur Sariette, that I should make a present of this comic-opera mystery, this burlesque adventure, this story in which we both cut somewhat pitiable figures, to a set of spiteful journalists? Do you wish to cover me with ridicule?"

The result of the colloquy was that the two gentlemen agreed to change all the locks in the library. Estimates were asked for and workmen called in. For six weeks the d'Esparvieu household rang from morning till night with the sound of hammers, the hum of centre-bits, and the grating of files. Fires were always going in the abode of the philosophers and globes, and the people of thehouse were simply sickened by the smell of heated oil. The old, smooth, easy-running locks were replaced, on the cupboards and doors of the rooms, by stubborn and tricky fastenings. There was nothing but combinations of locks, letter-padlocks, safety-bolts, bars, chains, and electric alarm-bells.

All this display of ironmongery inspired fear. The lock-cases glistened, and there was much grinding of bolts. To gain access to a room, a cupboard, or a drawer, it was necessary to know a certain number, of which Monsieur Sariette alone was cognisant. His head was filled with bizarre words and tremendous numbers, and he got entangled among all these cryptic signs, these square, cubic, and triangular figures. He himself couldn't get the doors and the cupboards undone, yet every morning he found them wide open, and the books thrown about, ransacked, and hidden away. In the gutter of the Rue Servandoni a policeman picked up a volume of Salomon Reinach on the identity of Barabbas and Jesus Christ. As it bore the book-plate of the d'Esparvieu library he returned it to the owner.

Monsieur René d'Esparvieu, not even deigning to inform Monsieur Sariette of the fact, made up his mind to consult a magistrate, a friend in whom he had complete confidence, to wit, a certain Monsieur des Aubels, Counsel at the Law Courts, who had put through many an important affair. He was a little plump man, very red, very bald, with a cranium that shone like a billiard ball. He entered the library one morning feigning to come as a book-lover, but he soon showed that he knew nothing about books. While all the busts of the ancient philosophers were reflected in his shining pate, he put divers insidious questions to Monsieur Sariette, who grew uncomfortable and turned red, for innocence is easily flustered. From that moment Monsieur des Aubels had a mighty suspicion that Monsieur Sariette was the perpetrator of the very thefts he denounced with horror; and it immediately occurred to him to seek out the accomplices of the crime. As regards motives, he did not trouble about them; motives are always to be found. Monsieur des Aubels told Monsieur René d'Esparvieu that, if he liked, he would have the house secretly watched by a detective from the Prefecture.

"I will see that you get Mignon," he said. "He is an excellent servant, assiduous and prudent."

By six o'clock next morning Mignon was already walking up and down outside the d'Esparvieus' house, his head sunk between his shoulders, wearing love-locks which showed from under the narrow brim of his bowler hat, his eye cocked over his shoulder. He wore an enormous dull-black moustache, his hands and feet were huge; in fact, his whole appearance was distinctly memorable. He paced regularly up and down from the nearest of the big rams' head pillars which adorn the Hôtel de la Sordière to the end of the Rue Garancière, towards the apse of St. Sulpice Church and the dome of the Chapel of the Virgin.

Henceforth it became impossible to enter or leave the d'Esparvieus' house without feeling that one's every action, that one's very thoughts, were being spied upon. Mignon was a prodigious person endowed with powers that Nature denies to other mortals. He neither ate nor slept. At all hours of the day and night, in wind and rain, he was to be found outside the house, and no one escaped the X-rays of his eye. One felt pierced through and through, penetrated to the very marrow, worse than naked, bare as a skeleton. It was the affair of a moment; the detective did not even stop, but continued his everlasting walk. It became intolerable. Young Maurice threatened to leave the paternal roof if he was to be so radiographed. His mother and his sister Berthe complained of his piercing look; it offended the chaste modesty of their souls. Mademoiselle Caporal, young Léon d'Esparvieu's governess, felt an indescribable embarrassment. Monsieur René d'Esparvieu was sick of the whole business. He never crossed his own threshold without crushing his hat over his eyes to avoid the investigating ray and without wishing old Sariette, the *fons et origo* of all the evil, at the devil. The intimates of the household, such as Abbé Patouille and Uncle Gaétan, made themselves scarce; visitors gave up calling, tradespeople hesitated about leaving their goods, the carts belonging to the big shops scarcely dared stop. But it was among the domestics that the spying roused the most disorder.

The footman, afraid, under the eye of the police, to go and join the cobbler's wife over her solitary labours in the afternoon, found the house unbearable and gave notice. Odile, Madame d'Esparvieu's lady's-maid, not daring, as was her custom after her mistress had retired, to introduce Octave, the handsomest of the neighbouring bookseller's clerks, to her little room upstairs, grew melancholy, irritable and nervous, pulled her mistress's hair while dressing it, spoke insolently, and made advances to Monsieur Maurice. The cook, Madame Malgoire, a serious matron of some fifty years, having no more visits from Auguste, the wine-merchant's man in the Rue Servandoni, and being incapable of suffering a privation so contrary to her temperament, went mad, sent up a raw rabbit to table, and announced that the Pope had asked her hand in marriage. At last, after a fortnight of superhuman assiduity, contrary to all known laws of organic life, and to the essential conditions of animal economy, Mignon, the detective, having observed nothing abnormal, ceased his surveillance and withdrew without a word, refusing to accept a gratuity. In the library the dance of the books became livelier than ever.

"That is all right," said Monsieur des Aubels. "Since nothing comes in nor goes out, the evil-doer must be in the house."

The magistrate thought it possible to discover the criminal without police-warrant or enquiry. On a date agreed upon at midnight, he had the floor of the library, the treads of the stairs, the vestibule, the garden path leading to Monsieur Maurice's summer-house, and the entrance hall of the latter, all covered with a coating of talc.

The following morning Monsieur des Aubels, assisted by a photographer from the Prefecture, and accompanied by Monsieur René d'Esparvieu and Monsieur Sariette, came to take the imprints. They found nothing in the garden, the wind had blown away the coating of talc; nothing in the summer-house either. Young Maurice told them he thought it was some practical joke and that he had brushed away the white dust with the hearth-brush. The real truth was, he had effaced the traces left by the boots of Odile, the lady's-maid. On the stairs and in the library the very light print of a bare foot could be discerned, it seemed to have sprung into the air and to have touched the ground at rare intervals and without any pressure. They discovered five of these traces. The clearest wasto be found in the abode of the busts and spheres, on the edge of the table where the books were piled. The photographer took several negatives of this imprint.

"This is more terrifying than anything else," murmured Monsieur Sariette.

Monsieur des Aubels did not hide his surprise.

Three days later the anthropometrical department of the Prefecture returned the proofs exhibited to them, saying that they were not in the records.

After dinner Monsieur René showed the photographs to his brother Gaétan, who examined them with profound attention, and after a long silence exclaimed:

"No wonder they have not got this at the Prefecture; it is the foot of a god or of an athlete of antiquity. The sole that made this impression is of a perfection unknown to our races and our climates. It exhibits toes of exquisite grace, and a divine heel."

René d'Esparvieu cried out upon his brother for a madman.

"He is a poet," sighed Madame d'Esparvieu.

"Uncle," said Maurice, "you'll fall in love with this foot if you ever come across it."

"Such was the fate of Vivant Denon, who accompanied Bonaparte to Egypt," replied Gaétan. "At Thebes, in a tomb violated by the Arabs, Denon found the little foot of a mummy of marvellous beauty. He contemplated it with extraordinary fervour, 'It is the foot of a young woman,' he pondered, 'of a princess—of a charming creature. No covering has ever marred its perfect shape.' Denon admired, adored, and loved it. You may see a drawing of this little foot in Denon's atlas of his journey to Egypt, whose leaves one could turn over upstairs, without going further afield, if only Monsieur Sariette would ever let us see a single volume of his library."

Sometimes, in bed, Maurice, waking in the middle of the night, thought he heard the sound of pages being turned over in the next room, and the thud of bound volumes falling on the floor.

One morning at five o'clock he was coming home from the club, after a night of bad luck, and while he stood outside the door of the summer-house, hunting in his pocket for his keys, his ears distinctly heard a voice sighing:

"Knowledge, whither dost thou lead me? Thought, whither dost thou lure me?"

But entering the two rooms he saw nothing, and told himself that his ears must have deceived him.

CHAPTER VIII

WHICH SPEAKS OF LOVE, A SUBJECT WHICH ALWAYS GIVES PLEASURE, FOR A TALE WITHOUT LOVE IS LIKE BEEF WITHOUT MUSTARD: AN INSIPID DISH

NOTHING ever astonished Maurice. He never sought to know the causes of things and dwelt tranquilly in the world of appearances. Not denying the eternal truth, he nevertheless followed vain things as his fancy led him.

Less addicted to sport and violent exercise than most young people of his generation, he followed unconsciously the old erotic traditions of his race. The French were ever the most gallant of men, and it were a pity they should lose this advantage. Maurice preserved it. He was in love with no woman, but, as St. Augustine said, he loved to love. After paying the tribute that was rightly due to the imperishable beauty and secret arts of Madame de la Berthelière, he had enjoyed the impetuous caresses of a young singer called Luciole. At present he was joylessly experiencing the primitive perversity of Odile, his mother's lady's-maid, and the tearful adoration of the beautiful Madame Boittier. And he felt a great void in his heart.

It chanced that one Wednesday, on entering the drawing-room where his mother entertained her friends—who were, generally speaking, unattractive and austere ladies, with a sprinkling of old men and very young people—he noticed, in this intimate circle, Madame des Aubels, the wife of the magistrate at the Law Courts, whom Monsieur d'Esparvieu had vainly consulted on the mysterious ransacking of his library. She was young, he found her pretty, and not without cause. Gilberte had been modelled by the Genius of the Race, and no other genius had had a part in the work.

Thus all her attributes inspired desire, and nothing in her shape or her being aroused any other sentiment.

The law of attraction which draws world to world moved young Maurice to approach this delicious creature, and under its influence he offered to escort her to the tea-table. And when Gilberte was served with tea, he said:

"We should hit it off quite well together, you and I, don't you think?"

He spoke in this way, according to modern usage, so as to avoid inane compliments and to spare a woman the boredom of listening to one of those old declarations of love which, containing nothing but what is vague and undefined, require neither a truthful nor an exact reply.

And profiting by the fact that he had an opportunity of conversing secretly with Madame des Aubels for a few minutes, he spoke urgently and to the point. Gilberte, so far as one could judge, was made rather to awaken desire than to feel it. Nevertheless, she well knew that her fate was to love, and she followed it willingly and with pleasure. Maurice did not particularly displease her. She would have preferred him to be an orphan, for experience had taught her how disappointing it sometimes is to love the son of the house.

"Will you?" he said by way of conclusion.

35

She pretended not to understand, and with her little *foie-gras* sandwich raised half-way to her mouth she looked at Maurice with wondering eyes.

"Will I *what*?" she asked.

"You know quite well."

Madame des Aubels lowered her eyes, and sipped her tea, for her prudishness was not quite vanquished. Meanwhile Maurice, taking her empty cup from her hand, murmured:

"Saturday, five o'clock, 126 Rue de Rome, on the ground-floor, the door on the right, under the arch. Knock three times."

Madame des Aubels glanced severely and imperturbably at the son of the house, and with a self-possessed air rejoined the circle of highly respectable women to whom the Senator Monsieur Le Fol was explaining how artificial incubators were employed at the agricultural colony at St. Julienne.

The following Saturday, Maurice, in his ground-floor flat, awaited Madame des Aubels. He waited her in vain. No light hand came to knock three times on the door under the arch. And Maurice gave way to imprecation, inwardly calling the absent one a jade and a hussy. His fruitless wait, his frustrated desires, rendered him unjust. For Madame des Aubels in not coming where she had never promised to go hardly deserved these names; but we judge human actions by the pleasure or pain they cause us.

Maurice did not put in an appearance in his mother's drawing-room until a fortnight after the conversation at the tea-table. He came late. Madame des Aubels had been there for half an hour. He bowed coldly to her, took a seat some way off, and affected to be listening to the talk.

"Worthily matched," a rich male voice was saying; "the two antagonists were well calculated to render the struggle a terrible and uncertain one. General Bol, with unprecedented tenacity, maintained his position as though he were rooted in the very soil. General Milpertuis, with an agility truly superhuman, kept carrying out movements of the most dazzling rapidity around his immovable adversary. The battle continued to be waged with terrible stubbornness. We were all in an agony of suspense...."

It was General d'Esparvieu describing the autumn manœuvres to a company of breathlessly interested ladies. He was talking well and his audience were delighted. Proceeding to draw a comparison between the French and German methods, he defined their distinguishing characteristics and brought out the conspicuous merits of both with a lofty impartiality. He did not hesitate to affirm that each system had its advantages, and at first made it appear to his circle of wondering, disappointed, and anxious dames, whose countenances were growing increasingly gloomy, that France and Germany were practically in a position of equality. But little by little, as the strategist went on to give a clearer definition of the two methods, that of the French began to appear flexible, elegant, vigorous, full of grace, cleverness, and verve; that of the Germans heavy, clumsy, and undecided. And slowly and surely the faces of the ladies began to clear and to light up with joyous smiles. In order to dissipate any lingering shadows of misgiving from the minds of these wives, sisters, and sweethearts, the General gave them to understand that we were in a position to make use of the German method when it suited us, but that the Germans could not avail themselves of the French method. No sooner had he delivered himself of these sentiments than he was button-holed by Monsieur le Truc de Ruffec, who was engaged in founding a patriotic society known as "Swordsmen All," of which the object was to regenerate France and ensure her superiority over all her adversaries. Even children in the cradle were to be enrolled, and Monsieur le Truc de Ruffec offered the honorary presidency to General d'Esparvieu.

Meanwhile Maurice was appearing to be interested in a conversation that was taking place between a very gentle old lady and the Abbé Lapetite, Chaplain to the Dames du Saint Sang. The old lady, severely tried of late by illness and the loss of friends, wanted to know how it was that people were unhappy in this world.

"How," she asked Abbé Lapetite, "do you explain the scourges that afflict mankind? Why are there plagues, famines, floods, and earthquakes?"

"It is surely necessary that God should sometimes remind us of his existence," replied Abbé Lapetite, with a heavenly smile.

Maurice appeared keenly interested in this conversation. Then he seemed fascinated by Madame Fillot-Grandin, quite a personable young woman, whose simple innocence, however, detracted all piquancy from her beauty, all savour from her bodily charms. A very sour, shrill-voiced old lady, who, affecting the dowdy, woollen weeds of poverty, displayed the pride of a great lady in theworld of Christian finance, exclaimed in a squeaky voice:

"Well, my dear Madame d'Esparvieu, so you have had trouble here. The papers speak darkly of robbery, of thefts committed in Monsieur d'Esparvieu's valuable library, of stolen letters...."

"Oh," said Madame d'Esparvieu, "if we are to believe all the newspapers say...."

"Oh, so, dear Madame, you have got your treasures back. All's well that ends well."

"The library is in perfect order," asserted Madame d'Esparvieu. "There is nothing missing."

"The library is on the floor above this, is it not?" asked young Madame des Aubels, showing an unexpected interest in the books.

Madame d'Esparvieu replied that the library occupied the whole of the second floor, and that they had put the least valuable books in the attics.

"Could I not go and look at it?"

The mistress of the house declared that nothing could be easier. She called to her son:

"Maurice, go and do the honours of the library to Madame des Aubels."

Maurice rose, and without uttering a word, mounted to the second floor in the wake of Madame des Aubels.

He appeared indifferent, but inwardly he rejoiced, for he had no doubt that Gilberte had feigned her ardent desire to inspect the library simply to see him in secret. And, while affecting indifference, he promised himself to renew those offers which, this time, would not be refused.

Under the romantic bust of Alexandre d'Esparvieu, they were met by the silent shadow of a little wan, hollow-eyed old man, who wore a settled expression of mute terror.

"Do not let us disturb you, Monsieur Sariette," said Maurice. "I am showing Madame des Aubels round the library."

Maurice and Madame des Aubels passed on into the great room where against the four walls rose presses filled with books and surmounted by bronze busts of poets, philosophers, and orators of antiquity. All was in perfect order, an order which seemed never to have been disturbed from the beginning of things.

Only, a black void was to be seen in the place which, only the evening before, had been filled by an unpublished manuscript of Richard Simon. Meanwhile, by the side of the young couple walked Monsieur Sariette, pale, faded, and silent.

"Really and truly, you have not been nice," said Maurice, with a look of reproach at Madame des Aubels.

She signed to him that the librarian might over-hear. But he reassured her.

"Take no notice. It is old Sariette. He has become a complete idiot." And he repeated: "No, you have not been at all nice. I awaited you. You did not come. You have made me unhappy."

After a moment's silence, while one heard the low melancholy whistling of asthma in poor Sariette's bronchial tubes, young Maurice continued insistently:

"You are wrong."

"Why wrong?"

"Wrong not to do as I ask you."

"Do you still think so?"

"Certainly."

"You meant it seriously?"

"As seriously as can be."

Touched by his assurance of sincere and constant feeling, and thinking she had resisted sufficiently, Gilberte granted to Maurice what she had refused him a fortnight ago.

They slipped into an embrasure of the window, behind an enormous celestial globe whereon were graven the Signs of the Zodiac and the figures of the stars, and there, their gaze fixed on the Lion, the Virgin, and the Scales, in the presence of a multitude of Bibles, before the works of the Fathers, both Greek and Latin, beneath the casts of Homer, Æschylus, Sophocles, Euripides, Herodotus, Thucydides, Socrates, Plato, Aristotle, Demosthenes, Cicero, Virgil, Horace, Seneca, and Epictetus, they exchanged vows of love and a long kiss on the mouth.

Almost immediately Madame des Aubels bethought herself that she still had some calls to pay, and that she must make her escape quickly, for love had not made her lose all sense of her own importance. But she had barely crossed the landing with Maurice when they heard a hoarse cry and saw Monsieur Sariette plunge madly downstairs, exclaiming as he went:

"Stop it, stop it; I saw it fly away! It escaped from the shelf by itself. It crossed the room ... there it is—there! It's going downstairs. Stop it! It has gone out of the door on the ground floor!"

"What?" asked Maurice.

Monsieur Sariette looked out of the landing window, murmuring horror-struck:

"It's crossing the garden! It's going into the summer-house. Stop it, stop it!"

"But what is it?" repeated Maurice—"in God's name, what is it?"

"My Flavius Josephus," exclaimed Monsieur Sariette. "Stop it!"

And he fell down unconscious.

"You see he is quite mad," said Maurice to Madame des Aubels, as he lifted up the unfortunate librarian.

Gilberte, a little pale, said she also thought she had seen something in the direction indicated by the unhappy man, something flying.

Maurice had seen nothing, but he had felt what seemed like a gust of wind.

He left Monsieur Sariette in the arms of Hippolyte and the housekeeper, who had both hastened to the spot on hearing the noise.

The old gentleman had a wound in his head.

"All the better," said the housekeeper; "this wound may save him from having a fit."

Madame des Aubels gave her handkerchief to stop the blood, and recommended an arnica compress.

CHAPTER IX

WHEREIN IT IS SHOWN THAT, AS AN ANCIENT GREEK POET SAID, "NOTHING IS SWEETER THAN APHRODITE THE GOLDEN"

ALTHOUGH he had enjoyed Madame des Aubels' favours for six whole months, Maurice still loved her. True they had had to separate during the summer. For lack of funds of his own he had had to go to Switzerland with his mother, and then to stop with the whole family at the Château d'Esparvieu. She had spent the summer with her mother at Niort, and the autumn with her husband at a little Normandy seaside place, so that they had hardly seen each other four or five times. But since the winter, kindly to lovers, had brought them back to town again, Maurice had been receiving her twice a week in his little flat in the Rue de Rome, and received no one else. No other woman had inspired him with feelings of such constancy and fidelity. What augmented his pleasure was that he believed himself loved, and indeed he was not unpleasing.

He thought that she did not deceive him, not that he had any reason to think so, but it appeared right and fitting that she should be content with him alone. What annoyed him was that she always kept him waiting, and was unpunctual in coming to their meeting-place; she was invariably late,—at times very late.

Now on Saturday, January 30th, since four o'clock in the afternoon, Maurice had been awaiting Madame des Aubels in the little pink room, where a bright fire was burning. He was gaily clad in a suit of flowered pyjamas, smoking Turkish cigarettes. At first he dreamt of receiving her with long kisses, with hitherto unknown caresses. A quarter of an hour having passed, he meditated serious and affectionate reproaches, then after an hour of disappointed waiting he vowed he would meet her with cold disdain.

At length she appeared, fresh and fragrant.

"It was scarcely worth while coming," he said bitterly, as she laid her muff and her little bag on the table and untied her veil before the wardrobe mirror.

Never, she told her beloved, had she had such trouble to get away. She was full of excuses, which he obstinately rejected. But no sooner had she the good sense to hold her tongue than he ceased his reproaches, and then nothing detracted from the longing with which she inspired him.

The curtains were drawn, the room was bathed in warm shadows lit by the dancing gleams of the fire. The mirrors in the wardrobe and on the chimney-piece shone with mysterious lights. Gilberte, leaning on her elbow, head on hand, was lost in thought. A little jeweller, a trustworthy and intelligent man, had shown her a wonderfully pretty pearl and sapphire bracelet; it was worth a great deal, and was to be had for a mere nothing. He had got it from a *cocotte* down on her luck, who was in a hurry to dispose of it. It was a rare chance; it would be a huge pity to let it slip.

"Would you like to see it, darling? I will ask the little man to let me have it to show you."

Maurice did not actually decline the proposal. But it was clear that he took no interest in the wonderful bracelet. "When small jewellers come across a great bargain, they keep it to themselves, and do not allow their customers to profit by it. Moreover, jewellery means nothing just now. Well-bred women have given up wearing it. Everyone goes in for sport, and jewellery does not go with sport."

Maurice spoke thus, contrary to truth, because having given his mistress a fur coat, he was in no hurry to give her anything more. He was not stingy, but he was careful with his money. His people did not give him a very large allowance, and his debts grew bigger every day. By satisfying the wishes of his inamorata too promptly he feared to arouse others still more pressing. The bargain seemed less wonderful to him than to Gilberte; besides, he liked to take the initiative in choosing his gifts. Above all, he thought that if he gave her too many presents he would be no longer sure of being loved for himself.

Madame des Aubels felt neither contempt nor surprise at this attitude; she was gentle and temperate, she knew men, and judged that one must take them as one found them, that for the most part they do not give very willingly, and that a woman should know how to make them give.

Suddenly a gas lamp was lighted in the street, and shone through the gaps in the curtains.

"Half-past six," she said. "We must be on the move."

Pricked by the touch of Time's fleeting wing, Maurice was conscious of reawakened desires and reanimated powers. A white and radiant offering, Gilberte, with her head thrown back, her eyes half closed, her lips apart, sunk in dreamy languor, was breathing slowly and placidly, when suddenly she started up with a cry of terror.

"Whatever is that?"

"Stay still," said Maurice, holding her back in his arms.

In his present mood, had the sky fallen it would not have troubled him. But in one bound she escaped from him. Crouching down, her eyes filled with terror, she was pointing with her finger at a figure which appeared in a corner of the room, between the fire-place and the wardrobe with the mirror. Then, unable to bear the sight, and nearly fainting, she hid her face in her hands.

CHAPTER X

WHICH FAR SURPASSES IN AUDACITY THE IMAGINATIVE FLIGHTS OF DANTE AND MILTON

MAURICE at length turned his head, saw the figure, and perceiving that it moved, was also frightened. Meanwhile, Gilberte was regaining her senses. She imagined that what she had seen was some mistress whom her lover had hidden in the room. Inflamed with anger and disgust at the idea of such treachery, boiling with indignation, and glaring at her supposed rival, she exclaimed:

"A woman ... a naked woman too! You bring me into a room where you allow your women to come, and when I arrive they have not had time to dress. And you reproach me with arriving late! Your impudence is beyond belief! Come, send the creature packing. If you wanted us both here together, you might at least have asked me whether it suited me...."

Maurice, wide-eyed and groping for a revolver that had never been there, whispered in her ear:

"Be quiet ... it is no woman. One can scarcely see, but it is more like a man."

She put her hands over her eyes again and screamed harder than ever.

"A man! Where does he come from? A thief. An assassin! Help! Help! Kill him.... Maurice, kill him! Turn on the light. No, don't turn on the light...."

She made a mental vow that should she escape from this danger she would burn a candle to the Blessed Virgin. Her teeth chattered.

The figure made a movement.

"Keep away!" cried Gilberte. "Keep away!"

She offered the burglar all the money and jewels she had on the table if he would consent not to stir. Amid her surprise and terror the idea assailed her that her husband, dissembling his suspicions, had caused her to be followed, had posted witnesses, and had had recourse to the Commissaire de Police. In a flash she distinctly saw before her the long painful future, the glaring scandal, the pretended disdain, the cowardly desertion of her friends, the just mockery of society, for it is indeed ridiculous to be found out. She saw the divorce, the loss of her position and of her rank. She saw the dreary and narrow existence with her mother, when no one would make love to her, for men avoid women who fail to give them the security of the married state. And all this, why? Why this ruin, this disaster? For a piece of folly, for a mere nothing. Thus in a lightning flash spoke the conscience of Gilberte des Aubels.

"Have no fear, Madame," said a very sweet voice.

Slightly reassured, she found strength to ask:

"Who are you?"

"I am an angel," replied the voice.

"What did you say?"

"I am an angel. I am Maurice's guardian angel."

"Say it again. I am going mad. I do not understand...."

Maurice, without understanding either, was indignant. He sprang forward and showed himself; with his right hand armed with a slipper he made a threatening gesture, and said in a rough voice:

"You are a low ruffian; oblige me by going the way you came."

"Maurice d'Esparvieu," continued the sweet voice, "He whom you adore as your Creator has stationed by the side of each of the faithful a good angel, whose mission it is to counsel and protect him; it is the invariable opinion of the Fathers, it is founded on many passages in the Bible, the Church admits it unanimously, without, however, pronouncing anathema upon those who hold a contrary opinion. You see before you one of these angels, yours, Maurice. I was commanded to watch over your innocence and to guard your chastity."

"That may be," said Maurice; "but you are certainly no gentleman. A gentleman would not permit himself to enter a room at such a moment. To be plain, what the deuce are you doing here?"

"I have assumed this appearance, Maurice, because, having henceforth to move among mankind, I have to make myself like them. The celestial spirits possess the power of assuming a form which renders them apparent to the eye and to the touch. This shape is real, because it is apparent, and all the realities in the world are but appearances."

Gilberte, pacified at length, was arranging her hair on her forehead.

The Angel pursued:

"The celestial spirits adopt, according to their fancy, one sex or the other, or both at once. But they cannot disguise themselves at any moment, according to their caprice or fantasy. Their metamorphoses are subject to constant laws, which you would not understand. Thus I have neither desire nor power to transform myself under your eyes, for your amusement or my own, into a lion, a tiger, a fly, or into a sycamore-shaving like the young Egyptian whose story was found in a tomb. I cannot change myself into an ass as did Lucius with the pomade of the youthful Photis. For in my wisdom I had fixed beforehand the hour of my apparition to mankind, nothing could hasten or delay it."

Impatient for enlightenment, Maurice asked for the second time:

"Still, what are you up to here?"

Joining her voice to his, Madame des Aubels asked: "Yes, indeed, what are you doing here?"

The Angel replied:

"Man, lend your ear. Woman, hear my voice. I am about to reveal to you a secret on which hangs the fate of the Universe. In rebellion against Him whom you hold to be the Creator of all things visible and invisible, I am preparing the Revolt of the Angels."

"Do not jest," said Maurice, who had faith and did not allow holy things to be played with.

But the Angel answered reproachfully: "What makes you think, Maurice, that I am frivolous and given to vain words?"

"Come, come," said Maurice, shrugging his shoulders. "You are not going to revolt against
_____"

He pointed to the ceiling—not daring to finish.

But the Angel continued:

"Do you not know that the sons of God have already revolted and that a great battle took place in the heavens?"

"That was a long time ago," said Maurice, putting on his socks.

Then the Angel replied:

"It was before the creation of the world. But nothing has changed since then in the heavens. The nature of the Angels is no different now from what it was originally. What they did then they could do again now."

"No! It is not possible. It is contrary to faith. If you were an angel, a good angel as you make out you are, it would never occur to you to disobey your Creator."

"You are in error, Maurice, and the authority of the Fathers condemns you. Origen lays it down in his homilies that good angels are fallible, that they sin every day and fall from Heaven like flies. Possibly you may be tempted to reject the authority of this Father, despite his knowledge of the Scriptures, because he is excluded from the Canon of the Saints. If this be so, I would remind you of the second chapter of Revelation, in which the Angels of Ephesus and Pergamos are rebuked for that they kept not ward over their church. You will doubtless contend that the angels to whom the Apostle here refers are, properly speaking, the Bishops of the two cities in question, and that he calls them angels on account of their ministry. It may be so, and I cede the point. But with what arguments, Maurice, would you counter the opinion of all those Doctors and Pontiffs whose unanimous teaching it is that angels may fall from good into evil? Such is the statement made by Saint Jerome in his Epistle to Damasus...."

"Monsieur," said Madame des Aubels, "go away, I beg you."

But the Angel hearkened not, and continued:

"Saint Augustine, in his *True Religion*, Chapter XIII; Saint Gregory, in his *Morals*, Chapter XXIV; Isidore——"

"Monsieur, let me get my things on; I am in a hurry."

"In his treatise on *The Greatest Good*, Book I, Chapter XII; Bede on Job——"

"Oh, please, Monsieur ..."

"Chapter VIII; John of Damascus on *Faith*, Book II, Chapter III. Those, I think, are sufficiently weighty authorities, and there is nothing for it, Maurice, but to admit your error. What has led you astray is that you have not duly considered my nature, which is free, active, and mobile, like that of all the angels, and that you have merely observed the grace and felicity with which you deem me so richly endowed. Lucifer possessed no less, yet he rebelled."

"But what on earth are you rebelling for?" asked Maurice.

"Isaiah," answered the child of light, "Isaiah has already asked, before you: '*Quomodo cecidisti de cœlo, Lucifer, qui mane oriebaris?*' Hearken, Maurice. Before Time was, the Angels rose up to win dominion over Heaven, the most beautiful of the Seraphim revolted through pride. As for me, it is science that has inspired me with the generous desire for freedom. Finding myself near you, Maurice, in a house containing one of the vastest libraries in the world, I acquired a taste for reading and a love of study. While, fordone with the toils of a sensual life, you lay sunk in heavy slumber, I surrounded myself with books, I studied, I pondered over their pages, sometimes in one of the rooms of the library, under the busts of the great men of antiquity, sometimes at the far end of the garden, in the room in the summer-house next to your own."

On hearing these words, young d'Esparvieu exploded with laughter and beat the pillow with his fist, an infallible sign of uncontrollable mirth.

"Ah ... ah ... ah! It was you who pillaged papa's library and drove poor old Sariette off his head. You know, he has become completely idiotic."

"Busily engaged," continued the Angel, "in cultivating for myself a sovereign intelligence, I paid no heed to that inferior being, and when he thought to offer obstacles to my researches and to disturb my work I punished him for his importunity.

"One particular winter's night in the abode of the philosophers and globes I let fall a volume of great weight on his head, which he tried to tear from my invisible hand. Then more recently, raising, with a vigorous arm composed of a column of condensed air, a precious manuscript of Flavius Josephus, I gave the imbecile such a fright, that he rushed out screaming on to the landing and (to borrow a striking expression from Dante Alighieri) fell even as a dead body falls. He was well rewarded, for you gave him, Madame, to staunch the blood from his wound, your little scented handkerchief. It was the day, you may remember, when behind a celestial globe you exchanged a kiss on the mouth with Maurice."

"Monsieur," said Madame des Aubels, with a frown, "I cannot allow you...."

But she stopped short, deeming it was an inopportune moment to appear over-exacting on a matter of decorum.

"I had made up my mind," continued the Angel impassively, "to examine the foundations of belief. I first attacked the monuments of Judaism, and I read all the Hebrew texts."

"You know Hebrew, then?" exclaimed Maurice.

"Hebrew is my native tongue: in Paradise for a long time we have spoken nothing else."

"Ah, you are a Jew. I might have deduced it from your want of tact."

The Angel, not deigning to hear, continued in his melodious voice: "I have delved deep into Oriental antiquities and also into those of Greece and Rome. I have devoured the works of theologians, philosophers, physicists, geologists, and naturalists. I have learnt. I have thought. I have lost my faith."

"What? You no longer believe in God?"

"I believe in Him, since my existence depends on His, and if He should fail to exist, I myself should fall into nothingness. I believe in Him, even as the Satyrs and the Mænads believed in Dionysus and for the same reason. I believe in the God of the Jews and the Christians. But I deny that He created the world; at the most He organised but an inferior part of it, and all that He touched bears the mark of His rough and unforeseeing touch. I do not think He is either eternal or infinite, for it is absurd to conceive of a being who is not bounded by space or time. I think Him limited, even very limited. I no longer believe Him to be the only God. For a long time He did not believe it Himself; in the beginning He was a polytheist; later, His pride and the flattery of His worshippers made Him a monotheist. His ideas have little connection; He is less powerful than He is thought to be. And, to speak candidly, He is not so much a god as a vain and ignorant demiurge. Those who, like myself, know His true nature, call Him Ialdabaoth."

"What's that you say?"

"Ialdabaoth."

"Ialdabaoth. What's that?"

"I have already told you. It is the demiurge whom, in your blindness, you adore as the one and only God."

"You're mad. I don't advise you to go and talk rubbish like that to Abbé Patouille."

"I am not in the least sanguine, my dear Maurice, of piercing the dense night of your intellect. I merely tell you that I am going to engage Ialdabaoth in conflict with some hopes of victory."

"Mark my words, you won't succeed."

"Lucifer shook His throne, and the issue was for a moment in doubt."

"What is your name?"

"Abdiel for the angels and saints, Arcade for mankind."

"Well, my poor Arcade, I regret to see you going to the bad. But confess that you are jesting with us. I could at a pinch understand your leaving Heaven for a woman. Love makes us commit the greatest follies. But you will never make me believe that you, who have seen God face to face, ultimately found the truth in old Sariette's musty books. No, you will never get me to believe that!"

"My dear Maurice, Lucifer was face to face with God, yet he refused to serve Him. As to the kind of truth one finds in books, it is a truth that enables us sometimes to discern what things are not, without ever enabling us to discover what they are. And this poor little truth has sufficed to prove to me that He in whom I blindly believed is not believable, and that men and angels have been deceived by the lies of Ialdabaoth."

"There is no Ialdabaoth. There is God. Come, Arcade, do the right thing. Renounce these follies, these impieties, dis-incarnate yourself, become once more a pure Spirit, and resume your office of guardian angel. Return to duty. I forgive you, but do not let us see you again."

"I should like to please you, Maurice. I feel a certain affection for you, for my heart is soft. But fate henceforth calls me elsewhere towards beings capable of thought and action."

"Monsieur Arcade," said Madame des Aubels, "withdraw, I implore you. It makes me horribly shy to be in this position before two men. I assure you I am not accustomed to it."

CHAPTER XI

RECOUNTS IN WHAT MANNER THE ANGEL, ATTIRED IN THE CAST-OFF GARMENTS OF A SUICIDE, LEAVES THE YOUTHFUL MAURICE WITHOUT A HEAVENLY GUARDIAN

REASSURE yourself, Madame," replied the apparition, "your position is not as risky as you say. You are not confronted with two men, but with one man and an angel."

45

She examined the stranger with an eye which, piercing the gloom, was anxiously surveying a vague but by no means negligible indication, and asked:

"Monsieur, is it quite certain that you are an angel?"

The apparition prayed her to have no doubt about it, and gave some precise information as to his origin.

"There are three hierarchies of celestial spirits, each composed of nine choirs; the first comprises the Seraphim, Cherubim, and the Thrones; the second, the Dominations, the Virtues, and the Powers; the third, the Principalities, the Archangels, and the Angels properly so called. I belong to the ninth choir of the third hierarchy."

Madame des Aubels, who had her reasons for doubting this, expressed at least one:

"You have no wings."

"Why should I, Madame? Am I bound to resemble the angels on your holy-water stoups? Those feathery oars that beat the waves of the air in rhythmic cadences are not always worn by the heavenly messengers on their shoulders. Cherubim may be apterous. That all too beautiful angelic pair who spent an anxious night in the house of Lot compassed about by an Oriental horde—they had no wings! No, they appeared just like men, and the dust of the road covered their feet, which the patriarch washed with pious hand. I would beg you to observe, Madame, that according to the Science of Organic Metamorphosis created by Lamarck and Darwin, the wings of birds have been successively transformed into fore-feet in the case of quadrupeds and into arms in the case of the Linnæan primates. And you may remember, Maurice, that by a rather annoying reversion to type, Miss Kate, your English nurse, who used to be so fond of giving you a whipping, had arms very like the pinions of a plucked fowl. One may say, then, that a being possessing both arms and wings is a monster and belongs to the department of Teratology. In Paradise we have Cherubim and Kerûbs in the shape of winged bulls, but those are the clumsy inventions of an inartistic god. It is nevertheless true, quite true, that the Victories of the Temple of Athena Nike on the Athenian Acropolis are beautiful, and possess both arms and wings; it is also true that the Victory of Brescia is beautiful, with her outstretched arms and her long wings folded on her mighty loins. It is one of the miracles of Greek genius to have known how to create harmonious monsters. The Greeks never err. The Moderns always."

"Yet on the whole," said Madame des Aubels, "you have not the look of a pure Spirit."

"Nevertheless, I am one, Madame, if ever there was one. And it ill becomes you, who have been baptised, to doubt it. Several of the Fathers, such as St. Justin, Tertullian, Origen, and Clement of Alexandria thought that the Angels were not purely spiritual, but possessed a body formed of some subtle material. This opinion has been rejected by the Church; hence I am merely Spirit. But what is spirit and what is matter? Formerly they were contrasted as being two opposites, and now your human science tends to reunite them as two aspects of the same thing. It teaches that everything proceeds from ether and everything returns to it, that the same movement transforms the waves of air into stones and minerals, and that the atoms scattered throughout illimitable space, form, by the varying speed of their orbits, all the substance of this material world."

But Madame des Aubels was not listening. She had something on her mind, and to put an end to her suspense, she asked:

"How long have you been here?"

"I came with Maurice."

"Well—that's a nice thing!" said she, shaking her head. But the Angel continued with heavenly serenity:

"Everything in the Universe is circular, elliptical, or hyperbolic, and the same laws which rule the stars govern this grain of dust. In the original and native movement of its substance, my body is spiritual, but it may affect, as you perceive, this material state, by changing the rhythm of its elements."

Having thus spoken he sat down in a chair on Madame des Aubels' black stockings.

A clock struck outside.

"Good heavens, seven o'clock!" exclaimed Gilberte. "What am I to say to my husband? He thinks I am at that tea-party in the Rue de Rivoli. We are dining with the La Verdelières to-night. Go away immediately, Monsieur Arcade. I must get ready to go. I have not a second to lose."

The Angel replied that he would have willingly obeyed Madame des Aubels had he been in a state to show himself decently in public, but that he could not dream of appearing out of doors without any clothes. "Were I to walk naked in the street," he added, "I should offend a nation attached to its ancient habits, habits which it has never examined. They are the basis of all moral systems. Formerly," he added, "the angels, in revolt like myself, manifested themselves to Christians under grotesque and ridiculous appearances, black, horned, hairy, and cloven-footed. Pure stupidity! They were the laughing-stock of people of taste. They merely frightened old women and children and met with no success."

"It is true he cannot go out as he is," said Madame des Aubels with justice.

Maurice tossed his pyjamas and his slippers to the celestial messenger. Regarded as outdoor habiliments they were not adequate. Gilberte pressed her lover to run at once in quest of other clothes. He proposed to go and get some from the concierge. She was violently opposed to this. It would, she said, be madly imprudent to drag the concierge into such an affair.

"Do you want them to know that ..." she exclaimed.

She pointed to the Angel and was silent.

Young d'Esparvieu went out to seek a clothes-shop.

Meanwhile, Gilberte, who could not delay any longer for fear of causing a horrible society scandal, turned on the light and dressed before the Angel. She did it without any awkwardness, for she knew how to adapt herself to circumstances; and she took it that in such an unheard-of encounter in which heaven and earth were mingled in unutterable confusion it was permissible to retrench in modesty.

Moreover, she knew that she possessed a good figure and had garments as dainty as the fashion demanded. As the apparition's sense of delicacy would not permit him to don Maurice's pyjamas, Gilberte could not help observing by the lamp-light that her suspicions were well-founded, and that angels have the same appearance as men. Curious to know if the appearance were real or imaginary she asked the child of light if Angels were like monkeys, who, to win women, merely lack money.

"Yes, Gilberte," replied Arcade, "Angels are capable of loving mortals. It is the teaching of the Scriptures. It is said in the Seventh Book of Genesis, 'When men became numerous on the face of the earth, and daughters were born to them, the sons of God saw that the daughters of men were beautiful, and they took as wives all those which pleased them.'"

"Good heavens," cried Gilberte all at once, "I shall never be able to fasten my dress; it hooks down the back."

When Maurice entered the room he found the Angel on his knees tying the shoes of the woman taken in *flagrante delicto*.

Taking her muff and her bag off the table she said:

"I have not forgotten anything? No. Good-night, Monsieur Arcade. Good-night, Maurice. I shall not forget to-day." And she vanished like a dream.

"Here," said Maurice, throwing the Angel a bundle of clothes.

The young man, having seen some dismal rags lying among clarionettes and clyster-pipes in the window of a second-hand shop, had bought for nineteen francs the cast-off suit of some wretched sable-clad mortal who had committed suicide. The Angel, with native majesty, took the garments and put them on. Worn by him, they took on an unexpected elegance. He took a step to the door.

"So you are leaving me," said Maurice. "It's settled, then? I very much fear that, some day, you will bitterly regret this hasty action."

"I must not look back. Adieu, Maurice."

Maurice timidly slipped five louis into his hand.

"Adieu, Arcade."

But when the Angel had passed through the door, and all that was to be seen of him in the door-way was his uplifted heel, Maurice called him back.

"Arcade! I never thought of it! I have no guardian angel now!"

"Quite true, Maurice, you have one no longer."

"Then what will become of me? One must have a guardian angel. Tell me,—are there not grave drawbacks,—is there no danger in not having one?"

"Before replying, Maurice, I must ask you if you wish me to speak to you according to your belief, which formerly was my own, according to the teaching of the Church and the Catholic faith, or according to natural philosophy."

"I don't care a straw for your natural philosophy. Answer me according to the religion I believe in, and which I profess, and in which I wish to live and die."

"Very well, my dear Maurice. The loss of your guardian angel will probably deprive you of certain spiritual succour, of certain celestial grace. I am expressing to you the unvarying opinion of the Church on the matter. You will lack an assistance, a support, a consolation which would have guided and confirmed you in the way of salvation. You will have less strength to avoid sin, and as it was you hadn't much. In fact, in spiritual matters, you will be without strength and without joy. Adieu, Maurice; when you see Madame des Aubels, please remember me to her."

"You are going?"

"Farewell."

Arcade disappeared, and Maurice in the depths of an arm-chair sat for a long time with his head in his hands.

CHAPTER XII

WHEREIN IT IS SET FORTH HOW THE ANGEL MIRAR, WHEN BEARING GRACE AND CONSOLATION TO THOSE DWELLING IN THE NEIGHBOURHOOD OF THE CHAMPS ÉLYSÉES IN PARIS, BEHELD A MUSIC-HALL SINGER NAMED BOUCHOTTE AND FELL IN LOVE WITH HER

THROUGH streets filled with brown fog, pierced with white and yellow lights, where horses exhaled their smoking breath and motors radiated their rapid search-lights, the angel made his way, and, mingling with the black flood of foot-passengers which rolled unceasingly along, proceeded across the town from north to south till he came to the lonely boulevards on the left bank of the river. Not far from the old walls of Port Royal, a small restaurant flings night by night athwart the pavement the clouded rays of its streaming windows. Coming to a halt there, Arcade entered a room full of warm, savoury odours, pleasing to the unfortunate beings faint with cold and hunger. Glancing round him he beheld Russian Nihilists, Italian Anarchists, refugees, conspirators, revolutionaries from every quarter of the globe, picturesque old faces with tumbled masses of hair and beard that swept downwards even as the torrent and the waterfall sweep over their rocky bed. There were young faces of virginal coldness, expressions sombre and wild, pale eyes of infinite sweetness, drawn faces, and, in a corner, there were two Russian women, one extremely lovely, the other hideous, but both resembling each other in their indifference to ugliness and to beauty. But failing to find the face he sought, for there were no angels in the room, he sat down at a small vacant marble table.

Angels, when driven by hunger, eat as do the animals of this earth, and their food, transformed by digestive heat, becomes one with their celestial substance. Seeing three angels under the oaks of Mamre, Abraham offered them cakes, kneaded by Sarah, an whole calf, butter and milk, and they ate. Lot, on receiving two angels in his house, ordered unleavened bread to be baked, and they did eat. Arcade was given a tough beef-steak by a seedy waiter, and he did eat. Nevertheless, his dreams were of the sweet leisure, of the repose, of the delightful studies he had quitted, of the heavy task he had undertaken, of the toil, the weariness, the perils which he would have to endure, and his soul was sad and his heart troubled.

As he was finishing his modest repast, a young man of poor appearance and thinly clad entered the room, and rapidly surveying the tables approached the angel and greeted him by the name of Abdiel, because he himself was a celestial spirit.

"I knew you would answer my call, Mirar," replied Arcade, addressing his angelic brother in his turn by the name he formerly bore in heaven. But Mirar was remembered no more in heaven since he, an Archangel, had left the service of God. He was called Théophile Belais on earth, and to earn his bread gave music lessons to small children in the day-time and at night played the violin in dancing saloons.

"It is you, dear Abdiel?" replied Théophile. "So here we are reunited in this sad world. I am pleased to see you again. All the same I pity you, for we lead a hard life here."

But Arcade answered:

"Friend, your exile draws to an end. I have great plans. I will confide them to you and associate you with them."

49

And Maurice's guardian angel, having ordered two coffees, revealed his ideas and his projects to his companion: he told how, during his visit on earth, he had abandoned himself to researches little practised by celestial spirits and had studied theologies, cosmogonies, the system of the Universe, theories of matter, modern essays on the transformation and loss of energy. Having, he explained, studied Nature, he had found her in perpetual conflict with the teachings of the Master he served. This Master, greedy of praise, whom he had for a long time adored, appeared to him now as an ignorant, stupid, and cruel tyrant. He had denied Him, blasphemed Him, and was burning to combat Him. His plan was to recommence the revolt of the angels. He wished for war, and hoped for victory.

"But," he added, "it is necessary above all to know our strength and that of our adversary." And he asked if the enemies of Ialdabaoth were numerous and powerful on earth.

Théophile looked wonderingly at his brother. He appeared not to understand the questions addressed him.

"Dear compatriot," he said, "I came at your invitation because it was the invitation of an old comrade. But I do not know what you expect of me, and I fear I shall be unable to help you in anything. I take no hand in politics, neither do I stand forth as a reformer. I am not like you, a spirit in revolt, a freethinker, a revolutionary. I remain faithful, in the depths of my soul, to the Celestial Creator. I still adore the Master I no longer serve, and I lament the days when shrouding myself with my wings I formed with the multitude of the children of light a wheel of flame around His throne of glory. Love, profane love has alone separated me from God. I quitted heaven to follow a daughter of men. She was beautiful and sang in music-halls."

They rose. Arcade accompanied Théophile, who was living at the other end of the town, at the corner of the Boulevard Rochechouart and the Rue de Steinkerque. While walking through the deserted streets he who loved the singer told his brother of his love and his sorrows.

His fall, which dated from two years back, had been sudden. Belonging to the eighth choir of the third hierarchy he was a bearer of grace to the faithful who are still to be found in large numbers in France, especially among the higher ranks of the officers of the army and navy.

"One summer night," he said, "as I was descending from Heaven, to distribute consolations, the grace of perseverance and of good deaths to divers pious persons in the neighbourhood of the Étoile, my eyes, although well accustomed to immortal light, were dazzled by the fiery flowers with which the Champs Élysées were sown. Great candelabra, under the trees, marking the entrances to cafés and restaurants, gave the foliage the precious glitter of an emerald. Long garlands of luminous pearl surrounded the open-air enclosures where a crowd of men and women sat closely packed listening to the sounds of a lively orchestra, whose strains reached my ears confusedly.

"The night was warm, my wings were beginning to grow tired. I descended into one of the concerts and sat down, invisible, among the audience. At this moment, a woman appeared on the stage, clad in a short spangled frock. Owing to the reflection of the footlights and the paint on her face all that was visible of the latter was the expression and the smile. Her body was supple and voluptuous.

"She sang and danced.... Arcade, I have always loved dancing and music, but this creature's thrilling voice and insidious movements created in me an uneasiness I had never known before. My colour came and went. My eyelids drooped, my tongue clove to my mouth. I could not leave the spot."

And Théophile related, groaning, how, possessed by desire for this woman, he did not return to Heaven again, but, taking the shape of a man, lived an earthly life, for it is written: "In those days the sons of God saw that the daughters of men were beautiful."

A fallen angel, having lost his innocence along with the vision of God, Théophile at heart still retained his simplicity of soul. Clad in rags, filched from the stall of a Jewish hawker, he went to seek the woman he loved. She was called Bouchotte and lodged in a small house in Montmartre. He flung himself at her feet and told her she was adorable, that she sang delightfully, that he loved her madly, that, for her, he would renounce his family and his country, that he was a musician and had nothing to eat. Touched by such youthful ingenuousness, candour, poverty, and love, she fed, clothed, and loved him.

However, after long and painful struggles, he procured employment as a music-teacher, and made some money, which he brought to his mistress, keeping nothing for himself. From that time forward she loved him no longer. She despised him for earning so little and did not conceal her indifference, weariness, and disgust. She overwhelmed him with reproaches, irony, and abuse, in spite of which she kept him, for she had had experience of worse partners and was used to domestic quarrels. For the rest, she led a busy, serious, and rather hard life as artist and woman. Théophile loved her as he had loved her the first night, and he suffered.

"She overworks herself," he told his celestial brother, "that is what makes her so hard to please, but I am certain she loves me. I hope soon to give her more comfort."

And he spoke at length of an operetta at which he was working and which he hoped to have brought out at a Paris theatre. A young poet had given him the libretto. It was the story of Aline, queen of Golconda, after an eighteenth-century tale.

"I am strewing it profusely with melodies," said Théophile; "my music comes from my heart. My heart is an inexhaustible source of melody. Unfortunately nowadays people like recondite arrangements, difficult scoring. They accuse me of being too fluid, too limpid, of not imparting enough colour to my style, not aiming at stronger effects in harmony and more vigorous contrasts. Harmony, harmony!... No doubt it has given its merits, but it does not appeal to the heart. It is melody which carries us away and ravishes us and brings smiles and tears to our eyes." At these words he smiled and wept to himself. Then he continued with emotion:

"I am a fountain of melody. But the orchestration! there's the rub! In Paradise, you know, Arcade, in the matter of instruments, we only possess the harp, the psaltery, and the hydraulic organ."

Arcade was only listening to him with half an ear. He was meditating plans which filled his soul and swelled his heart.

"Do you know any angels in revolt?" he asked his companion. "As for me, I know only one, Prince Istar, with whom I have exchanged a few letters and who offered to share his attic with me while I was finding a lodging in this town, where I believe rents are very high."

Of angels in revolt Théophile knew none. When he met a fallen spirit who had formerly been one of his comrades he shook him by the hand, for he was a faithful friend. Sometimes he saw Prince Istar. But he avoided all those bad angels who shocked him by the violence of their opinions and whose conversations plagued him to death.

"Then you don't approve of me?" asked the impulsive Arcade.

"Friend, I neither approve of you nor blame you. I understand nothing of the ideas which trouble you. Neither do I think it good for an artist to concern himself with politics. One has quite sufficient to occupy oneself with one's art."

He loved his profession, and had hopes of "arriving" one day, but theatrical ways disgusted him. The only chance he saw of having his piece played was to take one or two—perhaps three —collaborators, who, without having done any work, would sign their names and share the profits. Soon Bouchotte would fail to find engagements. When she offered her services in some small hall the manager began by asking her how many shares she was taking in the business. Such customs, thought Théophile, were deplorable.

CHAPTER XIII

WHEREIN WE HEAR THE BEAUTIFUL ARCHANGEL ZITA UNFOLD HER LOFTY DESIGNS AND ARE SHOWN THE WINGS OF MIRAR, ALL MOTH-EATEN, IN A CUPBOARD

THUS talking, the two archangels had reached the Boulevard Rochechouart. As his eye lighted on a tavern, whence, through the mist, the light fell golden on the pavement, Théophile suddenly bethought himself of the Archangel Ithuriel who, in the guise of a poor but beautiful woman, was living in wretched lodgings on La Butte and came every evening to read the papers at this tavern. The musician often met her there. Her name was Zita. Théophile had never been curious enough to enquire into the opinions entertained by this archangel, but it was generally supposed that she was a Russian nihilist, and he took her to be, like Arcade, an atheist and a revolutionary. He had heard remarkable tales about her. People said she was an hermaphrodite, and that as the active and passive principles were united within her in a condition of stable equilibrium, she was an example of a perfect being, finding in herself complete and continuous satisfaction, contented yet unfortunate in that she knew not desire.

"But," added Théophile, "I have my doubts about it. I believe she's a woman and subject to love, like everything else that has life and breath in the Universe. Besides, someone caught her one day kissing her hand to a strapping peasant fellow."

He offered to introduce his companion to her.

The two angels found her alone, reading. As they drew near she lifted her great eyes in whose deeps of molten gold little sparks of light were forever a-dance. Her brows were contracted into that austere fold which we see on the forehead of the Pythian Apollo; her nose was perfect and descended without a curve; her lips were compressed and imparted a disdainful and supercilious air to her whole countenance. Her tawny hair, with its gleaming lights, was carelessly adorned with the tattered remnants of a huge bird of prey, her garments lay about her in dark and shapeless folds. She was leaning her chin on a small ill-tended hand.

Arcade, who had but recently heard references made to this powerful archangel, showed her marked esteem, and placed entire confidence in her. He immediately proceeded to tell of the progress his mind had made towards knowledge and liberty, of his lucubrations in the d'Esparvieu library, of his philosophical reading, his studies of nature, his works on exegesis, his anger and his contempt when he recognised the deception of the demiurge, his voluntary exile among mankind, and, finally, of his project to stir up rebellion in Heaven. Ready to dare all against an odious master, whom he pursued with inextinguishable hatred, he expressed his profound happiness at finding in Ithuriel a mind capable of counselling and helping him in his great undertaking.

"You are not a very old hand at revolutions," said Zita, smiling.

Nevertheless, she doubted neither his sincerity nor the firmness of his declared resolve, and she congratulated him on his intellectual audacity.

"That is what is most lacking in our people," she said, "they do not think."

And she added almost immediately: "But on what can intelligence sharpen its wits, in a country where the climate is soft and existence made easy? Even here, where necessity calls for intellectual activity, nothing is rarer than a person who thinks."

"Nevertheless," replied Maurice's guardian angel, "man has created science. The important thing is to introduce it into Heaven. When the angels possess some notions of physics, chemistry, astronomy, and physiology; when the study of matter shows them worlds in an atom, and an atom in the myriads of planets; when they see themselves lost between these two infinities; when they weigh and measure the stars, analyse their composition, and calculate their orbits, they will recognise that these monsters work in obedience to forces which no intelligence can define, or that each star has its particular divinity, or indigenous god; and they will realise that the gods of Aldebaran, Betelgeuse, and Sirius are greater than Ialdabaoth. When at length they come to scrutinise with care the little world in which their lot is cast, and, piercing the crust of the earth, note the gradual evolution of its flora and fauna and the rude origin of man, who, under the shelter of rocks and in cave dwellings, had no God but himself; when they discover that, united by the bonds of universal kinship to plants, beasts, and men, they have successively indued all forms of organic life, from the simplest and the most primitive, until they became at length the most beautiful of the children of light, they will perceive that Ialdabaoth, the obscure demon of an insignificant world lost in space, is imposing on their credulity when he pretends that they issued from nothingness at his bidding; they will perceive that he lies in calling himself the Infinite, the Eternal, the Almighty, and that, so far from having created worlds, he knows neither their number nor their laws. They will perceive that he is like unto one of them; they will despise him, and, shaking off his tyranny, will fling him into the Gehenna where he has hurled those more worthy than himself."

"Do you think so?" murmured Zita, puffing out the smoke of her cigarette.... "Nevertheless, this knowledge by virtue of which you reckon to enfranchise Heaven, has not destroyed religious sentiment on earth. In countries where they have set up and taught this science of physics, of chemistry, astronomy, and geology, which you think capable of delivering the world, Christianity has retained almost all its sway. If the positive sciences have had such a feeble influence on the beliefs of mankind, it is not likely they will exercise a greater one on the opinions of the angels, and nothing is of such dubious efficacy as scientific propaganda."

"What!" exclaimed Arcade, "you deny that Science has given the Church its death-blow? Is it possible? The Church, at any rate, judges otherwise. Science, which you believe has no power over her, is redoubtable to her, since she proscribes it. From Galileo's dialogues to Monsieur Aulard's little manuals she has condemned all its discoveries. And not without reason.

"In former days, when she gathered within her fold all that was great in human thought, the Church held sway over the bodies as well as over the souls of men, and imposed unity of obedience by fire and sword. To-day her power is but a shadow and the elect among the great minds have withdrawn from her. That is the state to which Science has reduced her."

"Possibly," replied the beautiful archangel, "but how slowly, with what vicissitudes, at the price of what efforts, of what sacrifices!"

Zita did not absolutely condemn scientific propaganda, but she anticipated no prompt or certain results from it. For her it was not so much a question of enlightening the angels; the important thing was to enfranchise them. In her opinion one only exerted a strong influence on individuals, whoever they might be, by rousing their passions, and appealing to their interests.

"Persuade the angels that they will cover themselves with glory by overthrowing the tyrant, and that they will be happier once they are free; that is the most practical policy to attempt, and, for my own part, I am devoting all my energies to its fulfilment. It is certainly no light task, because the Kingdom of Heaven is a military autocracy and there is no public opinion in it. Nevertheless, I do not despair of starting an intellectual movement. I do not wish to boast, but no one is more closely acquainted than I with the different classes of angelic society."

Throwing away her cigarette, Zita pondered for a moment, then, amid the click of ivory balls on the billiard table, the clinking of glasses, the curt voices of the players announcing their points, the monotonous answers of the waiters to their customers, the Archangel enumerated the entire population of the spirits of light.

"We must not count on the Dominations, the Virtues, nor the Powers, which compose the celestial lower middle class. I have no need to tell you, for you know it as well as I, how selfish, base, and cowardly the middle classes are. As to the great dignitaries, the Ministers, the Generals, Thrones, Cherubim, and Seraphim, you know what they are; they will take no action. Let us, however, once prove ourselves the stronger, and we shall have them with us. For if autocrats do not readily acquiesce in their own downfall, once overthrown, all their forces recoil upon themselves. It will be well to work the Army. Entirely loyal as the Army is, it will allow itself to be influenced by a clever anarchist propaganda. But our greatest and most constant efforts ought to be brought to bear upon the angels of your own category, Arcade; the guardian angels, who dwell upon earth in such great numbers. They fill the lowest ranks of the hierarchy, are for the most part discontented with their lot, and more or less imbued with the ideas of the present century."

She had already conferred with the guardian angels of Montmartre, Clignancourt, and Filles-du-Calvaire. She had devised the plan of a vast association of Spirits on Earth with the view of conquering Heaven.

"To accomplish this task," she said, "I have established myself in France. But not because I had the folly to believe myself freer in a republic than in a monarchy. Quite the contrary, for there is no country where the liberty of the individual is less respected than in France. But the people are indifferent to everything connected with religion; nowhere else, therefore, should I enjoy such tranquillity."

She invited Arcade to unite his efforts to hers, and when they separated at the door of the *brasserie* the steel shutter was already making its groaning descent.

"Above all," said Zita, "you must meet the gardener. I will take you to his rustic home one day."

Théophile, who had slumbered during all this talk, begged his friend to come home with him and smoke a cigarette. He lived quite near in the small street opposite, leading off the Boulevard. Arcade would see Bouchotte, she would please him.

They climbed up five flights of stairs. Bouchotte had not yet returned. A tin of sardines lay open on the piano. Red stockings coiled about the arm-chairs.

"It's a little place, but it's comfortable," said Théophile.

And gazing out of the window which looked out on the russet-coloured night, with its myriad lights, he added, "One can see the *Sacré Cœur*." His hand on Arcade's shoulder, he repeated several times, "I am glad to see you."

Then, dragging his former companion in glory into the kitchen passage, he put down his candlestick, drew a key from his pocket, opened a cupboard, and, raising a linen covering, disclosed two large white wings.

"You see," he said, "I have preserved them. From time to time, when I am alone, I go and look at them; it does me good."

And he dabbed his reddened eyes. He stood awhile, overcome by silent emotion. Then, holding the candle near the long pinions which were moulting their down in places, he murmured, "They are eaten away."

"You must put some pepper on them," said Arcade.

"I have done so," replied the angelic musician, sighing. "I have put pepper, camphor, and powder on them. But nothing does any good."

CHAPTER XIV

WHICH REVEALS THE CHERUB TOILING FOR THE WELFARE OF HUMANITY AND CONCLUDES IN AN ENTIRELY NOVEL MANNER WITH THE MIRACLE OF THE FLUTE

THE first night of his incarnation Arcade slept at the angel Istar's, in a garret in that narrow, gloomy Rue Mazarine which wallows along beneath the shadow of the old Institute of France. Istar, who had been expecting him, had pushed against the wall the shattered retorts, cracked pots, broken bottles, and odds and ends of iron stoves, which made up the furniture of his room, and spread his clothes on the floor to lie on, leaving his guest his folding-bed with its straw mattress.

The celestial spirits differ from one another in appearance according to the hierarchy and the choir to which they belong, and according to their own particular nature. They are all beautiful; but in different fashion, and they do not all offer to the eye the soft contours and dimpling smiles of childhood with its rosy lights and pearly tints. Nor do they all adorn themselves with eternal youth, that indefinable beauty that Greek art in its decline has imparted to its most lovingly handled marbles, and whereof Christian painters have so often timidly essayed to give us veiled and softened imitations. In some of them the chin glows with tufts of hair, and the limbs are furnished with such vigorous muscles that it seems as if serpents were writhing beneath the skin. Some have no wings, others possess two, four, or six; others again are formed entirely of conjoined pinions. Many, and these not the least illustrious, take the form of superb monsters, such as the Centaurs of fable; nay, one may even see some who are living chariots, and wheels of fire. A member of the highest celestial hierarchy, Istar belonged to the choir of Cherubim or Kerûbs who see above them the Seraphim alone. In common with all the angelic spirits of his rank he had formerly borne in Heaven the bodily shape of a winged bull surmounted by the head of a horned and bearded man, and carrying between his loins the attributes of generous fecundity. He was vaster and more vigorous than any animal on earth, and when he stood erect with outspread wings he covered with his shadow sixty archangels.

Such was Istar in his native home. There he radiated strength and sweetness. His heart was full of courage and his soul benevolent. Moreover, in those days he loved his lord. He believed him to be good and yielded him faithful service. But even while guarding the portals of his

Master, he used to ponder unceasingly on the punishment of the rebellious angels and the curse of Eve. His mind worked slowly but profoundly. When, after a long course of centuries, he persuaded himself that Ialdabaoth in creating the world had created evil and death, he ceased to adore and to serve him. His love changed to hatred, his veneration to contempt. He shouted his execrations in his face, and fled to earth.

Embodied in human form and reduced to the stature of the sons of Adam, he still retained some characteristics of his former nature. His big protruding eyes, his beaked nose, his thick lips framed in a black beard which descended in curls on to his chest recalled those Cherubs of the tabernacle of Iahveh, of which the bulls of Nineveh afford us a pretty accurate representation. He bore the name of Istar on earth as well as in Heaven, and although exempt from vanity and free from all social prejudice, he was immensely desirous of showing himself sincere and truthful in all things. He therefore proclaimed the illustrious rank in which his birth had placed him in the celestial hierarchy and translated into French his title of Cherub by the equivalent one of Prince, calling himself Prince Istar. Seeking shelter among mankind he had developed an ardent love for them. While awaiting the coming of the hour when he should deliver Heaven from bondage, he dreamed of the salvation of regenerate humanity and was eager to consummate the destruction of this wicked world, in order to raise upon its ashes, to the sound of the lyre, a city radiant with happiness and love. A chemist in the pay of a dealer in nitrates, he lived very frugally. He wrote for newspapers with advanced views on liberty, spoke at public meetings, and had got himself sentenced several times to several months' imprisonment for anti-militarism.

Istar greeted his brother Arcade cordially, approved of his rupture with the party of crime, and informed him of the descent of fifty of the children of light who, at the present moment, formed a colony near Val de Grace, imbued with a really excellent spirit.

"It is simply raining angels in Paris," he said, laughing. "Every day some dignitary of the sacred palace falls on one's head, and soon the Sultan of the Cherubs will have no one to make into Vizirs or guards but the little unbreeched vagabonds of his pigeon coops."

Soothed by the good news, Arcade fell asleep, full of happiness and hope.

He awoke in the early dawn and saw Prince Istar bending over his furnaces, his retorts, and his test tubes. Prince Istar was working for the good of humanity.

Every morning when Arcade woke he saw Prince Istar fulfilling his work of tenderness and love. Sometimes the Kerûb, huddled up with his head in his hands, would softly murmur a few chemical formulæ; at others, drawing himself up to his full height, like a dark naked column, with his head, his arms, nay, his entire bust clean out of the sky-light window, he would deposit his melting-pot on the roof, fearing the perquisition with which he was constantly menaced. Moved by an immense pity for the miseries of the world wherein he dwelt in exile, conscious perhaps of the rumours to which his name gave rise, inebriated with his own virtue, he played the part of apostle to the Human Race, and neglecting the task he had undertaken in coming to earth, he forgot all about the emancipation of the angels. Arcade, who, on the contrary, dreamed of nothing else but of conquering Heaven and returning thither in triumph, reproached the Cherub with forgetting his native land.

Prince Istar, with a great frank, uncouth laugh, acknowledged that he had no preference for angels over men.

"If I am doing my best," he replied to his celestial brother, "if I am doing my best to stir up France and Europe, it is because the day is dawning which will behold the triumph of the social revolution. It is a pleasure to cast one's seed on ground so well prepared. The French having

56

passed from feudalism to monarchy, and from monarchy to a financial oligarchy, will easily pass from a financial oligarchy to anarchy."

"How erroneous it is," retorted Arcade, "to believe in great and sudden changes in the social order in Europe! The old order is still young in strength and power. The means of defence at her disposal are formidable. On the other hand, the proletariat's plan of defensive organisation is of the vaguest description and brings merely weakness and confusion to the struggle. In our celestial country all goes quite otherwise. Beneath an apparently unchangeable exterior all is rotten within. A mere push would suffice to overturn an edifice which has not been touched for millions of centuries. Out-worn administration, out-worn army, out-worn finance, the whole thing is more worm-eaten than either the Russian or Persian autocracy."

And the kindly Arcade adjured the Cherub to fly first to the aid of his brethren who, though dwelling amid the soft clouds with the sound of citterns and their cups of paradisal wine around them, were in more wretched plight than mankind bowed over the grudging earth. For the latter have a conception of justice, while the angels rejoice in iniquity. He exhorted him to deliver the Prince of Light and his stricken companions and to re-establish them in their ancient honours.

Prince Istar allowed himself to be convinced.

He promised to put the sweet persuasiveness of his words and the excellent formulæ of his explosives at the service of the celestial revolution. He gave his promise.

"To-morrow," he said.

And when the morrow came he continued his anti-militarist propaganda at Issy-les-Moulineaux. Like the Titan Prometheus, Istar loved mankind.

Arcade, suffering from all the desires to which the sons of Adam are subjected, found himself lacking in resources to satisfy them. Istar gave him a start in a printing house in the Rue de Vaugirard where he knew the foreman. Arcade, thanks to his celestial intelligence, soon knew how to set up type and became, in a short time, a good compositor.

After standing all day in the whirring workroom, holding the composing-stick in his left hand, and swiftly drawing the little leaden signs from the case in the order required by the copy fixed in the *visorium*, he would go and wash his hands at the pump and dine at the corner bar, a newspaper propped up before him on the marble table. Being now no longer invisible, he could not make his way into the d'Esparvieu library, and was thus debarred from allaying his ardent thirst for knowledge at that inexhaustible source. He went, of an evening, to read at the library of Ste. Geneviève on the famous hill of learning, but there were only ordinary books to be had there; greasy things, covered with ridiculous annotations, and lacking many pages.

The sight of women troubled and unsettled him. He would remember Madame des Aubels and her charm, and, although he was handsome, he was not loved, because of his poverty and his workaday clothes. He saw much of Zita, and took a certain pleasure in going for walks with her on Sundays along the dusty roads which edge the grass-grown trenches of the fortifications. They wandered, the pair of them, by wayside inns, market-gardens, and green retreats, propounding and discussing the vastest plans that ever stirred the world, and, occasionally, as they passed along by some travelling circus, the steam organ of the merry-go-round would furnish an accompaniment to their words as they breathed fire and fury against Heaven.

Zita used often to say:

"Istar means well, but he's a simple fellow. He believes in the goodness of men and things. He undertakes the destruction of the old world and imagines that anarchy of itself will create order and harmony. You, Arcade, you believe in Science; you deem that men and angels are capable of understanding, whereas, in point of fact, they are only creatures of sentiment. You may be quite sure thatnothing is to be obtained from them by appealing to their intelligence; one must rouse their interests and their passions."

Arcade, Istar, Zita, and three or four other angelic conspirators occasionally foregathered in Théophile Belais' little flat, where Bouchotte gave them tea. Though she did not know that they were rebellious angels, she hated them instinctively, and feared them, for she had had a Christian education, albeit she had sadly failed to keep it up.

Prince Istar alone pleased her; she thought there was something kind-hearted and an air of natural distinction about him. He stove in the sofa, broke down the arm-chairs, and tore corners off sheets of music to make notes, which he thrust into pockets invariably crammed with pamphlets and bottles. The musician used to gaze sorrowfully at the manuscript of his operetta, *Aline, Queen of Golconda*, with its corners all torn off. The prince also had a habit of giving Théophile Belais all sorts of things to take care of—mechanical contrivances, chemicals, bits of old iron, powders, and liquids which gave off noisome smells. Théophile Belais put them cautiously away in the cupboard where he kept his wings, and the responsibility weighed heavily upon him.

Arcade was much pained at the disdain of those of his fellows who had remained faithful. When they met him as they went on their sacred errands they regarded him as they passed by with looks of cruel hatred or of pity that was crueller still.

He used to visit the rebel angels whom Prince Istar pointed out to him, and usually met with a good reception, but as soon as he began to speak of conquering Heaven, they did not conceal the embarrassment and displeasure he caused them. Arcade perceived that they had no desire to be disturbed in their tastes, their affairs, and their habits. The falsity of their judgment, the narrowness of their minds, shocked him; and the rivalry, the jealousy they displayed towards one another deprived him of all hope of uniting them in a common cause. Perceiving how exile debases the character and warps the intellect, he felt his courage fail him.

One evening, when he had confessed his weariness of spirit to Zita, the beautiful archangel said:

"Let us go and see Nectaire; Nectaire has remedies of his own for sadness and fatigue."

She led him into the woods of Montmorency and stopped at the threshold of a small white house, adjoining a kitchen garden, laid waste by winter, where far back in the shadows the light shone on forcing-frames and cracked glass melon shades.

Nectaire opened the door to his visitors, and, after quieting the growls of a big mastiff which protected the garden, led them into a low room warmed by an earthenware stove.

Against the whitewashed wall, on a deal board, among the onions and seeds, lay a flute ready to be put to the lips. A round walnut table bore a stone tobacco-jar, a pipe, a bottle of wine and some glasses. The gardener offered each of his guests a cane-seated chair, and himself sat down on a stool by the table.

He was a sturdy old man; thick grey hair stood up on his head, he had a furrowed brow, a snub-nose, a red face, and a forked beard.

The big mastiff stretched himself at his master's feet, rested his short black muzzle on his paws, and closed his eyes. The gardener poured out some wine for his guests, and when they had drunk and talked a little, Zita said to Nectaire:

"Please play your flute to us, you will give pleasure to my friend whom I have brought to see you."

The old man immediately consented. He put the boxwood pipe to his lips,—so clumsy was it that it looked as if the gardener had fashioned it himself,—and preluded with a few strange runs. Then he developed rich melodies in which the thrills sparkled like diamonds and pearls on a velvet ground. Touched by cunning fingers, animated with creative breath, the rustic pipe sang like a silver flute. There were no over-shrill notes and the tone was always even and pure. One seemed to be listening to the nightingale and the Muses singing together, the soul of Nature and the soul of Man. And the old man ordered and developed his thoughts in a musical language full of grace and daring. He told of love, of fear, of vain quarrels, of all-conquering laughter, of the calm light of the intellect, of the arrows of the mind piercing with their golden shafts the monsters of Ignorance and Hate. He told also of Joy and Sorrow bending their twin heads over the earth and of Desire which brings worlds into being.

The whole night listened to the flute of Nectaire. Already the evening star was rising above the paling horizon.

There they sat; Zita with hands clasped about her knees, Arcade, his head leaning on his hand, his lips apart. Motionless they listened. A lark, which had awakened hard by in a sandy field, lured by these novel sounds, rose swiftly in the air, hovered a few seconds, then dropped at one swoop into the musician's orchard. The neighbouring sparrows, forsaking the crannies of the mouldering walls, came and sat in a row on the window-ledge whence notes came welling forth that gave them more delight than oats or grains of barley. A jay, coming for the first time out of his wood, folded his sapphire wings on a leafless cherry tree. Beside the drain-head, a large black rat, glistening with the greasy water of the sewers, sitting on his hind legs, raised his short arms and slender fingers in amazement. A field-mouse, that dwelt in the orchard, was seated near him. Down from the tiles came the old tom-cat, who retained the grey fur, the ringed tail, the powerful loins, the courage, and the pride of his ancestors. He pushed against the half-open door with his nose and approaching the flute-player with silent tread, sat gravely down, pricking his ears that had been torn in many a nocturnal combat; the grocer's white cat followed him, sniffing the vibrant air and then, arching her back and closing her blue eyes, listened in ravishment. Mice, swarming in crowds from under the boards, surrounded them, and fearing neither tooth nor claw, sat motionless, their pink hands folded voluptuously on their bosoms. Spiders that had strayed far from their webs, with waving legs, gathered in a charmed circle on the ceiling. A small grey lizard, that had glided on to the doorstep, stayed there, fascinated, and, in the loft, the bat might have been seen hanging by her nails, head down, now half-awakened from her winter sleep, swaying to the rhythm of the marvellous flute.

CHAPTER XV

WHEREIN WE SEE YOUNG MAURICE BEWAILING THE LOSS OF HIS GUARDIAN ANGEL, EVEN IN HIS MISTRESS'S ARMS, AND WHEREIN WE HEAR THE ABBÉ PATOUILLE REJECT AS VAIN AND ILLUSORY ALL NOTIONS OF A NEW REBELLION OF THE ANGELS

A FORTNIGHT had elapsed since the angel's apparition in the flat. For the first time Gilberte arrived before Maurice at the rendezvous. Maurice was gloomy, Gilberte sulky. So far as they were concerned Nature had resumed her drab monotony. They eyed each other languidly, and kept glancing towards the angle between the wardrobe with the mirror and the window, where recently the pale shade of Arcade had taken shape, and where now the blue cretonne of the hangings was the only thing visible. Without giving him a name (it was unnecessary) Madame des Aubels asked:

"You have not seen him since?"

Slowly, sadly, Maurice turned his head from right to left, and from left to right.

"You look as if you missed him," continued Madame des Aubels. "But come, confess that he gave you a terrible fright, and that you were shocked at his unconventionally."

"Certainly he was unconventional," said Maurice without any resentment.

"Tell me, Maurice, is it nothing to you now to be with me alone?... You need an angel to inspire you. That is sad, for a young man like you!"

Maurice appeared not to hear, and asked gravely:

"Gilberte, do you feel that your guardian angel is watching over you?"

"I, not at all. I have never thought of him, and yet I am not without religion. In the first place, people who have none are like animals. And then one cannot go straight without religion. It is impossible."

"Exactly, that's just it," said Maurice, his eyes on the violet stripes of his flowerless pyjamas; "when one has one's guardian angel one does not even think about him, and when one has lost him one feels very lonely."

"So you miss this...."

"Well, the fact is...."

"Oh, yes, yes, you miss him. Well, my dear, the loss of such a guardian angel as that is no great matter. No, no! he is not worth much, that Arcade of yours. On that famous day, while you were out getting him some clothes, he was ever so long fastening my dress, and I certainly felt his hand.... Well, at any rate, don't trust him."

Maurice dreamily lit a cigarette. They spoke of the six days' bicycle race at the winter velodrome, and of the aviation show at the motor exhibition at Brussels, without experiencing the slightest amusement. Then they tried love-making as a sort of convenient pastime, and succeeded in becoming moderately absorbed in it; but at the very moment when she might have been expected to play a part more in accordance with a mutual sentiment, she exclaimed with a sudden start:

"Good Heavens! Maurice, how stupid of you to tell me that my guardian angel can see me. You cannot imagine how uncomfortable the idea makes me."

Maurice, somewhat taken aback, recalled, a little roughly, his mistress's wandering thoughts.

She declared that her principles forbade her to think of playing a round game with angels.

Maurice was longing to see Arcade again and had no other thought. He reproached himself for suffering him to depart without discovering where he was going, and he cudgelled his brains night and day thinking how to find him again.

On the bare chance, he put a notice in the personal column of one of the big papers, running thus:

"Arcade. Come back to your Maurice."

Day after day went by, and Arcade did not return.

One morning, at seven o'clock, Maurice went to St. Sulpice to hear Abbé Patouille say Mass, then, as the priest was leaving the sacristy, he went up to him and asked to be heard for a moment.

They descended the steps of the church together and in the bright morning light walked round the fountain of the *Quatre Évêques*. In spite of his troubled conscience and the difficulty of presenting so extraordinary a case with any degree of credibility, Maurice related how the angel Arcade had appeared to him and had announced his unhappy resolve to separate from him and to stir up a new revolt of the spirits of glory. And young d'Esparvieu asked the worthy ecclesiastic how to find his celestial guardian again, since he could not bear his absence, and how to lead his angel back to the Christian faith. Abbé Patouille replied in a tone of affectionate sorrow that his dear child had been dreaming, that he took a morbid hallucination for reality, and that it was not permissible to believe that good angels may revolt.

"People have a notion," he added, "that they can lead a life of dissipation and disorder with impunity. They are wrong. The abuse of pleasure corrupts the intelligence and impairs the understanding. The devil takes possession of the sinner's senses, penetrating even to his soul. He has deceived you, Maurice, by a clumsy artifice."

Maurice objected that he was not in any way a victim of hallucinations, that he had not been dreaming, that he had seen his guardian angel with his eyes and heard him with his ears.

"Monsieur l'Abbé," he insisted, "a lady who happened to be with me at the time,—I need not mention her name,—also saw and heard him. And, moreover, she felt the angel's fingers straying ... well, anyhow, she felt them.... Believe me, Monsieur l'Abbé, nothing could be more real, more positively certain than this apparition. The angel was fair, young, very handsome. His clear skin seemed, in the shadow, as if bathed in milky light. He spoke in a pure, sweet voice."

"That, alone, my child," the Abbé interrupted quickly, "proves you were dreaming. According to all the demonologies, bad angels have a hoarse voice, which grates like a rusty lock, and even if they did contrive to give a certain look of beauty to their faces, they cannot succeed in imitating the pure voice of the good spirits. This fact, attested by numerous witnesses, is established beyond all doubt."

"But, Monsieur l'Abbé, I saw him. I saw him sit down, stark naked, in an arm-chair on a pair of black stockings. What else do you want me to tell you?"

The Abbé Patouille appeared in no way disturbed by this announcement.

"I say once more, my son," he replied, "that these unhappy illusions, these dreams of a deeply troubled soul, are to be ascribed to the deplorable state of your conscience. I believe, moreover, that I can detect the particular circumstance that has caused your unstable mind thus to come to grief. During the winter in company with Monsieur Sariette and your Uncle Gaétan, you came, in an evil frame of mind, to see the Chapel of the Holy Angels in this church, then undergoing repair. As I observed on that occasion, it is impossible to keep artists too closely to the rules of Christian art; they cannot be too strongly enjoined to respect Holy Writ and its authorized interpreters. Monsieur Eugène Delacroix did not suffer his fiery genius to be controlled by tradition. He brooked no guidance and, here, in this chapel he has painted pictures which in common parlance we call lurid, compositions of a violent, terrible nature which, far from inspiring the soul with peace, quietude, and calm, plunge it into a state of agitation. In them the angels are depicted with wrathful countenances, their features are sombre and uncouth. One might take them to be Lucifer and his companions meditating their revolt. Well, my son, it was these pictures, acting upon a mind already weakened and undermined by every kind of dissipation, that have filled it with the trouble to which it is at present a prey."

61

But Maurice would have none of it.

"Oh, no! Monsieur l'Abbé," he cried, "it is not Eugène Delacroix's pictures that have been troubling me. I didn't so much as look at them. I am completely indifferent to that kind of art."

"Well, then, my son, believe me: there is no truth, no reality, in any of the story you have just related to me. Your guardian angel has certainly not appeared to you."

"But, Abbé," replied Maurice, who had the most absolute confidence in the evidence of the senses, "I saw him tying up a woman's shoe-laces and putting on the trousers of a suicide."

And stamping his feet on the asphalt, Maurice called as witnesses to the truth of his words the sky, the earth, all nature, the towers of St. Sulpice, the walls of the great seminary, the Fountain of the *Quatre Évêques*, the public lavatory, the cabmen's shelter, the taxis and motor 'buses' shelter, the trees, the passers-by, the dogs, the sparrows, the flower-seller and her flowers.

The Abbé made haste to end the interview.

"All this is error, falsehood, and illusion, my child," said he. "You are a Christian: think as a Christian,—a Christian does not allow himself to be seduced by empty shadows. Faith protects him against the seduction of the marvellous, he leaves credulity to freethinkers. There are credulous people for you—freethinkers! There is no humbug they will not swallow. But the Christian carries a weapon which dissipates diabolical illusions,—the sign of the Cross. Reassure yourself, Maurice,—you have not lost your guardian angel. He still watches over you. It lies with you not to make this task too difficult nor too painful for him. Good-bye, Maurice. The weather is going to change, for I feel a burning in my big toe."

And Abbé Patouille went off with his breviary under his arm, hobbling along with a dignity that seemed to foretell a mitre.

That very day, Arcade and Zita were leaning over the parapet of La Butte, gazing down on the mist and smoke that lay floating over the vast city.

"Is it possible," said Arcade, "for the mind to conceive all the pain and suffering that lie pent within a great city? It is my belief that if a man succeeded in realising it, the weight of it would crush him to the earth."

"And yet," answered Zita, "every living being in that place of torment is enamoured of life. It is a great enigma!

"Unhappy, ill-fated, while they live, the idea of ceasing to be is, nevertheless, a horror to them. They look not for solace in annihilation, it does not even bring them the promise of rest. In their madness they even look upon nothingness with terror: they have peopled it with phantoms. Look you at these pediments, these towers and domes and spires that pierce the mist and rear on high their glittering crosses. Men bow in adoration before the demiurge who has given them a life that is worse than death, and a death that is worse than life."

Zita was for a long time lost in thought. At length she broke silence, saying:

"There is something, Arcade, that I must confess to you. It was no desire for a purer justice or wiser laws that hurried Ithuriel earthward. Ambition, a taste for intrigue, the love of wealth and honour, all these things made Heaven, with its calm, unbearable to me, and I longed to mingle with the restless race of men. I came, and by an art unknown to nearly all the angels, I learned how to fashion myself a body which, since I could change it as the fancy seized me, to

62

whatsoever age and sex I would, has permitted me to experience the most diverse and amazing of human destinies. A hundred times I took a position of renown among the leaders of the day, the lords of wealth and princes of nations. I will not reveal to you, Arcade, the famous names I bore; know only that I was pre-eminent in learning, in the fine arts, in power, wealth, and beauty, among all the nations of the world. At last, it was but a few years since, as I was journeying in France, under the outward semblance of a distinguished foreigner, I chanced to be roaming at evening through the forest of Montmorency, when I heard a flute unfolding all the sorrows of Heaven. The purity and sadness of its notes rent my very soul. Never before had I hearkened to aught so lovely. My eyes were wet with tears, my bosom full of sobs, as I drew near and beheld, on the skirts of a glade, an old man like to a faun, blowing on a rustic pipe. It was Nectaire. I cast myself at his feet, imprinted kisses on his hands and on his lips divine, and fled away....

"From that day forth, conscious of the littleness of human achievements, weary of the tumult and the vanity of earthly things, ashamed of my vast and profitless endeavours, and deciding to seek out a loftier aim for my ambition, I looked upwards towards my skiey home and vowed I would return to it as a Deliverer. I rid myself of titles, name, wealth, friends, the horde of sycophants and flatterers and, as Zita the obscure, set to work in indigence and solitude, to bring freedom into Heaven."

"And I," said Arcade, "I too have heard the flute of Nectaire. But who is this old gardener who can thus woo from a rude wooden pipe notes that are so moving and so beautiful?"

"You will soon know," answered Zita.

CHAPTER XVI

WHEREIN MIRA THE SEERESS, ZÉPHYRINE, AND THE FATAL AMÉDÉE ARE SUCCESSIVELY BROUGHT UPON THE SCENE, AND WHEREIN THE NOTION OF EURIPIDES THAT THOSE WHOM ZEUS WISHES TO CRUSH HE FIRST MAKES MAD, IS ILLUSTRATED BY THE TERRIBLE EXAMPLE OF MONSIEUR SARIETTE

DISAPPOINTED at his failure to enlighten an ecclesiastic renowned for his clarity of mind, and frustrated in the hope of finding his angel again on the high road of orthodoxy, Maurice took it into his head to resort to occultism and resolved to go and consult a seer. He would have undoubtedly applied to Madame de Thèbes, but he had already questioned her on the occasion of his early love troubles, and her replies showed such wisdom that he no longer believed her to be a soothsayer. He therefore had recourse to a fashionable medium, Madame Mira. He had heard many examples quoted of the extraordinary insight of this seeress, but it was necessary to present Madame Mira with some object which the absent one had either touched or worn and to which her translucent gaze had to be attracted. Maurice, trying to remember what the angel had touched since his ill-fated incarnation, recollected that in his celestial nudity he had sat down in an arm-chair on Madame des Aubels' black stockings and that he had afterwards helped that lady to dress.

Maurice asked Gilberte for one of the talismans required by the clairvoyante. But Gilberte could not give him a single one, unless, as she said, she herself were to play the part of the talisman. For the angel had, in her case, displayed the greatest indiscretion, and such agility that it was impossible always to forestall his enterprise. On hearing this confession, which nevertheless told him nothing new, Maurice lost his temper with the angel, calling him by the names of the lowest animals and swearing he would give him a good kick when he got him within reach of his foot. But his fury soon turned against Madame des Aubels; he accused her of having provoked the insolence she now denounced, and in his wrath he referred to her by all the

63

zoological symbols of immodesty and perversity. His love for Arcade was rekindled in his heart, and burned with a more ardent flame than ever, and the deserted youth, with outstretched arms and bended knees, invoked his angel with sobs and lamentations.

During his sleepless nights it occurred to him that perhaps the books the angel had turned over before his incarnation might serve as a talisman. One morning, therefore, Maurice went up to the library and greeted Monsieur Sariette, who was cataloguing under the romantic gaze of Alexandre d'Esparvieu. Monsieur Sariette smiled, but his face was deathly pale. Now that an invisible hand no longer upset the books placed under his charge, now that tranquillity and order once more reigned in the library, Monsieur Sariette was happy, but his strength diminished day by day. There was little left of him but a frail and contented shadow.

"One dies, in full content, of sorrow past."

"Monsieur Sariette," said Maurice, "you remember that time when your books were disarranged every night, how armfuls disappeared, how they were dragged about, turned over, ruined, and sent rolling helter-skelter as far as the gutter in the Rue Palatine. Those were great days! Point out to me, Monsieur Sariette, the books which suffered most."

This proposition threw Monsieur Sariette into a melancholy stupor, and Maurice had to repeat his request three times before he could make the aged librarian understand. At length he pointed to a very ancient Talmud from Jerusalem as having been frequently touched by those unseen hands. An apocryphal Gospel of the third century, consisting of twenty papyrus sheets, had also quitted its place time after time. Gassendi's Correspondence too seemed to have been well thumbed.

"But," added Monsieur Sariette, "the book to which the mysterious visitant devoted the most particular attention was undoubtedly a little copy of *Lucretius* adorned with the arms of Philippe de Vendôme, Grand Prieur de France, with autograph annotations by Voltaire, who, as is well known, frequently visited the Temple in his younger days. The fearsome reader who caused me such terrible anxiety never grew weary of this *Lucretius* and made it his bedside book, as it were. His taste was sound, for it's a gem of a thing. Alas! the monster made a blot of ink on page 137 which perhaps the chemists with all the science at their disposal will be powerless to erase."

And Monsieur Sariette heaved a profound sigh. He repented having said all this when young d'Esparvieu asked him for the loan of the precious *Lucretius*. Vainly did the jealous custodian affirm that the book was being repaired at the binder's and was not available. Maurice made it clear that he wasn't to be taken in like that. He strode resolutely into the abode of the philosophers and the globes and seating himself in an arm-chair said:

"I am waiting."

Monsieur Sariette suggested his having another edition. There were some that, textually, were more correct, and were, therefore, preferable from the student's point of view. He offered him Barbou's edition, or Coustelier's, or, better still, a French translation. He could have the Baron des Coutures' version—which was perhaps a little old-fashioned—or La Grange's, or those in the Nisard and Panckouke series; or, again, there were two versions of striking elegance, one in verse and the other in prose, both from the pen of Monsieur de Pongerville of the French Academy.

"I don't need a translation," said Maurice proudly. "Give me the Prior de Vendôme's copy."

Monsieur Sariette went slowly up to the cupboard in which the jewel in question was contained. The keys were rattling in his trembling hand. He raised them to the lock and withdrew them again immediately and suggested that Maurice should have the common *Lucretius* published by Garnier.

"It's very handy," said he with an engaging smile.

But the silence with which this proposal was received made it clear that resistance was useless. He slowly drew forth the volume from its place, and having taken the precaution to see that there wasn't a speck of dust on the table-cloth, he laid it tremblingly thereon before the great-grandson of Alexandre d'Esparvieu.

Maurice began to turn the leaves, and when he got to page 137 he saw the stain which had been made with violet ink. It was about the size of a pea.

"Ay, that's it," said old Sariette, who had his eye on the *Lucretius* the whole time; "that's the trace those invisible monsters left behind them."

"What, there were several of them, Monsieur Sariette?" exclaimed Maurice.

"I cannot tell. But I don't know whether I have a right to have this blot removed since, like the blot Paul Louis Courier made on the Florentine manuscript, it constitutes a literary document, so to speak."

Scarcely were the words out of the old fellow's mouth when the front door bell rang and there was a confused noise of voices and footsteps in the next room. Sariette ran forward at the sound and collided with Père Guinardon's mistress, old Zéphyrine, who, with her tousled hair sticking up like a nest of vipers, her face aflame, her bosom heaving, her abdominal part like an eiderdown quilt puffed out by a terrific gale, was choking with grief and rage. And amid sobs and sighs and groans and all the innumerable sounds which, on earth, make up the mighty uproar to which the emotions of living beings and the tumult of nature give rise, she cried:

"He's gone, the monster! He's gone off with her. He's cleared out the whole shanty and left me to shift for myself with eighteenpence in my purse."

And she proceeded to give a long and incoherent account of how Michel Guinardon had abandoned her and gone to live with Octavie, the bread-woman's daughter, and she let loose a torrent of abuse against the traitor.

"A man whom I've kept going with my own money for fifty years and more. For I've had plenty of the needful and known plenty of the upper ten and all. I dragged him out of the gutter and now this is what I get for it. He's a bright beauty, that friend of yours. The lazy scoundrel. Why, he had to be dressed like a child, the drunken contemptible brute. You don't know him yet, Monsieur Sariette. He's a forger. He turns out Giottos, Giottos, I tell you, and Fra Angelicos and Grecos, as hard as he can and sells them to art-dealers—yes, and Fragonards too, and Baudouins. He's a debauchee, and doesn't believe in God! That's the worst of the lot, Monsieur Sariette, for without the fear of God...."

Long did Zéphyrine continue to pour forth vituperations. When at last her breath failed her, Monsieur Sariette availed himself of the opportunity to exhort her to be calm and bring herself to look on the bright side of things. Guinardon would come back. A man doesn't forget anyone he's lived and got on well with for fifty years——

These two observations only goaded her to a fresh outburst, and Zéphyrine swore she would never forget the slight that had been put on her; she swore she would never have the monster back with her any more. And if he came to ask her to forgive him on his knees, she would let him grovel at her feet.

"Don't you understand, Monsieur Sariette, that I despise and hate him, that he makes me sick?"

Sixty times she voiced these lofty sentiments; sixty times she vowed she would never have Guinardon back with her again, that she couldn't bear the sight of him, even in a picture.

Monsieur Sariette made no attempt to oppose a resolve which, after protestations such as these, he regarded as unshakable. He did not blame Zéphyrine in the least. He even supported her. Unfolding to the deserted one a purer future, he told her of the frailty of human sentiment, exhorted her to display a spirit of renunciation and enjoined her to show a pious resignation to the will of God.

"Seeing, in truth, that your friend is so little worthy of affection ..."

He was not suffered to continue. Zéphyrine flew at him, and shaking him furiously by the collar of his frock-coat, she yelled, half choking with rage: "So little worthy of affection! Michel! Ah! my boy, you find another more kind, more gay, more witty, you find another like him, always young, yes, always. Not worthy of affection! Anyone can see you don't know anything about love, you old duffer."

Taking advantage of the fact that Père Sariette was thus deeply engaged, young d'Esparvieu slipped the little *Lucretius* into his pocket, and strolled deliberately past the crouching librarian, bidding him adieu with a little wave of the hand.

Armed with his talisman, he hastened to the Place des Ternes, to interview Madame Mira. She received him in a red drawing-room where neither owl nor frog nor any of the paraphernalia of ancient magic were to be found. Madame Mira, in a prune-coloured dress, her hair powdered, though already past her prime, was of very good appearance. She spoke with a certain elegance and prided herself on discovering hidden things by the help alone of Science, Philosophy, and Religion. She felt the morocco binding, feigning to close her eyes, and looking meanwhile through the narrow slit between her lids at the Latin title and the coat of arms which conveyed nothing to her.

Accustomed to receive as tokens such things as rings, handkerchiefs, letters, and locks of hair, she could not conceive to what sort of individual this singular book could belong. By habitual and mechanical cunning she disguised her real surprise under a feigned surprise.

"Strange!" she murmured, "strange! I do not see quite clearly ... I perceive a woman...."

As she let fall this magic word, she glanced furtively to see what sort of an effect it had and beheld on her questioner's face an unexpected look of disappointment. Perceiving that she was off the track, she immediately changed her oracle:

"But she fades away immediately. It is strange, strange! I have a confused impression of some vague form, a being that I cannot define," and having assured herself by a hurried glance that, this time, her words were going down, she expatiated on the vagueness of the person and on the mist that enveloped him.

However, the vision grew clearer to Madame Mira, who was following a clue step by step.

"A wide street ... a square with a statue ... a deserted street,—stairs. He is there in a bluish room—he is a young man, with pale and careworn face. There are things he seems to regret, and which he would not do again did they still remain undone."

But the effort at divination had been too great. Fatigue prevented the clairvoyante from continuing her transcendental researches. She spent her remaining strength in impressively recommending him who consulted her to remain in intimate union with God if he wished to regain what he had lost and succeed in his attempts.

On leaving Maurice placed a louis on the mantelpiece and went away moved and troubled, persuaded that Madame Mira possessed supernatural faculties, but unfortunately insufficient ones.

At the bottom of the stairs he remembered he had left the little *Lucretius* on the table of the pythoness, and, thinking that the old maniac Sariette would never get over its loss, went up to recover possession of it.

On re-entering the paternal abode his gaze lighted upon a shadowy and grief-stricken figure. It was old Sariette, who in tones as plaintive as the wail of the November wind began to beg for his *Lucretius*. Maurice pulled it carelessly out of his great-coat pocket.

"Don't flurry yourself, Monsieur Sariette," said he. "There the thing is."

Clasping the jewel to his bosom the old librarian bore it away and laid it gently down on the blue table-cloth, thinking all the while where he might safely hide his precious treasure, and turning over all sorts of schemes in his mind as became a zealous curator. But who among us shall boast of his wisdom? The foresight of man is short, and his prudence is for ever being baffled. The blows of fate are ineluctable; no man shall evade his doom. There is no counsel, no caution that avails against destiny. Hapless as we are, the same blind force which regulates the courses of atom and of star fashions universal order from our vicissitudes. Our ill-fortune is necessary to the harmony of the Universe. It was the day for the binder, a day which the revolving seasons brought round twice a year, beneath the sign of the Ram and the sign of the Scales. That day, ever since morning, Monsieur Sariette had been making things ready for the binder. He had laid out on the table as many of the newly purchased paper-bound volumes as were deemed worthy of a permanent binding or of being put in boards, and also those books whose binding was in need of repair, and of all these he had drawn up a detailed and accurate list. Punctually at five o'clock, old Amédée, the man from Léger-Massieu's, the binder in the Rue de l'Abbaye, presented himself at the d'Esparvieu library and, after a double check had been carried out by Monsieur Sariette, thrust the books he was to take back to his master into a piece of cloth which he fastened into knots at the four corners and hoisted on to his shoulder. He then saluted the librarian with the following words, "Good night, all!" and went downstairs.

Everything went off on this occasion as usual. But Amédée, seeing the *Lucretius* on the table, innocently put it into the bag with the others, and took it away without Monsieur Sariette's perceiving it. The librarian quitted the home of the Philosophers and Globes in entire forgetfulness of the book whose absence had been causing him such horrible anxiety all day long. Some people may take a stern view of the matter and call this a lapse, a defection of his better nature. But would it not be more accurate to say that fate had decided that things should come to pass in this manner, and that what is called chance, and is in fact but the regular order of nature, had accomplished this imperceptible deed which was to have such awful consequences in the sight of man? Monsieur Sariette went off to his dinner at the *Quatre Évêques*, and read his paper *La Croix*. He was tranquil and serene. It was only the next morning when he entered the abode of the Philosophers and Globes that he remembered the *Lucretius*. Failing to see it on the table he looked for it everywhere, but without success. It never entered his head that Amédée might have taken it away by mistake. What he did think was that the invisible visitant had returned, and he was mightily disturbed.

The unhappy curator, hearing a noise on the landing, opened the door and found it was little Léon, who, with a gold-braided *képi*stuck on his head, was shouting "Vive la France" and hurling dusters and feather-brooms and Hippolyte's floor polish at imaginary foes. The child preferred this landing for playing soldiers to any other part of the house, and sometimes he would stray into the library. Monsieur Sariette was seized with the sudden suspicion that it was he who had taken the *Lucretius* to use as a missile and he ordered him, in threatening tones, to give it back. The child denied that he had taken it, and Monsieur Sariette had recourse to cajolery.

"Léon, if you bring me back the little red book, I will give you some chocolates."

The child grew thoughtful; and in the evening, as Monsieur Sariette was going downstairs, he met Léon, who said:

"There's the book!"

And, holding out a much-torn picture-book called *The Story of Gribouille*, demanded his chocolates.

A few days later the post brought Maurice the prospectus of an enquiry agency managed by an ex-employee at the Prefecture of Police; it promised celerity and discretion. He found at the address indicated a moustached gentleman morose and careworn, who demanded a deposit and promised to find the individual.

The ex-police official soon wrote to inform him that very onerous investigations had been commenced and asked for fresh funds. Maurice gave him no more and resolved to carry on the search himself. Imagining, not without some likelihood, that the angel would associate with the wretched, seeing that he had no money, and with the exiled of all nations—like himself, revolutionaries—he visited the lodging-houses at St. Ouen, at la Chapelle, Montmartre, and the Barrière d'Italie. He sought him in the doss-houses, public-houses where they give you plates of tripe, and others where you can get a sausage for three sous; he searched for him in the cellars at the Market and at Père Momie's.

Maurice visited the restaurants where nihilists and anarchists take their meals. There he came across men dressed as women, gloomy and wild-looking youths, and blue-eyed octogenarians who laughed like little children. He observed, asked questions, was taken for a spy, had a knife thrust into him by a very beautiful woman, and the very next day continued his search in beer-houses, lodging-houses, houses of ill-fame, gambling-hells down by the fortifications, at the receivers of stolen goods, and among the "apaches."

Seeing him thus pale, harassed, and silent, his mother grew worried.

"We must find him a wife," she said. "It is a pity that Mademoiselle de la Verdelière has not a bigger fortune."

Abbé Patouille did not hide his anxiety.

"This child," he said, "is passing through a moral crisis."

"I am more inclined to think," replied Monsieur René d'Esparvieu, "that he is under the influence of some bad woman. We must find him an occupation which will absorb him and flatter his vanity. I might get him appointed Secretary to the Committee for the Preservation of Country Churches, or Consulting Counsel to the Syndicate of Catholic Plumbers."

CHAPTER XVII

WHEREIN WE LEARN THAT SOPHAR, NO LESS EAGER FOR GOLD THAN MAMMON, LOOKED UPON HIS HEAVENLY HOME LESS FAVOURABLY THAN UPON FRANCE, A COUNTRY BLESSED WITH A SAVINGS BANK AND LOAN DEPARTMENTS, AND WHEREIN WE SEE, YET ONCE AGAIN, THAT WHOSO IS POSSESSED OF THIS WORLD'S GOODS FEARS THE EVIL EFFECTS OF ANY CHANGE

MEANWHILE Arcade led a life of obscure toil. He worked at a printer's in the Rue St. Benoît, and lived in an attic in the Rue Mouffetard. His comrades having gone on strike, he left the workroom and devoted his day to his propaganda. So successful was he that he won over to the side of revolt fifty thousand of those guardian angels who, as Zita had surmised, were discontented with their condition and imbued with the spirit of the times. But lacking money, he lacked liberty, and could not employ his time as he wished in instructing the sons of Heaven. So, too, Prince Istar, hampered by want of funds, manufactured fewer bombs than were needed, and these less fine. Of course he prepared a good many small pocket machines. He had filled Théophile's rooms with them, and not a day passed but he forgot some and left them lying about on the seats in various cafés. But a nice bomb, easily handled and capable of destroying many big mansions, cost him from twenty to twenty-five thousand francs; and Prince Istar only possessed two of this kind. Equally bent on procuring funds, Arcade and Istar both went to make a request for money from a celebrated financier named Max Everdingen, who, as everyone knows, is the managing director of the biggest banking concern in France and indeed in the whole world. What is not so well known is that Max Everdingen was not born of woman, but is a fallen angel. Nevertheless, such is the truth. In Heaven he was named Sophar, and guarded the treasures of Ialdabaoth, a great collector of gold and precious stones. In the exercise of this function Sophar contracted a love of riches which could not be satisfied in a state of society in which banks and stock exchanges are alike unknown. His heart flamed with an ardent love for the god of the Hebrews to whom he remained faithful during a long course of centuries. But at the commencement of the twentieth century of the Christian era, casting his eyes down from the height of the firmament upon France, he saw that this country, under the name of a Republic, was constituted as a plutocracy and that, under the appearance of a democratic government, high finance exercised sovereign sway, untrammelled and unchecked.

Henceforth life in the Empyrean became intolerable to him. He longed for France as for the promised land, and one day, bearing with him all the precious stones he could carry, he descended to earth and established himself in Paris. This angel of cupidity did good business there. Since his materialisation his face had lost its celestial aspect; it reproduced the Semitic type in all its purity, and one could admire the lines and the puckers which wrinkle the faces of bankers and which are to be seen in the money-changers of Quintin Matsys.

His beginnings were humble and his success amazing. He married an ugly woman and they saw themselves reflected in their children as in a mirror. Baron Max Everdingen's large mansion, which rears itself on the heights of the Trocadéro, is crammed with the spoils of Christian Europe.

The Baron received Arcade and Prince Istar in his study,—one of the most modest rooms in his mansion. The ceiling is decorated with a fresco of Tiepolo, taken from a Venetian palace. The bureau of the Regent, Philip of Orleans, is in this room, which is full of cabinets, show-cases, pictures, and statues.

Arcade allowed his gaze to wander over the walls.

"How comes it, my brother Sophar," said he, "that you, in spite of your Jewish heart, obey so ill the commandment of the Lord your God who said: 'Thou shalt have no graven images'? for here I see an Apollo of Houdon's and a Hebe of Lemoine's, and several busts by Caffieri. And, like Solomon in his old age, O son of God, you set up in your dwelling-place the idols of strange nations: for such are this Venus of Boucher, this Jupiter of Rubens, and those nymphs that are indebted to Fragonard's brush for the gooseberry jam which smears their gleaming limbs. And here in this single show-case, Sophar, you keep the sceptre of St. Louis, six hundred pearls of Marie Antoinette's broken necklace, the imperial mantle of Charles V, the tiara wrought by Ghiberti for Pope Martin V, the Colonna, Bonaparte's sword—and I know not what besides."

"Mere trifles," said Max Everdingen.

"My dear Baron," said Prince Istar, "you even possess the ring which Charlemagne placed on a fairy's finger and which was thought to be lost. But let us discuss the business on which we have come. My friend and I have come to ask you for money."

"I can well believe it," replied Max Everdingen. "Everyone wants money, but for different reasons. What do you want money for?"

Prince Istar replied simply:

"To stir up a revolution in France."

"In France!" repeated the Baron, "in France? Well, I shall give you no money for that, you may be quite sure."

Arcade did not disguise the fact that he had expected greater liberality and more generous help from a celestial brother.

"Our project," he said, "is a vast one. It embraces both Heaven and Earth. It is settled in every detail. We shall first bring about a social revolution in France, in Europe, on the whole planet; then we shall carry war into the heavens, where we shall establish a peaceful democracy. And to reduce the citadels of Heaven, to overturn the mountain of God, to storm celestial Jerusalem, a vast army is needful, enormous resources, formidable machines, and electrophores of a strength yet unknown. It is our intention to commence with France."

"You are madmen!" exclaimed Baron Everdingen; "madmen and fools! Listen to me. There is not one single reform to carry out in France. All is perfect, finally settled, unchangeable. You hear?—unchangeable." And to add force to his statement, Baron Everdingen banged his fist three times on the Regent's bureau.

"Our points of view differ," said Arcade sweetly. "*I* think, as does Prince Istar, that everything should be changed in this country. But what boots it to dispute the matter? Moreover, it is too late. We have come to speak to you, O my brother Sophar, in the name of five hundred thousand celestial spirits, all resolved to commence the universal revolution to-morrow."

Baron Everdingen exclaimed that they were crazy, that he would not give a *sou*, that it was both criminal and mad to attack the most admirable thing in the world, the thing which renders earth more beautiful than heaven—Finance. He was a poet and a prophet. His heart thrilled with holy enthusiasm; he drew attention to the French Savings Bank, the virtuous Savings Bank, that chaste and pure Savings Bank like unto the Virgin of the Canticle who, issuing from the depths of the country in rustic petticoat, bears to the robust and splendid Bank—her bridegroom, who awaits her—the treasures of her love; and drew a picture of the Bank, enriched with the gifts of its spouse, pouring on all the nations of the world torrents of gold, which, of themselves, by a thousand invisible channels return in still greater abundance to the blessed land from which they sprung.

"By Deposit and Loan," he went on, "France has become the New Jerusalem, shedding her glory over all the nations of Europe, and the Kings of the Earth come to kiss her rosy feet. And that is what you would fain destroy? You are both impious and sacrilegious."

Thus spoke the angel of finance. An invisible harp accompanied his voice, and his eyes darted lightning.

Meanwhile Arcade, leaning carelessly against the Regent's bureau, spread out under the Banker's eyes various ground-plans, underground-plans, and sky-plans of Paris with red crosses indicating the points where bombs should be simultaneously placed in cellars and catacombs, thrown on public ways, and flung by a flotilla of aeroplanes. All the financial establishments, and notably the Everdingen Bank and its branches, were marked with red crosses.

The financier shrugged his shoulders.

"Nonsense! you are but wretches and vagabonds, shadowed by all the police of the world. You are penniless. How can you manufacture all the machines?"

By way of reply, Prince Istar drew from his pocket a small copper cylinder, which he gracefully presented to Baron Everdingen.

"You see," said he, "this ordinary-looking box. It is only necessary to let it fall on the ground immediately to reduce this mansion with its inmates to a mass of smoking ashes, and to set a fire going which would devour all the Trocadéro quarter. I have ten thousand like that, and I make three dozen a day."

The financier asked the Cherub to replace the machine in his pocket, and continued in a conciliatory tone:

"Listen to me, my friends. Go and start a revolution at once in Heaven, and leave things alone in this country. I will sign a cheque for you. You can procure all the material you need to attack celestial Jerusalem."

And Baron Everdingen was already working up in his imagination a magnificent deal in electrophores and war-material.

CHAPTER XVIII

WHEREIN IS BEGUN THE GARDENER'S STORY, IN THE COURSE OF WHICH WE SHALL SEE THE DESTINY OF THE WORLD UNFOLDED IN A DISCOURSE AS BROAD AND MAGNIFICENT IN ITS VIEWS AS BOSSUET'S DISCOURSE ON THE HISTORY OF THE UNIVERSE IS NARROW AND DISMAL

THE gardener bade Arcade and Zita sit down in an arbour walled with wild bryony, at the far end of the orchard.

"Arcade," said the beautiful Archangel, "Nectaire will perhaps reveal to you to-day the things you are burning to know. Ask him to speak."

Arcade did so and old Nectaire, laying down his pipe, began as follows:—

"I knew him. He was the most beautiful of all the Seraphim. He shone with intelligence and daring. His great heart was big with all the virtues born of pride: frankness, courage, constancy in trial, indomitable hope. Long, long ago, ere Time was, in the boreal sky where gleam the seven magnetic stars, he dwelt in a palace of diamond and gold, where the air was ever tremulous with the beating of wings and with songs of triumph. Iahveh, on his mountain, was jealous of Lucifer. You both know it: angels like unto men feel love and hatred quicken within them. Capable, at times, of generous resolves, they too often follow their own interests and yield to fear. Then, as now, they showed themselves, for the most part, incapable of lofty thoughts, and in the fear of the Lord lay their sole virtue. Lucifer, who held vile things in proud disdain, despised this rabble of commonplace spirits for ever wallowing in a life of feasts and pleasure. But to those who were possessed of a daring spirit, a restless soul, to those fired with a wild love of liberty, he proffered friendship, which was returned with adoration. These latter deserted in a mass the mountain of God and yielded to the Seraph the homage which That Other would fain have kept for himself alone.

"I ranked among the Dominations, and my name, Alaciel, was not unknown to fame. To satisfy my mind—that was ever tormented with an insatiable thirst for knowledge and understanding—I observed the nature of things, I studied the properties of minerals, air, and water. I sought out the laws which govern nature, solid or ethereal, and after much pondering I perceived that the Universe had not been formed as its pretended Creator would have us believe; I knew that all that exists, exists of itself and not by the caprice of Iahveh; that the world is itself its own creator and the spirit its own God. Henceforth I despised Iahveh for his imposture, and I hated him because he showed himself to be opposed to all that I found desirable and good: liberty, curiosity, doubt. These feelings drew me towards the Seraph. I admired him, I loved him. I dwelt in his light. When at length it appeared that a choice had to be made between him and That Other I ranged myself on the side of Lucifer and knew no other aim than to serve him, no other desire than to share his lot.

"War having become inevitable, he prepared for it with indefatigable vigilance and all the resourcefulness of a far-seeing mind. Making the Thrones and Dominations into Chalybes and Cyclopes, he drew forth iron from the mountains bordering his domain; iron, which he valued more than gold, and forged weapons in the caverns of Heaven. Then in the desert plain of the North he assembled myriads of Spirits, armed them, taught them, and drilled them. Although prepared in secret, the enterprise was too vast for his adversary not to be soon aware of it. It might in truth be said that he had always foreseen and dreaded it, for he had made a citadel of his abode and a warlike host of his angels, and he gave himself the name of the God of Hosts. He made ready his thunderbolts. More than half of the children of Heaven remained faithful to him; thronging round him he beheld obedient souls and patient hearts. The Archangel Michael, who knew not fear, took command of these docile troops. Lucifer, as soon as he saw that his army could gain no more in numbers or in warlike skill, moved it swiftly against the foe, and promising his angels riches and glory marched at their head towards the mountain upon whose summit stands the Throne of the Universe. For three days our host swept onward over the ethereal plains. Above our heads streamed the black standards of revolt. And now, behold, the Mountain of God shone rosy in the orient sky and our chief scanned with his eyes the glittering ramparts. Beneath the sapphire walls the foe was drawn up in battle array, and, while we marched clad in our iron and bronze, they shone resplendent in gold and precious stones.

"Their gonfalons of red and blue floated in the breeze, and lightning flashed from the points of their lances. In a little while the armies were only sundered one from the other by a narrow strip of level and deserted ground, and at this sight even the bravest shuddered as they thought that there in bloody conflict their fate would soon be sealed.

72

"Angels, as you know, never die. But when bronze and iron, diamond point or flaming sword tear their ethereal substance, the pain they feel is more acute than men may suffer, for their flesh is more exquisitely delicate; and should some essential organ be destroyed, they fall inert and, slowly decomposing, are resolved into clouds and during long æons float insensible in the cold ether. And when at length they resume spirit and form they fail to recover full memory of their past life. Therefore it is but natural that angels shrink from suffering, and the bravest among them is troubled at the thought of being reft of light and sweet remembrance. Were it otherwise the angelic race would know neither the delight of battle nor the glory of sacrifice. Those who, before the beginning of Time, fought in the Empyrean for or against the God of Armies, would have taken part without honour in mock battles, and it would not now become me to say to you, my children, with rightful pride:

"'Lo, I was there!'

"Lucifer gave the signal for the onset and led the assault. We fell upon the enemy, thinking to destroy him then and there and carry the sacred citadel at the first onslaught. The soldiers of the jealous God, less fiery, but no whit less firm than ours, remained immovable. The Archangel Michael commanded them with the calmness and resolution of a mighty spirit. Thrice we strove to break through their lines, thrice they opposed to our ironclad breast the flaming points of their lances, swift to pierce the stoutest cuirass. In millions the glorious bodies fell. At length our right wing pierced the enemy's left and we beheld the Principalities, the Powers, the Virtues, the Dominations, and the Thrones turn and flee in full career; while the Angels of the Third Choir, flying distractedly above them, covered them with a snow of feathers mingled with a rain of blood. We sped in pursuit of them amid the débris of chariots and broken weapons, and we spurred their nimble flight. Suddenly a storm of cries amazed us. It grew louder and nearer. With desperate shrieks and triumphal clamour the right wing of the enemy, the giant archangels of the Most High, had flung themselves upon our left flank and broken it. Thus we were forced to abandon the pursuit of the fugitives and hasten to the rescue of our own shattered troops. Our prince flew to rally them, and re-established the conflict. But the left wing of the enemy, whose ruin he had not quite consummated, no longer pressed by lance or arrow, regained courage, returned, and faced us yet again. Night fell upon the dubious field. While under the shelter of darkness, in the still, silent air stirred ever and anon by the moans of the wounded, his forces were resting from their toils, Lucifer began to make ready for the next day's battle. Before dawn the trumpets sounded the reveille. Our warriors surprised the enemy at the hour of prayer, put them to rout, and long and fierce was the carnage that ensued. When all had either fallen or fled, the Archangel Michael, none with him save a few companions with four wings of flame, still resisted the onslaughts of a countless host. They fell back ceaselessly opposing their breasts to us, and Michael still displayed an impassible countenance. The sun had run a third of its course when we commenced to scale the Mountain of God. An arduous ascent it was: sweat ran from our brows, a dazzling light blinded us. Weighed down with steel, our feathery wings could not sustain us, but hope gave us wings that bore us up. The beautiful Seraph, pointing with glittering hand, mounting ever higher and higher, showed us the way. All day long we slowly clomb the lofty heights which at evening were robed in azure, rose, and violet. The starry host appearing in the sky seemed as the reflection of our own arms. Infinite silence reigned above us. We went on, intoxicated with hope; all at once from the darkened sky lightning darted forth, the thunder muttered, and from the cloudy mountain-top fell fire from Heaven. Our helmets, our breast-plates were running with flames, and our bucklers broke under bolts sped by invisible hands. Lucifer, in the storm of fire, retained his haughty mien. In vain the lightning smote him; mightier than ever he stood erect, and still defied the foe. At length, the thunder, making the mountain totter, flung us down pell-mell, huge fragments of sapphire and ruby crashing down with us as we fell, and we rolled inert, swooning, for a period whose duration none could measure.

"I awoke in a darkness filled with lamentations. And when my eyes had grown accustomed to the dense shadows I saw round me my companions in arms, scattered in thousands on the sulphurous ground, lit by fitful gleams of livid light. My eyes perceived but fields of lava, smoking craters, and poisonous swamps.

"Mountains of ice and shadowy seas shut in the horizon. A brazen sky hung heavy on our brows. And the horror of the place was such that we wept as we sat, crouched elbow on knee, our cheeks resting on our clenched hands.

"But soon, raising my eyes, I beheld the Seraph standing before me like a tower. Over his pristine splendour sorrow had cast its mantle of sombre majesty.

"'Comrades,' said he, 'we must be happy and rejoice, for behold we are delivered from celestial servitude. Here we are free, and it were better to be free in Hell than serve in Heaven. We are not conquered, since the will to conquer is still ours. We have caused the Throne of the jealous God to totter; by our hands it shall fall. Arise, therefore, and be of good heart.'

"Thereupon, at his command, we piled mountain upon mountain and on the topmost peak we reared engines which flung molten rocks against the divine habitations. The celestial host was taken unaware and from the abodes of glory there issued groans and cries of terror. And even then we thought to re-enter in triumph on our high estate, but the Mountain of God was wreathed with lightnings, and thunderbolts, falling on our fortress, crushed it to dust. After this fresh disaster, the Seraph remained awhile in meditation, his head buried in his hands. At length he raised his darkened visage. Now he was Satan, greater than Lucifer. Steadfast and loyal the angels thronged about him.

"'Friends,' he said, 'if victory is denied us now, it is because we are neither worthy nor capable of victory. Let us determine wherein we have failed. Nature shall not be ruled, the sceptre of the Universe shall not be grasped, Godhead shall not be won, save by knowledge alone. We must conquer the thunder; to that task we must apply ourselves unwearyingly. It is not blind courage (no one this day has shown more courage than have you) which will win us the courts of Heaven; but rather study and reflection. In these silent realms where we are fallen, let us meditate, seeking the hidden causes of things; let us observe the course of Nature; let us pursue her with compelling ardour and all-conquering desire; let us strive to penetrate her infinite grandeur, her infinite minuteness. Let us seek to know when she is barren and when she brings forth fruit; how she makes cold and heat, joy and sorrow, life and death; how she assembles and disperses her elements, how she produces both the light air we breathe and the rocks of diamond and sapphire whence we have been precipitated, the divine fire wherewith we have been scarred and the soaring thought which stirs our minds. Torn with dire wounds, scorched by flame and by ice, let us render thanks to Fate which has sedulously opened our eyes, and let us rejoice at our lot. It is through pain that, suffering a first experience of Nature, we have been roused to know her and to subdue her. When she obeys us we shall be as gods. But even though she hide her mysteries for ever from us, deny us arms and keep the secret of the thunder, we still must needs congratulate ourselves on having known pain, for pain has revealed to us new feelings, more precious and more sweet than those experienced in eternal bliss, and inspired us with love and pity unknown to Heaven.'

"These words of the Seraph changed our hearts and opened up fresh hope to us. Our hearts were filled with a great longing for knowledge and love.

"Meanwhile the Earth was coming into being. Its immense and nebulous orb took on hourly more shape and more certainty of outline. The waters which fed the seaweed, the madrepores and shellfish and bore the light flotilla of the nautilus upon their bosom, no longer covered it in its entirety; they began to sink into beds, and already continents appeared, where, on the warm slime, amphibious monsters crawled. Then the mountains were overspread with forests, and divers races of animals commenced to feed on the grass, the moss, the berries on the trees, and on the acorns. Then there took possession of cavernous shelters under the rocks, a being who was cunning to wound with a sharpened stone the savage beasts, and by his ruses to overcome the ancient denizens of forest, plain, and mountain.

"Man entered painfully on his kingdom. He was defenceless and naked. His scanty hair afforded him but little protection from the cold. His hands ended in nails too frail to do battle with the claws of wild beasts, but the position of his thumb, in opposition to the rest of his fingers, allowed him easily to grasp the most diverse objects and endowed him with skill in default of strength. Without differing essentially from the rest of the animals, he was more capable than any others of observing and comparing. As he drew from his throat various sounds, it occurred to him to designate by a particular inflexion of the voice whatever impinged upon his mind, and by this sequence of different sounds he was enabled to fix and communicate his ideas. His miserable lot and his painstaking spirit aroused the sympathy of the vanquished angels, who discerned in him an audacity equalling their own, and the germ of the pride that was at once their glory and their bane. They came in large numbers to be near him, to dwell on this young earth whither their wings wafted them in effortless flight. And they took pleasure in sharpening his talents and fostering his genius. They taught him to clothe himself in the skins of wild beasts, to roll stones before the mouths of caves to keep out the tigers and bears. They taught him how to make the flame burst forth by twirling a stick among the dried leaves and to foster the sacred fire upon the hearth. Inspired by the ingenious spirits he dared to cross the rivers in the hollowed trunks of cleft trees, he invented the wheel, the grinding-mill, and the plough; the share tore up the earth and the wound brought forth fruit, and the grain offered to him who ground it divine nourishment. He moulded vessels in clay, and out of the flint he fashioned various tools.

"In fine, taking up our abode among mankind, we consoled them and taught them. We were not always visible to them, but of an evening, at the turn of the road, we would appear to them under forms often strange and weird, at times dignified and charming, and we adopted at will the appearance of a monster of the woods and waters, of a venerable old man, of a beautiful child, or of a woman with broad hips. Sometimes we would mock them in our songs or test their intelligence by some cunning prank. There were certain of us of a rather turbulent humour who loved to tease their women and children, but though lowly folk, they were our brothers, and we were never loath to come to their aid. Through our care their intelligence developed sufficiently to attain to mistaken ideas, and to acquire erroneous notions of the relations of cause and effect. As they supposed that some magic bond existed between the reality and its counterfeit presentment, they covered the walls of their caves with figures of animals and carved in ivory images of the reindeer and the mammoth in order to secure as prey the creatures they represented. Centuries passed by with infinite slowness while their genius was coming to birth. We sent them happy thoughts in dreams, inspired them to tame the horse, to castrate the bull, to teach the dog to guard the sheep. They created the family and the tribe. It came to pass one day that one of their wandering tribes was assailed by ferocious hunters. Forthwith the young men of the tribe formed an enclosed ring with their chariots, and in it they shut their women, children, old people, cattle, and treasures, and from the platform of their chariots they hurled murderous stones at their assailants. Thus was formed the first city. Born in misery and condemned to do murder by the law of Iahveh, man put his whole heart into doing battle, and to war he was indebted for his noblest virtues. He hallowed with his blood that sacred love of country which should (if man fulfils his destiny to the very end) enfold the whole earth in peace. One of us, Dædalus, brought him the axe, the plumb-line, and the sail. Thus we rendered the existence of mortals less hard and difficult. By the shores of the lakes they built dwellings of osier, where they might enjoy a meditative quiet unknown to the other inhabitants of the earth, and when they had learned to appease their hunger without too painful efforts we breathed into their hearts the love of beauty.

"They raised up pyramids, obelisks, towers, colossal statues which smiled stiff and uncouth, and genetic symbols. Having learnt to know us or trying at least to divine what manner of beings we were, they felt both friendship and fear for us. The wisest among them watched us with sacred awe and pondered our teaching. In their gratitude the people of Greece and of Asia consecrated to us stones, trees, shadowy woods; offered us victims, and sang us hymns; in fact we became gods in their sight, and they called us Horus, Isis, Astarte, Zeus, Cybele, Demeter, and Triptolemus. Satan was worshipped under the names of Evan, Dionysus, Iacchus, and Lenæus. He showed in his various manifestations all the strength and beauty which it is given to mortals to conceive. His eyes had the sweetness of the wood-violet, his lips were brilliant with the ruby-red of the pomegranate, a down finer than the velvet of the peach covered his cheeks and his chin: his fair hair, wound like a diadem and knotted loosely on the crown of his head, was encircled with ivy. He charmed the wild beasts, and penetrating into the deep forests drew to him all wild spirits, every thing that climbed in trees and peered through the branches with wild and timid gaze. On all these creatures fierce and fearful, that lived on bitter berries and beneath whose hairy breasts a wild heart beat, half-human creatures of the woods—on all he bestowed loving-kindness and grace, and they followed him drunk with joy and beauty. He planted the vine and showed mortals how to crush the grapes underfoot to make the wine flow. Magnificent and benign, he fared across the world, a long procession following in his train. To bear him company I took the form of a satyr; from my brow sprang two budding horns. My nose was flat and my ears were pointed. Glands, like those of the goat, hung on my neck, a goat's tail moved with my moving loins, and my hairy legs ended in a black cloven hoof which beat the ground in cadence.

"Dionysus fared on his triumphal march over the world. In his company I passed through Lydia, the Phrygian fields, the scorching plains of Persia, Media bristling with hoar-frost, Arabia Felix, and rich Asia where flourishing cities were laved by the waves of the sea. He proceeded on a car drawn by lions and lynxes, to the sound of flutes, cymbals, and drums, invented for his mysteries. Bacchantes, Thyades, and Mænads, girt with the dappled fawn-skin, waved the thyrsus encircled with ivy. He bore in his train the Satyrs, whose joyous troop I led, Sileni, Pans, and Centaurs. Under his feet flowers and fruit sprang to life, and striking the rocks with his wand he made limpid streams gush forth. In the month of the Vintage he visited Greece, and the villagers ran forth to meet him, stained with the green and ruddy juices of the plants, they wore masks of wood, or bark, or leaves; in their hands they bore earthen cups, and danced wanton dances. Their womenfolk, imitating the companions of the God, their heads wreathed with green smilax, fastened round their supple loins skins of fawn or goat. The virgins twined about their throats garlands of fig leaves, they kneaded cakes of flour, and bore the Phallus in the mystic basket. And the vine-dressers, all daubed with lees of wine, standing up in their wains and bandying mockery or abuse with the passers-by, invented Tragedy.

"Truly, it was not in dreaming beside a fountain, but by dint of strenuous toil that Dionysus taught them to grow plants and to make them bring forth succulent fruits. And while he pondered the art of transforming the rough woodlanders into a race that should love music and submit to just laws, more than once over his brow, burning with the fire of enthusiasm, did melancholy and gloomy fever pass. But his profound knowledge and his friendship for mankind enabled him to triumph over every obstacle. O days divine! Beautiful dawn of life! We led the

Bacchanals on the leafy summits of the mountains and on the yellow shores of the seas. The Naiads and the Oreads mingled with us at our play. Aphrodite at our coming rose from the foam of the sea to smile upon us."

CHAPTER XIX

THE GARDENER'S STORY, CONTINUED

THEN men had learned to cultivate the earth, to herd cattle, to enclose their holy places within walls, and to recognise the gods by their beauty, I withdrew to that smiling land girdled with dark woods and watered by the Stymphalos, the Olbios, the Erymanthus, and the proud Crathis, swollen with the icy waters of the Styx, and there, in a green valley at the foot of a hill planted with arbutus, olive, and pine, beneath a cluster of white poplars and plane trees, by the side of a stream flowing with soft murmur amid tufted mastic trees, I sang to the shepherds and the nymphs of the birth of the world, the origin of fire, of the tenuous air, of water and of earth. I told them how primeval men had lived wretched and naked in the woods, before the ingenious spirits had taught them the arts; of God, too, I sang to them, and why they gave Dionysus Semele to mother, because his desire to befriend mankind was born amid the thunder.

"It was not without effort that this people, more pleasing than all the others in the eyes of the gods, these happy Greeks, achieved good government and a knowledge of the arts. Their first temple was a hut composed of laurel branches; their first image of the gods, a tree; their first altar, a rough stone stained with the blood of Iphigenia. But in a short time they brought wisdom and beauty to a point that no nation had attained before them, that no nation has since approached. Whence comes it, Arcade, this solitary marvel on the earth? Wherefore did the sacred soil of Ionia and of Attica bring forth this incomparable flower? Because nor priesthood, nor dogma, nor revelation ever found a place there, because the Greeks never knew the jealous God.

"It was his own grace, his own genius that the Greek enthroned and deified as his God, and when he raised his eyes to the heavens it was his own image that he saw reflected there. He conceived everything in due measure; and to his temples he gave perfect proportion. All therein was grace, harmony, symmetry, and wisdom; all were worthy of the immortals who dwelt within them and who under names of happy choice, in realised shapes, figured forth the genius of man. The columns which bore the marble architrave, the frieze and the cornice were touched with something human, which made them venerable; and sometimes one might see, as at Athens and at Delphi, beautiful young girls strong-limbed and radiant upstaying the entablature of treasure house and sanctuary. O days of splendour, harmony, and wisdom!

"Dionysus resolved to repair to Italy, whither he was summoned under the name of Bacchus by a people eager to celebrate his mysteries. I took passage in his ship decked with tendrils of the vine, and landed under the eyes of the two brothers of Helen at the mouth of the yellow Tiber. Already under the teaching of the god, the inhabitants of Latium had learned to wed the vine to the young stripling elm. It was my pleasure to dwell at the foot of the Sabine hills in a valley crowned with trees and watered with pure springs. I gathered the verbena and the mallow in the meadows. The pale olive-trees twisting their perforated trunks on the slope of the hill gave me of their unctuous fruit. There I taught a race of men with square heads, who had not, like the Greeks, a fertile mind, but whose hearts were true, whose souls were patient, and who reverenced the gods. My neighbour, a rustic soldier, who for fifteen years had bowed under the burden of his haversack, had followed the Roman eagle over land and sea, and had seen the enemies of the sovereign people flee before him. Now he drove his furrow with his two red oxen, starred with white between their spreading horns, while beneath the cabin's thatch his spouse, chaste and sedate of mien, pounded garlic in a bronze mortar and cooked the beans upon the sacred hearth, And I, his friend, seated near by under an oak, used to lighten his labours with the sound of my flute, and smile on his little children, when the sun, already low in the sky, was lengthening the shadows, and they returned from the wood all laden with branches. At the garden gate where the pears and pumpkins ripened, and where the lily and the evergreen acanthus bloomed, a figure of Priapus carved out of the trunk of a fig tree menaced thieves with his formidable emblem, and the reeds swaying with the wind over his head scared away the plundering birds. At new moon the pious husbandman made offering of a handful of salt and barley to his household gods crowned with myrtle and with rosemary.

"I saw his children grow up, and his children's children, who kept in their hearts their early piety and did not forget to offer sacrifice to Bacchus, to Diana, and to Venus, nor omit to pour fresh wines and scatter flowers into the fountains. But slowly they fell away from their old habits of patient toil and simplicity.

"I heard them complain when the torrent, swollen with many rains, compelled them to construct a dyke to protect the paternal fields, and the rough Sabine wine grew unpleasing to their delicate palate. They went to drink the wines of Greece at the neighbouring tavern; and the hours slipped unheeded by, while within the arbour shade they watched the dance of the flute player, practised at swaying her supple limbs to the sound of the castanets.

"Lulled by murmuring leaves and whispering streams, the tillers of the soil took sweet repose, but between the poplars we saw along borders of the sacred way vast tombs, statues, and altars arise, and the rolling of the chariot wheels grew more frequent over the worn stones. A cherry sapling brought home by a veteran told us of the far-distant conquests of a Consul, and odes sung to the lyre related the victories of Rome, mistress of the world.

"All the countries where the great Dionysus had journeyed, changing wild beasts into men, and making the fruit and grain bloom and ripen beneath the passing of his Mænads, now breathed the Pax Romana. The nursling of the she-wolf, soldier and labourer, friend of conquered nations, laid out roads from the margin of the misty sea to the rocky slopes of the Caucasus; in every town rose the temple of Augustus and of Rome, and such was the universal faith in Latin justice that in the gorges of Thessaly or on the wooded borders of the Rhine, the slave, ready to succumb under his iniquitous burden, called aloud on the name of Cæsar.

"But why must it be that on this ill-starred globe of land and water, all should perish and die and the fairest things be ever the most fleeting? O adorable daughters of Greece! O Science! O Wisdom! O Beauty! kindly divinities, you were wrapt in heavy slumber ere you submitted to the outrages of the barbarians, who already in the marshy wastes of the North and on the lonely steppes, ready to assail you, bestrode bare-backed their little shaggy horses.

"While, dear Arcade, the patient legionary camped by the borders of the Phasis and the Tanais, the women and the priests of Asia and of monstrous Africa invaded the Eternal City and troubled the sons of Remus with their magic spells. Until now, Iahveh, the persecutor of the laborious demons, was unknown to the world that he pretended to have created, save to certain miserable Syrian tribes, ferocious like himself, and perpetually dragged from servitude to servitude. Profiting by the Roman peace which assured free travel and traffic everywhere, and favoured the exchange of ideas and merchandise, this old God insolently made ready to conquer the Universe. He was not the only one, for the matter of that, to attempt such an undertaking. At the same time a crowd of gods, demiurges, and demons, such as Mithra, Thammuz, the good Isis, and Eubulus, meditated taking possession of the peace-enfolded world. Of all the spirits, Iahveh appeared the least prepared for victory. His ignorance, his cruelty, his ostentation, his Asiatic luxury, his disdain of laws, his affectation of rendering himself invisible, all these things were calculated to offend those Greeks and Latins who had absorbed the teaching of Dionysus and the Muses. He himself felt he was incapable of winning the allegiance of free men and of cultivated minds, and he employed cunning. To seduce their souls he invented a fable which, although not so ingenious as the myths wherewith we have surrounded the spirits of our disciples of old, could, nevertheless, influence those feebler intellects which are to be found everywhere in great masses. He declared that men having committed a crime against him, an hereditary crime, should pay the penalty for it in their present life and in the life to come (for mortals vainly imagine that their existence is prolonged in hell); and the astute Iahveh gave out that he had sent his own son to earth to redeem with his blood the debt of mankind. It is not credible that a penalty should redress a fault, and it is still less credible that the innocent should pay for the guilty. The sufferings of the innocent atone for nothing, and do but add one evil to another. Nevertheless, unhappy creatures were found to adore Iahveh and his son, the expiator, and to announce their mysteries as good tidings. We should not be surprised at this folly. Have we not seen many times indeed human beings who, poor and naked, prostrate themselves before all the phantoms of fear, and rather than follow the teaching of well-disposed demons, obey the commandments of cruel demiurges? Iahveh, by his cunning, took souls as in a net. But he did not gain therefrom, for his glorification, all that he expected. It was not he, but his son, who received the homage of mankind, and who gave his name to the new cult. He himself remained almost unknown upon earth."

CHAPTER XX

THE GARDENER'S STORY, CONTINUED

THE new superstition spread at first over Syria and Africa; it won over the seaports where the filthy rabble swarm, and, penetrating into Italy, infected at first the courtesans and the slaves, and then made rapid progress among the middle classes of the towns. But for a long while the country-side remained undisturbed. As in the past, the villagers consecrated a pine tree to Diana, and sprinkled it every year with the blood of a young boar; they propitiated their Lares with the sacrifice of a sow, and offered to Bacchus—benefactor of mankind—a kid of dazzling whiteness, or if they were too poor for this, at least they had a little wine and a little flour from the vineyard and from the fields for their household gods. We had taught them that it sufficed to approach the altar with clean hands, and that the gods rejoiced over a modest offering.

"Nevertheless, the reign of Iahveh proclaimed its advent in a hundred places by its extravagances. The Christians burnt books, overthrew temples, set fire to the towns, and carried on their ravages as far as the deserts. There, thousands of unhappy beings, turning their fury against themselves, lacerated their sides with points of steel. And from the whole earth the sighs of voluntary victims rose up to God like songs of praise.

"My shadowy retreat could not escape for long from the fury of their madness.

"On the summit of the hill which overlooked the olive woods, brightened daily with the sounds of my flute, had stood since the earliest days of the Pax Romana, a small marble temple, round as the huts of our forefathers. It had no walls, but on a base of seven steps, sixteen columns rose in a circle with the acanthus on the capitals, bearing a cupola of white tiles. This cupola sheltered a statue of Love fashioning his bow, the work of an Athenian sculptor. The child seemed to breathe, joy was welling from his lips, all his limbs were harmonious and polished. I honoured this image of the most powerful of all the gods, and I taught the villagers to bear to him as an offering a cup crowned with verbena and filled with wine two summers old.

"One day, when seated as my custom was at the feet of the god, pondering precepts and songs, an unknown man, wild-looking, with unkempt hair, approached the temple, sprang at one bound up the marble steps, and with savage glee exclaimed:

"'Die, poisoner of souls, and joy and beauty perish with you.' He spoke thus, and drawing an axe from his girdle raised it against the god. I stayed his arm, I threw him down, and trampled him under my feet.

"'Demon,' he cried desperately, 'suffer me to overturn this idol, and you may slay me afterwards.'

"I heeded not his atrocious plea, but leaned with all my might on his chest, which cracked under my knee, and, squeezing his throat with my two hands, I strangled the impious one.

"While he lay there, with purple face and lolling tongue, at the feet of the smiling god, I went to purify myself at the sacred stream. Then leaving this land, now the prey of the Christian, I passed through Gaul and gained the banks of the Saône, whither Dionysus had, in days gone by, carried the vine. The god of the Christians had not yet been proclaimed to this happy people. They worshipped for its beauty a leafy beech-tree, whose honoured branches swept the ground, and they hung fillets of wool thereon. They also worshipped a sacred stream and set up images of clay in a dripping grotto. They made offering of little cheeses and a bowl of milk to the Nymphs of the woods and mountains.

"But soon an apostle of sorrow was sent to them by the new God. He was drier than a smoked fish. Although attenuated with fasting and watching, he taught with unabated ardour all manner of gloomy mysteries. He loved suffering, and thought it good; his anger fell upon all that was beautiful, comely, and joyous. The sacred tree fell beneath his hatchet. He hated the Nymphs, because they were beautiful, and he flung imprecations at them when their shining limbs gleamed among the leaves at evening, and he held my melodious flute in aversion. The poor wretch thought that there were certain forms of words wherewith to put to flight the deathless spirits that dwell in the cool groves, and in the depths of the woods and on the tops of the mountains. He thought to conquer us with a few drops of water over which he had pronounced certain words and made certain gestures. The Nymphs, to avenge themselves, appeared to him at nightfall and inflamed him with desire which the foolish knave thought animal; then they fled, their laughter scattered like grain over the fields, while their victim lay tossing with burning limbs on his couch of leaves. Thus do the divine nymphs laugh at exorcisers, and mock the wicked and their sordid chastity.

"The apostle did not do as much harm as he wished, because his teaching was given to the simple souls living in obedience to Nature, and because the mediocrity of most of mankind is such that they gain but little from the principles inculcated in them. The little wood in which I dwelt belonged to a Gaul of senatorial family, who retained some traces of Latin elegance. He loved his young freed-woman and shared with her his bed of broidered purple. His slaves cultivated his garden and his vineyard; he was a poet and sang, in imitation of Ausonius, Venus whipping her son with roses. Although a Christian, he offered me milk, fruit, and vegetables as if I were the genius of the place. In return I charmed his idle moments with the music of my flute, and I gave him happy dreams. In fact, these peaceful Gauls knew very little of Iahveh and his son.

"But now behold fires looming on the horizon, and ashes driven by the wind fall within our forest glades. Peasants come driving a long file of waggons along the roads or urging their flocks before them. Cries of terror rise from the villages, 'The Burgundians are upon us!'

"Now one horseman is seen, lance in hand, clad in shining bronze, his long red hair falling in two plaits on his shoulders. Then come two, then twenty, then thousands, wild and blood-stained; old men and children they put to the sword, ay, even aged grandams whose grey hairs cleave to the soles of the slaughterer's boots, mingled with the brains of babes new-born. My young Gaul and his young freed-woman stain with their blood the couch broidered with narcissi. The barbarians burn the basilicas to roast their oxen whole, shatter the amphoræ, and drain the wine in the mud of the flooded cellars. Their women accompany them, huddled, half naked, in their war chariots. When the Senate, the dwellers in the cities, and the leaders of the churches had perished in the flames, the Burgundians, soddened with wine, lay down to slumber beneath the arcades of the Forum. Two weeks later one of them might have been seen smiling in his shaggy beard at the little child whom, on the threshold of their dwelling, his fair-haired spouse gathers in her arms; while another, kindling the fire of his forge, hammers out his iron with measured stroke; another sings beneath the oak tree to his assembled comrades of the gods and heroes of his race; and yet others spread out for sale stones fallen from Heaven, aurochs' horns, and amulets. And the former inhabitants of the country, regaining courage little by little, crept from the woods where they had fled for refuge, and returned to rebuild their burnt-down cabins, plough their fields, and prune their vines.

"Once more life resumed its normal course; but those times were the most wretched that mankind had yet experienced. The barbarians swarmed over the whole Empire. Their ways were uncouth, and as they nurtured feelings of vengeance and greed, they firmly believed in the ransom of sin.

"The fable of Iahveh and his son pleased them, and they believed it all the more easily in that it was taught them by the Romans whom they knew to be wiser than themselves, and to whose arts and mode of life they yielded secret admiration. Alas! the heritage of Greece and Rome had fallen into the hands of fools. All knowledge was lost. In those days it was held to be a great merit to sing among the choir, and those who remembered a few sentences from the Bible passed for prodigious geniuses. There were still poets as there were birds, but their verse went lame in every foot. The ancient demons, the good genii of mankind, shorn of their honours, driven forth, pursued, hunted down, remained hidden in the woods. There, if they still showed themselves to men, they adopted, to hold them in awe, a terrible face, a red, green, or black skin, baleful eyes, an enormous mouth fringed with boars' teeth, horns, a tail, and sometimes a human face on their bellies. The nymphs remained fair, and the barbarians, ignorant of the winsome names they bore in other days, called them fairies, and, imputing to them a capricious character and puerile tastes, both feared and loved them.

"We had suffered a grievous fall, and our ranks were sadly thinned; nevertheless we did not lose courage and, maintaining a laughing aspect and a benevolent spirit, we were in those direful days the real friends of mankind. Perceiving that the barbarians grew daily less sombre and less ferocious, we lent ourselves to the task of conversing with them under all sorts of disguises. We incited them, with a thousand precautions, and by prudent circumlocutions, not to acknowledge the old Iahveh as an infallible master, not blindly to obey his orders, and not to fear his menaces. When need was, we had recourse to magic. We exhorted them unceasingly to study nature and to strive to discover the traces of ancient wisdom.

"These warriors from the North—rude though they were—were acquainted with some mechanical arts. They thought they saw combats in the heavens; the sound of the harp drew tears from their eyes; and perchance they had souls capable of greater things than the degenerate Gauls and Romans whose lands they had invaded. They knew not how to hew stone or to polish marble; but they caused porphyry and columns to be brought from Rome and from Ravenna; their chief men took for their seal a gem engraved by a Greek in the days when Beauty reigned supreme. They raised walls with bricks, cunningly arranged like ears of corn, and succeeded in building quite pleasing-looking churches with cornices upheld by consoles depicting grim faces, and heavy capitals whereon were represented monsters devouring one another.

"We taught them letters and sciences. A mouthpiece of their god, one Gerbert, took lessons in physics, arithmetic, and music with us, and it was said that he had sold us his soul. Centuries passed, and man's ways remained violent. It was a world given up to fire and blood. The successors of the studious Gerbert, not content with the possession of souls (the profits one gains thereby are lighter than air), wished to possess bodies also. They pretended that their universal and prescriptive monarchy was held from a fisherman on the lake of Tiberias. One of them thought for a moment to prevail over the loutish Germanus, successor to Augustus. But finally the spiritual had to come to terms with the temporal, and the nations were torn between two opposing masters.

"Nations took shape amid horrible tumult. On every side were wars, famines, and internecine conflicts. Since they attributed the innumerable ills that fell upon them to their God, they called him the Most Good, not by way of irony, but because to them the best was he who smote the hardest. In those days of violence, to give myself leisure for study I adopted a *rôle* which may surprise you, but which was exceedingly wise.

"Between the Saône and the mountains of Charolais, where the cattle pasture, there lies a wooded hill sloping gently down to fields watered by a clear stream. There stood a monastery celebrated throughout the Christian world. I hid my cloven feet under a robe and became a monk in this Abbey, where I lived peacefully, sheltered from the men at arms who to friend or foe alike showed themselves equally exacting. Man, who had relapsed into childhood, had all his lessons to learn over again. Brother Luke, whose cell was next to mine, studied the habits of animals and taught us that the weasel conceives her young within her ear. I culled simples in the fields wherewith to soothe the sick, who until then were made by way of treatment to touch the relics of saints. In the Abbey were several demons similar to myself whom I recognised by their cloven feet and by their kindly speech. We joined forces in our endeavours to polish the rough mind of the monks.

"While the little children played at hop-scotch under the Abbey walls our friends the monks devoted themselves to another game equally unprofitable, at which, nevertheless, I joined them, for one must kill time,—that, when one comes to think of it, is the sole business of life. Our game was a game of words which pleased our coarse yet subtle minds, set school fulminating against school, and put all Christendom in an uproar. We formed ourselves into two opposing camps. One camp maintained that before there were apples there was the Apple; that before there were popinjays there was the Popinjay; that before there were lewd and greedy monks there was the Monk, Lewdness and Greed; that before there were feet and before there were posteriors in this world the kick in the posterior must have had existence for all eternity in the bosom of God. The other camp replied that, on the contrary, apples gave man the idea of the apple; popinjays the idea of the popinjay; monks the idea of the monk, greed and lewdness, and that the kick in the posterior existed only after having been duly given and received. The players grew heated and came to fisticuffs. I was an adherent of the second party, which satisfied my reason better, and which was, in fact, condemned by the Council of Soissons.

"Meanwhile, not content with fighting among themselves, vassal against suzerain, suzerain against vassal, the great lords took it into their heads to go and fight in the East. They said, as well as I can remember, that they were going to deliver the tomb of the son of God.

"They said so, but their adventurous and covetous spirit excited them to go forth and seek lands, women, slaves, gold, myrrh, and incense. These expeditions, need it be said, proved disastrous; but our thick-headed compatriots brought back with them the knowledge of certain

82

crafts and oriental arts and a taste for luxury. Henceforth we had less difficulty in making them work and in putting them in the way of inventions. We built wonderfully beautiful churches, with daringly pierced arches, lancet-shaped windows, high towers, thousands of pointed spires, which, rising in the sky towards Iahveh, bore at one and the same time the prayers of the humble and the threats of the proud, for it was all as much our doing as the work of men's hands; and it was a strange sight to see men and demons working together at a cathedral, each one sawing, polishing, collecting stones, graving, on capital and on cornice, nettles, thorns, thistles, wild parsley, and wild strawberry,—carving faces of virgins and saints and weird figures of serpents, fishes with asses' heads, apes scratching their buttocks; each one, in fact, putting his own particular talent,—mocking, sublime, grotesque, modest, or audacious,—into the work and making of it all a harmonious cacophony, a rapturous anthem of joy and sorrow, a Babel of victory. At our instigation the carvers, the gold-smiths, the enamellers, accomplished marvels and all the sumptuary arts flourished at once; there were silks at Lyons, tapestries at Arras, linen at Rheims, cloth at Rouen. The good merchants rode on their palfreys to the fairs, bearing pieces of velvet and brocade, embroideries, orfrays, jewels, vessels of silver, and illuminated books. Strollers and players set up their trestles in the churches and in the public squares, and represented, according to their lights, simple chronicles of Heaven, Earth, and Hell. Women decked themselves in splendid raiment and lisped of love.

"In the spring when the sky was blue, nobles and peasants were possessed with the desire to make merry in the flower-strewn meadows. The fiddler tuned his instrument, and ladies, knights and demoiselles, townsfolk, villagers and maidens, holding hands, began the dance. But suddenly War, Pestilence, and Famine entered the circle, and Death, tearing the violin from the fiddler's hands, led the dance. Fire devoured village and monastery. The men-at-arms hanged the peasants on the sign-posts at the cross-roads when they were unable to pay ransom, and bound pregnant women to tree-trunks, where at night the wolves came and devoured the fruit within the womb. The poor people lost their senses. Sometimes, peace being re-established, and good times come again, they were seized with mad, unreasoning terror, abandoned their homes, and rushed hither and thither in troops, half naked, tearing themselves with iron hooks, and singing. I do not accuse Iahveh and his son of all this evil. Many ill things occurred without him and even in spite of him. But where I recognise the instigation of the All Good (as they called him) was in the custom instituted by his pastors, and established throughout Christendom, of burning, to the sound of bells and the singing of psalms, both men and women who, taught by the demons, professed, concerning this God, opinions of their own."

CHAPTER XXI

THE GARDENER'S STORY, CONCLUDED

IT seemed as if science and thought had perished for all eternity, and that the earth would never again know peace, joy, and beauty.

"But one day, under the walls of Rome, some workmen, excavating the earth on the borders of an ancient road, found a marble sarcophagus which bore carved on its sides simulacra of Love and the triumphs of Bacchus.

"The lid being raised, a maiden appeared whose face shone with dazzling freshness. Her long hair spread over her white shoulders, she was smiling in her sleep. A band of citizens, thrilled with enthusiasm, raised the funeral couch and bore it to the Capitol. The people came in crowds to contemplate the ineffable beauty of the Roman maiden and stood around in silence, watching for the awakening of the divine soul held within this form of adorable beauty.

"And it came to pass that the City was so greatly stirred by this spectacle that the Pope, fearing, not without reason, the birth of a pagan cult from this radiant body, caused it to be removed at night and secretly buried. The precaution was vain, the labour fruitless. After so many centuries of barbarism, the beauty of the antique world had appeared for a moment before the eyes of men; it was long enough for its image, graven on their hearts, to inspire them with an ardent desire to love and to know.

"Henceforth, the star of the God of the Christians paled and sloped to its decline. Bold navigators discovered worlds inhabited by numerous races who knew not old Iahveh, and it was suspected that he was no less ignorant of them, since he had given them no news of himself or of his son the expiator. A Polish Canon demonstrated the true motions of the earth, and it was seen that, far from having created the world, the old demiurge of Israel had not even an inkling of its structure. The writings of philosophers, orators, jurisconsults, and ancient poets were dragged from the dust of the cloisters and passing from hand to hand inspired men's minds with the love of wisdom. The Vicar of the jealous God, the Pope himself, no longer believed in Him whom he represented on earth. He loved the arts and had no other care than to collect ancient statues and to rear sumptuous buildings wherein were displayed the orders of Vitruvius re-established by Bramante. We began to breathe anew. Already the old gods, recalled from their long exile, were returning to dwell upon earth. There they found once more their temples and their altars. Leo, placing at their feet the ring, the three crowns, and the keys, offered them in secret the incense of sacrifices. Already Polyhymnia, leaning on her elbow, had begun to resume the golden thread of her meditations; already, in the gardens, the comely Graces and the Nymphs and Satyrs were weaving their mazy dances, and at length the earth had joy once more within its grasp. But, O calamity, unlucky fate,—most tragic circumstance! A German monk, all swollen with beer and theology, rose up against this renaissance of paganism, hurled menaces against it, shattered it, and prevailed single handed against the Princes of the Church. Inciting the nations, he called upon them to undertake a reform which saved that which was about to be destroyed. Vainly did the cleverest among us try to turn him from his work. A subtle demon, on earth called Beelzebub, marked him out for attack, now embarrassing him with learned controversial argument, now tormenting him with cruel mockery. The stubborn monk hurled his ink-pot at his head and went on with his dismal reformation. What ultimately happened? The sturdy mariner repaired, calked, and refloated the damaged ship of the Church. Jesus Christ owes it to this shaveling that his shipwreck was delayed for perhaps more than ten centuries. Henceforth things went from bad to worse. In the wake of this loutish monk, this beer-swiller and brawler, came that tall, dry doctor from Geneva, who, filled with the spirit of the ancient Iahveh, strove to bring the world back again to the abominable days of Joshua and the Judges of Israel. A maniac was he, filled with cold fury, a heretic and a burner of heretics, the most ferocious enemy of the Graces.

"These mad apostles and their mad disciples made even demons like myself, even the horned devils, look back longingly on the time when the Son with his Virgin Mother reigned over the nations dazzled with splendours: cathedrals with their stone tracery delicate as lace, flaming roses of stained glass, frescoes painted in vivid colours telling countless wondrous tales, rich orfrays, glittering enamel of shrines and reliquaries, gold of crosses and of monstrances, waxen tapers gleaming like starry galaxies amid the gloom of vaulted arches, organs with their deep-toned harmonies. All this doubtless was not the Parthenon, nor yet the Panathenæa, but it gladdened eyes and hearts; it was, at all events, beauty. And these cursed reformers would not suffer anything either pleasing or lovable. You should have seen them climbing in black swarms over doorways, plinths, spires, and bell-towers, striking with senseless hammers those images in stone which the demons had carved working hand in hand with the master designers, those genial saints and dear, holy women, and the touching idols of Virgin Mothers pressing their suckling to their heart. For, to be just, a little agreeable paganism had slipped into the cult of the jealous God. These monsters of heretics were for extirpating idolatry. We did our best, my companions and I, to hamper their horrible work, and I, for one, had the pleasure of flinging down some dozens from the top of the porches and galleries on to the Cathedral Square, where their detestable brains got knocked out. The worst of it was that the Catholic Church also reformed herself and grew more mischievous than ever. In the pleasant land of France, the seminarists and the monks were inflamed with unheard-of fury against the ingenious demons and the men of learning. My prior was one of the most violent opponents of sound knowledge. For some time past my studious lucubrations had caused him anxiety, and perhaps he had caught sight of my cloven foot. The scoundrel searched my cell and found paper, ink, some Greek books newly printed, and some Pan-pipes hanging on the wall. By these signs he knew me for an evil spirit and had me thrown into a dungeon where I should have eaten the bread of suffering and drunk the waters of bitterness, had I not promptly made my escape by the window and sought refuge in the wooded groves among the Nymphs and the Fauns.

"Far and wide the lighted pyres cast the odour of charred flesh. Everywhere there were tortures, executions, broken bones, and tongues cut out. Never before had the spirit of Iahveh breathed forth such atrocious fury. However, it was not altogether in vain that men had raised the lid of the ancient sarcophagus and gazed upon the Roman Virgin.

"During this time of great terror when Papists and Reformers rivalled one another in violence and cruelty, amidst all these scenes of torture, the mind of man was regaining strength and courage. It dared to look up to the heavens, and there it saw, not the old Jew drunk with vengeance, but Venus Urania, tranquil and resplendent. Then a new order of things was born, then the great centuries came into being. Without publicly denying the god of their ancestors, men of intellect submitted to his mortal enemies, Science and Reason, and Abbé Gassendi relegated him gently to the far-distant abyss of first causes. The kindly demons who teach and console unhappy mortals, inspired the great minds of those days with discourses of all kinds, with comedies and tales told in the most polished fashion. Women invented conversation, the art of intimate letter-writing, and politeness. Manners took on a sweetness and a nobility unknown to preceding ages. One of the finest minds of that age of reason, the amiable Bernier, wrote one day to St. Evremond: 'It is a great sin to deprive oneself of a pleasure.' And this pronouncement alone should suffice to show the progress of intelligence in Europe. Not that there had not always been Epicureans but, unlike Bernier, Chapelle, and Molière, they had not the consciousness of their talent.

"Then even the very devotees understood Nature. And Racine, fierce bigot that he was, knew as well as such an atheistical physician as Guy Patin, how to attribute to divers states of the organs the passions which agitate mankind.

"Even in my abbey, whither I had returned after the turmoil, and which sheltered only the ignorant and the shallow thinker, a young monk, less of a dunce than the rest, confided to me that the Holy Spirit expresses itself in bad Greek to humiliate the learned.

"Nevertheless, theology and controversy were still raging in this society of thinkers. Not far from Paris in a shady valley there were to be seen solitary beings known as 'les Messieurs,' who called themselves disciples of St. Augustine, and argued with honest conviction that the God of the Scriptures strikes those who fear Him, spares those who confront Him, holds works of no account, and damns—should He so wish it—His most faithful servant; for His justice is not our justice, and His ways are incomprehensible.

"One evening I met one of these gentlemen in his garden, where he was pacing thoughtfully among the cabbage-plots and lettuce-beds. I bowed my horned head before him and murmured these friendly words: 'May old Jehovah protect you, sir. You know him well. Oh, how well you know him, and how perfectly you have understood his character.' The holy man thought he discerned in me a messenger from Hell, concluded he was eternally damned, and died suddenly of fright.

"The following century was the century of philosophy. The spirit of research was developed, reverence was lost; the pride of the flesh was diminished and the mind acquired fresh energy. Manners took on an elegance until then unknown. On the other hand, the monks of my order grew more and more ignorant and dirty, and the monastery no longer offered me any advantage now that good manners reigned in the town. I could bear it no longer. Flinging my habit to the nettles, I put a powdered wig on my horned brow, hid my goat's legs under white stockings, and cane in hand, my pockets stuffed with gazettes, I frequented the fashionable world, visited the modish promenades, and showed myself assiduously in the *cafés* where men of letters were to be found. I was made welcome in *salons* where, as a happy novelty, there were arm-chairs that fitted the form, and where both men and women engaged in rational conversation.

"The very metaphysicians spoke intelligibly. I acquired great weight in the town as an authority on matters of exegesis, and, without boasting, I was largely responsible for the Testament of the curé Meslier and *The Bible Explained*, brought out by the chaplains to the King of Prussia.

"At this time a comic and cruel misadventure befel the ancient Iahveh. An American Quaker, by means of a kite, stole his thunderbolts.

"I was living in Paris, and was at the supper where they talked of strangling the last of the priests with the entrails of the last of the kings. France was in a ferment; a terrible revolution broke out. The ephemeral leaders of the disordered State carried on a Reign of Terror amidst unheard-of perils. They were, for the most part, less pitiless and less cruel than the princes and judges instituted by Iahveh in the kingdoms of the earth; nevertheless, they appeared more ferocious, because they gave judgment in the name of Humanity. Unhappily they were easily moved to pity and of great sensibility. Now men of sensibility are irritable and subject to fits of fury. They were virtuous; they had moral laws, that is to say they conceived certain narrowly defined moral obligations, and judged human actions not by their natural consequences but by abstract principles. Of all the vices which contribute to the undoing of a statesman, virtue is the most fatal; it leads to murder. To work effectively for the happiness of mankind, a man must be superior to all morals, like the divine Julius. God, so ill-used for some time past, did not, on the whole, suffer excessively harsh treatment from these new men. He found protectors among them, and was adored under the name of the Supreme Being. One might even go so far as to say that terror created a diversion from philosophy and was profitable to the old demiurge, in that he appeared to represent order, public tranquillity, and the security of person and property.

"While Liberty was coming to birth amid the storm, I lived at Auteuil, and visited Madame Helvetius, where freethinkers in every branch of intellectual activity were to be met with. Nothing could be rarer than a freethinker, even after Voltaire's day. A man who will face death without trembling dare not say anything out of the ordinary about morals. That very same respect for Humanity which prompts him to go forth to his death, makes him bow to public opinion. In those days I enjoyed listening to the talk of Volney, Cabanis, and Tracy. Disciples of the great Condillac, they regarded the senses as the origin of all our knowledge. They called themselves ideologists, were the most honourable people in the world, and grieved the vulgar minds by refusing them immortality. For the majority of people, though they do not know what to do with this life, long for another that shall have no end. During the turmoil, our small philosophical society was sometimes disturbed in the peaceful shades of Auteuil by patrols of patriots. Condorcet, our great man, was an outlaw. I myself was regarded as suspect by the friends of the people, who, in spite of my rustic appearance and my frieze coat, believed me to be an aristocrat, and I confess that independence of thought is the proudest of all aristocracies.

"One evening while I was stealthily watching the dryads of Boulogne, who gleamed amid the leaves like the moon rising above the horizon, I was arrested as a suspect, and put in prison. It was a pure misunderstanding; but the Jacobins of those days, like the monks whose place they had usurped, laid great stress on unity of obedience. After the death of Madame Helvetius our society gathered together in the *salon* of Madame de Condorcet. Bonaparte did not disdain to chat with us sometimes.

"Recognizing him to be a great man, we thought him an ideologist like ourselves. Our influence in the land was considerable. We used it in his favour, and urged him towards the Imperial throne, thinking to display to the world a second Marcus Aurelius. We counted on him to establish universal peace; he did not fulfil our expectations, and we were wrong-headed enough to be wroth with him for our own mistake.

"Without any doubt he greatly surpassed all other men in quickness of intelligence, depth of dissimulation, and capacity for action. What made him an accomplished ruler was that he lived entirely in the present moment, and had no thoughts for anything beyond the immediate and actual reality. His genius was far-reaching and agile; his intelligence, vast in extent but common and vulgar in character, embraced humanity, but did not rise above it. He thought what every grenadier in the army thought; but he thought it with unprecedented force. He loved the game of chance, and it pleased him to tempt fortune by urging pigmies in their hundreds and thousands against each other. It was the game of a child as big as the world. He was too wily not to introduce old Iahveh into the game,—Iahveh, who was still powerful on earth, and who resembled him in his spirit of violence and domination. He threatened him, flattered him, caressed him, and intimidated him. He imprisoned his Vicar, of whom he demanded, with the knife at his throat, that rite of unction which, since the days of Saul of old, has bestowed might upon kings; he restored the worship of the demiurge, sang *Te Deums* to him, and made himself known through him as God of the earth, in small catechisms scattered broadcast throughout the Empire. They united their thunders, and a fine uproar they made.

"While Napoleon's amusements were throwing Europe into a turmoil, we congratulated ourselves on our wisdom, a little sad, withal, at seeing the era of philosophy ushered in with massacre, torture, and war. The worst is that the children of the century, fallen into the most distressing disorder, formed the conception of a literary and picturesque Christianity, which betokens a degeneracy of mind really unbelievable, and finally fell into Romanticism. War and Romanticism, what terrible scourges! And how pitiful to see these same people nursing a childish and savage love for muskets and drums! They did not understand that war, which trained the courage and founded the cities of barbarous and ignorant men, brings to the victor himself but ruin and misery, and is nothing but a horrible and stupid crime when nations are united together by common bonds of art, science, and trade.

"Insane Europeans who plot to cut each others' throats, now that one and the same civilisation enfolds and unites them all!

"I renounced all converse with these madmen and withdrew to this village, where I devoted myself to gardening. The peaches in my orchard remind me of the sun-kissed skin of the Mænads. For mankind I have retained my old friendship, a little admiration, and much pity, and I await, while cultivating this enclosure, that still distant day when the great Dionysus shall come, followed by his Fauns and his Bacchantes, to restore beauty and gladness to the world, and bring back the Golden Age. I shall fare joyously behind his car. And who knows if in that day of triumph mankind will be there for us to see? Who knows whether their worn-out race will not have already fulfilled its destiny, and whether other beings will not rise upon the ashes and ruins of what once was man and his genius? Who knows if winged beings will not have taken possession of the terrestrial empire? Even then the work of the good demons will not be ended,—they will teach a winged race arts and the joy of life."

CHAPTER XXII

WHEREIN WE ARE SHOWN THE INTERIOR OF A BRIC-A-BRAC SHOP, AND SEE HOW PÈRE GUINARDON'S GUILTY HAPPINESS IS MARRED BY THE JEALOUSY OF A LOVE-LORN DAME

PÈRE GUINARDON (as Zéphyrine had faithfully reported to Monsieur Sariette) smuggled out the pictures, furniture, and curios stored in his attic in the rue Princesse—his studio he called it—and used them to stock a shop he had taken in the rue de Courcelles. Thither he went to take up his abode, leaving Zéphyrine, with whom he had lived for fifty years, without a bed or a saucepan or a penny to call her own, except eighteenpence the poor creature had in her purse. Père Guinardon opened an old picture and curiosity shop, and in it he installed the fair Octavie.

The shop-front presented an attractive appearance: there were Flemish angels in green copes, after the manner of Gérard David, a Salomé of the Luini school, a Saint Barbara in painted wood of French workmanship, Limoges enamel-work, Bohemian and Venetian glass, dishes from Urbino. There were specimens of English point-lace which, if her tale was true, had been presented to Zéphyrine, in the days of her radiant girlhood, by the Emperor Napoleon III. Within, there were golden articles that glinted in the shadows, while pictures of Christ, the Apostles, high-bred dames, and nymphs also presented themselves to the gaze. There was one canvas that was turned face to the wall so that it should only be looked at by connoisseurs; and connoisseurs are scarce. It was a replica of Fragonard's *Gimblette*, a brilliant painting that looked as if it had barely had time to dry. Papa Guinardon himself remarked on the fact. At the far end of the shop was a king-wood cabinet, the drawers of which were full of all manner of treasures: water-colours by Baudouin, eighteenth-century books of illustrations, miniatures, and so forth.

But the real masterpiece, the marvel, the gem, the pearl of great price, stood upon an easel veiled from public view. It was a *Coronation of the Virgin* by Fra Angelico, an exquisitely delicate thing in gold and blue and pink. Père Guinardon was asking a hundred thousand francs for it. Upon a Louis XV chair beside an Empire work-table on which stood a vase of flowers, sat the fair Octavie, broidery in hand. She, having left her glistering rags behind her in the garret in the rue Princesse, no longer presented the appearance of a touched-up Rembrandt, but shone, rather, with the soft radiance and limpidity of a Vermeer of Delft, for the delectation of the connoisseurs who frequented the shop of Papa Guinardon. Tranquil and demure, she remained alone in the shop all day, while the old fellow himself was up aloft working away at the deuce knows what picture. About five o'clock he used to come downstairs and have a chat with the habitués of the establishment.

The most regular caller was the Comte Desmaisons, a thin, cadaverous man. A strand of hair issued from the deep hollow under each cheek-bone, and, broadening as it descended, shed upon his chin and chest torrents of snow in which he was for ever trailing his long, fleshless, gold-ringed fingers. For twenty years he had been mourning the loss of his wife, who had been carried off by consumption in the flower of her youth and beauty. Since then he had spent his whole life in endeavouring to hold converse with the dead and in filling his lonely mansion with second-rate paintings. His confidence in Guinardon knew no bounds. Another client who was a scarcely less frequent visitor to the shop was Monsieur Blancmesnil, a director of a large financial establishment. He was a florid, prosperous-looking man of fifty. He took no great interest in matters of art, and was perhaps an indifferent connoisseur, but, in his case, it was the fair Octavie, seated in the middle of the shop, like a song-bird in its cage, that offered the attraction.

Monsieur Blancmesnil soon established relations with her, a fact which Père Guinardon alone failed to perceive, for the old fellow was still young in his love-affair with Octavie. Monsieur Gaétan d'Esparvieu used to pay occasional visits to Père Guinardon's shop out of mere curiosity, for he strongly suspected the old man of being a first-rate "faker."

And then that doughty swordsman, Monsieur Le Truc de Ruffec, also came to see the old antiquary on one occasion, and acquainted him with a plan he had on foot. Monsieur Le Truc de Ruffec was getting up a little historical exhibition of small arms at the Petit Palais in aid of the fund for the education of the native children in Morocco and wanted Père Guinardon to lend him a few of the most valuable articles in his collection.

"Our first idea," he said, "was to organise an exhibition to be called 'The Cross and the Sword.' The juxtaposition of the two words will make the idea which has prompted our undertaking sufficiently clear to you. It was an idea pre-eminently patriotic and Christian which led us to associate the Sword, which is the symbol of Honour, with the Cross, which is the symbol of Salvation. It was hoped that our work would be graced by the distinguished patronage of the Minister of War and Monseigneur Cachepot. Unfortunately there were difficulties in the way, and the full realisation of the project had to be deferred. In the meantime we are limiting our exhibition to 'The Sword.' I have drawn up an explanatory note indicating the significance of the demonstration."

Having delivered himself of these remarks, Monsieur Le Truc de Ruffec produced a pocket-case stuffed full of papers. Picking out from a medley of judgment summonses and other odds and ends a little piece of very crumpled paper, he exclaimed, "Ah, here it is," and proceeded to read as follows: "'The Sword is a fierce Virgin; it is *par excellence* the Frenchman's weapon. And now, when patriotic sentiment, after suffering an all too protracted eclipse, is beginning to shine forth again more ardently than ever ...' and so forth; you see?"

And he repeated his request for some really fine specimen to be placed in the most conspicuous position in the exhibition to be held on behalf of the little native children of Morocco, of which General d'Esparvieu was to be honorary President.

Arms and armour were by no means Père Guinardon's strong point. He dealt principally in pictures, drawings, and books. But he was never to be taken unawares. He took down a rapier with a gilt colander-shaped hilt, a highly typical piece of workmanship of the Louis XIII-Napoleon III period, and presented it to the exhibition promoter, who, while contemplating it with respect, maintained a diplomatic silence.

"I have something better still in here," said the antiquary, and he produced from his inner shop—where it had been lying among the walking-sticks and umbrellas—a real demon of a sword, adorned with fleurs-de-lys, a genuine royal relic. It was the sword of Philippe-Auguste as worn by an actor at the *Odéon* when *Agnès de Méranie* was being performed in 1846. Guinardon held it point downwards, as though it were a cross, clasping his hands piously on the cross-bar. He looked as loyal as the sword itself.

"Have her for your exhibition," said he. "The damsel is well worth it. Bouvines is her name."

"If I find a buyer for it," said Monsieur Le True de Ruffec, twirling his enormous moustachios, "I suppose you will allow me a little commission?"

Some days later, Père Guinardon was mysteriously displaying a picture to the Comte Desmaisons and Monsieur Blancmesnil. It was a newly discovered work of El Greco, an amazingly fine example of the Master's later style. It represented a Saint Francis of Assisi standing erect upon Mont Alverno. He was mounting heavenward like a column of smoke, and was plunging into the regions of the clouds a monstrously narrow head that the distance rendered smaller still. In fine it was a real, very real, nay, too real El Greco. The two collectors were attentively scrutinizing the work, while Père Guinardon was belauding the depth of the shadows and the sublimity of the expression. He was raising his arms aloft to convey an idea of the greatness of Theotocopuli, who derived from Tintoretto, whom, however, he surpassed in loftiness by a hundred cubits.

"He was chaste and pure and strong; a mystic, a visionary."

Comte Desmaisons declared that El Greco was his favourite painter. In his inmost heart Blancmesnil was not so entirely struck with it.

The door opened, and Monsieur Gaétan quite unexpectedly appeared on the scene.

He gave a glance at the Saint Francis, and said:

"Bless my soul!"

Monsieur Blancmesnil, anxious to improve his knowledge, asked him what he thought of this artist who was now so much in vogue. Gaétan replied, glibly enough, that he did not regard El Greco as the eccentric, the madman that people used to take him for. It was rather his opinion that a defect of vision from which Theotocopuli suffered compelled him to deform his figures.

"Being afflicted with astigmatism and strabismus," Gaétan went on, "he painted the things he saw exactly as he used to see them."

Comte Desmaisons was not readily disposed to accept so natural an explanation, which, however, by its very simplicity, highly commended itself to Monsieur Blancmesnil.

Père Guinardon, quite beside himself, exclaimed:

"Are you going to tell me, Monsieur d'Esparvieu, that Saint John was astigmatic because he beheld a woman clothed with the sun, crowned with stars, with the moon about her feet; the Beast with seven heads and ten horns, and the seven angels robed in white linen that bore the seven cups filled with the wrath of the Living God?"

"After all," said Monsieur Gaétan, by way of conclusion, "people are right in admiring El Greco if he had genius enough to impose his morbidity of vision upon them. By the same token, the contortions to which he subjects the human countenance may give satisfaction to those who love suffering,—a class more numerous than is generally supposed."

"Monsieur," replied the Comte Desmaisons, stroking his luxuriant beard with his long, thin hand, "we must love those that love us. Suffering loves us and attaches itself to us. We must love it if life is to be supportable to us. In the knowledge of this truth lies the strength and value of Christianity. Alas! I do not possess the gift of Faith. It is that which drives me to despair."

The old man thought of her for whom he had been mourning twenty years, and forthwith his reason left him, and his thoughts abandoned themselves unresistingly to the morbid imaginings of gentle and melancholy madness.

Having, he said, made a study of psychic matters, and having, with the co-operation of a favourable medium, carried out experiments concerning the nature and duration of the soul, he had obtained some remarkable results, which, however, did not afford him complete satisfaction. He had succeeded in viewing the soul of his dead wife under the appearance of a transparent and gelatinous mass which bore not the slightest resemblance to his adored one. The most painful part about the whole experiment—which he had repeated over and over again—was that the gelatinous mass, which was furnished with a number of extremely slender tentacles, maintained them in constant motion in time to a rhythm apparently intended to make certain signs, but of what these movements were supposed to convey there was not the slightest clue.

During the whole of this narrative Monsieur Blancmesnil had been whispering in a corner with the youthful Octavie, who sat mute and still, with her eyes on the ground.

Now Zéphyrine had by no means made up her mind to resign her lover into the hands of an unworthy rival. She would often go round of a morning, with her shopping-basket on her arm, and prowl about outside the curio shop. Torn betwixt grief and rage, tormented by warring ideas, she sometimes thought she would empty a saucepanful of vitriol on the head of the faithless one; at others that she would fling herself at his feet, and shower tears and kisses on his precious hands. One day, as she was thus eyeing her Michel—her beloved but guilty Michel—she noticed through the window the fair and youthful Octavie, who was sitting with her embroidery at a table upon which, in a vase of crystal, a rose was swooning to death. Zéphyrine, in a transport of fury, brought down her umbrella on her rival's fair head, and called her a bitch and a trollop. Octavie fled in terror, and ran for the police, while Zéphyrine, beside herself with grief and love, kept digging away with her old gamp at the *Gimblette* of Fragonard, the fuliginous Saint Francis of El Greco, the virgins, the nymphs, and the apostles, and knocked the gilt off the Fra Angelico, shrieking all the while:

"All those pictures there, the El Greco, the Beato Angelico, the Fragonard, the Gérard David, and the Baudouins—Guinardon painted the whole lot of them himself, the wretch, the scoundrel! That Fra Angelico there, why I saw him painting it on my ironing-board, and that Gérard David he executed on an old midwife's sign-board. You and that bitch of yours, why, I'll do for the pair of you just as I'm doing for these pictures."

And tugging away at the coat of an aged collector who, trembling all over, had hidden himself in the darkest corner of the shop, she called him to witness to the crimes of Guinardon, perjurer and impostor. The police had simply to tear her out of the ruined shop. As she was being taken off to the station, followed by a great crowd of people, she raised her fiery eyes to Heaven, crying in a voice choked with sobs:

"But don't you know Michel? If you knew him, you would understand that it is impossible to live without him. Michel! He is handsome and good and charming. He is a very god. He is Love itself. I love him! I love him! I love him! I have known men high up in the world—Dukes, Ministers of State, and higher still. Not one of them was worthy to clean the mud off Michel's boots. My good, kind sirs, give him back to me again."

CHAPTER XXIII

WHEREIN WE ARE PERMITTED TO OBSERVE THE ADMIRABLE CHARACTER OF BOUCHOTTE, WHO RESISTS VIOLENCE BUT YIELDS TO LOVE. AFTER THAT LET NO ONE CALL THE AUTHOR A MISOGYNIST

ON coming away from the Baron Everdingen's, Prince Istar went to have a few oysters and a bottle of white wine at an eating-house in the Market. Then, being prudent as well as powerful, he paid a visit to his friend, Théophile Belais, for his pockets were full of bombs, and he wanted to secrete them in the musician's cupboard. The composer of *Aline, Queen of Golconda* was not at home. However, the Kerûb found Bouchotte busily working up the rôle of Zigouille; for the young artiste was booked to play the principal part in *Les Apaches*, an operetta that was then being rehearsed in one of the big music halls. The part in question was that of a street-walker who by her obscene gestures lures a passer-by into a trap, and then, while her victim is being gagged and bound, repeats with fiendish cruelty the lascivious motions by which he had been led astray. The part required that she should appear both as mime and singer, and she was in a state of high enthusiasm about it.

The accompanist had just left. Prince Istar seated himself at the piano, and Bouchotte resumed her task. Her movements were unseemly and delicious. Her tawny hair was flying in all directions in wild disordered curls; her skin was moist, it exhaled a scent of violets and alkaline salts which made the nostrils throb; even she herself felt the intoxication. Suddenly, inebriated with her intoxicating presence, Prince Istar arose, and with never a word or a look, caught her into his arms and drew her on to the couch, the little couch with the flowered tapestry which Théophile had procured at one of the big shops by promising to pay ten francs a month for a long term of years. Now Istar might have solicited Bouchotte's favours; he might have invited her to a rapid, and, withal, a mutual embrace, and, despite her preoccupation and excitement, she would not have refused him. But Bouchotte was a girl of spirit. The merest hint of coercion awoke all her untamable pride. She would consent of her own accord, yes; but be mastered, never! She would readily yield to love, curiosity, pity, to less than that even, but she would die rather than yield to force. Her surprise immediately gave place to fury. She fought her aggressor with all her heart and soul.

With nails, to which fury lent an added edge, she tore at the cheeks and eyelids of the Kerûb, and, though he held her as in a vice, she arched herself so stiffly and made such excellent play with knee and elbow, that the human-headed bull, blinded with blood and rage, was sent crashing into the piano which gave forth a prolonged groan, while the bombs, tumbling out of his pockets, fell on the floor with a noise like thunder. And Bouchotte, with dishevelled locks, and one breast bare, beautiful and terrible, stood brandishing the poker over the prostrate giant, crying:

"Be off with you, or I'll put your eyes out!"

Prince Istar went to wash himself in the kitchen, and plunged his gory visage into a basin where some haricot beans lay soaking; then he withdrew without anger or resentment, for he had a noble soul.

Scarcely had he gone when the door-bell rang. Bouchotte, calling upon the absent maid in vain, slipped on a dressing-gown and opened the door herself. A young man, very correct in appearance and rather good-looking, bowed politely, and apologising for having to introduce himself, gave his name. It was Maurice d'Esparvieu.

Maurice was still seeking his guardian angel. Upheld by a desperate hope, he sought him in the queerest places. He enquired for him at the houses of sorcerers, magicians, and thaumaturgists, who in filthy hovels lay bare the ineffable secrets of the future, and who, though masters of all the treasures of the earth, wear trousers without any seats to them, and eat pigs' brains. That very day, having been to a back street in Montmartre to consult a priest of Satan, who practised black magic by piercing waxen images, Maurice had gone on to Bouchotte's, having been sent by Madame de la Verdelière, who, being about to give a fête in aid of the fund for the Preservation of Country Churches, was anxious to secure Bouchotte's services, since she had suddenly become—no one knew why—a fashionable artiste.

Bouchotte invited the visitor to sit down on the little flowered couch; at his request she seated herself beside him, and our young man of fashion explained to the singer what Madame de la Verdelière desired of her. The lady wished Bouchotte to sing one of those *apache* songs which were giving such delight in the fashionable world. Unfortunately Madame de la Verdelière could only offer a very modest fee, one out of all proportion to the merits of the artiste, but then it was for a good cause.

Bouchotte agreed to take part, and accepted the reduced fee with the accustomed liberality of the poor towards the rich and of artists towards society people. Bouchotte was not a selfish girl; the work for the preservation of country churches interested her. She remembered with sobs and tears her first communion, and she still retained her faith. When she passed by a church she wanted to enter it, especially in the evening. And so she did not love the Republic which had done its utmost to destroy both the Church and the Army. Her heart rejoiced to see the re-birth of national sentiment. France was lifting up her head. What was most applauded in the music halls were songs about the soldiers and the kind nuns. Meanwhile Maurice inhaled the odour of her tawny hair, the subtle bitter perfume of her body, all the odours of her person, and desire grew in him. He felt her near him on the little couch, very warm and very soft. He complimented the artiste on her great talent. She asked him what he liked best in all her repertory. He knew nothing about it, still he made replies that satisfied her. She had dictated them herself without knowing it. The vain creature spoke of her talent, of her success, as she wished others to speak of them. She never ceased talking of her triumphs, yet withal she was candour itself. Maurice in all sincerity praised Bouchotte's beauty, her fresh skin, her purity of line. She attributed this advantage to the fact that she never made up and never "put messes on her face." As to her figure, she admitted that there was enough everywhere and none too much, and to illustrate this assertion she passed her hand over all the contours of her charming body, rising lightly to follow the delightful curves on which she reposed.

Maurice was quite moved by it. It began to grow dark; she offered to light up. He begged her to do nothing of the sort.

Their talk, at first gay and full of laughter, grew more intimate and very sweet, with a certain languor in its tone. It seemed to Bouchotte that she had known Monsieur Maurice d'Esparvieu for a long time, and holding him for a man of delicacy, she gave him her confidence. She told him that she was by nature a good woman, but that she had had a grasping and unscrupulous mother. Maurice recalled her to the consideration of her own beauty, and exalted by subtle flattery the excellent opinion she had of herself. Patient and calculating, in spite of the burning desire growing in him, he aroused and increased in the desired one the longing to be still further admired. The dressing-gown opened and slipped down of its own accord, the living satin of her shoulders gleamed in the mysterious light of evening. He—so prudent, so clever, so adroit,—let her sink in his arms, ardent and half swooning before she had even perceived she had granted anything at all. Their breath and their murmurs intermingled. And the little flowery couch sighed in sympathy with them.

When they recovered the power to express their feelings in words, she whispered in his ear that his cheek was even softer than her own.

He answered, holding her embraced:

"It is charming to hold you like this. One would think you had no bones."

She replied, closing her eyes:

"It is because I love you. Love seems to dissolve my bones; it makes me as soft and melting as a pig's foot *à la Ste. Menebould.*"

93

Hereupon Théophile came in, and Bouchotte called upon him to thank Monsieur Maurice d'Esparvieu, who had been amiable enough to be the bearer of a handsome offer from Madame la Comtesse de la Verdelière.

The musician was happy, feeling the quiet and peace of the house after a day of fruitless applications, of colourless lessons, of failure and humiliation. Three new collaborators had been thrust upon him who would add their signatures to his on his operetta, and receive their share of the author's rights, and he had been told to introduce the tango into the Court of Golconda. He pressed young d'Esparvieu's hand and dropped wearily on to the little couch, which, being now at the end of its strength, gave way at the four legs and suddenly collapsed.

And the angel, precipitated to the ground, rolled terror-struck on to the watch, match-box and cigarette-case that had fallen from Maurice's pocket, and on to the bombs Prince Istar had left behind him.

CHAPTER XXIV

CONTAINING AN ACCOUNT OF THE VICISSITUDES THAT BEFEL THE "LUCRETIUS" OF THE PRIOR DE VENDÔME

LÉGER-MASSIEU, successor to Léger senior, the binder, whose establishment was in the rue de l'Abbaye, opposite the old Hôtel of the Abbés of Saint Germain-des-Prés, in the hotbed of ancient schools and learned societies, employed an excellent but by no means numerous staff of workmen, and served with leisurely deliberation a clientèle who had learned to practise the virtue of patience. Six weeks had elapsed since he had received the parcel of books that had been despatched by Monsieur Sariette, but still Léger-Massieu had not yet put the work in hand. It was not until fifty-three days had come and gone, that, after calling over the books against the list that had been drawn up by Monsieur Sariette, the binder gave them out to his workmen. The little *Lucretius* with the Prior de Vendôme's arms not being mentioned on the list, it was assumed that it had been sent by another customer.

And as it did not figure on any list of goods received it remained shut up in a cupboard, from which Léger-Massieu's son, the youthful Ernest, one day surreptitiously abstracted it, and slipped it into his pocket. Ernest was in love with a neighbouring seamstress whose name was Rose. Rose was fond of the country, and liked to hear the birds singing in the woods, and in order to procure the wherewithal to take her to Chatou one Sunday and give her a dinner, Ernest parted with the *Lucretius* for ten francs to old Moranger, a second-hand dealer in the rue Saint X——, who displayed no great curiosity regarding the origin of his acquisitions. Old Moranger handed over the volume, the very same day, to Monsieur Poussard, an expert in books, of the faubourg Saint Germain, for sixty francs. The latter removed the stamp which disclosed the ownership of the matchless copy, and sold it for five hundred francs to Monsieur Joseph Meyer, the well-known collector, who handed it straight away for three thousand francs to Monsieur Ardon, the bookseller, who immediately transferred it to Monsieur R——, the great Parisian bibliopolist, who gave six thousand for it, and sold it again a fortnight later at a handsome profit to Madame la Comtesse de Gorce. Well known in the higher ranks of Parisian society, the lady in question is what was called in the seventeenth century a "curieuse," that is to say, a lover of pictures, books, and china. In her mansion in the Avenue d'Jéna she possesses collections of works of art which bear witness to the diversity of her knowledge and the excellence of her taste. During the month of July, while the Comtesse de Gorce was away at her château at Sarville in Normandy, the house in the Avenue d'Jéna, being unoccupied, was visited one night by a thief said to belong to a gang known as "The Collectors," who made works of art the special objects of their raids.

The police enquiry elicited the fact that the marauder had reached the first floor by means of the waste-pipe, that he had then climbed over the balcony, forced a shutter with a jemmy, broken a pane of glass, turned the window-fastener, and made his way into the long gallery. There he broke open several cupboards and possessed himself of whatever took his fancy. His booty consisted for the most part of small but valuable articles, such as gold caskets, a few ivory carvings of the fourteenth century, two splendid fifteenth-century manuscripts, and a volume which the Countess's secretary briefly described as "a morocco-bound book with a coat of arms on it," and which was none other than the *Lucretius* from the d'Esparvieu library.

The malefactor, who was supposed to be an English cook, was never discovered. But, two months or so after the theft, a well-dressed, clean-shaven young man passed down the rue de Courcelles, in the dimness of twilight, and went to offer the Prior de Vendôme's *Lucretius* to Père Guinardon. The antiquary gave him four shillings for it, examined it carefully, recognised its interest and its beauty, and put it in the king-wood cabinet, where he kept his special treasures.

Such were the vicissitudes which, in the course of a single season, befel this thing of beauty.

CHAPTER XXV

WHEREIN MAURICE FINDS HIS ANGEL AGAIN

THE performance was over. Bouchotte in her dressing-room was taking off her make-up, when the door opened softly and old Monsieur Sandraque, her protector, came in, followed by a troop of her other admirers. Without so much as turning her head, she asked them what they meant by coming and staring at her like a pack of imbeciles, and whether they thought they were in a tent at the Neuilly Fair, looking at the freak woman.

"Now, then, ladies and gentlemen," she rattled on derisively, "just put a penny in the box for the young lady's marriage-portion, and she'll let you feel her legs,—all made of marble!"

Then, with an angry glance at the admiring throng, she exclaimed: "Come, off you go! Look alive!"

She sent them all packing, her sweetheart Théophile among them,—the pale-faced, long-haired, gentle, melancholy, short-sighted, and dreamy Théophile.

But recognizing her little Maurice, she gave him a smile. He approached her, and leaning over the back of the chair on which she was seated, congratulated her on her playing and singing, duly performing a kiss at the end of every compliment. She did not let him escape thus, and with reiterated enquiries, pressing solicitations, feigned incredulity, obliged him to repeat his stock panegyrics three or four times over, and when he stopped she seemed so disappointed that he was forced to take up the strain again immediately. He found it trying, for he was no connoisseur, but he had the pleasure of kissing her plump curved shoulders all golden in the light, and of catching glimpses of her pretty face in the mirror over the toilet-table.

"You were delicious."

"Really?... you think so?"

"Adorable ... div——"

Suddenly he gave a loud cry. His eyes had seen in the mirror a face appear at the back of the dressing-room. He turned swiftly round, flung his arms about Arcade, and drew him into the corridor.

"What manners!" exclaimed Bouchotte, gasping.

But, pushing his way through a troop of performing dogs, and a family of American acrobats, young d'Esparvieu dragged his angel towards the exit.

He hurried him forth into the cool darkness of the boulevard, delirious with joy and wondering whether it was all too good to be true.

"Here you are!" he cried; "here you are! I have been looking for you a long time, Arcade,— or Mirar if you like,—and I have found you at last. Arcade, you have taken my guardian angel from me. Give him back to me. Arcade, do you love me still?"

Arcade replied that in accomplishing the super-angelic task he had set himself he had been forced to crush under foot friendship, pity, love, and all those feelings which tend to soften the soul; but that, on the other hand, his new state, by exposing him to suffering and privation, disposed him to love Humanity, and that he felt a certain mechanical friendship for his poor Maurice.

"Well, then," exclaimed Maurice, "if only you love me, come back to me, stay with me. I cannot do without you. While I had you with me I was not aware of your presence. But no sooner did you depart than I felt a horrible blank. Without you I am like a body without a soul. Do you know that in the little flat in the rue de Rome, with Gilberte by my side, I feel lonely, I miss you sorely, and long to see you and to hear you as I did that day when you made me so angry. Confess I was right, and that your behaviour on that occasion was not that of a gentleman. That you, you of so high an origin, so noble a mind, could commit such an indiscretion is extraordinary, when one comes to think about it. Madame des Aubels has not yet forgiven you. She blames you for having frightened her by appearing at such an inconvenient moment, and for being insolent and forward while hooking her dress and tying her shoes. I, I have forgotten everything. I only remember that you are my celestial brother, the saintly companion of my childhood. No, Arcade, you must not, you cannot leave me. You are my angel; you are my property."

Arcade explained to young d'Esparvieu that he could no longer be guiding angel to a Christian, having himself gone down into the pit. And he painted a horrible picture of himself; he described himself as breathing hatred and fury; in fact, an infernal spirit.

"All nonsense!" said Maurice, smiling, his eyes big with tears.

"Alas! our ideas, our destiny, everything tends to part us, Maurice. But I cannot stifle the tenderness I feel for you, and your candour forces me to love you."

"No," sighed Maurice. "You do not love me. You have never loved me. In a brother or a sister such indifference would be natural; in a friend it would be ordinary; in a guardian angel it is monstrous. Arcade, you are an abominable being. I hate you."

"I have loved you dearly, Maurice, and I still love you. You trouble my heart which I deemed encased in triple bronze. You show me my own weakness. When you were a little innocent boy I loved you as tenderly and purely as Miss Kate, your English governess, who caressed you with so much fervour. In the country, when the thin bark of the plane trees peels off in long strips and discloses the tender green trunk, after the rains which make the fine sand run on the sloping paths, I showed you how with that sand, those strips of bark, a few wild flowers, and a spray of maidenhair fern to make rustic bridges, rustic shelters, terraces, and those gardens of Adonis, which last but an hour. During the month of May in Paris we raised an altar to the Virgin, and we burnt incense before it, the scent of which, permeating all the house, reminded Marcelline, the cook, of her village church and her lost innocence, and drew from her floods of tears; it also gave your mother a headache, your mother who, with all her wealth, was crushed with the *ennui* that is common to the fortunate ones of this world. When you went to college I interested myself in your progress, I shared your work and your play, I pondered with you over arduous problems in arithmetic, I sought the impenetrable meaning of a phrase of Julius Cæsar's. What fine games of prisoners' base and football we had together! More than once did we know the intoxication of victory, and our young laurels were not soaked in blood or tears. Maurice, I did all I could to protect your innocence, but I could not prevent your losing it at the age of fourteen. Afterwards I regretfully saw you loving women of all sorts, of divers ages, by no means beautiful, at least in the eyes of an angel. Saddened at the sight, I devoted myself to study; a fine library offered me resources rarely met with. I delved into the history of religions; you know the rest."

"But now, my dear Arcade," concluded young d'Esparvieu, "you have lost your position, your situation, you are entirely without resource. You have lost caste, you are off the lines, a vagabond, a bare-footed wanderer."

The Angel replied bitterly that, after all, he was a little better clad at present than when he was wearing the slops of a suicide.

Maurice alleged in excuse that when he dressed his naked angel in a suicide's slops, he was irritated with that angel's infidelity. But it was useless to dwell on the past or to recriminate. What was really needful was to consider what steps to take in future.

And he asked:

"Arcade, what do you think of doing?"

"Have I not already told you, Maurice? To fight with Him who reigns in the heavens, dethrone Him, and set up Satan in His stead."

"You will not do it. To begin with it is not the opportune moment. Opinion is not with you. You will not be in the swim, as papa says. Conservatism and authority are all the go nowadays. We like to be ruled, and the President of the Republic is going to parley with the Pope. Do not be obstinate, Arcade. You are not as bad as you say. At bottom you are like the rest of the world, you adore the good God."

"I thought I had already explained to you, Maurice, that He whom you consider God is actually but a demiurge. He is absolutely ignorant of the divine world above him, and in all good faith believes himself to be the true and only God. You will find in the *History of the Church*, by Monsignor Duchesne—Vol. I, page 162—that this proud and narrow-minded demiurge is named Ialdabaoth. My child, so as not to ruffle your prejudices and to deal gently with your feelings in future, that is the name I shall give him. If it should happen that I should speak of him to you, I shall call him Ialdabaoth. I must leave you. Adieu."

"Stay——"

"I cannot."

"I shall not let you go thus. You have deprived me of my guardian angel. It is for you to repair the injury you have caused me. Give me another one."

Arcade objected that it was difficult for him to satisfy such a demand. That having quarrelled with the sovereign dispenser of guardian Spirits, he could obtain nothing from that quarter.

"My dear Maurice," he added, smiling, "ask for one yourself from Ialdabaoth."

"No,—no,—no," exclaimed Maurice. "You have taken away my guardian angel,—give him back to me."

"Alas! I cannot."

"Is it, Arcade, because you are a revolutionary that you cannot?"

"Yes."

"An enemy of God?"

"Yes."

"A Satanic spirit?"

"Yes."

"Well, then," exclaimed young Maurice, "I will be your guardian angel,—I will not leave you."

And Maurice d'Esparvieu took Arcade to have some oysters at P——'s.

CHAPTER XXVI

THE CONCLAVE

THAT day, convoked by Arcade and Zita, the rebellious angels met together on the banks of the Seine at La Jonchère, in a deserted and tumble-down entertainment-hall that Prince Istar had hired from a pot-house keeper called Barattan. Three hundred angels crowded together in the stalls and boxes. A table, an arm-chair, and a collection of small chairs were arranged on the stage, where hung the tattered remnants of a piece of rustic scenery. The walls, coloured in distemper with flowers and fruit, were cracked and stained with damp, and were crumbling away in flakes. The vulgar and poverty-stricken appearance of the place rendered the grandeur of the passions exhibited therein all the more striking.

When Prince Istar asked the assembly to form its Committee, and first of all to elect a President, the name that was renowned throughout the world entered the minds of all present, but a religious respect sealed their lips; and after a moment's silence, the absent Nectaire was elected by acclamation. Having been invited to take the chair between Zita and an angel of Japan, Arcade immediately began as follows:

"Sons of Heaven! My comrades! You have freed yourselves from the bonds of celestial servitude—you have shaken off the thrall of him called Iahveh, but to whom we should here accord his veritable name of Ialdabaoth, for he is not the creator of the worlds, but merely an ignorant and barbarous demiurge, who having obtained possession of a minute portion of the Universe has therein sown suffering and death. Sons of Heaven, tell me, I charge you, whether you will combat and destroy Ialdabaoth?"

All with one voice made answer:

"We will!"

And many speaking all together swore they would scale the mountain of Ialdabaoth, and hurl down the walls of jasper and porphyry, and plunge the tyrant of Heaven into eternal darkness.

But a voice of crystal pierced through the sullen murmur.

"Tremble, ye impious, sacrilegious madmen! The Lord hath already lifted his dread arm to smite you!"

It was a loyal angel who, with an impulse of faith and love, envying the glory of confessors and martyrs, jealous and eager, like his God himself, to emulate man in the beauty of sacrifice, had flung himself in the midst of the blasphemers, to brave them, to confound them, and to fall beneath their blows. The assembly turned upon him with furious unanimity. Those nearest to him overwhelmed him with blows. He continued to cry, in a clear, ringing voice, "Glory to God! Glory to God! Glory to God!"

A rebel seized him by the neck and strangled his praises of the Almighty in his throat. He was thrown to the ground, trampled underfoot. Prince Istar picked him up, took him by the wings between his fingers, then rising like a column of smoke, opened a ventilator, which no one else could have reached, and passed the faithful angel through it. Order was immediately restored.

"Comrades," continued Arcade, "now that we have affirmed our stern resolve, we must examine the possible plans of campaign, and choose the best. You will therefore have to consider if we should attack the enemy in full force, or whether it were better, by a lengthy and assiduous propaganda, to win the inhabitants of Heaven to our cause."

"War! War!" shouted the assembled host.

And it seemed as if one could hear the sound of trumpets and the rolling of drums.

Théophile, whom Prince Istar had dragged to the meeting, rose, pale and unstrung, and, speaking with emotion, said:

"Brethren, do not take ill what I am about to say; for it is the friendship I have for you that inspires me. I am but a poor musician. But, believe me, all your plans will come to naught before the Divine Wisdom which has foreseen everything."

Théophile Belais sat down amid hisses. And Arcade continued:

"Ialdabaoth foresees everything. I do not contest it. He foresees everything, but in order to leave us our free will he acts towards us absolutely as if he foresaw nothing. Every instant he is surprised, disconcerted; the most probable events take him unawares. The obligation which he has undertaken, to reconcile with his prescience the liberty of both men and angels, throws him constantly into inextricable difficulties and terrible dilemmas. He never sees further than the end of his nose. He did not expect Adam's disobedience, and so little did he anticipate the wickedness of men that he repented having made them, and drowned them in the waters of the Flood, and all the animals as well, though he had no fault to find with the animals. For blindness he is only to be compared with Charles X, his favourite king. If we are prudent it will be easy to take him by surprise. I think that these observations will be calculated to reassure my brother."

Théophile made no reply. He loved God, but he was fearful of sharing the fate of the faithful angel.

One of the best-informed Spirits of the assembly, Mammon, was not altogether reassured by the remarks of his brother Arcade.

"Bethink you," said this Spirit, "Ialdabaoth has little general culture, but he is a soldier—to the marrow of his bones. The organisation of Paradise is a thoroughly military organisation. It is founded on hierarchy and discipline. Passive obedience is imposed there as a fundamental law. The angels form an army. Compare this spot with the Elysian Fields which Virgil depicts for you. In the Elysian Fields reign liberty, reason, and wisdom. The happy shades hold converse together in the groves of myrtle. In the Heaven of Ialdabaoth there is no civil population. Everyone is enrolled, numbered, registered. It is a barracks and a field for manœuvres. Remember that."

Arcade replied that they must look at their adversary in his true colours, and that the military organisation of Paradise was far more reminiscent of the villages of King Koffee than of the Prussia of Frederick the Great.

"Already," said he, "at the time of the first revolt, before the beginning of Time, the conflict raged for two days, and Ialdabaoth's throne was made to totter. Nevertheless, the demiurge gained the victory. But to what did he owe it? To the thunderstorm which happened to come on during the conflict. The thunderbolts falling on Lucifer and his angels struck them down, bruised and blackened, and Ialdabaoth owed his victory to the thunderbolts. Thunder is his sole weapon. He abuses its power. In the midst of thunder and lightning he promulgates his laws. 'Fire goeth before him,' says the Prophet. Now Seneca, the philosopher, said that the thunderbolt in its fall brings peril to very few, but fear to all. This remark was true enough for men of the first century of the Christian era; it is no longer so for the angels of the twentieth; all of which goes to prove that, in spite of his thunder, he is not very powerful; it was acute terror that made men rear him a tower of unbaked brick and bitumen. When myriads of celestial spirits, furnished with machines which modern science puts at their disposal, make an assault upon the heavens, think you, comrades, that the old master of the solar system surrounded with his angels, armed as in the time of Abraham, will be able to resist them? To this day the warriors of the demiurge wear helmets of gold and shields of diamond. Michael, his best captain, knows no other tactics than the hand-to-hand combat. To him Pharaoh's chariots are still the latest thing, and he has never heard of the Macedonian phalanx."

And young Arcade lengthily prolonged the parallel between the armed herds of Ialdabaoth and the intelligent fighting men of the rebel army. Then the question of pecuniary resources arose.

Zita asserted that there was enough money to commence war, that the electrophores were in order, that an initial victory would obtain them credit.

The discussion continued, amid turbulence and confusion. In this parliament of angels, as in the synods of men, empty words flowed in abundance. Disturbances grew more violent and more frequent as the time for putting the resolution drew near. It was beyond question that supreme command would be entrusted to him who had first raised the flag of revolt. But as everyone aspired to act as Lucifer's Lieutenant, each in describing the kind of fighting man to be preferred drew a portrait of himself. Thus Alcor, the youngest of the rebellious angels, arose and spoke rapidly as follows:

"In Ialdabaoth's army, happily for us, the officers obtain their posts by seniority. This being the case, there is little likelihood of the command falling into the hands of a military genius, for men are not made leaders by prolonged habits of obedience, and close attention to minutiæ is not a good apprenticeship for the evolution of vast plans of campaign. If we consult ancient and modern history, we shall see that the greatest leaders were kings like Alexander and Frederick, aristocrats like Cæsar and Turenne, or men impatient of red-tape like Bonaparte. A routine man will always be poor or second-rate. Comrades, let us appoint intelligent leaders, men in the prime of life, to command us. An old man may retain the habit of winning victories, but only a young man can acquire it!"

Alcor then gave place to an angel of the philosophic order, who mounted the rostrum and spoke thus:

"War never was an exact science, a clearly defined art. The genius of the race, or the brain of the individual, has ever modified it. Now how are we to define the qualities necessary for a general in command in the war of the future, where one must consider greater masses and a larger number of movements than the intelligence of man can conceive? The multiplication of technical means, by infinitely multiplying the opportunities for mistake, paralyses the genius of those in command. At a certain stage in the progress of military science, a stage which our models, the Europeans, are about to reach, the cleverest leader and the most ignorant become equalized by reason of their incapacity. Another result of great modern armaments is, that the law of numbers tends to rule with inflexible rigour. It is of course true that ten angels in revolt are worth more than ten angels of Ialdabaoth; it is not at all certain that a million rebellious angels are worth more than a million of Ialdabaoth's angels. Great numbers, in war as elsewhere, annihilate intelligence and individual superiority in favour of a sort of exceedingly rudimentary collective soul."

A buzz of conversation drowned the voice of the philosophic angel, and he concluded his speech in an atmosphere of general indifference.

The tribune then resounded with calls to arms and promises of victory. The sword was held up to praise, the sword which defends the right. The triumph of the angels in revolt was celebrated twenty times beforehand, to the plaudits of a delirious crowd.

Cries of "War!" rose to the silent heavens; "Give us war!"

In the midst of these transports Prince Istar hoisted himself on to the platform, and the floor creaked under his weight.

"Comrades," said he, "you wish for victory, and it is a very natural desire, but you must be mouldy with literature and poetry if you expect to obtain it from war. The idea of making war can nowadays only enter the brain of a sottish bourgeois or a belated romantic. What is war? A burlesque masquerade in the midst of which fatuous patriots sing their stupid dithyrambs. Had Napoleon possessed a practical mind he would not have made war; but he was a dreamer, intoxicated with Ossian. You cry, 'Give us war!' You are visionaries. When will you become thinkers? The thinkers do not look for power and strength from any of the dreams which constitute military art: tactics, strategy, fortifications, artillery, and all that rubbish. They do not believe in war, which is a phantasy; they believe in chemistry, which is a science. They know the way to put victory into an algebraic formula."

And drawing from his pocket a small bottle, which he held up to the meeting, Prince Istar exclaimed:

"Victory—it is here!"

CHAPTER XXVII

WHEREIN WE SHALL SEE REVEALED A DARK AND SECRET MYSTERY AND LEARN HOW IT COMES ABOUT THAT EMPIRES ARE OFTEN HURLED AGAINST EMPIRES, AND RUIN FALLS ALIKE UPON THE VICTORS AND THE VANQUISHED; AND THE WISE READER (IF SUCH THERE BE—WHICH I DOUBT) WILL MEDITATE UPON THIS IMPORTANT UTTERANCE: "A WAR IS A MATTER OF BUSINESS"

THE Angels had dispersed. At the foot of the slopes at Meudon, seated on the grass, Arcade and Zita watched the Seine flowing by the willows.

"In this world," said Arcade, "in this world, which we call a cosmos, though it is but a microcosm, no thinking being can imagine that he is able to destroy even one atom. At the utmost, all we can hope for is that we shall succeed in modifying, here and there, the rhythm of some group of atoms and the arrangement of certain cells. That, when one thinks of it, must be the limit of our great enterprise. And when we shall have set up the Contradictor in the place of Ialdabaoth, we shall have done no more.... Zita, is the evil in the nature of things or in their arrangement? That is what we ought to know. Zita, I am profoundly troubled——"

"Arcade," replied Zita, "if to act we had to know the secret of Nature, one would never act at all. And neither would one live—since to live is to act. Arcade, is your resolution failing you already?"

Arcade assured the beautiful angel that he was resolved to plunge the demiurge into eternal darkness.

A motor-car passed by on the road, followed by a long trail of dust. It stopped before the two angels, and the hooked nose of Baron Everdingen appeared at the window.

"Good morning, my celestial friends, good morning," said the capitalist. "Sons of Heaven, I am pleased to meet you. I have a word of importance to say to you. Do not remain idle—do not go to sleep. Arm! Arm! You may be surprised by Ialdabaoth. You have a big war-fund. Employ it without stint. I have just learnt that the Archangel Michael has given large orders in Heaven for thunderbolts and arrows. If you take my advice you will procure fifty thousand more electrophores. I will take the order. Good day, angels. Long live the celestial country!"

And Baron Everdingen flew by the flowery shores of Louveciennes in the company of a pretty actress.

"Is it true that they are taking up arms at the demiurge's?" asked Arcade.

"It may be," replied Zita, "that up there another Baron Everdingen is inciting to arms."

The guardian angel of young Maurice remained pensive for some moments. Then he murmured:

"Can it be that we are the sport of financiers?"

"Pooh!" said the beautiful archangel. "War is a business. It has always been a business."

Then they discussed at length the means of executing their immense enterprise. Rejecting disdainfully the anarchistic proceedings of Prince Istar, they conceived a formidable and sudden invasion of the kingdom of Heaven by their enthusiastic and well-drilled troops.

Now Barattan, the innkeeper of La Jonchère, who had let the entertainment-hall to the rebellious angels, was in the employ of the secret police. In the reports he furnished to the Prefecture he denounced the members of this secret meeting as meditating an attack on a certain person whom they described as obtuse and cruel, and whom they called *Alaballotte*. The agent believed this to be a pseudonym denoting either the President of the Republic or the Republic itself. The conspirators had unanimously given voice to threats against *Alaballotte*, and one of them, a very dangerous individual, well-known in anarchist circles, who had already several convictions against him on account of writings and speeches of a seditious nature, and who was known as Prince Istar or the *Quéroube*, had brandished a bomb of very small calibre which seemed to contain a formidable machine. The other conspirators were unknown to Barattan, notwithstanding the fact that he frequented revolutionary circles. Many among them were very young men, mere beardless youths. There were two who, it appeared, had spoken with conspicuous vehemence; a certain Arcade, dwelling in the Rue St. Jacques, and a woman of easy virtue called Zita, living at Montmartre, both without visible means of subsistence.

The affair seemed sufficiently serious to the Prefect of Police to make him think it necessary to confer without delay with the President of the Council.

The Third Republic was then going through one of those climacteric periods during which the French nation, enamoured of authority and worshipping force, gave itself up for lost because it was not governed enough, and clamoured loudly for a saviour. The President of the Council, and Minister of Justice, was only too eager to be that longed-for saviour. Still, for him to play that part it was first necessary that there should be a danger to face. Thus the news of a plot was highly welcome to him. He questioned the Prefect of Police on the character and importance of the affair. The Prefect of Police explained that the people seemed to have money, intelligence, and energy; but that they talked too much and were too numerous to undertake secret and concerted action. The Minister, leaning back in his arm-chair, pondered on the matter. The Empire writing-table at which he was seated, the ancient tapestry which covered the walls, the clock and the candelabra of the Restoration period—all, in this traditional setting, reminded him of those great principles of government which remain immutable throughout the succession of *régimes*, of stratagem and of bluff. After brief reflexion, he concluded that the plot must be allowed to grow and take shape, that it would even be fitting to nurse it, to embroider it, to colour it, and only to stifle it after having extracted every possible advantage from it.

He instructed the Prefect of Police to watch the affair closely, to render him an account of what went on from day to day, and to confine himself to the rôle of informer.

"I rely on your well-known prudence; observe, and do not intervene."

The Minister lit a cigarette. He quite reckoned, with the help of this plot, on silencing the Opposition, strengthening his own influence, diminishing that of his colleagues, humiliating the President of the Republic, and becoming the saviour of his country.

The Prefect of Police undertook to follow the ministerial instructions, vowing inwardly all the while to act in his own way. He had a watch put upon the individuals pointed out by Barattan, and commanded his agents not to intervene, come what might. Perceiving that he was a marked man, Prince Istar—who united prudence with strength—withdrew the bombs from the gutter outside his window where he had hidden them, and changing from motor 'bus to tube, from tube to motor 'bus, and choosing the most cunningly circuitous route, at length deposited his machines with the angelic musician.

Every time he left his house in the Rue St. Jacques, Arcade found a man of exaggerated smartness at his door, with yellow gloves and in his tie a diamond bigger than the Regent. Being a stranger to the things of this world, the rebellious angel paid no attention to the circumstance.

But young Maurice d'Esparvieu, who had undertaken the task of guarding his guardian-angel, viewed this gentleman with uneasiness, for he equalled in assiduity and surpassed in vigilance that Monsieur Mignon who had formerly allowed his inquisitive gaze to wander from the rams' heads on the Hôtel de la Sordière in the Rue Garancière to the apse of the church of St. Sulpice. Maurice came two and three times a day to see Arcade in his furnished rooms, warning him of the danger, and urging him to change his abode.

Every evening he took his angel to night restaurants, where they supped with ladies of easy virtue. There young d'Esparvieu would foretell the issue of some coming glove-fight, and afterwards exert himself to demonstrate to Arcade the existence of God, the necessity for religion, and the beauties of Christianity, and adjure him to renounce his impious and criminal undertakings wherefrom, he said, he would reap but bitterness and disappointment.

"For really," said the young apologist, "if Christianity were false it would be known."

The ladies approved of Maurice's religious sentiments, and when the handsome Arcade uttered some blasphemy in language they could understand, they put their hands to their ears and bade him be silent, for fear of being struck down with him. For they believed that God, in his omnipotence and sovereign goodness, taking sudden vengeance against those who insulted him, was quite capable of striking down the innocent with the guilty without meaning it.

Sometimes the angel and his guardian took supper with the angelic musician. Maurice, who remembered from time to time that he was Bouchotte's lover, was displeased to see Arcade taking liberties with the singer. She had allowed him to do so ever since the day when, the angelic musician having had the little flowery couch repaired, Arcade and Bouchotte had made it a foundation for their friendship. Maurice, who loved Madame des Aubels a great deal, also loved Bouchotte a little, and was rather jealous of Arcade. Now jealousy is a feeling natural to man and beast, and causes them, however slight the attack, keen unhappiness. Therefore, suspecting the truth, which Bouchotte's temperament and the angel's character made sufficiently obvious, he overwhelmed Arcade with sarcasm and abuse, reproaching him with the immorality of his ways. Arcade answered, tranquilly, that it was difficult to subject physiological impulses to perfectly defined rules, and that moralists encountered great difficulties in the case of certain natural necessities.

"Moreover," added Arcade, "I freely acknowledge that it is almost impossible systematically to constitute a natural moral law. Nature has no principles. She furnishes us with no reason to believe that human life is to be respected. Nature, in her indifference, makes no distinction between good and evil."

"You see, then," replied Maurice, "that religion is necessary."

"Moral law," replied the angel, "which is supposed to be revealed to us, is drawn in reality from the grossest empiricism. Custom alone regulates morals. What Heaven prescribes is merely the consecration of ancient customs. The divine law, promulgated amid fireworks on some Mount Sinai, is never anything but the codification of human prejudice. And from this fact—namely, that morals change—religions which endure for a long time, such as Judæo-Christianity, vary their moral law."

"At any rate," said Maurice, whose intelligence was swelling visibly, "you will grant me that religion prevents much profligacy and crime?"

"Except when it promotes crime—as, for instance, the murder of Iphigenia."

"Arcade," exclaimed Maurice, "when I hear you argue, I rejoice that I am not an intellectual."

Meanwhile Théophile, with his head bent over the piano, his face hidden by the long fair veil of his hair, bringing down from on high his inspired hands on to the keys, was playing and singing the full score of *Aline, Queen of Golconda*.

Prince Istar used to come to their friendly reunions, his pockets filled with bombs and bottles of champagne, both of which he owed to the liberality of Baron Everdingen. Bouchotte received the Kerûb with pleasure, since she saw in him the witness and the trophy of the victory she had gained on the little flowered couch. He was to her as the severed head of Goliath in the hands of the youthful David. And she admired the prince for his cleverness as an accompanist, his vigour, which she had subdued, and his prodigious capacity for drink.

One night, when young d'Esparvieu took his angel home in his car from Bouchotte's house to the lodgings in the Rue St. Jacques, it was very dark; before the door the diamond in the spy's necktie glittered like a beacon; three cyclists standing in a group under its rays made off in divers directions at the car's approach. The angel took no notice, but Maurice concluded that Arcade's movements interested various important people in the State. He judged the danger to be pressing, and at once made up his mind.

The next morning he came to seek the suspect, to take him to the Rue de Rome. The angel was in bed. Maurice urged him to dress and to follow him.

"Come," said he. "This house is no longer safe for you. You are watched. One of these days you will be arrested. Do you wish to sleep in gaol? No? Well, then, come. I will put you in a safe place."

The spirit smiled with some little compassion on his naïve preserver.

"Do you not know," he said, "that an angel broke open the doors of the prison where Peter was confined, and delivered the apostle? Do you believe me, Maurice, to be inferior in power to that heavenly brother of mine, and do you suppose that I am unable to do for myself what he did for the fisherman of the lake of Tiberias?"

"Do not count on it, Arcade. He did it miraculously."

"Or by a stroke of luck, as a modern historian of the Church has it. But no matter. I will follow you. Just allow me to burn a few letters and to make a parcel of some books I shall need."

He threw some papers in the fire-place, put several volumes in his pockets, and followed his guide to the car, which was waiting for them not far off, outside the College of France. Maurice took the wheel. Imitating the Kerûb's prudence, he made so many windings and turnings, and so many rapid twists that he put all the swift and numerous cyclists, speeding in pursuit, off the scent. At length, having left wheelmarks in every direction all over the town, he stopped in the Rue de Rome, before the first-door flat, where the angel had first appeared.

On entering the dwelling which he had left eighteen months before to carry out his mission, Arcade remembered the irreparable past, and breathing in the scent used by Gilberte, his nostrils throbbed. He asked after Madame des Aubels.

"She is very well," replied Maurice. "A little plumper and very much more beautiful for it. She still bears you a grudge for your forward behaviour. I hope that she will one day forgive you, as I have forgiven you, and that she will forget your offence. But she is still very annoyed with you."

Young d'Esparvieu did the honours of his flat to his angel with the manners of a well-bred man and the tender solicitude of a friend. He showed him the folding bed which was opened every evening in the entrance hall and pushed into a dark cupboard in the morning. He showed him the dressing-table, with its accessories; the bath, the linen cupboard, the chest of drawers; gave him the necessary information regarding the heating and lighting; told him that his meals would be brought and the rooms cleaned by the concierge, and showed him which bell to press when he required that person's services. He told him also that he must consider himself at home, and receive whom he wished.

CHAPTER XXVIII

WHICH TREATS OF A PAINFUL DOMESTIC SCENE

SO long as Maurice confined his selection of mistresses to respectable women, his conduct had called forth no reproach. It was a different matter when he took up with Bouchotte. His mother, who had closed her eyes to liaisons which, though guilty, were elegant and discreet, was scandalised when it came to her ears that her son was openly parading about with a music-hall singer. By dint of much prying and probing, Berthe, Maurice's younger sister, had got to know of her brother's adventures, and she narrated them, without any indignation, to her young girl friends. His little brother Léon declared to his mother one day, in the presence of several ladies, that when he was big he, too, would go on the spree, like Maurice. This was a sore wound to the maternal heart of Madame d'Esparvieu.

About the same time there occurred a family event of a very grave nature which occasioned much alarm to Monsieur René d'Esparvieu. Drafts were presented to him signed in his name by his son. His writing had not been forged, but there was no doubt that it had been the son's intention to pass off the signature as his father's. It showed a perverted moral sense; whence it appeared that Maurice was living a life of profligacy, that he was running into debt and on the point of outraging the decencies. The paterfamilias talked the matter over with his wife. It was arranged that he should give his son a very severe lecture, hint at vigorous corrective measures, and that in due course the mother should appear with gentle and sorrowing mien and endeavour to soothe the righteous indignation of the father. This plan being agreed upon, Monsieur René d'Esparvieu sent for his son to come to him in his study. To add to the solemnity of the occasion, he had arrayed himself in his frock-coat. As soon as Maurice saw it he knew there was something serious in the wind. The head of the family was pale, and his voice shook a little (for he was a nervous man), as he declared that he would no longer put up with his son's irregular behaviour, and insisted on an immediate and absolute reform. No more wild courses, no more running into debt, no more undesirable companions, but work, steadiness, and reputable connexions.

Maurice was quite willing to give a respectful reply to his father, whose complaints, after all, were perfectly justified; but, unfortunately, Maurice, like his father, was shy, and the frock-coat which Monsieur d'Esparvieu had donned in order to discharge his magisterial duty with greater dignity seemed to preclude the possibility of any open and unconstrained intercourse. Maurice maintained an awkward silence, which looked very much like insolence, and this silence compelled Monsieur d'Esparvieu to reiterate his complaints, this time with additional severity. He opened one of the drawers in his historic bureau (the bureau on which Alexandre d'Esparvieu had written his "Essay on the Civil and Religious Institutions of the World"), and produced the bills which Maurice had signed.

"Do you know, my boy," said he, "that this is nothing more nor less than forgery? To make up for such grave misconduct as that——"

At this moment Madame d'Esparvieu, as arranged, entered the room attired in her walking-dress. She was supposed to play the angel of forgiveness, but neither her appearance nor her disposition was suitable to the part. She was harsh and unsympathetic. Maurice harboured within him the seeds of all the ordinary and necessary virtues. He loved his mother and respected her. His love, however, was more a matter of duty than of inclination, and his respect arose from habit rather than from feeling. Madame René d'Esparvieu's complexion was blotchy, and having powdered herself in order to appear to advantage at the domestic tribunal, the colour of her face suggested raspberries sprinkled over with sugar. Maurice, being possessed of some taste, could not help realising that she was ugly and rather repulsively so. He was out of tune with her, and when she began to go through all the accusations his father had brought against him, making them out to be blacker than ever, the prodigal turned away his head to conceal his irritation.

"Your Aunt de Saint-Fain," she went on, "met you in the street in such disgraceful company that she was really thankful that you forbore to greet her."

"Aunt de Saint-Fain!" Maurice broke out. "I like to hear her talking about scandals! Everyone knows the sort of life she has led, and now the old hypocrite wants to——"

He stopped. He had caught sight of his father, whose face was even more eloquent of sorrow than of anger. Maurice began to feel as though he had committed murder, and could not imagine how he had allowed such words to escape him. He was on the point of bursting into tears, falling on his knees, and imploring his father to forgive him, when his mother, looking up at the ceiling, said with a sigh:

"What offence can I have committed against God, to have brought such a wicked son into the world?"

This speech struck Maurice as a piece of ridiculous affectation, and it pulled him up with a jerk. The bitterness of contrition suddenly gave place to the delicious arrogance of wrong-doing. He plunged wildly into a torrent of insolence and revolt, and breathlessly delivered himself of utterances quite unfit for a mother's ear.

"If you will have it, mamma, rather than forbid me to continue my friendship with a talented lyrical artist, you would be better employed in preventing my elder sister, Madame de Margy, from appearing, night after night, in society and at the theatres with a contemptible and disgusting individual that everybody knows is her lover. You should also keep an eye on my little sister Jeanne, who writes objectionable letters to herself in a disguised hand, and then, pretending she has found them in her prayer-book, shows them to you with assumed innocence, to worry and alarm you. It would be just as well, too, if you prevented my little brother Léon, a child of seven, from being quite so much with Mademoiselle Caporal, and you might tell your maid...."

"Get out, sir, I will not have you in the house!" cried Monsieur René d'Esparvieu, white with anger, pointing a trembling finger at the door.

CHAPTER XXIX

WHEREIN WE SEE HOW THE ANGEL, HAVING BECOME A MAN, BEHAVES LIKE A MAN, COVETING ANOTHER'S WIFE AND BETRAYING HIS FRIEND. IN THIS CHAPTER THE CORRECTNESS OF YOUNG D'ESPARVIEU'S CONDUCT WILL BE MADE MANIFEST

THE angel was pleased with his lodging. He worked of a morning, went out in the afternoon, heedless of detectives, and came home to sleep. As in days gone by, Maurice received Madame des Aubels twice or thrice a week in the room in which they had seen the apparition.

All went very well until one morning Gilberte, having, the night before, left her little velvet bag on the table in the blue room, came to find it, and discovered Arcade stretched on the couch in his pyjamas, smoking a cigarette, and dreaming of the conquest of Heaven. She gave a loud scream.

"You, Monsieur! Had I thought to find you here, you may be quite sure I should not ... I came to fetch my little bag, which is in the next room. Allow me...." And she slipped past the angel, cautiously and quickly, as if he were a brazier.

Madame des Aubels that morning, in her pale green tailor-made costume, was deliciously attractive. Her tight skirt displayed her movements, and her every step was one of those miracles of Nature which fill men's hearts with amazement.

She reappeared, bag in hand.

"Once more—I ask your pardon.... I never dreamt that...."

Arcade begged her to sit down and to stay a moment.

"I never expected, Monsieur," said she, "that you would be doing the honours of this flat. I knew how dearly Monsieur d'Esparvieu loved you.... Nevertheless, I had no idea that...."

The sky had suddenly grown overcast. A brownish glare began to steal into the room. Madame des Aubels told him she had walked for her health's sake, but a storm was brewing, and she asked if a carriage could be called for her.

Arcade flung himself at Gilberte's feet, took her in his arms as one takes a precious piece of china, and murmured words which, being meaningless in themselves, expressed desire.

She put her hands over his eyes and on his lips, and exclaimed, "I hate you!"

And shaking with sobs, she asked for a drink of water. She was choking. The angel went to her assistance. In this moment of extreme peril she defended herself courageously. She kept saying: "No!... No!... I will not love you. I should love you too well...." Nevertheless she succumbed.

In the sweet familiarity which followed their mutual astonishment she said to him:

"I have often asked after you. I knew that you were an assiduous frequenter of the playhouses at Montmartre,—that you were often seen with Mademoiselle Bouchotte, who, nevertheless, is not at all pretty. I knew that you had become very smart, and that you were making a good deal of money. I was not surprised. You were born to succeed. The day of your"—and she pointed at the spot between the window and the wardrobe with the mirror—"apparition, I was vexed with Maurice for having given you a suicide's rags to wear. You pleased me.... Oh, it was not your good looks! Don't think that women are as sensitive as people say to outward attractions. We consider other things in love. There is a sort of—— Well, anyhow I loved you as soon as I saw you."

The shadows grew deeper.

She asked:

"You are not an angel, are you? Maurice believes you are; but he believes so many things, Maurice." She questioned Arcade with her eyes and smiled maliciously. "Confess that you have been fooling him, and that you are no angel?"

Arcade replied:

"I only aspire to please you; I will always be what you want me to be."

Gilberte decided that he was no angel; first, because one never is an angel; secondly, for more detailed reasons which drew her thoughts to the question of love. He did not argue the matter with her, and once again words were found inadequate to express their feelings.

Outside, the rain was falling thick and fast, the windows were streaming, lightning lit up the muslin curtains, and thunder shook the panes. Gilberte made the sign of the Cross and remained with her head hidden in her lover's bosom.

At this moment Maurice entered the room. He came in wet and smiling, confident, tranquil, happy, to announce to Arcade the good news that with his half-share in the previous day's race at Longchamps the angel had won twelve times his stake. Surprising the lady and the angel in their embrace, he became furious; anger gripped the muscles of his throat, his face grew red with blood, and the veins stood out on his forehead. He sprang with clenched fists towards Gilberte, and then suddenly stopped.

Interrupted motion was transformed into heat. Maurice fumed. His anger did not arm him, like Archilochus, with lyrical vengeance. He merely applied an offensive epithet to his unfaithful one.

Meanwhile she had recovered her dignified bearing. She rose, full of modesty and grace, and gave her accuser a look which expressed both offended virtue and loving forgiveness.

But as young d'Esparvieu continued to shower coarse and monotonous insults on her, she grew angry in her turn.

"You are a pretty sort of person, are you not?" she said. "Did I run after this Arcade of yours? It was you who brought him here, and in what a state, too! You had only one idea: to give me up to your friend. Well, Monsieur, you can do as you like—I am not going to oblige you."

Maurice d'Esparvieu replied simply, "Get out of it, you trollop!" And he made a motion as if to push her out. It pained Arcade to see his mistress treated so disrespectfully, but he thought he lacked the necessary authority to interfere with Maurice. Madame des Aubels, who had lost none of her dignity, fixed young d'Esparvieu with her imperious gaze, and said:

"Go and get me a carriage."

And so great is the power of woman over a well-bred soul, in a gallant nation, that the young Frenchman went immediately and told the concierge to call a taxi. Madame des Aubels, with a studied exhibition of charm in every movement, took leave of them, throwing Maurice the contemptuous look that a woman owes to him whom she has deceived. Maurice witnessed her departure with an outward expression of indifference he was far from feeling. Then he turned to the angel clad in the flowered pyjamas which Maurice himself had worn the day of the apparition; and this circumstance, trifling in itself, added fuel to the anger of the host who had been thus shamefully deceived.

"Well," he said, "you may pride yourself on being a despicable individual. You have behaved basely, and all for nothing. If the woman took your fancy, you had but to tell me. I was tired of her. I had had enough of her. I would have willingly left her to you."

He spoke thus to hide his pain, for he loved Gilberte more than ever, and the creature's treachery caused him great suffering. He pursued:

"I was about to ask you to take her off my hands. But you have followed your lower nature—you have behaved like a sweep."

If at this solemn moment Arcade had but spoken one word from his heart, Maurice would have burst into tears, and forgiven his friend and his mistress, and all three would have become content and happy once again. But Arcade had not been nourished on the milk of human kindness. He had never suffered, and did not know how to sympathise with suffering. He replied with frigid wisdom:

"My dear Maurice, that same necessity which orders and constrains the actions of living beings, produces effects that are often unexpected, and sometimes absurd. Thus it is that I have been led to displease you. You would not reproach me if you had a good philosophical understanding of nature; for you would then know that free-will is but an illusion, and that physiological affinities are as exactly determined as are chemical combinations, and, like them, may be summed up in a formula. I think that, in your case, it might be possible to inculcate these truths, but it would be a difficult task, and maybe they would not bring you the serenity which eludes you. It is fitting, therefore, that I should leave this spot, and——"

"Stay," said Maurice.

Maurice had a very clear sense of social obligations. He put honour, when he thought about it, above everything. So now he told himself very forcibly that the outrage he had suffered could only be wiped out with blood. This traditional idea instantly lent an unexpected nobility to his speech and bearing.

"It is I, Monsieur," said he, "who will quit this place, never to return. You will remain here, since you are a refugee. My seconds will wait upon you."

The angel smiled.

"I will receive them, if it gives you pleasure, but, bethink you, my dear Maurice, I am invulnerable. Celestial spirits even when they are materialised cannot be touched by point of sword or pistol shot. Consider, my dear Maurice, the awkward situation in which this fatal inequality puts me, and realise that in refusing to appoint seconds I cannot give as a reason my celestial nature,—it would be unprecedented."

"Monsieur," replied the heir of the Bussart d'Esparvieu, "you should have thought of that before you insulted me."

Out he marched haughtily; but no sooner was he in the street than he staggered like a drunken man. The rain was still falling. He walked unseeing, unhearing, at haphazard, dragging his feet in the gutters through pools of water, through heaps of mud. He followed the outer boulevards for a long time, and at length, fordone with weariness, lay down on the edge of a piece of waste land. He was muddied up to the eyes, mud and tears smeared his face, the brim of his hat was dripping with rain. A passer-by, taking him for a beggar, tossed him a copper. He picked it up, put it carefully in his waistcoat pocket, and set off to find his seconds.

CHAPTER XXX

WHICH TREATS OF AN AFFAIR OF HONOUR, AND WHICH WILL AFFORD THE READER AN OPPORTUNITY OF JUDGING WHETHER, AS ARCADE AFFIRMS, THE EXPERIENCE OF OUR FAULTS MAKES BETTER MEN AND WOMEN OF US

THE ground chosen for the combat was Colonel Manchon's garden, on the Boulevard de la Reine at Versailles. Messieurs de la Verdelière and Le Truc de Ruffec, who had both of them constant practice in affairs of honour and knew the rules with great exactness, assisted Maurice d'Esparvieu. No duel was ever fought in the Catholic world without Monsieur de la Verdelière being present; and, in making application to this swordsman, Maurice had conformed to custom, though not without a certain reluctance, for he had been notorious as the lover of Madame de la Verdelière; but Monsieur de la Verdelière was not to be looked upon as a husband. He was an institution. As to Monsieur Le Truc de Ruffec, honour was his only known profession and avowedly his sole resource, and when the matter was made the subject of ill-natured comment in Society, the question was asked what finer career than that of honour Monsieur Le Truc de Ruffec could possibly have adopted. Arcade's seconds were Prince Istar and Théophile. The celestial musician had not voluntarily nor with a good grace taken a hand in this affair. He had a horror of every kind of violence and disapproved of single combat. The report of pistols and the clash of swords were intolerable to him, and the sight of blood made him faint. This gentle son of Heaven had obstinately refused to act as second to his brother Arcade, and to bring him to the starting-point the Kerûb had had to threaten to break a bottle of panclastite over his head.

Besides the combatants, the seconds, and the doctors, the only people in the garden were a few officers from the barracks at Versailles and several reporters. Although young d'Esparvieu was known merely as a young man of family, and Arcade had never been heard of at all, the duel had attracted quite a large crowd of inquisitive individuals, and the windows of the adjoining houses were crammed with photographers, reporters, and Society people. What had aroused much curiosity was that a woman was known to be the cause of the quarrel. Many mentioned Bouchotte, but the majority said it was Madame des Aubels. It had been remarked upon, moreover, that duels in which Monsieur de la Verdelière acted as second drew all Paris.

The sky was a soft blue, the garden all a-bloom with roses, a blackbird was piping in a tree. Monsieur de la Verdelière, who, stick in hand, conducted the affair, laid the points of the swords together, and said:

"Allez, Messieurs."

Maurice d'Esparvieu attacked by doubling and beating the blade. Arcade retired, keeping his sword in line. The first engagement was without result. The seconds were under the impression that Monsieur d'Esparvieu was in a grievous state of nervous irritability, and that his adversary would wear him down. In the second encounter Maurice attacked wildly, spread out his arms, and exposed his breast. He attacked as he advanced, gave a straight thrust, and the point of his sword grazed Arcade on the shoulder. The latter was thought to be wounded. But the seconds ascertained with surprise that it was Maurice who had received a scratch on the wrist. Maurice asserted that he felt nothing, and Dr. Quille declared, after examination, that his client might continue the fight. After the regulation quarter of an hour the duel was resumed. Maurice attacked with fury. His adversary was obviously nursing him, and, what disturbed Monsieur de la Verdelière, seemed to be paying very little attention to his own defence. At the opening of the fifth bout, a black spaniel that had got into the garden no one knew how rushed out from a clump of rose-bushes, made its way on to the space reserved for the combatants, and, in spite of

111

sticks and cries, ran in between Maurice's legs. The latter seemed as though his arm were benumbed, merely gave a shoulder-thrust at his invulnerable opponent. He then delivered a straight lunge and impaled his arm on his adversary's sword, which made a deep wound just below the elbow.

Monsieur de la Verdelière stopped the fight, which had lasted an hour and a half. Maurice was conscious of a painful shock. They laid him down on a grassy bank against a wall covered with wistaria. While the surgeon was dressing the wound Maurice called Arcade and offered him his wounded hand. And when the victor, saddened with his victory, advanced, Maurice embraced him tenderly, saying:

"Be generous, Arcade; forgive my treachery. Now that we have fought, I can ask you to be reconciled with me."

He embraced his friend, weeping, and whispered in his ear:

"Come and see me, and bring Gilberte."

Maurice, who was still unreconciled with his parents, was taken to the little flat in the Rue de Rome. No sooner was he stretched on the bed at the far end of the bedroom where the curtains were drawn as on the day of the apparition, than he saw Arcade and Gilberte appear. He began to suffer greatly from his wound; his temperature was rising, but he was at peace, happy and contented. Angel and woman, both in tears, threw themselves at the foot of the bed. He took both their hands with his left, smiled on them, and kissed them tenderly.

"I am sure now that I shall never quarrel with either of you again; you will deceive me no more. I now know you are capable of anything."

Gilberte, weeping, swore that Maurice had been misled by appearances, that she had never betrayed him with Arcade, that she had never betrayed him at all. And in a great gush of sincerity she persuaded herself that this was so.

"You wrong yourself, Gilberte," replied the wounded man. "It did happen; it had to. And it is well. Gilberte, you were basely false to me with my best friend in this very room, and you were right. If you had not been we should not be here, reunited, all three of us, and I should not be at your side tasting the greatest happiness of my life. Oh, Gilberte, how wrong of you to deny a perfect and accomplished fact!"

"If you wish, my friend," replied Gilberte, a little acidly, "I will not deny it. But it will only be to please you."

Maurice made her sit down on the bed, and begged Arcade to be seated in the arm-chair.

"My friend," said Arcade, "I was innocent. I became man. Straightway I did evil. Then I became better."

"Do not let us exaggerate things," said Maurice. "Let's have a game of bridge."

Scarcely, however, had the patient seen three aces in his hand and called "no trumps," than his eyes began to swim, the cards slipped from his fingers, head fell heavily back on the pillow, and he complained of a violent headache. Almost immediately, Madame des Aubels went off to pay some calls, for she made a point of appearing in Society, in order that the calmness and confidence of her demeanour might give the lie to the various rumours that were current concerning her. Arcade saw her to the door, and, with a kiss, inhaled from her a delicate perfume which he brought back with him into the room where Maurice lay dozing.

"I am perfectly content," murmured the latter, "that things should have happened as they have."

"It was bound to be so," answered the Spirit. "All the other angels in revolt would have done as I did with Gilberte. 'Women,' saith the Apostle, 'should pray with their heads covered, because of the angels,' and the Apostle speaks thus because he knows that the angels are disturbed when they look upon them and see that they are beautiful. No sooner do they touch the earth than they desire to embrace mortal women and fulfil their desire. Their clasp is full of strength and sweetness, they hold the secret of those ineffable caresses which plunge the daughters of men into unfathomable depths of delight. Laying upon the lips of their happy victims a honey that burns like fire, making their veins flow with torrents of refreshing flames, they leave them raptured and undone."

"Stop your clatter, you unclean beast," cried the wounded one.

"One word more!" said the angel; "just one other word, my dear Maurice, to bear out what I say, and I will let you rest quietly. There's nothing like having sound references. In order to assure yourself that I am not deceiving you, Maurice, on this subject of the amorous embraces of angels and women, look up Justin, *Apologies*, I and II; Flavius Josephus, *Jewish Antiquities*, Book I, Chapter III; Athenagoras, *Concerning the Resurrection*; Lactantius, Book II, Chapter XV; Tertullian, *On the Veil of the Virgins*; Marcus of Ephesus in *Psellus*; Eusebius, *Præparatio Evangelica*, Book V, Chapter IV; Saint Ambrose, in his book on *Noah and the Ark*, Chapter V; Saint Augustine, in his *City of God*, Book XV, Chapter XXIII; Father Meldonat, the Jesuit, *Treatise on Demons*, page 248; Pierre Lebyer the King's Counsellor——"

"Arcade, please, for pity's sake, be quiet; do, please do, and send this dog away," cried Maurice, whose face was burning, and whose eyes were starting from his head; for in his delirium he thought he saw a black spaniel on his bed.

Madame de la Verdelière, who was assiduous in every modish and patriotic practice, was reckoned, in the best French society, as one of the most gracious of the great ladies interested in good works. She came herself to ask for news of Maurice, and offered to nurse the wounded man. But at the vehement instigation of Madame des Aubels, Arcade shut the door in her face. Expressions of sympathy were showered upon Maurice. Piled on the salver, visiting cards displayed their innumerable little dogs' ears. Monsieur Le Truc de Ruffec was one of the first to show his manly sympathy at the flat in the Rue de Rome, and, holding out his loyal hand, asked young d'Esparvieu as one honourable man to another for twenty-five louis to pay a debt of honour.

"Of course, my dear Maurice, that is the sort of thing one could not ask of everybody."

The same day Monsieur Gaétan came to press his nephew's hand. The latter introduced Arcade.

"This is my guardian angel, whose foot you thought so beautiful when you saw the print it had made on the tell-tale powder, uncle. He appeared to me last year in this very room. You don't believe it? Well, it is true, nevertheless."

Then turning towards the Spirit he said:

"What say you, Arcade? The Abbé Patouille, who is a great theologian and a good priest, does not believe that you are an angel; and Uncle Gaétan, who doesn't know his catechism and hasn't a scrap of religion in him, doesn't think so either. They deny you, the pair of them; the one because he has faith, the other because he hasn't. After that you may be sure that your history, if ever it comes to be narrated, will scarcely appear credible. Moreover, the man that took it into his head to tell your story would not be a man of taste, and would not come in for much approval. For your story is not a pretty one. I love you, but I sit in judgment upon you, too. Since you fell into atheism, you have become an abominable scoundrel. A bad angel, a bad friend, a traitor, and a homicide, for I suppose it was to bring about my death that you sent that black spaniel between my legs on the duelling-ground."

The angel shrugged his shoulders and, addressing Gaétan, said:

"Alas! Monsieur, I am not surprised at finding little credit in your eyes. I have been told that you have fallen out with the Judæo-Christian heaven, which is where I came from."

"Monsieur," answered Gaétan, "my faith in Jehovah is not sufficiently strong to enable me to believe in his angels."

"Monsieur, he whom you call Jehovah is really a coarse and ignorant demiurge, and his name is Ialdabaoth."

"In that case, Monsieur, I am perfectly ready to believe in him. He is a narrow-minded ignoramus, is he? Then belief in his existence offers me no further difficulty. How is he getting on?"

"Badly! We are going to lay him low next month."

"Don't make too sure of that, Monsieur. You remind me of my brother-in-law, Cuissart, who has been expecting to hear of the fall of the Republic for the past thirty years."

"You see, Arcade," exclaimed Maurice, "Uncle Gaétan thinks as I do. He knows you won't succeed."

"And, pray, Monsieur Gaétan, what makes you think I shall not succeed?"

"Your Ialdabaoth is still very powerful in this world, if he isn't in the other. In days gone by he used to be upheld by his priests, by those who believed in him. Now he is supported by those who do not believe in him, by the philosophers. A pedant of a fellow called Picrochole has recently come on the scene who wants to make a bankrupt of science in order to do a good turn to the Church. And just lately Pragmatism has been invented for the express purpose of gaining credit for religion in the minds of rationalists."

"You have been studying Pragmatism?"

"Not I! I was frivolous once, and I went in for metaphysics. I read Hegel and Kant. I have become serious with years, and now I only trouble myself about things evident to the senses: what the eye can see or what the ear can hear. Man is summed up in Art. All the rest is moonshine."

Thus the conversation went on until evening; it was marked by obscenities that would have brought a blush—I will not say to a cuirassier, for cuirassiers are frequently chaste, but even to a Parisienne.

Monsieur Sariette came to see his old pupil. When he entered the room the bust of Alexandre d'Esparvieu seemed to take shape behind the librarian's bald head. He drew near the bed. In the place of blue curtains, mirrored wardrobe, and chimney-piece, there straightway came into view the heavy-laden bookcases of the room of the globes and busts, and the air was heavy with piles of papers, records, and files. Monsieur Sariette could not be dissociated from his library; one could not conceive of him or even see him apart from it. He himself was paler, more vague, more shadowy, and more a creature of the fancy than the fancies he evoked.

Maurice, who had grown very quiet, was sensible of this mark of friendship.

"Sit down, Monsieur Sariette,—you know Madame des Aubels. May I introduce Arcade to you,—my guardian angel. It was he who, while yet invisible, pillaged your library for two years, made you lose all desire for food and drink, and drove you to the verge of madness. He it was who moved piles of books from the room of the busts to my summer-house one day; under your very nose, he took away I know not what precious volumes; and was the cause of your falling on the staircase; another day he took a volume of Salomon Reinach's, and, forced to go out with me (for he never left me, as I have learnt later), he let the volume drop in the gutter of the Rue Princesse. Forgive him, Monsieur Sariette,—he had no pockets. He was invisible. I bitterly regret, Monsieur Sariette, that all your old books were not devoured by fire or swallowed up by a flood. They made my angel lose his head. He became man, and now knows neither faith nor obedience to laws. It is I, now, who am his guardian angel. God knows how it will all end."

While listening to this speech, Monsieur Sariette's face took on an expression of infinite, irreparable, eternal sadness; the sadness of a mummy. Rising to take his leave, the sorrowful librarian murmured in Arcade's ear:

"The poor child is very ill. He is delirious."

Maurice called the old man back.

"Do stay, Monsieur Sariette. You shall have a game of bridge with us. Monsieur Sariette, listen to my advice. Do not do as I did—do not keep bad company. You will be lost. I shudder at the mere thought. Monsieur Sariette, do not go yet. I have something very important to ask you. When you come again, bring me a book on the truth of religion, so that I may study it. I must restore to my guardian-angel the faith which he has lost."

CHAPTER XXXI

WHEREIN WE ARE LED TO MARVEL AT THE READINESS WITH WHICH AN HONEST MAN OF TIMID AND GENTLE NATURE CAN COMMIT A HORRIBLE CRIME

PROFOUNDLY distressed by the dark utterances of young Maurice, Monsieur Sariette took a motor-omnibus, and went to see Père Guinardon, his friend, his only friend, the one person in the whole world whom it gave him pleasure to see and hear. When Monsieur Sariette entered the shop in the Rue de Courcelles, Guinardon was alone, dozing in the depths of an antique arm-chair. His face, surrounded by his curly hair and luxuriant beard, was crimson in hue. Little violet filaments spread a network about the fleshy part of his nose, to which the wines of Burgundy had imparted a purple tint; for there was no longer any disguising the fact, Père Guinardon drank. Two feet away from him, on the fair Octavie's work-table, a rose, all but withered, drooped in an empty vase, and in a basket a piece of embroidery was lying unfinished and neglected. The young Octavie's absences from the shop were growing more and more frequent, and Monsieur Blancmesnil never called when she was not there. The reason of this was that they were meeting three times a week at five o'clock in a house close to the Champs Élysées. Père Guinardon knew nothing of that. He did not know the full extent of his misfortune, but he suffered.

Monsieur Sariette shook his old friend by the hand; but he did not enquire for the young Octavie, for he refused to recognise the connexion. He would sooner have talked about Zéphyrine, who had been so cruelly deserted, and whom he hoped the old man would make his lawful wife. But Monsieur Sariette was prudent. He contented himself with asking Guinardon how he was.

"Perfectly well," was Guinardon's reply; but he felt ill, for either age and love-making had undermined his sturdy constitution, or else young Octavie's faithlessness had dealt her lover a fatal blow. "God be praised," he went on, "I still retain my powers of mind and body. I am chaste. Be chaste, Sariette. Chastity is strength."

That evening Père Guinardon had taken some specially valuable books out of the king-wood cabinet to show to a distinguished bibliophile, Monsieur Victor Meyer, and after the latter's departure he had dropped off to sleep without putting them back in their places. Books had an attraction for Monsieur Sariette, and seeing these particular volumes on the marble top of the cabinet, he began to examine them with interest. The first one he looked at was *La Pucelle*, in morocco, with the English continuation. Doubtless it pained his patriotic and Christian heart to admire its text and illustrations, but a good copy was always virtuous and pure in his sight. Continuing to chat very affectionately with Guinardon, he picked up, one by one, the books which the antiquary had, for one reason or another—binding, illustrations, distinguished ownership, or scarcity—added to his stock.

Suddenly a glorious shout of joy and love broke from his lips. He had discovered the *Lucretius* of the Prior de Vendôme, his *Lucretius*, and he was clasping it to his bosom.

"Once again I behold you," he sighed, as he pressed it to his lips.

At first Père Guinardon could not quite make out what his old friend was talking about; but when the latter declared to him that the volume was from the d'Esparvieu collection, that it belonged to him, Sariette, and that he was going to take it away without further ado, the antiquary completely woke up, got on his legs, declared emphatically that the book belonged to him, Guinardon, by right of true and lawful purchase, and that he would not part with it unless he got five thousand francs for it cash down.

"You don't take in what I am telling you," answered Sariette. "The book belongs to the d'Esparvieu library; I must restore it to its place."

"*Pas de ça, Lisette*"—— hummed Guinardon.

"The book belongs to me, I tell you!"

"You are crazy, my good Sariette!"

And noticing that, as a matter of fact, the librarian had a wandering look in his eye, he took the book from him, and tried to change the conversation.

"Have you seen, Sariette, that the rascals are going to rip up the Palais Mazarin, and cover up the very heart and centre of the Old Town, the finest and most venerable place in the whole of Paris, with the deuce knows what works of art of theirs? They are worse than the Vandals, for the Vandals, although they destroyed the buildings of antiquity, did not replace them with hideous and disgusting erections and atrocious bridges like the Pont d'Alexandre. And your poor Rue Garancière, Sariette, has fallen a prey to the barbarians. What have they done with the pretty bronze mask of the Palace fountain?"

Monsieur Sariette never listened to a word of all this.

"Guinardon, you have not understood me. Now listen. This book belongs to the d'Esparvieu library. It was taken away, how or by whom I know not. Dreadful and mysterious things went on in that library. But, anyhow, the book was stolen. I need scarcely appeal to your sentiments of scrupulous probity, my dear friend. You would not like to be regarded as the receiver of stolen goods. Give me the book. I will return it to Monsieur d'Esparvieu, who will duly requite you; of that you may be sure. Rely on his generosity, and you will be acting like the downright good fellow that you are."

The antiquary smiled a bitter smile.

"Catch me relying on the generosity of that old curmudgeon of a d'Esparvieu. Why, he'd skin a flea to get its coat. Look at me, Sariette, old boy, and tell me if I look like a dunderhead. You know perfectly well that d'Esparvieu refused to give fifty francs in a second-hand shop for a portrait of Alexandre d'Esparvieu, the founder of the family, by Hersent, and that consequently the founder of the family has had to remain on the Boulevard Montparnasse, propped against a Jew hawker's stall, just opposite the cemetery, where all the dogs of the neighbourhood come and make water on him. Catch me trusting to Monsieur d'Esparvieu's liberality! You've got some bright ideas in your head, you have!"

"Very well, Guinardon, I myself will undertake to pay you any indemnity that a board of arbitrators may fix upon. Do you hear?"

"Now don't go and do the handsome for people who won't give you so much as a thank-you. This man, d'Esparvieu, has taken your knowledge, your energies, your whole life for a salary that even a valet wouldn't accept. So leave that idea alone. In any case it is too late. The book is sold."

"Sold? To whom?" asked Sariette in agonized tones.

"What does that matter? You'll never see it again. You'll hear no more about it; it's off to America."

"To America! The *Lucretius* with the arms of Philippe de Vendôme and marginalia in Voltaire's own hand! My *Lucretius* off to America!"

Père Guinardon began to laugh.

"My dear Sariette, you remind me of the Chevalier des Grieux when he learns that his darling mistress is to be transported to the Mississippi. 'My dear mistress going to the Mississippi!' says he."

"No! no!" answered Sariette, very pale, "this book shall not go to America. It shall return, as it ought, to the d'Esparvieu library. Let me have it, Guinardon."

The antiquary made a second attempt to put an end to an interview that now looked as if it might take an ugly turn.

"My good Sariette, you haven't told me what you think of my Greco. You never so much as glanced at it. It is an admirable piece of work all the same."

And Guinardon, putting the picture in a good light, went on:

"Now just look at Saint Francis here, the poor man of the Lord, the brother of Jesus. See how his fuliginous body rises heavenward like the smoke from an agreeable sacrifice, like the sacrifice of Abel."

"Give me the book, Guinardon," said Sariette, without turning his head; "give me the book."

The blood suddenly flew to Père Guinardon's head.

"That's enough of it," he shouted, as red as a turkey-cock, the veins standing out on his forehead.

And he dropped the *Lucretius* into his jacket pocket.

Straightway old Sariette flew at the antiquary, assailed him with sudden fury, and, frail and weakly as he was, butted him back into young Octavie's arm-chair.

Guinardon, in furious amazement, belched forth the most horrible abuse on the old maniac and gave him a punch that sent him staggering back four paces against the *Coronation of the Virgin*, by Fra Angelico, which fell down with a crash. Sariette returned to the charge, and tried to drag the book out of the pocket in which it lay hid. This time Père Guinardon would really have floored him had he not been blinded by the blood that was rushing to his head, and hit sideways at the work-table of his absent mistress. Sariette fastened himself on to his bewildered adversary, held him down in the arm-chair, and with his little bony hands clutched him by the neck, which, red as it was already, became a deep crimson. Guinardon struggled to get free, but the little fingers, feeling the mass of soft, warm flesh about them, embedded themselves in it with delicious ecstasy. Some unknown force made them hold fast to their prey. Guinardon's throat began to rattle, saliva was oozing from one corner of his mouth. His enormous frame quivered now and again beneath the grasp; but the tremors grew more and more intermittent and spasmodic. At last they ceased. The murderous hands did not let go their hold. Sariette had to make a violent effort to loose them. His temples were buzzing. Nevertheless he could hear the rain falling outside, muffled steps going past on the pavement, newspaper men shouting in the distance. He could see umbrellas passing along in the dim light. He drew the book from the dead man's pocket and fled.

The fair Octavie did not go back to the shop that night. She went to sleep in a little entresol underneath the bric-a-brac stores which Monsieur de Blancmesnil had recently bought for her in this same Rue de Courcelles. The workman whose task it was to shut up the shop found the antiquary's body still warm. He called Madame Lenain, the concierge, who laid Guinardon on the couch, lit a couple of candles, put a sprig of box in a saucer of holy water, and closed the dead man's eyes. The doctor who was called in to certify the death ascribed it to apoplexy.

Zéphyrine, informed of what had happened by Madame Lenain, hastened to the house, and sat up all night with the body. The dead man looked as if he were sleeping. In the flickering light of the candles El Greco's Saint mounted upwards like a wreath of smoke, the gold of the Primitives gleamed in the shadows. Near the deathbed a little woman by Baudouin was plainly discernible giving herself a douche. All through the night Zéphyrine's lamentations could be heard fifty yards away.

"He's dead, he's dead!" she kept saying. "My friend, my divinity, my all, my love—— But no! he is not dead, he moves. It is I, Michel; I, your Zéphyrine. Awake, hear me! Answer me; I love you; if ever I caused you pain, forgive me. Dead! dead! O my God! See how beautiful he is. He was so good, so clever, so kind. My God! My God! My God! If I had been there he would not now be lying dead. Michel! Michel!"

When morning came she was silent. They thought she had fallen asleep. She was dead too.

CHAPTER XXXII

WHICH DESCRIBES HOW NECTAIRE'S FLUTE WAS HEARD IN THE TAVERN OF CLODOMIR

MADAME DE LA VERDELIÈRE having failed to force an *entrée* as sick-nurse, returned after several days had elapsed,—during the absence of Madame des Aubels,—to ask Maurice d'Esparvieu for his subscription to the French churches. Arcade led her to the bedside of the convalescent. Maurice whispered in the angel's ear:

"Traitor, deliver me from this ogress immediately, or you will be answerable for the evil which will soon befall."

"Be calm," said Arcade, with a confident air.

After the conventional complimentary flourishes, Madame de la Verdelière signed to Maurice to dismiss the angel. Maurice feigned not to understand. And Madame de la Verdelière disclosed the ostensible reason of her visit.

"Our churches," she said, "our beloved country churches,—what is to become of them?"

Arcade gazed at her angelically and sighed.

"They will disappear, Madame; they will fall into ruin. And what a pity! I shall be inconsolable. The church amid the villagers' cottages is like the hen amidst her chickens."

"Just so!" exclaimed Madame de la Verdelière with a delighted smile. "It is just like that."

"And the spires, Madame?"

"Oh, Monsieur, the spires!..."

"Yes, the spires, Madame, that stick up into the skies towards the little Cherubim, like so many syringes."

Madame de la Verdelière incontinently left the place.

That same day Monsieur l'Abbé Patouille came to offer the wounded man good counsel and consolation. He exhorted him to break with his bad companions and to be reconciled to his family.

He drew a picture of the sorrowful father, the mother in tears, ready to receive their long-lost child with open arms. Renouncing with manly effort a life of profligacy and deluding joys, Maurice would recover his peace and strength of mind, he would free himself from devouring chimeras, and shake off the Evil Spirit.

Young d'Esparvieu thanked Abbé Patouille for all his kindness, and made a protestation of his religious feelings.

"Never," said he, "have I had such faith. And never have I been in such need of it. Just imagine, Monsieur l'Abbé, I have to teach my guardian angel his catechism all over again, for he has quite forgotten it!"

Monsieur l'Abbé Patouille heaved a deep sigh, and exhorted his dear child to pray, there being no other resource but prayer for a soul assailed by the Devil.

"Monsieur l'Abbé," asked Maurice, "may I introduce my guardian angel to you? Do stay a moment; he has gone to get me some cigarettes."

"Unhappy child!"

And Abbé Patouille's fat cheeks drooped in token of affliction. But almost immediately they plumped up again, as a sign of light-heartedness. For in his heart there was matter for rejoicing. Public opinion was improving. The Jacobins, the Freemasons, the Coalitionists were everywhere in disgrace. The Smart Set led the way. The Académie Française was of the right way of thinking. The number of Christian schools was increasing by leaps and bounds. The young men of the Quartier Latin were submitting to the Church, and the École Normale exhaled the perfume of the seminary. The Cross was gaining the day; but money was wanted,—more money, always money.

After six weeks' rest, Maurice was allowed by his doctor to take a drive. He wore his arm in a sling. His mistress and his friend went with him. They drove to the Bois, and took a gentle pleasure in looking upon the grass and the trees. They smiled on everything and everything smiled on them. As Arcade had said, their faults had made them better. By the unlooked-for ways of jealousy and anger, Maurice had attained to calm and kindliness. He still loved Gilberte and he loved her with an indulgent love. The angel still desired her as much as ever, but having once possessed her, his desire had lost the sting of curiosity. Gilberte forbore trying to please, and thereby pleased the more. They drank milk at the Cascade, and found it good. They were all three innocent. Arcade forgot the injustice of the old tyrant of the world. But he was soon to be reminded of it.

On entering his friend's house, he found Zita awaiting him, looking like a statue in ivory and gold.

"You excite my pity," she said to him. "The day is at hand the like of which has never dawned since the beginning of Time, and perhaps will never dawn again before the Sun enters with all its train into the constellation of Hercules. We are on the eve of surprising Ialdabaoth in his palace of porphyry, and you, who are burning to deliver the heavens, who were so eager to enter in triumph into your emancipated country,—you suddenly forget your noble purpose and fall asleep in the arms of the daughters of men. What pleasure can you find in intercourse with these unclean little animals, composed, as they are, of elements so unstable that they may be said to be in a state of constant evanescence? O Arcade! I was indeed right to distrust you. You are but an intellectual; you do but feel idle curiosity. You are incapable of action."

"You misjudge me, Zita," replied the angel. "It is the nature of the sons of heaven to love the daughters of men. Corruptible though it be, the material part of women and of flowers charms the senses none the less. But not one of these little animals can make me forget my hatred and my love, and I am ready to rise up against Ialdabaoth."

Zita expressed her satisfaction at seeing him in this resolute mood. She urged him to pursue the accomplishment of this vast undertaking with undiminished ardour. Nothing must be hurried or deferred.

"A great action, Arcade, is made up of a multitude of small ones; the most majestic whole is composed of a thousand minute details. Let us neglect nothing."

She had come to take him to a meeting where his presence was required. They were to take a census of the revolutionaries.

She added but one word:

"Nectaire will be there."

When Maurice saw Zita, he deemed her lacking in attraction. She failed to please him because she was perfectly beautiful and because true beauty always caused him painful surprise. Zita inspired him with antipathy when he learned that she was an angel in revolt and that she had come to seek Arcade to take him away among the conspirators.

The poor child tried to retain his companion by all the means that his wit and the circumstances afforded him. If his guardian angel would only remain with him, he would take him to a magnificent boxing-match, to a "revue" where he would witness the apotheosis of Poincaré, or, lastly, to a certain house he knew of where he would behold women remarkable for their beauty, talents, vices, or deformities. But the angel would not allow himself to be tempted, and said he was going with Zita.

"What for?"

"To plot the conquest of the skies."

"Still the same nonsense! The conquest of—— but there, I proved to you that it was neither possible nor desirable."

"Good night, Maurice."

"You are going? Well, I will accompany you."

And Maurice, his arm in a sling, went with Arcade and Zita all the way to Clodomir's restaurant at Montmartre, where the tables were laid in an arbour in the garden.

Prince Istar and Théophile were already there, with a little creature who looked like a child, and was, in fact, a Japanese angel.

"We are only waiting for Nectaire," said Zita.

And at that moment the old gardener noiselessly appeared. He took his seat, and his dog lay down at his feet. French cooking is the best in the world. It is a glory that will transcend all others when humanity has grown wise enough to put the spit above the sword. Clodomir served the angels, and the mortal who was with them, with a soup made of cabbages and bacon, a loin of pork and kidneys cooked in wine, thereby proving himself a real Montmartre cook, and showing that he had not been spoilt by the Americans, who corrupt the most excellent *chefs* of the City of Restaurants.

Clodomir brought forth some Bordeaux, which, though unrecorded among the renowned vintages of Médoc, gave evidence by its choice and delicate aroma of the high nobility of its origin. We must not omit to chronicle that, after this wine and many others had been drunk, the cellarman, in solemn state, produced a Burgundy choice and rare, full-bodied yet not heavy, generous yet delicate, rich with the true Burgundian mellowness, a noble and, withal, a somewhat heady wine, that brought delight alike to mind and sense.

"Hail to thee, Dionysus, greatest of the Gods!" cried old Nectaire, raising his glass on high. "I drink to thee who wilt restore the Golden Age, and give again to mortal men, who will become heroes as of old, the grapes which the Lesbians used to cull, long since, from the vines of Methymna; who wilt restore the vineyards of Thasus, the white clusters of Lake Mareotis, the storehouses of Falernus, the vines of the Tmolus, and the wine of Phanae, of all wines the king. And the juice thereof shall be divine, and, as in old Silenus' day, men shall grow drunk with Wisdom and with Love."

When the coffee was served, Prince Istar, Zita, Arcade, and the Japanese angel took it in turns to give an account of the forces assembled against Ialdabaoth. Angels, in exchanging eternal bliss for the sufferings of an earthly life, grow in intelligence, acquire the means of going astray and the faculty of self-contradiction. Consequently their meetings, like those of men, are tumultuous and confused. Did one of them deal in figures, the others immediately called them in question. They could not add one number to another without quarrelling, and arithmetic itself, subjected to passion, lost its certitude. The Kerûb, who had brought with him the pious Théophile, waxed indignant when he heard the musician praising the Lord, and rained down such blows on his head as would have felled an ox. But the head of a musician is harder than a bucranium, and the blows which Théophile received did not avail to modify that angel's notion of divine providence. Arcade, having at great length set up his scientific idealism in opposition to Zita's pragmatism, the beautiful archangel told him that he argued badly.

"And you are surprised at that!" exclaimed young Maurice's guardian angel. "I argue, like you, in the language of human beings. And what is human language but the cry of the beasts of the forests or the mountains, complicated and corrupted by arrogant anthropoids. How then, Zita, can one be expected to argue well with a collection of angry or plaintive sounds like that? Angels do not reason at all; men, being superior to the angels, reason imperfectly. I will not mention the professors who think to define the absolute with the aid of cries that they have inherited from the pithecanthropoid monkeys, marsupials, and reptiles, their ancestors! It is a colossal joke! How it would amuse the demiurge, if he had any brains!"

It was a beautiful starlight night. The gardener was silent.

"Nectaire," said the beautiful archangel, "play to us on your flute, if you are not afraid that the Earth and Heaven will be stirred to their depths thereby."

Nectaire took up his flute. Young Maurice lighted a cigarette. The flame burnt brightly for a moment, casting back the sky and its stars into the shadows, and then died out. And Nectaire sang of the flame on his divine flute. The silvery voice soared aloft and sang:

"That flame was a whole universe which fulfilled its destiny in less than a minute. Suns and planets were formed therein. Venus Urania apportioned the orbits of the wandering spheres in those infinite spaces. Beneath the breath of Eros—the first of the gods,—plants, animals, and thoughts sprang into being. In the twenty seconds which hurried by betwixt the life and death of those worlds, civilizations were unfolded, and empires sank in long decline. Mothers shed tears, and songs of love, cries of hatred, and sighs of victims rose upward to the silent skies.

"In proportion to its minuteness, that universe lasted as long as this one—whereof we see a few atoms glittering above our heads—has lasted or will last. They are, one no less than the other, but a gleam in the Infinite."

As the clear, pure notes welled up into the charmed air, the earth melted into a soft mist, the stars revolved rapidly in their orbits, the Great Bear fell asunder, its parts flew far and wide. Orion's belt was shattered; the Pole Star forsook its magnetic axis. Sirius, whose incandescent flame had lit up the far horizon, grew blue, then red, flickered, and suddenly died out. The shaken constellations formed new signs which were extinguished in their turn. By its incantations the magic flute had compressed into one brief moment the life and the movement of this universe which seems unchanging and eternal both to men and angels. It ceased, and the heavens resumed their immemorial aspect. Nectaire had vanished. Clodomir asked his guests if they were pleased with the cabbage soup which, in order that it might be strong, had been kept simmering for twenty-four hours on the fire, and he sang the praises of the Beaujolais which they had drunk.

The night was mild. Arcade, accompanied by his guardian angel, Théophile, Prince Istar, and the Japanese angel, escorted Zita home.

CHAPTER XXXIII

HOW A DREADFUL CRIME PLUNGES PARIS INTO A STATE OF TERROR

THE city was asleep. Their footsteps rang loudly on the deserted pavement. Having reached the corner of the Rue Feutrier, half-way up Montmartre, the little company halted before the dwelling of the beautiful angel. Arcade was talking about the Thrones and Dominations with Zita, who, her finger on the bell, could not make up her mind to ring. Prince Istar was tracing the mechanism of a new sort of bomb on the pavement with the end of his stick, and bellowed so loudly that he woke the sleeping citizens and stirred into activity the amatory passions of the neighbouring Pasiphaës. Théophile was singing the barcarole from the second act of *Aline, Queen of Golconda* at the top of his voice. Maurice, his arm in a sling, was fencing left-handed with the Japanese, striking sparks from the pavement, and crying "A hit! a hit!" in a piercing voice.

Meanwhile Inspector Grolle at the corner of the next street was dreaming. He had the bearing of a Roman legionary and displayed all the characteristics of that proudly servile race, who, ever since men first took to building cities, have been the mainstay of Empires and the support of ruling houses. Inspector Grolle was very strong, but very tired. He suffered from an arduous profession and from lack of food. He was a man devoted to duty, but still a man, and he was unable to resist the wiles, the charms, and the blandishments of the gay ladies whom he met in swarms in the shadows along the empty streets and round about pieces of waste ground; he loved them. He loved like a soldier under arms. It tired him, but courage conquered fatigue. Though he had not yet reached the middle of Life's way, he longed for sweet repose and peaceful country pursuits. At the corner of the Rue Muller, on this mild night, he stood lost in thought. He was dreaming of the house where he was born, of the little olive wood, of his father's bit of ground, of his old mother, bent with long and heavy labour, whom he would never see again. Roused from his reverie by the nocturnal tumult, Inspector Grolle turned the corner of the street, and looked rather unfavourably at the band of loiterers, wherein his social instinct suspected enemies of law and order. He was patient and resolute. After a lengthy silence, he said, with awe-inspiring calm:

"Move on, there!"

But Maurice and the Japanese angel were fencing and heard nothing. The musician heard nothing but his own melodies. Prince Istar was absorbed in the explanation of explosive formulæ. Zita was discussing with Arcade the greatest enterprise that had ever been conceived since the solar system issued from its original nebula,—and thus they all remained unconscious of their surroundings.

"Move on, I tell you!" repeated Inspector Grolle.

This time the angels heard the solemn word of warning, but either through indifference or contempt, they neglected to obey, and continued their talk, their songs, and their cries.

"So you want to be taken up, do you?" shouted Inspector Grolle, clapping his great hand on Prince Istar's shoulder.

The Kerûb was indignant at this vile contact, and with one blow from his formidable fist sent the Inspector flying into the gutter. But Constable Fesandet was already running to his comrade's aid, and they both fell upon the Prince, whom they belaboured with mechanic fury, and whom, notwithstanding his strength and weight, they would perchance have dragged all bleeding to the police station, had not the Japanese angel overset them one after the other without effort, and reduced them to writhing and shrieking in the mud, before Maurice, Arcade, and Zita had time to intervene. As to the angelic musician, he stood apart trembling, and invoked the heavens.

At this moment two bakers who were kneading their dough in a neighbouring cellar ran out at the noise, in their white aprons, stripped to the waist. With an instinctive feeling for social solidarity they took the side of the downfallen police. Théophile conceived a just fear at the sight of them, and fled away; they caught him and were about to hand him over to the guardians of the peace, when Arcade and Zita tore him from their hands. The fight continued, unequal and terrible, between the two angels and the two bakers. Like an athlete of Lysippus in strength and beauty, Arcade smothered his heavy adversary in his arms. The beautiful archangel drove her dagger into the baker who had attacked her. A dark stream of blood flowed down over his hairy chest, and the two white-capped supporters of the law sank to the ground.

Constable Fesandet had fainted face downwards in the gutter. But Inspector Grolle, who had got up, blew a blast on his whistle loud enough to be heard at the neighbouring police-station, and sprang upon young Maurice, who, having but one arm with which to defend himself, fired his revolver with his left hand at the inspector, who put his hand to his heart, staggered, and dropped down. He gave a long sigh, and the shadows of eternity darkened his eyes.

Meanwhile, windows opened one by one, and heads looked out on the street. A sound of heavy steps approached. Two policemen on bicycles debouched upon the street. Thereupon Prince Istar flung a bomb which shook the ground, put out the gas, shattered some of the houses, and enveloped the flight of young Maurice and the angels in a dense smoke.

Arcade and Maurice came to the conclusion that the safest thing to do after this adventure was to return to the little flat in the Rue de Rome. They would certainly not be sought for immediately and probably not at all, the bomb thrown by the Kerûb having fortunately wiped out all witnesses of the affair. They fell asleep towards dawn, and they had not yet awoke at ten o'clock in the morning when the concierge brought their tea. While eating his toast and butter and slice of ham, young d'Esparvieu remarked to the angel:

"I used to think that a murder was something very extraordinary. Well, I was mistaken. It is the simplest, the most natural action in the world."

"And of most ancient tradition," replied the angel. "For long centuries it was both usual and necessary for man to kill and despoil his fellows. It is still recommended in warfare. It is also honourable to attempt human life in certain definite circumstances, and people approved when you wanted to assassinate me, Maurice, because it appeared to you that I had been intimate with your mistress. But killing a police-inspector is not the action of a man of fashion."

"Be silent," exclaimed Maurice, "be silent, scoundrel! I killed the poor Inspector instinctively, not knowing what I was doing. I am grieved to my heart about it. But it is not I, it is you who are the guilty one; you who are the murderer. It was you who lured me along this path of revolt and violence which leads to the pit. You have been my undoing. You have sacrificed my peace of mind, my happiness, to your pride and your wickedness, and all in vain; for I warn you, Arcade, you will not succeed in what you are undertaking."

The concierge brought in the newspapers. On seeing them Maurice grew pale. They announced the outrage in the Rue de Ramey in huge headlines:

"An Inspector killed—Two cyclist policemen and two bakers seriously wounded—Three houses blown up, numerous victims."

Maurice let the paper drop, and said in a weak, plaintive voice:

"Arcade, why did you not slay me in the little garden at Versailles amidst the roses, to the song of the blackbirds?"

Meanwhile terror reigned in Paris. In the public squares, and in the crowded streets, house-wives, string-bag in hand, grew pale as they listened to the story of the crime, and consigned the perpetrators to the most dreadful punishment. Shop-keepers, standing at the doors of their shops, put it all down to the anarchists, syndicalists, socialists, and radicals, and demanded that special measures should be taken against them.

The more thoughtful people recognized the handiwork of the Jew and the German, and demanded the expulsion of all aliens. Many vaunted the ways of America and advocated lynching. In addition to the printed news sinister rumours became current. Explosions had been heard at various places; everywhere bombs had been discovered; everywhere individuals, taken for malefactors, had been struck down by the popular arm and given up to justice, torn to ribbons. On the Place de la République a drunkard who was crying "Down with the police" was torn to pieces by the crowd.

The President of the Council and Minister of Justice held long conferences with the Prefect of Police, and they agreed to take immediate action. In order to allay the excitement of the Parisians, they arrested five or six hooligans out of the thirty thousand which the Capital contains. The chief of the Russian police, believing he recognised in this attack the methods of the Nihilists, demanded, on behalf of his Government, that a dozen refugees should be given up. The demand was immediately granted. Proceedings were also taken for certain individuals to be extradited to ensure the safety of the King of Spain.

On learning of these energetic measures, Paris breathed once more, and the evening papers congratulated the Government. There was excellent news of the wounded. They were out of danger and identified as their assailants all who were brought before them.

True, Inspector Grolle was dead; but two Sisters of Mercy kept vigil at his side, and the President of the Council came and laid the Cross of Honour on the breast of this victim of duty.

At night there were panics. In the Avenue de la Révolte the police, noticing a travelling acrobat's caravan on a piece of waste ground, took it for the retreat of a band of robbers. They whistled for help, and when they were a goodly number, attacked the caravan. Some worthy citizens joined them; fifteen thousand revolver-shots were fired, the caravan was blown up with dynamite, and among the débris they found the corpse of a monkey.

CHAPTER XXXIV

WHICH CONTAINS AN ACCOUNT OF THE ARREST OF BOUCHOTTE AND MAURICE, OF THE DISASTER WHICH BEFELL THE D'ESPARVIEU LIBRARY, AND OF THE DEPARTURE OF THE ANGELS

MAURICE D'ESPARVIEU passed a terrible night. At the least sound he seized his revolver that he might not fall alive into the hands of justice. When morning came he snatched the newspapers from the hands of the concierge, devoured them greedily, and gave a cry of joy; he had just read that Inspector Grolle having been taken to the Morgue for the post-mortem, the police-surgeons had only discovered bruises and contusions of a very superficial nature, and stated that death had been brought about by the rupture of an aneurism of the aorta.

"You see, Arcade," he exclaimed triumphantly; "you see I am not an assassin. I am innocent. I could never have imagined how extremely agreeable it is to be innocent."

Then he grew thoughtful, and—no unusual phenomenon—reflection dissipated his gaiety.

"I am innocent,—but there is no disguising the fact," he said, shaking his head, "I am one of a band of malefactors. I live with miscreants. You are in your right place there, Arcade, for you are deceitful, cruel, and perverse. But I come of good family and have received an excellent education, and I blush for it."

"I also," said Arcade, "have received an excellent education."

"Where was that?"

"In Heaven."

"No, Arcade, no; you never had any education. If good principles had been inculcated into you, you would still hold them. Such principles are never lost. In my childhood I learnt to revere my family, my country, my religion. I have not forgotten the lesson and I never shall. Do you know what shocks me most in you? It is not your perversity, your cruelty, your black ingratitude; it is not your agnosticism, which may be borne with at a pinch; it is not your scepticism, though it is very much out of date (for since the national awakening there is no longer any scepticism in France);—no, what disgusts me in you is your lack of taste, the bad style of your ideas, the inelegance of your doctrines. You think like an intellectual, you speak like a freethinker, you have theories which reek of radicalism and Combeism and all ignoble systems. Get along with you! you disgust me. Arcade, my old friend, Arcade, my dear angel, Arcade, my beloved child, listen to your guardian angel! Yield to my prayers, renounce your mad ideas; become good, simple, innocent, and happy once more. Put on your hat, come with me to Nôtre-Dame. We will say a prayer and burn a candle together."

Meanwhile public opinion was still active in the matter; the leading papers, the organs of the national awakening, in articles of real elevation and real depth, unravelled the philosophy of this monstrous attack which was revolting to the conscience. They discovered the real origin, the indirect but effective cause in the revolutionary doctrines which had been disseminated unchecked, in the weakening of social ties, the relaxing of moral discipline, in the repeated appeals to every appetite, to every greedy desire. It would be needful, so as to cut down the evil at its root, to repudiate as quickly as possible all such chimeras and Utopias as syndicalism, the income-tax, etc., etc., etc. Many newspapers, and these not the least important, pointed out that the recrudescence of crime was but the natural fruit of impiety and concluded that the salvation of society lay in an unanimous and sincere return to religion. On the Sunday which followed the crime the congregations in the churches were noticed to be unusually large.

Judge Salneuve, who was entrusted with the task of investigation, first examined the persons arrested by the police, and lost his way among attractive but illusory clues; however, the report of the detective Montremain, which was laid before him, put him on the right road, and soon led him to recognise the miscreants of La Jonchère as the authors of the crime of the Rue de Ramey. He ordered a search to be made for Arcade and Zita, and issued a warrant against Prince Istar, on whom the detectives laid hands as he was leaving Bouchotte's, where he had been depositing some bombs of new design. The Kerûb, on learning the detectives' intentions, smiled broadly and asked them if they had a powerful motor-car. On their replying that they had one at the door, he assured them that was all he wanted. Thereupon he felled the two detectives on the stairs, walked up to the waiting car, flung the chauffeur under a motor-'bus which was opportunely passing, and seized the steering wheel under the eyes of the terrified crowd.

That same evening Monsieur Jeancourt, the Police Magistrate, entered Théophile's rooms just when Bouchotte was swallowing a raw egg to clear her voice, for she was to sing her new song, "They haven't got any in Germany," at the "National Eldorado" that evening. The musician was absent. Bouchotte received the Magistrate, and received him with a hauteur which intensified the simplicity of her attire; Bouchotte was *en déshabille*. The worthy Magistrate seized the score of *Aline, Queen of Golconda*, and the love-letters which the singer carefully preserved in the drawer of the table by her bed, for she was an orderly young woman. He was about to withdraw when he espied a cupboard, which he opened with a careless air, and found machines capable of blowing up half Paris, and a pair of large white wings, whose nature and use appeared inexplicable to him. Bouchotte was invited to complete her toilette, and, in spite of her cries, was taken off to the police-station.

Monsieur Salneuve was indefatigable. After the examination of the papers seized in Bouchotte's house, and acting on the information of Montremain, he issued a warrant for the arrest of young d'Esparvieu, which was executed on Wednesday, the 27th May, at seven o'clock in the morning, with great discretion. For three days Maurice had neither slept nor eaten, loved nor lived. He had not a moment's doubt as to the nature of the matutinal visit. At the sight of the police magistrate a strange calm fell on him. Arcade had not returned to sleep in the flat. Maurice begged the magistrate to wait for him, dressed with care, and then accompanied the magistrate a calmness of mind which was barely disturbed when the door of the Conciergerie closed on him. Alone in his cell, he climbed upon the table to look out. His tranquillity was due to his weariness of spirit, to his numbed senses, and to the fact that he no longer stood in fear of arrest. His misfortune endowed him with superior wisdom. He felt he had fallen into a state of grace. He did not think too highly or too humbly of himself, but left his cause in the hands of God. With no desire to cover up his faults, which he would not hide even from himself, he addressed himself in mind to Providence, to point out that if he had fallen into disorder and rebellion it was to lead his erring angel back into the straight path. He stretched himself on the couch and slept in peace.

On hearing of the arrest of a music-hall singer and of a young man of fashion, both Paris and the provinces felt painful surprise. Deeply stirred by the tragic accounts which the leading newspapers were bringing out, the general idea was that the sort of people the authorities ought to bring to justice were ferocious anarchists, all reeking and dripping from deeds of blood and arson; but they failed to understand what the world of Art and Fashion should have to do with such things. At this news, which he was one of the last to hear, the President of the Council and Keeper of the Seals started up in his chair. The Sphinxes that adorned it were less terrible than he, and in the throes of his angry meditation he cut the mahogany of his imperial table with his penknife, after the manner of Napoleon. And when Judge Salneuve, whose attendance he had commanded, appeared before him, the President flung his penknife in the grate, as Louis XIV flung his cane out of the window in the presence of Lauzun; and it cost him a supreme effort to master himself and to say in a voice of suppressed fury:

"Are you mad? Surely I said often enough that I meant the plot to be anarchist, anti-social, fundamentally anti-social and anti-governmental, with a shade of syndicalism. I have made it clear enough that I wanted it kept within these lines; and what do you go and make of it?... The vengeance of anarchists and aspirants to freedom? Whom do you arrest? A singer adored of the nationalist public, and the son of a man highly esteemed in the Catholic party, who receives our bishops and has the *entrée* to the Vatican; a man who may be one day sent as ambassador to the Pope. At one blow you alienate one hundred and sixty Deputies and forty Senators of the Right on the very eve of a motion to discuss the question of religious pacification; you embroil me with my friends of to-day, with my friends of to-morrow. Was it to find out if you were in the same dilemma as des Aubels that you seized the love-letters of young Maurice d'Esparvieu? I can put your mind at rest on that point. You are, and all Paris knows it. But it is not to avenge your personal affronts that you are on the Bench."

"Monsieur le Garde des Sceaux," murmured the Judge, nearly apoplectic and in a choked voice. "I am an honest man."

"You are a fool ... and a provincial. Listen to me; if Maurice d'Esparvieu and Mademoiselle Bouchotte are not released within half an hour I will crush you like a piece of glass. Be off!"

Monsieur René d'Esparvieu went himself to fetch his son from the Conciergerie and took him back to the old house in the Rue Garancière. The return was triumphant. The news had been disseminated that Maurice had with generous imprudence interested himself in an attempt to restore the monarchy, and that Judge Salneuve, the infamous freemason, the tool of Combes and André, had tried to compromise the young man by making him out to be an accomplice of a band of criminals.

That was what Abbé Patouille seemed to think, and he answered for Maurice as for himself. It was known, moreover, that breaking with his father, who had rallied to the support of the Republic, young d'Esparvieu was on the high road to becoming an out-and-out Royalist. The people who had an inside knowledge of things saw in his arrest the vengeance of the Jews. Was not Maurice a notorious anti-Semite? Catholic youths went forth to hurl imprecations at Judge Salneuve under the windows of his residence in the Rue Guénégaud, opposite the Mint.

On the Boulevard du Palais a band of students presented Maurice with a branch of palm. Maurice made a charming reply.

Maurice was overcome with emotion when he beheld the old house in which his childhood had been spent, and fell weeping into his mother's arms.

It was a great day, unhappily marred by one painful incident. Monsieur Sariette, who had lost his reason as a consequence of the shocking events that had taken place in the Rue de Courcelles, had suddenly become violent. He had shut himself up in the library, and there he had remained for twenty-four hours, uttering the most horrible cries, and, turning a deaf ear alike to threats and entreaties, refused to come out. He had spent the night in a condition of extreme restlessness, for all night long the lamp had been seen passing rapidly to and fro behind the curtains. In the morning, hearing Hippolyte shouting to him from the court below, he opened the window of the Hall of the Spheres and the Philosophers, and heaved two or three rather weighty tomes on to the old valet's head. The whole of the domestic staff—men, women, and boys—hurried to the spot, and the librarian proceeded to throw out books by the armful on to their heads. In view of the gravity of the situation, Monsieur René d'Esparvieu did not disdain to intervene. He appeared in night-cap and dressing-gown, and attempted to reason with the poor lunatic, whose only reply was to pour forth torrents of abuse on the man whom till then he had worshipped as his benefactor, and to endeavour to crush him beneath all the Bibles, all the Talmuds, all the sacred books of India and Persia, all the Greek Fathers, and all the Latin Fathers, Saint John Chrysostom, Saint Gregory Nazianzen, Saint Augustine, Saint Jerome, all the apologists, ay! and under the *Histoire des Variations*, annotated by Bossuet himself! Octavos, quartos, folios came crashing down, and lay in a sordid heap on the courtyard pavement. The letters of Gassendi, of Père Mersenne, of Pascal, were blown about hither and thither by the wind. The lady's-maid who had stooped down to rescue some of the sheets from the gutter got a blow on the head from an enormous Dutch atlas. Madame René d'Esparvieu had been terrified by the ominous sounds, and appeared on the scene without waiting to apply the finishing touches of powder and paint. When he caught sight of her, old Sariette became more violent than ever. Down they came one after another as hard as he could pelt them; the busts of the poets, philosophers, and historians of antiquity—Homer, Æschylus, Sophocles, Euripides, Herodotus, Thucydides, Socrates, Plato, Aristotle, Demosthenes, Cicero, Virgil, Horace, Seneca, Epictetus—all lay scattered on the ground. The celestial sphere and the terrestrial globe descended with a terrifying crash that was followed by a ghastly hush, broken only by the shrill laughter of little Léon, who was looking down on the scene from a window above. A locksmith having opened the library door, all the household hastened to enter, and found the aged Sariette entrenched behind piles of books, busily engaged in tearing and slashing away at the *Lucretius* of the Prior de Vendôme annotated in Voltaire's own hand. They had to force a way through the barricade. But the maniac, perceiving that his stronghold was being invaded, fled away and escaped on to the roof. For two whole hours he gave vent to shouts and yells that were heard far and wide. In the Rue Garancière the crowd kept growing bigger and bigger. All had their eyes fixed on the unhappy creature, and whenever he stumbled on the slates, which cracked beneath him, they gave a shout of terror. In the midst of the crowd, the Abbé Patouille, who expected every moment to see him hurled into space, was reciting the prayers for the dying, and making ready to give him the absolution *in extremis*. There was a cordon of police round the house keeping order. Someone summoned the fire-brigade, and the sound of their approach was soon heard. They placed a ladder against the wall of the house, and after a terrific struggle managed to secure the maniac, who in the course of his desperate resistance had one of the muscles of his arm torn out. He was immediately removed to an asylum.

Maurice dined at home, and there were smiles of tenderness and affection when Victor, the old butler, brought on the roast veal. Monsieur l'Abbé Patouille sat at the right hand of the Christian mother, unctuously contemplating the family which Heaven had so plentifully blessed. Nevertheless, Madame d'Esparvieu was ill at ease. Every day she received anonymous letters of so insulting and coarse a nature that she thought at first they must come from a discharged footman. She now knew they were the handiwork of her youngest daughter, Berthe, a mere child! Little Léon, too, gave her pain and anxiety. He paid no attention to his lessons, and was given to bad habits. He showed a cruel disposition. He had plucked his sister's canaries alive; he stuck innumerable pins into the chair on which Mademoiselle Caporal was accustomed to sit, and had stolen fourteen francs from the poor girl, who did nothing but cry and dab her eyes and nose from morning till night.

No sooner was dinner over than Maurice rushed off to the little dwelling in the Rue de Rome, impatient to meet his angel again. Through the door he heard a loud sound of voices, and saw assembled in the room where the apparition had taken place, Arcade, Zita, the angelic musician, and the Kerûb, who was lying on the bed, smoking a huge pipe, carelessly scorching pillows, sheets, and coverlets. They embraced Maurice, and announced their departure. Their faces shone with happiness and courage. Alone, the inspired author of *Aline, Queen of Golconda*, shed tears and raised his terrified gaze to heaven. The Kerûb forced him into the party of rebellion by setting before him two alternatives: either to allow himself to be dragged from prison to prison on earth, or to carry fire and sword into the palace of Ialdabaoth.

Maurice perceived with sorrow that the earth had scarcely any hold over them. They were setting out filled with immense hope, which was quite justifiable. Doubtless they were but a few combatants to oppose the innumerable soldiers of the sultan of the heavens; but they counted on compensating for the inferiority of their numbers by the irresistible impetus of a sudden attack. They were not ignorant of the fact that Ialdabaoth, who flatters himself on knowing all things, sometimes allows himself to be taken by surprise. And it certainly looked as if the first attack would have taken him unawares had it not been for the warning of the archangel Michael. The celestial army had made no progress since its victory over the rebels before the beginning of Time.

As regards armaments and material it was as out of date as the army of the Moors. Its generals slumbered in sloth and ignorance. Loaded with honours and riches, they preferred the delights of the banquet to the fatigues of war. Michael, the commander-in-chief, ever loyal and brave, had lost, with the passing of centuries, his fire and enthusiasm. The conspirators of 1914, on the other hand, knew the very latest and the most delicate appliances of science for the art of destruction. At length all was ready and decided upon. The army of revolt, assembled by corps each a hundred thousand angels strong, on all the waste places of the earth—steppes, pampas, deserts, fields of ice and snow—was ready to launch itself against the sky. The angels, in modifying the rhythm of the atoms of which they are composed, are able to traverse the most varied mediums. Spirits that have descended on to the earth, being formed, since their incarnation, of too compact a substance, can no longer fly of themselves, and to rise into ethereal regions and then insensibly grow volatilized, have need of the assistance of their brothers, who, though revolutionaries like themselves, nevertheless, stayed behind in the Empyrean and remained, not immaterial (for all is matter in the Universe), but gloriously untrammelled and diaphanous. Certes, it was not without painful anxiety that Arcade, Istar, and Zita prepared themselves to pass from the heavy atmosphere of the earth to the limpid depths of the heavens. To plunge into the ether there is need to expend such energy that the most intrepid hesitate to take flight. Their very substance, while penetrating this fine medium, must in itself grow fine-spun, become vaporised, and pass from human dimensions to the volume of the vastest clouds which have ever enveloped the earth. Soon they would surpass in grandeur the uttermost planets, whose orbits they, invisible and imponderable, would traverse without disturbing.

In this enterprise—the vastest that angels could undertake—their substance would be ultimately hotter than the fire and colder than the ice, and they would suffer pangs sharper than death.

Maurice read all the daring and the pain of the undertaking in the eyes of Arcade.

"You are going?" he said to him, weeping.

"We are going, with Nectaire, to seek the great archangel to lead us to victory."

"Whom do you call thus?"

"The priests of the demiurge have made him known to you in their calumnies."

"Unhappy being," sighed Maurice.

Arcade embraced him, and Maurice felt the angel's tears as they dropped upon his cheek.

CHAPTER XXXV

AND LAST, WHEREIN THE SUBLIME DREAM OF SATAN IS UNFOLDED

CLIMBING the seven steep terraces which rise up from the bed of the Ganges to the temples muffled in creepers, the five angels reached, by half-obliterated paths, the wild garden filled with perfumed clusters of grapes and chattering monkeys, and, at the far end thereof, they discovered him whom they had come to seek. The archangel lay with his elbow on black cushions embroidered with golden flames. At his feet crouched lions and gazelles. Twined in the trees, tame serpents turned on him their friendly gaze. At the sight of his angelic visitors his face grew melancholy. Long since, in the days when, with his brow crowned with grapes and his sceptre of vine-leaves in his hand, he had taught and comforted mankind, his heart had many times been heavy with sorrow; but never yet, since his glorious downfall, had his beautiful face expressed such pain and anguish.

Zita told him of the black standards assembled in crowds in all the waste places of the globe; of the deliverance premeditated and prepared in the provinces of Heaven, where the first revolt had long ago been fomented.

"Prince," she went on, "your army awaits you. Come, lead it on to victory."

"Friends," replied the great archangel, "I was aware of the object of your visit. Baskets of fruit and honeycombs await you under the shade of this mighty tree. The sun is about to descend into the roseate waters of the Sacred River. When you have eaten, you will slumber pleasantly in this garden, where the joys of the intellect and of the senses have reigned since the day when I drove hence the spirit of the old Demiurge. To-morrow I will give you my answer."

Night hung its blue over the garden. Satan fell asleep. He had a dream, and in that dream, soaring over the earth, he saw it covered with angels in revolt, beautiful as gods, whose eyes darted lightning. And from pole to pole one single cry, formed of a myriad cries, mounted towards him, filled with hope and love. And Satan said:

"Let us go forth! Let us seek the ancient adversary in his high abode." And he led the countless host of angels over the celestial plains. And Satan was cognizant of what took place in the heavenly citadel. When news of this second revolt came thither, the Father said to the Son:

"The irreconcilable foe is rising once again. Let us take heed to ourselves, and in this, our time of danger, look to our defences, lest we lose our high abode."

And the Son, consubstantial with the Father, replied:

"We shall triumph under the sign that gave Constantine the victory."

Indignation burst forth on the Mountain of God. At first the faithful Seraphim condemned the rebels to terrible torture, but afterwards decided on doing battle with them. The anger burning in the hearts of all inflamed each countenance. They did not doubt of victory, but treachery was feared, and eternal darkness had been at once decreed for spies and alarmists.

There was shouting and singing of ancient hymns and praise of the Almighty. They drank of the mystic wine. Courage, over-inflated, came near to giving way, and a secret anxiety stole into the inner depths of their souls. The archangel Michael took supreme command. He reassured their minds by his serenity. His countenance, wherein his soul was visible, expressed contempt for danger. By his orders, the chiefs of the thunderbolts, the Kerûbs, grown dull with the long interval of peace, paced with heavy steps the ramparts of the Holy Mountain, and, letting the gaze of their bovine eyes wander over the glittering clouds of their Lord, strove to place the divine batteries in position. After inspecting the defences, they swore to the Most High that all was in readiness. They took counsel together as to the plan they should follow. Michael was for the offensive. He, as a consummate soldier, said it was the supreme law. Attack, or be attacked, —there was no middle course.

"Moreover," he added, "the offensive attitude is particularly suitable to the ardour of the Thrones and Dominations."

Beyond that, it was impossible to obtain a word from the valiant chief, and this silence seemed the mark of a genius sure of himself.

As soon as the approach of the enemy was announced, Michael sent forth three armies to meet them, commanded by the archangels Uriel, Raphael, and Gabriel. Standards, displaying all the colours of the Orient, were unfurled above the ethereal plains, and the thunders rolled over the starry floors. For three days and three nights was the lot of the terrible and adorable armies unknown on the Mountain of God. Towards dawn on the fourth day news came, but it was vague and confused. There were rumours of indecisive victories; of the triumph now of this side, now of that. There came reports of glorious deeds which were dissipated in a few hours.

The thunderbolts of Raphael, hurled against the rebels, had, it was said, consumed entire squadrons. The troops commanded by the impure Zita were thought to have been swallowed up in the whirlwind of a tempest of fire. It was believed that the savage Istar had been flung headlong into the gulf of perdition so suddenly that the blasphemies begun in his mouth had been forced backwards with explosive results. It was popularly supposed that Satan, laden with chains of adamant, had been plunged once again into the abyss. Meanwhile, the commanders of the three armies had sent no messages. Mutterings and murmurs, mingling with the rumours of glory, gave rise to fears of an indecisive battle, a precipitate retreat. Insolent voices gave out that a spirit of the lowest category, a guardian angel, the insignificant Arcade, had checked and routed the dazzling host of the three great archangels.

There were also rumours of wholesale defection in the Seventh Heaven, where rebellion had broken out before the beginning of Time, and some had even seen black clouds of impious angels joining the armies of the rebels on Earth. But no one lent an ear to the odious rumours, and stress was laid on the news of victory which ran from lip to lip, each statement readily finding confirmation. The high places resounded with hymns of joy; the Seraphim celebrated on harp and psaltery Sabaoth, God of Thunder. The voices of the elect united with those of the angels in glorifying the Invisible and at the thought of the bloodshed that the ministers of holy wrath had caused among the rebels, sighs of relief and jubilation were wafted from the Heavenly Jerusalem towards the Most High. But the beatitude of the most blessed, having swelled to the utmost limit before due time, could increase no more, and the very excess of their felicity completely dulled their senses.

The songs had not yet ceased when the guards watching on the ramparts signalled the approach of the first fugitives of the divine army; Seraphim on tattered wing, flying in disorder, maimed Kerûbs going on three feet. With impassive gaze, Michael, prince of warriors, measured the extent of the disaster, and his keen intelligence penetrated its causes. The armies of the living God had taken the offensive, but by one of those fatalities in war which disconcert the plans of the greatest captains, the enemy had also taken the offensive, and the effect was evident. Scarcely were the gates of the citadel opened to receive the glorious but shattered remnants of the three armies, when a rain of fire fell on the Mountain of God. Satan's army was not yet in sight, but the walls of topaz, the cupolas of emerald, the roofs of diamond, all fell in with an appalling crash under the discharge of the electrophores. The ancient thunderclouds essayed to reply, but the bolts fell short, and their thunders were lost in the deserted plains of the skies.

Smitten by an invisible foe, the faithful angels abandoned the ramparts. Michael went to announce to his God that the Holy Mountain would fall into the hands of the demon in twenty-four hours, and that nothing remained for the Master of the Heavens but to seek safety in flight. The Seraphim placed the jewels of the celestial crown in coffers. Michael offered his arm to the Queen of Heaven, and the Holy Family escaped from the palace by a subterranean passage of porphyry. A deluge of fire was falling on the citadel. Regaining his post once more, the glorious archangel declared that he would never capitulate, and straightway advanced the standards of the living God. That same evening the rebel host made its entry into the thrice-sacred city. On a fiery steed Satan led his demons. Behind him marched Arcade, Istar, and Zita. As in the ancient revels of Dionysus, old Nectaire bestrode his ass. Thereafter, floating out far behind, followed the black standards.

The garrison laid down their arms before Satan. Michael placed his flaming sword at the feet of the conquering archangel.

"Take back your sword, Michael," said Satan. "It is Lucifer who yields it to you. Bear it in defence of peace and law." Then letting his gaze fall on the leaders of the celestial cohorts, he cried in a ringing voice:

"Archangel Michael, and you, Powers, Thrones, and Dominations, swear all of you to be faithful to your God."

"We swear it," they replied with one voice.

And Satan said:

"Powers, Thrones, and Dominations, of all past wars, I wish but to remember the invincible courage that you displayed and the loyalty which you rendered to authority, for these assure me of the steadfastness of the fealty you have just sworn to me."

The following day, on the ethereal plain, Satan commanded the black standards to be distributed to the troops, and the winged soldiers covered them with kisses and bedewed them with tears.

And Satan had himself crowned God. Thronging round the glittering walls of Heavenly Jerusalem, apostles, pontiffs, virgins, martyrs, confessors, the whole company of the elect, who during the fierce battle had enjoyed delightful tranquillity, tasted infinite joy in the spectacle of the coronation.

The elect saw with ravishment the Most High precipitated into Hell, and Satan seated on the throne of the Lord. In conformity with the will of God which had cut them off from sorrow they sang in the ancient fashion the praises of their new Master.

And Satan, piercing space with his keen glance, contemplated the little globe of earth and water where of old he had planted the vine and formed the first tragic chorus. And he fixed his gaze on that Rome where the fallen God had founded his empire on fraud and lie. Nevertheless, at that moment a saint ruled over the Church. Satan saw him praying and weeping. And he said to him:

"To thee I entrust my Spouse. Watch over her faithfully. In thee I confirm the right and power to decide matters of doctrine, to regulate the use of the sacraments, to make laws and to uphold purity of morals. And the faithful shall be under obligation to conform thereto. My Church is eternal, and the gates of hell shall not prevail against it. Thou art infallible. Nothing is changed."

And the successor of the apostles felt flooded with rapture. He prostrated himself, and with his forehead touching the floor, replied:

"O Lord, my God, I recognise Thy voice! Thy breath has been wafted like balm to my heart. Blessed be Thy name. Thy will be done on Earth, as it is in Heaven. Lead us not into temptation, but deliver us from evil."

And Satan found pleasure in praise and in the exercise of his grace; he loved to hear his wisdom and his power belauded. He listened with joy to the canticles of the cherubim who celebrated his good deeds, and he took no pleasure in listening to Nectaire's flute, because it celebrated nature's self, yielded to the insect and to the blade of grass their share of power and love, and counselled happiness and freedom. Satan, whose flesh had crept, in days gone by, at the idea that suffering prevailed in the world, now felt himself inaccessible to pity. He regarded suffering and death as the happy results of omnipotence and sovereign kindness. And the savour of the blood of victims rose upward towards him like sweet incense. He fell to condemning intelligence and to hating curiosity. He himself refused to learn anything more, for fear that in acquiring fresh knowledge he might let it be seen that he had not known everything at the very outset. He took pleasure in mystery, and believing that he would seem less great by being understood, he affected to be unintelligible. Dense fumes of Theology filled his brain. One day, following the example of his predecessor, he conceived the notion of proclaiming himself one god in three persons. Seeing Arcade smile as this proclamation was made, he drove him from his presence. Istar and Zita had long since returned to earth. Thus centuries passed like seconds. Now, one day, from the altitude of his throne, he plunged his gaze into the depths of the pit and saw Ialdabaoth in the Gehenna where he himself had long lain enchained. Amid the everlasting gloom Ialdabaoth still retained his lofty mien. Blackened and shattered, terrible and sublime, he glanced upwards at the palace of the King of Heaven with a look of proud disdain, then turned away his head. And the new god, as he looked upon his foe, beheld the light of intelligence and love pass across his sorrow-stricken countenance. And lo! Ialdabaoth was now contemplating the Earth and, seeing it sunk in wickedness and suffering, he began to foster thoughts of kindliness in his heart. On a sudden he rose up, and beating the ether with his mighty arms, as though with oars, he hastened thither to instruct and to console mankind. Already his vast shadow shed upon the unhappy planet a shade soft as a night of love.

And Satan awoke bathed in an icy sweat.

Nectaire, Istar, Arcade, and Zita were standing round him. The finches were singing.

"Comrades," said the great archangel, "no—we will not conquer the heavens. Enough to have the power. War engenders war, and victory defeat.

"God, conquered, will become Satan; Satan, conquering, will become God. May the fates spare me this terrible lot; I love the Hell which formed my genius. I love the Earth where I have done some good, if it be possible to do any good in this fearful world where beings live but by rapine. Now, thanks to us, the god of old is dispossessed of his terrestrial empire, and every thinking being on this globe disdains him or knows him not. But what matter that men should be no longer submissive to Ialdabaoth if the spirit of Ialdabaoth is still in them; if they, like him, are jealous, violent, quarrelsome, and greedy, and the foes of the arts and of beauty? What matter that they have rejected the ferocious Demiurge, if they do not hearken to the friendly demons who teach all truths; to Dionysus, Apollo, and the Muses? As to ourselves, celestial spirits, sublime demons, we have destroyed Ialdabaoth, our Tyrant, if in ourselves we have destroyed Ignorance and Fear."

And Satan, turning to the gardener, said:

"Nectaire, you fought with me before the birth of the world. We were conquered because we failed to understand that Victory is a Spirit, and that it is in ourselves and in ourselves alone that we must attack and destroy Ialdabaoth."

THE END

The Gods are Athirst

I

Evariste Gamelin, painter, pupil of David, member of the Section du Pont-Neuf, formerly Section Henri IV, had betaken himself at an early hour in the morning to the old church of the Barnabites, which for three years, since 21st May 1790, had served as meeting-place for the General Assembly of the Section. The church stood in a narrow, gloomy square, not far from the gates of the Palais de Justice. On the façade, which consisted of two of the Classical orders superimposed and was decorated with inverted brackets and flaming urns, blackened by the weather and disfigured by the hand of man, the religious emblems had been battered to pieces, while above the doorway had been inscribed in black letters the Republican catchword of "Liberty, Equality, Fraternity or Death." Évariste Gamelin made his way into the nave; the same vaults which had heard the surpliced clerks of the Congregation of St. Paul sing the divine offices, now looked down on red-capped patriots assembled to elect the Municipal magistrates and deliberate on the affairs of the Section. The Saints had been dragged from their niches and replaced by the busts of Brutus, Jean-Jacques and Le Peltier. The altar had been stripped bare and was surmounted by the Table of the Rights of Man.

It was here in the nave that twice a week, from five in the evening to eleven, were held the public assemblies. The pulpit, decorated with the colours of the Nation, served as tribune for the speakers who harangued the meeting. Opposite, on the Epistle side, rose a platform of rough planks, for the accommodation of the women and children, who attended these gatherings in considerable numbers.

On this particular morning, facing a desk planted underneath the pulpit, sat in red cap and *carmagnole* complete the joiner from the Place Thionville, the *citoyen* Dupont senior, one of the twelve forming the Committee of Surveillance. On the desk stood a bottle and glasses, an ink-horn, and a folio containing the text of the petition urging the Convention to expel from its bosom the twenty-two members deemed unworthy.

Évariste Gamelin took the pen and signed.

"I was sure," said the carpenter and magistrate, "I was sure you would come and give in your name, *citoyen* Gamelin. You are the real thing. But the Section is lukewarm; it is lacking in virtue. I have proposed to the Committee of Surveillance to deliver no certificate of citizenship to any one who has failed to sign the petition."

"I am ready to sign with my blood," said Gamelin, "for the proscription of these federalists, these traitors. They have desired the death of Marat: let them perish."

"What ruins us," replied Dupont senior, "is indifferentism. In a Section which contains nine hundred citizens with the right to vote there are not fifty attend the assembly. Yesterday we were eight and twenty."

"Well then," said Gamelin, "citizens must be obliged to come under penalty of a fine."

"Oh, ho!" exclaimed the joiner frowning, "but if they all came, the patriots would be in a minority.... *Citoyen* Gamelin, will you drink a glass of wine to the health of all good sansculottes?..."

On the wall of the church, on the Gospel side, could be read the words, accompanied by a black hand, the forefinger pointing to the passage leading to the cloisters: "*Comité civil, Comité de surveillance, Comité de bienfaisance.*" A few yards further on, you came to the door of the erstwhile sacristy, over which was inscribed: *Comité militaire.*

Gamelin pushed this door open and found the Secretary of the Committee within; he was writing at a large table loaded with books, papers, steel ingots, cartridges and samples of saltpetre-bearing soils.

"Greeting, *citoyen* Trubert. How are you?"

"I?... I am perfectly well."

The Secretary of the Military Committee, Fortuné Trubert, invariably made this same reply to all who troubled about his health, less by way of informing them of his welfare than to cut short any discussion on the subject. At twenty-eight, he had a parched skin, thin hair, hectic cheeks and bent shoulders. He was an optician on the Quai des Orfèvres, and owned a very old house which he had given up in '91 to a superannuated clerk in order to devote his energies to the discharge of his municipal duties. His mother, a charming woman, whose memory a few old men of the neighbourhood still cherished fondly, had died at twenty; she had left him her fine eyes, full of gentleness and passion, her pallor and timidity. From his father, optician and mathematical instrument maker to the King, carried off by the same complaint before his thirtieth year, he inherited an upright character and an industrious temperament.

Without stopping his writing:

"And you, *citoyen*," he asked, "how are you?"

"Very well. Anything new?"

"Nothing, nothing. You can see,—we are all quiet here."

"And the situation?"

"The situation is just the same."

The situation was appalling. The finest army of the Republic blockaded in Mayence; Valenciennes besieged; Fontenay taken by the Vendéens; Lyons rebellious; the Cévennes in insurrection, the frontier open to the Spaniards; two-thirds of the Departments invaded or revolted; Paris helpless before the Austrian cannon, without money, without bread!

Fortuné Trubert wrote on calmly. The Sections being instructed by resolution of the Commune to carry out the levy of twelve thousand men for La Vendée, he was drawing up directions relating to the enrolment and arming of the contingent which the "Pont-Neuf," erstwhile "Henri IV," was to supply. All the muskets in store were to be handed over to the men requisitioned for the front; the National Guard of the Section would be armed with fowling-pieces and pikes.

"I have brought you here," said Gamelin, "the schedule of the church-bells to be sent to the Luxembourg to be converted into cannon."

Évariste Gamelin, albeit he had not a penny, was inscribed among the active members of the Section; the law accorded this privilege only to such citizens as were rich enough to pay a contribution equivalent in amount to three days' work, and demanded a ten days' contribution to qualify an elector for office. But the Section du Pont-Neuf, enamoured of equality and jealous of its independence, regarded as qualified both for the vote and for office every citizen who had paid out of his own pocket for his National Guard's uniform. This was Gamelin's case, who was an *active* citizen of his Section and member of the Military Committee.

Fortuné Trubert laid down his pen:

"*Citoyen* Évariste," he said, "I beg you to go to the Convention and ask them to send us orders to dig up the floor of cellars, to wash the soil and flag-stones and collect the saltpetre. It is not everything to have guns, we must have gunpowder too."

A little hunchback, a pen behind his ear and a bundle of papers in his hand, entered the erstwhile sacristy. It was the *citoyen* Beauvisage, of the Committee of Surveillance.

"*Citoyens*," he announced, "we have bad news: Custine has evacuated Landau."

"Custine is a traitor!" cried Gamelin.

"He shall be guillotined," said Beauvisage.

Trubert, in his rather breathless voice, expressed himself with his habitual calmness:

"The Convention has not instituted a Committee of Public Safety for fun. It will enquire into Custine's conduct. Incompetent or traitor, he will be superseded by a General resolved to win the victory,—and *ça ira!*"

He turned over a heap of papers, scrutinizing them with his tired eyes:

"That our soldiers may do their duty with a quiet mind and stout heart, they must be assured that the lot of those they leave behind at home is safeguarded. If you are of the same opinion, *citoyen* Gamelin, you will join me in demanding, at the next assembly, that the Committee of Benevolence concert measures with the Military Committee to succour the families that are in indigence and have a relative at the front."

He smiled and hummed to himself: "*Ça ira! ça ira!...*"

Working twelve and fourteen hours a day at his table of unpainted deal for the defence of the fatherland in peril, this humble Secretary of the Sectional Committee could see no disproportion between the immensity of the task and the meagreness of his means for performing it, so filled was he with a sense of the unity in a common effort between himself and all other patriots, so intimately did he feel himself one with the Nation at large, so merged was his individual life in the life of a great People. He was of the sort who combine enthusiasm with long-suffering, who, after each check, set about organizing the victory that is impossible, but is bound to come. And verily they *must* win the day. These men of no account, who had destroyed Royalty and upset the old order of things, this Trubert, a penniless optician, this Évariste Gamelin, an unknown dauber, could expect no mercy from their enemies. They had no choice save between victory and death. Hence both their fervour and their serenity.

Quitting the Barnabites, Évariste Gamelin set off in the direction of the Place Dauphine, now renamed the Place de Thionville in honour of a city that had shown itself impregnable.

Situated in the busiest quarter of Paris, the *Place* had long lost the fine stateliness it had worn a hundred years ago; the mansions forming its three sides, built in the days of Henri IV in one uniform style, of red brick with white stone dressings, to lodge splendour-loving magistrates, had had their imposing roofs of slate removed to make way for two or three wretched storeys of lath and plaster or had even been demolished altogether and replaced by shabby whitewashed houses, and now displayed only a series of irregular, poverty-stricken, squalid fronts, pierced with countless narrow, unevenly spaced windows enlivened with flowers in pots, birdcages, and rags hanging out to dry. These were occupied by a swarm of artisans, jewellers, metal-workers, clockmakers, opticians, printers, laundresses, sempstresses, milliners, and a few grey-beard lawyers who had not been swept away in the storm of revolution along with the King's courts.

It was morning and springtime. Golden sunbeams, intoxicating as new wine, played on the walls and flashed gaily in at garret casements. Every sash of every window was thrown open, showing the housewives' frowsy heads peeping out. The Clerk of the Revolutionary Tribunal, who had just left his house on his way to Court, distributed amicable taps on the cheeks of the children playing under the trees. From the Pont-Neuf came the crier's voice denouncing the treason of the infamous Dumouriez.

Évariste Gamelin lived in a house on the side towards the Quai de l'Horloge, a house that dated from Henri IV and would still have preserved a not unhandsome appearance but for a mean tiled attic that had been added on to heighten the building under the last but one of the *tyrants*. To adapt the lodging of some erstwhile dignitary of the *Parlement* to the exigencies of the bourgeois and artisan households that formed its present denizens, endless partitions and false floors had been run up. This was why the *citoyen* Remacle, concierge and jobbing tailor, perched in a sort of 'tween-decks, as low ceilinged as it was confined in area. Here he could be seen through the glass door sitting cross-legged on his work-bench, his bowed back within an inch of the floor above, stitching away at a National Guard's uniform, while the *citoyenne* Remacle, whose cooking stove boasted no chimney but the well of the staircase, poisoned the other tenants with the fumes of her stew-pots and frying-pans, and their little girl Joséphine, her face smudged with treacle and looking as pretty as an angel, played on the threshold with Mouton, the joiner's dog. The *citoyenne*, whose heart was as capacious as her ample bosom and broad back, was reputed to bestow her favours on her neighbour the *citoyen* Dupont senior, who was one of the twelve constituting the Committee of Surveillance. At any rate her husband had his strong suspicions, and from morning to night the house resounded with the racket of the alternate squabbles and reconciliations of the pair. The upper floors were occupied by the *citoyen* Chaperon, gold and silver-smith, who had his shop on the Quai de l'Horloge, by a health officer, an attorney, a goldbeater, and several employés at the Palais de Justice.

Évariste Gamelin climbed the old-fashioned staircase as far as the fourth and last storey, where he had his studio together with a bedroom for his mother. At this point ended the wooden stairs laid with tiles that took the place of the grand stairway of the more important floors. A ladder clamped to the wall led to a cock-loft, from which at that moment emerged a stout man with a handsome, florid, rosy-cheeked face, climbing painfully down with an enormous package clasped in his arms, yet humming gaily to himself: *J'ai perdu mon serviteur.*

Breaking off his song, he wished a polite good-day to Gamelin, who returned him a fraternal greeting and helped him down with his parcel, for which the old man thanked him.

"There," said he, shouldering his burden again, "you have a batch of dancing-dolls which I am going to deliver straight away to a toy-merchant in the Rue de la Loi. There is a whole tribe of them inside; I am their creator; they have received of me a perishable body, exempt from joys and sufferings. I have not given them the gift of thought, for I am a benevolent God."

It was the *citoyen* Brotteaux, once farmer of taxes and *ci-devant* noble; his father, having made a fortune in these transactions, had bought himself an office conferring a title on the possessor. In the good old times Maurice Brotteaux had called himself Monsieur des Ilettes and used to give elegant suppers which the fair Madame de Rochemaure, wife of a King's *procureur*, enlivened with her bright glances,—a finished gentlewoman whose loyal fidelity was never impugned so long as the Revolution left Maurice Brotteaux in possession of his offices and emoluments, his hôtel, his estates and his noble name. The Revolution swept them all away. He made his living by painting portraits under the archways of doors, making pancakes and fritters on the Quai de la Mégisserie, composing speeches for the representatives of the people and giving dancing lessons to the young *citoyennes*. At the present time, in his garret into which you climbed by a ladder and where a man could not stand upright, Maurice Brotteaux, the proud owner of a glue-pot, a ball of twine, a box of water-colours and sundry clippings of paper, manufactured dancing-dolls which he sold to wholesale toy-dealers, who resold them to the pedlars who hawked them up and down the Champs-Élysées at the end of a pole,—glittering magnets to draw the little ones' eyes. Amidst the calamities of the State and the disaster that overwhelmed himself, he preserved an unruffled spirit, reading for the refreshment of his mind in his Lucretius, which he carried with him wherever he went in the gaping pocket of his plum-coloured surtout.

Évariste Gamelin pushed open the door of his lodging. It offered no resistance, for his poverty spared him any trouble about lock and key; when his mother from force of habit shot the bolt, he would tell her: "Why, what's the good? Folks don't steal spiders'-webs,—nor my pictures, neither." In his workroom were piled, under a thick layer of dust or with faces turned to the wall, the canvases of his student years,—when, as the fashion of the day was, he limned scenes of gallantry, depicting with a sleek, timorous brush emptied quivers and birds put to flight, risky pastimes and reveries of bliss, high-kilted goose-girls and shepherdesses with rose-wreathed bosoms.

But it was not a genre that suited his temperament. His cold treatment of such like scenes proved the painter's incurable purity of heart. Amateurs were right: Gamelin had no gifts as an erotic artist. Nowadays, though he was still short of thirty, these subjects struck him as dating from an immemorial antiquity. He saw in them the degradation wrought by Monarchy, the shameful effects of the corruption of Courts. He blamed himself for having practised so contemptible a style and prostituted his genius to the vile arts of slavery. Now, citizen of a free people, he occupied his hand with bold charcoal sketches of Liberties, Rights of Man, French Constitutions, Republican Virtues, the People as Hercules felling the Hydra of Tyranny, throwing into each and all his compositions all the fire of his patriotism. Alas! he could not make a living by it. The times were hard for artists. No doubt the fault did not lie with the Convention, which was hurling its armies against the kings gathered on every frontier, which, proud, unmoved, determined in the face of the coalesced powers of Europe, false and ruthless to itself, was rending its own bosom with its own hands, which was setting up terror as the order of the day, establishing for the punishment of plotters a pitiless tribunal to whose devouring maw it was soon to deliver up its own members; but which through it all, with calm and thoughtful brow, the patroness of science and friend of all things beautiful, was reforming the calendar, instituting technical schools, decreeing competitions in painting and sculpture, founding prizes to encourage artists, organizing annual exhibitions, opening the Museum of the Louvre, and, on the model of Athens and Rome, endowing with a stately sublimity the celebration of National festivals and public obsequies. But French Art, once so widely appreciated in England, and Germany, in Russia, in Poland, now found every outlet to foreign lands closed. Amateurs of painting, dilettanti of the fine arts, great noblemen and financiers, were ruined, had emigrated or were in hiding. The men the Revolution had enriched, peasants who had bought up National properties, speculators, army-contractors, gamesters of the Palais-Royal, durst not at present show their wealth, and did not care a fig for pictures, either. It needed Regnault's fame or the youthful Gérard's cleverness to sell a canvas. Greuze, Fragonard, Houin were reduced to indigence. Prud'hon could barely earn bread for his wife and children by drawing subjects which Copia reproduced in stippled engravings. The patriot painters Hennequin, Wicar, Topino-Lebrun were starving. Gamelin, without means to meet the expenses of a picture, to hire a model or buy colours, abandoned his vast canvas of *The Tyrant pursued in the Infernal Regions by the Furies*, after barely sketching in the main outlines. It blocked up half the studio with its half-finished, threatening shapes, greater than life-size, and its vast brood of green snakes, each darting forth two sharp, forked tongues. In the foreground, to the left, could be discerned Charon in his boat, a haggard, wild-looking figure,—a powerful and well conceived design, but of the schools, schooly. There was far more of genius and less of artificiality in a canvas of smaller dimensions, also unfinished, that hung in the best lighted corner of the studio. It was an Orestes whom his sister Electra was raising in her arms on his bed of pain. The maiden was putting back with a moving tenderness the matted hair that hung over her brother's eyes. The head of the hero was tragic and fine, and you could see a likeness in it to the painter's own countenance.

Gamelin cast many a mournful look at this composition; sometimes his fingers itched with the craving to be at work on it, and his arms would be stretched longingly towards the boldly sketched figure of Electra, to fall back again helpless to his sides. The artist was burning with enthusiasm, his soul aspired to great achievements. But he had to exhaust his energy on pot-boilers which he executed indifferently, because he was bound to please the taste of the vulgar and also because he had no skill to impress trivial things with the seal of genius. He drew little allegorical compositions which his comrade Desmahis engraved cleverly enough in black or in colours and which were bought at a low figure by a print-dealer in the Rue Honoré, the *citoyen* Blaise. But the trade was going from bad to worse, declared Blaise, who for some time now had declined to purchase anything.

This time, however, made inventive by necessity, Gamelin had conceived a new and happy thought, as *he* at any rate believed,—an idea that was to make the print-seller's fortune, and the engraver's and his own to boot. This was a "patriotic" pack of cards, where for the kings and queens and knaves of the old style he meant to substitute figures of Genius, of Liberty, of Equality and the like. He had already sketched out all his designs, had finished several and was eager to pass on to Desmahis such as were in a state to be engraved. The one he deemed the most successful represented a soldier dressed in the three-cornered hat, blue coat with red facings, yellow breeches and black gaiters of the Volunteer, seated on a big drum, his feet on a pile of cannon-balls and his musket between his knees. It was the *citizen of hearts* replacing the *ci-devant* knave of hearts. For six months and more Gamelin had been drawing soldiers with never-failing gusto. He had sold some of these while the fit of martial enthusiasm lasted, while others hung on the walls of the room, and five or six, water-colours, colour-washes and chalks in two tints, lay about on the table and chairs. In the days of July, '92, when in every open space rose platforms for enrolling recruits, when all the taverns were gay with green leaves and resounded to the shouts of "Vive la Nation! freedom or death!" Gamelin could not cross the Pont-Neuf or pass the Hôtel de Ville without his heart beating high at sight of the beflagged marquee in which magistrates in tricolour scarves were inscribing the names of volunteers to the sound of the *Marseillaise*. But for him to join the Republic's armies would have meant leaving his mother to starve.

Heralded by a grievous sound of puffing and panting the old *citoyenne*, Gamelin's widowed mother, entered the studio, hot, red and out of breath, the National cockade hanging half unpinned in her cap and on the point of falling out. She deposited her basket on a chair and still standing, the better to get her breath, began to groan over the high price of victuals.

A shopkeeper's wife till the death of her husband, a cutler in the Rue de Grenelle-Saint-Germain, at the sign of the Ville de Châtellerault, now reduced to poverty, the *citoyenne* Gamelin lived in seclusion, keeping house for her son the painter. He was the elder of her two children. As for her daughter Julie, at one time employed at a fashionable milliner's in the Rue Honoré, the best thing was not to know what had become of her, for it was ill saying the truth, that she had emigrated with an aristocrat.

"Lord God!" sighed the *citoyenne*, showing her son a loaf baked of heavy dun-coloured dough, "bread is too dear for anything; the more reason it should be made of pure wheat! At market neither eggs nor green-stuff nor cheese to be had. By dint of eating chestnuts, we're like to grow into chestnuts."

After a long pause, she began again:

"Why, I've seen women in the streets who had nothing to feed their little ones with. The distress is sore among poor folks. And it will go on the same till things are put back on a proper footing."

"Mother," broke in Gamelin with a frown, "the scarcity we suffer from is due to the unprincipled buyers and speculators who starve the people and connive with our foes over the border to render the Republic odious to the citizens and to destroy liberty. This comes of the Brissotins' plots and the traitorous dealings of your Pétions and Rolands. It is well if the federalists in arms do not march on Paris and massacre the patriot remnant whom famine is too slow in killing! There is no time to lose; we must tax the price of flour and guillotine every man who speculates in the food of the people, foments insurrection or palters with the foreigner. The Convention has set up an extraordinary tribunal to try conspirators. Patriots form the court; but will its members have energy enough to defend the fatherland against our foes? There is hope in Robespierre; he is virtuous. There is hope above all in Marat. He loves the people, discerns its true interests and promotes them. He was ever the first to unmask traitors, to baffle plots. He is incorruptible and fearless. He, and he alone, can save the imperilled Republic."

The *citoyenne* Gamelin shook her head, paying no heed to the cockade that fell out of her cap at the gesture.

"Have done, Évariste; your Marat is a man like another and no better than the rest. You are young and your head is full of fancies. What you say to-day of Marat, you said before of Mirabeau, of La Fayette, of Pétion, of Brissot."

"Never!" cried Gamelin, who was genuinely oblivious.

After clearing one end of the deal table of the papers and books, brushes and chalks that littered it, the *citoyenne* laid out on it the earthenware soup-bowl, two tin porringers, two iron forks, the loaf of brown bread and a jug of thin wine.

Mother and son ate the soup in silence and finished their meal with a small scrap of bacon. The *citoyenne*, putting *her* titbit on her bread, used the point of her pocket knife to convey the pieces one by one slowly and solemnly to her toothless jaws and masticated with a proper reverence the victuals that had cost so dear.

She had left the best part on the dish for her son, who sat lost in a brown study.

"Eat, Évariste," she repeated at regular intervals, "eat,"—and on her lips the word had all the solemnity of a religious commandment.

She began again with her lamentations on the dearness of provisions, and again Gamelin demanded taxation as the only remedy for these evils.

But she shrilled:

"There is no money left in the country. The *émigrés* have carried it all off with them. There is no confidence left either. Everything is desperate."

"Hush, mother, hush!" protested Gamelin. "What matter our privations, our hardships of a moment? The Revolution will win for all time the happiness of the human race."

The good dame sopped her bread in her wine; her mood grew more cheerful and she smiled as her thoughts returned to her young days, when she used to dance on the green in honour of the King's birthday. She well remembered too the day when Joseph Gamelin, cutler by trade, had asked her hand in marriage. And she told over, detail by detail, how things had gone,—how her mother had bidden her: "Go dress. We are going to the Place de Grève, to Monsieur Bienassis' shop, to see Damiens drawn and quartered," and what difficulty they had to force their way through the press of eager spectators. Presently, in Monsieur Bienassis' shop, she had seen Joseph Gamelin, wearing his fine rose-pink coat and had known in an instant what he would be at. All the time she sat at the window to see the regicide torn with red-hot pincers, drenched with molten lead, dragged at the tail of four horses and thrown into the flames, Joseph Gamelin had stood behind her chair and had never once left off complimenting her on her complexion, her hair and her figure.

She drained the last drop in her cup and continued her reminiscences of other days:

"I brought you into the world, Évariste, sooner than I had expected, by reason of a fright I had when I was big. It was on the Pont-Neuf, where I came near being knocked down by a crowd of sightseers hurrying to Monsieur de Lally's execution. You were so little at your birth the surgeon thought you would not live. But I felt sure God would be gracious to me and preserve your life. I reared you to the best of my powers, grudging neither pains nor expense. It is fair to say, my Évariste, that you showed me you were grateful and that, from childhood up, you tried your best to recompense me for what I had done. You were naturally affectionate and tender-hearted. Your sister was not bad at heart; but she was selfish and of unbridled temper. Your compassion was greater than ever was hers for the unfortunate. When the little ragamuffins of the neighbourhood robbed birds' nests in the trees, you always fought hard to rescue the nestlings from their hands and restore them to the mother, and many a time you did not give in till after you had been kicked and cuffed cruelly. At seven years of age, instead of wrangling with bad boys, you would pace soberly along the street saying over your catechism; and all the poor people you came across you insisted on bringing home with you to relieve their needs, till I was forced to whip you to break you of the habit. You could not see a living creature suffer without tears. When you had done growing, you turned out a very handsome lad.

To my great surprise, you appeared not to know it,—how different from most pretty boys, who are full of conceit and vain of their good looks!"

His old mother spoke the truth. Évariste at twenty had had a grave and charming cast of countenance, a beauty at once austere and feminine, the countenance of a Minerva. Now his sombre eyes and pale cheeks revealed a melancholy and passionate soul. But his gaze, when it fell on his mother, recovered for a brief moment its childish softness.

She went on:

"You might have profited by your advantages to run after the girls, but you preferred to stay with me in the shop, and I had sometimes to tell you not to hang on always to my apron-strings, but to go and amuse yourself with your young companions. To my dying day I shall always testify that you have been a good son, Évariste. After your father's death, you bravely took me and provided for me; though your work barely pays you, you have never let me want for anything, and if we are at this moment destitute and miserable, I cannot blame you for it. The fault lies with the Revolution."

He raised his hand to protest; but she only shrugged and continued:

"I am no aristocrat. I have seen the great in the full tide of their power, and I can bear witness that they abused their privileges. I have seen your father cudgelled by the Duc de Canaleilles' lackeys because he did not make way quick enough for their master. I could never abide *the Austrian*—she was too haughty and too extravagant. As for the King, I thought him good-hearted, and it needed his trial and condemnation to alter my opinion. In fact, I do not regret the old régime,—though I have had some agreeable times under it. But never tell me the Revolution is going to establish equality, because men will never be equal; it is an impossibility, and, let them turn the country upside down to their heart's content, there will still be great and small, fat and lean in it."

As she talked, she was busy putting away the plates and dishes. The painter had left off listening. He was thinking out a design,—for a sansculotte, in red cap and *carmagnole*, who was to supersede the discredited knave of spades in his pack of cards.

There was a sound of scratching on the door, and a girl appeared,—a country wench, as broad as she was long, red-haired and bandy-legged, a wen hiding the left eye, the right so pale a blue it looked white, with monstrous thick lips and teeth protruding beyond them.

She asked Gamelin if he was Gamelin the painter and if he could do her a portrait of her betrothed, Ferrand (Jules), a volunteer serving with the Army of the Ardennes.

Gamelin replied that he would be glad to execute the portrait on the gallant warrior's return.

But the girl insisted gently but firmly that it must be done at once.

The painter protested, smiling in spite of himself as he pointed out that he could do nothing without the original.

The poor creature was dumfounded; she had not foreseen the difficulty. Her head drooping over the left shoulder, her hands clasped in front of her, she stood still and silent as if overwhelmed by her disappointment. Touched and diverted by so much simplicity, and by way of distracting the poor, lovesick creature's grief, the painter handed her one of the soldiers he had drawn in water-colours and asked her if he was like that, her sweetheart in the Ardennes.

She bent her doleful look on the sketch, and little by little her eye brightened, sparkled, flashed, and her moon face beamed out in a radiant smile.

"It is his very likeness," she cried at last. "It is the very spit of Jules Ferrand, it is Jules Ferrand to the life."

Before it occurred to the artist to take the sheet of paper out of her hands, she folded it carefully with her coarse red fingers into a tiny square, slipped it over her heart between her stays and her shift, handed the painter an *assignat* for five livres, and wishing the company a very good day, hobbled light-heartedly to the door and so out of the room.

III

In the afternoon of the same day Évariste set out to see the *citoyen* Jean Blaise, printseller, as well as dealer in ornamental boxes, fancy goods and games of all sorts, in the Rue Honoré, opposite the Oratoire and near the office of the Messageries, at the sign of the *Amour peintre*. The shop was on the ground floor of a house sixty years old, and opened on the street by a vaulted arch the keystone of which bore a grotesque head with horns. The semicircle beneath the arch was occupied by an oil-painting representing "the Sicilian or Cupid the Painter," after a composition by Boucher, which Jean Blaise's father had put up in 1770 and which sun and rain had been doing their best to obliterate ever since. On either side of the door a similar arched opening, with a nymph's head on the keystone arch glazed with the largest panes to be got, exhibited for the benefit of the public the prints in vogue at the time and the latest novelties in coloured engravings. To-day's display included a series of scenes of gallantry by Boilly, treated in his graceful, rather stiff way, *Leçons d'amour conjugal*, *Douces résistances* and the like, which scandalized the Jacobins and which the rigid moralists denounced to the Society of Arts, Debucourt's *Promenade publique*, with a dandy in canary-coloured breeches lounging on three chairs, a group of horses by the young Carle Vernet, pictures of air balloons, the *Bain de Virginie* and figures after the antique.

Amid the stream of citizens that flowed past the shop it was the raggedest figures that loitered longest before the two fascinating windows. Easily amused, delighting in pictures and bent on getting their share, if only through the eyes, of the good things of this world, they stood in open-mouthed admiration, whereas the aristocrats merely glanced in, frowned and passed on.

The instant he came within sight of the house, Évariste fixed his eyes on one of the row of windows above the shop, the one on the left hand, where there was a red carnation in a flower-pot behind a balcony of twisted ironwork. It was the window of Élodie's chamber, Jean Blaise's daughter. The print-dealer lived with his only child on the first floor of the house.

Évariste, after halting a moment as if to get his breath in front of the *Amour peintre*, turned the hasp of the shop-door. He found the *citoyenne* Élodie within; she had just sold a couple of engravings by Fragonard *fils* and Naigeon, carefully selected from a number of others, and before locking up the *assignats* received in payment in the strong-box, was holding them one after the other between her fine eyes and the light, to scrutinize the delicate lines and intricate curves of engraving and the watermark. She was naturally suspicious, for as much forged paper was in circulation as true, which was a great hindrance to commerce. As in former days, in the case of such as copied the King's signature, forgers of the national currency were punished by death; yet plates for printing *assignats* were to be found in every cellar, the Swiss smuggled in counterfeits by the million, whole packets were put in circulation in the inns, the English landed bales of them every day on our coasts, to ruin the Republic's credit and bring good patriots to destitution. Élodie was in terror of accepting bad paper, and still more in terror of passing it and being treated as an accomplice of Pitt, though she had a firm belief in her own good luck and felt pretty sure of coming off best in any emergency.

Évariste looked at her with the sombre gaze that speaks more movingly of love than the most smiling face. She returned his gaze with a mocking curl of the lips and an arch gleam in the dark eyes,—an expression she wore because she knew he loved her and liked to know it and because such a look provokes a lover, makes him complain of ill-usage, brings him to the speaking point, if he has not spoken already, which was Évariste's case.

Before depositing the *assignats* in the strong-box, she produced from her work-basket a white scarf, which she had begun to embroider, and set to work on it. At once industrious and a coquette, she knew instinctively how to ply her needle so as to fascinate an admirer and make a pretty thing for her wearing at one and the same time; she had quite different ways of working according to the person watching her,—a nonchalant way for those she would lull into a gentle languor, a capricious way for those she was fain to see in a more or less despairing mood. For Évariste, she bent with an air of painstaking absorption over her scarf, for she wanted to stir a sentiment of serious affection in his heart.

Élodie was neither very young nor very pretty. She might have been deemed plain at the first glance. She was a brunette, with an olive complexion; under the broad white kerchief knotted carelessly about her head, from which the dark lustrous ringlets escaped, her eyes of fire gleamed as if they would burn their orbits. Her round face with its prominent cheek-bones, laughing lips and rather broad nose, that gave it a wild-wood, voluptuous expression, reminded the painter of the faun of the Borghese, a cast of which he had seen and been struck with admiration for its freakish charm. A faint down of moustache accentuated the curve of the full lips. A bosom that seemed big with love was confined by a crossed kerchief in the fashion of the year. Her supple waist, her active limbs, her whole vigorous body expressed in every movement a wild, delicious freedom. Every glance, every breath, every quiver of the warm flesh called for love and promised passion. There, behind the tradesman's counter, she seemed rather a dancing nymph, a bacchante of the opera, stripped of her lynx skin and thyrsus, imprisoned, and travestied by a magician's spell under the modest trappings of a housewife by Chardin.

"My father is not at home," she told the painter; "wait a little, he will not be long."

In the small brown hands the needle travelled swiftly over the fine lawn.

"Is the pattern to your taste, Monsieur Gamelin?"

It was not in Gamelin's nature to pretend. And love, exaggerating his confidence, encouraged him to speak quite frankly.

"You embroider cleverly, *citoyenne*; but, if I am to say what I think, the pattern you have traced is not simple enough or bold enough, and smacks of the affected taste that in France governed too long the ornamentation of dress and furniture and woodwork; all those rosettes and wreaths recall the pretty, finikin style that was in favour under the tyrant. There is a new birth of taste. Alas! we have much leeway to make up. In the days of the infamous Louis XV the art of decoration had something Chinese about it. They made pot-bellied cabinets with drawer handles grotesque in their contortions, good for nothing but to be thrown on the fire to warm good patriots. Simplicity alone is beautiful. We must hark back to the antique. David designs beds and chairs from the Etruscan vases and the wall-paintings of Herculaneum."

"Yes, I have seen those beds and chairs," said Élodie, "they are lovely. Soon we shall want no other sort. I am like you, I adore the antique."

"Well, then, *citoyenne*," returned Évariste, "if you had limited your pattern to a Greek border, with ivy leaves, serpents or crossed arrows, it would have been worthy of a Spartan maiden ... and of you. But you can still keep this design by simplifying it, reducing it to the plain lines of beauty."

She asked her preceptor what should be picked out.

He bent over the work, and the girl's ringlets swept lightly over his cheek. Their hands met and their breaths mingled. For an instant Évariste tasted an ecstatic bliss, but to feel Élodie's lips so close to his own filled him with fear, and dreading to alarm her modesty, he drew back quickly.

The *citoyenne* Blaise was in love with Évariste Gamelin; she thought his great ardent eyes superb no less than the fine oval of his pale face, and his abundant black locks, parted above the brow and falling in showers about his shoulders; his gravity of demeanour, his cold reserve, his severe manner and uncompromising speech which never condescended to flattery, were equally to her liking. She was in love, and therefore believed him possessed of supreme artistic genius that would one day blossom forth in incomparable masterpieces and make his name world-famous,—and she loved him the better for the belief. The *citoyenne* Blaise was no prude on the score of masculine purity and her scruples were not offended because a man should satisfy his passions and follow his own tastes and caprices; she loved Évariste, who was virtuous; she did not love him because he was virtuous, albeit she appreciated the advantage of his being so in that she had no cause for jealousy or suspicion or any fear of rivals in his affections.

Nevertheless, for the time being, she deemed his reserve a little overdone. If Racine's "Aricie," who loved "Hippolyte," admired the youthful hero's untameable virtue, it was with the hope of winning a victory over it, and she would quickly have bewailed a sternness of moral fibre that had refused to be softened for her sake. At the first opportunity she more than half declared her passion to constrain him to speak out himself. Like her prototype the tender-hearted "Aricie," the *citoyenne* Blaise was much inclined to think that in love the woman is bound to make the advances. "The fondest hearts," she told herself, "are the most fearful; they need help and encouragement. Besides, they are so simple a woman can go half way and even further without their even knowing it, if only she lets them fancy the credit is theirs of the bold attack and the glorious victory." What made her more confident of success was the fact that she knew for a certainty (and indeed there was no doubt about it) that Évariste, before ever the Revolution had made him a hero, had loved a mistress like any ordinary mortal, a very unheroic creature, no other than the *concierge* at the Academy of Painting. Élodie, who was a girl of some experience, quite realised that there are different sorts of love. The sentiment Évariste inspired in her heart was profound enough for her to dream of making him the partner of her life. She was very ready to marry him, but hardly expected her father would approve the union of his only daughter with a poor and unknown artist. Gamelin had nothing, while the printseller turned over large sums of money. The *Amour peintre* brought him in large profits, the share market larger still, and he was in partnership with an army contractor who supplied the cavalry of the Republic with rushes in place of hay and mildewed oats. In a word, the cutler's son of the Rue Saint-Dominique was a very insignificant personage beside the publisher of engravings, a man known throughout Europe, related to the Blaizots, Basans and Didots, and an honoured guest at the houses of the *citoyens* Saint-Pierre and Florian. Not that, as an obedient daughter should, she held her father's consent to be an indispensable preliminary to her settlement in life. The latter, early left a widower, and a man of a self-indulgent, volatile temper, as enterprising with women as he was in business, had never paid much heed to her and had left her to develop at her own sweet will, untrammelled whether by parental advice or parental affection, more careful to ignore than to safeguard the girl's behaviour, whose passionate temperament he appreciated as a connoisseur of the sex and in whom he recognized charms far and away more seductive than a pretty face. Too generous-hearted to be circumspect, too clever to come to harm, cautious even in her caprices, passion had never made her forget the social proprieties. Her father was infinitely grateful for this prudent behaviour, and as she had inherited from him a good head for business and a taste for money-making, he never troubled himself as to the mysterious reasons that deterred a girl so eminently marriageable from entering that estate and kept her at home, where she was as good as a housekeeper and four clerks to him. At twenty-seven she felt old enough and experienced enough to manage her own concerns and had no need to ask the advice or consult the wishes of a father still a young man, and one of so easy-going and careless a temper. But for her to marry Gamelin, Monsieur Blaise must needs contrive a future for a son-in-law with such poor prospects, give him an interest in the business, guarantee him regular work as he did to several artists already—in fact, one way or another, provide him with a livelihood; and such a favour was out of the question, she considered, whether for the one to offer or the other to accept, so small was the bond of sympathy between the two men.

The difficulty troubled the girl's tender heart and wise brain. She saw nothing to alarm her in a secret union with her lover and in taking the author of nature for sole witness of their mutual troth. Her creed found nothing blameworthy in such a union, which the independence of her mode of life made possible and which Évariste's honourable and virtuous character gave her good hopes of forming without apprehension as to the result. But Gamelin was hard put to it to live and provide his old mother with the barest necessaries, and it did not seem as though in so straitened an existence room could well be found for an amour even when reduced to the simplicity of nature. Moreover, Évariste had not yet spoken and declared his intentions, though certainly the *citoyenne* Blaise hoped to bring him to this before long.

She broke off her meditations, and the needle stopped at the same moment.

"*Citoyen* Évariste," she said, "I shall not care for the scarf, unless you like it too. Draw me a pattern, please. Meanwhile, I will copy Penelope and unravel what I have done in your absence."

He answered in a tone of sombre enthusiasm:

"I promise you I will, *citoyenne*. I will draw you the brand of the tyrannicide Harmodius,—a sword in a wreath,"—and pulling out his pencil, he sketched in a design of swords and flowers in the sober, unadorned style he admired. And as he drew, he expounded his views of art:

"A regenerated People," he declared, "must repudiate all the legacies of servitude, bad taste, bad outline, bad drawing. Watteau, Boucher, Fragonard worked for tyrants and for slaves. Their works show no feeling for good style or purity of line, no love of nature or truth. Masks, dolls, fripperies, monkey-tricks,—nothing else! Posterity will despise their frivolous productions. In a hundred years all Watteau's pictures will be banished to the garrets and falling to pieces from neglect; in 1893 struggling painters will be daubing their studies over Boucher's canvases. David has opened the way; he approaches the Antique, but he has not yet reached true simplicity, true grandeur, bare and unadorned. Our artists have many secrets still to learn from the friezes of Herculaneum, the Roman bas-reliefs, the Etruscan vases."

He dilated at length on antique beauty, then came back to Fragonard, whom he abused with inexhaustible venom:

"Do you know him, *citoyenne*?"

Élodie nodded.

"You likewise know good old Greuze, who is ridiculous enough, to be sure, with his scarlet coat and his sword. But he looks like a wise man of Greece beside Fragonard. I met him, a while ago, the miserable old man, trotting by under the arcades of the Palais-Égalité, powdered, genteel, sprightly, spruce, hideous. At sight of him, I longed that, failing Apollo, some sturdy friend of the arts might hang him up to a tree and flay him alive like Marsyas as an everlasting warning to bad painters."

Élodie gave him a long look out of her dancing, wanton eyes.

"You know how to hate, Monsieur Gamelin, are we to conclude you know also how to lo...?"

"Is that you, Gamelin?" broke in a tenor voice; it was the *citoyen* Blaise just come back to his shop. He advanced, boots creaking, charms rattling, coat-skirts flying, an enormous black cocked hat on his head, the corners of which touched his shoulders.

Élodie, picking up her work-basket, retreated to her chamber.

"Well, Gamelin!" inquired the *citoyen* Blaise, "have you brought me anything new?"

"May be," declared the painter,—and proceeded to expound his ideas.

"Our playing cards present a grievous and startling contrast with our present ways of thinking. The names of knave and king offend the ears of a patriot. I have designed and executed a reformed, Revolutionary pack in which for kings, queens, and knaves are substituted Liberties, Equalities, Fraternities; the aces in a border of fasces, are called Laws.... You call Liberty of clubs, Equality of spades, Fraternity of diamonds, Law of hearts. I venture to think my cards are drawn with some spirit; I propose to have them engraved on copper by Desmahis, and to take out letters of patent."

So saying and extracting from his portfolio some finished designs in water-colour, the artist handed them to the printseller.

The *citoyen* Blaise declined to take them, and turning away:

"My lad," he sneered, "take 'em to the Convention; they will perhaps accord you a vote of thanks. But never think to make a *sol* by your new invention which is not new at all. You're a day behind the fair. Your Revolutionary pack of cards is the third I've had brought me. Your comrade Dugourc offered me last week a picquet set with four Geniuses of the People, four Liberties, four Equalities. Another was suggested, with Sages and Heroes, Cato, Rousseau, Hannibal,—I don't know what all!... And these cards had the advantage over yours, my friend, in being coarsely drawn and cut on wood blocks—with a penknife. How little you know the world to dream that players will use cards designed in the taste of David and engraved à la

148

Bartolozzi! And then again, what a strange mistake to think it needs all this to-do to suit the old packs to the new ideas. Out of their own heads, the good sansculottes can find a corrective for what offends them, saying, instead of 'king'—'The Tyrant!' or just 'The fat pig!' They go on using the same old filthy cards and never buy new ones. The great market for playing-cards is the gaming-hells of the Palais-Égalité; well, I advise you to go there and offer the croupiers and punters there your Liberties, your Equalities, your ... what d'ye call 'em?... Laws of hearts ... and come back and tell me what sort of a reception they gave you!"

The *citoyen* Blaise sat down on the counter, filliped away sundry grains of snuff from his nankeen breeches and looking at Gamelin with an air of gentle pity:

"Let me give you a bit of advice, *citoyen*; if you want to make your living, drop your patriotic packs of cards, leave your revolutionary symbols alone, have done with your Hercules, your hydras, your Furies pursuing guilt, your Geniuses of Liberty, and paint me pretty girls. The people's ardour for regeneration grows lukewarm with time, but men will always love women. Paint me women, all pink and white, with little feet and tiny hands. And get this into your thick skull that nobody cares a fig about the Revolution or wants to hear another word about it."

But Évariste drew himself up in indignant protest:

"What! not hear another word of the Revolution!... But, why surely, the restoration of liberty, the victories of our armies, the chastisement of tyrants are events that will startle the most remote posterity. How could we not be struck by such portents?... What! the sect of the*sansculotte* Jesus has lasted well-nigh eighteen centuries, and the religion of Liberty is to be abolished after barely four years of existence!"

But Jean Blaise resumed in a tone of superiority:

"You walk in a dream; *I* see life as it is. Believe me, friend, the Revolution is a bore; it lasts over long. Five years of enthusiasm, five years of fraternal embraces, of massacres, of fine speeches, of *Marseillaises*, of tocsins, of 'hang up the aristocrats,' of heads promenaded on pikes, of women mounted astride of cannon, of trees of Liberty crowned with the red cap, of white-robed maidens and old men drawn about the streets in flower-wreathed cars; of imprisonments and guillotinings, of proclamations, and short commons, of cockades and plumes, swords and *carmagnoles*—it grows tedious! And then folk are beginning to lose the hang of it all. We have gone through too much, we have seen too many of the great men and noble patriots whom you have led in triumph to the Capitol only to hurl them afterwards from the Tarpeian rock,—Necker, Mirabeau, La Fayette, Bailly, Pétion, Manuel, and how many others! How can we be sure you are not preparing the same fate for your new heroes?... Men have lost all count."

"Their names, *citoyen* Blaise; name them, these heroes we are making ready to sacrifice!" cried Gamelin in a tone that recalled the print-dealer to a sense of prudence.

"I am a Republican and a patriot," he replied, clapping his hand on his heart. "I am as good a Republican as you, as ardent a patriot as you,*citoyen* Gamelin. I do not suspect your zeal nor accuse you of any backsliding. But remember that my zeal and my devotion to the State are attested by numerous acts. Here you have my principles: I give my confidence to every individual competent to serve the Nation. Before the men whom the general voice elects to the perilous honour of the Legislative office, such as Marat, such as Robespierre, I bow my head; I am ready to support them to the measure of my poor ability and offer them the humble co-operation of a good citizen. The Committees can bear witness to my ardour and self-sacrifice. In conjunction with true patriots, I have furnished oats and fodder to our gallant cavalry, boots for our soldiers. This very day I am despatching from Vernon a convoy of sixty oxen to the Army of the South through a country infested with brigands and patrolled by the emissaries of Pitt and Condé. I do not talk; I act."

Gamelin calmly put back his sketches in his portfolio, the strings of which he tied and then slipped it under his arm.

"It is a strange contradiction," he said through his clenched teeth, "to see men help our soldiers to carry through the world the liberty they betray in their own homes by sowing discontent and alarm in the soul of its defenders.... Greeting and farewell, *citoyen* Blaise."

Before turning down the alley that runs alongside the Oratoire, Gamelin, his heart big with love and anger, wheeled round for a last look at the red carnations blossoming on a certain window-sill.

He did not despair; the fatherland would yet be saved. Against Jean Blaise's unpatriotic speeches he set his faith in the Revolution. Still he was bound to recognize that the tradesman had some show of reason when he asserted that the people of Paris had lost its old interest in public events. Alas! it was but too manifest that to the enthusiasm of the early days had little by little succeeded a widespread indifference, that never again would be seen the mighty crowds, unanimous in their ardour, of '89, never again the millions, one in heart and soul, that in '90 thronged round the altar of the *fédérés*. Well, good citizens must show double zeal and courage, must rouse the people from its apathy, bidding it choose between liberty and death.

Such were Gamelin's thoughts, and the memory of Élodie was a spur to his confidence.

Coming to the Quais, he saw the sun setting in the distant west behind lowering clouds that were like mountains of glowing lava; the roofs of the city were bathed in a golden light; the windows flashed back a thousand dazzling reflections. And Gamelin pictured the Titans forging out of the molten fragments of by-gone worlds Diké, the city of brass.

Not having a morsel of bread for his mother or himself, he was dreaming of a place at the limitless board that should have all the world for guests and welcome regenerated humanity to the feast. Meantime, he tried to persuade himself that the fatherland, as a good mother should, would feed her faithful child. Shutting his mind against the gibes of the printseller, he forced himself to believe that his notion of a Revolutionary pack of cards was a novel one and a good one, and that with these happily conceived sketches of his he held a fortune in the portfolio under his arm. "Desmahis," he told himself, "shall engrave them. We will publish for ourselves the new patriotic toy and we are sure to sell ten thousand packs in a month, at twenty *sols* apiece."

In his impatience to realize the project, he strode off at once for the Quai de la Ferraille, where Desmahis lived over a glazier's shop.

The entrance was through the shop. The glazier's wife informed Gamelin that the *citoyen* Desmahis was not in, a fact that in no wise surprised the painter, who knew his friend was of a vagabond and dissipated humour and who marvelled that a man could engrave so much and so well as he did while showing so little perseverance. Gamelin made up his mind to wait a while for his return and the woman offered him a chair. She was in a black mood and began to grumble at the badness of trade, though she had always been told that the Revolution, by breaking windows, was making the glaziers' fortunes.

150

Night was falling; so abandoning his idea of waiting for his comrade, Gamelin took his leave of his hostess of the moment. As he was crossing the Pont-Neuf, he saw a detachment of National Guards debouch from the Quai des Morfondus. They were mounted and carried torches. They were driving back the crowd, and amid a mighty clatter of sabres escorting a cart driving slowly on its way to the guillotine with a man whose name no one knew, a *ci-devant* noble, the first prisoner condemned by the newly constituted Revolutionary Tribunal. He could be seen by glimpses between the guardsmen's hats, sitting with hands tied behind his back, his head bared and swaying from side to side, his face to the cart's tail. The headsman stood beside him lolling against the rail. The passers-by had stopped to look and were telling each other it was likely one of the fellows who starved the people, and staring with eyes of indifference. Gamelin, coming closer, caught sight of Desmahis among the spectators; he was struggling to push a way through the press and cut across the line of march. He called out to him and clapped a hand on his shoulder,—and Desmahis turned his head. He was a young man with a handsome face and a stalwart person. In former days, at the Academy, they used to say he had the head of Bacchus on the torso of Hercules. His friends nicknamed him "Barbaroux" because of his likeness to that representative of the people.

"Come here," Gamelin said to him, "I have something of importance to say to you, Desmahis."

"Leave me alone," the latter answered peevishly, muttering some half-heard explanation, looking out as he spoke for a chance of darting across:

"I was following a divine creature, in a straw hat, a milliner's wench, with her flaxen hair down her back; that cursed cart has blocked my way.... She has gone on ahead, she is at the other end of the bridge by now!"

Gamelin endeavoured to hold him back by his coat skirts, swearing his business was urgent.

But Desmahis had already slipped away between horses, guards, swords and torches, and was in hot pursuit of the milliner's girl.

IV

It was ten o'clock in the forenoon. The April sun bathed the tender leafage of the trees in light. A storm had cleared the air during the night and it was deliciously fresh and sweet. At long intervals a horseman passing along the Allée des Veuves broke the silence and solitude. On the outskirts of the shady avenue, over against a rustic cottage known as *La Belle Lilloise*, Évariste sat on a wooden bench waiting for Élodie. Since the day their fingers had met over the embroidery and their breaths had mingled, he had never been back to the *Amour peintre*. For a whole week his proud stoicism and his timidity, which grew more extreme every day, had kept him away from Élodie. He had written her a letter conceived in a key of gravity, at once sombre and ardent, in which, explaining the grievance he had against the *citoyen* Blaise, but saying no word of his love and concealing his chagrin, he announced his intention of never returning to her father's shop, and was now showing greater steadfastness in keeping this resolution than a woman in love was quite likely to approve.

A born fighter whose bent was to defend her property under all circumstances, Élodie instantly turned her mind to the task of winning back her lover. At first she thought of going to see him at the studio in the Place de Thionville. But knowing his touchy temper and judging from his letter that he was sick and sore, she feared he might come to regard daughter and father with the same angry displeasure and make a point of never seeing her again; so she deemed it wiser to invite him to a sentimental, romantic rendezvous which he could not well decline, where she would have ample time to cajole and charm him and where solitude would be her ally to fascinate his senses and overcome his scruples.

At this period, in all the English gardens and all the fashionable promenades, rustic cottages were to be found, built by clever architects, whose aim it was to flatter the taste of the city folk for a country life. The *Belle Lilloise* was occupied as a house of light refreshment; its exterior bore a look of poverty that was part of the *mise en scène* and it stood on the fragments, artistically imitated, of a fallen tower, so as to unite with the charm of rusticity the melancholy appeal of a ruined castle. Moreover, as though a peasant's cot and a shattered donjon were not enough to stir the sensibilities of his customers, the owner had raised a tomb beneath a weeping-willow,—a column surmounted by a funeral urn and bearing the inscription: "Cléonice to her faithful Azor." Rustic cots, ruined keeps, imitation tombs,—on the eve of being swept away, the aristocracy had erected in its ancestral parks these symbols of poverty, of decadence and of death. And now the patriot citizen found his delight in drinking, dancing, making love in sham hovels, under the broken vaults, a sham in their very ruin, of sham cloisters and surrounded by a sham graveyard; for was not he too, like his betters, a lover of nature, a disciple of Jean-Jacques? was not his heart stuffed as full as theirs with sensibility and the philosophy of humanity?

Reaching the rendezvous before the appointed time, Évariste waited, measuring the minutes by the beating of his heart as by the pendulum of a clock. A patrol passed, guarding a convoy of prisoners. Ten minutes after a woman dressed all in pink, carrying a bouquet as the fashion was, escorted by a gentleman in a three-cornered hat, red coat, striped waistcoat and breeches, slipped into the cottage, both so very like the gallants and dames of the ancien régime one was bound to think with the *citoyen* Blaise that mankind possesses characteristics Revolutions cannot change.

A few minutes later, coming from Rueil or Saint-Cloud, an old woman carrying a cylindrical box, painted in brilliant colours, arrived and sat down beside Gamelin, on his bench. She put down her box in front of her, and he saw that the lid had a turning needle fixed on it; the poor woman's trade was to hold a lottery in the public gardens for the children to try their luck at. She also dealt in "ladies' pleasures," an old-fashioned sweetmeat which she sold under a new name; whether because the time-honoured title of "forget-me-nots" called up inappropriate ideas of unhappiness and retribution or that folks had just got tired of it in course of time, "forget-me-nots" were now yclept "ladies' pleasures."

The old dame wiped the sweat from her forehead with a corner of her apron and broke out into railings against heaven, upbraiding God for injustice when he made life so hard for his creatures. Her husband kept a tavern on the river-bank at Saint-Cloud, while she came in every day to the Champs Élysées, sounding her rattle and crying: "*Ladies' pleasures*, come buy, come buy!" And with all this toil the old couple could not scrape enough together to end their days in comfort.

Seeing the young man beside her disposed to commiserate with her, she expounded at great length the origin of her misfortunes. It was all the Republic; by robbing the rich, it was taking the bread out of poor people's mouths. And there was no hoping for a better state of affairs. Things would only go from bad to worse,—she knew that from many tokens. At Nanterre a woman had had a baby born with a serpent's head; the lightning had struck the church at Rueil and melted the cross on the steeple; a were-wolf had been seen in the woods of Chaville. Masked men were poisoning the springs and throwing plague powders in the air to cause diseases....

Évariste saw Élodie spring from a carriage and run forward. The girl's eyes flashed in the clear shadow cast by her straw hat; her lips, as red as the carnations she held in her hand, were wreathed in smiles. A scarf of black silk, crossed over the bosom, was knotted behind the back. Her yellow gown displayed the quick movements of the knees and showed a pair of low-heeled shoes below the hem. The hips were almost entirely unconfined; the Revolution had enfranchised the waists of its *citoyennes*. For all that, the skirts, still puffed out below the loins, marked the curves by exaggerating them and veiled the reality beneath an artificial amplitude of outline.

He tried to speak but could not find his voice, and was chagrined at his failure, which Élodie preferred to the most eloquent greeting. She noticed also and looked upon it as a good omen, that he had tied his cravat with more than usual pains.

She gave him her hand.

"I wanted to see you," she began, "and talk to you. I did not answer your letter; I did not like it and I did not think it worthy of you. It would have been more to my taste if it had been more outspoken. It would be to malign your character and common sense to suppose you do not mean to return to the *Amour peintre* because you had a trifling altercation there about politics with a man many years your senior. Rest assured you have no cause to fear my father will receive you ill whenever you come to see us again. You do not know him; he has forgotten both what he said to you and what you said in reply. I do not say there is any great bond of sympathy between you two; but he bears no malice; I tell you frankly he pays no great heed to you ... nor to me. He thinks only of his own affairs and his own pleasures."

She stepped towards the shrubberies surrounding the *Belle Lilloise*, and he followed her with something of repugnance, knowing it to be the trysting-place of mercenary lovers and amours of a day. She selected the table furthest out of sight.

"How many things I have to tell you, Évariste. Friendship has its rights; you do not forbid me to exercise them? I have much to say about you ... and something about myself, if you will let me."

The landlord having brought a carafe of lemonade, she filled their glasses herself with the air of a careful housewife; then she began to tell him about her childhood, described her mother's beauty, which she loved to dilate upon both as a tribute to the latter's memory and as the source of her own good looks, and boasted of her grandparents' sturdy vigour, for she was proud of her bourgeois blood. She related how at sixteen she had lost this mother she adored and had entered on a life without anyone to love or rely upon. She painted herself as she was, a vehement, passionate nature, full of sensibility and courage, and concluded:

"Oh, Évariste, my girlhood was so sad and lonely I cannot but know what a prize is a heart like yours, and I will not surrender, I give you fair warning, of my own free will and without an effort to retain it, a sympathy on which I trusted I might count and which I held dear."

Évariste gazed at her tenderly.

"Can it be, Élodie, that I am not indifferent to you? Can I really think...?"

He broke off, fearing to say too much and thereby betray so trusting a friendliness.

153

She gave him a little confiding hand that half-peeped out of the long narrow sleeve with its lace frillings. Her bosom rose and fell in long-drawn sighs.

"Credit me, Évariste, with all the sentiments you would have me feel for you, and you will not be mistaken in the dispositions of my heart."

"Élodie, Élodie, you say that? will you still say it when you know ..."—he hesitated.

She dropped her eyes; and he finished the sentence in a whisper:

"... when you know I love you?"

As she heard the declaration, she blushed,—with pleasure. Yet, while her eyes still spoke of a tender ecstasy, a quizzical smile flickered in spite of herself about one corner of her lips. She was thinking:

"And he imagines he proposed first!... and he is afraid perhaps of offending me!..."

Then she said to him fondly:

"So you had never seen, dear heart, that I loved you?"

They seemed to themselves to be alone, the only two beings in the universe. In his exaltation, Évariste raised his eyes to the firmament flashing with blue and gold:

"See, the sky is looking down at us! It is benign; it is adorable, as you are, beloved; it has your brightness, your gentleness, your smile."

He felt himself one with all nature, it formed part and parcel of his joy and triumph. To his eyes, it was to celebrate his betrothal that the chestnut blossoms lit their flaming candles, the poplars burned aloft like giant torches.

He exulted in his strength and stature. She, with her softer as well as finer nature, more pliable and more malleable, rejoiced in her very weakness and, his subjection once secured, instantly bowed to his ascendancy; now she had brought him under her slavery, she acknowledged him for the master, the hero, the god, burned to obey, to admire, to offer her homage. In the shade of the shrubbery he gave her a long, ardent kiss, which she received with head thrown back and, clasped in Évariste's arms, felt all her flesh melt like wax.

They went on talking a long time of themselves, forgetful of the universe. Évariste abounded mainly in vague, high thoughts, which filled Élodie with ecstasy. She spoke sweetly of things of practical utility and personal interest. Then, presently, when she felt she could stay no longer, she rose with a decided air, gave her lover the three red carnations from the flower in her balcony and sprang lightly into the cabriolet in which she had driven there. It was a hired carriage, painted yellow, hung on very high wheels and certainly had nothing out of the common about it, or the coachman either. But Gamelin was not in the habit of hiring carriages and his friends were hardly more used to such an indulgence. To see the great wheels whirling her away gave him a strange pang and a painful presentiment assailed him; by a sort of hallucination of the mind, the hack horse seemed to be carrying Élodie away from him beyond the bounds of the actual world and present time towards a city of wealth and pleasure, towards abodes of luxury and enjoyment, which he would never be able to enter.

The carriage disappeared. Évariste recovered his calm by degrees; but a dull anguish remained and he felt that the hours of tender abandonment he had just lived would never be his again.

He returned by the Champs Élysées, where women in light summer dresses were sitting on wooden chairs, talking or sewing, while their children played under the trees. A woman selling "ladies' pleasures,"—*her* box was shaped like a drum—reminded him of the one he had spoken to in the Allée des Veuves, and it seemed as if a whole epoch of his life had elapsed between the two encounters. He crossed the Place de la Révolution. In the Tuileries gardens he caught the distant roar of a host of men, a sound of many voices shouting in accord, so familiar in those great days of popular enthusiasm which the enemies of the Revolution declared would never dawn again. He quickened his pace as the noise grew louder and louder, reached the Rue Honoré and found it thronged with a crowd of men and women yelling: "Vive la République! Vive la Liberté!" The walls of the gardens, the windows, the balconies, the very roofs were black with lookers-on waving hats and handkerchiefs. Preceded by a sapper, who cleared a way for the procession, surrounded by Municipal Officers, National Guards, gunners, gendarmes, huzzars, advanced slowly, high above the backs of the citizens, a man of a bilious complexion, a wreath of oak-leaves about his brow, his body wrapped in an old green surtout with an ermine collar. The women threw him flowers, while he cast about him the piercing glance of his jaundiced eyes, as though, in this enthusiastic multitude he was still searching out enemies of the people to denounce, traitors to punish. As he went by, Gamelin bent his head and joining his voice to a hundred thousand others, shouted his:

"Vive Marat!"

The triumphant hero entered the Hall of the Convention like Fate personified. While the crowd slowly dispersed Gamelin sat on a stone post in the Rue Honoré and pressed his hand over his heart to check its wild beating. What he had seen filled him with high emotion and burning enthusiasm.

He loved and worshipped Marat, who, sick and fevered, his veins on fire, eaten up by ulcers, was wearing out the last remnants of his strength in the service of the Republic, and in his own poor house, closed to no man, welcomed him with open arms, conversed eagerly with him of public affairs, questioned him sometimes on the machinations of evil-doers. He rejoiced that the enemies of *the Just*, conspiring for his ruin, had prepared his triumph; he blessed the Revolutionary Tribunal, which acquitting the Friend of the People had given back to the Convention the most zealous and most immaculate of its legislators. Again his eyes could see the head racked with fever, garlanded with the civic crown, the features instinct with virtuous pride and pitiless love, the worn, ravaged, powerful face, the close-pressed lips, the broad chest, the strong man dying by inches who, raised aloft in the living chariot of his triumph, seemed to exhort his fellow-citizens: "Be ye like me,—patriots to the death!"

The street was empty, darkening with the shadows of approaching night; the lamplighter went by with his cresset, and Gamelin muttered to himself:

"Yes, to the death!"

V

By nine in the morning Évariste reached the gardens of the Luxembourg, to find Élodie already therBe seated on a bench waiting for him.

155

It was a month ago they had exchanged their vows and since then they had seen each other every day, either at the *Amour peintre* or at the studio in the Place de Thionville. Their meetings had been very tender, but at the same time characterized by a certain reserve that checked their expansiveness,—a reserve due to the staid and virtuous temper of the lover, a theist and a good citizen, who, while ready to make his beloved mistress his own before the law or with God alone for witness according as circumstances demanded, would do nothing save publicly and in the light of day. Élodie knew the resolution to be right and honourable; but, despairing of a marriage that seemed impossible from every point of view and loath to outrage the prejudices of society, she contemplated in her inmost heart a liaison that could be kept a secret till the lapse of time gave it sanction. She hoped one day to overcome the scruples of a lover she could have wished less scrupulous, and meantime, unwilling to postpone some necessary confidences as to the past, she had asked him to meet her for a lover's talk in a lonely corner of the gardens near the Carthusian Priory.

She threw him a tender look, took his hand frankly, invited him to share the bench and speaking slowly and thoughtfully:

"I esteem you too well, Évariste, to hide anything from you. I believe myself worthy of you; I should not be so were I not to tell you everything. Hear me and be my judge. I have no act to reproach myself with that is degrading or base, or even merely selfish. I have only been weak and credulous.... Do not forget, dear Évariste, the difficult circumstances in which I found myself. You know how it was with me; I had lost my mother, my father, still a young man, thought only of his own amusement and neglected me. I had a feeling heart, nature has dowered me with a loving temper and a generous soul; it was true she had not denied me a firm will and a sound judgment, but in those days what ruled my conduct was passion, not reason. Alas! it would be the same again to-day, if the two were not in harmony; I should be driven to give myself to you, beloved, heart and soul, and for ever!"

She expressed herself in firm, well-balanced phrases. She had well thought over what she would say, having long ago made up her mind to this confession for several reasons—because she was naturally candid, because she found pleasure in following Rousseau's example, and because, as she told herself reasonably enough:

"One day Évariste must fathom a secret which is known to others as well as myself. A frank avowal is best. It is unforced and therefore to my credit, and only tells him what some time or other he would discover to my shame."

Soft-hearted as she was and amenable to nature's promptings, she did not feel herself to be very much to blame, and this made her confession the easier; besides which, she had no intention of telling more than was absolutely requisite.

"Ah!" she sighed, "why did I not know you, Évariste, in the days when I was alone and forsaken?"

Gamelin had taken her request quite literally when Élodie asked him to be her judge. Primed at once by nature and the education of books for the exercise of domestic justice, he sat ready to receive Élodie's admissions.

As she still hesitated, he motioned to her to proceed. Then she began speaking very simply:

"A young man, who with many defects of character combined some good qualities, and only showed the latter, found me to his taste and courted me with a perseverance that was surprising

156

in such a case; he was in the flower of his youth, full of charm and the idol of a bevy of charming women who made no attempt to hide their adoration. It was not his good looks nor even his brilliance that appealed to me.... He touched my heart by the tokens of true love he gave me, and I do think he loved me truly. He was tender, impassioned. I asked no pledge save of his heart, and alas! his heart was fickle.... I blame no one but myself; it is my confession I am making, not his. I lay nothing to his charge, for indeed he is become a stranger to me. Ah! believe me, Évariste, I swear it, he is no more to me than if he had never existed."

She had finished, but Gamelin vouchsafed no answer. He folded his arms, a steadfast, sombre look settling in his eyes. His mistress and his sister Julie were running together in his thoughts. Julie too had hearkened to a lover; but, unlike, altogether unlike, he thought, the unhappy Élodie, *she* had let him have his will and carry her off, not misled by the promptings of a tender heart, but to enjoy, far from her home and friends, the sweets of luxury and pleasure. He was a stern moralist; he had condemned his sister and he was half inclined to condemn his mistress.

Élodie resumed in a very pleading voice:

"I was full of Jean-Jacques' philosophy; I believed men were naturally honest and honourable. My misfortune was to have encountered a lover who was not formed in the school of nature and natural morality, and whom social prejudice, ambition, self-love, a false point of honour had made selfish and treacherous."

The words produced the effect she had calculated on. Gamelin's eyes softened. He asked:

"Who was your seducer? Is he a man I know?"

"You do not know him."

"Tell me his name."

She had foreseen the question and was firmly resolved not to answer it.

She gave her reasons:

"Spare me, I beseech you. For your peace of mind as for my own, I have already said too much."

Then, as he still pressed her:

"In the sacred name of our love, I refuse to tell you anything to give you a definite notion of this stranger. I will not give your jealousy a shape to feed on; I will not bring a harassing shadow between you and me. I have not forgotten the man's name, but I will never let you know it."

Gamelin insisted on knowing the name of the seducer,—that was the word he employed all through, for he felt no doubt Élodie had been seduced, cajoled, trifled with. He could not so much as conceive any other possibility,—that she had obeyed an overmastering desire, an irresistible craving, listened to the tempter's voice in the shape of her own flesh and blood; he could not find it credible that the fair victim, a creature of hot passion and a fond heart, had offered herself a willing sacrifice; to satisfy his ideal, she must needs have been overborne by force or fraud, constrained by sheer violence, caught in snares spread about her steps on every

157

side. He questioned her in guarded terms, but with a close, searching, embarrassing persistency. He asked her how the liaison began, if it was long or short, tranquil or troubled, under what circumstances it was broken off. And his enquiries came back again and again to the means the fellow had used to cajole her, as if these must surely have been extraordinary and unheard of. But all his cross-examination was in vain. She kept her own counsel with a gentle, deprecatory obstinacy, her lips tightly pressed together and tears welling in her eyes.

Presently, however, Évariste having asked where the man was now, she told him:

"He has left the Kingdom—France, I mean," she corrected herself in an instant.

"An *émigré*!" ejaculated Gamelin.

She looked at him, speechless, at once reassured and disheartened to see him create in his own mind a truth in accordance with his political passions and of his own motion give his jealousy a Jacobin complexion.

In actual fact Élodie's lover was a little lawyer's clerk, a very pretty lad, half Adonis, half guttersnipe, whom she had adored and the thought of whom, though three years had gone by since, still thrilled her nerves. Rich old women were his particular game, and he deserted Élodie for a woman of the world of a certain age who could and did recompense his merits. Having, after the abolition of offices, attained a post in the Mairie of Paris, he was now a *sansculotte* dragoon and the hanger-on of a *ci-devant* Countess.

"A noble! an *émigré*!" muttered Gamelin, whom she took good care not to undeceive, never having been desirous he should know the whole truth. "And he deserted you like a dastard?"

She nodded in answer. He clasped her to his heart:

"Dear victim of the vile corruption of monarchies, my love shall avenge his villainy! Heaven grant, I may meet the scoundrel! I shall not fail to know him!"

She turned away, at one and the same time saddened and smiling,—and disappointed. She would fain have had him wiser in the lore of love, with more of the natural man about him, more perhaps even of the brute. She felt he forgave so readily only because his imagination was cold and the secret she had revealed awoke in him none of the mental pictures that torture sensuous natures,—in a word, that he saw her seduction solely under a moral and social aspect.

They had risen, and while they walked up and down the shady avenues of the gardens, he informed her that he only esteemed her the more because she had suffered wrong, Élodie entertained no such high claims; however, take him as he was, she loved him, and admired the brilliant artistic genius she divined in him.

As they left the Luxembourg, they came upon crowds thronging the Rue de l'Égalité and the whole neighbourhood of the Théâtre de la Nation. There was nothing to surprise them in this; for several days great excitement had prevailed in the most patriotic Sections; denunciations were rife against the Orleans faction and the Brissotin plotters, who were conspiring, it was said, to bring about the ruin of Paris and the massacre of good Republicans. Gamelin himself a short time back had signed a petition from the Commune demanding the expulsion of the Twenty-one.

Just before passing under the arcade, joining the theatre to the neighbouring house, they had to find their way through a group of citizens *en carmagnole* who were listening to a harangue from a young soldier mounted on the top of the gallery. He looked as beautiful as the Eros of Praxiteles in his helmet of panther-skin. This fascinating warrior was charging the People's Friend with indolence:

"Marat, you are asleep," he was crying, "and the federalists are forging fetters to bind us."

Hardly had Élodie cast eyes on the orator before she turned rapidly to Évariste and begged him to get her away. The crowd, she declared, frightened her and she was afraid of fainting in the crush.

They parted in the Place de la Nation, swearing an oath of eternal fidelity.

That same morning early the *citoyen* Brotteaux had made the *citoyenne* Gamelin the magnificent present of a capon. It would have been an act of indiscretion for him to mention how he had come by it; as a fact, he had it of a *Dame de la Halle* at the Pointe Eustache for whom he sometimes acted as amanuensis, and as everybody knows, these "Ladies of the Market" cherished Royalist sympathies and were in correspondence with the *émigrés*. The *citoyenne* Gamelin had received the gift with heartfelt gratitude. Such dainties were scarce ever seen then; victuals grew dearer every day. The people feared a famine; the aristocrats, they said, wished it, and the "corner" makers were at work to bring it about.

The *citoyen* Brotteaux, being invited to eat his share of the capon at the midday dinner, appeared in due course and congratulated his hostess on the rich aroma of cooking that assailed his nostrils. Indeed a noble smell of rich, savoury broth filled the painter's studio.

"You are very obliging, sir," replied the good dame. "To prepare the digestion for your capon, I have made a vegetable soup with a slice of fat bacon and a big beef bone. There's nothing like a marrowbone, sir, to give soup a flavour."

"The maxim does you honour, *citoyenne*," returned the old man. "And you will be doing wisely to put back again to-morrow and the day after, all the week, in fact, to put back again, I say, this precious bone in the pot, which it will continue to flavour. The wise woman of Panzoust always did so; she used to make a soup of green cabbages with a rind of rusty bacon and an old *savorados*. That is what in her country, which is also mine, they call the medullary bone, the most tasty and most succulent of all bones."

"This lady you speak of, sir," remarked the *citoyenne* Gamelin, "was she not rather a saving soul, to make the same bone serve so many times over?"

"Oh! she lived in a small way," explained Brotteaux, "she was poor, albeit a prophetess."

At that moment, Évariste Gamelin returned, agitated by the confession he had heard and determined to know who was Élodie's betrayer, to avenge at one and the same time the Republic's wrong and his own on the miscreant.

After the usual greetings had been exchanged, the *citoyen* Brotteaux resumed the thread of his discourse:

"It is seldom those who make a trade of foretelling the future grow rich. Their impostures are too soon found out and their trickery renders them odious. But indeed we should be bound to detest them much worse if they prophesied truly. A man's life would be intolerable if he knew what is to befall him. He would be aware of calamities to come and suffer their pains in advance, while he would get no joy of present blessings whose end he would foresee. Ignorance is a necessary condition of human happiness, and it must be owned that in most cases we fulfil it well. We know almost nothing about ourselves; absolutely nothing about our neighbours. Ignorance constitutes our peace of mind; self-deception our felicity."

The *citoyenne* Gamelin set the soup on the table, said the Benedicite and seated her son and her guest at the board. She stood up herself to eat, declining the chair the *citoyen* Brotteaux offered her beside him; she said she knew what good manners required of a woman.

VI

Ten o'clock in the forenoon. Not a breath of wind. It was the hottest July ever known. In the narrow Rue de Jérusalem a hundred or so citizens of the Section were waiting in queue at the baker's door, under the eye of four National Guards who stood at ease smoking their pipes.

The National Convention had decreed the *maximum*,—and instantly corn and flour had disappeared. Like the Israelites in the wilderness, the Parisians had to rise before daybreak if they wished to eat. The crowd was lined up, men, women and children tightly packed together, under a sky of molten lead. The heat beat down on the rotting foulness of the kennels and exaggerated the stench of unwashed, sweating humanity. All were pushing, abusing their neighbours, exchanging looks fraught with every sort of emotion one human being can feel for another,—dislike, disgust, interest, attraction, indifference. Painful experience had taught them there was not bread enough for everybody; so the late comers were always trying to push forward, while those who lost ground complained bitterly and indignantly and vainly claimed their rights. Women shoved and elbowed savagely to keep their place or squeeze into a better. When the press grew too intolerable, cries rose of "Stop pushing there!" while each and all protested they could not help it—it was someone else pushing them.

To obviate these daily scenes of disorder, the officials appointed by the Section had conceived the notion of fastening a rope to the shop-door which each applicant held in his proper order; but hands at such close quarters *would* come in contact on the rope and a struggle would result. Whoever lost hold could never recover it, while the disappointed and the mischievously inclined sometimes cut the cord. In the end the plan had to be abandoned.

On this occasion there was the usual suffocation and confusion. While some swore they were dying, others indulged in jokes or loose remarks; all abused the aristocrats and federalists, authors of all the misery. When a dog ran by, wags hailed the beast as Pitt. More than once a loud slap showed that some *citoyenne* in the line had resented with a vigorous hand the insolence of a lewd admirer, while, pressed close against her neighbour, a young servant girl, with eyes half shut and mouth half open, stood sighing in a sort of trance. At any word, or gesture, or attitude of a sort to provoke the sportive humour of the coarse-minded populace, a knot of young libertines would strike up the *Ça-ira* in chorus, regardless of the protests of an old Jacobin, highly indignant to see a dirty meaning attached to a refrain expressive of the Republican faith in a future of justice and happiness.

160

His ladder under his arm, a billsticker appeared to post up on a blank wall facing the baker's a proclamation by the Commune apportioning the rations of butcher's-meat. Passers-by halted to read the notice, still sticky with paste. A cabbage vendor going by, basket on back, began calling out in her loud cracked voice:

"They'm all gone, the purty oxen! best rake up the guts!"

Suddenly such an appalling stench of putrefaction rose from a sewer near by that several people were turned sick; a woman was taken ill and handed over in a fainting condition to a couple of National Guards, who carried her off to a pump a few yards away. All held their noses, and fell to growling and grumbling, exchanging conjectures each more ghastly and alarming than the last. What was it? a dead animal buried thereabouts, a dead fish, perhaps, put in for mischief's sake, or more likely a victim of the September massacres, some noble or priest, left to rot in a cellar.

"They buried them in cellars, eh?"

"They got rid of 'em anywhere and anyhow."

"It will be one of the Châtelet prisoners. On the 2nd I saw three hundred in a heap on the Port au Change."

The Parisians dreaded the vengeance of these aristocrats who were like to poison them with their dead bodies.

Évariste Gamelin joined the line; he was resolved to spare his old mother the fatigues of the long wait. His neighbour, the *citoyen*Brotteaux, went with him, calm and smiling, his Lucretius in the baggy pocket of his plum-coloured coat.

The good old fellow enjoyed the scene, calling it a bit of low life worthy the brush of a modern Teniers.

"These street-porters and goodwives," he declared, "are more amusing than the Greeks and Romans our painters are so fond of nowadays. For my part, I have always admired the Flemish style."

One fact he was too sensible and tactful to mention—that he had himself owned a gallery of Dutch masters rivalled only by Monsieur de Choiseul's in the number and excellence of the examples.

"Nothing is beautiful save the Antique," returned the painter, "and what is inspired by it. Still, I grant you these low-life scenes by Teniers, Jan Steen or Ostade are better stuff than the frills and furbelows of Watteau, Boucher, or Van Loo; humanity is shown in an ugly light, but it is not degraded as it is by a Baudouin or a Fragonard."

A hawker went by bawling:

"*Bulletin of the Revolutionary Tribunal!*... list of the condemned!"

"One Revolutionary Tribunal is not enough," said Gamelin, "there should be one in every town ... in every town, do I say?—nay, in every village, in every hamlet. Fathers of families, citizens, one and all, should constitute themselves judges. At a time when the enemy's cannon is at her gates and the assassin's dagger at her throat, the Nation must hold mercy to be parricide. What! Lyons, Marseilles, Bordeaux in insurrection, Corsica in revolt, La Vendée on fire, Mayence and Valenciennes in the hands of the Coalition, treason in the country, town and camp, treason sitting on the very benches of the National Convention, treason assisting, map in hand, at the council board of our Commanders in the field!... The fatherland is in danger—and the guillotine must save her!"

"I have no objection on principle to make to the guillotine," replied Brotteaux. "Nature, my only mistress and my only instructress, certainly offers me no suggestion to the effect that a man's life is of any value; on the contrary, she teaches in all kinds of ways that it is of none. The sole end and object of living beings seems to be to serve as food for other beings destined to the same end. Murder is of natural right; therefore, the penalty of death is lawful, on condition it is exercised from no motives either of virtue or of justice, but by necessity or to gain some profit thereby. However, I must have perverse instincts, for I sicken to see blood flow, and this defect of character all my philosophy has failed so far to correct."

"Republicans," answered Évariste, "are humane and full of feeling. It is only despots hold the death penalty to be a necessary attribute of authority. The sovereign people will do away with it one day. Robespierre fought against it, and all good patriots were with him; the law abolishing it cannot be too soon promulgated. But it will not have to be applied till the last foe of the Republic has perished beneath the sword of law and order."

Gamelin and Brotteaux had by this time a number of late comers behind them and amongst these several women of the Section, including a stalwart, handsome *tricoteuse*, in head-kerchief and sabots, wearing a sword in a shoulder belt, a pretty girl with a mop of golden hair and a very tumbled neckerchief, and a young mother, pale and thin, giving the breast to a sickly infant.

The child, which could get no milk, was screaming, but its voice was weak and stifled by its sobs. Pitifully small, with a pallid, unhealthy skin and inflamed eyes, the mother gazed at it with mingled anxiety and grief.

"He is very young," observed Gamelin, turning to look at the unhappy infant groaning just at his back, half stifled amid the crowd of new arrivals.

"He is six months, poor love!... His father is with the army; he is one of the men who drove back the Austrians at Condé. His name is Dumonteil (Michel), a draper's assistant by trade. He enlisted at a booth they had established in front of the Hôtel de Ville. Poor lad, he was all for defending his country and seeing the world.... He writes telling me to be patient. But pray, how am I to feed Paul (he's called Paul, you know) when I can't feed myself?"

"Oh, dear!" exclaimed the pretty girl with the flaxen hair, "we've got another hour before us yet, and to-night we shall have to repeat the same ceremony over again at the grocer's. You risk your life to get three eggs and a quarter of a pound of butter."

"Butter!" sighed the *citoyenne* Dumonteil, "why, it's three months since I've seen a scrap!"

And a chorus of female voices rose, bewailing the scarcity and dearness of provisions, cursing the *émigrés* and devoting to the guillotine the Commissaries of Sections who were ready to give good-for-nothing minxes, in return for unmentionable services, fat hens and four-pound loaves. Alarming stories passed round of cattle drowned in the Seine, sacks of flour emptied in the sewers, loaves of bread thrown into the latrines.... It was all those Royalists, and

162

Rolandists, and Brissotins, who were starving the people, bent on exterminating every living thing in Paris!

All of a sudden the pretty, fair-haired girl with the rumpled neckerchief broke into shrieks as if her petticoats were afire. She was shaking these violently and turning out her pockets, vociferating that somebody had stolen her purse.

At news of the petty theft, a flood of indignation swept over this crowd of poor folks, the same who had sacked the mansions of the Faubourg Saint-Germain and invaded the Tuileries without appropriating the smallest thing, artisans and housewives, who would have burned down the Palace of Versailles with a light heart, but would have thought it a dire disgrace if they had stolen the value of a pin. The young rakes greeted the pretty girl's loss with some ribald jokes, that were immediately drowned under a burst of public indignation. There was some talk of instant execution—hanging the thief to the nearest lamp-post, and an investigation was begun, where everyone spoke at once and nobody would listen to a word of reason. The tall *tricoteuse*, pointing her finger at an old man, strongly suspected of being an unfrocked monk, swore it was the "Capuchin" yonder who was the cut-purse. The crowd believed her without further evidence and raised a shout of "Death! death!"

The old man so unexpectedly exposed to the public vengeance was standing very quietly and soberly just in front of the *citoyen* Brotteaux. He had all the look, there was no denying it, of a *ci-devant* cleric. His aspect was venerable, though the face was changed and drawn by the terrors the poor man had suffered from the violence of the crowd and the recollection of the September days that were still vivid in his imagination. The fear depicted on his features stirred the suspicion of the populace, which is always ready to believe that only the guilty dread its judgments, as if the haste and recklessness with which it pronounces them were not enough to terrify even the most innocent.

Brotteaux had made it a standing rule never to go against the popular feeling of the moment, above all when it was manifestly illogical and cruel, "because in that case," he would say, "the voice of the people was the voice of God." But Brotteaux proved himself untrue to his principles; he asseverated that the old man, whether he was a Capuchin or not, could not have robbed the *citoyenne*, having never gone near her for one moment.

The crowd drew its own conclusion,—the individual who spoke up for the thief was of course his accomplice, and stern measures were proposed to deal with the two malefactors, and when Gamelin offered to guarantee Brotteaux' honesty, the wisest heads suggested sending *him* along with the two others to the Sectional headquarters.

But the pretty girl gave a cry of delight; she had found her purse again. The statement was received with a storm of hisses, and she was threatened with a public whipping,—like a Nun.

"Sir," said the ex-monk, addressing Brotteaux, "I thank you for having spoken in my defence. My name is of no concern, but I had better tell you what it is; I am called Louis de Longuemare. I am in truth a Regular; but not a Capuchin, as those women would have it. There is the widest difference; I am a monk of the Order of the Barnabites, which has given Doctors and Saints without number to the Church. It is only a half-truth to refer its origin to St. Charles Borromeo; we must account as the true founder the Apostle St. Paul, whose cipher it bears on its arms. I have been compelled to quit my cloister, now headquarters of the Section du Pont-Neuf, and adopt a secular habit.

163

"Nay, Father," said Brotteaux, scrutinizing Monsieur de Longuemare's frock, "your dress is token enough that you have not forsworn your profession; to look at it, one might think you had reformed your Order rather than forsaken it. It is your good heart makes you expose yourself in these austere habiliments to the insults of a godless populace."

"Yet I cannot very well," replied the ex-monk, "wear a blue coat, like a roisterer at a dance!"

"What I mention, Father, about your dress is by way of paying homage to your character and putting you on your guard against the risks you run."

"On the contrary, sir, it would be much better to inspirit me to confess my faith. For indeed, I am only too prone to fear danger. I have abandoned my habit, sir, which is a sort of apostasy; I would fain not have deserted, had it been possible, the House where God granted me for so many years the grace of a peaceable and retired life. I got leave to stay there, and I still continued to occupy my cell, while they turned the church and cloister into a sort of petty *hôtel de ville* they called the Section. I saw, sir, I saw them hack away the emblems of the Holy Verity; I saw the name of the Apostle Paul replaced by a convicted felon's cap. Sometimes I was actually present at the confabulations of the Section, where I heard amazing errors propounded. At last I quitted this place of profanation and went to live on the pension of a hundred pistoles allowed me by the Assembly in a stable that stood empty, the horses having been requisitioned for the service of the armies. There I sing Mass for a few of the faithful, who come to the office to bear witness to the eternity of the Church of Jesus Christ."

"For my part, Father," replied the other, "if you care to know my name, I am called Brotteaux, and I was a publican in former days."

"Sir," returned the Père Longuemare, "I was aware by St. Matthew's example that one may look for good counsel from a publican."

"Father, you are too obliging."

"*Citoyen* Brotteaux," remarked Gamelin, "pray admire the virtues of the people, more hungry for justice than for bread; consider how everyone here is ready to lose his place to chastise the thief. These men and women, victims of such poverty and privation, are of so stern a probity they cannot tolerate a dishonest act."

"It must indeed be owned," replied Brotteaux, "that in their hearty desire to hang the pilferer, these folks were like to do a mischief to this good cleric, to his champion and to his champion's champion. Their avarice itself and their selfish eagerness to safeguard their own welfare were motives enough; the thief in attacking one of them threatened all; self-preservation urged them to punish him.... At the same time, it is like enough the most part of these workmen and goodwives are honest and keep their hands off other folk's goods. From the cradle these sentiments have been instilled in them by their father and mother, who have whipped them well and soundly and inculcated the virtues through their backside."

Gamelin did not conceal the fact from his old neighbour that he deemed such language unworthy of a philosopher.

"Virtue," said he, "is natural to mankind; God has planted the seed of it in the heart of mortals."

Old Brotteaux was a sceptic and found in his atheism an abundant source of self-satisfaction.

"I see this much, *citoyen* Gamelin, that, while a Revolutionary for what is of this world, you are, where Heaven is concerned, of a conservative, or even a reactionary temper. Robespierre and Marat are the same to you. For me, I find it strange that Frenchmen, who will not put up with a mortal king any longer, insist on retaining an immortal tyrant, far more despotic and ferocious. For what is the Bastille, or even the *Chambre Ardente* beside Hellfire? Humanity models its gods on its tyrants, and you, who reject the original, preserve the copy!"

"Oh! *citoyen!*" protested Gamelin, "are you not ashamed to hold such language? how can you confound the dark divinities born of ignorance and fear with the Author of Nature? Belief in a benevolent God is necessary for morality. The Supreme Being is the source of all the virtues and a man cannot be a Republican if he does not believe in God. Robespierre knew this, who, as we all remember, had the bust of the philosopher Helvétius removed from the Hall of the Jacobins, because he had taught Frenchmen the lessons of slavery by preaching atheism.... I hope, at least, *citoyen* Brotteaux, that, as soon as the Republic has established the worship of Reason, you will not refuse your adhesion to so wise a religion!"

"I love reason, but I am no fanatic in my love," was Brotteaux's answer. "Reason is our guide and beacon-light; but when you have made a divinity of it, it will blind you and instigate you to crime,"—and he proceeded to develop his thesis, standing both feet in the kennel, as he had once been used to perorate, seated in one of Baron d'Holbach's gilt armchairs, which, as he was fond of saying, formed the basis of natural philosophy.

"Jean Jacques Rousseau," he proceeded, "who was not without talents, particularly in music, was a scampish fellow who professed to derive his morality from Nature while all the time he got it from the dogmas of Calvin. Nature teaches us to devour each other and gives us the example of all the crimes and all the vices which the social state corrects or conceals. We should love virtue; but it is well to know that this is simply and solely a convenient expedient invented by men in order to live comfortably together. What we call morality is merely a desperate enterprise, a forlorn hope, on the part of our fellow creatures to reverse the order of the universe, which is strife and murder, the blind interplay of hostile forces. She destroys herself, and the more I think of things, the more convinced I am that the universe is mad. Theologians and philosophers, who make God the author of Nature and the architect of the universe, show Him to us as illogical and ill-conditioned. They declare Him benevolent, because they are afraid of Him, but they are forced to admit that His acts are atrocious. They attribute a malignity to him seldom to be found even in mankind. And that is how they get human beings to adore Him. For our miserable race would never lavish worship on just and benevolent deities from which they would have nothing to fear; they would feel only a barren gratitude for their benefits. Without purgatory and hell, your good God would be a mighty poor creature."

"Sir," said the Père Longuemare, "do not talk of Nature; you do not know what Nature is."

"Egad, I know it as well as you do, Father."

"You cannot know it, because you have not religion, and religion alone teaches us what Nature is, wherein it is good, and how it has been made evil. However, you must not expect me to answer you; God has vouchsafed me, to refute your errors, neither eloquence nor force of intellect. I should only be afraid, by my inadequate replies, of giving you occasion to blaspheme and further reasons for hardening your heart. I feel a strong desire to help you; yet the sole fruit of my importunate efforts would be to...."

The discussion was cut short by a tremendous shout coming from the head of the column to warn the whole regiment of famished citizens that the baker was opening his doors. The line began to push forward, but very, very slowly. A National Guard on duty admitted the purchasers one by one. The baker, his wife and boy presided over the sale, assisted by two Civil Commissaries. These, wearing a tricoloured riband round the left arm, saw that the customers belonged to the Section and were given their proper share in proportion to the number of mouths to be filled.

The *citoyen* Brotteaux made the quest of pleasure the one and only aim of life, holding that the reason and the senses, the sole judges when gods there were none, were unable to conceive any other. Accordingly, finding the painter's remarks somewhat overfull of fanaticism, and the Monk's of simplicity, to please his taste, this wise man, bent on squaring his behaviour with his views and relieving the tedium of waiting, drew from the bulging pocket of his plum-coloured coat his Lucretius, now as always his chiefest solace and faithful comforter. The binding of red morocco was chafed by hard wear, and the *citoyen* Brotteaux had judiciously erased the coat of arms that once embellished it,—three islets or, which his father the financier had bought for good money down. He opened the book at the passage where the poet philosopher, who is for curing men of the futile and mischievous passion of love, surprises a woman in the arms of her serving-women in a state bound to offend all a lover's susceptibilities. The *citoyen* Brotteaux read the lines, though not without casting a surreptitious glance at the golden pate of the pretty girl in front of him and enjoying a sniff of the heady perfume of the little slut's hot skin. The poet Lucretius was a wise man, but he had only one string to his bow; his disciple Brotteaux had several.

So he read on, taking two steps forward every quarter of an hour. His ear, soothed by the grave and cadenced numbers of the Latin Muse, was deaf to the women's scolding about the monstrous prices of bread and sugar and coffee, candles and soap. In this calm and unruffled mood he reached the threshold of the bakehouse. Behind him, Évariste Gamelin could see over his head the gilt cornsheaf surmounting the iron grating that filled the fanlight over the door.

When his turn came to enter the shop, he found the hampers and lockers already emptied; the baker handed him the only scrap of bread left, which did not weigh two pounds. Évariste paid his money, and the gate was slammed on his heels, for fear of a riot and the people carrying the place by storm.

But there was no need to fear; these poor folks, trained to obedience alike by their old-time oppressors and by their liberators of to-day, slunk off with drooping heads and dragging feet.

As he reached the corner of the street, Gamelin caught sight of the *citoyenne* Dumonteil, seated on a stone post, her nursling in her arms. She sat there quite still; her face was colourless and her tearless eyes seemed to see nothing. The infant was sucking her finger voraciously. Gamelin stood a while in front of her, abashed and uncertain what to do. She did not appear to see him.

He stammered something, then pulled out his pocket-knife, a clasp-knife with a horn handle, cut his loaf in two and laid half on the young mother's knee. She looked up at him in wonder; but he had already turned the corner of the street.

On reaching home, Évariste found his mother sitting at the window darning stockings. With a light laugh he put his half of the bread in her hand.

"You must forgive me, mother dear; I was tired out with standing about and exhausted by the heat, and out in the street there as I trudged home, mouthful by mouthful I have gobbled up half of our allowance. There's barely your share left,"—and as he spoke, he made a pretence of shaking the crumbs off his jacket.

VII

Employing a very old-fashioned locution, the *citoyenne* Gamelin had declared: "that by dint of eating chestnuts they would be turning into chestnuts." As a matter of fact, on that day, the 13th July, she and her son had made their midday dinner on a basin of chestnut porridge. As they were finishing this austere repast, a lady pushed open the door and the room was flooded in an instant with the splendour of her presence and the fragrance of her perfumes. Évariste recognised the *citoyenne* Rochemaure. Thinking she had mistaken the door and meant her visit for the *citoyen* Brotteaux, her friend of other days, he was already preparing to point her out the *ci-devant* aristocrat's garret or perhaps summon Brotteaux and so spare an elegant woman the task of scrambling up a mill-ladder; but she made it clear at once that the *citoyen* Évariste Gamelin and no other was the person she had come to see by announcing that she was happy to find him at home and was his servant to command.

They were not entirely strangers to each other, having met more than once in David's studio, in a box at the Assembly Hall, at the Jacobins, at Venua's restaurant. On these occasions she had been struck by his good looks and youth and interesting air.

Wearing a hat beribboned like a fairing and plumed like the head-piece of a Representative on mission, the *citoyenne* Rochemaure was wigged, painted, patched and scented. But her complexion was young and fresh behind all these disguises; these extravagant artificialities of fashion only betokened a frantic haste to enjoy life and the feverishness of these dreadful days when the morrow was so uncertain. Her corsage, with wide facings and enormous basques and all ablaze with huge steel buttons, was blood-red, and it was hard to tell, so aristocratic and so revolutionary at one and the same time was her array, whether it was the colours of the victims or of the headsman that she sported. A young officer, a dragoon, accompanied her.

Dandling her long cane by its handle of mother-o'-pearl, a tall, fine woman, of generous proportions and ample bosom, she made the circuit of the studio, and putting up to her grey eyes her double quizzing-glasses of gold, examined the painter's canvases with many smiles and exclamations of delight, admiring the handsome artist and flattering him in hopes of a return in kind.

"What," asked the *citoyenne*, "is that picture—it is so nobly conceived, so touching—of a gentle, beautiful woman standing by a young man lying sick?"

Gamelin told her it was meant to represent *Orestes tended by his sister Electra*, and that, had he been able to finish it, it might perhaps have been the least unsatisfactory of his works.

"The subject," he went on to say, "is taken from the *Orestes* of Euripides. I had read, in a translation of this tragedy made years ago, a scene that filled me with admiration,—the one where the young Electra, raising her brother on his bed of pain, wipes away the froth that gathers on his lips, puts aside the locks that blind his eyes and beseeches the brother she loves to hearken to what she will tell him while the Furies are at peace for the moment.... As I read and re-read this translation, I seemed to be aware of a kind of fog that shrouded the forms of Greek perfection, a fog I could not drive away. I pictured the original text to myself as more nervous and pitched in a different accent. Feeling a keen desire to get a precise idea of the thing, I went to Monsieur Gail, who was the Professor of Greek at the Collège de France (this was in '91), and begged him to expound the scene to me word by word. He did what I asked, and I then saw that the Ancients are much more simple and homely than people think. Thus, for instance, Electra says to Orestes: 'Dear brother, what joy it gave me to see thee sleep! Shall I help thee to rise?' And Orestes answers: 'Yes, help me, take me in thy arms, and wipe away the spume that still clings about my mouth and eyes. Put thy bosom against mine and part from my brow my tangled hair, for it blinds my eyes....' My mind still full of this poetry, so young and vivid, ringing with these simple, strong phrases, I sketched the picture you see there, *citoyenne*."

The painter, who, as a rule, spoke so sparingly of his works, waxed eloquent on the subject of this one. At an encouraging gesture from the *citoyenne* Rochemaure, who lifted her quizzing-glasses in token of attention, he continued:

"Hennequin has depicted the madness of Orestes in masterly fashion. But Orestes appeals to us still more poignantly in his sorrow than when he is distraught. What a fate was his! It was filial piety, obedience to a sacred obligation, drove him to commit his dreadful deed,—a sin the gods cannot but pardon, but which men will never condone. To avenge outraged justice, he has repudiated Nature, has made himself a monster, has torn out his own heart. But his spirit remains unbroken under the weight of his horrible, yet innocent crime.... That is what I would fain have exhibited in my group of brother and sister." He stepped up to the canvas and looked at it not without satisfaction.

"Parts of the picture," he said, "are pretty nearly finished; the head and arm of Orestes, for instance."

"It is an admirable composition.... And Orestes reminds me of you, *citoyen* Gamelin."

"You think he is like me?" exclaimed the painter, with a grave smile.

She took the chair Gamelin offered her. The young dragoon stood beside her, his hand on the back of the chair on which she sat. Which showed plainly that the Revolution was an accomplished fact, for under the ancien régime, no man would ever, in company, have touched so much as with the tip of a finger, the seat occupied by a lady. In those days a gentleman was trained and broken in to the laws of politeness, sometimes pretty hard laws, and taught to understand that a scrupulous self-restraint in public places gives a peculiar zest to the sweet familiarity of the boudoir, and that to lose your respectful awe of a woman, you must first have that feeling.

Louise Masché de Rochemaure, daughter of a Lieutenant of the King's Hunt, widow of a Procureur and, for twenty years, the faithful mistress of the financier Brotteaux des Ilettes, had fallen in with the new ideas. She was to be seen, in July, 1790, digging the soil of the Champ de Mars. Her strong inclination to side with the powers that be had carried her readily enough along a political path that started with the Feuillants and led by way of the Girondins to end on the summit of *the Mountain*, while at the same time a spirit of compromise, a passion for conversion and a certain aptitude for intrigue still attached her to the aristocratic and anti-revolutionary party. She was to be met everywhere,—at coffee houses and theatres, fashionable restaurants, gaming-saloons, drawing-rooms, newspaper offices and ante-chambers of Committees. The Revolution yielded her a hundred satisfactions,—novelty and amusement, smiles and pleasures, business ventures and profitable speculations. Combining political with amorous intrigue, playing the harp, drawing landscapes, singing ballads, dancing Greek dances, giving supper parties, entertaining pretty women, such as the Comtesse de Beaufort and the actress Mademoiselle Descoings, presiding all night long over a *trente-et-un* or *biribi* table and

168

an adept at *rouge et noir*, she still found time to be charitable to her friends. Inquisitive and interfering, giddy-pated and frivolous, she understood men but knew nothing of the masses; as indifferent to the creed she professed as to the opinions she felt bound to repudiate, understanding nothing whatever of all that was happening in the country, she was enterprising, intrepid, and full of audacity from sheer ignorance of danger and an unbounded confidence in the efficacy of her charms.

The soldier who escorted her was in the heyday of youth. A brazen helmet decorated with a panther skin and the crest set off with a crimson cock's-comb shaded his fresh young face and displayed a long and terrific mane that swept his back. His red jacket was cut short and square, barely reaching to the waist, the better to show off his elegant figure. In his girdle he carried an enormous sabre, the hilt of which was a glittering eagle's beak. A pair of flapped breeches of sky blue moulded the fine muscles of his legs and was braided in rich arabesques of a darker blue on the thighs. He might have been a dancer dressed for some warlike and dashing rôle, in *Achilles at Scyros* or *Alexander's Wedding-feast*, in a costume designed by a pupil of David with the one idea of accentuating every line of the shape.

Gamelin had a vague recollection of having seen him before. He was, in fact, the same young soldier he had come upon a fortnight previously haranguing the people from the arcades of the Théâtre de la Nation.

The *citoyenne* Rochemaure introduced him by name:

"The *citoyen* Henry, Member of the Revolutionary Committee of the Section of the Rights of Man."

She had him always at her heels,—a mirror of gallantry and a living and walking guarantee of patriotism.

The *citoyenne* complimented Gamelin on his talents and asked him if he would be willing to design a card for a protégée of hers, a fashionable milliner. He would, of course, choose an appropriate *motif*,—a woman trying on a scarf before a cheval glass, for instance, or a young workwoman carrying a band-box on her arm.

She had heard several artists mentioned as competent to execute a little matter of the sort,— Fragonard *fils*, young Ducis, as well as a certain Prudhomme; but she would rather apply to the *citoyen* Évariste Gamelin. However, she made no definite proposal on this head and it was evident she had mentioned the commission merely by way of starting the conversation. In truth she had come for something quite different. She wanted the *citoyen* Gamelin to do her a favour; knowing he was a friend of the *citoyen* Marat, she had come to ask him to introduce her to the Friend of the People, with whom she desired an interview.

Gamelin replied that he was too insignificant an individual to present her to Marat, besides which, she had no need of anyone to be her sponsor; Marat, albeit overwhelmed with business, was not the inaccessible person he was said to be,—and, added Gamelin:

"He will receive you, *citoyenne*, if you are in distress; his great heart makes him compassionate to all who suffer. He will likewise receive you if you have any revelation to make concerning the public weal; he has vowed his days to the unmasking of traitors."

The *citoyenne* Rochemaure answered that she would be happy to greet in Marat an illustrious citizen, who had rendered great services to his country, who was capable of rendering greater still, and that she was anxious to bring the legislator in question into relation with friends of hers of good repute and good will, philanthropists favoured by fortune and competent to provide him with new means of satisfying his ardent affection for humanity.

"It is very desirable," she concluded, "to make the rich co-operate in securing public prosperity."

In actual fact, the *citoyenne* had promised the banker Morhardt to arrange a dinner where he and Marat should meet.

Morhardt, a Swiss like the Friend of the People, had entered into a combination with several deputies of the Convention, Julien (of Toulouse), Delaunay (of Angers) and the ex-Capuchin Chabot, to speculate in the shares of the *Compagnie des Indes*. The game was very simple,—to bring down the price of these shares to 650 livres by proposing motions pointing in the direction of confiscation, in order to buy up the greatest possible number at this figure and then push them up to 4,000 or 5,000 livres by dint of proposals of a reassuring nature. But for Chabot, Julien, Delaunay, their little ways were too notorious, while suspicions were rife of Lacroix, Fabre d'Églantine, and even Danton. The arch-speculator, the Baron de Batz, was looking for new confederates in the Convention and had advised Morhardt to sound Marat.

This idea of the anti-revolutionary speculators was not so extravagant as might have been supposed at the first blush. It was always the way of these gentry to form alliance with those in power at the moment, and by virtue of his popularity, his pen, his character, Marat was a power to be reckoned with. The Girondists were near shipwreck; the Dantonists, battered by the hurricane, had lost their hold on the helm. Robespierre, the idol of the people, was a man jealous of his scrupulous honesty, full of suspicion, impossible to approach. The great thing was to get round Marat, to secure his good will against the day when he should be dictator—and everything pointed to this consummation,—his popularity, his ambition, his eagerness to recommend heroic measures. And it might be, after all, Marat would re-establish order, the finances, the prosperity of the country. More than once he had risen in revolt against the zealots who were for outbidding him in fanaticism; for some time past he had been denouncing the demagogues as vehemently as the moderates. After inciting the people to sack the "cornerers'" shops and hang them over their own counters, he was now exhorting the citizens to be calm and prudent. He was growing into an administrator.

In spite of certain rumours disseminated against him as against all the other chiefs of the Revolution, these pirates of the money-market did not believe he could be corrupted, but they did know him to be vain and credulous, and they hoped to win him over by flattery and still more by a condescending friendliness which they looked upon as the most seductive form of flattery from men like themselves. They counted, thanks to him, on blowing hot and cold on all the securities they might wish to buy and sell, and making him serve their interests while supposing himself to be acting solely for the public good.

Great as a go-between, albeit she was still of an age for amours on her own account, the *citoyenne* Rochemaure had made it her mission to bring together the legislator-journalist and the banker, and in her extravagant imagination she already saw the man of the underworld, the man whose hands were yet red with the blood of the September massacres, a partner in the game of the financiers whose agent she was; she pictured him drawn by his very warmth of feeling and unsophisticated candour into the whirlpool of speculation, a recruit to the côterie she loved of "corner" makers, contractors, foreign emissaries, gamblers, and women of gallantry.

She insisted on the *citoyen* Gamelin taking her to see the Friend of the People, who lived quite near, in the Rue des Cordeliers, near the church. After some little show of reluctance, the painter acceded to the *citoyenne's* wishes.

The dragoon Henry was invited to join them in the visit, but declined, declaring he meant to keep his liberty of action, even towards the *citoyen* Marat, who, he felt no doubt, had rendered services to the Republic, but was weakening nowadays; had he not, in his news sheet, counselled resignation as the proper thing for the people of Paris?

And the young man, in a sweet voice, broken by long-drawn sighs, deplored the fate of the Republic, betrayed by the men in whom she had put her trust,—Danton rejecting the notion of a tax on the rich, Robespierre opposing the permanence of the Sections, Marat, whose pusillanimous counsels were paralyzing the enthusiasm of the citizens.

"Ah!" he cried, "how feeble such men appear beside Leclerc and Jacques Roux!... Roux! Leclerc! *ye* are the true friends of the people!"

Gamelin did not hear these remarks, which would have angered him; he had gone into the next room to don his blue coat.

"You may well be proud of your son," observed the *citoyenne* Rochemaure, addressing the *citoyenne* Gamelin. "He is a great man; talent and character both make him so."

In answer, the widow Gamelin gave a good account of her son, yet without making much boast of him before a lady of high station, for she had been taught in her childhood that the first duty of the lowly is humility towards the great. She was of a complaining bent, having indeed only too good cause and finding in such jeremiads a salve for her griefs. She was garrulous in her revelations of all the hardships she had to bear to any whom she supposed in a position to relieve them, and Madame de Rochemaure seemed to belong to that class. She made the most, therefore, of this favourable opportunity and told a long and breathless story of their distresses, —how mother and son were both dying of slow starvation. Pictures could not be sold any more; the Revolution had killed business dead. Victuals were scarce and too dear for words....

The good dame poured out her lamentations with all the loose-lipped volubility her halting tongue was capable of, so as to get them all finished by the time her son, whose pride would not brook such whining, should reappear. She was bent on attaining her object in the shortest possible time,—that of touching a lady whom she deemed rich and influential, and enlisting her sympathy in her boy's future. She felt sure that Évariste's good looks were an asset on her side to move the heart of a well-born lady. And so they were; the *citoyenne* Rochemaure proved tender-hearted and was melted to think of Évariste's and his mother's sufferings. She made plans to alleviate them; she had rich men amongst her friends and would get them to buy the artist's pictures.

"The truth is," she added, with a smile, "there is still money in France, but it keeps in hiding."

Better still, now Art was ruined, she would obtain Évariste a post in Morhardt's bank or with the Brothers Perregaux, or a place as clerk in the office of an army contractor.

Then she reflected that this was not what a man of his character needed; and, after a moment's thought, she nodded in sign that she had hit the nail on the head:

"There are still several jurymen left to be appointed on the Revolutionary Tribunal. Juryman, magistrate, that is the thing to suit your son. I have friendly relations with the Committee of Public Safety. I know Robespierre the elder personally; his brother frequently sups at my house. I will speak to them. I will get a word said to Montané, Dumas, Fouquier."

The *citoyenne* Gamelin, bursting with excitement and gratitude, put a finger to her lip; Évariste was coming back into the studio.

He escorted the *citoyenne* Rochemaure down the gloomy staircase, the steps of which, whether of wood or tiled, were coated with an ancient layer of dirt.

On the Pont-Neuf, where the sun, now near its setting, threw a lengthened shadow from the pedestal that had borne the Bronze Horse and was now gay with the National colours, a crowd of men and women of the people gathered in little groups were listening to some tale that was being told them. Consternation reigned and a heavy silence, broken at intervals by groans and fierce cries. Many were making off at a rapid pace in the direction of the Rue de Thionville, erstwhile Rue Dauphine; Gamelin joined one of these groups and heard the news—that Marat had just been assassinated.

Little by little the tidings were confirmed and particulars became known; he had been murdered in his bath by a woman who had come expressly from Caen to commit the crime.

Some thought she had escaped; but the majority declared she had been arrested.

There they stood like sheep without a shepherd, thinking sadly:

"Marat, the tender-hearted, the humane, Marat our benefactor, is no longer there to guide us, Marat who was never deceived, who saw through every subterfuge and never feared to reveal the truth!... What can we do, what is to become of us? We have lost our adviser, our champion, our friend." They knew very well whence the blow had come, and who had directed the woman's arm. They groaned aloud:

"Marat has been struck down by the same criminal hands that are bent on our extermination. His death is the signal for the slaughter of all good patriots."

Different reports were current, as to the circumstances of the tragic event and the last words of the victim; endless questions were asked concerning the assassin, all that anyone knew was that it was a young woman sent by those traitors, the federalists. Baring teeth and nails, the *citoyennes* devoted the culprit to condign punishment; deeming the guillotine too merciful a death, they demanded this monster of iniquity should be scourged, broken on the wheel, torn limb from limb, and racked their brains to invent new tortures.

An armed body of National Guards was haling to the Section headquarters a man of determined mien. His clothes were in tatters, and streams of blood trickled down his white face. He had been overheard saying that Marat had earned his fate by his constant incitements to pillage and massacre, and it was only with great difficulty that the Guards had saved him from the fury of the populace. A hundred fingers pointed him out as the accomplice of the assassin, and threats of death followed him as he was led away.

Gamelin was stunned by the blow. A few hot tears blistered his burning eyes. With the grief he felt as a disciple mingled solicitude for the popular idol, and these combined feelings tore at his heart-strings. He thought to himself:

"After Le Peltier, after Bourdon, Marat!... I foresee the fate of the patriots; massacred on the Champ de Mars, at Nancy, at Paris, they will perish one and all." And he thought of Wimpfen, the traitor, who only a while before was marching on Paris, and who, had he not been stopped at Vernon, by the gallant patriots, would have devoted the heroic city to fire and slaughter.

And how many perils still remained, how many criminal designs, how many treasonable plots, which only Marat's perspicacity and vigilance could unravel and foil! Now he was dead, who was there to denounce Custine loitering in idleness in the Camp of Cæsar and refusing to relieve Valenciennes, Biron tarrying inactive in the Lower Vendée letting Saumur be taken and Nantes blockaded, Dillon betraying the Fatherland in the Argonne?...

Meantime, all about him, rose momentarily higher the sinister cry:

"Marat is dead; the aristocrats have killed him!"

As he was on his way, his heart bursting with grief and hate and love, to pay a last mark of respect to the martyr of liberty, an old countrywoman, wearing the coif of the Limousin peasantry, accosted him to ask if the Monsieur Marat who had been murdered was not Monsieur le Curé Mara, of Saint-Pierre-de-Queyroix.

VIII

It was the eve of the Festival, a calm, bright evening, and Élodie hanging on Évariste's arm, was strolling with him about the *Champ de la Fédération*. Workmen were hastily completing their task of erecting columns, statues, temples, a "mountain," an altar of the Fatherland. Huge symbolic figures, Hercules (representing the people) brandishing his club, Nature suckling the Universe from her inexhaustible breasts, were rising at a moment's notice in the capital that, tortured by famine and fear, was listening for the dreaded sound of the Austrian cannon on the road from Meaux. La Vendée was making good its check before Nantes by a series of startling victories. A ring of fire and flame and hate was drawn about the great revolutionary city.

And meantime, she was preparing a superb welcome, like the sovereign state of a vast empire, for the deputies of the primary Assemblies which had accepted the Constitution. Federalism was on its knees; the Republic, one and indivisible, would surely vanquish all its enemies.

Waving his arm towards the thronged expanse:

"There it was," cried Évariste, "that on the 17th July, '91, the infamous Bailly ordered the people to be shot down at the foot of the altar of the fatherland. Passavant, the grenadier, who witnessed the massacre, returned to his house, tore his coat from his back and cried: 'I have sworn to die with Liberty; Liberty is no more, and I fulfil my oath,'—and blew out his brains."

All this time artists and peaceful citizens were examining the preparations for the festival, their faces showing as joyless a joy in life as their lives were dull and joyless; to their minds the mightiest events shrank into insignificance and grew as insipid as they were themselves. Couple by couple they went, carrying in their arms or holding by the hand or letting them run on in front children as unprepossessing as their parents and promising to grow up no whit happier, who in due course would give birth to children of their own as poor in spirit and looks as they. Yet now and again a young girl would pass, tall and fair and desirable, rousing in young men a not ignoble passion to possess, and in the old regret for the bliss they had missed.

Near the *École Militaire* Évariste pointed out to his companion the Egyptian statues designed by David on Roman models of the age of Augustus, and they overheard a Parisian, an old man with powdered hair, ejaculate to himself:

"Egad! you might think yourself on the banks of the Nile!"

It was three days since Élodie had seen her lover, and serious events had befallen meantime at the *Amour peintre*. The *citoyen* Blaise had been denounced to the Committee of General Security for fraudulent dealings in the matter of supplies to the armies. Fortunately for himself, the print-dealer was well known in his Section; the Committee of Surveillance of the *Section des Piques* had stood guarantee of his patriotism with the general committee and had completely justified his conduct.

This alarming incident Élodie now recounted in trembling accents, concluding:

"We are quiet now, but the alarm was a hot one. A little more and my father would have been clapped in prison. If the danger had lasted a few hours more, I should have come to you, Évariste, to make interest for him among your influential friends."

Évariste vouchsafed no reply to this, but Élodie was very far from realizing all his silence portended.

They went on hand in hand along the banks of the river, discoursing of their mutual fondness in the phrases of Julie and Saint-Preux; the good Jean-Jacques gave them the colours to paint and prank their love withal.

The Municipality of Paris had wrought a miracle,—abundance reigned for a day in the famished city. A fair was installed on the *Place des Invalides*, beside the Seine, where hucksters in booths sold sausages, saveloys, chitterlings, hams decked with laurels, Nanterre cakes, gingerbreads, pancakes, four-pound loaves, lemonade and wine. There were stalls also for the sale of patriotic songs, cockades, tricolour ribands, purses, pinchbeck watch-chains and all sorts of cheap gewgaws. Stopping before the display of a petty jeweller, Évariste selected a silver ring having a head of Marat in relief with a silk handkerchief wound about the brows, and put it on Élodie's finger.

The same evening Gamelin proceeded to the Rue de l'Arbre-Sec to call on the *citoyenne* Rochemaure, who had sent for him on pressing business. She received him in her bedchamber, reclining on a couch in a seductive dishabille.

While the *citoyenne's* attitude expressed a voluptuous languor, everything about her spoke of her accomplishments, her diversions, her talents,—a harp beside an open harpsichord, a guitar on a chair, an embroidering frame with a square of satin stretched on it, a half-finished miniature on a table among papers and books, a bookcase in dire disorder as if rifled by the hand of a fair reader as eager to know as to feel.

She gave him her hand to kiss, and addressed him:

"Greeting, sir juryman!... This very day Robespierre the elder gave me a letter in your favour to be handed to the President Herman, a very well turned letter, pretty much to this effect:

"I bring to your notice the *citoyen* Gamelin, commendable alike for his talents and for his patriotism. I have made it my duty to make known to you a patriot whose principles are good and his conduct steadfast in the right line of revolution. You will not let slip the opportunity of being useful to a Republican.... This letter I carried there and then to the President Herman, who received me with an exquisite politeness and signed your appointment on the spot. The thing is done."

After a moment's pause:

"*Citoyenne*," said Gamelin, "though I have not a morsel of bread to give my mother, I swear on my honour I accept the duties of a juror only to serve the Republic and avenge her on her foes."

The *citoyenne* thought this but a cold way of expressing gratitude and considered the sentiment high-flown. The young man was no adept, she suspected, at graceful courtesies. But she was too great an admirer of youth not to excuse some little lack of polish. Gamelin was a handsome fellow, and that was merit enough in her eyes. "We will form him," she said to herself. So she invited him to her suppers to which she welcomed her friends every evening after the theatre.

"You will meet at my house men of wit and talent,—Elleviou, Talma, the *citoyen* Vigée, who turns bouts-rimés with a marvellous aptitude. The *citoyen* François read us his 'Paméla' the other day, the piece rehearsing at the present moment at the *Théâtre de la Nation*. The style is elegant and chaste, as everything is that comes from the *citoyen* François' pen. The plot is touching; it brought tears to all our eyes. It is the young *citoyenne* Lange who is to take the part of 'Paméla.'"

"I believe it if you say so, *citoyenne*," answered Gamelin, "but the *Théâtre de la Nation* is scarcely National and it is hard on the *citoyen*François that his works should be produced on the boards degraded by the contemptible verses of a Laya; the people has not forgotten the scandal of the *Ami des Lois*...."

"Nay, *citoyen* Gamelin, say what you will of Laya; he is none of my friends."

It was not purely out of kindness that the *citoyenne* had employed her credit to get Gamelin appointed to a much envied post; after what she had done for him and what peradventure she might come to do for him in the future, she counted on binding him closely to her interests and in that way securing for herself a protector connected with a tribunal she might one day or another have to reckon with; for the fact is, she was in constant correspondence with the French provinces and foreign countries, and at that date such a circumstance was ground enough for suspicion.

"Do you often go to the theatre, *citoyen*?"

As she asked the question, Henry, the dragoon, entered the room, looking more charming than the youthful Bathyllus. A brace of enormous pistols was passed through his belt.

He kissed the fair *citoyenne's* hand. Turning to him:

175

"There stands the *citoyen* Évariste Gamelin," she said, "for whose sake I have spent the day at the Committee of General Security, and who is an ungrateful wretch. Scold him for me."

"Ah! *citoyenne*," cried the young soldier, "you have seen our Legislators at the Tuileries. What an afflicting sight! Is it seemly the Representatives of a free people should sit beneath the roof of a despot? The same lustres that once shone on the plots of Capet and the orgies of Antoinette now illumine the deliberations of our law-makers. 'Tis enough to make Nature shudder."

"Pray, congratulate the *citoyen* Gamelin," was all her answer, "he is appointed juryman on the Revolutionary Tribunal."

"My compliments, *citoyen*!" said Henry. "I am rejoiced to see a man of your character invested with these functions. But, to speak truth, I have small confidence in this systematic justice, set up by the moderates of the Convention, in this complaisant Nemesis that is considerate to conspirators and merciful to traitors, that hardly dares strike a blow at the Federalists and fears to summon *the Austrian* to the bar. No, it is not the Revolutionary Tribunal will save the Republic. They are very culpable, the men who, in the desperate situation we are in, have arrested the flowing torrent of popular justice!"

"Henry," interrupted the *citoyenne* Rochemaure, "pass me that scent bottle, please...."

On reaching home, Gamelin found his mother and old Brotteaux playing a game of piquet by the light of a smoky tallow-candle. At the moment the old woman was calling "sequence of kings" without the smallest scruple.

When she heard her son was appointed juryman, she kissed him in a transport of triumph, thinking what an honour it was for both of them and that henceforth they would have plenty to eat every day.

"I am proud and happy," she declared, "to be the mother of a juryman. Justice is a fine thing, and of all the most necessary; without justice the weak would be harassed every moment of their lives. And I think you will give right judgment, Évariste, my own boy; for from a child I have found you just and kind-hearted in all concerns. You could never endure wrong-doing and always tried what you could to hinder violence. You compassionated the unfortunate and that is the finest jewel in a juror's crown.... But tell me, Évariste, how are you dressed in your grand tribunal?"

Gamelin informed her that the judges wore a hat with black plumes, but that the jury had no special costume, that they were dressed in their every-day attire.

"It would be better," returned the good woman, "if they wore wig and gown; it would inspire more respect. Though you are mostly dressed carelessly, you are a handsome man and you set off your clothes; but the majority of men need some fine feathers to make them look imposing; yes, the jury should have wigs and gowns."

The *citoyenne* had heard say that the duties of a juror of the Tribunal carried a salary; and she had no hesitation in asking the question whether the emoluments were enough to live respectably on, for a juryman, she opined, ought to cut a good figure in the world.

She was pleased to hear that each juror received an allowance of eighteen livres for every sitting and that the multiplicity of crimes against the security of the State obliged the court to sit very frequently.

Old Brotteaux gathered up the cards, rose from the table and addressing Gamelin:

"*Citoyen*," he said, "you are invested with an august and redoubtable office. I congratulate you on lending the light of your integrity to a tribunal more trustworthy and less fallible perhaps than any other, because it searches out good and evil, not in themselves and in their essence, but solely in relation to tangible interests and plain and obvious sentiments. You will have to determine betwixt hate and love, which is done spontaneously, not betwixt truth and falsehood, to discriminate which is impossible for the feeble mind of man. Giving judgment after the impulses of your heart, you will run no risk of mistake, inasmuch as the verdict will be good provided it satisfy the passions that are your sacred law. But, all the same, if I was your President, I should imitate Bridoie, I should appeal to the arbitrament of the dice. In matters of justice it is still the surest plan."

IX

Evariste Gamelin was to enter on his duties on the 14th September, when the reorganization of the Tribunal was complete, according to which it was henceforth subdivided into four sections with fifteen jurors for each. The prisons were full to overflowing; the Public Prosecutor was working eighteen hours a day. Defeats in the field, revolts in the provinces, conspiracies, plots, betrayals, the Convention had one panacea for them all,—terror. The Gods were athirst.

The first act of the new juror was to pay a visit of ceremony to the President Herman, who charmed him by the amiability of his conversation and the courtesy of his bearing. A compatriot and friend of Robespierre's, whose sentiments he shared, he showed every sign of a feeling and virtuous temper. He was deeply attached to those humane sentiments, too long foreign to the heart of our judges, that redound to the everlasting glory of a Dupaty and a Beccaria. He looked with complacency on the greater mildness of modern manners as evidenced, in judicial matters, by the abolition of torture and of ignominious or cruel forms of punishment. He was rejoiced to see the death penalty, once so recklessly inflicted and employed till quite lately for the repression of the most trifling offences, applied less frequently and reserved for heinous crimes. For his own part, he agreed with Robespierre and would gladly have seen it abolished altogether, except only in cases touching the public safety. At the same time, he would have deemed it treason to the State not to adjudge the punishment of death for crimes against the National Sovereignty.

All his colleagues were of like mind; the old Monarchical idea of reasons of State still inspired the Revolutionary Tribunal. Eight centuries of absolute power had moulded the magisterial conscience, and it was by the principles of Divine Right that the Court even now tried and sentenced the enemies of Liberty.

The same day Évariste Gamelin sought an interview with the Public Prosecutor, the *citoyen* Fouquier, who received him in the Cabinet where he used to work with his clerk of the court. He was a sturdily built man, with a rough voice, catlike eyes, bearing in his pock-marked face and leaden complexion marks of the mischief wrought by a sedentary and indoor life on a vigorous constitution adapted to the open air and violent exercise. Towering piles of papers shut him in like the walls of a tomb, and it was plain to see he was in his element amid all these dreadful documents that seemed like to bury him alive. His conversation was that of a hard-working magistrate, a man devoted to his task and whose mind never left the narrow groove of his official duties. His fiery breath reeked of the brandy he took to keep up his strength; but the liquor seemed never to fly to his brain, so clear-headed, albeit entirely commonplace, was every word he uttered.

He lived in a small suite of rooms in the Palais de Justice with his young wife, who had given him twin boys. His wife, an aunt Henriette and the maid-servant Pélagie made up the whole household. He was good and kind to these women. In a word, he was an excellent person in his family and professional relations, with a scarcity of ideas and a total lack of imagination.

Gamelin could not help being struck unpleasantly by the close resemblance in temper and ways of thought between the new magistrates and their predecessors under the old régime. In fact, they were of the old régime; Herman had held the office of Advocate General to the Council of Artois; Fouquier was a former Procureur at the Châtelet. They had preserved their character, whereas Gamelin believed in a Revolutionary palingenesis.

Quitting the precincts of the court, he passed along the great gallery of the Palace and halted in front of the shops where articles of every sort and kind were exposed for sale in the most attractive fashion. Standing before the *citoyenne* Ténot's stall, he turned over sundry historical, political, and philosophical works:—"The Chains of Slavery," "An Essay on Despotism," "The Crimes of Queens." "Very good!" he thought, "here is Republican stuff!" and he asked the woman if she sold a great many of these books. She shook her head:

"The only things that sell are songs and romances,"—and pulling a duodecimo volume out of a drawer:

"Here," she told him, "here we have something good."

Évariste read the title: "La Religieuse en chemise," "The Nun in dishabille!"

Before the next shop he came upon Philippe Desmahis, who, with a tender, conquering-hero air, among the *citoyenne* Saint-Jorre's perfumes and powders and sachets, was assuring the fair tradeswoman of his undying love, promising to paint her portrait and begging her to vouchsafe him a moment's talk that evening in the Tuileries gardens. There was no resisting him; persuasion sat on his lips and beamed from his eye. The *citoyenne* Saint-Jorre was listening without a word, her eyes on the ground, only too ready to believe him.

Wishing to familiarize himself with the awful duties imposed on him, the new juror resolved to mingle with the throng and look on at a case before the Tribunal as a member of the general public. He climbed the great stairs on which a vast crowd was seated as in an amphitheatre and pushed his way into the ancient Hall of the Parlement of Paris.

This was crammed to suffocation; some General or other was taking his trial. For in those days, as old Brotteaux put it, "the Convention, copying the example of His Britannic Majesty's Government, made a point of arraigning beaten Generals, in default of traitorous Generals, the latter taking good care not to stand their trial. Not that a beaten General," Brotteaux would add, "is necessarily criminal, for in the nature of things there must be one in every battle. But there's nothing like condemning a General to death for giving encouragement to others."

Several had already appeared before the Tribunal; they were all alike, these empty-headed, opinionated soldiers with the brains of a sparrow in an ox's skull. This particular commander was pretty nearly as ignorant of the sieges and battles of his own campaign as the magistrates who were questioning him; both sides, prosecution and defence, were lost in a fog of effectives, objectives, munitions and ammunitions, marches and counter-marches. But the mass of citizens listening to these obscure and never-ending details could see behind the half-witted soldier the bare and bleeding breast of the fatherland enduring a thousand deaths; and by look and voice urged the jurymen, sitting quietly on their bench, to use their verdict as a club to fell the foes of the Republic.

Évariste was firmly convinced of one thing,—what they had to strike at in the pitiful creature was the two dread monsters that were battening on the fatherland, revolt and defeat. What a to-do to discover if this particular soldier was innocent or guilty! When La Vendée was recovering heart, when Toulon was surrendering to the enemy, when the army of the Rhine was recoiling before the victors of Mayence, when the Army of the North, cowering in Cæsar's Camp, might be taken at a blow by the Imperialists, the English, the Dutch, now masters of Valenciennes, the one important thing was to teach the Generals of the Republic to conquer or to die. To see yonder feeble-witted muddle-pated veteran losing himself under cross-examination among his maps as he had done before in the plains of Northern France, Gamelin longed to yell "death! death!" with the rest, and fled from the Hall of Audience to escape the temptation.

At the meeting of the Section, the newly appointed juryman received the congratulations of the President Olivier, who made him swear on the old high altar of the Barnabites, now altar of the fatherland, to stifle in his heart, in the sacred name of humanity, every human weakness.

Gamelin, with uplifted right hand, invoked as witness of his oath the august shade of Marat, martyr of Liberty, whose bust had lately been set up against a pillar of the erstwhile church, facing that of Le Peltier.

There was some applause, interrupted by cries of protest. The meeting was a stormy one; at the entrance of the nave stood a group of members of the Section, armed with pikes and shouting clamorously:

"It is anti-republican," declared the President, "to carry arms at a meeting of free citizens,"— and he ordered the muskets and pikes to be deposited there and then in the erstwhile sacristy.

A hunchback, with blazing eyes and lips drawn back so as to show the teeth, the *citoyen* Beauvisage, of the Committee of Vigilance, mounted to the pulpit, now become the speakers' tribune and surmounted by a red cap of liberty.

"The Generals are betraying us," he vociferated, "and surrendering our armies to the enemy. The Imperialists are pushing forward their cavalry around Péronne and Saint-Quentin. Toulon has been given up to the English, who are landing fourteen thousand men there. The foes of the Republic are busy with plots in the very bosom of the Convention. In the capital conspiracies without number are afoot to deliver *the Austrian*. At this very moment while I speak there runs a rumour that the Capet brat has escaped from the Temple and is being borne in triumph to Saint-Cloud by those who would fain re-erect the tyrant's throne in his favour. The dearness of food, the depreciation of the *assignats* are the direct result of manœuvres carried out in our own homes, beneath our very eyes, by the agents of the foreigners. In the name of public safety I call upon the new juryman, our fellow-citizen, to show no pity to conspirators and traitors."

As he left the tribune, cries rose among the audience: "Down with the Revolutionary Tribunal! Down with the Moderates!"

A stout, rosy-faced man, the *citoyen* Dupont senior, a joiner living in the Place de Thionville, mounted the Tribune, announcing that he wished to ask a question of the new juror. Then he demanded of Gamelin what attitude he meant to take up in the matter of the Brissotins and of the widow Capet.

Évariste was timid and unpractised in public speaking. But indignation gave him eloquence. He rose with a pale face and said in a voice of suppressed emotion:

"I am a magistrate. I am responsible to my conscience only. Any promise I might make you would be against my duty, which is to speak in the Court and hold my peace elsewhere. I have ceased to know you. It is mine to give judgment; I know neither friends nor enemies."

The meeting, made up like all meetings of divers elements and subject to sudden and incalculable moods, approved these sentiments. But the *citoyen* Dupont returned to the charge; he could not forgive Gamelin for having secured a post he had coveted himself.

"I understand," he said, "I even approve the juror's scruples. They say he is a patriot; it is for him to examine his conscience and see if it permits him to sit on a tribunal intended to destroy the enemies of the Republic and resolved to spare them. There are circumstances in which a good citizen is bound to repudiate all complicity. Is it not averred that more than one juror of this tribunal has let himself be corrupted by the gold of the accused, and that the President Montané falsified the procedure to save the head of the woman Corday?"

At the words the hall resounded with vehement applause. The vaults were still reverberating with the uproar when Fortuné Trubert mounted the tribune. He had grown thinner than ever in the last few months. His face was pale and the cheek-bones seemed ready to pierce the reddened skin; his eyes had a glassy look under the inflamed lids.

"*Citoyens,*" he began, in a weak, breathless voice that yet had a strangely penetrating quality, "we cannot suspect the Revolutionary Tribunal without at the same time suspecting the Convention and the Committee of Public Safety from which it derives its powers. The*citoyen* Beauvisage has alarmed us, showing us the President Montané tampering with the course of justice in favour of a culprit. Why did he not add, to relieve our fears, that on the denunciation of the Public Prosecutor, Montané has been dismissed his office and thrown into prison?... Is it impossible to watch over the public safety without casting suspicion on all and sundry? Is there no talent, no virtue left in the Convention? Robespierre, Couthon, Saint-Just, are not these honest men? It is a notable thing that the most violent language is held by individuals who have never been known to fight for the Republic. They could speak no otherwise if they wish to render her hateful.*Citoyens*, less talk, say I, and more work! It is with shot and shell and not with shouting that France will be saved. One-half the cellars of the Section have not been dug up. Not a few citizens still hold considerable quantities of bronze. We would remind the rich that patriotic gifts are for them the most potent guarantees. I recommend to your generosity the wives and daughters of our soldiers who are covering themselves with glory on the frontiers and on the Loire. One of these, the hussar Pommier (Augustin), formerly a cellarman's lad in the Rue de Jérusalem, on the 10th of last month, before Condé, when watering the troop horses, was set upon by six Austrian cavalrymen; he killed two of them and brought in the others prisoners. I ask the Section to declare that Pommier (Augustin) has done his duty."

This speech was applauded and the Sectionaries dispersed with cries of "Vive la République!"

Left alone in the nave with Trubert, Gamelin pressed the latter's hand.

"Thank you. How are you?"

"I? Oh! Very well, very well!" replied Trubert, coughing and spitting blood into his handkerchief. "The Republic has many enemies without and within, and our own Section counts a not inconsiderable number of them. It is not with loud talk but with iron and laws that empires are founded ... good night, Gamelin; I have letters to write."

And he disappeared, his handkerchief pressed to his lips, into the old-time sacristy.

The widow Gamelin, her cockade now and henceforth fastened more carefully in her hood, had from one day to the next assumed a fine, consequential air, a Republican haughtiness and the dignified carriage suitable to the mother of a juror of the State.

The veneration for the law in which she had been brought up, the admiration with which the magistrate's gown and cassock had from a child inspired her, the holy terror she had always experienced at sight of those to whom God had delegated on earth His divine right of life and death, these feelings made her regard as an august and worshipful and holy being the son whom till yesterday she had thought of as little more than a child. To her simple mind the conviction of the continuity of justice through all the changes of the Revolution was as strong as was that of the legislators of the Convention regarding the continuity of the State under varying systems of government, and the Revolutionary Tribunal appeared to her every whit as majestic as any of the time-honoured jurisdictions she had been taught to revere.

The *citoyen* Brotteaux showed the young magistrate an interest mingled with surprise and a reluctant deference. His views were the same as the widow Gamelin's as to the continuity of justice under successive governments; but, in flat contradiction to that good lady's attitude, his scorn for the Revolutionary Tribunals was on a par with his contempt for the courts of the ancien régime. Not daring to express his opinions openly and unable to make up his mind to say nothing, he indulged in a string of paradoxes which Gamelin understood just well enough to suspect the anti-patriotism that underlay them.

"The august tribunal whereon you are soon to take your seat," he told him on one occasion, "was instituted by the French Senate for the security of the Republic; and it was for certain a magnanimous thought on the part of our legislators to set up a court to try our enemies. I appreciate its generosity, but I doubt its wisdom. It would have shown greater astuteness, it seems to me, if they had struck down in the dark the more irreconcilable of their adversaries and won over the rest by gifts and promises. A tribunal strikes slowly and effects more harm than it inspires fear; its first duty is to make an example. The mischief yours does is to unite together all whom it terrifies and make out of a mass of contradictory interests and passions a great party capable of common and effective action. You sow fear broadcast, and it is terror more than courage that produces heroes; I pray, *citoyen*, you may not one day see prodigies of terror arrayed against you!"

The engraver Desmahis, in love that week with a light o' love of the Palais-Égalité named Flora, a brown-locked giantess, had nevertheless found five minutes to congratulate his comrade and tell him that such an appointment was a great compliment to the fine arts.

Élodie herself, though without knowing it she detested everything revolutionary and who dreaded official functions as the most dangerous of rivals, the most likely to estrange her lover's affections, the tender Élodie was impressed by the glamour attaching to a magistrate called upon to pronounce judgment in matters of life and death. Besides which, Évariste's promotion as a juryman was followed by other fortunate results that filled her loving heart with satisfaction; the *citoyen* Jean Blaise made a point of calling at the studio in the Place de Thionville and embraced the young juror affectionately in a burst of manly sympathy.

Like all the anti-revolutionaries, he had a great respect for the authorities established by the Republic, and ever since he had been denounced for fraud in connection with his supplies for the army, the Revolutionary Tribunal had inspired him with a wholesome dread. He felt himself to be a person too much in the public eye and mixed up in too many transactions to enjoy perfect security; so the *citoyen*Gamelin struck him as a friend worth cultivating. When all was said, one was a good citizen and on the side of justice.

He gave the painter magistrate his hand, declaring himself his true friend and a true patriot, a well-wisher of the arts and of liberty. Gamelin forgot his injuries and pressed the hand so generously offered.

"*Citoyen* Évariste Gamelin," said Jean Blaise, "I appeal to you as a friend and as a man of talent. I am going to take you to-morrow for two days' jaunt in the country; you can do some drawing and we can enjoy a talk."

Several times every year the print-dealer was in the habit of making a two or three days' expedition of this sort in the company of artists who made drawings, according to his suggestions, of landscapes and ruins. He was quick to see what would please the public and these little journeys always resulted in some picturesque bits which were then finished at home and cleverly engraved; prints in red or colours were struck off from these, and brought in a good profit to the *citoyen* Blaise. From the same sketches he had over-doors and panels executed, which sold as well or better than the decorative works of Hubert Robert.

On this occasion he had invited the *citoyen* Gamelin to accompany him to sketch buildings after nature, so much had the juror's office increased the painter's importance in his eyes. Two other artists were of the party, the engraver Desmahis, who drew well, and an almost unknown man, Philippe Dubois, an excellent designer in the style of Robert. According to custom, the *citoyenne* Élodie with her friend the*citoyenne* Hasard accompanied the artists. Jean Blaise, an adept at combining pleasure with profit, had also extended an invitation to the*citoyenne* Thévenin, an actress at the Vaudeville, who was reputed to be on the best of terms with him.

X

On Saturday at seven in the morning the *citoyen* Blaise, in a black cocked-hat, scarlet waistcoat, doe-skin breeches, and boots with yellow tops, rapped with the handle of his riding-whip at the studio door. The *citoyenne* Gamelin was in the room in polite conversation with the *citoyen* Brotteaux, while Évariste stood before a bit of looking-glass knotting his high white cravat.

"A pleasant journey, Monsieur Blaise!" the *citoyenne* greeted him. "But, as you are going to paint landscapes, why don't you take Monsieur Brotteaux, who is a painter?"

"Well, well," said Jean Blaise, "will you come with us, *citoyen* Brotteaux?"

On being assured he would not be intruding, Brotteaux, a man of a sociable temper and fond of all amusements, accepted the invitation.

The *citoyenne* Élodie had climbed the four storeys to embrace the widow Gamelin, whom she called her good mother. She was in white from head to foot, and smelt of lavender.

An old two-horsed travelling *berline* stood waiting in the Place, with the hood down. Rose Thévenin occupied the back seat with Julienne Hasard. Élodie made the actress sit on the right, took the left-hand place herself and put the slim Julienne between the two of them. Brotteaux settled himself, back to the horses, facing the *citoyenne* Thévenin; Philippe Dubois, opposite the *citoyenne* Hasard; Évariste opposite Élodie. As for Philippe Desmahis, he planted his athletic figure on the box, on the coachman's left, and proceeded to amaze that worthy with a traveller's tale about a country in America where the trees bore chitterlings and saveloys by way of fruit.

The *citoyen* Blaise, who was a capital rider, took the road on horseback, going on in front to escape the dust from the *berline*.

As the wheels rattled merrily over the suburban roads the travellers began to forget their cares, and at sight of the green fields and trees and sky, their minds turned to gay and pleasant thoughts. Élodie dreamed she was surely born to rear poultry with Évariste, a country justice, to help her, in some village on a river bank beside a wood. The roadside elms whirled by as they sped along. Outside the villages the peasants' mastiffs dashed out to intercept the carriage and barked at the horses, while a fat spaniel, lying in the roadway, struggled reluctantly to its feet; the fowls scattered and fled; the geese in a close-packed band waddled slowly out of the way. The children, with their fresh morning faces, watched the company go by. It was a hot day and a cloudless sky. The parched earth was thirsting for rain. They alighted just outside Villejuif. On their way through the little town, Desmahis went into a fruiterer's to buy cherries for the overheated *citoyennes*. The shop-keeper was a pretty woman, and Desmahis showed no signs of reappearing. Philippe Dubois shouted to him, using the nickname his friends constantly gave him:

"Ho there! Barbaroux!... Barbaroux!"

At this hated name the passers-by pricked up their ears and faces appeared at every window. Then, when they saw a young and handsome man emerge from the shop, his jacket thrown open, his neckerchief flying loose over a muscular chest, and carrying over his shoulder a basket of cherries and his coat at the end of a stick, taking him for the proscribed girondist, a posse of *sansculottes* laid violent hands on him. Regardless of his indignant protests, they would have haled him to the town-hall, had not old Brotteaux, Gamelin, and the three young women borne testimony that the *citoyen* was named Philippe Desmahis, a copper-plate engraver and a good Jacobin. Even then the suspect had to show his *carte de civisme*, which he had in his pocket by great good luck, for he was very heedless in such matters. At this price he escaped from the hands of these patriotic villagers without worse loss than one of his lace ruffles, which had been torn off; but this was a trifle after all. He even received the apologies of the National Guards who had hustled him the most savagely and who now spoke of carrying him in triumph to the Hôtel de Ville.

A free man again and with the *citoyennes* Élodie, Rose, and Julienne crowding round him, Desmahis looked at Philippe Dubois—he did not like the man and suspected him of having played him a practical joke—with a wry smile, and towering above him by a whole head:

"Dubois," he told him, "if you call me Barbaroux again, I shall call you Brissot; he is a little fat man with a silly face, greasy hair, an oily skin and damp hands. They'll be perfectly sure you are the infamous Brissot, the people's enemy; and the good Republicans, filled with horror and loathing at sight of you, will hang you from the nearest lamp-post. You hear me?"

The *citoyen* Blaise, who had been watering his horse, announced that he had arranged the affair, though it was quite plain to everybody that it had been arranged without him.

The company got in again, and as they drove on, Desmahis informed the coachman that in this same plain of Longjumeau several inhabitants of the Moon had once come down, in shape and colour much like frogs, only very much bigger. Philippe Dubois and Gamelin talked about their art. Dubois, a pupil of Regnault, had been to Rome, where he had seen Raphael's tapestries, which he set above all the masterpieces of the world. He admired Correggio's colouring, Annibale Caracci's invention, Domenichino's drawing, but thought nothing comparable in point of style with the pictures of Pompeio Battoni. He had been in touch at Rome with Monsieur Ménageot and Madame Lebrun, who had both pronounced against the Revolution; so the less said of them the better. But he spoke highly of Angelica Kauffmann, who had a pure taste and a fine knowledge of the Antique.

Gamelin deplored that the apogee of French painting, belated as it was, for it only dated from Lesueur, Claude and Poussin and corresponded with the decadence of the Italian and Flemish schools, had been succeeded by so rapid and profound a decline. This he attributed to the degraded state of manners and to the Academy, which was the expression of that state. But the Academy had been happily abolished, and under the influence of new canons, David and his school were creating an art worthy of a free people. Among the young painters, Gamelin, without a trace of envy, gave the first place to Hennequin and Topino-Lebrun. Philippe Dubois preferred his own master Regnault to David, and founded his hopes for the future of painting on that rising artist Gérard.

Meantime Élodie complimented the *citoyenne* Thévenin on her red velvet toque and white gown. The actress repaid the compliment by congratulating her two companions on their toilets and advising them how to do better still; the thing, she said, was to be more sparing in ornaments and trimmings.

"A woman can never be dressed too simply," was her dictum. "We see this on the stage, where the costume should allow every pose to be appreciated. That is its true beauty and it needs no other."

"You are right, my dear," replied Élodie. "Only there is nothing more expensive in dress than simplicity. It is not always out of bad taste we add frills and furbelows; sometimes it is to save our pockets."

They discussed eagerly the autumn fashions,—frocks entirely plain and short-waisted.

"So many women disfigure themselves through following the fashion!" declared Rose Thévenin. "In dressing every woman should study her own figure."

"There is nothing beautiful save draperies that follow the lines of the figure and fall in folds," put in Gamelin. "Everything that is cut out and sewn is hideous."

These sentiments, more appropriate in a treatise of Winckelmann's than in the mouth of a man talking to Parisiennes, met with the scorn they deserved, being entirely disregarded.

"For the winter," observed Élodie, "they are making quilted gowns in Lapland style of taffeta and muslin, and coats *à la Zulime*, round-waisted and opening over a stomacher *à la Turque*."

"Nasty cheap things," declared the actress, "you can buy them ready made. Now I have a little seamstress who works like an angel and is not dear; I'll send her to see you, my dear."

So they prattled on trippingly, eagerly discussing and appraising different fine fabrics—striped taffeta, self-coloured china silk, muslin, gauze, nankeen.

And old Brotteaux, as he listened to them, thought with a pensive pleasure of these veils that hide women's charms and change incessantly,—how they last for a few years to be renewed eternally like the flowers of the field. And his eyes, as they wandered from the three pretty women to the cornflowers and the poppies in the wheat, were wet with smiling tears.

They reached Orangis about nine o'clock and stopped before the inn, the *Auberge de la Cloche*, where the Poitrines, husband and wife, offered accommodation for man and beast. The *citoyen* Blaise, who had repaired any disorder in his dress, helped the *citoyennes* to alight. After ordering dinner for midday, they all set off, preceded by their paintboxes, drawing-boards, easels, and parasols, which were carried by a village lad, for the meadows near the confluence of the Orge and the Yvette, a charming bit of country giving a view over the verdant plain of Longjumeau and bounded by the Seine and the woods of Sainte-Geneviève.

Jean Blaise, the leader of the troop of artists, was bandying funny stories with the *ci-devant* financier, tales that brought in without rhyme or reason Verboquet the Open-handed, Catherine Cuissot the pedlar, the demoiselles Chaudron, the fortune-teller Galichet, as well as characters of a later time like Cadet-Rousselle and Madame Angot.

Évariste, inspired with a sudden love of nature, as he saw a troop of harvesters binding their sheaves, felt the tears rise to his eyes, while visions of concord and affection filled his heart. For his part, Desmahis was blowing the light down of the seeding dandelions into the *citoyennes'* hair. All three loved posies, as town-bred girls always do, and were busy in the meadows plucking the mullein, whose blossoms grow in spikes close round the stem, the campanula, with its little blue-bells hanging in rows one above another, the slender twigs of the scented vervain, wallwort, mint, dyer's weed, milfoil—all the wild flowers of late summer. Jean-Jacques had made botany the fashion among townswomen, so all three knew the name and symbolism of every flower. As the delicate petals, drooping for want of moisture, wilted in her hands and fell in a shower about her feet, the *citoyenne* Élodie sighed:

"They are dying already, the poor flowers!"

All set to work and strove to express nature as they saw her; but each saw her through the eyes of a master. In a short time Philippe Dubois had knocked off in the style of Hubert Robert a deserted farm, a clump of storm-riven trees, a dried-up torrent. Évariste Gamelin found a landscape by Poussin ready made on the banks of the Yvette. Philippe Desmahis was at work before a pigeon-cote in the picaresque manner of Callot and Duplessis. Old Brotteaux who piqued himself on imitating the Flemings, was drawing a cow with infinite care. Élodie was sketching a peasant's hut, while her friend Julienne, who was a colourman's daughter, set her palette. A swarm of children pressed about her, watching her paint, whom she would scold out of her light at intervals, calling them pestering gnats and giving them lollipops. The *citoyenne* Thévenin, picking out the pretty ones, would wash their faces, kiss them and put flowers in their hair. She fondled them with a gentle air of melancholy, because she had missed the joy of motherhood,—as well as to heighten her fascinations by a show of tender sentiment and to practise herself in the art of pose and grouping.

She was the only member of the party neither drawing nor painting. She devoted her attention to learning a part and still more to charming her companions, flitting from one to another, book in hand, a bright, entrancing creature.

"No complexion, no figure, no voice, no nothing," declared the women,—and she filled the earth with movement, colour and harmony. Faded, pretty, tired, indefatigable, she was the joy of the expedition. A woman of ever-varying moods, but always gay, sensitive, quick-tempered and yet easy-going and accommodating, a sharp tongue with the most polished utterance, vain, modest, true, false, delightful; if Rose Thévenin enjoyed no triumphant success, if she was not worshipped as a goddess, it was because the times were out of joint and Paris had no more incense, no more altars for the Graces. The *citoyenne* Blaise herself, who made a face when she spoke of her and used to call her "my step-mother," could not see her and not be subjugated by such an array of charms.

They were rehearsing *Les Visitandines* at the Théâtre Feydeau, and Rose was full of self-congratulation at having a part full of "naturalness." It was this quality she strove after, this she sought and this she found.

"Then we shall not see 'Paméla'?" asked Desmahis.

The Théâtre de la Nation was closed and the actors packed off to the Madelonnettes and to Pélagie.

"Do you call that liberty?" cried Rose Thévenin, raising her beautiful eyes to heaven in indignant protest.

"The players of the Théâtre de la Nation are aristocrats, and the *citoyen* François' piece tends to make men regret the privileges of the noblesse."

"Gentlemen," said Rose Thévenin, "have you patience to listen only to those who flatter you?"

As midday approached everybody began to feel pangs of hunger and the little band marched back to the inn.

Évariste walked beside Élodie, smilingly recalling memories of their first meetings:

"Two young birds had fallen out of their nests on the roof on to the sill of your window. You brought the little creatures up by hand; one of them lived and in due time flew away. The other died in the nest of cotton-wool you had made him. 'It was the one I loved best,' I remember you said. That day, Élodie, you were wearing a red bow in your hair."

186

Philippe Dubois and Brotteaux, a little behind the rest, were talking of Rome, where they had both been, the latter in '72, the other towards the last days of the Academy. Brotteaux indeed had never forgotten the Princess Mondragone, to whom he would most certainly have poured out his plaints but for the Count Altieri, who always followed her like her shadow. Nor did Philippe Dubois fail to mention that he had been invited to dine with Cardinal de Bernis and that he was the most obliging host in the world.

"I knew him," said Brotteaux, "and I may add without boasting that I was for some while one of his most intimate friends; he had a taste for low society. He was an amiable man, and for all his affectation of telling fairy tales, there was more sound philosophy in his little finger than in the heads of all you Jacobins, who are for making us virtuous and God-fearing by Act of Parliament. Upon my word I prefer our simple-minded theophagists who know not what they say nor yet what they do, to these mad law-menders, who make it their business to guillotine us in order to render us wise and virtuous and adorers of the Supreme Being who has created them in His likeness. In former days I used to have Mass said in the Chapel at Les Ilettes by a poor devil of a Curé who used to say in his cups: 'Don't let's speak ill of sinners; we live by 'em, we priests, unworthy as we are!' You must agree, sir, this prayer-monger held sound maxims of government. We should adopt his principles, and govern men as being what they are and not what we should like them to be."

Rose Thévenin had meantime drawn closer to the old man. She knew he had lived on a grand scale, and the thought of this gilded the *ci-devant* financier's present poverty, which she deemed less humiliating as being due to general causes, the result of the public bankruptcy. She saw in him, with curiosity not unmixed with respect, the survival of one of those open-handed millionaires of whom her elder comrades of the stage spoke with sighs of unfeigned regret. Besides, the old fellow in his plum-coloured coat, so threadbare and so well brushed, pleased her by his agreeable address.

"Monsieur Brotteaux," she said to him, "we know how once upon a time, in a noble park, on moonlight nights, you would slip into the shade of myrtle groves with actresses and dancing-girls to the far-off shrilling of flutes and fiddles.... Alas! they were more lovely, were they not, your goddesses of the Opera and the Comédie-Française, than we of to-day, we poor little National actresses?"

"Never think it, Mademoiselle," returned Brotteaux, "but believe me, if one like you had been known in those days, she would have moved alone, as sovereign queen without a rival (little as she would have desired such solitude), in the park you are obliging enough to form so flattering a picture of...."

It was quite a rustic inn, this Hôtel de la Cloche. A branch of holly hung over the great waggon doors that opened on a courtyard where fowls were always pecking about in the damp soil. On the far side of this stood the house itself, consisting of a ground floor and one storey above, crowned by a high-pitched tiled roof and with walls almost hidden under old climbing rose-trees covered with blossom. To the right, trimmed fruit-trees showed their tops above the low garden wall. To the left was the stable, with an outside manger and a barn supported by wooden pillars. A ladder leaned against the wall. Here again, under a shed crowded with agricultural implements and stumps of trees, a white cock was keeping an eye on his hens from the top of a broken-down cabriolet. The courtyard was enclosed on this side by cow-sheds, in front of which rose in mountainous grandeur a dunghill which at this moment a girl as broad as she was long, with straw-coloured hair, was turning over with a pitchfork. The liquid manure filled her sabots and bathed her bare feet, and you could see the heels rise out of her shoes every now and then as yellow as saffron. Her petticoats were kilted and revealed the filth on her enormous calves and thick ankles. While Philippe Desmahis was staring at her, surprised and tickled by the whimsicalities of nature in framing this odd example of breadth without length, the landlord shouted:

"Ho, there! Tronche, my girl! go fetch some water!"

She turned her head, showing a scarlet face and a vast mouth in which one huge front tooth was missing. It had needed nothing less than a bull's horn to effect a breach in that powerful jaw. She stood there grinning, pitchfork on shoulder. Her sleeves were rolled up and her arms, as thick as another woman's thighs, gleamed in the sun.

The table was laid in the farm kitchen, where a brace of fowls was roasting,—they were almost done to a turn,—under the hood of the open fireplace, above which hung two or three old fowling-pieces by way of ornament. The bare whitewashed room, twenty feet long, was lighted only through the panes of greenish glass let into the door and by a single window, framed in roses, near which the grandmother sat turning her spinning-wheel. She wore a coif and a lace frilling in the fashion of the Regency. Her gnarled, earth-stained fingers held the distaff. Flies clustered about her lids without her trying to drive them away. As a child in her mother's arms, she had seen Louis XIV go by in his coach.

Sixty years ago she had made the journey to Paris. In a weak sing-song voice she told the tale to the three young women, standing in front of her, how she had seen the Hôtel de Ville, the Tuileries and the Samaritaine, and how, when she was crossing the Pont-Royal, a barge loaded with apples for the Marché du Mail had broken up, the apples had floated down the current and the river was all red with the rosy-cheeked fruit.

She had been told of the changes that had occurred of late in the kingdom, and in particular of the coil there was betwixt the curés who had taken the oath and the nonjuring curés. She knew likewise there had been wars and famines and portents in the sky. She did not believe the King was dead. They had contrived his escape, she *would* have it, by a subterranean passage, and had handed over to the headsman in his stead a man of the common people.

At the old woman's feet, in his wicker cradle, Jeannot, the last born of the Poitrines, was cutting his teeth. The *citoyenne* Thévenin lifted the cradle and smiled at the child, which moaned feebly, worn out with feverishness and convulsions. It must have been very ill, for they had sent for the doctor, the *citoyen* Pelleport, who, it is true, being a deputy-substitute to the Convention, asked no payment for his visits.

The *citoyenne* Thévenin, an innkeeper's daughter herself, was in her element; not satisfied with the way the farm-girl had washed the plates and dishes, she gave an extra wipe to the crockery and glass, an extra polish to the knives and forks. While the *citoyenne* Poitrine was attending to the soup, which she tasted from time to time as a good cook should, Élodie was cutting up into slices a four-pound loaf hot from the oven. Gamelin, when he saw what she was doing, addressed her:

"A few days ago I read a book written by a young German whose name I have forgotten, and which has been very well translated into French. In it you have a beautiful young girl named Charlotte, who, like you, Élodie, was cutting bread and butter, and like you, cutting it gracefully, and so prettily that at the sight the young Werther fell in love with her."

"And it ended in their marrying?" asked Élodie.

"No," replied Évariste; "it ended in Werther's death by violence."

They dined well, they were all very hungry; but the fare was indifferent. Jean Blaise complained bitterly; he was a great trencherman and made it a rule of conduct to feed well; and no doubt what urged him to elaborate his gluttony into a system was the general scarcity. In every household the Revolution had overturned the cooking pot. The common run of citizens had nothing to chew upon. Clever folks like Jean Blaise, who made big profits amid the general wretchedness, went to the cookshop where they showed their astuteness by stuffing themselves to repletion. As for Brotteaux who, in this year II of liberty, was living on chestnuts and bread-crusts, he could remember having supped at Grimod de la Reynière's at the near end of the Champs Élysées. Eager to win the repute of an accomplished gourmand he reeled off, sitting there before Dame Poitrine's bacon and cabbages, a string of artful kitchen recipes and wise gastronomic maxims. Presently, when Gamelin protested that a Republican scorns the pleasures of the table, the old financier, always a lover of antiquity, gave the young Spartan the true recipe for the famous black broth.

After dinner, Jean Blaise, who never forgot business, set his itinerant academy to make studies and sketches of the inn, which struck him as quite romantic in its dilapidation. While Philippe Desmahis and Philippe Dubois were drawing the cow-houses the girl Tronche came out to feed the pigs. The *citoyen* Pelleport, officer of health, who at the same moment appeared at the door of the farm kitchen where he had been bestowing his professional services on the Poitrine baby, stepped up to the artists and after complimenting them on their talents, which were an honour to the whole nation, pointed to the Tronche girl in the middle of her porkers:

"You see that creature," he said, "it is not one girl, it is two girls. I speak by the letter, understand that. I was amazed at the extraordinary massiveness of her bony framework and I examined her, to discover she had most of the bones in duplicate—in each thigh two femurs welded together, in each shoulder a double humerus. Some of her muscles are likewise in duplicate. It is a case, in my view, of a pair of twins associated or rather confounded together. It is an interesting phenomenon. I notified Monsieur Saint-Hilaire of the facts, and he thanked me. It is a monster you see before you, *citoyens*. The people here call her 'the girl Tronche'; they should say 'the girls Tronches,' for there are two of them. Nature has these freaks.... Good evening, *citoyens*; we shall have a storm to-night...."

After supper by candle-light, the Academy Blaise adjourned to the courtyard where they were joined by a son and daughter of the house in a game of blindman's-buff, in which the young folks, both men and women, displayed a feverish energy sufficiently accounted for by the high spirits proper to their age without seeking an explanation in the wild and precarious times in which they lived. When it was quite dark, Jean Blaise proposed children's games in the farm kitchen. Élodie suggested the game of "hunt my heart," and this was agreed to unanimously. Under the girl's direction Philippe Desmahis traced in chalk, on different pieces of furniture, on doors and walls, seven hearts, that is to say one less than there were players, for old Brotteaux had obligingly joined the rest. They danced round in a ring singing "La Tour, prends garde!" and at a signal from Élodie, each ran to put a hand on a heart. Gamelin in his absent-minded clumsiness was too late to find one vacant, and had to pay a forfeit, the little knife he had bought for six sous at the fair of Saint-Germain and with which he had cut the loaf for his mother in her poverty. The game went on, and one after the other Blaise, Élodie, Brotteaux and Rose Thévenin failed to touch a heart; each paid a forfeit in turn—a ring, a reticule, a little morocco-bound book, a bracelet. Then the forfeits were raffled on Élodie's lap, and each player had to redeem his property by showing his society accomplishments—singing a song or reciting a poem. Brotteaux chose the speech of the patron saint of France in the first canto of the *Pucelle*:

"Je suis Denis et saint de mon métier,J'aime la Gaule,..."

The *citoyen* Blaise, though a far less well-read man, replied without hesitation with Richemond's ripost:
"Monsieur le Saint, ce n'était pas la peineD'abandonner le céleste domaine...."

At that time everybody was reading and re-reading with delight the masterpiece of the French Ariosto; the most serious of men smiled over the loves of Jeanne and Dunois, the adventures of Agnès and Monrose and the exploits of the winged ass. Every man of cultivation knew by heart the choice passages of this diverting and philosophical poem. Évariste Gamelin himself, stern-tempered as he was, when he recovered his twopenny knife from Élodie's lap, recited the going down of Grisbourdon into hell, with a good deal of spirit. The *citoyenne*Thévenin sang without accompaniment Nina's ballad:

"*Quand le bien-aimé reviendra.*"

Desmahis sang to the tune of *La Faridondaine*:
"Quelques-uns prirent le cochonDe ce bon saint Antoine,Et lui mettant un capuchon,Ils en firent un moine.Il n'en coûtait que la façon...."

All the same Desmahis was in a pensive mood. For the moment he was ardently in love with all the three women with whom he was playing forfeits, and was casting burning looks of soft appeal at each in turn. He loved Rose Thévenin for her grace, her supple figure, her clever acting, her roving glances, and her voice that went straight to a man's heart; he loved Élodie, because he recognized instinctively her rich endowment of temperament and her kind, complaisant humour; he loved Julienne Hasard, despite her colourless hair, her pale eyelashes, her freckles and her thin bust, because, like Dunois in Voltaire's *Pucelle*, he was always ready, in his generosity, to give the least engaging a token of love—and the more so in this instance because she appeared to be for the moment the most neglected, and therefore the most amenable to his attentions. Without a trace of vanity, he was never sure of these being agreeable; nor yet was he ever sure of their not being. So he never omitted to offer them on the chance. Taking advantage of the opportunities offered by the game of forfeits, he made some tender speeches to Rose Thévenin, who showed no displeasure, but could hardly say much in return under the jealous eyes of the*citoyen* Jean Blaise. He spoke more warmly still to the *citoyenne* Élodie, whom he knew to be pledged to Gamelin, but he was not so exacting as to want a heart all to himself. Élodie could never care for him; but she thought him a handsome fellow and did not altogether succeed in hiding the fact from him. Finally, he whispered his most ardent vows in the ear of the *citoyenne* Hasard, which she received with an air of bewildered stupefaction that might equally express abject submission or chill indifference. And Desmahis did not believe she was indifferent to him.

The inn contained only two bedrooms, both on the first floor and opening on the same landing. That to the left, the better of the two, boasted a flowered paper and a looking-glass the size of a man's hand, the gilt frame of which had been blackened by generations of flies since the days when Louis XIV was a child. In it, under sprigged muslin curtains, stood two beds with down pillows, coverlets and counterpanes. This room was reserved for the three *citoyennes*.

When the time came to retire, Desmahis and the *citoyenne* Hasard, each holding a bedroom candlestick, wished each other good-night on the landing. The amorous engraver quickly passed a note to the colourman's daughter, beseeching her to come to him, when everybody was asleep, in the garret, which was over the *citoyennes'* chamber.

With judicious foresight, he had taken care in the course of the day to study the lie of the land and explore the garret in question, which was full of strings of onions, apples and pears left there to ripen with a swarm of wasps crawling over them, chests and old trunks. He had even noticed an old bed of sacking, decrepit and now disused, as far as he could see, and a palliasse, all ripped up and jumping with fleas.

Facing the *citoyennes'* room was another of very modest dimensions containing three beds, where the men of the party were to sleep, in such comfort as they might. But Brotteaux, who was a Sybarite, betook himself to the barn to sleep among the hay. As for Jean Blaise, he had disappeared. Dubois and Gamelin were soon asleep. Desmahis went to bed; but no sooner had the silence of night, like a stagnant pool, enveloped the house, than the engraver got up and climbed the wooden staircase, which creaked under his bare feet. The door of the garret stood ajar. From within came a breath of stifling hot air, mingled with the acrid smell of rotting fruit. On the broken-down bed of sacking lay the girl Tronche, fast asleep with her mouth open.

Desmahis returned to his room, where he slept soundly and peacefully till daybreak.

On the morrow, after a last day's work, the itinerant Academy took the road back to Paris. When Jean Blaise paid mine host in assignats, the *citoyen* Poitrine complained bitterly that he never saw what he called "square money" nowadays, and promised a fine candle to the beggar who'd bring back the "yellow boys" again.

He offered the *citoyennes* their pick of flowers. At his orders, the girl Tronche mounted on a ladder in her sabots and kilted skirts, giving a full view of her noble, much-bespattered calves, and was indefatigable in cutting blossoms from the climbing roses that covered the wall. From her huge hands the flowers fell in showers, in torrents, in avalanches, into the laps of Élodie, Julienne, and Rose Thévenin, who held out their skirts to catch them. The carriage was full of them. The whole party, when they got back at nightfall, carried armfuls home, and their sleeping and waking were perfumed with their fragrance.

XI

In the forenoon of the 7th September the *citoyenne* Rochemaure, on her way to visit Gamelin, the new juror, whose interest she wished to solicit on behalf of an acquaintance, who had been denounced as a suspect, encountered on the landing the *ci-devant* Brotteaux des Ilettes, who had been her lover in the old happy days. Brotteaux was just starting to deliver a gross of dancing-dolls of his manufacture to the toy-merchant in the Rue de la Loi; for their more convenient carriage he had hit on the idea of tying them at the end of a pole, as the street hawkers do with their commodities. His manners were always chivalrous towards women, even to those whose fascination for him had been blunted by long familiarity, as could hardly fail to be the case with Madame de Rochemaure,—unless indeed he found her appetizing with the added seasoning of betrayal, absence, unfaithfulness and fat. Be this as it may, he now greeted her on the sordid stairs with their cracked tiles as courteously as he had ever done on the steps before the entrance-door of Les Ilettes, and begged her to do him the honour of entering his garret. She climbed the ladder nimbly enough and found herself under a timbering, the sloping beams of which supported a tiled roof pierced with a skylight. It was impossible to stand upright. She sat down on the only chair there was in the wretched place; after a brief glance at the broken tiling, she asked in a tone of surprise and sorrow:

"Is this where you live, Maurice? You need have little fear of intruders. One must be an imp or a cat to find you here."

"I am cramped for space," returned the *ci-devant* millionaire; "and I do not deny the fact that sometimes it rains on my pallet. It is a trifling inconvenience. And on fine nights I can see the moon, symbol and confidant of men's loves. For the moon, Madame, since the world began, has been apostrophized by lovers, and at her full, with her pale round face, she recalls to the fond swain's mind the object of his desires."

"I know," sighed the *citoyenne*.

"When their time comes the cats make a fine pandemonium in the rain gutter yonder. But we must forgive love if it makes them caterwaul and swear on the tiles, seeing how it fills the lives of men with torments and villanies."

Both had had the tact to greet each other as friends who had parted the night before to take their night's rest, and though grown strangers to each other, they conversed with a good grace and on a footing of friendliness.

At the same time Madame de Rochemaure seemed pensive. The Revolution, which had for a long while been pleasant and profitable to her, was now a source of anxiety and disquietude; her suppers were growing less brilliant and less merry. The notes of her harp no longer charmed the cloud from sombre faces. Her play-tables were forsaken by the most lavish punters. Many of her cronies, now numbered among the suspects, were in hiding; her lover, Morhardt the financier, was under arrest, and it was on his behalf she had come to sound the juror Gamelin. She was suspect herself. A posse of National Guards had made a search at her house, had turned out the drawers of her cabinets, prised up boards in her floor, thrust their bayonets into her mattresses. They had found nothing, had made their apologies and drunk her wine. But they had come very near lighting on her correspondence with an *émigré*, Monsieur d'Expilly. Certain friends he had among the Jacobins had warned her that Henry, her handsome favourite, was beginning to compromise his party by his violent language, which was too extravagant to be sincere.

Elbows on knees and head on fist, she sat buried in thought; then turning to her old lover sitting on the palliasse, she asked:

"What do you think of it all, Maurice?"

"I think these good gentry give a philosopher and an amateur of the shows of life abundant matter for reflection and amusement; but that it would be better for you, my dear, if you were out of France."

"Maurice, where will it land us?"

"That is what you asked me, Louise, one day we were driving on the banks of the Cher, on the road to Les Ilettes; the horse, you remember, had taken the bit in his teeth and was galloping off with us at a frantic pace. How inquisitive women are! to-day, for the second time, you want to know where we are going to. Ask the fortune-tellers. I am not a wizard, sweetheart. And philosophy, even the soundest, is of small help for revealing the future. These things will have an end; everything has. One may foresee divers issues. The triumph of the Coalition and the entry of the allies into Paris. They are not far off; yet I doubt if they will get there. These soldiers of the Republic take their beatings with a zest nothing can extinguish. It may be Robespierre will marry Madame Royale and have himself proclaimed Protector of the Kingdom during the minority of Louis XVII."

"You think so!" exclaimed the *citoyenne*, agog to have a hand in so promising an intrigue.

"Again it may be," Brotteaux went on, "that La Vendée will win the day and the rule of the priests be set up again over heaps of ruins and piles of corpses. You cannot conceive, dear heart, the empire the clergy still wields over the masses of the foolish,... I beg pardon, I meant to say, —of 'the Faithful'; it was a slip of the tongue. The most likely thing, in my poor opinion, is that the Revolutionary Tribunal will bring about the destruction of the régime it has established; it is a menace over too many heads. Those it terrifies are without number; they will unite together, and to destroy it they will destroy the whole system of government. I think you have got our young friend Gamelin posted to this court. He is virtuous; he will be implacable. The more I think of it, fair friend, the more convinced I am that this Tribunal, set up to save the Republic, will destroy it. The Convention has resolved to have, like Royalty, its *Grands Jours*, its *Chambre Ardente*, and to provide for its security by means of magistrates appointed by itself and by it kept in subjection. But how inferior are the Convention's *Grands Jours* to those of the Monarchy, and its *Chambre Ardente* to that of Louis XIV! The Revolutionary Tribunal is dominated by a sentiment of mean-spirited justice and common equality that will quickly make it odious and ridiculous and will disgust everybody. Do you know, Louise, that this tribunal, which is about to cite to its bar the Queen of France and twenty-one legislators, yesterday condemned a servant-girl convicted of crying: 'Vive le Roi!' with malicious intent and in the hope of destroying the Republic? Our judges, with their black hats and plumes, are working on the model of that William Shakespeare, so dear to the heart of Englishmen, who drags in coarse buffooneries in the middle of his most tragic scenes."

"Ah, well! Maurice," asked the *citoyenne*, "are you still as fortunate as ever with women?"

"Alas!" replied Brotteaux, "the doves flock to the bright new dovecote and light no more on the ruined tower."

"You have not changed.... Good-bye, dear friend,—till we meet again."

The same evening the dragoon Henry, paying a visit uninvited at Madame de Rochemaure's, found her in the act of sealing a letter on which he read the address of the *citoyen* Rauline at Vernon. The letter, he knew, was for England. Rauline used to receive Madame de Rochemaure's communications by a postilion of the posting-service and send them on to Dieppe by the hands of a fishwife. The master of a fishing-smack delivered them under cover of night to a British ship cruising off the coast; an *émigré*, Monsieur d'Expilly, received them in London and passed them on, if he thought it advisable, to the Cabinet of Saint James's.

Henry was young and good looking; Achilles was not such a paragon of grace and vigour when he donned the armour Ulysses offered him. But the *citoyenne* Rochemaure, once so enraptured by the charms of the young hero of the Commune, now looked askance at him; her mood had changed since the day she was told how the young soldier had been denounced at the Jacobins as one whose zeal outran discretion and that he might compromise and ruin her. Henry thought it might not break his heart perhaps to leave off loving Madame de Rochemaure; but he was piqued to have fallen in her good graces. He counted on her to meet sundry expenses in which the service of the Republic had involved him. Last but not least, remembering to what extremities women will proceed and how they go in a flash from the most ardent tenderness to the coldest indifference, and how easy they find it to sacrifice what once they held dear and destroy what once they adored, he began to suspect that some day his fascinating mistress might have him thrown into prison to get rid of him. Common prudence urged him to regain his lost ascendancy and to this end he had come armed with all his fascinations. He came near, drew away, came near again, hovered round her, ran from her, in the approved fashion of seduction in the ballet. Then he threw himself in an armchair and in his irresistible voice, his voice that went straight to women's hearts, he extolled the charms of nature and solitude and with a lovelorn sigh proposed an expedition to Ermenonville.

Meanwhile she was striking chords on her harp and looking about her with an expression of impatience and boredom. Suddenly Henry got up with a gesture of gloomy resolution and informed her that he was starting for the army and in a few days would be before Maubeuge.

Without a sign either of scepticism or surprise she nodded her approval.

"You congratulate me on my decision?"

"I do indeed."

She was expecting a new admirer who was infinitely to her taste and from whom she hoped to reap great advantages,—a contrast in every way to the old, a Mirabeau come to life again, a Danton rehabilitated and turned army-contractor, a lion who talked of pitching every patriot into the Seine. She was on tenter-hooks, thinking to hear the bell ring at any moment.

To hasten Henry's departure, she fell silent, yawned, fingered a score, and yawned again. Seeing he made no move to go, she told him she had to go out and withdrew into her dressing-room.

He called to her in a broken voice:

"Farewell, Louise!... Shall I ever see you again?"—and his hands were busy fumbling in the open writing-desk.

When he reached the street, he opened the letter addressed to the *citoyen* Rauline and read it with absorbed attention. Indeed it drew a curious picture of the state of public feeling in France. It spoke of the Queen, of the actress Rose Thévenin, of the Revolutionary Tribunal and a host of confidential remarks emanating from that worthy, Brotteaux des Ilettes, were repeated in it.

Having read to the end and restored the missive to his pocket, he stood hesitating a few moments; then, like a man who has made up his mind and says to himself "the sooner the better," he turned his steps to the Tuileries and found his way into the antechamber of the Committee of General Security.

———————————————

The same day, at three o'clock of the afternoon, Évariste Gamelin was seated on the jurors' bench along with fourteen colleagues, most of whom he knew, simple-minded, honest, patriotic folks, savants, artists or artisans,—a painter like himself, an artist in black-and-white, both men of talent, a surgeon, a cobbler, a *ci-devant* marquis, who had given high proofs of patriotism, a printer, two or three small tradesmen, a sample lot in a word of the inhabitants of Paris. There they sat, in the workman's blouse or bourgeois coat, with their hair close-cropped *à la Titus* or clubbed *à la catogan*; there were cocked-hats tilted over the eyes, round hats clapped on the back of the head, red caps of liberty smothering the ears. Some were dressed in coat, flapped waistcoat and breeches, as in olden days, others in the *carmagnole* and striped trousers of the sansculottes. Wearing top-boots or buckled shoes or sabots, they offered in their persons every variety of masculine attire prevalent at that date. Having all of them occupied their places on several previous occasions, they seemed very much at their ease, and Gamelin envied them their unconcern. His own heart was thumping, his ears roaring; a mist was before his eyes and everything about him took on a livid tinge.

When the usher announced the opening of the sitting, three judges took their places on a raised platform of no great size in front of a green table. They wore hats cockaded and crowned with great black plumes and the official cloak with a tricolour riband from which a heavy silver medal was suspended on the breast. In front of them at the foot of the daïs, sat the deputy of the Public Prosecutor, similarly attired. The clerk of the court had a seat between the judges' bench and the prisoner's chair, at present unoccupied. To Gamelin's eyes these men wore a different aspect from that of every day; they seemed nobler, graver, more alarming, albeit their bearing was commonplace enough as they turned over papers, beckoned to an usher or leant back to listen to some communication from a juryman or an officer of the court.

Above the judges' heads hung the tables of the Rights of Man; to their right and left, against the old feudal walls, the busts of Le Peltier Saint-Fargeau and Marat. Facing the jury bench, at the lower end of the hall, rose the public gallery. The first row of seats was filled by women, who all, fair, brown and grey-haired alike, wore the high coif with the pleated tucker shading their cheeks; the breast, which invariably, as decreed by the fashion of the day, showed the amplitude of the nursing mother's bosom, was covered with a crossed white kerchief or the rounded bib of a blue apron. They sat with folded arms resting on the rail of the tribune. Behind them, scattered about the rising tiers, could be seen a sprinkling of citizens dressed in the varied garb which at that date gave every gathering so striking and picturesque a character. On the right hand, near the doors, behind a broad barrier, a space was reserved where the public could stand. On this occasion it was nearly empty. The business that was to occupy the attention of this particular section of the tribunal interested only a few spectators, while doubtless the other sections sitting at the same hour would be hearing more exciting cases.

This fact somewhat reassured Gamelin; his heart was like to fail him as it was, and he could not have endured the heated atmosphere of one of the great days. His eyes took in the most trifling details of the scene,—the cotton-wool in the *greffier's* ear and a blot of ink on the Deputy Prosecutor's papers. He could see, as through a magnifying glass, the capitals of the pillars sculptured at a time when all knowledge of the classical orders was forgotten and which crowned the Gothic columns with wreaths of nettle and holly. But wherever he looked, his gaze came back again and again to the fatal chair; this was of an antiquated make, covered in red Utrecht velvet, the seat worn and the arms blackened with use. Armed National Guards stood guarding every door.

At last the accused appeared, escorted by grenadiers, but with limbs unbound, as the law directed. He was a man of fifty or thereabouts, lean and dry, with a brown face, a very bald head, hollow cheeks and thin livid lips, dressed in an out-of-date coat of a sanguine red. No doubt it was fever that made his eyes glitter like jewels and gave his cheeks their shiny, varnished look. He took his seat. His legs, which he crossed, were extraordinarily spare and his great knotted hands met round the knees they clasped. His name was Marie-Adolphe Guillergues, and he was accused of malversation in the supply of forage to the Republican troops. The act of indictment laid to his charge numerous and serious offences, of which no single one was positively certain. Under examination, Guillergues denied the majority of the

195

charges and explained the rest in a light favourable to himself. He spoke in a cold, precise way, with a marked ability and gave the impression of being a dangerous man to have business dealings with. He had an answer for everything. When the judge asked him an embarrassing question, his face remained unmoved and his voice confident, but his two hands, folded on his breast, kept twitching in an agony. Gamelin was struck by this and whispered to the colleague sitting next him, a painter like himself:

"Watch his thumbs!"

The first witness to depose alleged a number of most damaging facts. He was the mainstay of the prosecution. Those on the other hand who followed showed themselves well disposed to the prisoner. The Deputy of the Public Prosecutor spoke strongly, but did not go beyond generalities. The advocate for the defence adopted a tone of bluff conviction of his client's innocence that earned the accused a sympathy he had failed to secure by his own efforts. The sitting was suspended and the jury assembled in the room set apart for deliberation. There, after a confused and confusing discussion, they found themselves divided in two groups about equal in number. On the one side were the unemotional, the lukewarm, the men of reason, whom no passion could stir, on the other the kind who let their feelings guide them, who prove all but inaccessible to argument and only consult their heart. These always voted guilty. They were the true metal, pure and unadulterated; their only thought was to save the Republic and they cared not a straw for anything else. Their attitude made a strong impression on Gamelin who felt he was of the same kidney himself.

"This Guillergues," he thought to himself, "is a cunning scamp, a villain who has speculated in the forage supplied to our cavalry. To acquit him is to let a traitor escape, to be false to the fatherland, to devote the army to defeat." And in a flash Gamelin could see the Hussars of the Republic, mounted on stumbling horses, sabred by the enemy's cavalry.... "But if Guillergues was innocent...?"

Suddenly he remembered Jean Blaise, likewise suspected of bad faith in the matter of supplies. There were bound to be many others acting like Guillergues and Blaise, contriving disaster, ruining the Republic! An example must be made. But if Guillergues was innocent...?

"There are no proofs," said Gamelin, aloud.

"There never are," retorted the foreman of the jury, shrugging his shoulders; he was good metal, pure metal!

In the end, there proved to be seven votes for condemnation, eight for acquittal.

The jury re-entered the hall and the sitting was resumed. The jurors were required to give reasons for their verdict, and each spoke in turn facing the empty chair. Some were prolix, others confined themselves to a sentence; one or two talked unintelligible gabble.

When Gamelin's turn came, he rose and said:

"In presence of a crime so heinous as that of robbing the defenders of the fatherland of the sinews of victory, we need formal proofs which we have not got."

By a majority of votes the accused was declared not guilty.

Guillergues was brought in again and stood before his judges amid a hum of sympathy from the spectators which conveyed the news of his acquittal to him. He was another man. His features had lost their harshness, his lips were relaxed again. He looked venerable; his face bore the impression of innocence. The President read out in tones of emotion the verdict releasing the prisoner; the audience broke into applause. The gendarme who had brought Guillergues in threw himself into his arms. The President called him to the daïs and gave him the embrace of brotherhood. The jurors kissed him, while Gamelin's eyes rained hot tears.

The courtyard of the Palais, dimly lighted by the last rays of the setting sun, was filled with a howling, excited crowd. The four sections of the Tribunal had the day before pronounced thirty sentences of death, and on the steps of the Great Stairway a throng of *tricoteuses* squatted to see the tumbrils start. But Gamelin, as he descended the steps among the press of jurors and spectators, saw nothing, heard nothing but his own act of justice and humanity and the self-congratulation he felt at having recognized innocence. In the courtyard stood Élodie, all in white, smiling through her tears; she threw herself into his arms and lay there half fainting. When she had recovered her voice, she said to him:

"Évariste, you are noble, you are good, you are generous! In the hall there, your voice, so gentle and manly, went right through me with its magnetic waves. It electrified me. I gazed at you on your bench, I could see no one but you. But you, dear heart, you never guessed I was there? Nothing told you I was present? I sat in the gallery in the second row to the right. By heaven! how sweet it is to do the right! you saved that unhappy man's life. Without you, it was all over with him; he was as good as dead. You have given him back to life and the love of his friends. At this moment he must bless you. Évariste, how happy I am and how proud to love you!"

Arm in arm, pressed close to one another, they went along the streets; their bodies felt so light they seemed to be flying.

They went to the *Amour peintre*. On reaching the Oratoire:

"Better not go through the shop," Élodie suggested.

She made him go in by the main coach-door and mount the stairs with her to the suite of rooms above. On the landing she drew out of her reticule a heavy iron key.

"It might be the key of a prison," she exclaimed, "Évariste, you are going to be my prisoner."

They crossed the dining-room and were in the girl's bedchamber.

Évariste felt upon his the ardent freshness of Élodie's lips. He pressed her in his arms; with head thrown back and swooning eyes, her hair flowing loose over her relaxed form, half fainting, she escaped his hold and ran to shoot the bolt....

The night was far advanced when the *citoyenne* Blaise opened the outer door of the flat for her lover and whispered to him in the darkness.

"Good-bye, sweetheart! it is the hour my father will be coming home. If you hear a noise on the stairs, go up quick to the higher floor and don't come down till all danger is over of your being seen. To have the street-door opened, give three raps on the *concierge's* window. Good-bye, my life, good-bye, my soul!"

When he found himself in the street, he saw the window of Élodie's chamber half unclose and a little hand pluck a red carnation, which fell at his feet like a drop of blood.

XII

One evening when old Brotteaux arrived in the Rue de la Loi bringing a gross of dancing-dolls for the *citoyen* Caillou, the toy-merchant, the latter, a soft-spoken, polite man as a rule, stood there stiff and stern among his dolls and punch-and-judies and gave him a far from gracious welcome.

"Have a care, *citoyen* Brotteaux," he began, "have a care! There is a time to laugh, and a time to be serious; jokes are not always in good taste. A member of the Committee of Security of the Section, who inspected my establishment yesterday, saw your dancing-dolls and deemed them anti-revolutionary."

"He was jesting!" declared Brotteaux.

"Not so, *citoyen*, not at all. He is not the man to joke. He said in these little fellows the National representatives were insidiously mimicked, that in particular one could discover caricatures of Couthon, Saint-Just and Robespierre, and he seized the lot. It is a dead loss to me, to say nothing of the grave risks to which I am exposed."

"What! these Harlequins, these Gilles, these Scaramouches, these Colins and Colinettes, which I have painted the same as Boucher used to fifty years ago, how should they be parodies of Couthons and Saint-Justs? No sensible man could imagine such a thing."

"It is possible," replied the *citoyen* Caillou, "that you acted without malice, albeit we must always distrust a man of parts like you. But it is a dangerous game. Shall I give you an instance? Natoile, who runs a little outdoor theatre in the Champs Élysées, was arrested the day before yesterday for anti-patriotism, because he made Polichinelle poke fun at the Convention."

"Now listen to me," Brotteaux urged, raising the cloth that covered his little dangling figures; "just look at these masks and faces, are they anything else whatever but characters in plays and pastorals? How could you let yourself be persuaded, *citoyen* Caillou, that I was making fun of the National Convention?"

Brotteaux was dumfounded. While allowing much for human folly, he had not thought it possible it could ever go so far as to suspect his Scaramouches and Colinettes. Repeatedly he protested their innocence and his; but the *citoyen* Caillou would not hear a word.

"*Citoyen* Brotteaux, take your dolls away. I esteem you, I honour you, but I do not mean to incur blame or get into trouble because of you. I intend to remain a good citizen and to be treated as such. Good evening, *citoyen* Brotteaux; take your dolls away."

The old man set out again for home, carrying his suspects over his shoulder at the end of a pole, an object of derision to the children, who took him for the hawker of rat-poison. His thoughts were gloomy. No doubt, he did not live only by his dancing-dolls; he used to paint portraits at twenty *sols* apiece, under the archways of doors or in one of the market halls, among the darners and old-clothes menders, where he found many a young recruit starting for the front and wanting to leave his likeness behind for his sweetheart. But these petty tasks cost him endless pains, and he was a long way from making as good portraits as he did dancing-dolls. Sometimes, too, he acted as amanuensis for the Market dames, but this meant mixing himself

198

up in Royalist plots, and the risks were heavy. He remembered there lived in the Rue Neuve-des-Petits-Champs, near the erstwhile Place Vendôme, another toy-merchant, Joly by name, and he resolved to go next day to offer him the goods the chicken-hearted Caillou had declined.

A fine rain began to fall. Brotteaux who feared its effects on his marionettes, quickened his pace. As he crossed the Pont-Neuf and was turning the corner of the Place de Thionville, he saw by the light of a street-lamp, sitting on a stone post, a lean old man who seemed utterly exhausted with fatigue and hunger, but still preserved his venerable appearance. He was dressed in a tattered surtout, had no hat and appeared over sixty. Approaching the poor wretch, Brotteaux recognised the Père Longuemare, the same he had saved from hanging six months before while both of them were waiting in queue in front of the bakery in the Rue de Jérusalem. Feeling bound to the monk by the service he had already done him, Brotteaux stepped up to him and made himself known as the publican who had stood beside him among the common herd, one day of great scarcity, and asked him if he could not be of some use to him.

"You seem wearied, Father. Take a taste of cordial,"—and Brotteaux drew from the pocket of his plum-coloured coat a flask of brandy, which lay there alongside his Lucretius.

"Drink. And I will help you to get back to your house."

The Père Longuemare pushed away the flask with his hand and tried to rise, but only to fall back again in his seat.

"Sir," he said in a weak but firm voice, "for three months I have been living at Picpus. Being warned they had come to arrest me at my lodging, yesterday at five o'clock of the afternoon, I did not return home. I have no place to go to; I am wandering the streets and am a little fatigued."

"Very well, Father," proposed Brotteaux, "do me the honour to share my garret."

"Sir," replied the Barnabite, "you know, I suppose, I am a suspect."

"I am one too," said Brotteaux, "and my marionettes into the bargain, which is the worst thing of all. You see them exposed under this flimsy cloth to the fine rain that chills our bones. For, I must tell you, Father, that after having been a publican, I now make dancing-dolls for a living."

The Père Longuemare took the hand the *ci-devant* financier extended to him and accepted the hospitality offered. Brotteaux, in his garret, served him a meal of bread and cheese and wine, which last he had put to cool in the rain-gutter, for was he not a Sybarite?

Having appeased his hunger:

"Sir," said the Père Longuemare, "I ought to inform you of the circumstances that led to my flight and left me to die on yonder post where you found me. Driven from my cloister, I lived on the scanty allowance the Assembly had assigned to me; I gave lessons in Latin and Mathematics and I wrote pamphlets on the persecution of the Church of France. I have even composed a work of some length, to prove that the Constitutional oath of the Priests is subversive of Ecclesiastical discipline. The advances made by the Revolution deprived me of all my pupils, while I could not get my pension because I had not the certificate of citizenship required by law. This certificate I went to the Hôtel de Ville to claim, in the conviction I was well entitled to it. Member of an order founded by the Apostle Paul himself, who boasted the title of Roman citizen, I always piqued myself on behaving after his example as a good French citizen, a respecter of all human laws which are not in opposition to the Divine. I presented my demand to Monsieur Colin, pork-butcher and Municipal officer, in charge of the delivery of certificates of the sort. He questioned me as to my calling. I told him I was a Priest. He asked me if I was married, and on my answering that I was not, he told me that was the worse for me. Finally, after a variety of questions, he asked me if I had proved my citizenship on the 10th August, the 2nd September and the 31st May. 'No certificates can be given,' he added, 'except to such as have proved their patriotism by their behaviour on these three occasions.' I could not give him an answer that would satisfy him. However, he took down my name and address and promised me to make prompt enquiry into my case. He kept his word, and as the result of his enquiry two Commissioners of the Committee of General Security of Picpus, supported by an armed band, presented themselves at my lodging in my absence to conduct me to prison. I do not know of what crime I am accused. But you will agree with me one must pity Monsieur Colin, whose wits are so clouded he holds it a reproach to an ecclesiastic not to have made display of his patriotism on the 10th August, the 2nd September, and the 31st May. A man capable of such a notion is surely deserving of commiseration."

"*I* am in the same plight, I have no certificate," observed Brotteaux. "We are both suspects. But you are weary. To bed, Father. We will discuss plans to-morrow for your safety."

He gave the mattress to his guest and kept the palliasse for himself; but the monk in his humility demanded the latter with so much urgency that his wish had to be complied with; otherwise he would have slept on the boards.

These arrangements completed, Brotteaux blew out the candle both to save tallow and as a wise precaution.

"Sir," the monk addressed him, "I am thankful for what you are doing for me; but alas! it is of small moment to you whether I am grateful or no. May God account your act meritorious! *That* is of infinite concern for you. But God pays no heed to what is not done for his glory and is merely the outcome of purely natural virtue. Wherefore I beseech you, sir, to do for Him what you were led to do for me."

"Father," answered Brotteaux, "never trouble yourself on this head and do not think of gratitude. What I am doing now, the merit of which you exaggerate,—is not done for any love of you; for indeed, albeit you are a lovable man, Father, I know you too little to love you. Nor yet do I act so for love of humanity; for I am not so simple as to think with 'Don Juan' that humanity has rights; indeed this prejudice, in a mind so emancipated as his, grieves me. I do it out of that selfishness which inspires mankind to perform all their deeds of generosity and self-sacrifice, by making them recognize themselves in all who are unfortunate, by disposing them to commiserate their own calamities in the calamities of others and by inciting them to offer help to a mortal resembling themselves in nature and destiny, so that they think they are succouring themselves in succouring him. I do it also for lack of anything better to do; for life is so desperately insipid we must find distraction at any cost, and benevolence is an amusement, of a mawkish sort, one indulges in for want of any more savoury; I do it out of pride and to get an advantage over you; I do it, in a word, as part of a system and to show you what an atheist is capable of."

"Do not calumniate yourself, sir," replied the Père Longuemare. "I have received of God more marks of grace than He has accorded you hitherto; but I am not as good a man as you, and am greatly your inferior in natural merits. But now let me take an advantage too over you. Not knowing me, you cannot love me. And I, sir, without knowing you, I love you better than myself; God bids me do so."

Having so said, the Père Longuemare knelt down on the floor, and after repeating his prayers, stretched himself on his palliasse and fell peacefully asleep.

XIII

Evariste Gamelin occupied his place as juror of the Tribunal for the second time. Before the opening of the sitting, he discussed with his colleagues the news that had arrived that morning. Some of it was doubtful, some untrue; but part was authentic—and appalling; the armies of the coalition in command of all the roads and marching *en masse* on Paris, La Vendée triumphant, Lyons in insurrection, Toulon surrendered to the English, who were landing fourteen thousand men there.

For him and his fellow magistrates these were not only events of interest to all the world, but so many matters of domestic concern. Foredoomed to perish in the ruin of the fatherland, they made the public salvation their own proper business. The Nation's interests, thus entangled with their own, dictated their opinions and passions and conduct.

Gamelin, where he sat on the jury bench, was handed a letter from Trubert, Secretary of the Committee of Defence; it was to notify his appointment as Commissioner of Supplies of Powder and Saltpetre:

"You will excavate all the cellars in the Section in order to extract the substances necessary for the manufacture of powder. To-morrow perhaps the enemy will be before Paris; the soil of the fatherland must provide us with the lightning we shall launch against our aggressors. I send you herewith a schedule of instructions from the Convention regarding the manipulation of saltpetres. Farewell and brotherly greeting."

At that moment the accused was brought in. He was one of the last of the defeated Generals whom the Convention delivered over one after the other to the Tribunal, and the most insignificant. At sight of him Gamelin shuddered; once again he seemed to see the same soldier whom three weeks before, looking on as a spectator, he had seen sentenced and sent to the guillotine. The man was the same, with his obstinate, opinionated look; the procedure was the same. He gave his answers in a cunning, brutish way that ruined the effect even of the most convincing. His cavilling and chicanery and the accusations he levelled against his subordinates, made you forget he was fulfilling the honourable task of defending his honour and his life. Everything was uncertain, every statement disputed,—position of the armies, total of forces engaged, munitions of war, orders given, orders received, movements of troops; nobody knew anything. It was impossible to make head or tail of these confused, nonsensical, aimless operations which had ended in disaster; defending counsel and the accused himself were as much in the dark as were accuser, judges, and jury, and strange to say, not a soul would admit, whether to himself or to other people, that this was the case. The judges took a childish delight in drawing plans and discussing problems of tactics and strategy, while the prisoner constantly betrayed his inborn predilection for crooked ways.

The arguments dragged on endlessly. And all the time Gamelin could see on the rough roads of the north the ammunition wagons stogged in the mire and the guns capsized in the ruts, and along all the ways the broken and beaten columns flying in disorder, while from all sides the enemy's cavalry was debouching by the abandoned defiles. And from this host of men betrayed he could hear a mighty shout going up in accusation of the General. When the hearing closed, darkness was falling on the hall, and the head of Marat gleamed half-seen like a phantom above the President's head. The jury was called upon to give judgment, but was of two minds. Gamelin, in a hoarse, strangled voice, but in resolute accents, declared the accused guilty of treason against the Republic, and a murmur of approval rose from the crowd, a flattering unction to his youthful virtue. The sentence was read by the light of torches which cast a lurid, uncertain gleam on the prisoner's hollow temples beaded with drops of sweat. Outside the doors, on the steps crowded with the customary swarm of cockaded harridans, Gamelin could hear his name, which the habitués of the Tribunal were beginning to know, passed from mouth to mouth, and was assailed by a bevy of *tricoteuses* who shook their fists in his face, demanding the head of *the Austrian*.

The next day Évariste had to give judgment on the fate of a poor woman, the widow Meyrion. She distributed bread from house to house and tramped the streets pushing a little hand-cart and carrying a wooden tally hung at her waist, on which she cut notches with her knife representing the number of the loaves she had delivered. Her gains amounted to eight sous a day. The deputy of the Public Prosecutor displayed an extraordinary virulence towards the wretched creature, who had, it appears, shouted "Vive le Roi!" on several occasions, uttered anti-revolutionary remarks in the houses where she called to leave the daily dole of bread, and been mixed up in a plot for the escape of the woman Capet. In answer to the Judge's question she admitted the facts alleged against her; whether fool or fanatic, she professed Royalist sentiments of the most enthusiastic sort and waited her doom.

The Revolutionary Tribunal made a point of proving the triumph of Equality by showing itself just as severe for street-porters and servant maids as for the aristocrats and financiers. Gamelin could conceive no other system possible under a popular government. He would have deemed it a mark of contempt, an insult to the people, to exclude it from punishment. That would have been to consider it, so to speak, as unworthy of chastisement by the law. Reserved for aristocrats only, the guillotine would have appeared to him in the light of an iniquitous privilege. In his thoughts he was beginning to erect chastisement into a religious and mystic dogma, to assign it a virtue, a merit of its own; he conceived that society owes punishment to criminals and that it is doing them an injustice to cheat them of this right. He declared the woman Meyrion guilty and deserving of death, only regretting that the fanatics, more culpable than herself, who had brought her to her ruin, were not there to share her fate.

Every evening almost Évariste attended the meetings of the Jacobins, who assembled in the former chapel of the Dominicans, commonly known as Jacobins, in the Rue Honoré. In a courtyard, in which stood a tree of Liberty, a poplar whose leaves shook and rustled all day in the wind, the chapel, built in a poor, clumsy style and surmounted by a heavy roof of tiles, showed its bare gable, pierced by a round window and an arched doorway, above which floated the National colours, the flagstaff crowned with the cap of Liberty. The Jacobins, like the Cordeliers, and the Feuillants, had appropriated the premises and taken the name of the dispossessed monks. Gamelin, once a regular attendant at the sittings of the Cordeliers, did not find at the Jacobins the familiar sabots, carmagnoles and rallying cries of the Dantonists. In Robespierre's club administrative reserve and bourgeois gravity were the order of the day. The Friend of the People was no more, and since his death Évariste had followed the lessons of Maximilien whose thought ruled the Jacobins, and thence, through a thousand affiliated societies was disseminated over all France. During the reading of the minutes, his eyes wandered over the bare, dismal walls, which, after sheltering the spiritual sons of the arch-inquisitor of heresy, now looked down on the assemblage of zealous inquisitors of crimes against the fatherland.

There, without pomp or ceremony, sat the body that was the chiefest power of the State and ruled by force of words. It governed the city, the empire, dictated its decrees to the Convention itself. These artisans of the new order of things, so respectful of the law that they continued Royalists in 1791 and would fain have been Royalists still on the King's return from Varennes, so obstinate in their attachment to the Constitution, friends of the established order of the State even after the massacres of the Champ-de-Mars, and never revolutionaries against the Revolution, heedless of popular agitation, cherished in their dark and puissant soul a love of the fatherland that had given birth to fourteen armies and set up the guillotine. Évariste was lost in admiration of their vigilance, their suspicious temper, their reasoned dogmatism, their love of system, their supremacy in the art of governing, their sovereign sanity.

The public that formed the audience gave no token of their presence save a low, long-drawn murmur as of one voice, like the rustling of the leaves of the tree of Liberty that stood outside the threshold.

That day, the 11th Vendémiaire, a young man, with a receding brow, a piercing eye, a sharp prominent nose, a pointed chin, a pock-marked face, a look of cold self-possession, mounted the tribune slowly. His hair was white with powder and he wore a blue coat that displayed his slim figure. He showed the precise carriage and moved with the cadenced step that made some say in mockery that he was like a dancing-master and earned him from others the name of the "French Orpheus." Robespierre, speaking in a clear voice, delivered an eloquent discourse against the enemies of the Republic. He belaboured with metaphysical and uncompromising arguments Brissot and his accomplices. He spoke at great length, in free-flowing harmonious periods. Soaring in the celestial spheres of philosophy, he launched his lightnings at the base conspirators crawling on the ground.

Évariste heard and understood. Till then he had blamed the Gironde; were they not working for the restoration of the monarchy or the triumph of the Orleans faction, were they not planning the ruin of the heroic city that had delivered France from her fetters and would one day deliver the universe? Now, as he listened to the sage's voice, he discerned truths of a higher and purer compass; he grasped a revolutionary metaphysic which lifted his mind above coarse, material conditions into a region of absolute, unqualified convictions, untrammelled by the errors of the senses. Things are in their nature involved and full of confusion; the complexity of circumstances is such that we lose our way amongst them. Robespierre simplified them to his mind, put good and evil before him in clear and precise formulas. Federalism,—indivisibility; unity and indivisibility meant salvation, federalism, damnation. Gamelin tasted the ineffable joy of a believer who knows the word that saves and the word that destroys the soul. Henceforth the Revolutionary Tribunal, as of old the ecclesiastical courts, would take cognizance of crime absolute, of crime definable in a word. And, because he had the religious spirit, Évariste welcomed these revelations with a sombre enthusiasm; his heart swelled and rejoiced at the thought that, henceforth, he had a talisman to discern betwixt crime and innocence, he possessed a creed! Ye stand in lieu of all else, oh, treasures of faith!

The sage Maximilien enlightened him further as to the perfidious intent of those who were for equalizing property and partitioning the land, abolishing wealth and poverty and establishing a happy mediocrity for all. Misled by their specious maxims, he had originally approved their designs, which he deemed in accord with the principles of a true Republican. But Robespierre, in his speeches at the Jacobins, had unmasked their machinations and convinced him that these men, disinterested as their intentions appeared, were working to overthrow the Republic, that they were alarming the rich only to rouse against the lawful authority powerful and implacable foes. Once private property was threatened, the whole population, the more ardently attached to its possessions the less of these it owned, would turn suddenly against the Republic. To terrify vested interests is to conspire against the State. These men who, under pretence of securing universal happiness and the reign of justice, proposed a system of equality and community of goods as a worthy object of good citizens' endeavours, were traitors and malefactors more dangerous than the Federalists.

But the most startling revelation he owed to Robespierre's wisdom was that of the crimes and infamies of atheism. Gamelin had never denied the existence of God; he was a deist and believed in a Providence that watches over mankind; but, admitting that he could form only a very vague conception of the Supreme Being and deeply attached to the principle of freedom of conscience, he was quite ready to allow that right-thinking men might follow the example of Lamettrie, Boulanger, the Baron d'Holbach, Lalande, Helvétius, the *citoyen* Dupuis, and deny God's existence, on condition they formulated a natural morality and found in themselves the sources of justice and the rules of a virtuous life. He had even felt himself in sympathy with the atheists, when he had seen them vilified and persecuted. Maximilien had opened his mind and unsealed his eyes. The great man by his virtuous eloquence had taught him the true character of atheism, its nature, its objects, its effects; he had shown him how this doctrine, conceived in the drawing-rooms and boudoirs of the aristocracy, was the most perfidious invention the enemies of the people had ever devised to demoralize and enslave it; how it was a criminal act to uproot from the heart of the unfortunate the consoling thought of a Providence to reward and compensate and give them over without rein or bit to the passions that degrade men and make vile slaves of them; how, in fine, the monarchical Epicureanism of a Helvétius led to immorality, cruelty, and every wickedness. Now that he had learnt these lessons from the lips of a great man and a great citizen, he execrated the atheists—especially when they were of an open-hearted, joyous temper, like his old friend Brotteaux.

———————————

In the days that followed Évariste had to give judgment one after the other on a *ci-devant* convicted of having destroyed wheat-stuffs in order to starve the people, three *émigrés* who had returned to foment civil war in France, two ladies of pleasure of the Palais-Égalité, fourteen Breton conspirators, men, women, old men, youths, masters, and servants. The crime was proven, the law explicit. Among the guilty was a girl of twenty, adorable in the heyday of her young beauty under the shadow of the doom so soon to overwhelm her, a fascinating figure. A blue bow bound her golden locks, her lawn kerchief revealed a white, graceful neck.

Évariste was consistent in casting his vote for death, and all the accused, with the one exception of an old gardener, were sent to the scaffold.

The following week Évariste and his section mowed down sixty-three heads—forty-five men and eighteen women.

The judges of the Revolutionary Tribunal drew no distinction between men and women, in this following a principle as old as justice itself. True, the President Montané, touched by the bravery and beauty of Charlotte Corday, had tried to save her by paltering with the procedure of the trial and had thereby lost his seat, but women as a rule were shown no favour under examination, in strict accordance with the rule common to all the tribunals. The jurors feared them, distrusting their artful ways, their aptitude for deception, their powers of seduction. They were the match of men in resolution, and this invited the Tribunal to treat them in the same way. The majority of those who sat in judgment, men of normal sensuality or sensual on occasion, were in no wise affected by the fact that the prisoner was a woman. They condemned or acquitted them as their conscience, their zeal, their love, lukewarm or vehement, for the Republic dictated. Almost always they appeared before the court with their hair carefully dressed and attired with as much elegance as the unhappy conditions allowed. But few of them were young and still fewer pretty. Confinement and suspense had blighted them, the harsh light of the hall betrayed their weariness and the anguish they had endured, beating down on faded lids, blotched and pimpled cheeks, white, drawn lips. Nevertheless, the fatal chair more than once held a young girl, lovely in her pallor, while a shadow of the tomb veiled her eyes and made her beauty the more seductive. That the sight had the power to melt some jurymen and irritate others, who should deny? That, in the secret depraved heart of him, one of these magistrates may have pried into the most sacred intimacies of the fair body that was to his morbid fancy at the same moment a living and a dead woman's, and that, gloating over voluptuous and ghoulish imaginings he may have found an atrocious pleasure in giving over to the headsman those dainty, desirable limbs,—this is perhaps a thing better left unsaid, but one which no one can deem impossible who knows what men are. Évariste Gamelin, cold and pedantic in his artistic creed, could see no beauty but in the Antique; he admired beauty, but it hardly stirred his senses. His classical taste was so severe he rarely found a woman to his liking; he was as insensible to the charms of a pretty face as he was to Fragonard's colouring and Boucher's drawing. He had never known desire save under the form of deep passion.

Like the majority of his colleagues in the Tribunal, he thought women more dangerous than men. He hated the *ci-devant* princesses, the creatures he pictured to himself in his horrified dreams in company with Elisabeth and *the Austrian* weaving plots to assassinate good patriots; he even hated all those fair mistresses of financiers, philosophers, and men of letters whose only crime was having enjoyed the pleasures of the senses and the mind and lived at a time when it was sweet to live. He hated them without admitting the feeling to himself, and when he had one before him at the bar, he condemned her out of pique, convinced all the while that he was dooming her justly and rightly for the public good. His sense of honour, his manly modesty, his cold, calculated wisdom, his devotion to the State, his virtues in a word, pushed under the knife heads that might well have moved men's pity.

But what is this, what is the meaning of this strange prodigy? Once the difficulty was to find the guilty, to search them out in their lair, to drag the confession of their crime from reluctant lips. Now, there is no hunting with a great pack of sleuth-hounds, no pursuing a timid prey; lo! from all sides come the victims to offer themselves a voluntary sacrifice. Nobles, virgins, soldiers, courtesans, flock to the Tribunal, dragging their condemnation from dilatory judges, claiming death as a right which they are impatient to enjoy. Not enough the multitude with which the zeal of the informers has crowded the prisons and which the Public Prosecutor and his myrmidons are wearing out their lives in haling before the Tribunal; punishment must likewise be provided for those who refuse to wait. And how many others, prouder and more pressing yet, begrudging their judges and headsmen their death, perish by their own hand! The mania of killing is equalled by the mania to die. Here, in the Conciergerie, is a young soldier, handsome, vigorous, beloved; he leaves behind him in the prison an adorable mistress; she bade him "Live for me!"—he will live neither for her nor love nor glory. He lights his pipe with his act of accusation. And, a Republican, for he breathes liberty through every pore, he turns Royalist that he may die. The Tribunal tries its best to save him, but the accused proves the stronger; judges and jury are forced to let him have his way.

Évariste's mind, naturally of an anxious, scrupulous cast, was filled to overflowing through the lessons he learned at the Jacobins and the contemplation of life with suspicions and alarms. At night, as he paced the ill-lighted streets on his way to Élodie's, he fancied through every cellar-grating he passed he caught a glimpse of a plate for printing off forged assignats; in the dark recesses of the baker's and grocer's empty shops he imagined storerooms bursting with provisions fraudulently held back for a rise in prices; looking in at the glittering windows of the eating-houses, he seemed to hear the talk of the speculators plotting the ruin of the country as they drained bottles of Beaune and Chablis; in the evil-smelling alleys he could see the very prostitutes trampling underfoot the National cockade to the applause of elegant young roisterers; everywhere he beheld conspirators and traitors. And he thought: "Against so many foes, secret or declared, oh! Republic thou hast but one succour; Saint Guillotine, save the fatherland!..."

Élodie would be waiting for him in her little blue chamber above the *Amour peintre*. To let him know he might come in, she used to set on the window-sill her little watering-can beside the pot of carnations. Now he filled her with horror, he seemed like a monster to her; she was afraid of him,—and she adored him. All the night, clinging together in a frantic embrace, the bloody-minded lover and the amorous girl exchanged in silence frenzied kisses.

XIV

Rising at dawn, the Père Longuemare, after sweeping out the room, departed to say his Mass in a chapel in the Rue d'Enfer served by a nonjuring priest. There were in Paris thousands of similar retreats, where the refractory clergy gathered together clandestinely little troops of the faithful. The police of the Sections, vigilant and suspicious as they were, kept their eyes shut to these hidden folds, from fear of the exasperated flock and moved by some lingering veneration for holy things. The Barnabite made his farewells to his host who had great difficulty in persuading him to come back to dine, and only succeeded in the end by promising that the cheer would be neither plentiful nor delicate.

Brotteaux, when left to himself, kindled a little earthenware stove; then, while he busied himself with preparations for the Monk's and the Epicurean's meal, he read in his Lucretius and meditated on the conditions of human beings.

As a sage and a philosopher, he was not surprised that these wretched creatures, silly playthings of the forces of nature, found themselves more often than not in absurd and painful situations; but he was weak and illogical enough to believe that the Revolutionaries were more wicked and more foolish than other men, thereby falling into the error of the metaphysician. At the same time he was no Pessimist and did not hold that life was altogether bad. He admired Nature in several of her departments, especially the celestial mechanism and physical love, and accommodated himself to the labours of life, pending the arrival of the day, which could not be far off, when he would have nothing more either to fear or to desire.

He coloured some dancing-dolls with painstaking care and made a Zerline that was very like Rose Thévenin. He liked the girl and his Epicureanism highly approved of the arrangement of the atoms of which she was composed.

These tasks occupied him till the Barnabite's return.

"Father," he announced, as he opened the door to admit him, "I told you, you remember, that our fare would be meagre. We have nothing but chestnuts. The more reason, therefore, they should be well seasoned."

"Chestnuts!" cried Père Longuemare, smiling, "there is no more delicious dish. My father, sir, was a poor gentleman of the Limousin, whose whole estate consisted of a pigeon-cote in ruins, an orchard run wild and a clump of chestnut-trees. He fed himself, his wife and his twelve children on big green chestnuts, and we were all strong and sturdy. I was the youngest and the most turbulent; my father used to declare, by way of jesting, he would have to send me to America to be a filibuster.... Ah! sir, how fragrant your chestnut soup smells! It takes me back to the table where my mother sat smiling, surrounded by her troop of little ones."

The repast ended, Brotteaux set out for Joly's, the toy-merchant in the Rue Neuve-des-Petits-Champs, who took the dancing-dolls Caillou had refused, and ordered—not another gross of them like the latter, but a round twenty-four dozen to begin with.

On reaching the erstwhile Rue Royale and turning into the Place de la Révolution, Brotteaux caught sight of a steel triangle glittering between two wooden uprights; it was the guillotine. An immense crowd of light-hearted spectators pressed round the scaffold, waiting the arrival of the loaded carts. Women were hawking Nanterre cakes on a tray hung in front of them and crying their wares; sellers of cooling drinks were tinkling their little bells; at the foot of the Statue of Liberty an old man had a peep-show in a small booth surmounted by a swing on which a monkey played its antics. Underneath the scaffold some dogs were licking yesterday's blood, Brotteaux turned back towards the Rue Honoré.

Regaining his garret, where the Barnabite was reading his breviary, he carefully wiped the table and arranged his colour-box on it alongside the materials and tools of his trade.

"Father," he said, "if you do not deem the occupation unworthy of the sacred character with which you are invested, I will ask you to help me make my marionettes. A worthy tradesman, Joly by name, has this very morning given me a pretty heavy order. Whilst I am painting these figures already put together, you will do me a great service by cutting out heads, arms, legs, and bodies from the patterns here. Better you could not find; they are after Watteau and Boucher."

"I agree with you, sir," replied Longuemare, "that Watteau and Boucher were well fitted to create such-like baubles; it had been more to their glory if they had confined themselves to innocent figures like these. I should be delighted to help you, but I fear I may not be clever enough for that."

The Père Longuemare was right to distrust his own skill; after sundry unsuccessful attempts, the fact was patent that his genius did not lie in the direction of cutting out pretty shapes in thin cardboard with the point of a penknife. But when, at his suggestion, Brotteaux gave him some string and a bodkin, he showed himself very apt in endowing with motion the little creatures he had failed to make and teaching them to dance. He had a happy knack, by way of trying them afterwards, of making them each execute three or four steps of a gavotte, and when they rewarded his pains, a smile would flicker on his stern lips.

One time when he was pulling the string of a Scaramouch to a dance tune:

"Sir," he observed, "this little travesty reminds me of a quaint story. It was in 1746, when I was completing my noviciate under the care of the Père Magitot, a man well on in years, of deep learning and austere morals. At that period, you perhaps remember, dancing figures, intended in the first instance to amuse children, exercised over women and even over men, both young and old, an extraordinary fascination; they were all the rage in Paris. The fashionable shops were crammed with them; they were to be found in the houses of people of quality, and it was nothing out of the way to see a grave and reverend senior dancing his doll in the streets and public gardens. The Père Magitot's age, character, and sacred profession did not avail to guard him against infection. Every time he saw anyone busy jumping his cardboard mannikin, his fingers itched with impatience to be at the same game,—an impatience that soon grew well nigh intolerable. One day when he was paying a visit of importance on a matter involving the interests of the whole Order to Monsieur Chauvel, advocate in the courts of the Parlement, noticing one of these dancers hanging from the chimney-piece, he felt a terrible temptation to pull its string, which he only resisted at the cost of a tremendous effort. But this frivolous ambition pursued him everywhere and left him no peace. In his studies, in his meditations, in his prayers, at church, at chapter, in the confessional and in the pulpit, he was possessed by it. After some days of dreadful agony of mind, he laid bare his extraordinary case to the General of the Order, who happened fortunately to be in Paris at the moment. He was an eminent ecclesiastic of Milan, a Doctor and Prince of the Church. His counsel to the Père Magitot was to satisfy a craving, innocent in its inception, importunate in its consequences and inordinate in its excess, which threatened to super induce the gravest disorders in the soul which was afflicted with it. On the advice, or more strictly by the order of the General, the Père Magitot returned to Monsieur Chauvel's house, where the advocate received him, as on the first occasion, in his cabinet. There, finding the dancing figure still fastened in the same place, he ran excitedly to the chimney-piece and begged his host to do him a favour,—to let him pull the string. The lawyer gave him his permission very readily, and informed him in confidence that sometimes he set Scaramouch (that was the doll's name) dancing while he was studying his briefs, and that, only the night before, he had modulated on Scaramouch's movements the peroration of his speech in defence of a woman falsely accused of poisoning her husband. The Père Magitot seized the string with trembling fingers and saw Scaramouch throw his limbs wildly about under his manipulation like one possessed of devils in the agonies of exorcism."

"Your tale does not surprise me, father," Brotteaux told him, "We see such cases of obsession; but it is not always cardboard figures that occasion it."

The Père Longuemare, who was religious by profession, never talked about religion, while Brotteaux was for ever harping on the subject. He was conscious of a bond of sympathy between himself and the Barnabite, and took a delight in embarrassing and disturbing his peace of mind with objections against divers articles of the Christian faith.

Once when they were working together making Zerlines and Scaramouches:

"When I consider," remarked Brotteaux, "the events which have brought us to the point at which we stand, I am in doubt as to which party, in the general madness, has been the most insane; sometimes, I am greatly tempted to believe it was that of the Court."

"Sir," answered the Monk, "all men lose their wits like Nebuchadnezzar, when God forsakes them; but no man in our days ever plunged so deep in ignorance and error as the Abbé Fauchet, no man was so fatal as he to the kingdom. God must needs have been sorely exasperated against France to send her Monsieur l'Abbé Fauchet!"

"I imagine we have seen other evil-doers besides poor, unhappy Fauchet."

"The Abbé Gregoire too, was full of malice."

"And Brissot, and Danton, and Marat, and a hundred others, what of them, Father?"

"Sir, they are laics; the laity could never incur the same responsibilities as the clergy. They do not work evil from so high a standpoint, and their crimes are not of universal bearing."

"And your God, Father, what say you of His behaviour in the present Revolution?"

"I do not understand you, sir."

"Epicurus said: Either God wishes to hinder evil and cannot, or He can and does not wish to, or He cannot nor does he wish to, or He does wish to and can. If He wishes to and cannot, He is impotent; if He can and does not wish to, He is perverse; if He cannot nor does He wish to, He is impotent and perverse; if He does wish to and can, why does He not, tell me that, Father!"— and Brotteaux cast a look of triumph at his interlocutor.

"Sir," retorted the Monk, "there is nothing more contemptible than these difficulties you raise. When I look into the reasoning of infidels, I seem to see ants piling up a few blades of grass as a dam against the torrent that sweeps down from the mountains. With your leave, I had rather not argue with you; I should have too many excellent reasons and too few wits to apply them. Besides, you will find your refutation in the Abbé Guénée and twenty other apologists. I will only say that what you quote from Epicurus is foolishness; because God is arraigned in it as if he was a man, with a man's moral code. Well! sir, the sceptics, from Celsus down to Bayle and Voltaire, have cajoled fools with such-like paradoxes."

"See, Father," protested Brotteaux, "to what lengths your faith makes you go. Not satisfied with finding all truth in your Theology, you likewise refuse to discover any in the works of so many noble intellects who thought differently from yourselves."

"You are entirely mistaken, sir," replied Longuemare. "On the contrary, I believe that nothing could ever be altogether false in a man's thoughts. The atheists stand on the lowest rung of the ladder of knowledge; but even there, gleams of sense are to be found and flashes of truth, and even when darkness is thick about him, a man may lift up his eyes to God, and He will put understanding in his heart; was it not so with Lucifer?"

"Well, sir," said Brotteaux, "I cannot match your generosity and I am bound to tell you I cannot find in all the works of the Theologians one atom of good sense."

At the same time he would repudiate any desire to attack religion, which he deemed indispensable for the nations; he could only wish it had for its ministers philosophers instead of controversialists. He deplored the fact that the Jacobins were for replacing it by a newer and more pestilent religion, the cult of liberty, equality, the republic, the fatherland. He had observed this, that it is in the vigour of their youth religions are the fiercest and most cruel, and grow milder as they grow older. He was anxious, therefore, to see Catholicism preserved; it had devoured many victims in the times of its vigour, but nowadays, burdened by the weight of years and with enfeebled appetite, it was content with roasting four or five heretics in a hundred years.

"As a matter of fact," he concluded, "I have always got on very well with your God-eaters and Christ-worshippers. I kept a chaplain at Les Ilettes, where Mass was said every Sunday and all my guests attended. The philosophers were the most devout while the opera girls showed the most fervour. I was prosperous then and had crowds of friends."

"Friends," exclaimed the Père Longuemare, "friends! Ah! sir, do you really think they loved you, all these philosophers and all these courtesans, who have degraded your soul in such wise that God himself would find it hard to know it for one of the temples built by Him for His glory?"

The Père Longuemare lived for a week longer at the publican's without being interfered with. As far as possible he observed the discipline of his House and every night at the canonical hours would rise from his palliasse to kneel on the bare boards and recite the offices. Though both were reduced to a diet of wretched scraps, he duly observed fasts and abstinence. A smiling but pitiful spectator of these austerities, Brotteaux one day asked him:

"Do you really believe that God finds any satisfaction in seeing you endure cold and hunger as you do?"

"God himself," was the Monk's answer, "has given us the example of suffering."

On the ninth day since the Barnabite had come to share the philosopher's garret, the latter sallied forth at twilight to deliver his dancing-dolls to Joly, the toy-merchant of the Rue Neuve-des-Petits-Champs. He was on his way back overjoyed at having sold them all, when, as he was crossing the erstwhile Place du Carrousel, a girl in a blue satin pelisse trimmed with ermine, running by with a limping gait, threw herself into his arms and held him fast in the way suppliants have had since the world began.

She was trembling and her heart was beating so fast and loud it could be plainly heard. Wondering to see one of her common sort look so pathetic, Brotteaux, a veteran amateur of the stage, thought how Mademoiselle Raucourt, if she could have seen her, might have learnt something from her bearing.

She spoke in breathless tones, lowering her voice to a whisper for fear of being overheard by the passers-by:

"Take me with you, *citoyen*, and hide me, for the love of pity!... They are in my room in the Rue Fromenteau. While they were coming upstairs, I ran for refuge into Flora's room,—she is my next-door neighbour,—and leapt out of the window into the street, that is how I sprained my ankle.... They are coming; they want to put me in prison and kill me.... Last week they killed Virginie."

Brotteaux understood, of course, that the child was speaking of the delegates of the Revolutionary Committee of the Section or else the Commissaries of the Committee of General Security. At that time the Commune had as *procureur* a man of virtue, the *citoyen* Chaumette who regarded the ladies of pleasure as the direct foes of the Republic and harassed them unmercifully in his efforts to regenerate the Nation's morals. To tell the truth, the young ladies of the Palais-Égalité were no great patriots. They regretted the old state of things and did not always conceal the fact. Several had been guillotined already as conspirators, and their tragic fate had excited no little emulation among their fellows.

The *citoyen* Brotteaux asked the suppliant what offence she had been guilty of to bring down on herself a warrant of arrest.

She swore she had no notion, that she had done nothing anyone could blame her for.

"Well then, my girl," Brotteaux told her, "you are not suspect; you have nothing to fear. Be off with you to bed and leave me alone."

At this she confessed everything:

"I tore out my cockade and shouted: 'Vive le roi!'"

He walked down to the river-side and she kept by his side along the deserted *quais*. Clinging to his arm she went on:

"It is not that I care for him particularly, the King, you know; I never knew him, and I daresay he wasn't very much different from other men. But they are bad people. They are cruel to poor girls. They torment and vex and abuse me in every kind of way; they want to stop me following my trade. I have no other trade. You may be sure, if I had, I should not be doing what I do.... What is it they want? They are so hard on poor humble folks, the milkman, the charcoalman, the water carrier, the laundress. They won't rest content till they've set all poor people against them."

He looked at her; she seemed a mere child. She was no longer afraid; she was almost smiling, as she limped along lightly at his side. He asked her her name. She said she was called Athenaïs and was sixteen.

Brotteaux offered to see her safe to anywhere she wished to go. She did not know a soul in Paris; but she had an aunt, in service at Palaiseau, who would take her in.

Brotteaux made up his mind at once.

"Come with me, my child," he ordered, and led the way home, with her hanging on his arm.

On his arrival, he found the Père Longuemare in the garret reading his breviary.

Holding Athenaïs by the hand, he drew the other's attention to her:

"Father," he said, "here is a girl from the Rue Fromenteau who has been shouting: 'Vive le roi!' The revolutionary police are on her track. She has nowhere to lay head. Will you allow the girl to pass the night here?"

The Père Longuemare closed his breviary.

"If I understand you right," he said, "you ask me, sir, if this young girl, who is like myself subject to be molested under a warrant of arrest, may be suffered, for her temporal salvation, to spend the night in the same room as I?"

"Yes, Father."

"By what right should I object? and why must I suppose myself affronted by her presence? am I so sure that I am any better than she?"

He established himself for the night in an old broken-down armchair, declaring he should sleep excellently in it. Athenaïs lay on the mattress. Brotteaux stretched himself on the palliasse and blew out the candle.

The hours and half-hours sounded one after the other from the church towers, but the old man could not sleep; he lay awake listening to the mingled breathing of the man of religion and the girl of pleasure. The moon rose, symbol and witness of his old-time loves, and threw a silvery ray into the attic, illuminating the fair hair and golden lashes, the delicate nose and round, red mouth of Athenaïs, who lay sound asleep.

"Truly," he thought to himself, "a terrible enemy for the Republic!"

When Athenaïs awoke, the day was breaking. The Monk had disappeared. Brotteaux was reading Lucretius under the skylight, learning from the maxims of the Latin poet to live without fears and without desires; but for all this he felt himself at the moment devoured with regrets and disquietudes.

Opening her eyes, Athenaïs was dumfounded to see the roof beams of a garret above her head. Then she remembered, smiled at her preserver and extended towards him with a caressing gesture her pretty little dirty hands.

Rising on her elbow, she pointed to the dilapidated armchair in which the Monk had passed the night.

"He is not there?... He has not gone to denounce me, has he?"

"No, no, my child. You could not find a more honest soul than that old madman."

Athenaïs asked in what the old fellow's madness consisted; and when Brotteaux informed her it was religion, she gravely reproached him for speaking so, declaring that men without faith were worse than the beasts that perish and that for her part she often prayed to God, hoping He would forgive her her sins and receive her in His blessed mercy.

Then, noticing that Brotteaux held a book in his hand, she thought it was a book of the Mass and said:

"There you see, you too, you say your prayers! God will reward you for what you have done for me."

Brotteaux having told her that it was not a Mass-book, and that it had been written before ever the Mass had been invented in the world, she opined it was an *Interpretation of Dreams*, and asked if it did not contain an explanation of an extraordinary dream she had had. She could not read and these were the only two sorts of books she had heard tell of.

Brotteaux informed her that this book was only by way of explaining the dream of life. Finding this a hard saying, the pretty child did not try to understand it and dipped the end of her nose in the earthenware crock that replaced the silver basins Brotteaux had once been accustomed to use. Next, she arranged her hair before her host's shaving-glass with scrupulous care and gravity. Her white arms raised above her head, she let fall an observation from time to time with long intervals between:

"You, you were rich once."

"What makes you think that?"

"I don't know. But you *were* rich,—and you are an aristocrat, I am certain of it."

She drew from her pocket a little Holy Virgin of silver in a round ivory shrine, a bit of sugar, thread, scissors, a flint and steel, two or three cases for needles and the like, and after selecting what she required, sat down to mend her skirt, which had got torn in several places.

"For your own safety, my child, put this in your cap!" Brotteaux bade her, handing her a tricolour cockade.

"I will do that gladly, sir," she agreed, "but it will be for the love of you and not for love of the Nation."

When she was dressed and had made herself look her best, taking her skirt in both hands, she dropped a curtsey as she had been taught to do in her village, and addressing Brotteaux:

"Sir," she said, "I am your very humble servant."

She was prepared to oblige her benefactor in all ways he might wish, but she thought it more becoming that he asked for no favour and she offered none; it seemed to her a pretty way to part so, and what good manners required.

Brotteaux slipped a few assignats into her hand to pay her coach-hire to Palaiseau. It was the half of his fortune, and, albeit he was notorious for his lavishness towards women, it was the first time he had ever made so equal a partition of his goods with any of the sex.

She asked him his name.

"I am called Maurice."

It was with reluctance he opened the garret door for her:

"Good-bye, Athenaïs."

She kissed him. "Monsieur Maurice," she said, "when you think of me, if ever you do, call me Marthe; that is the name I was christened, the name they called me by in the village.... Good-bye and thank you.... Your very humble servant, Monsieur Maurice."

XV

The prisons were full to bursting and must be emptied; the work of judging, judging, must go on without truce or respite. Seated against the tapestried walls with their fasces and red caps of liberty, like their fellows of the fleurs-de-lis, the judges preserved the same gravity, the same dreadful calm, as their Royal predecessors. The Public Prosecutor and his Deputies, worn out with fatigue, consumed with the fever of sleeplessness and brandy, could only shake off their exhaustion by a violent effort; their broken health made them tragic figures to look upon. The jurors, divers in character and origin, some educated, others ignorant, craven or generous, gentle or violent, hypocritical or sincere, but all men who, knowing the fatherland and the Republic in danger, suffered or feigned to suffer the same anguish, to burn with the same ardour; all alike primed to atrocities of virtue or of fear, they formed but one living entity, one single head, dull and irritable, one single soul, a beast of the apocalypse that by the mere exercise of its natural functions produced a teeming brood of death. Kind-hearted or cruel by caprice of sensibility, when shaken momentarily by a sudden pang of pity, they would acquit with streaming eyes a prisoner whom an hour before they would have condemned to the guillotine with taunts. The further they proceeded with their task, the more impetuously did they follow the impulses of their heart.

Judge and jury toiled, fevered and half asleep with overwork, distracted by the excitement outside and the orders of the sovereign people, menaced by the threats of the *sansculottes* and *tricoteuses* who crowded the galleries and the public enclosure, relying on insane evidence, acting on the denunciations of madmen, in a poisonous atmosphere that stupefied the brain, set ears hammering and temples beating and darkened the eyes with a veil of blood. Vague rumours were current among the public of jurors bought by the gold of the accused. But to these the jury as a body replied with indignant protest and merciless condemnations. In truth they were men neither worse nor better than their fellows. Innocence more often than not is a piece of good fortune rather than a virtue; any other who should have consented to put himself in their place would have acted as they did and accomplished to the best of his commonplace soul these appalling tasks.

Antoinette, so long expected, sat at last in the fatal chair, in a black gown, the centre of such a concentration of hate that only the certainty of what the sentence would be made the court observe the forms of law. To the deadly questions the accused replied sometimes with the instinct of self-preservation, sometimes with her wonted haughtiness, and once, thanks to the hideous suggestion of one of her accusers, with the noble dignity of a mother. The witnesses were confined to outrage and calumny; the defence was frozen with terror. The tribunal, forcing itself to respect the rules of procedure, was only waiting till all formalities were completed to hurl the head of *the Austrian* in the face of Europe.

Three days after the execution of Marie Antoinette Gamelin was called to the bedside of the *citoyen* Fortuné Trubert, who lay dying, within thirty paces of the Military Bureau where he had worn out his life, on a pallet of sacking, in the cell of some expelled Barnabite father. His livid face was sunk in the pillow. His eyes, which already were almost sightless, turned their glassy pupils upon his visitor; his parched hand grasped Évariste's and pressed it with unexpected vigour. Three times he had vomited blood in two days. He tried to speak; his voice, at first hoarse and feeble as a whisper, grew louder, deeper:

"Wattignies! Wattignies!... Jourdan has forced the enemy into their camp ... raised the blockade at Maubeuge.... We have retaken Marchiennes, *ça ira* ... *ça ira* ..." and he smiled.

These were no dreams of a sick man, but a clear vision of the truth that flashed through the brain so soon to be shrouded in eternal darkness. Hereafter the invasion seemed arrested; the Generals were terrorized and saw that the one best thing for them to do was to be victorious. Where voluntary recruiting had failed to produce what was needed, a strong and disciplined army, compulsion was succeeding. One effort more, and the Republic would be saved.

After a half hour of semi-consciousness, Fortuné Trubert's face, hollow-cheeked and worn by disease, lit up again and his hands moved.

He lifted his finger and pointed to the only piece of furniture in the room, a little walnut-wood writing-desk. The voice was weak and breathless, but the mind quite unclouded:

"Like Eudamidas," he said, "I bequeath my debts to my friend,—three hundred and twenty livres, of which you will find the account ... in that red book yonder ... good-bye, Gamelin. Never rest; wake and watch over the defence of the Republic. *Ça ira.*"

The shades of night were deepening in the cell. The difficult breathing of the dying man was the only sound, and his hands scratching on the sheet.

At midnight he uttered some disconnected phrases:

"More saltpetre.... See the muskets are delivered. Health? Oh! excellent.... Get down the church-bells...."

He breathed his last at five in the morning.

By order of the Section his body lay in state in the nave of the erstwhile church of the Barnabites, at the foot of the Altar of the Fatherland, on a camp bed, covered with a tricolour flag and the brow wreathed with an oak crown.

Twelve old men clad in the Roman toga, with palms in their hands, twelve young girls wearing long veils and carrying flowers, surrounded the funeral couch. At the dead man's feet stood two children, each holding an inverted torch. One of them Évariste recognized as his *concierge's* little daughter Joséphine, who in her childish gravity and beauty reminded him of those charming genii of Love and Death the Romans used to sculpture on their tombs.

The funeral procession made its way to the Cemetery of Saint-André-des-Arts to the strains of the *Marseillaise* and the *Ça-ira*.

As he laid the kiss of farewell on Fortuné Trubert's brow, Évariste wept. His tears flowed in self-pity, for he envied his friend who was resting there, his task accomplished.

On reaching home, he received notice that he was posted a member of the Council General of the Commune. After standing as candidate for four months, he had been elected unopposed, after several ballots, by some thirty suffrages. No one voted nowadays; the Sections were deserted; rich and poor alike only sought to shirk the performance of public duties. The most momentous events had ceased to rouse either enthusiasm or curiosity; the newspapers were left unread. Out of the seven hundred thousand inhabitants of the capital Évariste doubted if as many as three or four thousand still preserved the old Republican spirit.

The same day the Twenty-one came up for trial. Innocent or guilty of the calamities and crimes of the Republic, vain, incautious, ambitious and impetuous, at once moderate and violent, feeble in their fear as in their clemency, quick to declare war, slow to carry it out, haled before the Tribunal to answer for the example they had given, they were not the less the first and the most brilliant children of the Revolution, whose delight and glory they had been. The judge who will question them with artful bias; the pallid accuser yonder who, where he sits behind his little table, is planning their death and dishonour; the jurors who will presently try to stifle their defence; the public in the galleries which overwhelms them with howls of insult and abuse,—all, judge, jury, people, have applauded their eloquence in other days, extolled their talents and their virtues. But judge, jury, people have short memories now.

Once Évariste had made Vergniaud his god, Brissot his oracle. But he had forgotten; if any vestige of his old wonder still lingered in his memory, it was to think that these monsters had seduced the noblest citizens.

Returning to his lodging after the sitting, Gamelin heard heart-breaking cries as he entered the house. It was little Joséphine; her mother was whipping her for playing in the Place with good-for-nothing boys and dirtying the fine white frock she had worn for the obsequies of the *citoyen* Trubert.

XVI

After three months during which he had made a daily holocaust of victims, illustrious or insignificant, to the fatherland, Évariste had a case that interested him personally; there was one prisoner he made it his special business to track down to death.

Ever since he had sat on the juror's bench, he had been eagerly watching, among the crowd of culprits who appeared before him, for Élodie's seducer; of this man he had elaborated in his busy fancy a portrait, some details of which were accurate. He pictured him as young, handsome, haughty, and felt convinced he had fled to England. He thought he had discovered him in a young *émigré* named Maubel, who, having come back to France and been denounced by his host, had been arrested in an inn at Passy; Fouquier-Tinville was in charge of the prosecution,—among a thousand others. Letters had been found on him which the accusation regarded as proofs of a plot concocted between Maubel and the agents of Pitt, but which were in fact only letters written to the *émigré* by a banking-house in London which he had entrusted with certain funds. Maubel, who was young and good-looking, seemed to be mainly occupied in affairs of gallantry. His pocket-book afforded a clue to some correspondence with Spain, then at war with France; but these communications were really of a purely private nature, and if the court of preliminary enquiry did not ignore the bill, it was only in virtue of the maxim that justice should never be in too great a hurry to release a prisoner.

Gamelin was handed a report of Maubel's first semi-private examination and he was struck by what it revealed of the young man's character, which he took to agree with what he believed to be that of Élodie's betrayer. Thereafter he spent long hours in the private room of the Clerk of the Court, poring eagerly over the papers relating to this case. His suspicion received a remarkable confirmation on his discovering in a note-book belonging to the *émigré*, but long out of date, the address of the *Amour peintre*, in company, it is true, with those of the *Green Monkey*, the *Dauphin's Head*, and several more print and picture shops. But when he was informed that in this same note-book had been found three or four petals of a red carnation carefully wrapped in a piece of silk paper, remembering how the red carnation was Élodie's favourite flower, the one she cultivated on her window-sill, wore in her hair and used to give (he had reason to know) as a love-token, Évariste's last doubts vanished. Being now convinced he knew the facts, he resolved to question Élodie, though without letting her know the circumstances that had led him to discover the culprit.

As he was climbing the stairs to his lodgings, he perceived even on the lower landings a stifling smell of fruit, and on reaching the studio, found Élodie helping the *citoyenne* Gamelin to make quince preserve. While the old housewife was kindling the stove and turning over in her mind ways of saving the fuel and moist sugar without prejudicing the quality of the preserves, the *citoyenne* Blaise, seated in a straw-bottomed chair, with an apron of brown holland and her lap full of the golden fruit, was peeling the quinces, quartering and throwing them into a shallow copper basin. The strings of her coif were thrown back over her shoulders, the meshes of her black hair coiled above her moist forehead; from her whole person breathed a domestic charm and an intimate grace that induced gentle thoughts and voluptuous dreams of tranquil pleasures.

Without stirring from her seat, she lifted her beautiful eyes, that gleamed like molten gold, to her lover's face, and said:

"See, Évariste, we are working for you. We mean you to have a store of delicious quince jelly to last you the winter; it will settle your stomach and make your heart merry."

But Gamelin, stepping nearer, uttered a name in her ear:

"Jacques Maubel...."

At that moment Combalot the cobbler showed his red nose at the half-open door. He had brought, along with some pairs of shoes he had re-heeled, the bill for the repairs.

For fear of being taken for a bad citizen, he made a point of using the new calendar. The *citoyenne* Gamelin, who liked to see clearly what was what in her accounts, was all astray among the *Fructidors* and *Vendémiaires*. She heaved a sigh.

"Jesus!" she complained, "they want to alter everything,—days, months, seasons of the year, the sun and the moon! Lord God, Monsieur Combalot, what ever is this pair of over-shoes down for the 8 Vendémiaire?"

"*Citoyenne*, just cast your eye over your almanac, and you'll get the hang of it."

She took it down from the wall, glanced at it and immediately turning her head another way.

"It hasn't a Christian look!" she cried in a shocked tone.

"Not only that, *citoyenne*," said the cobbler, "but now we have only three Sundays in the month instead of four. And that's not all; we shall soon have to change our ways of reckoning. There will be no more farthings and half-farthings, everything will be regulated by distilled water."

At the words the *citoyenne* Gamelin, whose lips were trembling, threw up her eyes to the ceiling and sighed out:

"They are going too far!"

And, while she was lost in lamentations, looking like the holy women in a wayside calvary, a bad coal that had caught alight in the fire when her attention was diverted, began to fill the studio with a poisonous smother which, added to the stifling smell of quinces, was like to make the air unbreathable.

Élodie complained that her throat was tickling her and begged to have the window opened. But, directly the *citoyen* Combalot had taken his leave and the *citoyenne* Gamelin had gone back to her stove, Évariste repeated the same name in the girl's ear:

"Jacques Maubel," he reiterated.

She looked up at him in some surprise, and very quietly, still going on cutting a quince in quarters:

"Well!... Jacques Maubel...?"

"He is the man."

"The man! what man?"

"You once gave him a red carnation."

She declared she did not understand and asked him to explain himself.

"That aristocrat! that *émigré*! that scoundrel!"

She shrugged her shoulders, and denied with the most natural air that she had never known a Jacques Maubel.

It was true; she *had* never known anyone of the name.

She denied she had ever given red carnations to anybody but Évariste; but perhaps, on this point, her memory was not very good.

He had little experience of women and was far from having fully fathomed Élodie's character; still, he deemed her quite capable of cajoling and deceiving a cleverer man than himself.

"Why deny?" he asked. "I know all."

Again she asseverated she had never known anybody called Maubel. And, having done peeling the quinces, she asked for a basin of water, because her fingers were sticky. This Gamelin brought her, and, as she washed her hands, she repeated her denials.

Again he repeated that he knew, and this time she made no reply.

She did not guess the object of her lover's question and she was a thousand miles from suspecting that this Maubel, whom she had never heard spoken of before, was to appear before the Revolutionary Tribunal; she could make nothing of the suspicions with which she was assailed, but she knew them to be unfounded. For this reason, having very little hope of dissipating them, she had very little wish to do so either. She ceased to deny having known Maubel, preferring to leave her jealous lover to go astray on a false trail, when from one moment to the next, the smallest incident might start him on the right road. Her little lawyer's clerk of former days, now grown into a patriot dragoon and lady-killer, had quarrelled by now with his aristocratic mistress. Whenever he met Élodie in the street, he would gaze at her with a glance that seemed to say:

"Come, my beauty! I feel sure I am going to forgive you for having betrayed you, and I am really quite ready to take you back into favour." She made no further attempt therefore to cure what she called her lover's crotchets, and Gamelin remained firm in the conviction that Jacques Maubel was Élodie's seducer.

Through the days that ensued the Tribunal devoted its undivided attention to the task of crushing Federalism, which, like a hydra, had threatened to devour Liberty. They were busy days; and the jurors, worn out with fatigue, despatched with the utmost possible expedition the case of the woman Roland, instigator and accomplice of the crimes of the Brissotin faction.

218

Meantime Gamelin spent every morning at the Courts to press on Maubel's trial. Some important pieces of evidence were to be found at Bordeaux; he insisted on a Commissioner being sent to ride post to fetch them. They arrived at last. The deputy of the Public Prosecutor read them, pulled a face and told Évariste:

"It is not good for much, your new evidence! there is nothing in it! mere fiddle-faddle.... If only it was certain that this *ci-devant* Comte de Maubel ever really emigrated...!"

In the end Gamelin succeeded. Young Maubel was served with his act of accusation and brought before the Revolutionary Tribunal on the 19 Brumaire.

From the first opening of the sitting the President showed the gloomy and dreadful face he took care to assume for the hearing of cases where the evidence was weak. The Deputy Prosecutor stroked his chin with the feather of his pen and affected the serenity of a conscience at ease. The Clerk read the act of accusation; it was the hollowest sham the Court had ever heard so far.

The President asked the accused if he had not been aware of the laws passed against the *émigrés*.

"I was aware of them and I observed them," answered Maubel, "and I left France provided with passports in proper form."

As to the reasons for his journey to England and his return to France he had satisfactory explanations to offer. His face was pleasant, with a look of frankness and confidence that was agreeable. The women in the galleries looked at the young man with a favourable eye. The prosecution maintained that he had made a stay in Spain at the time that Nation was at war with France; he averred he had never left Bayonne at that period. One point alone remained obscure. Among the papers he had thrown in the fire at the time of his arrest, and of which only fragments had been found, some words in Spanish had been deciphered and the name of "Nieves."

On this subject Jacques Maubel refused to give the explanations demanded; and, when the President told him that it was in the accused's own interest to clear up the point, he answered that a man ought not always to do what his own interest requires.

Gamelin only thought of convicting Maubel of a crime; three times over he pressed the President to ask the accused if he could explain about the carnation the dried petals of which he hoarded so carefully in his pocket-book.

Maubel replied that he did not consider himself obliged to answer a question that had no concern with the case at law, as no letter had been found concealed in the flower.

The jury retired to the hall of deliberations, favourably impressed towards the young man whose mysterious conduct appeared chiefly connected with a lover's secrets. This time the good patriots, the purest of the pure themselves, would gladly have voted for acquittal. One of them, a *ci-devant* noble, who had given pledges to the Revolution, said:

"Is it his birth they bring up against him? I, too, I have had the misfortune to be born in the aristocracy."

"Yes, but you have left them," retorted Gamelin, "and he has not."

219

And he spoke with such vehemence against this conspirator, this emissary of Pitt, this accomplice of Coburg, who had climbed the mountains and sailed the seas to stir up enemies to Liberty, he demanded the traitor's condemnation in such burning words, that he awoke the never-resting suspicions, the old stern temper of the patriot jury.

One of them told him cynically:

"There are services that cannot well be refused between colleagues."

The verdict of death was recorded by a majority of one.

The condemned man heard his sentence with a quiet smile. His eyes, which had been gazing unconcernedly about the hall, as they fell on Gamelin's face, took on an expression of unspeakable contempt.

No one applauded the decision of the court.

Jacques Maubel was taken back to the Conciergerie; here he wrote a letter while he waited the hour of execution, which was to take place the same evening, by torchlight:

My dear sister,—The tribunal sends me to the scaffold, affording me the only joy I have been able to appreciate since the death of my adored Nieves. They have taken from me the only relic I had left of her, a pomegranate flower, which they called, I cannot tell why, a carnation.

I loved the arts; at Paris, in happier times, I made a collection of paintings and engravings, which are now in a sure place, and which will be delivered to you so soon as this is possible. I pray you, dear sister, to keep them in memory of me.

He cut a lock of his hair, enclosed it in the letter, which he folded and wrote outside:

To the citoyenne Clémence Dezeimeries, née Maubel, La Réole.

He gave all the silver he had on him to the turnkey, begging him to forward this letter to its destination, asked for a bottle of wine, which he drank in little sips while waiting for the cart....

After supper Gamelin ran to the *Amour Peintre* and burst into the blue chamber where every night Élodie was waiting for him.

"You are avenged," he told her. "Jacques Maubel is no more. The cart that took him to his death has just passed beneath your window, escorted by torch-bearers."

She understood:

"Wretch! it is you have killed him, and he was not my lover. I did not know him.... I have never seen him.... What was this man? He was young, amiable ... innocent. And you have killed him, wretch! wretch!"

She fell in a faint. But, amid the shadows of this momentary death, she felt herself overborne by a flood at once of horror and voluptuous ecstasy. She half revived; her heavy lids lifted to show the whites of the eyes, her bosom swelled, her hands beat the air, seeking for her lover. She pressed him to her in a strangling embrace, drove her nails into the flesh, and gave him with her bleeding lips, without a word, without a sound, the longest, the most agonized, the most delicious of kisses.

She loved him with all her flesh, and the more terrible, cruel, atrocious she thought him, the more she saw him reeking with the blood of his victims, the more consuming was her hunger and thirst for him.

XVII

The 24 Frimaire, at ten in the forenoon, under a clear bright sun that was melting the ice formed in the night, the *citoyens* Guénot and Delourmel, delegates of the Committee of General Security, proceeded to the Barnabites and asked to be conducted to the Committee of Surveillance of the Section, in the Capitular hall, whose only occupant for the moment was the *citoyen* Beauvisage, who was piling logs on the fire. But they did not see him just at first because of his short, thickset stature.

In a hunchback's cracked voice the *citoyen* Beauvisage begged the delegates to seat themselves and put himself entirely at their service.

Guénot then asked him if he knew a *ci-devant* Monsieur des Ilettes, residing near the Pont-Neuf.

"It is an individual," he added, "whose arrest I am instructed to effect,"—and he exhibited the order from the Committee of General Security.

Beauvisage, after racking his memory for a while, replied that he knew no individual of that name, that the suspect in question might not be an inhabitant of his Section, certain portions of the *Sections du Muséum, de l'Unité, de Marat-et-Marseille* being likewise in the near neighbourhood of the Pont-Neuf; that, if he did live in the Section, it must be under another name than that borne on the Committee's order; that, nevertheless, it would not be long before they laid hands on him.

"Let's lose no time," urged Guénot. "Our vigilance was aroused in this case by a letter from one of the man's accomplices that was intercepted and put into the hands of the Committee a fortnight ago, but which the *citoyen* Lacroix took action upon only yesterday evening. We are overdone with business; denunciations flow in from every quarter in such abundance one does not know which to attend to."

"Denunciations," replied Beauvisage proudly, "are coming in freely, too, to the Committee of Vigilance of our Section. Some make these revelations out of patriotism, others lured by the bait of a bank-bill for a hundred *sols*. Many children denounce their parents, whose property they covet."

"This letter," resumed Guénot, "emanates from a *ci-devant* called Rochemaure, a woman of gallantry, at whose house they played *biribi*, and is addressed to one *citoyen* Rauline; but is really for an *émigré* in the service of Pitt. I have brought it with me to communicate to you the portion relating to this man des Ilettes."

He drew the letter from his pocket.

"It begins with copious details as to those members of the Convention who might, according to the woman's tale, be gained over by the offer of a sum of money or the promise of a well-paid post under a new Government, more stable than the present. Then comes the following passage:

"I have just returned from a visit to Monsieur des Ilettes, who lives near the Pont-Neuf in a garret where you must be either a cat or an imp to get at him; he is reduced to earning a living by making punch-and-judies. He is a man of judgment, for which reason I report to you, sir, the main gist of his conversation. He does not believe that the existing state of things will last long. Nor does he foresee its being ended by the victory of the coalition, and events appear to justify his opinion; for, as you are aware, sir, for some time past tidings from the front have been bad. He would rather seem to believe in the revolt of the poor and the women of the humbler classes, who remain still deeply attached to their religion. He holds that the widespread alarm caused by the Revolutionary Tribunal will soon reunite all France against the Jacobins. 'This tribunal,' he said, in his joking way, 'which sentences the Queen of France and a bread-hawker, is like that William Shakespeare the English admire so much, etc....' He thinks it not impossible that Robespierre may marry Madame Royale and have himself named Protector of the Kingdom.

"I should be grateful to you, sir, if you would transmit me the amount owing to me, that is to say one thousand pounds sterling, by the channel you are in the habit of using; but whatever you do, do not write to Monsieur Morhardt; he has lately been arrested, thrown into prison, etc., etc...."

"This worthy des Ilettes makes dancing-dolls, it appears," observed Beauvisage, "that is a valuable clue ... though certainly there are many petty trades of the sort carried on in the Section."

"That reminds me," said Delourmel, "I promised to bring home a doll for my little girl Nathalie, my youngest, who is ill with scarlatina. The fever is not a dangerous one, but it demands careful nursing, and Nathalie, a very forward child for her age, and with a very active brain, has but delicate health."

"I," remarked Guénot, "I have only a boy. He plays hoop with barrel-hoops and makes little montgolfier balloons by inflating paper bags."

"Very often," Beauvisage put in his word, "it is with articles that are not toys at all that children like best to play. My nephew Émile, a little chap of seven, a very intelligent child, amuses himself all day long with little wooden bricks with which he builds houses.... Do you snuff,*citoyens*?"—and Beauvisage held out his open snuff-box to the two delegates.

"Now we must set about nabbing our rascal," said Delourmel, who had long moustaches and great eyes that rolled in his head. "I feel quite in the mood this morning for a dish of aristocrat's lights and liver, washed down with a glass of white wine."

Beauvisage suggested to the delegates going to the Place Dauphine to see if his colleague Dupont senior was at his shop there; he would be sure to know this man, des Ilettes.

So they set off in the keen morning air, accompanied by four grenadiers of the Section.

"Have you seen '*The Last Judgment of Kings*' played?" Delourmel asked his companions; "the piece is worth seeing. The author shows you all the Kings of Europe on a desert island where they have taken refuge, at the foot of a volcano which swallows them up. It is a patriotic work."

At the corner of the Rue du Harlay Delourmel's eye was caught by a little cart, as brilliantly painted as a reliquary, which an old woman was pushing, wearing over her coif a hat of waxed cloth.

"What is that old woman selling?" he asked.

The old dame answered for herself:

"Look, gentlemen, make your choice. I have beads and rosaries, crosses, St. Anthonys, holy cerecloths, St. Veronica handkerchiefs, *Ecce homos*, *Agnus Deis*, hunting-horns and rings of St. Hubert, and articles of devotion of every sort and kind."

"Why, it is the very arsenal of fanaticism!" cried Delourmel in horror,—and he proceeded to a summary examination of the poor woman, who made the same answer to every question:

"My son, it's forty years I have been selling articles of devotion."

Another Delegate of the Committee of General Security, noticing a blue-coated National Guard passing, directed him to convey the astonished old woman to the Conciergerie.

The *citoyen* Beauvisage pointed out to Delourmel that it would have been more in the competence of the Committee of Surveillance to arrest the woman and bring her before the Section; that in any case, one never knew nowadays what attitude to take up towards the old religion so as to act up to the views of the Government, and whether it was best to allow everything or forbid everything.

On nearing the joiner's shop, the delegates and the commissary could hear angry shouts mingling with the hissing of the saw and the grinding of the plane. A quarrel had broken out between the joiner, Dupont senior, and his neighbour Remacle, the porter, because of the*citoyenne* Remacle, whom an irresistible attraction was for ever drawing into the recesses of the workshop, whence she would return to the porter's lodge all covered with shavings and saw-dust. The injured porter bestowed a kick on Mouton, the carpenter's dog, which at that very moment his own little daughter Joséphine was nursing lovingly in her arms. Joséphine was furious and burst into a torrent of imprecations against her father, while the carpenter shouted in a voice of exasperation:

"Wretch! I tell you you shall not beat my dog."

"And I," retorted the porter brandishing his broom, "I tell you you shall *not*...."

He did not finish the sentence; the joiner's plane had hurtled close past his head.

The instant he caught sight of the *citoyen* Beauvisage and the attendant delegates, he rushed up to him and cried:

"*Citoyen* Commissary you are my witness, this villain has just tried to murder me."

The *citoyen* Beauvisage, in his red cap, the badge of his office, put out his long arms in the attitude of a peacemaker, and addressing the porter and the joiner:

223

"A hundred *sols*," he announced, "to whichever of you will inform us where to find a suspect, wanted by the Committee of General Security, a *ci-devant* named des Ilettes, a maker of dancing-dolls."

With one accord porter and carpenter designated Brotteaux's lodging, the only quarrel now between them being who should have the assignat for a hundred *sols* promised the informer.

Delourmel, Guénot, and Beauvisage, followed by the four grenadiers, Remacle the porter, Dupont the carpenter, and a dozen little scamps of the neighbourhood filed up the stairs which shook under their tread, and finally mounted the ladder to the attics.

Brotteaux was in his garret busy cutting out his dancing figures, while the Père Longuemare sat facing him, stringing their scattered limbs on threads, smiling to himself to see rhythm and harmony thus growing under his fingers.

At the sound of muskets being grounded on the landing, the monk trembled in every limb, not that he was a whit less courageous than Brotteaux, who never moved a muscle, but the habit of respect for human conventions had never disciplined him to assume an attitude of self-composure. Brotteaux gathered from the *citoyen* Delourmel's questions the quarter from which the blow had come and saw too late how unwise it is to confide in women. He obeyed the *citoyen* Commissary's order to go with him, first picking up his Lucretius and his three shirts.

"The *citoyen*," he said, pointing to the Père Longuemare, "is an assistant I have taken to help me make my marionettes. His home is here."

But the monk failing to produce a certificate of citizenship, was put under arrest along with Brotteaux.

As the procession filed past the porter's door, the *citoyenne* Remacle, leaning on her broom, looked at her lodger with the eyes of virtue beholding crime in the clutches of the law. Little Joséphine, dainty and disdainful, held back Mouton by his collar when the dog tried to fawn on the friend who had often given him a lump of sugar. A gaping crowd filled the Place de Thionville.

At the foot of the stairs Brotteaux came face to face with a young peasant woman who was on the point of going up. She carried a basket on her arm full of eggs and in her hand a flat cake wrapped in a napkin. It was Athenaïs, who had come from Palaiseau to present her saviour with a token of her gratitude. When she observed a posse of magistrates and four grenadiers and "Monsieur Maurice" being led away a prisoner, she stopped in consternation and asked if it was really true; then she stepped up to the Commissary and said in a gentle voice:

"You are not taking him to prison? it can't be possible.... Why! you don't know him! God himself is not better or kinder."

The *citoyen* Delourmel pushed her away and beckoned to the grenadiers to come forward. Then Athenaïs let loose a torrent of the foulest abuse, the filthiest and most abominable invective, at the magistrates and soldiers, who thought that all the rinsings of the Palais-Royal and the Rue Fromenteau were being emptied over their devoted heads. After which, in a voice that filled the whole Place de Thionville and sent a shudder through the throng of curious onlookers:

224

"Vive le roi! Vive le roi!" she yelled.

XVIII

The *citoyenne* Gamelin was devoted to old Brotteaux, and taking him altogether, thought him the best and greatest man she had ever known. She had not bidden him good-bye when he was arrested, because she would not have dared to defy the powers that be and because in her lowly estate she looked upon cowardice as a duty. But she had received a blow she could not recover from.

She could not eat and lamented she had lost her appetite just when she had at last the means to satisfy it. She still admired her son; but she durst not let her mind dwell on the appalling duties he was engaged upon and congratulated herself she was only an ignorant woman who had no call to judge his conduct.

The poor mother had found a rosary at the bottom of a trunk; she hardly knew how to use it, but often fumbled the beads in her trembling fingers. She had lived to grow old without any overt exercise of her religion, but she had always been a pious woman, and she would pray to God all day long, in the chimney corner, to save her boy and that good, kind Monsieur Brotteaux. Élodie often came to see her; they durst not look each other in the eyes, and sitting side by side they would talk at random of indifferent matters.

One day in Pluviose, when the snow, falling in heavy flakes, darkened the sky and deadened the noises of the city, the *citoyenne* Gamelin, who was alone in the lodging heard a knock at the door. She started violently; for months now the slightest noise had set her trembling. She opened the door. A young man of eighteen or twenty walked in, his hat on his head. He was dressed in a bottle-green box-coat, the triple collar of which covered his bust and descended to the waist. He wore top-boots of an English cut. His chestnut hair fell in ringlets about his shoulders. He stepped into the middle of the studio, as if wishful that all the light admitted by the snow-encumbered skylight might fall on him, and stood there some moments without moving or speaking.

At last, in answer to the *citoyenne* Gamelin's look of amazement:

"Don't you know your daughter?"

The old dame clasped her hands:

"Julie!... It is you.... Good God! is it possible?..."

"Why, yes, it is I. Kiss me, mother."

The *citoyenne* Gamelin pressed her daughter to her bosom, and dropped a tear on the collar of the box-coat. Then she began again in an anxious voice:

"You, in Paris!..."

"Ah! mother, but why did I not come alone! For myself, they will never know me in this dress."

It was a fact the box-coat sufficiently disguised her shape, and she did not look very different from a great many very young men, who, like her, wore their hair long and parted in two

225

masses on the forehead. Her features, which were delicately cut and charming, but burnt by the sun, drawn with fatigue, worn with anxiety, had a bold, masculine expression. She was slim, with long straight limbs and an easy carriage; only the clear treble of her voice could have betrayed her sex.

Her mother asked her if she was hungry. She said she would be glad of something to eat, and when bread, wine and ham had been set before her, she fell to, one elbow on the table, with a pretty gluttony, like Ceres in the hut of the old woman Baubo.

Then, the glass still at her lips:

"Mother," she asked, "do you know when my brother will be back? I have come to speak to him."

The good woman looked at her daughter in embarrassment and said nothing.

"I must see him. My husband was arrested this morning and taken to the Luxembourg."

By this name of "husband" she designated Fortuné de Chassagne, a *ci-devant* noble and officer in Bouillé's regiment. He had first loved her when she was a work-girl at a milliner's in the Rue des Lombards, and had carried her away with him to England, whither he had fled after the 10th August. He was her lover; but she thought it more becoming to speak of him as her husband before her mother. Indeed, she told herself that the hardships they had shared had surely united them in a wedlock consecrated by suffering.

More than once they had spent the night side by side on a bench in one of the London parks and gathered up scraps of broken bread under the table in the taverns in Piccadilly.

Her mother could find no answer and gazed at her mournfully.

"Don't you hear what I say, mother? Time presses, I must see Évariste at once; he, and he only, can save Fortuné's life."

"Julie," answered her mother at last, "it is better you should not speak to your brother."

"Why, what do you mean, mother?"

"I mean what I say, it is better you do not speak to your brother about Monsieur de Chassagne."

"But, mother, I must!"

"My child, Évariste can never forgive Monsieur de Chassagne for his treatment of you. You know how angrily he used to speak of him, what names he called him."

"Yes, he called him seducer," said Julie with a little hissing laugh, shrugging her shoulders.

"My child, it was a mortal blow to his pride. Évariste has vowed never again to mention Monsieur de Chassagne's name, and for two years now he has not breathed one word of him or of you. But his feelings have not altered; you know him, he can never forgive you."

"But, mother, as Fortuné has married me ... in London...."

The poor mother threw up her eyes and hands:

"Fortuné is an aristocrat, an *émigré*, and that is cause enough to make Évariste treat him as an enemy."

"Mother, give me a direct answer. Do you mean that if I ask him to go to the Public Prosecutor and the Committee of General Security and take the necessary steps to save Fortuné's life, do you mean that he will not consent?... But, mother, he would be a monster if he refused!"

"My child, your brother is an honest man and a good son. But do not ask him, oh! do not ask him to intercede for Monsieur de Chassagne.... Listen to me, Julie. He does not confide his thoughts to me and, no doubt, I should not be competent to understand them ... but he is a juror; he has principles; he acts as his conscience dictates. Do not ask him anything, Julie."

"Ah! I see you know him now. You know that he is cold, callous, that he is a bad man, that ambition and vainglory are his only guides. And you always loved him better than me. When we lived together, all three of us, you set him up as my pattern to copy. His staid demeanour and grave speech impressed you; you thought he possessed all the virtues. And me, me you always blamed, you gave me all the vices, because I was frank and free, and because I climbed trees. You could never endure me. You loved nobody but him. There, I hate him, your model Évariste; he is a hypocrite."

"Hush, Julie! I have been a good mother to you as well as to him. I had you taught a trade. It has been no fault of mine that you are not an honest woman and did not marry in your station. I loved you tenderly and I love you still. I forgive you and I love you. But do not speak ill of Évariste. He is a good son. He has always taken care of me. When you left me, my child, when you abandoned your trade and forsook your shop, to go and live with Monsieur de Chassagne, what would have become of me without him? I should have died of hunger and wretchedness."

"Do not talk so, mother; you know very well we would have cherished you with all affection, Fortuné and I, if you had not turned your face from us, at Évariste's instigation. Never tell me! he is incapable of a kindly action. It was to make me odious in your eyes that he made a pretence of caring for you. He! love you?... Is he capable of loving anyone? He has neither heart nor head. He has no talent, not a scrap. To paint, a man must have a softer, tenderer nature than his."

She threw a glance round the canvases in the studio, which she found to be no better and no worse than when she left her home.

"There you see his soul! he has put it in his pictures, cold and sombre as it is. His Orestes, his Orestes with the dull eye and cruel mouth, and looking as if he had been impaled, is himself all over.... But, mother, cannot you understand at all? I cannot leave Fortuné in prison. You know these Jacobins, these patriots, all Évariste's crew. They will kill him. Mother, little mother, darling mother, I cannot have them kill him. I love him! I love him! He has been so good to me, and we have been so unhappy together. Look, this box-coat is one of his coats. I had never a shift left. A friend of Fortuné's lent me a jacket and I got a post with an eating-house keeper at Dover, while he worked at a barber's. We knew quite well that to return to France was to risk our lives; but we were asked if we would go to Paris to carry out an important mission.... We agreed,—we would have accepted a mission to hell! Our travelling expenses were paid and we were given a letter of exchange on a Paris banker. We found the offices closed; the banker is in prison and going to be guillotined. We had not a brass farthing. All the individuals with whom we were in correspondence and to whom we could appeal are fled or imprisoned. Not a door to knock at. We slept in a stable in the Rue de la Femme-sans-tête. A charitable bootblack, who slept on the same straw with us there, lent my lover one of his boxes, a brush and a pot of blacking three quarters empty. For a fortnight Fortuné made his living and mine by blacking shoes in the Place de Grève.

"But on Monday a Member of the Commune put his foot on the box to have his boots polished. He had been a butcher once, a man Fortuné had before now given a kick behind to for selling meat of short weight. When Fortuné raised his head to ask for his two sous, the rascal recognized him, called him aristocrat, and threatened to have him arrested. A crowd collected, made up of honest folks and a few blackguards, who began to shout "*Death to the émigré!*" and called for the gendarmes. At that moment I came up with Fortuné's bowl of soup. I saw him taken off to the Section and shut up in the church of Saint-Jean. I tried to kiss him, but they hustled me away. I spent the night like a dog on the church steps.... They took him away this morning...."

Julie could not finish, her sobs choked her.

She threw her hat on the floor and fell on her knees at her mother's feet.

"They took him away this morning to the Luxembourg prison. Mother, mother, help me to save him; have pity on your child!"

Drowned in her tears, she threw open her box-coat and, the better to prove herself a woman and a wife, bared her bosom; seizing her mother's hands, she held them close over her throbbing breasts.

"My darling, my daughter, Julie, my Julie!" sobbed the widow Gamelin,—and pressed her streaming cheeks to the girl's.

For some moments they clung together without a word. The poor mother was racking her brains for some way of helping her daughter, and Julie was watching the kind look in those tearful eyes.

"Perhaps," thought Évariste's mother, "perhaps, if I speak to him, he will be melted. He is good, he is tender-hearted. If politics had not hardened him, if he had not been influenced by the Jacobins, he would never have had these cruel feelings, that terrify me because I cannot understand them."

She took Julie's head in her two hands:

"Listen, my child. I will speak to Évariste. I will sound him, get him to see you and hear your story. The sight of you might anger him; his first impulse might be to turn against you.... And then, I know him; this costume would offend him; he is uncompromising in everything that touches morals, that shocks the proprieties. *I* was a bit startled to see my Julie dressed as a man."

"Oh! mother, the emigration and the fearful disorders of the kingdom have made these disguises quite a common thing. They are adopted in order to follow a trade, to escape recognition, to get a borrowed passport or a certificate approved. In London I saw young Girey dressed as a girl,—and he made a very pretty girl; you must own, mother, *that* is a more scandalous disguise than mine."

"My poor child, you have no need to justify yourself in my eyes, whether in this or any other thing. I am your mother; for me you will always be blameless. I will speak to Évariste, I will say...."

She broke off. She knew what her son was; she felt it in her heart, but she would not believe it, she *would* not know it.

"He is kind-hearted. He will do it for my sake ... for your sake, he will do what I ask him."

The two women, weary to the death, fell silent. Julie sank asleep, her head pillowed on the knees where she had rested as a child, while the mother, the rosary between her hands, wept, like another *mater dolorosa*, over the calamities she felt drawing stealthily nearer and nearer in the silence of this day of snow when everything was hushed, footsteps and carriage wheels and the very heaven itself.

Suddenly, with a keenness of hearing sharpened by anxiety, she caught the sound of her son's steps on the stairs.

"Évariste!" she cried. "Hide"—and she hurried the girl into the bedroom.

"How are you to-day, mother dear?"

Évariste hung up his hat on its peg, changed his blue coat for a working jacket and sat down before his easel. For some days he had been working at a sketch in charcoal of a Victory laying a wreath on the brow of a dead soldier, who had died for the fatherland. Once the subject would have called out all his enthusiasm, but the Tribunal consumed all his days and absorbed his whole soul, while his hand had lost its knack from disuse and had grown heavy and inert.

He hummed over the *Ça ira*.

"I hear you singing," said the *citoyenne* Gamelin; "you are light-hearted, Évariste?"

"We have reason to be glad, mother; there is good news. La Vendée is crushed, the Austrians beaten, the Army of the Rhine has forced the lines of Lautern and of Wissembourg. The day is at hand when the Republic triumphant will show her clemency. Why must the conspirators' audacity increase the mightier the Republic waxes in strength, and traitors plot to strike the fatherland a blow in the dark at the very moment her lightnings overwhelm the enemies that assail her openly?"

The *citoyenne* Gamelin, as she sat knitting a stocking, was watching her son's face over her spectacles.

"Berzélius, your old model, has been to ask for the ten livres you owed him; I paid him. Little Joséphine has had a belly-ache from eating too much of the preserves the carpenter gave her. So I made her a drop of herb tea.... Desmahis has been to see you; he was sorry he did not find you in. He wanted to engrave a design by you. He thinks you have great talent. He is a fine fellow; he looked at your sketches and admired them."

"When peace is re-established and conspiracy suppressed," said the painter, "I shall begin on my Orestes again. It is not my way to flatter myself; but that head is worthy of David's brush."

He outlined with a majestic sweep the arm of his Victory.

"She holds out palms," he said. "But it would be finer if her arms themselves were palms."

"Évariste!"

"Mother?"

"I have had news ... guess, of whom...."

"I do not know."

"Of Julie ... of your sister.... She is not happy."

"It would be a scandal if she were."

"Do not speak so, my son, she is your sister. Julie is not a bad woman; she had a good disposition, which misfortune has developed. She loves you. I can assure you, Évariste, that she only desires a hard-working, exemplary life and her fondest wish is to be reconciled to her friends. There is nothing to prevent your seeing her again. She has married Fortuné Chassagne."

"She has written to you?"

"No."

"How, then, have you had news of her, mother?"

"It was not by letter, Évariste; it was...."

He sprang up and stopped her with a savage cry:

"Not another word, mother! Do not tell me they have both returned to France.... As they are doomed to perish, at least let it not be at my hands. For their own sake, for yours, for mine, let me not know they are in Paris.... Do not force the knowledge on me; otherwise...."

"What do you mean, my son? you would think, you would dare...?"

"Mother, hear what I say; if I knew my sister Julie to be in that room ..." (and he pointed at the closed door), "I should go instantly to denounce her to the Committee of Vigilance of the Section."

The poor mother, her face as white as her coif, dropped her knitting from her trembling hands and sighed in a voice fainter than the faintest whisper:

"I would not believe it, but I see it now; my boy is a monster...."

As pale as she, the froth gathering on his lips, Évariste fled from the house and ran to find at Élodie's side forgetfulness, sleep, the delicious foretaste of extinction.

XIX

While the Père Longuemare and the girl Athenaïs were examined at the Section, Brotteaux was led off between two gendarmes to the Luxembourg, where the door-keeper refused to admit him, declaring he had no room left. The old financier was next taken to the Conciergerie and brought into the Gaoler's office, quite a small room, divided in two by a glazed partition.

230

While the clerk was inscribing his name in the prison registers, Brotteaux could see through the panes two men lying each on a tattered mattress, both as still as death and with glazed eyes that seemed to see nothing. Plates, bottles and bits of broken bread and meat littered the floor round them. They were prisoners condemned to death and waiting for the cart to arrive.

The *ci-devant* Monsieur des Ilettes was thrust into a dungeon, where by the light of a lantern he could just make out two figures stretched on the ground, one savage-looking and hideously mutilated, the other graceful and pleasing. The two prisoners offered him a share of their straw, and this, rotten and swarming with vermin as it was, was better than having to lie on the earth, which was befouled with excrement. Brotteaux sank down on a bench in the pestiferous darkness and sat there, his head against the wall, speechless and motionless. So intense was his agony of mind he would have dashed out his brains against the stones if he had had the strength. He could not breathe. His eyes swam, and a long-drawn murmur, as soft as silence, filled his ears. He felt his whole being bathed in a delicious semi-consciousness. For one incomparable moment everything was harmony, serenity, light, fragrance, sweetness. Then he ceased to know or feel anything.

When he returned to himself, the first notion that entered his head was to regret his coma and, a philosopher even in the stupor of despair, he reflected how he had had to plunge to the depths of an underground dungeon, there to await execution, to enjoy the most exquisite of all voluptuous sensations he had ever tasted. He tried hard to lose consciousness again, but without success; on the contrary, little by little he felt the poisonous air of the dungeon fill his lungs and bring with it, along with the fever of life, a full consciousness of his intolerable wretchedness.

Meantime his two companions regarded his silence as a cruel personal insult. Brotteaux, who was of a sociable turn, endeavoured to satisfy their curiosity; but when they discovered he was only what they called "a political," one of the mild sort whose crime was only a matter of words and opinions, they lost all respect and sympathy for him. The offences charged against these two prisoners had more grit; the older of the men was a murderer, the other had been manufacturing forged assignats. Both made the best of their situation and even found some alleviations in it. Brotteaux's thoughts suddenly turned to the world above him,—how over his head all was noise and bustle, light and life, while the pretty shopwomen in the Palais de Justice behind their counters, loaded with perfumery and pretty knicknacks, smiled on their customers, happy people free to go where they pleased,—and the picture doubled his despair.

Night fell, unmarked in the darkness and silence of the dungeon, but yet gloomy and oppressive. One leg extended on his bench and his back propped against the wall, Brotteaux fell into a doze. And lo! he saw himself seated at the foot of a leafy beech, in which the birds were singing; the setting sun bathed the river in liquid fire and the clouds were edged with purple. The night wore through. A burning fever consumed him and he greedily drained his pitcher to the dregs, but the fetid water only increased his distress.

Next day the gaoler who brought the food promised Brotteaux, if he could afford the cost, to give him the privileges of a prisoner who pays for his accommodation, so soon as there should be room, and it was not likely to be long first. And so it turned out; two days later he invited the old financier to leave his dungeon. At every step he took upwards, Brotteaux felt life and vigour coming back to him, and when he saw a room with a red-tiled floor and in it a bed of sacking covered with a dingy woollen counterpane, he wept for joy. The gilded bed carved with doves billing and cooing that he had once had made for the prettiest of the dancers at the Opera had not seemed so desirable or promised him such delights.

This bed of sacking was in a large hall, very fairly clean, which held seventeen others like it, separated by high partitions of planks. The company that occupied these quarters, composed of ex-nobles, tradesmen, bankers, working-men, hit the old publican's taste well enough, for he could accommodate himself to persons of all qualities. He noticed that these, cut off like himself from every opportunity of pleasure and foredoomed to perish at the hand of the executioner, were of a very merry humour and showed a marked taste for wit and raillery. His bent was to think lightly of mankind, so he attributed the high spirits of his companions to the frivolity of their minds, which prevented them from looking seriously at their situation. Moreover, he was strengthened in his opinion by observing how the more intelligent among them were profoundly sad. He remarked before long, that, for the most part, wine and brandy supplied the inspiration of a gaiety that betrayed its source by its violent and sometimes almost insane character. They did not all possess courage; but all made a display of it. This caused Brotteaux no surprise; he was well aware how men will readily enough avow cruelty, passion, even avarice, but never cowardice, because such an admission would bring them, among savages and even in civilized society, into mortal danger. That is the reason, he reflected, why all nations are nations of heroes and all armies are made up of brave men only.

More potent, even, than wine and brandy were the rattle of weapons and keys, the clash of locks and bolts, the cry of sentries, the stamping of feet at the door of the Tribunal, to intoxicate the prisoners and fill their minds with melancholy, insanity, or frenzy. Some there were who cut their throat with a razor or threw themselves from a window.

Brotteaux had been living for three days in these privileged quarters when he learned through the turnkey that the Père Longuemare was languishing on the rotten verminous straw of the common prison with the thieves and murderers. He had him put on paying terms in the same room as himself, where a bed had fallen vacant. Having promised to pay for the monk, the old publican, who had no large sum of money about him, struck out the idea of making portraits at a crown apiece. By the help of a gaoler, he procured a supply of small black frames in which to put pretty little designs in hair which he executed with considerable cleverness. These productions sold well, being highly appreciated among people whose thoughts were set on leaving souvenirs to their friends.

The Père Longuemare kept a good heart and a high spirit. While waiting his summons to appear before the Revolutionary Tribunal, he was preparing his defence. Drawing no distinction between his own case and that of the Church, he promised himself to expose to his judges the disorders and scandals to which the Spouse of Christ was exposed by the Civil Constitution of the Clergy; he proposed to depict the eldest daughter of the Church waging sacrilegious war upon the Pope, the French clergy robbed, outraged, subjected to the odious domination of laics, the regulars, Christ's true army, despoiled and scattered. He cited St. Gregory the Great and St. Irenæus, quoted numerous articles of the Canon Law and whole paragraphs from the Decretals.

All day long he sat scribbling on his knees, at the foot of his bed, dipping stumps of pens worn to the feathers in ink, soot, coffee-grounds, covering with illegible writing candle-wrappers, packing-paper, newspapers, playing cards, even thinking of using his shirt for the same purpose after starching it. Leaf by leaf the pile grew; pointing to this mass of undecipherable scrawls, he would say:

"Ah! when I appear before my judges, I will inundate them with light."

Another day, casting a look of satisfaction on his defence, which grew bulkier day by day, and thinking of these magistrates he was burning to confound, he cried:

"I wouldn't like to be in *their* shoes!"

The prisoners whom fate had brought together in this prison-room were Royalists or Federalists, there was even a Jacobin amongst the rest; they held widely different views as to the right way of conducting the business of the State, but not one of them all preserved the smallest vestige of Christian beliefs. Feuillants, Constitutionals, Girondists, all, like Brotteaux, considered the Christians' God a very bad thing for themselves and an excellent one for the people; as for the Jacobins, they were for installing in the place of Jehovah a Jacobin god, anxious to refer the dispensation of Jacobinism on earth to a higher source. But as they could not conceive, either one or the other, of anybody being so absurd as to believe in any revealed religion, seeing that the Père Longuemare was no fool, they took him to be a knave. By way, no doubt, of preparing for martyrdom, he made confession of faith at every opportunity, and the more sincerity he displayed, the more like an impostor he seemed.

In vain Brotteaux stood surety for the monk's good faith; Brotteaux himself was reputed to believe only a part of what he said. His ideas were too singular not to appear affected and satisfied nobody entirely. He dubbed Jean-Jacques a dull, paltry rascal. Voltaire, on the other hand, he accounted among the divinely-gifted men, though not on the same level as the amiable Helvétius, or Diderot, or the Baron d'Holbach. In his opinion the greatest genius of the century was Boulanger. He also thought highly of the astronomer Lalande and of Dupuis, author of a *Memoir on the origin of the Constellations*.

The wits of the company made a thousand jokes at the poor Barnabite's expense, the point of which he never saw; his simplicity saved him from every pitfall. To drown the suspense that racked them and escape the torments of idleness, the prisoners played at draughts, cards and backgammon. No instrument of music was allowed. After supper they would sing, or recite verses. Voltaire's *La Pucelle* brought a little cheerfulness to these aching hearts, and the company never wearied of hearing the telling passages repeated. But, unable to distract their thoughts from the appalling vision that always loomed before their mind's eye, they strove sometimes to make a diversion of it, and in the chamber of the eighteen beds, before turning in for the night, they would play the game of the Revolutionary Tribunal. The parts were distributed according to tastes and aptitudes. While some represented the judges and prosecutor, others were the accused or the witnesses, others again the headsman and his men. The trials invariably wound up with the execution of the condemned, who were laid at full length on a bed, the neck underneath a plank. The scene then shifted to the infernal regions. The most agile of the troop, wrapped in white sheets, played spectres. There was a young *avocat* from Bordeaux, a man named Dubosc, short, dark, one-eyed, humpbacked, bandy-legged, the very black deuce in person, who used to come all horned and hoofed, to drag the Père Longuemare feet first out of his bed, announcing to the culprit that he was condemned to the everlasting flames of hell and doomed past redemption for having made of the Creator of the Universe a jealous being, a blockhead, and a bully, an enemy of human happiness and love.

"Ah! ha! ha!" the devil would scream discordantly, "so you taught, you old bonze, that God delights to see His creatures languish in contrition and deny themselves His dearest gifts. Impostor, hypocrite, sneak, sit on nails and eat egg-shells for all eternity!"

The Père Longuemare, for all reply, would observe that the speech showed the philosopher's cloven hoof behind the devil's and that the meanest imp of hell would never have talked such foolishness, having at least rubbed shoulders with Theology and for certain being less ignorant than an Encyclopædist.

But when the Girondist *avocat* called him a Capuchin, he turned scarlet with anger and declared that a man incapable of distinguishing a Barnabite from a Franciscan was too blind to see a fly in milk.

The Revolutionary Tribunal was always draining the prisons, which the Committees were as unceasingly replenishing; in three months the chamber of the eighteen was half full of new faces. The Père Longuemare lost his tormentor. The *avocat* Dubosc was haled before the Revolutionary Tribunal and condemned to death as a Federalist and for having conspired against the unity of the Republic. On leaving the court, he returned, as the prisoners always did, by a corridor that ran through the prison and opened on the room he had enlivened for three months with his gaiety. As he made his farewells to his companions, he maintained the same light tone and cheerful air that were habitual with him.

"Forgive me, sir," he said to the Père Longuemare, "for having hauled you feet foremost from your bed. I will never do it again."

Then, turning to old Brotteaux:

"Good-bye, I go before you into the land of nowhere. I gladly return to Nature the atoms of my composition, only hoping she will make a better use of them for the future, for it must be owned she did not make much of a job of me."

So he went on his way to the gaoler's room, leaving Brotteaux sorrowful and the Père Longuemare trembling and green as a leaf, more dead than alive to see the impious wretch laugh on the brink of the abyss.

When Germinal brought back the bright days, Brotteaux, who was of an ardent temperament, tramped down several times every day to the courtyard giving on the women's quarters, near the fountain where the female prisoners used to come of a morning to wash their linen. An iron railing separated the two barracks; but the bars were not so close together as to hinder hands joining and lips meeting. Under the kindly shade of night loving couples would press against the obstacle. At such times Brotteaux would retire discreetly to the staircase and, sitting on a step, would draw from the pocket of his plum-coloured surtout his little Lucretius and read, by the light of a lantern, some of the author's sternly consolatory maxims: "*Sic ubi non erimus....* When we shall have ceased to be, nothing will have power to move us, not even the heavens and earth and sea confounding their shattered fragments...." But, in the act of enjoying his exalted wisdom, Brotteaux would find himself envying the Barnabite this craze that veiled the universe from his eyes.

Month by month terror grew more intense. Every night the tipsy gaolers, their watch-dogs at their heels, would march from cell to cell, delivering acts of accusation, howling out names they mutilated, waking the prisoners and for twenty victims marked on their list terrifying two hundred. Along these corridors, reeking with bloody memories, passed every day, without a murmur, twenty, thirty, fifty condemned prisoners, old men, women, young men and maidens, so widely different in rank and character and opinion that the question rose involuntarily to the lips,—had they not been chosen by lot?

And the card playing went on, the Burgundy drinking, the making of plans, the assignations for after dark at the rails. The company, new almost to a man, now consisted in great part of "extremists" and "irreconcilables." But still the room of the eighteen beds remained the home of elegance and good breeding; barring two prisoners recently transferred from the Luxembourg to the Conciergerie and added to the company, by whom they were suspected of being spies, the *citoyens* Navette and Bellier by name, there were none but honest folk there who reposed a mutual trust in each other. Glass in hand, the victories of the Republic were celebrated by all. Amongst the rest were several poets, as there always are in any gathering of people with nothing to do. The most accomplished composed odes on the triumphs of the Army of the Rhine, which they recited with much mouthing. They were uproariously applauded. Brotteaux was the only lukewarm admirer of the victors and the bards who sang their victories.

"Since Homer began it," he observed one day, "it has always been a mania with poets, this extolling the powers of fighting-men. War is not an art, and luck alone decides the fate of battles. With two generals, both blockheads, face to face, one of them must inevitably be victorious. Wait till some day one of these warriors you make gods of swallows you all up like the stork in the fable who gobbles up the frogs. Ah! then he would be really and truly a God! For you can always tell the gods by their appetite."

Brotteaux's head had never been turned by the glamour of arms. He felt no triumph at the victories of the Republic, which he had foreseen. He did not like the new régime, which military success confirmed. He was a malcontent. Another would have been the same for less cause.

One morning it was announced that the Commissaries of the Committee of General Security were going to institute a search in the prisoners' quarters, that they would seize assignats, articles of gold and silver, knives, scissors; that similar proceedings had been taken at the Luxembourg, where letters, papers, and books had been taken possession of.

Thereupon everyone tried to think of some hiding place in which to secure whatever he held most precious. The Père Longuemare carried away his defence in armfuls to a rain-gutter, while Brotteaux slipped his Lucretius among the ashes on the hearth.

When the Commissaries, wearing tricolour ribands at their necks, arrived to carry out their perquisition, they found scarcely anything but such trifles as it had been deemed judicious to let them discover. On their departure, the Père Longuemare ran to his rain-pipe and rescued as much of his defence as wind and water had spared. Brotteaux pulled out his Lucretius from the fireplace all black with soot.

"Let us make the best of the present," he thought, "for I augur from sundry tokens that our time is straitly measured from henceforth."

One soft night in Prairial, while over the prison yard the moon riding high in a pale sky showed her two silver horns, the ex-financier, who, as his way was, sat reading Lucretius on a step of the stone stairs, heard a voice call him, a woman's voice, a delightful voice, which he did not know. He went down into the court and saw behind the railing a form which he recognized as little as he did the voice, but which reminded him, in its half-seen fascinating outlines, of all the women he had loved. A flood of silvery blue moonlight fell on it. Next instant Brotteaux recognized the pretty actress of the Rue Feydeau, Rose Thévenin.

"You here, my child! It is a joy to see you, but it stabs my heart. Since when have you been here, and why?"

"Since yesterday,"—and she added very low:

"I have been denounced as a Royalist. They accuse me of conspiring to set free the Queen. Knowing you were here, I tried at once to see you. Listen to me, dear friend ... you will let me call you so?... I know people in power; I have sympathizers, I am sure of it, on the Committee of Public Safety itself. I will set my friends to work; they will deliver me, and *I* will deliver you."

But Brotteaux in a voice that took on an accent of urgency:

"By everything you hold dear, my child, do nothing of the sort! Do not write, do not petition; ask nothing of anybody, I conjure you, let yourself be forgotten."

As she appeared unconvinced by what he said, he went on more beseechingly still:

"Not a word, Rose, let them forget you; there lies safety. Anything your friends might attempt would only hasten your undoing. Time is everything; only a short delay, a very short one, I hope, is needed to save you.... Above all, never try to melt the judges, the jurors, a Gamelin. They are not men, they are things; there is no arguing with things. Let them forget you; if you take my advice, sweetheart, I shall die happy, happy to have saved your life."

She answered:

"I will do as you say.... Never talk of dying...."

He shrugged his shoulders.

"My life is ended, my child. Do you live and be happy."

She took his hands and laid them on her bosom:

"Hear what I say, dear friend.... I have only seen you once for a day, and yet you are not indifferent to me. And if what I am going to tell you can renew your attachment to life, oh! believe my promise,—I will be for you ... whatever you shall wish me to be."

And they exchanged a kiss on the mouth through the bars.

XX

Evariste Gamelin, as he sat, one day that a long, tedious case was before the Tribunal, on the jury-bench in the stifling court, closed his eyes and thought:

"Evil-doers, by forcing Marat to hide in holes and corners, had turned him into a bird of night, the bird of Minerva, whose glance pierced the dark recesses where conspirators lurked. Now it is a blue eye, cold and calm, that discovers the enemies of the State and denounces traitors with a subtlety unknown even to the Friend of the People, now asleep for ever in the garden of the Cordeliers. The new saviour of the country, as zealous and more keen-sighted than the first, sees what no man before had seen and with a lifted finger spreads terror broadcast. He discerns the fine, imperceptible shades of difference that divide evil from good, vice from virtue, which but for him would have been confounded, to the hurt of the fatherland and freedom, he marks out before him the thin, inflexible line outside which lies, to the right hand and to the left, only error, crime, and wickedness. The Incorruptible teaches how men serve the foreigner equally by excess of zeal and by supineness, by persecuting the religious in the name of reason no less than by fighting in the name of religion against the laws of the Republic. Every whit as much as the villains who immolated Le Peltier and Marat, do they serve the foreigner who decree them divine honours, to compromise their memory. Agent of the foreigner whosoever repudiates the ideas of order, wisdom, opportunity; agent of the foreigner whosoever

236

outrages morals, scandalizes virtue, and, in the foolishness of his heart, denies God. Yes, fanatic priests deserve to die; but there is an anti-revolutionary way of combating fanaticism; abjurers, too, may be guilty of a crime. By moderation men destroy the Republic; by violence they do the same.

"August and terrible the functions of a judge,—functions defined by the wisest of mankind! It is not aristocrats alone, federalists, scoundrels of the Orleans faction, open enemies of the fatherland, that we must strike down. The conspirator, the agent of the foreigner is a Proteus, he assumes all shapes, he puts on the guise of a patriot, a revolutionary, an enemy of Kings; he affects the boldness of a heart that beats only for freedom; his voice swells, and the foes of the Republic tremble. His name is Danton; his violence is a poor cloak to his odious moderatism, and his base corruption is manifest at last. The conspirator, the agent of the foreigner is that fluent stammerer, the man who clapped the first cockade of revolution in his hat, that pamphleteer who, in his ironical and cruel patriotism, nicknamed himself, 'The procureur of the Lantern.' *His* name is Camille Desmoulins. He threw off the mask by defending the Generals, traitors to their country, and claiming measures of clemency criminal at such a time. There was Philippeaux, there was Hérault, there was the despicable Lacroix. There was the Père Duchesne, he, too, a conspirator and agent of the foreigner, the vile demagogue who degraded liberty, and whose filthy calumnies stirred sympathy for Antoinette herself. There was Chaumette, who yet was a mild man, popular, moderate, well-intentioned, and virtuous in the administration of the Commune; but he was an atheist! Conspirators, agents of the foreigner,—such were all those sansculottes in red cap and carmagnole and sabots who recklessly outbid the Jacobins in patriotism. Conspirator and agent of the foreigner was Anacharsis Cloots, 'orator of the human race,' condemned to die by all the Monarchies of the world; but everything was to be feared of him,—he was a Prussian.

"Now violent or moderate, all these evil-doers, all these traitors,—Danton, Desmoulins, Hébert, Chaumette,—have perished under the axe. The Republic is saved; a chorus of praises rises from all the Committees and the popular assemblies one and all to greet Maximilien and *the Mountain*. Good citizens cry aloud: 'Worthy representatives of a free people, in vain have the sons of the Titans lifted their proud heads; oh! mountain of blessing, oh! protecting Sinai, from thy tumultuous bosom has issued the saving lightning....'

"In this chorus the Tribunal has its meed of praise. How sweet a thing it is to be virtuous, and how dear to public gratitude, to the heart of the upright judge!

"Meanwhile, for a patriot heart, what food for amazement, what motives for anxiety! What! to betray the people's cause, it was not enough to have a Mirabeau, a La Fayette, a Bailly, a Pétion, a Brissot? We must likewise have the men who denounced these traitors. Can it be that all the patriots who made the Revolution only wrought to ruin her? that these heroes of the great days were but contriving with Pitt and Coburg to give the kingdom to the Orleans and set up a Regency under Louis XVII? What! Danton was another Monk. What! Chaumette and the Hébertists, falser than the Federalists who sent them to the guillotine, had conspired to destroy the State! But among those who hurried to their death the traitor Danton and the traitor Chaumette, will not the blue eye of Robespierre discover anon more perfidious traitors yet? What will be the end of this hideous concatenation of traitors betrayed and the revelations of the keen-sighted Incorruptible?..."

XXI

Meantime Julie Gamelin, in her bottle-green box-coat, went every day to the Luxembourg Gardens and there, on a bench at the end of one of the avenues, sat waiting for the moment when her lover should show his face at one of the dormers of the Palace. Then they would beckon to each other and talk together in a language of signs they had invented. In this way she learned that the prisoner occupied a fairly good room and had pleasant companions, that he wanted a blanket for his bed and a kettle and loved his mistress fondly.

She was not the only one to watch for the sight of a dear face at a window of the Palace now turned into a prison. A young mother not far from her kept her eyes fixed on a closed casement; then directly she saw it open, she would lift her little one in her arms above her head. An old lady in a lace veil sat for long hours on a folding-chair, vainly hoping to catch a momentary glimpse of her son, who, for fear of breaking down, never left his game of quoits in the courtyard of the prison till the hour when the gardens were closed.

During these long hours of waiting, whether the sky were blue or overcast, a man of middle age, rather stout and very neatly dressed, was constantly to be seen on a neighbouring bench, playing with his snuff-box and the charms on his watch-guard or unfolding a newspaper, which he never read. He was dressed like a bourgeois of the old school in a gold-laced cocked hat, a plum-coloured coat and blue waistcoat embroidered in silver. He looked well-meaning enough, and was something of a musician to judge by a flute, one end of which peeped from his pocket. Never for a moment did his eyes wander from the supposed stripling, on whom he bestowed continual smiles, and when he saw him leave his seat, he would get up himself and follow him at a distance. Julie, in her misery and loneliness, was touched by the discreet sympathy the good man manifested.

One day, as she was leaving the gardens, it began to rain; the old fellow stepped up to her and, opening his vast red umbrella, asked permission to offer her its shelter. She answered sweetly, in her clear treble, that she would be very glad. But at the sound of her voice and warned perhaps by a subtle scent of womanhood, he strode rapidly away, leaving the girl exposed to the rain-storm; she took in the situation, and, despite her gnawing anxieties, could not restrain a smile.

Julie lived in an attic in the Rue du Cherche-Midi and represented herself as a draper's shop-boy in search of employment; the widow Gamelin, at last convinced that the girl was running smaller risks anywhere else than at her home, had got her away from the Place de Thionville and the Section du Pont-Neuf, and was giving her all the help she could in the way of food and linen. Julie did her trifle of cooking, went to the Luxembourg to see her beloved prisoner and back again to her garret; the monotony of the life was a balm to her grief, and, being young and strong, she slept well and soundly the night through. She was of a fearless temper and broken in to an adventurous life; the costume she wore added perhaps a further spice of excitement, and she would sometimes sally out at night to visit a restaurateur's in the Rue du Four, at the sign of the Red Cross, a place frequented by men of all sorts and conditions and women of gallantry. There she read the papers or played backgammon with some tradesman's clerk or citizen-soldier, who smoked his pipe in her face. Drinking, gambling, love-making were the order of the day, and scuffles were not unfrequent. One evening a customer, hearing a trampling of hoofs on the paved roadway outside, lifted the curtain, and recognizing the Commandant-in-Chief of the National Guard, the *citoyen* Hanriot, who was riding past with his Staff, muttered between his teeth:

"There goes Robespierre's jackass!"

Julie overheard and burst into a loud guffaw.

But a moustachioed patriot took up the challenge roundly:

"Whoever says that," he shouted, "is a bl—sted aristocrat, and I should like to see the fellow sneeze into Samson's basket. I tell you General Hanriot is a good patriot who'll know how to defend Paris and the Convention at a pinch. That's why the Royalists can't forgive him."

Glaring at Julie, who was still laughing, the patriot added:

"You there, greenhorn, have a care I don't land you a kick in the backside to learn you to respect good patriots."

But other voices were joining in:

"Hanriot's a drunken sot and a fool!"

"Hanriot's a good Jacobin! Vive Hanriot!"

Sides were taken, and the fray began. Blows were exchanged, hats battered in, tables overturned, and glasses shivered; the lights went out and the women began to scream. Two or three patriots fell upon Julie, who seized hold of a settle in self-defence; she was brought to the ground, where she scratched and bit her assailants. Her coat flew open and her neckerchief was torn, revealing her panting bosom. A patrol came running up at the noise, and the girl aristocrat escaped between the gendarmes' legs.

Every day the carts were full of victims for the guillotine.

"But I cannot, I cannot let my lover die!" Julie would tell her mother.

She resolved to beg his life, to take what steps were possible, to go to the Committees and Public Departments, to canvas Representatives, Magistrates, to visit anyone who could be of help. She had no woman's dress to wear. Her mother borrowed a striped gown, a kerchief, a lace coif from the *citoyenne* Blaise, and Julie, attired as a woman and a patriot, set out for the abode of one of the judges, Renaudin, a damp, dismal house in the Rue Mazarine.

With trembling steps she climbed the wooden, tiled stairs and was received by the judge in his squalid cabinet, furnished with a deal table and two straw-bottomed chairs. The wall-paper hung in strips. Renaudin, with black hair plastered on his forehead, a lowering eye, tucked-in lips, and a protuberant chin, signed to her to speak and listened in silence.

She told him she was the sister of the *citoyen* Chassagne, a prisoner at the Luxembourg, explained as speciously as she could the circumstances under which he had been arrested, represented him as an innocent man, the victim of mischance, pleaded more and more urgently; but he remained callous and unsympathetic.

She fell at his feet in supplication and burst into tears.

No sooner did he see her tears than his face changed; his dark blood-shot eyes lit up, and his heavy blue jowl worked as if pumping up the saliva in his dry throat.

"*Citoyenne*, we will do what is necessary. You need have no anxiety,"—and opening a door, he pushed the petitioner into a little sitting-room, with rose-pink hangings, painted panels, Dresden china figures, a time-piece and gilt candelabra; for furniture it contained settees, and a sofa covered in tapestry and adorned with a pastoral group after Boucher. Julie was ready for anything to save her lover.

Renaudin had his way,—rapidly and brutally. When she got up, readjusting the *citoyenne's* pretty frock, she met the man's cruel mocking eye; instantly she knew she had made her sacrifice in vain.

"You promised me my brother's freedom," she said.

He chuckled.

"I told you, *citoyenne*, we would do what was necessary,—that is to say, we should apply the law, neither more nor less. I told you to have no anxiety,—and why should you be anxious? The Revolutionary Tribunal is always just."

She thought of throwing herself upon the man, biting him, tearing out his eyes. But, realizing she would only be consummating Fortuné Chassagne's ruin, she rushed from the house, and fled to her garret to take off Élodie's soiled and desecrated frock. All night she lay, screaming with grief and rage.

Next day, on returning to the Luxembourg, she found the gardens occupied by gendarmes, who were turning out the women and children. Sentinels were posted in the avenues to prevent the passers-by from communicating with the prisoners. The young mother, who used to come every day, carrying her child in her arms, told Julie that there was talk of plotting in the prisons and that the women were blamed for gathering in the gardens in order to rouse the people's pity in favour of aristocrats and traitors.

XXII

A mountain has suddenly sprung up in the garden of the Tuileries. Under a cloudless sky, Maximilien heads the procession of his colleagues in a blue coat and yellow breeches, carrying in his hand a bouquet of wheatears, cornflowers and poppies. He ascends the mountain and proclaims the God of Jean-Jacques to the Republic, which hears and weeps. Oh purity! oh sweetness! oh faith! oh antique simplicity! oh tears of pity! oh fertilizing dew! oh clemency! oh human fraternity!

In vain Atheism still lifts its hideous face; Maximilien grasps a torch; flames devour the monster and Wisdom appears, with one hand pointing to the sky, in the other holding a crown of stars.

On the platform raised against the façade of the Tuileries, Évariste, standing amid a throng of deeply-stirred spectators, sheds tears of joy and renders thanks to God. An era of universal felicity opens before his eyes.

He sighs:

"At last we shall be happy, pure, innocent, if the scoundrels suffer it."

Alas! the scoundrels have not suffered it. There must be more executions; more torrents of tainted blood must be shed. Three days after the festival celebrating the new alliance and the reconciliation of heaven and earth, the Convention promulgates the Law of Prairial which suppresses, with a sort of ferocious good-nature, all the traditional forms of Law, whatever has been devised since the time of the Roman jurisconsults for the safeguarding of innocence under suspicion. No more sifting of evidence, no more questioning of the accused, no more witnesses, no more counsel for the defence; love of the fatherland supplies everything that is needful. The prisoner, who bears locked up in his bosom his guilt or innocence, passes without a word allowed before the patriot jury, and it is in this brief moment they must unravel his case, often complicated and obscure. How is justice possible? How distinguish in an instant between the honest man and the villain, the patriot and the enemy of the fatherland...?

Disconcerted for the moment, Gamelin quickly learned his new duties and accommodated himself to his new functions. He recognized that this curtailment of formalities was genuinely characteristic of the new justice, at once salutary and terrifying, the administrators of which were no longer ermined pedants leisurely weighing the *pros* and *contras* in their Gothic balances, but good sansculottes judging by inspiration and seeing the whole truth in a flash. When guarantees and precautions would have undone everything, the impulses of an upright heart saved the situation. We must follow the promptings of Nature, the good mother who never deceives; the heart must teach us to do judgment, and Gamelin made invocation to the manes of Jean-Jacques:

"Man of virtue, inspire me with the love of men, the ardent desire to regenerate humankind!"

His colleagues, for the most part, felt with him. They were, first and foremost, simple people; and when the forms of law were simplified, they felt more comfortable. Justice thus abbreviated satisfied them; the pace was quickened, and no obstacles were left to fret them. They limited themselves to an inquiry into the opinions of the accused, not conceiving it possible that anyone could think differently from themselves except in pure perversity. Believing themselves the exclusive possessors of truth, wisdom, the quintessence of good, they attributed to their opponents nothing but error and evil. They felt themselves all-powerful; they envisaged God.

They saw God, these jurors of the Revolutionary Tribunal. The Supreme Being, acknowledged by Maximilien, flooded them with His flames of light. They loved, they believed.

The chair of the accused had been replaced by a vast platform able to accommodate fifty persons; the court only dealt with batches now. The Public Prosecutor would often confound under the same charge or implicate as accomplices individuals who met each other for the first time before the Tribunal. The latter, taking advantage of the terrible facilities accorded by the law of Prairial, sat in judgment on those supposed prison plots which, coming after the proscriptions of the Dantonists and the Commune, were made to seem their outcome by the insinuations of cunning adversaries. In fact, to let the world appreciate the two essential characteristics of a conspiracy fomented by foreign gold against the Republic,—to wit inopportune moderation on the one hand and self-interested excess of zeal on the other, they had united in the same condemnation two very different women, the widow of Camille Desmoulins, poor lovable Lucille, and the widow of the Hébertist Momoro, goddess of a day and jolly companion all her life. Both, to make the analogy complete, had been shut up in the same prison, where they had mingled their tears on the same bench; both, to round off the resemblance, had climbed the scaffold. Too ingenious the symbol,—a masterpiece of equilibrium, conceived doubtless by a lawyer's brain, and the honour of which was given to Maximilien. This representative of the people was accredited with every eventuality, happy or unhappy, that came about in the Republic, every change that was effected in the laws, in manners and morals, the very course of the seasons, the harvests, the incidence of epidemics. Unjust of course, but not unmerited the injustice, for indeed the man, the little, spruce, cat-faced dandy, was all powerful with the people....

That day the Tribunal was clearing off a batch of prisoners involved in the great plot, thirty or more conspirators from the Luxembourg, submissive enough in gaol, but Royalists or

Federalists of the most pronounced type. The prosecution relied almost entirely on the evidence of a single informer. The jurors did not know one word of the matter,—not so much as the conspirators' names. Gamelin, casting his eye over the prisoners' bench, recognized Fortuné Chassagne among the accused. Julie's lover, pale-faced and emaciated by long confinement and his features showing coarser in the glare of light that flooded the hall, still retained traces of his old grace and proud bearing. His eyes met Gamelin's and filled with scorn.

Gamelin, possessed by a calm fury, rose, asked leave to speak, and, fixing his eyes on the bust of Roman Brutus, which looked down on the Tribunal:

"*Citoyen* President," he said, "although there may exist between one of the accused and myself ties which, if they were made public, would be ties of married kinship, I hereby declare I do not decline to act. The two Bruti did not decline their duty, when for the salvation of the state and the cause of freedom, the one had to condemn a son, the other to strike down an adoptive father."

He resumed his seat.

"A fine scoundrel that," muttered Chassagne between his teeth.

The public remained cold, whether because it was tired of high-flown characters, or thinking that Gamelin had triumphed too easily over his feelings of family affection.

"*Citoyen* Gamelin," said the President, "by the terms of the law, every refusal must be formulated in writing within the twenty-four hours preceding the opening of the trial. In any case, you have no reason to refuse; a patriot jury is superior to human passions."

Each prisoner was questioned for three or four minutes, the examination resulting in a verdict of death in every instance. The jurors voted without a word said, by a nod of the head or by exclamation. When Gamelin's turn came to pronounce his opinion:

"All the accused," he declared, "are convicted, and the law is explicit."

As he was descending the stairway of the Palais de Justice, a young man dressed in a bottle-green box-coat, and who looked seventeen or eighteen years of age, stopped him abruptly as he went by. The lad wore a round hat, tilted on the back of his head, the brim framing his fine pale face in a dark aureole. Facing the juror, in a terrible voice vibrating with passion and despair:

"Villain, monster, murderer!" he screamed. "Strike me, coward! I am a woman! Have me arrested, have me guillotined, Cain! I am your sister,"—and Julie spat in his face.

The throng of *tricoteuses* and *sansculottes* was relaxing by this time in its Revolutionary vigilance; its civic zeal had largely cooled; Gamelin and his assailant found themselves the centre of nothing worse than uproar and confusion. Julie fought a way through the press and disappeared in the dark.

XXIII

Evariste Gamelin was worn out and could not rest; twenty times in the night he would awake with a start from a sleep haunted by nightmares. It was only in the blue chamber, in Élodie's arms, that he could snatch a few hours' slumber. He talked and cried out in his sleep and used often to awake her; but she could make nothing of what he said.

One morning, after a night when he had seen the Eumenides, he started awake, broken with terror and weak as a child. The dawn was piercing the window curtains with its wan arrows. Évariste's hair, lying tangled on his brow, covered his eyes with a black veil; Élodie, by the bedside, was gently parting the wild locks. She was looking at him now, with a sister's tenderness, while with her handkerchief she wiped away the icy sweat from the unhappy man's forehead. Then he remembered that fine scene in the *Orestes* of Euripides, which he had essayed to represent in a picture that, if he could have finished it, would have been his masterpiece—the scene where the unhappy Electra wipes away the spume that sullies her brother's lips. And he seemed to hear Élodie also saying in a gentle voice:

"Hear me, beloved brother, while the Furies leave you master of your reason ..."

And he thought:

"And yet I am no parricide. Far from it, it is filial piety has made me shed the tainted blood of the enemies of my fatherland."

XXIV

There seemed no end to these trials for conspiracy in the prisons. Forty-nine accused crowded the tiers of seats. Maurice Brotteaux occupied the right-hand corner of the topmost row,—the place of honour. He was dressed in his plum-coloured surtout, which he had brushed very carefully the day before and mended at the pocket where his little Lucretius had ended by fretting a hole. Beside him sat the woman Rochemaure, painted and powdered and patched, a brilliant and ghastly figure. They had put the Père Longuemare between her and the girl Athenaïs, who had recovered her look of youthful freshness at the Madelonnettes.

On the platform the gendarmes massed a number of other prisoners unknown to any of our friends, and who, as likely as not, knew nothing of each other,—yet accomplices one and all,— lawyers, journalists, *ci-devant* nobles, citizens, and citizens' wives. The *citoyenne*Rochemaure caught sight of Gamelin on the jurors' bench. He had not answered her urgent letters and repeated messages; still she had not abandoned hope and threw him a look of supplication, trying to appear fascinating and pathetic for him. But the young juror's cold glance robbed her of any illusion she might have entertained.

The Clerk read the act of accusation, which, succinct as was its reference to each individual, was a lengthy document because of the great number accused. It began by exposing in general outline the plot concocted in the prisons to drown the Republic in the blood of the Representatives of the nation and the people of Paris; then, coming to each severally, it went on:

"One of the most mischievous authors of this abominable conspiracy is the man Brotteaux, once known as des Ilettes, receiver of imposts under the tyrant. This person, who was remarkable, even in the days of tyranny, for his libertine behaviour, is a sure proof how dissoluteness and immorality are the greatest enemies of the liberty and happiness of peoples; as a fact, after misappropriating the public revenues and wasting in debauchery a noticeable part of the people's patrimony, the person in question connived with his former concubine, the woman Rochemaure, to enter into correspondence with the *émigrés* and traitorously keep the faction of the foreigner informed of the state of our finances, the movements of our troops, the fluctuations of public opinion.

"Brotteaux, who, at this period of his despicable life, was living in concubinage with a prostitute he had picked up in the mud of the Rue Fromenteau, the girl Athenaïs, easily suborned her to his purposes and made use of her to foment the counterrevolution by impudent and unpatriotic cries and indecent and traitorous speeches.

"Sundry remarks of this ill-omened individual will afford you a clear indication of his abject views and pernicious purpose. Speaking of the patriotic tribunal now called upon to punish him, he declared insultingly,—'The Revolutionary Tribunal is like a play of William Shakespeare, who mixes up with the most bloodthirsty scenes the most trivial buffooneries.' Then he was forever preaching atheism, as the surest means of degrading the people and driving it into immorality. In the prison of the Conciergerie, where he was confined, he used to deplore as among the worst of calamities the victories of our valiant armies, and tried to throw suspicion on the most patriotic Generals, crediting them with designs of tyrannicide. 'Only wait,' he would say in atrocious language which the pen is loath to reproduce, 'only wait till, some day, one of these warriors, to whom you owe your salvation, swallows you all up as the stork in the fable gobbled up the frogs.'

"The woman Rochemaure, a *ci-devant* noble, concubine of Brotteaux, is not less culpable than he. Not only was she in correspondence with the foreigner and in the pay of Pitt himself, but in complicity with swindlers, such as Jullien (of Toulouse) and Chabot, associates of the *ci-devant* Baron de Batz, she seconded that reprobate in all sorts of cunning machinations to depreciate the shares of the Company of the Indies, buy them in at a cheap price, and then raise the quotation by artifices of an opposite tendency, to the confusion and ruin of private fortunes and of the public funds. Incarcerated at La Bourbe and the Madelonnettes, she never ceased in prison to conspire, to dabble in stocks and shares and to devote herself to attempts at corruption, to suborn judges and jury.

"Louis Longuemare, ex-noble, ex-capuchin, had long been practised in infamy and crime before committing the acts of treason for which he has to answer here. Living in a shameful promiscuity with the girl Gorcut, known as Athenaïs, under Brotteaux's very roof, he is the accomplice of the said girl and the said *ci-devant* nobleman. During his imprisonment at the Conciergerie he has never ceased for one single day writing pamphlets aimed at the subversion of public liberty and security.

"It is right to say, with regard to Marthe Gorcut, known as Athenaïs, that prostitutes are the greatest scourge of public morality, which they insult, and the opprobrium of the society which they disgrace. But why speak at length of revolting crimes which the accused confesses shamelessly...?"

The accusation then proceeded to pass in review the fifty-four other prisoners, none of whom either Brotteaux, or the Père Longuemare, or the *citoyenne* Rochemaure, were acquainted with, except for having seen several of them in the prisons, but who were one and all included with the first named in "this odious plot, with which the annals of the nation can furnish nothing to compare."

The piece concluded by demanding the penalty of death for all the culprits.

Brotteaux was the first to be examined:

"You were in the plot?"

"No, I have been in no plots. Every word is untrue in the act of accusation I have just heard read."

"There, you see; you are plotting still, at this moment, to discredit the Tribunal,"—and the President went on to the woman Rochemaure, who answered with despairing protestations of innocence, tears and quibblings.

The Père Longuemare referred himself purely and entirely to God's will. He had not even brought his written defence with him.

All the questions put to him he answered in a spirit of resignation. Only, when the President spoke of him as a Capuchin, did the old Adam wake again in him:

"I am not a Capuchin," he said, "I am a priest and a monk of the Order of the Barnabites."

"It is the same thing," returned the President good-naturedly.

The Père Longuemare looked at him indignantly:

"One cannot conceive a more extraordinary error," he cried, "than to confound with a Capuchin a monk of this Order of the Barnabites which derives its constitutions from the Apostle Paul himself."

The remark was greeted with a burst of laughter and hooting from the spectators, at which the Père Longuemare, taking this derision to betoken a denial of his proposition, announced that he would die a member of this Order of St. Barnabas, the habit of which he wore in his heart.

"Do you admit," asked the President, "entering into plots with the girl Gorcut, known as Athenaïs, the same who accorded you her despicable favours?"

At the question, the Père Longuemare raised his eyes sorrowfully to heaven, but made no answer; his silence expressed the surprise of an unsophisticated mind and the gravity of a man of religion who fears to utter empty words.

"You, the girl Gorcut," the President asked, turning to Athenaïs, "do you admit plotting in conjunction with Brotteaux?"

Her answer was softly spoken:

"Monsieur Brotteaux, to my knowledge, has done nothing but good. He is a man of the sort we should have more of; there is no better sort. Those who say the contrary are mistaken. That is all I have to say."

The President asked her if she admitted having lived in concubinage with Brotteaux. The expression had to be explained to her, as she did not understand it. But, directly she gathered what the question meant, she answered, that would only have depended on him, but he had never asked her.

There was a laugh in the public galleries, and the President threatened the girl Gorcut to refuse her a hearing if she answered in such a cynical sort again.

At this she broke out, calling him sneak, sour face, cuckold, and spewing out over him, judges, and jury a torrent of invective, till the gendarmes dragged her from her bench and hustled her out of the hall.

The President then proceeded to a brief examination of the rest of the accused, taking them in the order in which they sat on the tiers of benches.

One, a man named Navette, pleaded that he could not have plotted in prison where he had only spent four days. The President observed that the point deserved to be considered, and begged the *citoyens* of the jury to make a note of it. A certain Bellier said the same, and the President made the same remark to the jury in his favour. This mildness on the judge's part was interpreted by some as the result of a praiseworthy scrupulosity, by others as payment due in recognition of their talents as informers.

The Deputy of the Public Prosecutor spoke next. All he did was to amplify the details of the act of accusation and then to put the question:

"Is it proven that Maurice Brotteaux, Louise Rochemaure, Louis Longuemare, Marthe Gorcut, known as Athenaïs, Eusèbe Rocher, Pierre Guyton-Fabulet, Marcelline Descourtis, etc., etc., are guilty of forming a conspiracy, the means whereof are assassination, starvation, the making of forged assignats and false coin, the depravation of morals and public spirit; the aim and object, civil war, the abolition of the National representation, the re-establishment of Royalty?"

The jurors withdrew into the chamber of deliberation. They voted unanimously in the affirmative, only excepting the cases of the afore-named Navette and Bellier, whom the President, and following his lead, the Public Prosecutor, had put, as it were, in a separate class by themselves.

Gamelin stated the motives for his decision thus:

"The guilt of the accused is self-evident; the safety of the Nation demands their chastisement, and they ought themselves to desire their punishment as the only means of expiating their crimes."

The President pronounced sentence in the absence of those it concerned. In these great days, contrary to what the law prescribed, the condemned were not called back again to hear their judgment read, no doubt for fear of the effects of despair on so large a number of prisoners. A needless apprehension, so extraordinary and so general was the submissiveness of the victims in those days! The Clerk of the Court came down to the cells to read the verdict, which was listened to with such silence and impassivity as made it a common comparison to liken the condemned of Prairial to trees marked down for felling.

The *citoyenne* Rochemaure declared herself pregnant. A surgeon, who was likewise one of the jury, was directed to see her. She was carried out fainting to her dungeon.

"Ah!" sighed the Père Longuemare, "these judges and jurors are men very deserving of pity; their state of mind is truly deplorable. They mix up everything and confound a Barnabite with a Franciscan."

The execution was to take place the same day at the *Barrière du Trone-Renversé*. The condemned, their toilet completed, hair cropped and shirt cut down at the neck, waited for the headsman, packed like cattle in the small room separated off from the Gaoler's office by a glazed partition.

When presently the executioner and his men arrived, Brotteaux, who was quietly reading his Lucretius, put the marker at the page he had begun, shut the book, stuffed it in the pocket of his coat, and said to the Barnabite:

"What enrages me, Reverend Father, is that I shall never convince you. We are going both of us to sleep our last sleep, and I shall not be able to twitch you by the sleeve and tell you: 'There you see; you have neither sensation nor consciousness left; you are inanimate. What comes after life is like what goes before.'"

He tried to smile; but an atrocious spasm of pain wrung his heart and vitals, and he came near fainting.

He resumed, however:

"Father, I let you see my weakness. I love life and I do not leave it without regret."

"Sir," replied the monk gently, "take heed, you are a braver man than I, and nevertheless death troubles you more. What does that mean, if not that I see the light, which you do not see yet?"

"Might it not also be," said Brotteaux, "that I regret life because I have enjoyed it better than you, who have made it as close a copy of death as possible?"

"Sir," said the Père Longuemare, his face paling, "this is a solemn moment. God help me! It is plain we shall die without spiritual aid. It must be that in other days I have received the sacraments lukewarmly and with a thankless heart, for Heaven to refuse me them to-day, when I have such pressing need of them."

The carts were waiting. The condemned were loaded into them pell-mell, with hands tied. The woman Rochemaure, whose pregnancy had not been verified by the surgeon, was hoisted into one of the tumbrils. She recovered a little of her old energy to watch the crowd of onlookers, hoping against hope to find rescuers amongst them. The throng was less dense than formerly, and the excitement less extreme. Only a few women screamed, "Death! death!" or mocked those who were to die. The men mostly shrugged their shoulders, looked another way, and said nothing, whether out of prudence or from respect of the laws.

A shudder went through the crowd when Athenaïs emerged from the wicket. She looked a mere child.

She bowed her head before the monk:

"Monsieur le Curé," she asked him, "give me absolution."

The Père Longuemare gravely recited the sacramental words in muttered tones; then:

"My daughter!" he added, "you have fallen into great disorders of living; but can I offer the Lord a heart as simple as yours? Would I were sure!"

She climbed lightly into the cart. And there, throwing out her bosom and proudly lifting her girlish head, she cried "Vive le Roi!"

She made a little sign to Brotteaux to show him there was a vacant place beside her. Brotteaux helped the Barnabite to get in and came and placed himself between the monk and the simple-hearted girl.

"Sir," said the Père Longuemare to the Epicurean philosopher, "I ask you a favour; this God in whom you do not yet believe, pray to Him for me. It is far from sure you are not nearer to Him than I am myself; a moment can decide this. A second, and you may be called by the Lord to be His highly favoured son. Sir, pray for me."

While the wheels were grinding over the pavement of the long Faubourg Antoine, the monk was busy, with heart and lips, reciting the prayers of the dying. Brotteaux's mind was fixed on recalling the lines of the poet of nature: *Sic ubi non erimus*.... Bound as he was and shaken in the vile, jolting cart, he preserved his calm and even showed a certain solicitude to maintain an easy posture. At his side, Athenaïs, proud to die like the Queen of France, surveyed the crowd with haughty looks, and the old financier, noting as a connoisseur the girl's white bosom, was filled with regret for the light of day.

XXV

While the carts, escorted by gendarmes, were rumbling along on their way to the Place du Trône Renversé, carrying to their death Brotteaux and his "accomplices," Évariste sat pensive on a bench in the garden of the Tuileries. He was waiting for Élodie. The sun, nearing its setting, shot its fiery darts through the leafy chestnuts. At the gate of the garden, Fame on her winged horse blew her everlasting trumpet. The newspaper hawkers were bawling the news of the great victory of Fleurus.

"Yes," thought Gamelin, "victory is ours. We have paid full price for it."

He could see the beaten Generals, disconsolate shades, trailing in the blood-stained dust of yonder Place de la Révolution where they perished. And he smiled proudly, reflecting that, but for the severities in which he had borne his share, the Austrian horses would to-day be gnawing the bark of the trees beside him.

He soliloquized:

"Life-giving terror, oh! blessed terror! Last year at this time, our heroic defenders were beaten and in rags, the soil of the fatherland was invaded, two-thirds of the departments in revolt. Now our armies, well equipped, well trained, commanded by able generals, are taking the offensive, ready to bear liberty through the world. Peace reigns over all the territory of the Republic.... Life-giving terror, oh! blessed terror! oh! saintly guillotine! Last year at this time, the Republic was torn with factions, the hydra of Federalism threatened to devour her. Now a united Jacobinism spreads over the empire its might and its wisdom...."

Nevertheless, he was gloomy. His brow was deeply lined, his mouth bitter. His thoughts ran: "We used to say: *To conquer or to die.* We were wrong; it is *to conquer and to die* we ought to say."

He looked about him. Children were building sand-castles. *Citoyennes* in their wooden chairs under the trees were sewing or embroidering. The passers-by, in coat and breeches of elegant cut and strange fashion, their thoughts fixed on their business or their pleasures, were making for home. And Gamelin felt himself alone amongst them; he was no compatriot, no contemporary of theirs. What was it had happened? How came the enthusiasm of the great years to have been succeeded by indifference, weariness, perhaps disgust? It was plain to see, these people never wanted to hear the Revolutionary Tribunal spoken of again and averted their eyes from the guillotine. Grown too painful a sight in the Place de la Révolution, it had been banished to the extremity of the Faubourg Antoine. There even, the passage of the tumbrils was greeted with murmurs. Voices, it was said, had been heard to shout: "Enough!"

Enough, when there were still traitors, conspirators! Enough, when the Committees must be reformed, the Convention purged! Enough, when scoundrels disgraced the National representation. Enough, when they were planning the downfall of *The Just!* For, dreadful thought, but only too true! Fouquier himself was weaving plots, and it was to ruin Maximilien that he had sacrificed with solemn ceremony fifty-seven victims haled to death in the red sheet of parricides. France was giving way to pity—and pity was a crime! Then we should have saved her in spite of herself, and when she cried for mercy, stopped our ears and struck! Alas! the fates had decided otherwise; the fatherland was for cursing its saviours. Well, let it curse, if only it may be saved!

"It is not enough to immolate obscure victims, aristocrats, financiers, publicists, poets, a Lavoisier, a Roucher, an André Chénier. We must strike these all-puissant malefactors who, with hands full of gold and dripping with blood, are plotting the ruin of *the Mountain*—the Fouchers, Talliens, Rovères, Carriers, Bourdons. We must deliver the State from all its enemies. If Hébert had triumphed, the Convention was overthrown, the Republic hastening to the abyss; if Desmoulins and Danton had triumphed, the Convention had lost its virtue, ready to surrender the Republic to the aristocrats, the money-jobbers and the Generals. If men like Tallien and Foucher, monsters gorged with blood and rapine, triumph, France is overwhelmed in a welter of crime and infamy ... Robespierre, awake; when criminals, drunken with fury and affright, plan your death and the death of freedom! Couthon, Saint-Just, make haste; why tarry ye to denounce the plots?

"Why! the old-time state, the Royal monster, assured its empire by imprisoning every year four hundred thousand persons, by hanging fifteen thousand, by breaking three thousand on the wheel—and the Republic still hesitates to sacrifice a few hundred heads for its security and domination! Let us drown in blood and save the fatherland...."

He was buried in these thoughts when Élodie hurried up to him, pale-faced and distraught:

"Évariste, what have you to say to me? Why not come to the *Amour peintre* to the blue chamber? Why have you made me come here?"

"To bid you an eternal farewell."

He had lost his wits, she faltered, she could not understand....

He stopped her with a very slight movement of the hand:

"Élodie, I cannot any more accept your love."

She begged him to walk on further; people could see them, overhear them, where they were.

He moved on a score of yards, and resumed, very quietly:

"I have made sacrifices to my country of my life and my honour. I shall die infamous; I shall have naught to leave you, unhappy girl, save an execrated memory.... We, love? Can anyone love me still?... Can I love?"

She told him he was mad; that she loved him, that she would always love him. She was ardent, sincere; but she felt as well as he, she felt better than he, that he was right. But she fought against the evidence of her senses.

He went on:

"I blame myself for nothing. What I have done, I would do again. I have made myself anathema for my country's sake. I am accursed. I have put myself outside humanity; I shall never re-enter its pale. No, the great task is not finished. Oh! clemency, forgiveness!—Do the traitors forgive? Are the conspirators clement? scoundrels, parricides multiply unceasingly; they spring up from underground, they swarm in from all our frontiers,—young men, who would have done better to perish with our armies, old men, children, women, with every mark of innocence, purity, and grace. They are offered up a sacrifice,—and more victims are ready for the knife!... You can see, Élodie, I must needs renounce love, renounce all joy, all sweetness of life, renounce life itself."

He fell silent. Born to taste tranquil joys, Élodie not for the first time was appalled to find, under the tragic kisses of a lover like Évariste, her voluptuous transports blended with images of horror and bloodshed; she offered no reply. To Évariste the girl's silence was as a draught of a bitter chalice.

"Yes, you can see, Élodie, we are on a precipice; our deeds devour us. Our days, our hours are years. I shall soon have lived a century. Look at this brow! Is it a lover's? Love!..."

"Évariste, you are mine, I will not let you go; I will not give you back your freedom."

She was speaking in the language of sacrifice. He felt it; she felt it herself.

"Will you be able, Élodie, one day to bear witness that I lived faithful to my duty, that my heart was upright and my soul unsullied, that I knew no passion but the public good; that I was born to feel and love? Will you say: 'He did his duty'? But no! You will not say it and I do not ask you to say it. Perish my memory! My glory is in my own heart; shame beleaguers me about. If you love me, never speak my name; eternal silence is best."

A child of eight or nine, trundling its hoop, ran just then between Gamelin's legs.

He lifted the boy suddenly in his arms:

"Child, you will grow up free, happy, and you will owe it to the infamous Gamelin. I am ferocious, that you may be happy. I am cruel, that you may be kind; I am pitiless, that to-morrow all Frenchmen may embrace with tears of joy."

He pressed the child to his breast.

"Little one, when you are a man, you will owe your happiness, your innocence to me; and, if ever you hear my name uttered, you will execrate it."

Then he put down the child, which ran away in terror to cling to its mother's skirts, who had hurried up to the rescue. The young mother, who was pretty and charming in her aristocratic grace, with her gown of white lawn, carried off the boy with a haughty look.

Gamelin turned his eyes on Élodie:

"I have held the child in my arms; perhaps I shall send the mother to the guillotine,"—and he walked away with long strides under the ordered trees.

Élodie stood a moment motionless, her eyes fixed on the ground. Then, suddenly, she darted after her lover, and frenzied, dishevelled, like a Mænad, she gripped him as if to tear him in pieces and cried in a voice choked with blood and tears:

"Well, then! me too, my beloved, send me to the guillotine; me too, lay me under the knife!"

And, at the thought of the knife at her neck, all her flesh melted in an ecstasy of horror and voluptuous transport.

XXVI

The sun of Thermidor was setting in a blood-red sky, while Évariste wandered, gloomy and careworn, in the Marbeuf gardens, now a National park frequented by the Parisian idlers. There were stalls for the sale of lemonade and ices; wooden horses and shooting-galleries were provided for the younger patriots. Under a tree, a little Savoyard in rags, with a black cap on his head, was making a marmot dance to the shrill notes of his hurdy-gurdy. A man, still young, slim-waisted, wearing a blue coat and his hair powdered, with a big dog at his heels, stopped to listen to the rustic music. Évariste recognized Robespierre. He found him paler, thinner, his face harder and drawn in folds of suffering. He thought to himself:

"What fatigues, how many griefs have left their imprint on his brow! How grievous a thing it is to work for the happiness of mankind! What are his thoughts at this moment? Does the sound of this mountain music perhaps distract him from the cares of government? Is he thinking that he has made a pact with Death and that the hour of reckoning is coming close? Is he dreaming of a triumphant return to the Committee of Public Safety, from which he withdrew, weary of being held in check, with Couthon and Saint-Just, by a seditious majority? Behind that impenetrable countenance what hopes are seething or what fears?"

But Maximilien smiled at the lad, in a gentle, kind voice asked him several questions about his native valley, the humble home and parents the poor child had left behind, tossed him a small piece of silver and resumed his stroll. After taking a few steps, he turned round again to call his dog; sniffing at the marmot, it was showing its teeth at the little creature that bristled up in defiance.

"To heel, Brount!" he called, "to heel!"—and he plunged among the dark trees.

Gamelin, out of respect, did not interrupt his lonely walk; but, as he gazed after the slender form disappearing in the darkness, he mentally addressed his hero in these impassioned words:

"I have seen thy sadness, Maximilien; I have understood thy thought. Thy melancholy, thy fatigue, even the look of fear that stamps thy face, everything says: 'Let the reign of terror end and that of fraternity begin! Frenchmen, be united, be virtuous, be good and kind. Love ye one another....' Well then, I will second your designs; that you, in your wisdom and goodness, may be able to put an end to our civil discord, to our fratricidal hate, turn the headsman into a gardener who will henceforth cut off only the heads of cabbages and lettuces. I will pave the way with my colleagues of the Tribunal that must lead to clemency by exterminating conspirators and traitors. We will redouble our vigilance and our severity. No culprit shall escape us. And when the head of the last enemy of the Republic shall have fallen under the knife, then it will be given thee to be merciful without committing a crime, then thou canst inaugurate the reign of innocence and virtue in all the land, oh! father of thy country!"

The Incorruptible was already almost out of sight. Two men in round hats and nankeen breeches, one of whom, a tall, lean man of a wild, unkempt aspect, had a blur on one eye and resembled Tallien, met him at the corner of an avenue, looked at him askance and passed on, pretending not to recognize him. When they had gone far enough to be out of hearing, they muttered under their breath:

"So there he goes, the King, the Pope, the God. For he is God; and Catherine Théot is his prophetess."

"Dictator, traitor, tyrant! the race of Brutus is not extinct."

"Tremble, malefactor! the Tarpeian rock is near the Capitol!"

The dog Brount ran towards the pair. They said no more and quickened their pace.

XXVII

Robespierre, awake! The hour is come, time presses,... soon it will be too late....

At last, on the 8 Thermidor, in the Convention, the Incorruptible rises, he is going to speak. Sun of the 31st May, is this to be a second day-spring? Gamelin waits and hopes. His mind is made up then! Robespierre is to drag from the benches they dishonour these legislators more guilty than the federalists, more dangerous than Danton.... No! not yet. "I cannot," he says, "resolve to clear away entirely the veil that hides this mystery of iniquity."

It is mere summer lightning that flashes harmlessly and without striking any one of the conspirators, terrifies all. Sixty of them at least for a fortnight had not dared sleep in their beds. Marat's way was to denounce traitors by their name, to point the finger of accusation at conspirators. The Incorruptible hesitates, and from that moment he is the accused....

That evening at the Jacobins, the hall is filled to suffocation, the corridors, the courtyard are crowded.

They are all there, loud-voiced friends and silent enemies. Robespierre reads them the speech the Convention had heard in affrighted silence, and the Jacobins greet it with excited applause.

"It is my dying testament," declares the orator. "You will see me drain the hemlock undismayed."

"I will drink it with you," answered David.

"All, we all will!" shout the Jacobins, and separate without deciding anything.

Évariste, while the death of *The Just* was preparing, slept the sleep of the Disciples in the garden of Gethsemane. Next day, he attended the Tribunal where two sections were sitting. That on which he served was trying twenty-one persons implicated in the conspiracy of the Lazare prison. The case was still proceeding when the tidings arrived:

"The Convention, after a six-hours' session, has decreed Maximilien Robespierre accused,—with him Couthon and Saint-Just; add Augustin Robespierre, and Lebas, who have demanded to share the lot of the accused. The five outlaws stand at the bar of the house."

News is brought that the President of the Section sitting in the next court, the *citoyen* Dumas, has been arrested on the bench, but that the case goes on. Drums can be heard beating the alarm, and the tocsin peals from the churches.

Évariste is still in his place when he is handed an order from the Commune to proceed to the Hôtel de Ville to sit in the General Council. To the sound of the rolling drums and clanging church bells, he and his colleagues record their verdict; then he hurries home to embrace his mother and snatch up his scarf of office. The Place de Thionville is deserted. The Section is afraid to declare either for or against the Convention. Wayfarers creep along under the walls, slip down side-streets, sneak indoors. The call of the tocsin and alarm-drums is answered by the noise of barring shutters and bolting doors. The *citoyen* Dupont senior has secreted himself in his shop; Remacle the porter is barricaded in his lodge. Little Joséphine holds Mouton tremblingly in her arms. The widow Gamelin bemoans the dearness of victuals, cause of all the trouble. At the foot of the stairs Évariste encounters Élodie; she is panting for breath and her black locks are plastered on her hot cheek.

"I have been to look for you at the Tribunal; but you had just left. Where are you going?"

"To the Hôtel de Ville."

"Don't go there! It would be your ruin; Hanriot is arrested ... the Sections will not stir. The *Section des Piques*, Robespierre's Section, will do nothing, I know it for a fact; my father belongs to it. If you go to the Hôtel de Ville, you are throwing away your life for nothing."

"You wish me to be a coward?"

"No! the brave thing is to be faithful to the Convention and to obey the Law."

"The law is dead when malefactors triumph."

"Évariste, hear me; hear your Élodie; hear your sister. Come and sit beside her and let her soothe your angry spirit."

He looked at her; never had she seemed so desirable in his eyes; never had her voice sounded so seductive, so persuasive in his ears.

"A couple of paces, only a couple of paces, dear Évariste!"—and she drew him towards the raised platform on which stood the pedestal of the overthrown statue. It was surrounded by benches occupied by strollers of both sexes. A dealer in fancy articles was offering his laces, a seller of cooling drinks, his portable cistern on his back, was tinkling his bell; little girls were showing off their airs and graces. The parapet was lined with anglers, standing, rod in hand, very still. The weather was stormy, the sky overcast. Gamelin leant on the low wall and looked down on the islet below, pointed like the prow of a ship, listening to the wind whistling in the tree-tops, and feeling his soul penetrated with an infinite longing for peace and solitude.

Like a sweet echo of his thoughts, Élodie's voice sighed in his ear:

"Do you remember, Évariste, how, at sight of the green fields, you wanted to be a country justice in a village? Yes, that would be happiness."

But above the rustling of the trees and the girl's voice, he could hear the tocsin and alarm-drums, the distant tramp of horses, and rumbling of cannon along the streets.

Two steps from them a young man, who was talking to an elegantly attired *citoyenne*, remarked:

"Have you heard the latest?... The Opera is installed in the Rue de la Loi."

Meantime the news was spreading; Robespierre's name was spoken, but in a shuddering whisper, for men feared him still. Women, when they heard the muttered rumour of his fall, concealed a smile.

Évariste Gamelin seized Élodie's hand, but dropped it again swiftly next moment:

"Farewell! I have involved you in my hideous fortunes, I have blasted your life for ever. Farewell! I pray you may forget me!"

"Whatever you do," she warned him, "do not go back home to-night. Come to the *Amour peintre*. Do not ring; throw a pebble at my shutters. I will come and open the door to you myself; I will hide you in the loft."

"You shall see me return triumphant, or you shall never see me more. Farewell!"

On nearing the Hôtel de Ville, he caught the well-remembered roar of the old great days rising to the grey heavens. In the Place de Grève a clash of arms, the glitter of scarfs and uniforms, Hanriot's cannon drawn up. He mounts the grand stairs and, entering the Council Hall, signs the attendance book. The Council General of the Commune, by the unanimous voice of the 491 members present, declares for the outlawed patriots.

The Mayor sends for the Table of the Rights of Man, reads the clause which runs, "When the Government violates the Rights of the people, insurrection is for the people the most sacred and the most indispensable of duties," and the first magistrate of Paris announces that the Commune's answer to the Convention's act of violence is to raise the populace in insurrection.

The members of the Council General take oath to die at their posts. Two municipal officers are deputed to go out on the Place de Grève and invite the people to join with their magistrates in saving the fatherland and freedom.

There is an endless looking for friends, exchanging news, giving advice. Among these Magistrates, artisans are the exception. The Commune assembled here is such as the Jacobin purge has made it,—judges and jurors of the Revolutionary Tribunal, artists like Beauvallet and Gamelin, householders living on their means and college professors, cosy citizens, well-to-do tradesmen, powdered heads, fat paunches, and gold watch-chains, very few sabots, striped trousers, carmagnole smocks and red caps.

These bourgeois councillors are numerous and determined, but, when all is said, they are pretty well all Paris possesses of true Republicans. They stand on guard in the city mansion-house, as on a rock of liberty, but an ocean of indifference washes round their refuge.

However, good news arrives. All the prisons where the proscribed had been confined open their doors and disgorge their prey. Augustin Robespierre, coming from La Force, is the first to enter the Hôtel de Ville and is welcomed with acclamation.

At eight o'clock it is announced that Maximilien, after a protracted resistance, is on his way to the Commune. He is eagerly expected; he is coming; he is here; a roar of triumph shakes the vault of the old Municipal Palace.

He enters, supported by twenty arms. It is he, the little man there, slim, spruce, in blue coat and yellow breeches. He takes his seat; he speaks.

At his arrival the Council orders the façade of the Hôtel de Ville to be illuminated there and then. It is there the Republic resides. He speaks in a thin voice, in picked phrases. He speaks lucidly, copiously. His hearers who have staked their lives on his head, see the naked truth, see it to their horror. He is a man of words, a man of committees, a wind-bag incapable of prompt action, incompetent to lead a Revolution.

They draw him into the Hall of Deliberation. Now they are all there, these illustrious outlaws, —Lebas, Saint-Just, Couthon. Robespierre has the word. It is midnight and past, he is still speaking. Meantime Gamelin in the Council Hall, his bent brow pressed against a window, looks out with a haggard eye and sees the lamps flare and smoke in the gloom. Hanriot's cannon are parked before the Hôtel de Ville. In the black Place de Grève surges an anxious crowd, in uncertainty and suspense. At half past twelve torches are seen turning the corner of the Rue de la Vannerie, escorting a delegate of the Convention, clad in the insignia of office, who unfolds a paper and reads by the ruddy light the decree of the Convention, the outlawry of the members of the insurgent Commune, of the members of the Council General who are its abettors and of all such citizens as shall listen to its appeal.

Outlawry, death without trial! The mere thought pales the cheek of the most determined. Gamelin feels the icy sweat on his brow. He watches the crowd hurrying with all speed from the Place. Turning his head, he finds that the Hall, packed but now with Councillors, is almost empty. But they have fled in vain; their signatures attest their attendance.

It is two in the morning. The Incorruptible is in the neighbouring Hall, in deliberation with the Commune and the proscribed representatives.

Gamelin casts a despairing look over the dark Square below. By the light of the lanterns he can see the wooden candles above the grocer's shop knocking together like ninepins; the street lamps shiver and swing; a high wind has sprung up. Next moment a deluge of rain comes down; the Place empties entirely; such as the fear of the Convention and its dread decree had not put to flight scatter in terror of a wetting. Hanriot's guns are abandoned, and when the lightning reveals the troops of the Convention debouching simultaneously from the Rue Antoine and from the Quai, the approaches to the Hôtel de Ville are utterly deserted.

At last Maximilien has resolved to make appeal from the decree of the Convention to his own Section,—the *Section des Piques.*

The Council General sends for swords, pistols, muskets. But now the clash of arms, the trampling of feet and the shiver of broken glass fill the building. The troops of the Convention sweep by like an avalanche across the Hall of Deliberation, and pour into the Council Chamber. A shot rings out; Gamelin sees Robespierre fall; his jaw is broken. He himself grasps his knife, the six-sous knife that, one day of bitter scarcity, had cut bread for a starving mother, the same knife that, one summer evening at a farm at Orangis, Élodie had held in her lap, when she cried the forfeits. He opens it, tries to plunge it into his heart, but the blade strikes on a rib, closes on the handle, the catch giving way, and two fingers are badly cut. Gamelin falls, the blood pouring from the wounds. He lies quite still, but the cold is cruel, and he is trampled underfoot in the turmoil of a fearful struggle. Through the hurly-burly he can distinctly hear the voice of the young dragoon Henry, shouting:

"The tyrant is no more; his myrmidons are broken. The Revolution will resume its course, majestic and terrible."

Gamelin fainted.

At seven in the morning a surgeon sent by the Convention dressed his hurts. The Convention was full of solicitude for Robespierre's accomplices; it would fain not have one of them escape the guillotine.

The artist, ex-juror, ex-member of the Council General of the Commune, was borne on a litter to the Conciergerie.

XXVIII

On the 10th, when Évariste, after a fevered night passed on the pallet-bed of a dungeon, awoke with a start of indescribable horror, Paris was smiling in the sunshine in all her beauty and immensity; new-born hope filled the prisoners' hearts; tradesmen were blithely opening their shops, citizens felt themselves richer, young men happier, women more beautiful, for the fall of Robespierre. Only a handful of Jacobins, a few *Constitutional* priests and a few old women trembled to see the Government pass into the hands of the evil-minded and corrupt. Delegates from the Revolutionary Tribunal, the Public Prosecutor and two judges, were on their way to the Convention to congratulate it on having put an end to the plots. By decree of the Assembly the scaffold was again to be set up in the Place de la Révolution. They wanted the wealthy, the fashionable, the pretty women to see, without putting themselves about, the execution of Robespierre, which was to take place that same day. The Dictator and his accomplices were outlawed; it only needed their identity to be verified by two municipal officers for the Tribunal to hand them over immediately to the executioner. But a difficulty arose; the verifications could not be made in legal form, the Commune as a body having been put outside the pale of law. The Assembly authorized identification by ordinary witnesses.

The triumvirs were haled to death, with their chief accomplices, amidst shouts of joy and fury, imprecations, laughter and dances.

The next day Évariste, who had recovered some strength and could almost stand on his legs, was taken from his cell, brought before the Tribunal, and placed on the platform where so many victims, illustrious or obscure, had sat in succession. Now it groaned under the weight of seventy individuals, the majority members of the Commune, some jurors, like Gamelin, outlawed like him. Again he saw the jury-bench, the seat where he had been accustomed to loll, the place where he had terrorized unhappy prisoners, where he had affronted the scornful eyes of Jacques Maubel and Maurice Brotteaux, the appealing glances of the *citoyenne* Rochemaure, who had got him his post as juryman and whom he had recompensed with a sentence of death. Again he saw, looking down on the daïs where the judges sat in three mahogany armchairs, covered in red Utrecht velvet, the busts of Chalier and Marat and that bust of Brutus which he had one day apostrophized. Nothing was altered, neither the axes, the fasces, the red caps of Liberty on the wall-paper, nor the insults shouted by the *tricoteuses* in the galleries to those about to die, nor yet the soul of Fouquier-Tinville, hard-headed, painstaking, zealously turning over his murderous papers, and, in his character of perfect magistrate, sending his friends of yesterday to the scaffold.

The *citoyens* Remacle, tailor and door-keeper, and Dupont senior, joiner, of the Place de Thionville, member of the Committee of Surveillance of the Section du Pont-Neuf, identified Gamelin (Évariste), painter, ex-juror of the Revolutionary Tribunal, ex-member of the Council General of the Commune. For their services they received an assignat of a hundred *sols* from the funds of the Section; but, having been neighbours and friends of the outlaw, they found it embarrassing to meet his eye. Anyhow, it was a hot day; they were thirsty and in a hurry to be off and drink a glass of wine.

Gamelin found difficulty in mounting the tumbril; he had lost a great deal of blood and his wounds pained him cruelly. The driver whipped up his jade and the procession got under way amid a storm of hooting.

Some women recognized Gamelin and yelled:

"Go your ways, drinker of blood! murderer at eighteen francs a day!... He doesn't laugh now; look how pale he is, the coward!"

They were the same women who used in other days to insult conspirators and aristocrats, extremists and moderates, all the victims sent by Gamelin and his colleagues to the guillotine.

The cart turned into the Quai des Morfondus, made slowly for the Pont-Neuf and the Rue de la Monnaie; its destination was the Place de la Révolution and Robespierre's scaffold. The horse was lame; every other minute the driver's whip whistled about its ears. The crowd of spectators, a merry, excited crowd, delayed the progress of the escort, fraternizing with the gendarmes, who pulled in their horses to a walk. At the corner of the Rue Honoré, the insults were redoubled. Parties of young men, at table in the fashionable restaurateurs' rooms on the mezzanine floor, ran to the windows, napkin in hand, and howled:

"Cannibals, man-eaters, vampires!"

The cart having plunged into a heap of refuse that had not been removed during the two days of civil disorder, the gilded youth screamed with delight:

"The waggon's mired.... Hurrah! The Jacobins in the jakes!"

Gamelin was thinking, and truth seemed to dawn on him.

"I die justly," he reflected. "It is just we should receive these outrages cast at the Republic, for we should have safeguarded her against them. We have been weak; we have been guilty of supineness. We have betrayed the Republic. We have earned our fate. Robespierre himself, the immaculate, the saint, has sinned from mildness, mercifulness; his faults are wiped out by his martyrdom. He was my exemplar, and I, too, have betrayed the Republic; the Republic perishes; it is just and fair that I die with her. I have been over sparing of blood; let my blood flow! Let me perish! I have deserved ..."

Such were his reflections when suddenly he caught sight of the signboard of the *Amour peintre*, and a torrent of bitter-sweet emotions swept tumultuously over his heart.

The shop was shut, the sun-blinds of the three windows on the mezzanine floor were drawn right down. As the cart passed in front of the window of the blue chamber, a woman's hand, wearing a silver ring on the ring-finger, pushed aside the edge of the blind and threw towards Gamelin a red carnation which his bound hands prevented him from catching, but which he adored as the token and likeness of those red and fragrant lips that had refreshed his mouth. His eyes filled with bursting tears, and his whole being was still entranced with the glamour of this farewell when he saw the blood-stained knife rise into view in the Place de la Révolution.

XXIX

It was Nivôse. Masses of floating ice encumbered the Seine; the basins in the Tuileries garden, the kennels, the public fountains were frozen. The North wind swept clouds of hoar frost before it in the streets. A white steam breathed from the horses' noses, and the city folk would glance in passing at the thermometer at the opticians' doors. A shop-boy was wiping the fog from the window-panes of the *Amour peintre*, while curious passers-by threw a look at the prints in vogue,—Robespierre squeezing into a cup a heart like a pumpkin to drink the blood, and ambitious allegorical designs with such titles as the Tigrocracy of Robespierre; it was all hydras, serpents, horrid monsters let loose on France by the tyrant. Other pictures represented the Horrible Conspiracy of Robespierre, Robespierre's Arrest, The Death of Robespierre.

That day, after the midday dinner, Philippe Desmahis walked into the *Amour peintre*, his portfolio under his arm, and brought the *citoyen*Jean Blaise a plate he had just finished, a stippled engraving of the Suicide of Robespierre. The artist's picaresque burin had made Robespierre as hideous as possible. The French people were not yet satiated with all the memorials which enshrined the horror and opprobrium felt for the man who was made scapegoat of all the crimes of the Revolution. For all that, the printseller, who knew his public, informed Desmahis that henceforward he was going to give him military subjects to engrave.

"We shall all be wanting victories and conquests,—swords, waving plumes, triumphant generals. Glory is to be the word. I feel it in me; my heart beats high to hear the exploits of our valiant armies. And when I have a feeling, it is seldom all the world doesn't have the same feeling at the same time. What we want is warriors and women, Mars and Venus."

"*Citoyen* Blaise, I have still two or three drawings of Gamelin's by me, which you gave me to engrave. Is it urgent?"

"Not a bit."

"By-the-bye, about Gamelin; yesterday, strolling in the Boulevard du Temple, I saw at a dealer's, who keeps a second-hand stall opposite the House of Beaumarchais, all that poor devil's canvases, amongst the rest his *Orestes and Electra*. The head of Orestes, who's like Gamelin, is really fine, I assure you.... The head and arm are superb.... The man told me he found no difficulty in getting rid of these canvases to artists who want to paint over them.... Poor Gamelin! He might have been a genius of the first order, perhaps, if he hadn't taken to politics."

258

"He had the soul of a criminal!" replied the *citoyen* Blaise. "I unmasked him, on this very spot, when his sanguinary instincts were still held in check. He never forgave me.... Oh! he was a choice blackguard."

"Poor fellow! he was sincere enough. It was the fanatics were his ruin."

"You don't defend him, I presume, Desmahis!... There's no defending him."

"No, *citoyen* Blaise, there's no defending him."

The *citoyen* Blaise tapped the gallant Desmahis' shoulder amicably, and observed:

"Times are changed. We can call you *Barbaroux* now the Convention is recalling the proscribed.... Now I think of it, Desmahis, engrave me a portrait of Charlotte Corday, will you?"

A woman, a tall, handsome brunette, enveloped in furs, entered the shop and bestowed on the *citoyen* Blaise a little discreet nod that implied intimacy. It was Julie Gamelin; but she no longer bore that dishonoured name, she preferred to be called the *citoyenne* widow Chassagne, and wore, under her mantle, a red tunic in honour of the red shirts of the terror. Julie had at first felt a certain repulsion towards Évariste's mistress; anything that had come near her brother was odious to her. But the *citoyenne* Blaise, after Évariste's death, had found an asylum for the unhappy mother in the attics of the *Amour peintre*. Julie had also taken refuge there; then she had got employment again at the fashionable milliner's in the Rue des Lombards. Her short hair *à la victime*, her aristocratic looks, her mourning weeds had won the sympathies of the gilded youth. Jean Blaise, whom Rose Thévenin had pretty well thrown over, offered her his homage, which she accepted. Still Julie was fond of wearing men's clothes, as in the old tragic days; she had a fine *Muscadin* costume made for her and often went, huge bâton and all complete, to sup at some tavern at Sèvres or Meudon with a girl friend, a little assistant in a fashion shop. Inconsolable for the loss of the young noble whose name she bore, this masculine-minded Julie found the only solace to her melancholy in a savage rancour; every time she encountered Jacobins, she would set the passers-by on them, crying "Death, death!" She had small leisure left to give to her mother, who alone in her room told her beads all day, too deeply shocked at her boy's tragic death to feel the grief that might have been expected. Rose was now the constant companion of Élodie who certainly got on amicably with her step-mothers.

"Where is Élodie?" asked the *citoyenne* Chassagne.

Jean Blaise shook his head; he did not know. He never did know; he made it a point of honour not to.

Julie had come to take her friend with her to see Rose Thévenin at Monceaux, where the actress lived in a little house with an English garden.

At the Conciergerie Rose Thévenin had made the acquaintance of a big army-contractor, the *citoyen* Montfort. She had been released first, by Jean Blaise's intervention, and had then procured the *citoyen* Montfort's pardon, who was no sooner at liberty than he started his old trade of provisioning the troops, to which he added speculation in building-lots in the Pépinière quarter. The architects Ledoux, Olivier and Wailly were erecting pretty houses in that district, and in three months the land had trebled in value. Montfort, since their imprisonment together in the Luxembourg, had been Rose Thévenin's lover; he now gave her a little house in the neighbourhood of Tivoli and the Rue du Rocher, which was very expensive,—and cost him nothing, the sale of the adjacent properties having already repaid him several times over. Jean Blaise was a man of the world, so he deemed it best to put up with what he could not hinder; he gave up Mademoiselle Thévenin to Montfort without ceasing to be on friendly terms with her.

Julie had not been long at the *Amour peintre* before Élodie came down to her in the shop, looking like a fashion plate. Under her mantle, despite the rigours of the season, she wore nothing but her white frock; her face was even paler than of old, and her figure thinner; her looks were languishing, and her whole person breathed voluptuous invitation.

The two women set off for Rose Thévenin's, who was expecting them. Desmahis accompanied them; the actress was consulting him about the decoration of her new house and he was in love with Élodie, who had by this time half made up her mind to let him sigh no more in vain. When the party came near Monceaux, where the victims of the Place de la Révolution lay buried under a layer of lime:

"It is all very well in the cold weather," remarked Julie; "but in the spring the exhalations from the ground there will poison half the town."

Rose Thévenin received her two friends in a drawing-room furnished *à l'antique*, the sofas and armchairs of which were designed by David. Roman bas-reliefs, copied in monochrome, adorned the walls above statues, busts and candelabra of imitation bronze. She wore a curled wig of a straw colour. At that date wigs were all the rage; it was quite common to include half a dozen, a dozen, a dozen and a half in a bride's trousseau. A gown *à la Cyprienne* moulded her body like a sheath. Throwing a cloak over her shoulders, she led her two friends and the engraver into the garden, which Ledoux was laying out for her, but which as yet was a chaos of leafless trees and plaster. She showed them, however, Fingal's grotto, a gothic chapel with a bell, a temple, a torrent.

"There," she said, pointing to a clump of firs, "I should like to raise a cenotaph to the memory of the unfortunate Brotteaux des Ilettes. I was not indifferent to him; he was a lovable man. The monsters slaughtered him; I bewailed his fate. Desmahis, you shall design me an urn on a column."

Then she added almost without a pause:

"It is heart-breaking.... I wanted to give a ball this week; but all the fiddles are engaged three weeks in advance. There is dancing every night at the *citoyenne* Tallien's."

After dinner Mademoiselle Thévenin's carriage took the three friends and Desmahis to the Théâtre Feydeau. All that was most elegant in Paris was gathered in the house—the women with hair dressed *à l'antique* or *à la victime*, in very low dresses, purple or white and spangled with gold, the men wearing very tall black collars and the chin disappearing in enormous white cravats.

The bill announced *Phèdre* and the *Chien du Jardinier*,—The Gardener's Dog. With one voice the audience demanded the hymn dear to the *muscadins* and the gilded youth, the *Réveil du peuple*,—The Awakening of the People.

The curtain rose and a little man, short and fat, took the stage; it was the celebrated Lays. He sang in his fine tenor voice:

Peuple français, peuple de frères!...

Such storms of applause broke out as set the lustres of the chandelier jingling. Then some murmurs made themselves heard, and the voice of a citizen in a round hat answered from the pit with the hymn of the Marseillaise:

Allons, enfants de la patrie....

The voice was drowned by howls, and shouts were raised:

"Down with the Terrorists! Death to the Jacobins!"

Lays was recalled and sang a second time over the hymn of the Thermidorians.

Peuple français, peuple de frères!...

In every play-house was to be seen the bust of Marat, surmounting a column or raised on a pedestal; at the Théâtre Feydeau this bust stood on a dwarf pillar on the "prompt" side, against the masonry-framing in the stage.

While the orchestra was playing the Overture of *Phèdre et Hippolyte*, a young *Muscadin*, pointing his cane at the bust, shouted:

"Down with Marat!"—and the whole house took up the cry: "Down with Marat! Down with Marat!"

Urgent voices rose above the uproar:

"It is a black shame that bust should still be there!"

"The infamous Marat lords it everywhere, to our dishonour! His busts are as many as the heads he wanted to cut off."

"Venomous toad!"

"Tiger!"

"Vile serpent!"

Suddenly an elegantly dressed spectator clambers on to the edge of his box, pushes the bust, oversets it. The plaster head falls in shivers on the musicians' heads amid the cheers of the audience, who spring to their feet and strike up the *Réveil du Peuple*:

Peuple français, peuple de frères!...

Among the most enthusiastic singers Élodie recognized the handsome dragoon, the little lawyer's clerk, Henry, her first love.

After the performance the gallant Desmahis called a cabriolet and escorted the *citoyenne* Blaise back to the *Amour peintre*.

In the carriage the artist took Élodie's hand between his:

"You know, Élodie, I love you?"

"I know it, because you love all women."

"I love them in you."

She smiled:

"I should be assuming a heavy task, spite of the wigs black, blonde and red, that are the rage, if I undertook to be all women, all sorts of women, for you."

"Élodie, I swear...."

"What! oaths, *citoyen* Desmahis? Either you have a deal of simplicity, or you credit me with overmuch."

Desmahis had not a word to say, and she hugged herself over the triumph of having reduced her witty admirer to silence.

At the corner of the Rue de la Loi they heard singing and shouting and saw shadows flitting round a brazier of live coals. It was a band of young bloods who had just come out of the Théâtre Français and were burning a guy representing the Friend of the People.

In the Rue Honoré the coachman struck his cocked hat against a burlesque effigy of Marat swinging from the cord of a street lantern.

The fellow, heartened by the incident, turned round to his fares and told them how, only last night, the tripe-seller in the Rue Montorgueil had smeared blood over Marat's head, declaring: "That's the stuff he liked," and how some little scamps of ten had thrown the bust into the sewer, and how the spectators had hit the nail on the head, shouting:

"That's the Panthéon for him!"

Meanwhile, from every eating-house and restaurateur's voices could be heard singing:

Peuple français, peuple de frères!...

"Good-bye," said Élodie, jumping out of the cabriolet.

But Desmahis begged so hard, he was so tenderly urgent and spoke so sweetly, that she had not the heart to leave him at the door.

"It is late," she said; "you must only stay an instant."

In the blue chamber she threw off her mantle and appeared in her white gown *à l'antique*, which displayed all the warm fulness of her shape.

"You are cold, perhaps," she said, "I will light the fire; it is already laid."

She struck the flint and put a lighted match to the fire.

Philippe took her in his arms with the gentleness that bespeaks strength, and she felt a strange, delicious thrill. She was already yielding beneath his kisses when she snatched herself from his arms, crying:

262

"Let me be."

Slowly she uncoiled her hair before the chimney-glass; then she looked mournfully at the ring she wore on the ring-finger of her left hand, a little silver ring on which the face of Marat, all worn and battered, could no longer be made out. She looked at it till the tears confused her sight, took it off softly and tossed it into the flames.

Then, her face shining with tears and smiles, transfigured with tenderness and passion, she threw herself into Philippe's arms.

The night was far advanced when the *citoyenne* Blaise opened the outer door of the flat for her lover and whispered to him in the darkness:

"Good-bye, sweetheart! It is the hour my father will be coming home. If you hear a noise on the stairs, go up quick to the higher floor and don't come down till all danger is over of your being seen. To have the street-door opened, give three raps on the *concierge's* window. Good-bye, my life, good-bye, my soul!"

The last dying embers were glowing on the hearth when Élodie, tired and happy, dropped her head on the pillow.

THE END

The White Stone

A FEW Frenchmen, united in friendship, who were spending the spring in Rome, were wont to meet amid the ruins of the disinterred Forum. They were Joséphin Leclerc, an Embassy Attaché on leave; M. Goubin, licencié ès lettres, an annotator; Nicole Langelier, of the old Parisian family of the Langeliers, printers and classical scholars; Jean Boilly, a civil engineer, and Hippolyte Dufresne, a man of leisure, and a lover of the fine arts.

Towards five o'clock of the afternoon of the first day of May, they wended their way, as was their custom, through the northern door, closed to the public, where Commendatore Boni, who superintended the excavations, welcomed them with quiet amenity, and led them to the threshold of his house of wood nestling in the shadow of laurel bushes, privet hedges and cytisus, and rising above the vast trench, dug down to the depth of the ancient Forum, in the cattle market of pontifical Rome.

Here, they pause awhile, and look about them.

Facing them rise the truncated shafts of the Columnæ Honorariæ, and where stood the Basilica of Julia, the eye rested on what bore the semblance of a huge draughts-board and its draughts. Further south, the three columns of the Temple of the Dioscuri cleave the azure of the skies with their blue-tinted volutes. On their right, surmounting the dilapidated Arch of Septimus Severus, the tall columns of the Temple of Saturn, the dwellings of Christian Rome, and the Women's Hospital display in tiers, their facings yellower and muddier than the waters of the Tiber. To their left stands the Palatine flanked by huge red arches and crowned with evergreen oaks. At their feet, from hill to hill, among the flagstones of the Via Sacra, narrow as a village street, spring from the earth an agglomeration of brick walls and marble foundations, the remains of buildings which dotted the Forum in the days of Rome's strength. Trefoil, oats, and the grasses of the field which the wind has sown on their lowered tops, have covered them with a rustic roof illumined by the crimson poppies. A mass of *débris*, of crumbling entablatures, a multitude of pillars and altars, an entanglement of steps and enclosing walls: all this indeed not stunted but of a serried vastness and within limits.

Nicole Langelier was doubtless reviewing in his mind the host of monuments confined in this famed space:

"These edifices of wise proportions and moderate dimensions," he remarked, "were separated from one another by narrow streets full of shade. Here ran the *vicoli* beloved in countries where the sun shines, while the generous descendants of Remus, on their return from hearing public speakers, found, along the walls of the temples, cool yet foul-smelling corners, whence the rinds of water-melons and castaway shells were never swept away, and where they could eat and enjoy their siesta. The shops skirting the square must certainly have emitted the pungent odour of onions, wine, fried meats, and cheese. The butchers' stalls were laden with meats, to the delectation of the hardy citizens, and it was from one of those butchers that Virginius snatched the knife with which he killed his daughter. There also were doubtless jewellers and vendors of little domestic tutelary deities, protectors of the hearth, the ox-stall, and the garden. The citizens' necessaries of life were all centred in this spot. The market and the shops, the basilicas, i.e., the commercial Exchanges and the civil tribunals; the Curia, that municipal council which became the administrative power of the universe; the prisons, whose vaults emitted their much dreaded and fetid effluvia, and the temples, the altars, of the highest necessity to the Italians who have ever some thing to beg of the celestial powers.

"Here it was, lastly, that during a long roll of centuries were accomplished the vulgar or strange deeds, almost ever flat and dull, oftentimes odious and ridiculous, at times generous, the agglomeration of which constitutes the august life of a people."

"What is it that one sees, in the centre of the square, fronting the commemorative pedestals?" inquired M. Goubin, who, primed with an eye-glass, had noticed a new feature in the ancient Forum, and was thirsting for information concerning it.

Joséphin Leclerc obligingly answered him that they were the foundations of the recently unearthed colossal statue of Domitian.

Thereupon he pointed out, one after the other, the monuments laid bare by Giacomo Boni in the course of his five years' fruitful excavations: the fountain and the well of Juturna, under the Palatine Hill; the altar erected on the site of Cæsar's funeral pile, the base of which spread itself at their feet, opposite the Rostra; the archaic stele and the legendary tomb of Romulus over which lies the black marble slab of the Comitium; and again, the Lacus Curtius.

The sun, which had set behind the Capitol, was striking with its last shafts the triumphal arch of Titus on the towering Velia. The heavens, where to the West the pearl-white moon floated, remained as blue as at midday. An even, peaceful, and clear shadow spread itself over the silent Forum. The bronzed navvies were delving this field of stones, while, pursuing the work of the ancient Kings, their comrades turned the crank of a well, for the purpose of drawing the water which still forms the bed where slumbered, in the days of pious Numa, the reed-fringed Velabrum.

They were performing their task methodically and with vigilance. Hippolyte Dufresne, who had for several months been a witness of their assiduous labour, of their intelligence and of their prompt obedience to orders, inquired of the director of the excavations how it was that he obtained such yeoman's work from his labourers.

"By leading their life," replied Giacomo Boni. "Together with them do I turn over the soil; I impart to them what we are together seeking for, and I impress on their minds the beauty of our common work. They feel an interest in an enterprise the grandeur of which they apprehend but vaguely. I have seen their faces pale with enthusiasm when unearthing the tomb of Romulus. I am their everyday comrade, and if one of them falls ill, I take a seat at his bedside. I place as great faith in them as they do in me. And so it is that I boast of faithful workmen."

"Boni, my dear Boni," exclaimed Joséphin Leclerc, "you know full well that I admire your labours, and that your grand discoveries fill me with emotion, and yet, allow me to say so, I regret the days when flocks grazed over the entombed Forum. A white ox, from whose massive head branched horns widely apart, chewed the cud in the unploughed field; a hind dozed at the foot of a tall column which sprang from the sward, and one mused: Here was debated the fate of the world. The Forum has been lost to poets and lovers from the day that it ceased to be the Campo Formio."

Jean Boilly dwelt on the value of these excavations, so methodically carried out, as a contribution towards a knowledge of the past. Then, the conversation having drifted towards the philosophy of the history of Rome:

"The Latins," he remarked, "displayed reason even in the matter of their religion. Their gods were commonplace and vulgar, but full of common sense and occasionally generous. If a comparison be drawn between this Roman Pantheon composed of soldiers, magistrates, virgins, and matrons and the deviltries painted on the walls of Etruscan tombs, reason and madness will be found in juxtaposition. The infernal scenes depicted in the mortuary chambers of Corneto represent the monstrous creations of ignorance and fear. They seem to us as grotesque as Orcagna's *Day of Judgment* in Santa Maria Novella at Florence, and the *Dantesque Hell* of the Campo Santo of Pisa, whereas the Latin Pantheon reflects for ever the image of a well-organised society. The gods of the Romans were like themselves, industrious and good citizens. They were useful deities, each one having its proper function. The very nymphs held civil and political offices.

"Look at Juturna, whose altar at the foot of the Palatine we have so frequently contemplated. She did not seem fated by her birth, her adventures, and her misfortunes to occupy a permanent post in the city of Romulus. An incensed Rutula, beloved by Jupiter, who rewarded her with immortality, when King Turnus fell by the hand of Æneas, as decreed by the Fates, she flung herself into the Tiber, to escape thus from the light of day, since it was denied her to perish with her royal brother. Long did the shepherds of Latium tell the story of the living nymph's lamentations from the depths of the river. In later years, the villagers of rural Rome, when looking down at night-time over the bank, imagined that they could see her by the moon's rays, lurking in her glaucous garments among the rushes. The Romans, however, did not leave her to the idle contemplation of her sorrows. They promptly conceived the idea of allotting to her an important duty, and entrusted her with the custody of their fountains, converting her into a municipal goddess. And so it is with all their divinities. The Dioscuri, whose temple lives in its beautiful ruins, the Dioscuri, the brothers of Helen, the sparkling *Gemini*, were put to good use by the Romans, as messengers of the State. The Dioscuri it was, who, mounted on a white charger, brought to Rome the news of the victory of Lake Regillus.

"The Italians asked of their gods only temporal and substantial benefits. In this respect, notwithstanding the Asiatic fears which have invaded Europe, their religious sentiment has not changed. That which they formally demanded from their gods and their genii, they nowadays expect from the Madonna and the Saints. Every parish possesses its Beatified patron, to whom requests are preferred just as in the case of a Deputy. There are Saints for the vine, for cereals, for cattle, for the colic, and for toothache. Latin imagination has repeopled Heaven with a multitude of living bodies, and has converted Judaic monotheism into a new polytheism. It has enlivened the Gospels with a copious mythology; it has re-established a familiar intercourse between the divine and the terrestrial worlds. The peasantry demand miracles of their protecting Saints, and hurl invectives at them if the miracle is slow of manifestation. The peasant who has in vain solicited a favour of the Bambino, returns to the chapel, and addressing on this occasion the Incoronata herself, exclaims:

"'I am not speaking to you, you whoreson, but to your sainted mother.'

"The women make the Madre di Dio a confidant of their love affairs. They believe with some show of reason that being a woman she understands, and that there is no need to be on a footing of delicacy with her. They have no fear of going too far—a proof of their piety. Hence we must view with admiration the prayer which a fine lass of the Genoese Riviera addressed to the Madonna: 'Holy Mother of God, who didst conceive without sin, grant me the grace of sinning without conceiving.'"

Nicole Langelier here remarked that the religion of the Romans lent itself to the evolution of Rome's policy.

"Bearing the stamp of a distinctly national character," he said, "it was, for all that, capable of penetrating the minds of foreign nations, and of winning them over by its sociable and tolerant spirit. It was an administrative religion propagating itself without effort together with the rest of the administration."

"The Romans loved war," said M. Goubin, who studiously avoided paradoxes.

"They loved not war for itself," was Jean Boilly's rejoinder. "They were far too reasonable for that. That military service was to them a hardship is revealed by certain signs. Monsieur Michel Bréal tells you that the word which primarily expressed the equipment of the soldier, *ærumna*, subsequently assumed the general meaning of lassitude, need, trouble, hardship, toil, pain, and distress. Those peasants were just as other peasants. They entered the ranks merely because compelled and forced thereto. Their very leaders, the wealthy proprietors, waged war neither for pleasure nor for glory. Previous to entering on a campaign, they consulted their interests twenty times over, and carefully computed the chances."

"True," said M. Goubin, "but their circumstances and the state of the world compelled them ever to be in arms. Thus it is that they carried civilisation to the far ends of the known world. War is above all an instrument of progress."

"The Latins," resumed Jean Boilly, "were agriculturists who waged agriculturists' wars. Their ambitions were ever agricultural. They exacted of the vanquished, not money, but soil, the whole or part of the territory of the subjugated confederation, generally speaking one-third, out of friendship, as they said, and because they were moderate in their desires. The farmer came and drove his plough over the spot where the legionary had a short while ago planted his pike. The tiller of the soil confirmed the soldier's conquests. Admirable soldiers, doubtless, well disciplined, patient, and brave, who fought and who were sometimes beaten just like any others; yet still more admirable peasants. If wonder is felt at their having conquered so many lands, still more is it to be wondered at that they should have kept them. The marvel of it is that in spite of the many battles they lost, these stubborn peasants never yielded an acre of soil, so to speak."

While this discussion was proceeding, Giacomo Boni was gazing with a hostile eye at the tall brick house standing to the north of the Forum on top of several layers of ancient substructures.

"We are about," he said, "to explore the Curia Julia. We shall soon, I hope, be in a position to break up the sordid building which covers its remains. It will not cost the State much to purchase it for the spade's work. Buried under nine mètres of soil on which stands the Convent of S. Adriano lie the flagstones of Diocletian, who restored the Curia for the last time. We shall surely find among the rubbish a number of the marble tables on which the laws were engraved. It is a matter of interest to Rome, to Italy, nay to the whole world, that the last vestiges of the Roman Senate should see the light of day."

Thereupon he invited his friends into his hut, as hospitable and rustic a one as that of Evander.

It constituted a single room wherein stood a deal table laden with black potteries and shapeless fragments giving out an earthy smell.

"Prehistorical treasures!" sighed Joséphin Leclerc. "And so, my good Giacomo Boni, not content with seeking in the Forum the monuments of the Emperors, those of the Republic, and those of the Kings, you must fain sink down into the soil which bore flora and fauna that have vanished, drive your spade into the quaternary, and the tertiary, penetrate the pliocene, the miocene, and the eocene; from Latin archæology you wander to prehistoric archæology and to palæontology. The salons are expressing alarm at the depths to which you are venturing. Countess Pasolini would like to know where you intend to stop, and you are represented in a little satirical sheet as coming out at the Antipodes, breathing the words: *Adesso va bene!*"

Boni seemed not to have heard.

He was examining with deep attention a clay vessel still damp and covered with ooze. His pale blue expressive eyes darkened while critically examining this humble work of man for some unrevealed trace of a mysterious past, but resumed their natural hue as the Commendatore's mind wandered off into a reverie.

"These remains which you have before you," he presently remarked, "these roughly hewn little wooden sarcophagi and these cinerary urns of black pottery and of house-like shape containing calcined bones were gathered under the Temple of Faustina, on the north-west side of the Forum.

"Black urns containing ashes, and skeletons resting in their coffins as if in a bed, are here to be met with side by side. The funeral rites of the Greeks and the Romans included both those of burial and of cremation. Over the whole of Europe, in prehistoric days, the two customs were simultaneously observed, in the same city and in the same tribe. Does this dual fashion of sepulture correspond with the ideals of two races? I am inclined to believe so."

Picking up, with reverential and almost ritual gesture, an urn shaped like a dwelling and containing a small quantity of ashes, he went on:

"The men who in immemorial times gave this form to clay, believed that the soul, being attached to the bones and the ashes, had need of a dwelling, but that it did not require a very large house wherein to live the abridged life of the dead. These men were of a noble race which came from Asia. The one whose light ashes I now hold lived before the days of Evander and of the shepherd Faustulus."

Then, making use of the phraseology of the ancients, he added:

"Those were the days when King Vitulus, King Calf as we should say, held peaceful sway over this country so pregnant with glory. Monotonous pastoral times reigned over the Ausonian plain. These men were, however, neither ignorant nor boorish. Much priceless knowledge had come to them from their forefathers. Both the ship and the oar were known to them. They practised the art of subjecting oxen to the yoke and of harnessing them to the pole. They kindled at will the divine flame. They gathered salt, wrought in gold, kneaded and baked vases of clay. Probably too they began to till the soil. They do say that the Latin shepherds became agricultural labourers in the fabled days of the Calf. They cultivated millet, wheat, and spelt. They stitched skins together with needles of bone. They wove and perchance made wool false to its whiteness by dyeing it various colours. By the phases of the moon did they measure time. They gazed upon the heavens but to discover in them what was in the world below. They saw in them the greyhound who watches for Diospiter the shepherd who tends the starry flock. The prolific clouds were to them the Sun's cattle, the cows supplying milk to the cerulean countryside. They worshipped the heavens as their Father, and the Earth as their Mother. At eventide, they heard the chariots of the gods, like themselves migratory, roll along the mountain roads with their ponderous wheels. They enjoyed the light of day and pondered with sadness over the life of the souls in the Kingdom of Shadows.

"We know that these massive-headed Aryans were fair, since their gods, made to their own image, were fair. Indra had locks like ears of wheat and a beard as tawny as the tiger's coat. The Greeks conceived the immortal gods with blue or glaucous eyes, and a head of golden hair. The goddess Roma was *flava et candida*:

"Were it possible to make a whole out of these calcined bony fragments, the result would be pure Aryan forms. In those massive and vigorous skulls, in those heads as square as the primary Rome which their sons were to build, you would recognise the ancestors of the patricians of the Commonwealth, the long flourishing stock which produced tribunes of the people, pontiffs, and consuls; you would be handling the magnificent mould of the robust brains which constructed religion, the family, the army, and the public laws of the most strongly organised city that ever existed."

Gently placing the bit of pottery on the rustic table, Giacomo Boni bends over a coffin the size of a cradle, a coffin dug out of the trunk of an oak, and similar in shape to the early canoes of man. He lifts up the thin covering of bark and sap-wood forming the lid of that funeral wherry, and brings to light bones as frail as a bird's skeleton. Of the body, there hardly remains the spinal column, and it would bear resemblance to one of the lowest of vertebrata, such as a big saurian, did not the fullness of the forehead reveal man. Coloured beads, which have become detached from a necklace, are scattered over these bones browned with age, washed by subterraneous waters, and exhumed from clayey soil.

"Look!" says Boni, "at this little boy who was not given the honours of cremation, but buried, and returned as a whole to the earth whence he sprung. He is not a son of headmen, nor a noble inheritor of the traits of a fair race. He belongs to the race indigenous to the Mediterranean, the race which became the Roman *plebs*, and which supplies Italy to the present day with subtile lawyers and calculating individuals. He was born in the Palatine City of the Seven Hills, in days seen dimly through the mist of heroic fables. It is a Romulean boy. In those days, the Valley of the Seven Hills was a morass, and the slopes of the Palatine were covered with reed-thatched huts only. A tiny lance was placed on the coffin to show that the child was a male. He was barely four years old when he fell asleep in death. Then his mother clothed him with a beautiful tunic clasped at the neck, around which she fastened a string of beads. The kinsmen did not begrudge him their offerings. They deposited on his tomb, in urns of black earthenware, milk, beans, and a bunch of grapes. I have collected these vessels and I have fashioned similar ones out of the same clay by the heat of a wood fire lit in the Forum at night. Previous to taking a last farewell of him, they ate and drank together a portion of their offerings; this funeral repast assuaged their sorrow. Child, thou who sleepest since the days of the god Quirinus, an Empire has passed over thy agrestic coffin, and the same stars which shone at thy birth are about to light up the skies above us. The unfathomable space which separates the hours of your life from those of our own constitutes but an imperceptible moment in the life of the Universe."

After a moment's silence, Nicole Langelier remarked:

"It is as difficult to distinguish amid a people the races composing it as to trace in the course of a river the streams which mingle with it. What constitutes, moreover, a race? Do any human races really exist? I see white men, red men, and black men. But, they do not constitute races; they are merely varieties of the same race, of the same species, which form together fruitful unions and intermingle without ceasing. *A fortiori*, the man of learning knows not several yellow races or several white races. Human beings invent, however, races in pursuance of their vanity, their hatred, or their greed. In 1871, France became dismembered by virtue of the rights

269

of the Germanic race, and yet no German race has an existence. The antiemites kindle the hatred of Christian peoples against the Jews, and still there is no Jewish race.

"What I state on the subject, Boni, is purely speculative, and not with the view of running counter to your ideas. How could one not believe you! Conviction has its home on your lips. Moreover, you blend in your thoughts the profound verities of poetry with the far-spreading truths of science. As you truly state, the shepherds who came from Bactriana peopled Greece and Italy. As you again say, they found there natives of the soil. In ancient days, a belief shared in common by Italians and Hellenes was that the first men who peopled their country were like Erectheus, born of Mother Earth. Nor do I pretend, my dear Boni, that you cannot trace through the centuries the antochthones of your Ausonia, and the immigrants from the Pamir; the former, intelligent and eloquent plebeians; the latter, patricians fully impregnated with courage and faith. For, when all is said, if there are not, properly speaking, several human races, and if still less so several white races, our species assuredly comprises distinct varieties oftentimes stamped with marked characteristics. Hence there is nothing to hinder two or more of these varieties living for a long time side by side without fusing, each one preserving its individual characteristics. Nay, these differences may occasionally, in lieu of vanishing with the course of time under the action of the plastic forces of nature, on the contrary become accentuated more strongly through the empire of immutable customs, and the stress of social institutions."

"*E proprio vero,*" said Boni in a low tone, as he replaced the oaken lid on the coffin of the Romulean child.

Then, begging his guests to be seated, he said to Nicole Langelier:

"I shall now hold you to your promise, and beg you to read to us that story of Gallio, at which I have seen you at work in your little room in the *Foro Traiano*. You make Romans speak in your script. This is the spot to hear your narrative, here in a corner of the Forum, close by the Via Sacra, between the Capitol and the Palatine. Tarry not with your reading, so as not to be overtaken by the twilight, and lest your voice be quickly drowned by the cries of the birds warning one another of approaching night."

The guests of Giacomo Boni welcomed the foregoing utterance with a murmur of approval, and Nicole Langelier, without waiting for more pressing entreaties, unrolled a manuscript and read aloud the following narrative.

II
GALLIO

IN the 804th year of the foundation of Rome, and the 13th of the principality of Claudius Cæsar, Junius Annæus Novatus was proconsul of Achaia. Born of a knightly family of Spanish origin, a son of Seneca the Rhetor and of the chaste Helvia, a brother of Annæus Mela, and of the famed Lucius Annæus, he bore the name of his adoptive father, the Rhetor Gallio, exiled by Tiberius. In his mother's veins flowed the same blood as that of Cicero, and he had inherited from his father, together with immense wealth, a love of letters and of philosophy. He studied the works of the Greeks even more assiduously than those of the Latins. His mind was a prey to noble aspiration. He was an interested student of nature and of what appertains to her. The activity of his intelligence was so keen that he enjoyed being read to while in his bath, and that, even when joining in the chase, he was wont to carry with him his tablets of wax and his stylus. During the leisure moments which he managed to secure in the intervals of most serious duties and most important works, he wrote books on subjects relating to nature, and composed tragedies.

His clients and his freedmen loudly proclaimed his gentleness. His was indeed a genial character. He had never been known to give way to a fit of anger. He looked upon violence as the worst and most unpardonable of weaknesses.

All deeds of cruelty were held in execration by him, save when their true character escaped him owing to the consecration of custom and of public opinion. He frequently discovered, amid the severities rendered sacred by ancestral usage and sanctified by the laws, revolting excesses against which he raised his voice in protest, and which he would have attempted to sweep away, had not the interests of the State and the common welfare been objected from all quarters. In those days, conscientious magistrates and honest functionaries were not few and far between throughout the Empire. There were indeed a number as honest and as impartial as Gallio himself, but it is to be doubted whether another could be found so humane.

Entrusted with the administration of that Greece despoiled of her riches, her pristine glory departed, and fallen from her freedom so full of life into an idle tranquillity, he remembered that she had formerly taught the world wisdom and the fine arts, and his treatment of her combined the vigilance of a guardian with the reverence of a son. He respected the liberties of the cities and the rights of individuals. He showed honour to those who were truly Greeks by birth and education, regretting that their numbers were sorely restricted, and that his authority extended for the greater part over an infamous rabble of Jews and Syrians; yet he remained equitable in dealing with these Asiatics, laying unction to his soul for what he considered a meritorious endeavour.

He dwelt in Corinth, the richest and most densely populated city of Roman Greece. His villa, built in the time of Augustus, enlarged and embellished since then by the pro-consuls who had governed the province in succession, stood on the furthermost western slopes of the Acrocorinthus, whose foliaged summit was crowned by the Temple of Venus and the groves where dwelt her priests. It was a somewhat spacious mansion surrounded by gardens studded with bushy trees, watered by springs, ornamented with statues, alcoves, gymnasia, baths, libraries, and altars consecrated to the gods.

He was strolling in it on a certain morn, according to his wont, with his brother Annæus Mela, discoursing on the order of nature and the vicissitudes of fortune. The sun was rising, hazy in its white splendour in the roseate heavens. The gentle undulations of the hills of the Isthmus concealed the Saronic shore, the Stadium, the sanctuary of the sports, and the eastern harbour of Cenchreæ. Between the fallow slopes of the Geranean range and the crimson twin-peaked Helicon, one could, however, obtain a glimpse of the quiescent blue waters of the Alcyonium Mare. In the distance, and to the north, glistened the three snow-capped summits of Parnassus. Gallio and Mela proceeded together as far as the edge of the elevated foreground. At their feet spread Corinth standing on an extensive plateau of pale yellow sand, and sloping gently towards the spumous fringe of the Gulf. The pavements of the forum, the columns of the basilica, the tiers of the hippodrome, the white steps of the porches sparkled, while the gilded roofs of the temples flashed dazzling rays. Vast and new, the town was intersected with straight-running streets. A wide road descended to the harbour of Lechæum, whose shore was fringed with warehouses and whose waters were covered with ships. To the west, the atmosphere reeked with the smoke of the iron-foundries, while the streams ran black from the pollution of the dye-houses, and on that side, forests of pine extending to the edge of the horizon, were lost to sight in the skies.

Gradually, the town awoke from its slumbers. The strident neighing of a horse rent the morning calm, and soon were heard the muffled rumblings of wheels, shouting of waggoners, and the chanting voices of women selling herbs. Emerging from their hovels amid the ruins of the Palace of Sisyphus, aged and blind hags bearing copper vessels on their heads, and led by children, wended their way to draw water from the Pirene fountain. On the flat roofs of the houses abutting the grounds of the proconsul, Corinthian women were spreading linen to dry, and one of them was castigating her child with leek-stalks. In the hollow road leading to the Acropolis, a semi-nude old bronze-coloured man, prodded the rump of an ass laden with salad herbs and chanted between the stumps of his teeth and in his unkempt beard, a slave-song:

> "Toil, little ass,
> As I have toiled.
> Much good will it do you:
> You may be sure of it."

Meanwhile, at the sight of the town resuming its daily labour, Gallio fell a-musing over the earlier Corinth, the lovely Ionian city, opulent and joyous until the day when she witnessed the massacre of her citizens by the soldiery of Mummius, her women, the noble daughters of Sisyphus, sold at auction, her palaces and temples the prey of flames, her walls razed to the ground, and her riches piled away into the Liburnian ships of the Consul.

"Hardly a century ago," he remarked, "the work wrought by Mummius still stood revealed in all its horror. The shore which you see, brother mine, was more of a desert than the Libyan sands. The divine Julius rebuilt the town wrecked by our arms, and peopled it with freedmen. On this very strand, where the illustrious Bacchiadæ formerly revelled in their haughty indolence, poor and rude Latins settled, and Corinth entered upon a new lease of life. She grew rapidly, and realised how to take advantage of her position. She levies tribute on all ships which, whether from the East or from the West, cast anchor in her two harbours of Lechæum and Cenchreæ. Her population and wealth increase apace under the ægis of the Roman peace.

"What blessings has not the Empire bestowed throughout the world! To the Empire is due the profound tranquillity which the countryside enjoys. The seas are swept of pirates, and the highways of robbers. From the befogged Ocean to the Permulic Gulf, from Gades to the Euphrates, the trading of merchandise proceeds in undisturbed security. The law protects the lives and property of all. Individual rights must not be infringed upon. Liberty has henceforth no other limits than its lines of defence, and is circumscribed for its own security alone. Justice and reason rule the world."

Unlike his two brothers, Annæus Mela had not intrigued for honours. Those who loved him, and their name was legion, for he was ever in his intercourse affable and extremely pleasant, attributed his detachment from public affairs to the moderation of a mind attracted by the blessings of tranquil obscurity, a mind which had no other care than the study of philosophy. But those who observed him with greater insight were under the impression that he was ambitious after his own fashion, and that like Mæcenas, he, a simple knight, was consumed with the envy of enjoying the same consideration as the consuls. Lastly, certain evil-minded individuals believed that they discerned in him the greed of the Senecas for the riches which they affected to despise, and thus did they explain to themselves that Mela had for a long time lived in obscurity in Betica, giving himself up entirely to the management of his vast estates, and that subsequently summoned to Rome by his brother the philosopher, he had devoted himself to the administration of the finances of the Empire, rather than go in the quest of high judiciary or military posts. His character could not be readily determined from his utterances, for he spoke the language of the Stoics, a language equally adapted for the concealment of the weaknesses of the mind and the revelation of the grandeur of one's sentiments. It was in those days the height of elegance to utter virtuous discourse. At any rate, there is no doubt that Mela spoke his thoughts.

He replied to his brother that, although not versed in public affairs like himself, he had had occasion to admire the power and wisdom of the Romans.

"They reveal themselves," he said, "in the most remote parts of our own Spain. But it is in a wild pass of the mountains of Thessaly that I have been made to appreciate at its highest the beneficent majesty of the Empire. I had come from Hypata, a town renowned for its cheeses, and whose women were notorious for witchcraft, and I had been riding for some hours along mountain paths, without coming across a human face. Overcome by the heat and fatigue, I tethered my horse to a tree by the road, and lay down under an arbutus-bush. I had been resting there a short while only, when there came along a lean old man bowed down under a load of branches. Utterly exhausted, he tottered in his steps, and just as he was about to fall, exclaimed: 'Cæsar.' On hearing such an invocation escape the lips of a poor woodcutter in this stony solitude, my heart overflowed with veneration for the tutelary City, which inspires, even unto the farthermost lands, the most rustic of minds with so great a conception of its sovereign providence. But sadness and a feeling of distress mingled with my admiration, brother mine, when I reflected upon the injury and insults to which the inheritance of Augustus and the fortune of Rome were exposed through men's folly and the vices of the century."

"I have witnessed on the spot, brother mine," replied Gallio, "the crimes and follies which sadden your mind. My cheek has blanched under the gaze of the victims of Caius from my seat in the Senate. I have held my peace, as I did not despair of better days. I am of the opinion that good citizens should serve the Republic under bad princes rather than shirk their duty in a useless death."

As Gallio was uttering these sentiments, two men, still in their youth and wearing the toga, came up to him. The one was Lucius Cassius, of a Roman family, plebeian but ancient, and having attained distinction. The other, Marcus Lollius, son and grandson of consuls, and moreover of a knightly family, which had sprung from the free town of Terracina. Both had frequented the schools of Athens, and acquired a knowledge of the laws of nature of which those Romans who had not been in Greece were totally ignorant.

At the present moment, they were studying in Corinth the management of public affairs, and the proconsul surrounded himself with them as an ornamental adjunct to his magistracy. Somewhat behind them, the Greek Apollodorus, wearing the short cape of the philosophers, bald of head, and with Socratic beard, sauntered along, with uplifted arm and gesticulating fingers, discussing with himself.

Gallio welcomed all three of them in kindly fashion.

"The rose of dawn is already fading," he said, "and the sun is beginning to shed its steeled darts. Come along, my good friends, to the coolness of the shady foliage beyond."

Saying this, he led them along the banks of a stream whose babbling murmur invited peaceful reflections, until they had reached an enclosure of verdant bushes in the midst of which lay in a hollow an alabaster basin filled with limpid waters on whose surface floated the feather of a dove, which had just bathed in them, and which was now cooing plaintively from a branch. They took their seats on a semicircular marble bench supported by griffins. Laurel and myrtle bushes blended their shadows about it. Statues encircled the enclosure. A wounded Amazon gracefully coiled her arm about her head. Grief appeared a thing of beauty on her lovely face. A shaggy Satyr was playing with a goat. A Venus, emerging from the bath, was drying her wetted limbs along which a shudder of pleasurable emotion seemed to run. Near by, a youthful Faun was smilingly placing a flute to his lips. His face was partly concealed by the branches, but his shining belly glistened amid the leafage.

"That Faun seems animated," remarked Marcus Lollius. "One could imagine that a gentle breathing was causing his bosom to heave."

"He is true to life, Marcus," said Gallio. "One expects to hear rustic melodies flow from his flute. A Greek slave carved him out of the marble, in imitation of an ancient model. The Greeks formerly excelled in the making of these fanciful statues. Several of their efforts in this style are justly renowned. There is no gainsaying it: they have found the means of giving august traits to the gods and of expressing in both marble and bronze the majesty of the masters of the world. Who but admires the Olympian Zeus? And yet, who would care to be Phidias!"

"No Roman would assuredly care to be Phidias," exclaimed Lollius, who was spending the fortune he had inherited from his ancestry in ornamenting his villa at Pausilypum with the masterpieces of Phidias and Myron brought over from Greece and Asia.

Lucius Cassius was of the same opinion. He argued with some warmth that the hands of a free man were not made to wield the sculptor's chisel or the painter's brush, and that no Roman citizen would condescend to the degrading work of casting bronze, hewing marble into shape, and painting forms on a wall.

He professed admiration for the manners of the ancient times, and vaunted at every opportunity the ancestral virtues.

"Men of the stamp of Curius and Fabricius cultivated their lettuce-beds, and slept under thatched roofs," he said. "They wot of no other statue than the Priapus carved in the heart of a box-tree, who, protruding his vigorous pale in the centre of their garden, threatened pilferers with a terrible and shameful punishment."

Mela, who was well versed in the annals of Rome, opposed to this opinion the example of an old patrician.

"In the days of the Republic," he pointed out, "that illustrious man, Caius Fabius, of a family issued from Hercules and Evander, limned with his own hand on the walls of the Temple of Salus paintings so highly prized that their recent loss, on the destruction of the temple by fire, has been considered a public misfortune. It is moreover related that he did not doff his toga when painting, thus to indicate that such work was not unworthy of a Roman citizen. He was given the surname of Pictor, which his descendants were proud to bear."

Lucius Cassius replied with vivacity:

"When painting victories in a temple, Caius Fabius had in mind those victories, and not the painting of them. No painters existed in Rome in those days. Anxious that the doughty deeds of his ancestors should for ever be present to the gaze of the Romans, he set an example to the artisans. But just as a pontiff or an ædile lays the first stone of an edifice, without exercising for that the trade of a mason or of an architect, Caius Fabius executed the first painting Rome boasted of, without it being permissible to number him with the workmen who earn their livelihood by painting on walls."

Apollodorus signified approval of this speech with a nod, and, stroking his philosophic beard, remarked:

"The sons of Ascanius are born to rule the world. Any other care would be unworthy of them."

Then, speaking at some length and in well-rounded sentences, he sang the praises of the Romans. He flattered them because he feared them. But in his innermost being, he felt nothing but contempt for their shallow intelligences so devoid of finesse. He beslavered Gallio with praise in these words:

"Thou hast ornamented this city with magnificent monuments. Thou hast assured the liberty of its Senate and of its people. Thou hast decreed excellent regulations for trade and navigation, and thou dispensest justice with even tempered equity. Thy statue shall stand in the Forum. The title shall be granted to you of the second founder of Corinth, or rather Corinth shall take from you the name of Annæa. All these things are worthy of a Roman, and worthy of Gallio. But, do not think that the Greeks have an exaggerated affection for the manual arts. If many of them are engaged in painting vases, in dyeing stuffs, and in modelling figures, it is through necessity. Ulysses constructed his bed and his ship with his own hands. At the same time, the Greeks proclaim that it is unworthy of a wise man to give himself up to futile and gross arts. In his youth, Socrates followed the trade of a sculptor, and modelled an image of the Charites still to be seen on the Acropolis of Athens. His skill was certainly not of a mediocre order, and, had he so wished, he could, like the most renowned artists, have portrayed an athlete throwing a discus or bandaging his head. But he abandoned like works to devote himself to the quest of wisdom, as commanded by the oracle. Henceforth, he attached himself to young men, not for the purpose of measuring the proportions of their bodies but solely to teach them that which is honest. He preferred those whose soul was beautiful to those of perfect form, differing in this respect from sculptors, painters and debauchees, who consider only external beauty, despising the inner comeliness. You are aware that Phidias engraved on the great toe of his Jupiter the name of an athlete, because he was handsome, and without considering whether he was pure."

"Hence it is," was Gallio's summing up, "that we do not sing the praises of sculptors, while bestowing them on their works."

"By Hercules!" exclaimed Lollius, "I do not know whether to admire most that Venus or that Faun. The goddess seems to reflect coolness from the water still dripping from her. She is truly the desire of gods and men; do you not fear, Gallio, that some night, a lout concealed in your grounds may subject her to an outrage similar to the one inflicted by a profane youth, so it is reported, on the Aphrodite of the Cnidians? The priestesses of her temple discovered one morning traces of the outrage on the body of the goddess, and travellers affirm that from that day until now she bears the indelible mark of her defilement. The audacity of the man and the patience of the Immortal One are to be wondered at."

"The crime did not remain unpunished," affirmed Gallio. "The sacrilegious profaner flung himself into the sea, and fell on the rocks a shapeless mass. He was never again seen."

"There can be no doubt," resumed Lollius, "that the Venus of Cnidus surpasses all others in beauty. But the artisan who carved the one in your grounds, Gallio, knew how to make marble plastic. Look at that Faun; he is laughing, and saliva moistens his teeth and his lips; his cheeks have the fresh bloom of the apple: his whole body glistens with youth. However, I prefer the Venus to the Faun."

Raising his right arm, Apollodorus said:

"Most gentle Lollius, just think a bit, and you will fain admit that a like preference is pardonable in an ignorant individual who follows his instincts and who reasons not, but that it is not permitted to one as wise as yourself. That Venus cannot be as beautiful as that Faun, for the body of woman enjoys a perfection lesser than that of man, and the copy of a thing which is less perfect can never equal in beauty the copy of a thing that is more perfect. No doubt can assuredly exist, Lollius, that the body of woman is less beautiful than that of man, since it contains a less beautiful soul. Women are vain, quarrelsome, their mind occupied with trifles and incapable of elevated thoughts, while sickness oftentimes obscures their intellect."

"And yet," remarked Gallio, "both in Rome and in Athens, virgins and matrons have been held worthy of presiding over sacred rites and of placing offerings on the altars. Nay more, the gods have at times selected virgins to give utterance to their oracular words, or to reveal the future to men. Cassandra wore the bands of Apollo about her head and prophesied the discomfiture of the Trojans. Juturna, to whom the love of a god gave immortality, was entrusted with the guardianship of the fountains of Rome."

"Quite true," replied Apollodorus. "But the gods sell dearly to virgins the privilege of interpreting their wishes, and of announcing future events. While conferring on them the power of seeing that which is hidden, they deprive them of their reason and inflict madness on them. I will, however, Gallio, grant you that some women are better than some men and that some men are less good than some women. This arises from the fact that the two sexes are not as distinct and separate from each other as one would believe, and that, quite on the contrary, there is something of man in many women, and of woman in many a man. The following is the explanation of this commingling:

"The ancestors of the men who nowadays people the earth sprang from the hands of Prometheus, who, to give them shape, kneaded the clay as does the potter. He did not confine himself to shaping with his hands a single couple. Far too prudent and too industrious to cause the entire human race to grow from one seed and from a single vessel, he undertook the manufacture of a multitude of women and men, in order to secure at once to humanity the advantage of numbers. In order better to carry out so difficult a work, he modelled separately at the outset all the parts which were to constitute both male and female bodies. He fashioned as many lungs, livers, hearts, brains, bladders, spleens, intestines, matrices and generative organs as were required, and, lastly, he made with subtle art, and in sufficient quantity, all the organs by means of which human beings might breathe freely, feed themselves, and enjoy the reproduction of the species. He forgot neither muscles, tendons, bones, blood nor fluids. He next cut out skins, intending to place in each one, as in a sack, the requisite articles. All these component parts of men and women were duly finished, and nothing remained but to put them together, when he was of a sudden invited to partake of supper at the residence of Bacchus. He went thither, crowned with roses, and indulged too freely in libations to the god, returning with tottering steps to his workshop. His brain befogged with the fumes of wine, his eyesight dimmed, and his hands shaky, he resumed his task, greatly to our misfortune. The distribution of organs among human beings seemed to him an easy enough pastime. He knew not what he was about, and was perfectly contented with his job, however badly he accomplished it. He was constantly and inadvertently allotting to woman that which was proper to man, and to man the things pertaining to woman.

"Thus it came about that our first parents were composed of ill-assorted pieces which did not harmonise. And, having mated by choice or at haphazard, they produced beings as incoherent as themselves. Thus has it come about, through the Titan's fault, that we see so many virile

276

women and so many effeminate men. This also explains the contradictory characteristics to be met with in the firmest of minds and how it is that the most determined character is perpetually false to itself. And, finally, this is why we are all at variance with our own selves."

Lucius Cassius expressed condemnation of this fable, because it did not teach man to conquer himself, but on the contrary induced him to yield to nature.

Gallio pointed out that the poets and philosophers gave a different interpretation as to the origin of the world and the creation of mankind.

"The fables told by the Greeks," he said, "should not be believed in too blindly, nor should we hold as truthful, Apollodorus, what they state in particular concerning the stones thrown by Pyrrha. The philosophers are not in accord among themselves as to the principle presiding over the creation of the world, and leave us in doubt as to whether the earth was produced by water, by air, or, as seems more credible, by the subtile heat. But the Greeks wish to know all things, and so they forge ingenious falsehood. How much better it is to confess our ignorance. The past is as much concealed from us as is the future; we are circumscribed by two dense clouds, in the forgetfulness of what was, and in the uncertainty of what shall be. And yet we suffer ourselves to be the playthings of an inquisitive desire to become acquainted with the causes of things, and a consuming anxiety incites us to ponder over the destinies of mankind and of the world."

"It is true," sighed Cassius, "that we are everlastingly striving to penetrate the impenetrable future. We toil at this quest with all our might, and call to our aid all kinds of means. Anon we think to attain our object by meditation; again, by prayer and ecstasy. Some of us consult the oracles of the gods; others, fearing not to do that which is forbidden, appeal to the augurs of Chaldæa, or try the Babylonian spells. Futile and sacrilegious curiosity! For, of what advantage would be to us the knowledge of future things, since they are inevitable! Nevertheless the wise men, still more so than the vulgar herd, feel the desire of delving into the future and of, so to speak, hurling themselves into it. It is doubtless because they hope thus to escape the present which inflicts on them so much that is sad and distasteful. Why should not the men of to-day be goaded with the desire of fleeing from these wretched times? We are living in an age replete with deeds of cowardice, abounding in ignominious acts, and fertile in crimes."

Cassius spoke at some length in depreciation of the times in which he lived. He lamented the fact that the Romans, fallen from their ancient virtues, no longer found any pleasure except in the consumption of the oysters of the Lucrine lake and of the birds of Phasis river, and that they had no taste except for mummers, chariot-drivers, and gladiators. He deplored the ills which the Empire was suffering from, the insolent luxury of the great, the contemptible avidity of the clients, and the savage depravity of the multitude.

Gallio and his brother agreed with him. They loved virtue. Nevertheless, they had nothing in common with the patricians of old who, having no other care than the fattening of their swine, and the performance of the sacred rites, conquered the world for the better administration of their farms. This nobility of the byre, instituted by Romulus and Remus, was long since extinct. The patrician families created by the divine Julius and by the Emperor Augustus, had passed away. Intelligent men from all the provinces of the Empire had stepped into their places. Romans in Rome, they were nowhere strangers. They greatly surpassed the old Cethegus family by their refined minds and humane feelings. They did not regret the Republic; they did not regret liberty, the recollection of which recalled simultaneously proscriptions and civil wars. They honoured Cato as the heroic figure of another age, without wishing to see so exalted a type of virtue arise on top of fresh ruins. They looked upon the Augustan epoch and the first years of Tiberius as the happiest the world had ever known, since the Golden Age had existed in the imagination of the poets only. They lamented the fact that the new order of things, which had promised the world a long reign of felicity, should have so promptly burdened Rome with an unheard of shame unknown even to the contemporaries of Marius and Sulla. They had, during the madness of Caius, seen the best citizens branded with a hot iron, sentenced to the mines, to labour on the roads, thrown to wild beasts, fathers compelled to be present at the agony of their children, and men shining by their virtues, such as Cremutius Cordus, suffer themselves to die of starvation, in order to cheat the tyrant of their death. To Rome's shame, be it said, Caligula respected neither his sisters nor the most illustrious dames. And, what filled these rhetors and philosophers with as great an indignation as the one they felt over the rape of the matrons and the assassination of the best citizens, were the crimes perpetrated by Caius against eloquence and letters. This madman had conceived the idea of destroying the poems of Homer, and had caused to be removed from all bookshelves the writings, the portraits, and the names of Virgil and of Livy. Finally, Gallio could not forgive him for having compared the style of Seneca to mortar without cement.

They dreaded Claudius in a somewhat lesser degree, but despised him the more for all that. They ridiculed his pumpkin-like head and his seal-like voice. That old savant was not a monster of wickedness. The worst they could reproach him with was his weakness. But, in the exercise of the sovereign power, such weakness became at times as cruel as the cruelty of Caius. They also bore domestic grievances against him. If Caius had held Seneca up to ridicule, Claudius had banished him to Corsica. It is true that he had subsequently recalled him to Rome and conferred a prætorship on him. But they showed him no gratitude for having thus carried out the behests of Agrippina, in ignorance of what he was commanding. Indignant but long suffering, they left it to the Empress to determine the fate of the aged man, and the choice of the new prince. Many rumours were current to the shame of the unchaste and cruel daughter of Germanicus. They heeded them not, and sang the praises of the illustrious woman to whom the Senecas owed the termination of their misfortune and their rise in honours. As will oftentimes happen, their convictions were in harmony with their interests. A painful experience of public life had left unshaken their trust in the *régime* established by the divine Augustus, a *régime* placed on a firmer basis by Tiberius, and under which they filled high positions. They were reckoning on a new master to redress the evils engendered by the masters of the Empire.

Gallio produced from the folds of his toga a roll of papyrus.

"Dear friends," he said, "I have learnt this morning, through letters from Rome, that our young prince has married Octavia, the daughter of Cæsar."

A murmur of approval greeted the news.

"We should indeed," continued Gallio, "congratulate ourselves over a union, by virtue of which the prince, combining with his former qualifications those of husband and of son-in-law, becomes henceforth the equal of Britannicus. My brother Seneca never ceases praising in his letters to me the eloquence and gentleness of his pupil who sheds lustre on his youth by pleading before the Senate in the presence of the Emperor. He has not yet completed his sixteenth year, yet he has already won the cases of three unfortunate or guilty cities—Ilion, Bolonia, and Apamea."

"He has not then," asked Lucius Cassius, "inherited the evil disposition of the Domitians, his ancestors?"

"Indeed he has not," replied Gallio. "It is Germanicus who lives anew in him."

Annæus Mela, who was not looked upon as a sycophant, joined in the praise of the son of Agrippina. His praises appeared affecting and sincere, since he pledged them, so to speak, on the head of his son, who was still of tender age.

"Nero is chaste, modest, of a kindly disposition, and religious. My little Lucan, who is dearer to me than my eyes, was his play- and school-mate. Together they practised declamation in the Greek and Latin languages. Together they attempted to indite verse. Never did Nero, in the course of these contests of skill at versification, manifest the slightest symptom of jealousy. Quite the contrary, he enjoyed praising his rival's verses, which, in spite of his tender age, revealed traces here and there of a consuming energy. He sometimes seemed happy to be surpassed by the nephew of his teacher. Such was the charming modesty of the prince of youth! Poets will some day compare the friendship of Nero and Lucan with that of Euryalus and Nisus."

"Nero," the proconsul went on to say, "displays with the ardour of youth a gentle and merciful spirit. Time will but strengthen such virtues.

"Claudius, when adopting him, has wisely acquiesced in the hope expressed by the Senate and the wish of the people. In so doing, he has removed from the Imperial succession a child overwhelmed by the shame of his mother, and has now, by giving Octavia to Nero, secured the accession of a youthful Cæsar whom Rome will delight in. The respectful son of an honoured mother, the zealous disciple of a philosopher, Nero, whose adolescence is illumined with the most agreeable qualities, Nero, our hope and the hope of the world, will remember, when clad in purple, the teachings of the Portico, and will rule the universe with justice and moderation."

"We welcome the omen," remarked Lollius. "May an era of happiness dawn upon the human race!"

"'Tis difficult to predict the future," said Gallio. "Still, we experience no doubts regarding the eternity of the City. The oracles have promised Rome an empire without end, and it would be sacrilegious not to put our faith in the gods. Shall I reveal to you my fondest hope? I joyfully expect the time when peace will reign for ever on the earth, following upon the chastising of the Parthians. Yes indeed, we may, without fear of deceiving ourselves, herald the end of war so hated by mothers. Who is there to disturb the Roman peace henceforth? Our eagles have spread to the confines of the universe. All the nations have experienced our strength and our mercy. The Arab, the Sabæan, the dweller on the slopes of the Hæmus, the Sarmatian who quenches his thirst with the blood of his steed, the Sygambri of the curly locks, the woolly-headed Ethiopian, all come in hordes to worship Rome their protectress. Whence would new barbarians spring? Is it likely that the icy plains of the North or the burning sands of Libya hold in store enemies of the Roman nation? All Barbarians, won over to our friendship, will lay down their arms, and Rome, the white-haired great-grandmother, tranquil in her old age, will see the nations respectfully grouped about her as her adopted children, dwelling in harmony and love."

All signified their approval of the foregoing sentiments, excepting Cassius, who shook his head in disagreement.

He felt a pride in his military ancestry while the glory of arms, so greatly extolled by poets and rhetors, kindled his enthusiasm.

"I doubt, my friend Gallio," he commented, "that nations will ever cease to hate and fear one another. To tell the truth, I should not desire such a consummation. Did war cease, what would become of strength of character, grandeur of soul, and love of country? Courage and devotion would be virtues out of date."

"Rest assured, Lucius," said Gallio, "that when men shall cease to conquer one another, they will strive to subdue their own selves. That is the most virtuous attempt they can make, and the most noble use to which they can put their bravery and magnanimity. Yes indeed, the august mother whose wrinkles and whose hairs, blanched by centuries, we worship, Rome, will establish universal peace. Then shall the enjoyment of life be realised. Life under certain conditions is worth living. Life is a tiny flame between two infinite shadows; 'tis our share of the divine essence. During the term of his life, a man is similar to the gods."

While Gallio was thus discoursing, a dove perched itself on the shoulder of the Venus, whose marble contours gleamed among the myrtles.

"My dear Gallio," said Lollius with a smile, "the bird of Aphrodite takes delight in thy words. They are gentle and full of gracefulness."

A slave approached, bearing cool wine, and the friends of the proconsul discoursed of the gods. Apollodorus was of opinion that it was not easy to grasp their nature. Lollius doubted their very existence.

"When thunder peals," he said, "it all depends upon the philosopher whether it is the cloud or the god who has thundered."

Cassius, however, did not countenance such thoughtless arguments. He believed in the gods of the Republic. While entertaining doubts as to the extent of their providence, he asserted their existence, as he did not wish to differ from humanity on an essential point. And to support his belief in the faith of his ancestors, he had recourse to an argument he had learnt from the Greeks.

"The gods exist," he said. "Men have formed their idea of what they are like. Now, it is impossible to conceive an image not based on reality. How would it be possible to see Minerva, Neptune, and Mercury, were there neither Mercury, nor Neptune, nor Minerva?"

"You have convinced me," said Lollius mockingly. "The old woman who sells honey-cakes in the Forum, outside the basilica, has seen the god Typhon, he with the shaggy head of an ass, and a monster belly. He threw her on her back, threw her clothes over her ears, chastised her while keeping time to each resounding blow, and left her for dead, after polluting her in a disgusting fashion. She has herself told how, even as Antiope, she had been favoured with the visit of an immortal god. It is certain that the god Typhon exists, since he committed an outrage on an old cake-selling hag."

"In spite of thy mockery, Marcus, I do not doubt the existence of the gods," resumed Cassius. "And I believe that they enjoy a human form, since it is under that form that they always show themselves to us, whether we slumber or whether we are awake."

"It would be better," remarked Apollodorus, "to say that men possess the divine form, since the gods existed before them."

"My dear Apollodorus," exclaimed Lollius. "You forget that Diana was first worshipped under the form of a tree, and that several important gods have the shape of an unhewn stone. Cybele is represented, not as a woman should be, with two breasts, but with several teats like a bitch or a sow. The sun is a god, but being too hot to assume the human form, he has taken the shape of a ball; he is a round god."

Annæus Mela gently censured this academic jesting.

"All that is related about the gods," he said, "should not be taken literally. The vulgar herd calls wheat Ceres, and wine Bacchus. But where is to be found the man crazy enough to believe that he drinks and eats a god? Let us indulge in a more exalted knowledge of the divine nature. The gods are but the several parts of nature, and they are all lost in one god, who is nature in its entirety."

The proconsul signified his approval of the words of his brother, and speaking in a serious strain, defined the attributes of divinity.

"God is the soul of the world; this soul spreads to all parts of the universe, infusing motion and life into it. This soul, a creative flame, penetrating the inert mass of matter, gave shape to the world, governing and preserving it. Divinity, an active force, is essentially good. The matter which it has put to good use, being inert and passive, is bad in certain of its parts. God has been powerless to change its nature. This explains the origin of the evil in the world. Our souls are particles of the divine fire into which they will some day be merged. Consequently, God is within us and he dwells in particular in the virtuous man whose soul is not hampered with gross materialism. This wise man, in whom God dwells, is God's equal. He should not implore him, but contain him within himself. And what madness it is to pray to God! What an act of impiety it is to petition him! It is tantamount to believing that it is possible to enlighten his intelligence, to change his heart, and to persuade him to mend his behaviour. It is displaying ignorance of the necessity governing his immutable wisdom. He is subjected to Destiny, or, to be more accurate, he is Destiny. His ways are laws to which he is like ourselves subjected. For once that he commands, he obeys for ever. Free and powerful in his submission, it is to himself that he shows obedience. All the happenings in the world are the manifestations of sovereign intentions originating with himself. His helplessness against himself is infinite."

Gallio's speech was applauded by his hearers. Apollodorus, however, craved permission to submit a few objections.

"You are right, Gallio," he said, "when you believe that Jupiter is at the mercy of Ananke and I hold with you that Ananke is the first among the immortal goddesses. But it appears to me that your god, above all admirable in his compass and his perpetuity, had better intentions than luck when he created the world, since he found nothing better wherewith to knead it than a rebellious and ingrate substance, and that the material betrays the workman. I cannot but feel for him over his discomfiture. The potters of Athens are more fortunate. They procure, for the purpose of making vases, a delicate and plastic clay which readily takes and preserves the contours they give it. Hence do their goblets and amphoræ present an agreeable form. Their curves are graceful, and the painter limns with ease figures pleasing to the eye, such as old Silenus bestriding his ass, the toilet of Aphrodite, and the chaste Amazons. When I come to think of it, Gallio, I am of the opinion that if your god was less fortunate than the potters of Athens, 'tis for the reason that he lacked wisdom and that he was a poor artisan. The material at his disposal was not of the best. Still, it was not devoid of all serviceable properties, as you have yourself confessed. Nothing is absolutely good or absolutely bad. A thing may be bad if put to a certain use, while it may be excellent in some other. It would be waste of time to plant olive-trees in the clay used in fashioning amphoræ. The tree of Pallas would not grow in the light and pure soil of which are made the beautiful vases which our victorious athletes receive, blushing the while with pride and modesty. It seems to me, Gallio, that your god, when fashioning the world with a material that was not suitable for the undertaking, was guilty of the mistake which a vine-dresser of Megara would be committing, were he to plant a vine in modelling clay, or were some worker in ceramics to select for the making of amphoræ the stony soil which affords nutriment to the clusters of the grape-vine. Your god, you say, made the universe. He ought certainly to have given form to some other thing, in order to make suitable use of his material. Since the substance, as you assert, proved rebellious to him, either through its inherent inertia, or through some other bad quality, should he have persisted in putting it to a use it could not respond to, and, as the saying goes, carve his bow out of a cypress? The secret of industry does not consist in accomplishing much, but in doing good work. Why did he not content himself with creating some small thing, say a gnat, or a drop of water, but finish it to perfection?

"I might add further remarks about your god, Gallio, and ask you, for instance, if you do not entertain a fear that from his constant rubbing against matter, he may wear out, just as a millstone becomes worn in the long run in the course of grinding wheat. But such questions are not to be solved in a hurry, and the time of a proconsul is precious. Permit me at least to say to you that you are not justified in believing that your god rules and preserves the world, since, according to your own admission, he deprived himself of intelligence after having become acquainted with all things; of will-power, after having willed all things, and of power, following upon his ability to do what he saw fit. Herein again lay, on his part, a serious mistake, for he was thus an instrument in depriving himself of the means of correcting his imperfect work. So far as I am concerned, I am inclined to believe that god is in reality, not the one you have conceived, but indeed the matter he discovered on a certain day, and which the Greeks have styled chaos. You are mistaken in your belief that matter is inert. It is ever in motion, and its perpetual activity keeps life a-going throughout the universe."

Thus spake the philosopher Apollodorus. Gallio, who had listened to his speech with some degree of impatience, denied that he had fallen a victim to the mistakes and contradictions with which the Greek charged him. But he failed in refuting successfully the arguments of his opponent, as his intellect was not a subtle one and because he demanded principally of philosophy the means of rendering men virtuous, and because he was interested in useful truths only.

"Try to grasp, Apollodorus," he said, "that God is none other than nature. Nature and himself are one. God and Nature are the two names of a single being, just as Novatus and Gallio designate one and the same man. God, if you prefer, is divine reason commingling with the earth. You need have no fear that he will wear out through this amalgamation, since his tenuous substance participates of the fire which consumes all matter while remaining unchanged.

"But should, nevertheless," proceeded Gallio, "my doctrine embrace ill-assorted ideas, do not blame me for it, my dear Apollodorus, but rather give me praise because I suffer a few contradictions to find a place in my mind. Were I not conciliatory as regards my own ideas, were I to confer upon a single system an exclusive preference, I could no longer tolerate the freedom of every opinion; having destroyed my own freedom of thought, I could not readily tolerate it in the case of others, and I should forfeit the respect due to every doctrine established or professed by a sincere man. The gods forbid that I should see my opinion prevail to the exclusion of any other, and exercise an absolute sway on other minds. Conjure up a picture, my dear friends, of the state of manners and morals, were a sufficient number of men firmly to believe that they were the sole possessors of the truth, if, by some impossible chance, they were thoroughly agreed as to that truth. A too narrow piety among the Athenians, who are nevertheless full of wisdom and of doubt, was the cause of the banishment of Anaxagoras and of the death of Socrates. What would happen were millions of men enslaved by one solitary idea concerning the nature of the gods? The genius of the Greeks and the prudence of our ancestors made allowance for doubt, and tolerated the worship of Jupiter under several names. No sooner should a powerful sect come on this ailing earth and proclaim that Jupiter has one name only, than blood would flow the world over, and no longer would there be but one Caius whose madness should threaten the human race with death. All the men of such a sect would be so many Caiuses. They would face death for a name. For a name, they would kill, since it is rather in the nature of men to kill than to die on behalf of what seems to them true and most excellent. Hence it is better to base public order on the diversity of opinions, than to seek to establish it on a universal consent to one and the same belief. A like unanimous consent could never be realised, and in seeking to obtain it, men would become stupid and maddened. For, indeed, the most patent truth is but a vain jangle of words to the men on whom it is attempted to impose it. You would compel me to believe a thing which you understand, but which passes my understanding. You would thus be forcing upon me not a thing that is intelligible, but one that is incomprehensible. And I am nearer you when holding a different belief, one which I understand. For, in that case, both of us are making use of our reason, and we both possess an intelligent comprehension of our own belief."

"Enough of all this," remarked Lollius. "Educated men will never combine for the purpose of stifling all other doctrines to the advantage of a single one. As to the vulgar herd, who cares to teach it that Jupiter has six hundred names, or a single one?"

Cassius, slow of utterance, and of a serious turn of mind, spoke next.

"Beware, Gallio," he said, "lest the existence of God, such as expounded by you, be not in contradiction with the beliefs of our forefathers. It matters little, after all, whether your arguments are better or worse than those of Apollodorus. What we have to consider is the fatherland. To its religion does Rome owe her virtues and her power. To destroy our gods is to compass our own destruction."

"You need not fear, my friend," rejoined Gallio with some show of animation, "have no fear, I repeat, that I deny in an insolent spirit the heavenly protectors of the Empire. The only divinity which the philosophers acknowledge embodies within itself all the gods, just as humanity embraces all men. The gods whose worship was instituted by the wisdom of our forefathers, Jupiter, Juno, Mars, Minerva, Quirinus, and Hercules, constitute the most august parts of the universal providence, and no less than the whole do these parts exist. No, indeed, I am not an impious man, nor inimical to the laws. None respects the sacred things more than Gallio."

No one seemed disposed to dispute these ideas. Thereupon Lollius, bringing the conversation back to its starting-point, remarked:

"We have been seeking to penetrate the veil of the future. What are man's destinies, according to you, my friends, after his demise?"

In reply to this question, Annæus Mela promised immortality to heroes and wise men, while denying it to the common of mankind.

"It passes belief," he said, "that misers, gluttons, and mean-spirited men should possess an immortal soul. Could so singular a privilege be the portion of coarse and silly oafs? I cannot entertain such a thought. It would be an insult to the majority of the gods to believe that they have decreed the immortality of the boor who wots only of his goats and cheeses, or of the freedman, richer than Crœsus, who had no other cares in the world than to check the accounts of his stewards. Why, good gods, should they be provided with a soul? What sort of a figure would they present among heroes and wise men in the Elysian fields? These wretches, like so many others here below, are incapable of realising humanity's short-spanned life. How could they realise a life of longer duration? Vulgar souls are snuffed out at the hour of death, or they may for a while whirl about our globe, to vanish in the dense strata of the atmosphere. Virtue only, by making man the equal of the gods, makes them participate in their immortality. To quote the poet:

"'Illustrious virtue never descends into the Stygian shades. Lead a hero's life, and the fates will not consign thee to the pitiless river of forgetfulness. When comes thy last day, glory will open to thee the path of heaven.'

"Let us realise our condition. We must all die, and all that we are must die. The man of shining virtue simply escapes the common destiny by becoming god, and by obtaining his admission into Olympus among the Heroes and the Gods."

"But he is not conscious of his own apotheosis," said Marcus Lollius. "There does not exist upon earth a slave or a barbarian who is not aware that Augustus is a god. But Augustus knows it not. Hence it is that our Cæsars journey reluctantly towards the constellations, and even now we see Claudius near with blanched face these shadowy honours."

Gallio shook his head, and remarked, "The poet Euripides has said:

"'We love the life which is revealed unto us upon earth, since we know of no other.'

"Everything that is related concerning the dead is open to doubt, and is bound up with fables and falsehoods. Nevertheless, I believe that virtuous men attain an immortality of which they are fully cognisant. Let it be clearly understood that they achieve it by their own efforts, and not as a recompense conferred by the gods. By what right should the immortal gods degrade a virtuous man to the extent of rewarding him? The leading of a blameless life is its own reward, and no prize is there worthy of virtue, which is its own reward. Let us leave to vulgar souls, that they may thereby sustain their wretched fortitude, the dread of punishment, and the hope of a reward. Let us love virtue for its own sake. Gallio, if what the poets tell of the infernal regions be true, if after your death you are arraigned before the tribunal of Minos, you may say to him: "Minos shall not judge me. By my actions have I been judged."'"

"How," inquired Apollodorus the philosopher, "can the gods give to men an immortality they themselves do not enjoy?"

Apollodorus, indeed, did not believe in the immortality of the gods, or rather that their sway over the world should be exercised for all time.

He proceeded to develop the reasons for his belief.

"The reign of Jupiter," he said, "began after the Golden Age. We know through the traditions preserved for us by the poets that the son of Saturn succeeded to his father in the governing of the world. Now, everything that had a beginning must have an end. It is foolish to suppose that anything finite in one part can be infinite in another. It would then become necessary to call it finite and infinite as a whole, which would be absurd. Anything possessed of an extreme point can be measured from that point itself, and could not in any way cease to be measured at any point of its extent, without changing its nature, and the proper of what is measurable is to be comprised between two extreme points. We may therefore make up our minds that the reign of Jupiter will end just as did that of Saturn. As Æschylus has said:

284

"'Jupiter is subordinate to Anankè. He cannot escape his fate.'"

Gallio thought the same, for reasons derived from the observation of nature.

"I consider with you, Apollodorus, that the reigns of the gods are not immortal, and the observation of the celestial phenomena inclines me to this belief. The heavens, as well as the earth, are subject to corruption, and the divine palaces, liable to ruin just as the dwellings of mankind, crumble under the weight of the centuries. I have seen stones fall from the aerial regions. They were blackened and corroded by fire, and bore testimony to a celestial conflagration.

"The bodies of the gods, Apollodorus, are not any more exempt from injury than their dwellings. If it be true, as Homer teaches, that the gods, inhabitants of Olympus, impregnate the flanks of goddesses and mortal women, it is assuredly because they are not themselves immortal, in spite of their life's span being greater than that of mankind, and hence it is patent that fate subjects them to the necessity of transmitting a life which they may not enjoy for ever.

"In truth," said Lollius, "it is hardly to be conceived that immortals should produce children in the same way as human beings and animals, or even that they should possess organs adapted to such a purpose. But perhaps the loves of the gods owe their origin to the mendacity of the poets."

Apollodorus persisted in his assertion that the reign of Jupiter would some day cease, supporting his opinion with subtle reasons. He prophesied that Prometheus would succeed the son of Saturn.

"Prometheus," replied Gallio, "was set free by Hercules with the consent of Jupiter, and he enjoys in Olympus the happiness he owes to his foresight and to his love of mankind. Nothing will ever happen to change his happy fate."

Apollodorus asked him:

"Who then, according to you, Gallio, shall inherit the thunder which sets the world a-quaking?"

"Although it may seem audacious to answer this question," replied Gallio, "I think I am competent to do so, and to name Jove's successor."

As he spoke, an officer of the basilica, whose duty it was to call cases, approached him, and informed him that some suitors were waiting for him in court.

The proconsul asked if the matter was one of paramount importance.

"It is a most petty case, Gallio," replied the officer of the basilica. "A man from the harbour of Cenchreæ has just dragged a stranger before your tribunal. They are both Jews and of humble condition. They are quarrelling over some barbarian custom or some gross superstition, as is the wont of Syrians. Here is the minute of their case. It is all Punic to the clerk who wrote it.

"The plaintiff sets forth, Gallio, that he is the head of the assembly of the Jews or, as one says in Greek, of the synagogue, and he begs justice of you against a man from Tarsus, who, recently settled at Cenchreæ, goes every Saturday to the synagogue, for the purpose of speaking against the Jewish law. 'It is a scandal and an abomination, which thou shalt put an end to,' says the plaintiff, and he clamours for the integrity of the privileges belonging to the children of Israel. The defendant claims for all those who believe his teachings adoption and incorporation into the family of a man named Abraham, and he threatens the plaintiff with the divine ire. You see, Gallio, that the case is a petty and ambiguous one. It rests with you to decide whether you will take the case yourself, or whether you will leave it to be judged by a lesser magistrate."

The proconsul's friends begged him not to disturb himself for so miserable an affair.

"I make it my duty," he said in response to their prayers, "to follow in this respect the rules laid down by the divine Augustus. I must therefore try personally, not only important cases, but also smaller ones, when the jurisprudence concerning them has not been determined. Certain light cases recur daily and are of importance, if only for their frequency. It is meet that I should personally try one of each class. A judgment rendered by a proconsul serves as an example, and establishes a precedent in law."

"You deserve praise, Gallio," said Lollius, "for the zeal you display in the fulfilment of your consular duties. But, acquainted as I am with your wisdom, I doubt whether it is agreeable for you to render justice. That which men honour with this title is really an administration of base prudence and of cruel revenge. Human laws are the daughters of fear and anger."

Gallio protested feebly against this definition. He did not admit that human laws bore the character of real justice, saying:

"The punishment of crime consists in its commission. The penalty added thereto by the laws is superfluous, and does not fit the crime. However, since through the fault of mankind laws there are, we should apply them equitably."

Thereupon he told the officer of the court that he would proceed to the tribunal very shortly, and, turning towards his friends, he said:

"To speak truly, I have a special reason for looking into this case with my own eyes. I must not neglect any opportunity of keeping an eye on these Jews of Cenchreæ, a turbulent, rancorous race, which shows contempt for the laws, and which it is not easy to hold in check. If ever the peace of Corinth should be troubled, it will be by them. This port, where all the ships of the East come to anchor, conceals amid a congested mass of warehouses and taverns, a countless horde of thieves, eunuchs, soothsayers, sorcerers, lepers, desecraters of graves, and assassins. It is the haunt of every abomination and of every form of superstition. Isis, Eschmoun, the Phœnician Venus, and the god of the Jews, are all worshipped there. I am alarmed at seeing those unclean Jews multiply, rather in the way of fishes than in that of mankind. They swarm about the miry streets of the harbour like crabs under the rocks."

"What is more dreadful is that they infest Rome to a like extent," exclaimed Lucius Cassius. "To great Pompey's own door must be laid the crime of introducing this plague of leprosy into the City. He it was who committed the wrong of not treating as did our ancestors the prisoners he brought from Judæa for his triumphal entry into the City, and they have peopled the right bank of the Tiber with their base spawn. Dwelling about the base of the Janiculum, amid the tanneries, the gut-works, and the fermenting-troughs, in the suburbs whither flock all the abominations and horrors of the world, they earn their livelihood at the vilest of trades, unloading lighters, selling rags and refuse, and exchanging matches for broken glasses. Their women tell fortunes in the houses of the wealthy; their children beg from the frequenters of Egeria's groves. As you rightly said, Gallio, hostile to the human race and to themselves, they are ever fomenting sedition. A few years back, the followers of a certain Chrestus or Cherestus raised bloody riots among the Jews. The Porta Portuensis was put to fire and sword, and Cæsar was compelled to exercise severe repression, in spite of his forbearance. He expelled from Rome the leaders of the movement."

"Full well do I know it," said Gallio. "Several of these exiles came to Cenchreæ, among others a Jew and a Jewess from the Pontus, who still dwell there, following some humble trade. I believe that they weave the coarse stuffs of Cilicia. I have not learnt anything noteworthy in regard to the partisans of Chrestus. As to Chrestus himself, I am ignorant of what has become of him, and whether he is still of this world."

"I am as ignorant on this score as you are, Gallio," resumed Lucius Cassius, "and no one will ever know it. These vile wretches do not so much as attain celebrity in the annals of crime. Moreover, there are so many slaves of the name of Chrestus that it would be no easy matter to distinguish a particular one amid the throng.

"It is but a trifling matter that the Jews should cause tumult within the low purlieus where their number and their lowliness protect them from supervision. They swarm through the city, they ingratiate themselves into families, and are everywhere a source of trouble. They shout in the Forum on behalf of the agitators who pay them, and these despicable foreigners incite the citizens to a hatred of one another. Too long have we endured their presence in popular assemblages, and for a long time now have public speakers avoided running counter to the opinion of these wretches, for fear of their insults. Obstinate in the observance of their barbarian law, they wish to subject others to it, and they find adepts among the Asiatics, and even among the Greeks. And, what is hardly to be credited, they impose their customs on the Latins themselves. There are, in the City, whole quarters where all the shops are closed on their Sabbath day. Oh the shame of Rome! And, while corrupting the lowly folk among whom they dwell, their kings, admitted into Cæsar's palace, insolently practise their superstitions, and set to all citizens a detestable and noted example. Thus do the Jews inoculate Italy on all sides with an oriental venom."

Annæus Mela, who had travelled over the whole of the Roman world, sought to make his friends realise the extent of the evil they deplored.

"The Jews corrupt the whole world," he said. "There is not a Greek city, there are hardly any barbarian towns where work does not cease on the seventh day, where lamps are not lit, where their keeping of fast-days is not followed, and where the abstaining from the flesh of certain animals is not observed in imitation of them.

"I have met in Alexandria an aged Jew not lacking in intelligence, who was even versed in Greek literature. He rejoiced at the progress of his religion in the Empire. 'In proportion to the knowledge foreigners acquire of our laws,' he told me, 'do they find them pleasant, and they conform readily to them, both Romans and Greeks, those who dwell on the mainland and the people of the isles, Eastern and Western nations, Europe and Asia.' The ancient one spoke perhaps with some degree of exaggeration. Still one sees a number of Greeks yielding to the beliefs of the Jews."

Apollodorus sharply denied such to be the case.

"The Greeks who judaise," he said, "are not to be met with except amid the dregs of the populace, and among the barbarians wandering about Greece, as brigands and tramps. The followers of the Stammerer may, however, have persuaded some few ignorant Greeks, by inducing them to believe that the ideas of Plato are to be found in the Hebrew scriptures. Such is the lie which they strive to spread."

"It is a fact," replied Gallio, "that the Jews recognise an only, invisible, almighty god, who has created the earth. But they are far from worshipping him with wisdom. They publicly proclaim that this god is the enemy of all that is not Jewish, and that he will not tolerate in his temple either the effigies of the other gods, or the statue of Cæsar, or his own images. They regard as impious those who fashion out of perishable matter a god the image of man. Various reasons, some of them good and in harmony with the ideas which we conceive in regard to the divine providence, are adduced why this god should not be given expression to in marble or in bronze. But what can be thought, dear Apollodorus, of a god sufficiently inimical to the Republic that he will not admit in his sanctuary the statues of the Prince? How conceive a god who takes offence at the honours rendered to other gods? And what opinion can one have of a nation which credits its gods with like sentiments! The Jews look upon the gods of the Latins, Greeks and Barbarians as hostile gods, and they carry superstition to the point of believing that they possess a full and complete knowledge of God, one to which nothing can be added, and from which nothing can be subtracted.

"As you are aware, my dear friends, it is not sufficient to tolerate every religion; we should honour them all, believe that all are sacred, that they are all coequal in the sincerity of those professing them, and that similar to arrows shot from various points towards the same goal, they all meet in the bosom of God. Alone the religion which only tolerates itself, cannot be endured. Were it to be permitted to spread, it would absorb all others. Nay, so unsociable a religion is not a religion, but rather an abligion, and no longer a bond that unites pious men, but one severing that sacred bond. It is the most impious of things. Can, indeed, a greater insult be offered to the deity than to worship it under a particular form, while at one and the same time dooming it to execration under all the other forms it assumes in the eyes of men?

"What! Because I sacrifice to Jupiter crowned with a bushel, I am to forbid a foreigner from sacrificing to a Jupiter whose head of hair, similar to the flower of the hyacinth, drops uncrowned over his shoulders; and that, impious man that I should be, I should still consider myself a worshipper of Jupiter! No, by all means no! The religious man bound to the immortal gods is equally bound to all men by the religion which embraces both the earth and the heavens. Odious is the error of the Jews who believe they are pious in that they worship their god alone!"

"They suffer themselves to be circumcised in his honour," spoke Annæus Mela. "In order that this mutilation should not be noticed, it is necessary, when frequenting the public baths, for them to conceal that which should neither be made a display of, nor covered as a thing of shame. For it is alike ridiculous for a man to pride himself on, or to be ashamed of, what he shares in common with all men. We have good cause to dread, my friends, the progress of Judaic customs in the Empire. There is, however, no cause to fear that Romans and Greeks will adopt circumcision. It passes belief that this custom is likely to make its way among the Barbarians who, however, would feel the disgrace of it to a lesser degree, since they are, for the greater part, absurd enough to reckon as disgraceful for a man to appear before his fellow men in a state of nudity."

"While I think of it!" exclaimed Lollius. "When our gentle Canidia, the flower of the matrons of the Esquiline, sends her beautiful slaves to the hot baths, she compels them to wear drawers, as she grudges everybody even a view of what is most dear to her about their bodies. By Pollux, she will be the cause of their being taken for Jews, an insulting supposition, even for a slave."

Lucius Cassius resumed, revealing the irritation which consumed him:

"I cannot say whether the Jewish folly will overtake the whole world. But it is past endurance that this madness should spread among the ignorant, that it should be tolerated in the Empire, that this fœtid race, which has descended to every form of turpitude, absurd and sordid in its manners and customs, impious and villainous in its laws, and execrated by the immortal gods, should be suffered to exist. The obscene Syrian is corrupting the City of Rome. We have cast aside with contempt our ancient usages, and the salutary methods of discipline of our ancestors. We no longer serve these masters of the earth, who conquered it for us. Which of us still believes in the haruspices? Who is there with any respect for the augurs? Who shows reverence to Mars and the divine Twins? Oh the sad neglect of our religious duties! Italy has repudiated her indigenous gods, and her tutelary genii. She is henceforth on all sides at the mercy of foreign superstitions, and is handed over defenceless to the impure horde of oriental priests. Alas, did Rome conquer the world only to be conquered by the Jews? Warnings have assuredly not been lacking. The overflowing of the Tiber and the grain famine are certainly not doubtful manifestations of the divine ire. No day passes without its sinister presage. The earth quakes, the sun is veiled, while lightning flashes in a clear sky. Wonders follow upon wonders. Birds of ill omen have been seen to perch on the summit of the Capitol. An ox has been heard to speak on the Etruscan shore. Women have brought forth monsters; a wailing voice has sounded amid the recreations of the theatre. The statue of Victory has dropped the reins of her chariot."

"The hosts of the celestial palaces," remarked Lollius, "have strange ways of making themselves heard. If they desire a little more incense, or sigh for a few more fat offerings, let them say so plainly, instead of expressing their wishes by means of thunder, clouds, crows, bronze statues, and two-headed children. Moreover, you must admit, Lucius, theirs is a far too one-sided part when they presage the evils threatening us, since, in the natural course of things, not a day goes by but what brings some individual or public misfortune."

Gallio exhibited distress at the sorrows of Cassius.

"Claudius," he remarked, "Claudius, although he is always dozing, has deeply felt this great peril. He has complained to the Senate of the contempt into which ancient usages have been suffered to fall. Alarmed at the progress of foreign superstitions, the Senate has, on his recommendation, re-established haruspices. But it is not sufficient that the observance of the ceremonial rites of worship should be restored; rather is it necessary once more to instil into men's hearts their primitive purity. The souls of virtuous men constitute the proper shrine of the gods in this world. Give a home within your hearts to past virtues once more, simplicity, good faith, love of the public welfare, and the gods will immediately re-enter them. You shall then yourselves be temples and altars."

He spoke, and, taking leave of his friends, entered his litter, which, for some little time past, had been awaiting him near a clump of myrtle-bushes to convey him to the tribunal.

His friends had risen from their seats, and leaving the grounds, followed leisurely behind him under a double portico, so disposed as to afford shadow at all hours of the day, and leading from the walls of the villa to the basilica where the proconsul dispensed justice.

By the way, Lucius Cassius expressed to Mela his regret at the oblivion into which the ancient methods of discipline had fallen.

Marcus Lollius, placing a hand on the shoulder of Apollodorus, said:

"It seems to me that neither our gentle Gallio nor Mela, nor even Cassius, have stated their reasons for their deep hatred of the Jews. I think I know, and I am going to tell you, most dear

Apollodorus. The Romans who offer up to the gods a white sow ornamented with white bands, execrate the Jews who refuse to partake of pork. It is not in vain that the fates sent to the pious Æneas a white female boar as a presage. Had the gods not studded with oaks the wild realms of Evander and Turnus, Rome would not be to-day the mistress of the world. The acorns of Latium fattened the swine whose flesh has alone appeased the insatiable hunger of the magnanimous descendants of Remus. Our Italians, whose bodies are built on boars and pigs, feel offended at the proud abstinence of the Jews, who persist in casting aside as unclean victuals the fat sounders, beloved of old Cato, which furnish food to the masters of the Universe."

Thus discoursing pleasantly, and enjoying the kindly shade, the four friends reached the furthermost end of the portico, when of a sudden the Forum appeared before them in a glitter of light.

At that early hour, it was all astir with the coming and going of noisy crowds. In the centre of the square stood a bronze Minerva on a pedestal on which were sculptured the Muses, and to the right and to the left stood a Mercury and a bronze Apollo, the work of Hermogenes of Cythera. A Neptune with a green beard arose from the centre of a basin. At the feet of the god, a dolphin vomited forth water.

The Forum was surrounded in all directions by monuments, the high columns and the arches of which revealed the Roman style of architecture. Facing the portico by way of which Mela and his friends had come, the Propylæ, surmounted by two gilded chariots, formed the boundary of the public square, and led, by way of marble steps, to the broad and straight road of the harbour of Lechæum. On either side of these heroic gates rose in kingly fashion the painted pediments of the sanctuaries, the Pantheon, and the temple of Artemis of Ephesus. The temple of Octavia, the sister of Augustus, dominated the Forum, and looked upon the sea.

Between it and the basilica ran an insignificant little street. The building rose over two stories of arcades supported by pillars flanked with Doric half-columns forming a square. The Roman style, which stamped its character upon all the other buildings of the city, was patent. There remained of the pristine Corinth nothing but the calcined ruins of an old temple.

The lower arcades of the basilica were open and served as shops to sellers of fruit, vegetables, oil, wine and fried foods, to bird-fanciers, jewellers, booksellers, and barbers. Money-changers sat at little tables laden with gold and silver coins. From the gloomy hollow of these stalls emerged shouts, laughter, hailings, the noise of disputes, and pungent odours. On the marble steps, wherever their slabs were tinted blue by the shade, loafers shook dice or tossed knuckle-bones, suitors paced to and fro with anxious mien, sailors gravely looked for the pleasures upon which they should squander their wages, while quidnuncs read news from Rome written for them by frivolous Greeks. Blended with this crowd of Corinthians and foreigners, numerous blind beggars persistently obtruded themselves, as well as callow and rouged youths, matchsellers and crippled sailors from whose necks depended a picture of the wreck of their ships. Doves flew in flocks from the roof of the basilica down to the large open spaces on which the sun shone, and picked up grain between the cracks of the heated flagstones.

A girl of twelve, dark and velvety as a pansy of Xanthus, placed on the ground her little brother, as yet unable to walk, put beside him a chipped bowl filled with porridge and a wooden spoon, saying to him:

"Eat, Comatas, eat and keep quiet, or that red horse will have you."

Then, holding an obolus in her hand, she ran towards the fish-dealer, whose wrinkled face and naked breast, the colour of saffron, appeared amid baskets lined with seaweed.

While she was thus engaged, a dove hovering about the little Comatas got its talons entangled in the child's locks. The boy began to cry, and to call his sister to his help, screaming in a voice choked with sobs:

"Joessa! Joessa!"

But Joessa heard him not. She was rummaging in the old man's baskets, amid the fish and the shell-fish, for something that would improve the taste of her stale bread. Naturally she did not pick out a peacock-fish or a smaris, whose flesh is most delicate, but which cost money. She brought away in the hollow of her gown, which she had tucked up, three handfuls of sea-urchins and sticklebacks.

Meanwhile little Comatas, his mouth wide open, and drinking his own tears, was still bawling:

"Joessa! Joessa!"

Unlike Jove's eagle, the bird of Venus did not carry off little Comatas into the glorious skies. It left him on the earth, taking with it in its flight, between its pink talons, three golden hairs from his matted locks.

The child, with cheeks glistening with tears and begrimed with dust, clenching his wooden spoon in his tiny fists, was sobbing beside his overturned bowl.

Annæus Mela, followed by his three friends, had reached the top of the basilica's steps. Alike heedless of the noise and stir of the idle multitude, he was imparting information to Cassius in regard to the future renovation of the universe.

"On a day determined by the gods," he said, "the things existing to-day, whose order and disposition claim our attention, will be destroyed. Stars will clash with stars, all matters composing the earth, the air, and the waters will be consumed in one conflagration. Human souls, imperceptible *débris* amid the universal destruction, will be resolved anew into their primitive elements. An entirely new world...."

As he uttered the words, Annæus Mela stumbled against a sleeper stretched out in the shade. It was an old man who had artistically gathered about his dust-covered body the ragged remnants of his cloak. His wallet, his sandals, and his stick lay beside him.

The proconsul's brother, ever courteous and kindly, even to men of the lowliest class, was about to apologise, but the recumbent individual did not allow him time to do so.

"Try and see where you put your feet, you brute," he exclaimed, "and give alms to the philosopher Posocharis."

"I perceive a wallet and a stick," smilingly replied the Roman, "but so far I do not see any philosopher."

Just as he was about to toss a piece of silver to Posocharis, Apollodorus stayed his hand, saying:

"Do not give him anything, Annæus. It is not a philosopher; nay, not even a man."

"But I am one," replied Mela, "if I give him money, and he is a man if he takes this coin. For, alone among all animals, man does both these things. And can you not see that for the sake of a small coin I satisfy myself that I am a better man than he? Your master teaches that he who gives is better than he who receives."

Posocharis took the coin. Then he hurled coarse invectives at Annæus Mela and his companions, stigmatising them as arrogant and as debauchees, and referring them to the jugglers and harlots who walked past them with undulating hips. Then, baring to the navel his hairy body, and drawing over his face his tattered cloak, he once more stretched himself out at full length on the pavement.

"Would it not interest you," asked Lollius of his companions, "to hear those Jews expound their dispute in the prætorium?"

They replied that they entertained no such curiosity, preferring to stroll under the portico, while waiting for the proconsul, who would doubtless not be long in coming out.

"I am with you, my friends," said Lollius. "We shall not miss anything very interesting."

"Moreover," he went on to say, "the Jews who have come from Cenchreæ to accompany the suitors are not all in the basilica. Here comes one who is recognisable by his beaked nose and his forked beard. He is in as fine a state of frenzy as Pythia herself."

Lollius was pointing with both look and finger at a lean stranger, poorly clad, who was vociferating under the portico, in the midst of a railing mob.

"Men of Corinth, you place a vain trust in your wisdom, which is naught but madness. You follow blindly the precepts of your philosophers who teach you death, and not life. You do not observe the natural law, and in order to punish you, God has delivered you unto unnatural vices...."

A sailor, who had just joined the group of spectators, recognised the man, for, with a shrug of the shoulders, he muttered:

"Why, 'tis Stephanas, the Jew of Cenchreæ, who brings once more some extraordinary piece of news from his trip to the skies, into which he ascended, if we are to credit him."

And Stephanas was teaching the people.

"The Christian is not bound by law and concupiscence. He is exempt from damnation through the mercy of God, who sent his only son to assume a sinful body, in order to destroy sin. But ye shall only be delivered if, breaking with the flesh, you live according to the spirit.

"The Jews observe the laws, and believe that they are saved by their works. But it is their faith which saves them, and not their works. Of what use is it to them to be circumcised in fact, if their heart is uncircumcised?

"Men of Corinth, glory in the faith, and ye shall be incorporated into the family of Abraham."

The mob was beginning to laugh and jeer at these obscure utterances. Still the Jew continued prophesying in hollow tones. He was announcing a great manifestation of wrath and the all-destroying fire which was to consume the earth.

"And these things shall come to pass in my lifetime," he cried, "and I shall witness them with mine own eyes. The hour has come for us to awaken from our sleep. The night has passed, and the day is dawning. The Saints will rejoice in Heaven, and those who have not believed in Jesus crucified shall perish."

Then, promising the resurrection of the body, he invoked Anastasis, amid the jeers of the hilarious crowd.

Just then, a leather-lunged man, Milo the baker, a member of the Corinthian Senate, who for some time past had been listening to the Jew with impatience, came up to him, took him by the arm, and shaking him roughly said:

"Cease, you wretch, spouting idle words. All this is children's fables and nonsense fit to capture a woman's mind. How canst thou, on the strength of thy dreams, indulge in such foolery, casting aside all that is beautiful, and taking pleasure in what is evil only, without even deriving any advantage from thy hatred? Renounce your strange phantasies, your perverse designs, your gloomy forebodings, lest a god abandon you to the crows, to punish you for your imprecations against this city and the Empire."

The citizens applauded Milo's speech.

"He speaks truly," they shouted. "Those Syrians have but one design: they seek to weaken our fatherland. They are the enemies of Cæsar."

A number of them abstracted from the fruiterers' stalls gourds and locust-beans, others picked up oyster-shells, and flung them at the apostle, who was still vaticinating.

Thrown down the steps of the portico, he wended his way through the Forum, shouting, amid a storm of hooting, insults, and blows, pelted with dirt, bleeding, and half naked:

"My Master has said it, we are the sweepings of the world."

And he exulted in his joy.

The children pursued him on the Cenchreæ road, yelling.

"Anastasis! Anastasis!"

Posocharis was not sleeping. Hardly had the friends of the proconsul gone away, when he raised himself upon his elbow. Seated on a step, a short distance from him, the swarthy Joessa was crunching between her teeth the shell of a sea-urchin. The cynic hailed her and showed her the glittering piece of silver he had just received. Then, having readjusted his rags and tatters, he rose, slipped his feet into his sandals, picked up his stick and wallet, and went down the steps. Joessa went up to him, relieved him of his wallet full of holes, which she gravely placed on her shoulder, as if to carry it as an offering to the august Cypris, and followed the old man.

Apollodorus saw them taking the Cenchreæ road with the object of reaching the cemetery of the slaves, and the place of execution conspicuous from afar by the swarms of crows which hovered over the crosses. The philosopher and the young girl knew there a clump of arbutus always deserted, and favourable to dalliance with Eros.

At the sight of this, Apollodorus, pulling Mela by the flap of his toga, remarked:

"Just look. No sooner has that cur received your alms than he decoys a child, in order to mate with her."

"Which goes to prove," answered Mela, "that I gave money to the kind of man who knows full well what to do with it."

Meanwhile, the brat Comatas, squatting on the heated flagstone and sucking his thumbs, was laughing at the sight of a pebble glistening in the sun.

"Besides," resumed Mela, "you must admit, Apollodorus, that the way in which Posocharis makes love is not a bit philosophical. The dog is assuredly wiser than our young debauchees of the Palatine, who love amid perfumes, tears, and laughter, with languor or with passion..."

As he spoke, a hoarse clamour arose in the prætorium, deafening to the ears of the Greek and the three Romans.

"By Pollux!" exclaimed Lollius, "the suitors whose case our friend Gallio is trying are shouting like dockers, and it seems to me that together with their growls a stench of sweat and onions reaches us."

"Nothing is more true," quoth Apollodorus. "But, were Posocharis a philosopher instead of the dog he is, far from sacrificing to the Venus of the cross-roads, he would flee from the whole breed of women, and attach himself solely to some youth, whose eternal comeliness he would contemplate merely as the expression of an inner beauty more noble and more precious."

"Love," resumed Mela, "is an abject passion. It disturbs the reason, destroys noble impulses, and diverts the most elevated ideas to the vilest cares. It has no place in a sensible mind. As the poet Euripides teaches us...."

Mela did not finish his sentence. Preceded by lictors, who pushed the crowd aside, the proconsul came out of the basilica, and went up to his friends.

"I have not been away from you long," he said. "The case which I was summoned to try was as meagre as could be, and ridiculous in the extreme. On entering the prætorium, I found it invaded by a motley crowd of the Jews who, in their sordid shops along the wharves of the harbour of Cenchreæ, sell carpets, stuffs, and petty articles of silver and gold jewellery to the sailors. The atmosphere was filled with their shrill yelping, and with a pungent odour of goat. It was with difficulty that I could grasp the meaning of their words, and it cost me an effort to understand that one of those Jews, Sosthenes by name, who styled himself the chief of the synagogue, was charging with impiety another Jew, the latter, repulsively ugly, bandy-legged, and blear-eyed, and named Paul or Saul, a native of Tarsus, who has for some time past been exercising in Corinth his trade of weaver, and has gone into partnership with certain Jews expelled from Rome, for the weaving of tent-cloths and Cilician garments in goat-hair. They all spoke at once, and in very bad Greek. I made out, however, that this Sosthenes imputed as a crime to this Paul that he had entered the house wherein the Jews of Corinth are in the habit of meeting every Saturday, and had spoken with the object of seducing his co-religionists, and of persuading them to worship their god in a fashion contrary to their law. I had heard enough. So having, not without difficulty, silenced them, I informed them that had they come to me to complain of some matter of wrong or of some deed of violence wherefrom they might have suffered injury, I should have listened to them with patience, and with all the necessary attention; but, since their case turned simply upon a question of words, and a disagreement in regard to their law, it concerned me not, and that I could not be judge of such matters. I thereupon dismissed them with these words: 'Settle your quarrels among yourselves, as best you see fit.'"

"What did they say to that?" asked Cassius. "Did they submit with good grace to so wise a decision?"

"It is not in the nature of brutes," replied the proconsul, "to relish wisdom. Those fellows greeted my decision with harsh murmurings of which, as you may well imagine, I took no notice. I left them shouting and struggling at the foot of the tribunal. From what I could see, most of the blows fell to the plaintiff. He will be left for dead, if my lictors do not interfere. These Jews from the harbour are great ignoramuses, and like most ignorant people, not enjoying the faculty of supporting with arguments the truth of what they believe, they know no other argument than kicks and fisticuffs.

"The friends of that little deformed and blear-eyed Jew named Paul seem to be particularly clever at that kind of controversy. Ye gods! How they got the better of the chief of the synagogue, raining blows on him, and trampling him under their feet! But I do not doubt that had the friends of Sosthenes been the stronger of the two parties, they would have treated Paul as the friends of Paul treated Sosthenes."

Mela congratulated the proconsul.

"You were right, brother mine, in sending those wretched litigants about their business."

"Could I do otherwise?" replied Gallio. "How could I have decided between that Sosthenes and that Paul who are the one as stupid and as rabid as the other?... If I treat them with contempt, do not, my friends, think that is because they are poor and humble, because Sosthenes reeks of salted fish, or for the reason that Paul's fingers have become worn in weaving carpets and tent-cloth. No, Philemon and Baucis were poor, yet worthy of the highest honours. The gods did not disdain being entertained at their frugal board. Wisdom raises a slave above his master. Nay, a virtuous slave is superior to the gods. If he is their equal in wisdom, he surpasses them in the beauty of the accomplishment. Those Jews are to be despised simply because they are boorish, and that no image of the divinity is reflected in them."

A smile overspread the countenance of Marcus Lollius at these word.

"Truly, the gods," he said, "would hardly frequent the Syrians who infest the harbours, amid the sellers of fruit and the strumpets."

"The Barbarians themselves," resumed the proconsul, "possess some knowledge of the gods. Not to mention the Egyptians, who, in the olden days, were men filled with piety, there is not in wealthy Asia a nation which has not worshipped Diana, Vulcan, Juno, or the mother of the Æneædes. They give these divinities strange names, confused forms, and sometimes offer up to them human sacrifices, but they recognise their power. Alone are the Jews ignorant of the providence of the gods. I know not whether that Paul, whom the Syrians also call Saul, is as superstitious as the others, and as obstinate in his errors. I know not what obscure idea he conceives of the immortal gods, and to tell the truth, I am not concerned to know it. What is there to be learned of those who know nothing! It amounts, to put it plainly, to educating oneself in ignorance. I gathered from some of his confused expressions in my presence and in reply to his accuser, that he joins issue with the priests of his nation, that he repudiates the religion of the Jews, and that he worships Orpheus under an assumed name which has escaped me. What makes me suppose this, is that he speaks with respect of a god, or rather of a hero, who is supposed to have descended into Hades, and to have reascended into the heavens, after having wandered among the pallid shades of the dead. He may perhaps have set himself to worship some subterranean Mercury. I should, however, feel more inclined to believe that he worships Adonis, for I think I heard him say that, following in the steps of the women of Byblos, he wept over the sufferings and the death of a god.

"These youthful gods, who die and come to life again, abound on Asiatic soil. The Syrian courtesans have brought several of them to Rome, and these celestial youths please, more than is proper, our respectable women. Our matrons do not blush to celebrate their mysterious rites in private. My Julia, so prudent and so self-contained, has repeatedly asked me how much should be believed of them. 'What kind of a god,' have I answered her with indignation, 'what can be the god who takes delight in the stealthy homage of a married dame? A woman should know no other friends than those of her husband. And do not the gods stand first in order among our friends?'"

"Does not this man of Tarsus," inquired the philosopher Apollodorus, "pay reverence rather to Typhon, whom the Egyptians call Sethon? It is said that a god with an ass's head is shown honour by a certain Jewish sect. This god can be no other than Typhon, and I should not be surprised if the weavers of Cenchreæ held a secret intercourse with the Immortal, who, according to our gentle Marcus, committed so disgusting an outrage on the old woman who sold cakes."

"I know not," resumed Gallio. "They do indeed say that a number of Syrians meet to celebrate in secret the worship of a god with a donkey's head. It may be that Paul is one of them. But what matters the Adonis, the Mercury, the Orpheus, or the Typhon of that Jew? He will never reign over any but the female fortune-tellers, the usurers, and the sordid traders who spoil the sailors in seaports. At the very utmost will he be able to win over, in the suburbs of the big cities, a few handfuls of slaves."

"Oho! Oho!" exclaimed Marcus Lollius in an outburst of laughter, "can you see that hideous Paul founding a religion of slaves? By Castor, it would indeed be a miraculous novelty! Should perchance the god of the slaves (may Jove avert the omen!) climb up into Olympus and expel therefrom the gods of the empire, what would he do in turn? In what way would he exercise his power over the astonished world? I should enjoy seeing him at work. He would no doubt keep up the Saturnalia during the entire course of the year. He would open to gladiators the road to the highest honours, establish the prostitutes of the Suburra in the temple of Vesta, and perhaps make of some wretched straggling village in Syria the capital of the world."

Lollius might have followed up his jest for some time had Gallio not interrupted him.

"Marcus," he said, "do not entertain the hope of witnessing these marvellous novelties. Although men are capable of stupendous acts of folly, it is not a little Jew weaver who could seduce them with his bad Greek and his tales about a Syrian Orpheus. The slaves' god could but foment uprisings and servile wars, which would be promptly put down in blood, and he would soon perish himself, together with his worshippers, in an amphitheatre, under the teeth of wild beasts, to the plaudits of the Roman people.

"Enough of Paul and Sosthenes. Their mind would not be of any help to us in the quest we were engaged upon ere they so untowardly interrupted us. We were seeking to know the future the gods have in store for us, not for you, dear friends, or for me in particular (for we are prepared to endure all that is to be), but for the fatherland and for the human race which we love and towards which we feel kindly. It is not that Jew weaver, with his inflamed eyelids, who could tell us, whatever Marcus may think, the name of the god who is to dethrone Jupiter."

Gallio broke off his speech to dismiss the lictors, who stood motionless in line before him, shouldering their fasces.

"We require neither the rods nor the axes," he remarked with a smile. "Speech is our only weapon. May the day come when the universe shall know no others. If you are not tired, my friends, let us walk towards the Pirene fountain. We shall find midway an old fig-tree under which, so it is related, the betrayed Medea meditated her cruel revenge. The Corinthians hold the tree in reverence, in memory of that jealous queen, and suspend votive tablets from its branches, for Medea never brought them but good. It has cleft the earth with its branches, which have thrown out roots, and it is still crowned with a luxuriant foliage. Seated in its shade, we can while away time with conversation till our bath-hour."

The children, weary of pursuing Stephanas, were playing at knuckle-bones by the roadside. The apostle was striding along rapidly, when he came across, near the place of execution, a band of Jews, who had come up from Cenchreæ to ascertain the judgment rendered by the proconsul in regard to the synagogue. They were friends of Sosthenes, and were greatly irritated against the Jew of Tarsus and his adherents because they sought to change the law. Noticing the man, who was wiping with his sleeve his eyes blinded with blood, they thought they recognised him, and one of them, pulling him by the beard, asked him if he were not Stephanas, the companion of Paul.

Proudly he answered:

"Behold him!"

He was quickly thrown to the ground, and trampled under foot. The Jews were picking up stones and shouting:

"He is a blasphemer! Stone him!"

A couple of the most zealous tore up the milestone sunk by the Romans, and were endeavouring to heave it at him. The stones fell with a dull thud on the skinny bones of the apostle, who yelled:

"Oh the delight of these wounds! Oh the joy of these sufferings! Oh the refreshment of this torture! I behold Jesus."

A few steps farther off, under an arbutus, and to the murmurings of a spring, old Posocharis was pressing in his arms the smooth flanks of Joessa. Annoyed at the disturbance, he growled with a choking voice, with head buried in the hair of the young girl:

"Begone, you low brutes, and do not trouble a philosopher's pastime."

After a few minutes, a centurion who was passing along the now deserted road, raised Stephanas from the ground, made him swallow a mouthful of wine, and gave him linen wherewith to bandage his wounds.

While this was going on, Gallio, sitting with his friends under Medea's tree, was saying:

"If you wish to know the successor of the master of gods and men, meditate the words of the poet:

"'Jove's spouse shall bring forth a son more powerful than his father.'

"This line designates, not the august Juno, but the most illustrious among the noble women with whom consorted the Olympian who so often changed his form and his loves. It seems to me assured that the government of the universe is to fall to the lot of Hercules. This opinion has long since taken root in my mind, by reasons derived not only from the poets, but from philosophers and men of science. I have, so to speak, greeted by anticipation the accession of the son of Alcmene, in the climax of my tragedy of *Hercules on Œta*, ending with the following words:

"'Hail, great conqueror of monsters, and pacifier of the world; be propitious unto us! Cast thy gaze upon the earth, and if some monster of a new kind strike terror into mankind, destroy it with a thunderbolt. Better than thy father wilt thou know how to hurl thunder.'

"I augur favourably of the coming reign of Hercules. During his life upon earth, he displayed a spirit patient and inclined to elevated thoughts. When the time comes for thunder to arm his hand, he will not suffer a new Caius to govern the Empire with impunity. Virtue, ancient simplicity, courage, innocence, and peace will reign with him. Thus do I prophesy."

And Gallio, having risen, took leave of his friends with these words:

"Fare ye well, and love me."

III

AS Nicole Langelier came to the end of his reading, the birds heralded by Giacomo Boni filled the deserted Forum with their friendly cries.

The sky was spreading over the Roman ruins the ash-tinted veil of evening; the young laurel-bushes planted along the Via Sacra lifted up into the diaphanous atmosphere their branches black as antique bronzes, while the flanks of the Palatine were clothed in azure.

"Langelier," spoke M. Goubin, who was not easily deceived, "you did not invent that story. The suit brought by Sosthenes against St. Paul before Gallio, proconsul of Achaia, is to be found in the *Acts of the Apostles*."

Nichole Langelier readily admitted the fact.

"The story is told," he said, "in chapter xviii., and occupies verses 12 to 17 inclusively, which I am able to read to you, for I copied them on to a sheet of my manuscript."

Whereupon he read:

"'12. And when Gallio was the deputy of Achaia, the Jews made insurrection with one accord against Paul, and brought him to the judgment seat,

"'13. Saying, This *fellow* persuadeth men to worship God contrary to the law.

"'14. And when Paul was now about to open *his* mouth, Gallio said unto the Jews, If it were a matter of wrong or wicked lewdness, O *ye* Jews, reason would that I should bear with you:

"'15. But if it be a question of words and names, and *of* your law, look ye *to it*; for I will be no judge of such *matters*.

"'16. And he drove them from the judgment seat.

"'17. Then all the Greeks took Sosthenes, the chief ruler of the synagogue, and beat *him* before the judgment seat. And Gallio cared for none of those things.'

"I have not invented anything," added Langelier. "Little is known of Annæus Mela, and of Gallio, his brother. It is, however, certain that they were numbered among the most intelligent men of their day. When Achaia, a senatorial province under Augustus, an imperial one under Tiberius, was restored to the Senate by Claudius, Gallio was sent thither as proconsul. He was doubtless indebted for the post to the influence of his brother Seneca; it is possible, however, that he was selected for his knowledge of Greek literature, and as a man agreeable to the Athenian professors, whose intellects the Romans admired. He was highly educated. He had written a book on physiological subjects, and, it is believed, some few tragedies. His works are all lost, unless something from his pen is to be met with in the collection of tragic recitations attributed without sufficient reasons to his brother the philosopher. I have assumed that he was a Stoic, and that he held in many respects the same opinions as his illustrious brother. But, while placing in his mouth words of virtue and rectitude, I have guarded against attributing any settled doctrine to him. The Romans of those days blended the ideas of Epicurus with those of Zenon. I was not incurring any great risk of being mistaken, when investing Gallio with this eclecticism. I have represented him as a kindly man. He was that, assuredly. Seneca has said of him that no one loved him in a lukewarm fashion. His gentleness was universal. He aspired to honours.

"Quite the contrary, his brother Annæus Mela held aloof from them. We have on that point the testimony of Seneca the philosopher, as well as that of Tacitus. When Helvia, the mother of the three Senecas, lost her husband, the most famed of her sons indited a small philosophical treatise for her. In a certain part of this work, he exhorts her to consider, in order to reconcile her to life, that there remain unto her sons like Gallio and Mela, differing as to character, but equally worthy of her affection.

"'Cast thine eyes upon my brothers,' he says, or words to that effect. 'Both shall, by the diversity of their virtues, charm thy weary moments. Gallio has attained honours through his talents. Mela has despised them in his wisdom. Derive enjoyment from the regard in which the one is held, from the calm of the other, and from the love of both. I know the inner sentiments of my brothers. Gallio seeks in dignities an ornament for thyself. Mela embraces a gentle and peaceful life in order to devote himself to thee.'

"A child during the principality of Nero, Tacitus did not know the Senecas. He merely collected what was currently said about them in his day. He states that if Mela held aloof from honours, it was through a refinement of ambition, and, a simple Roman knight, to rival the influence of the consular officers. After having administered in person the vast estates he possessed in Boetica, Mela came to Rome, and had himself appointed administrator of Nero's estate. The conclusion was drawn therefrom that he was shrewd in matters of business, and he was even suspected of not being as disinterested as he wished to appear. That may be. The Senecas, while parading their contempt for riches, were possessed of great wealth, and it is very hard to believe the tutor of Nero when, amid the luxury of his furniture and his gardens, he represents himself as faithful to his beloved poverty. Still, the three sons of Helvia were not ordinary souls. Mela had of Atilla, his wife, a son, Lucan the poet. It would seem that Lucan's talent reflected great lustre on his father's name. Letters were then held in high honour, and eloquence and poetry ranked above all things.

"Seneca, Mela, Lucan, and Gallio perished with the accomplices of Piso. Seneca the philosopher was already an aged man. Tacitus, who had not been a witness of his death, has portrayed the scene for us. We know how Nero's tutor opened his veins while in his bath, and how his young wife Paulina protested that she would die with him, and by a similar death. By Nero's order, Paulina's wrists, which had been opened at the veins, were bandaged. She lived, preserving thereafter a deathly pallor. Tacitus records that young Lucan, whilst under torture, denounced his mother. Even if there were confirmation of this infamous deed, the blame for it should be laid to the tortures he underwent. But there is certainly one reason for not believing it. If indeed pain extorted from Lucan the names of several of the conspirators, he did not pronounce that of Atilla, since Atilla was not molested at a time when every information was blindly credited.

"After the death of Lucan, Mela, with too great a haste and diligence, seized on the inheritance of his son. A friend of the young poet, who doubtless coveted the inheritance, became the accuser of Mela. It was alleged that the father had been initiated into the secret of the conspiracy, and a forged letter of Lucan was brought forth. Nero, after having read it, ordered it to be shown to Mela. Following the example set by his brother and so many of Nero's victims, Mela caused his veins to be opened, after having bequeathed a large sum of money to the freedmen of Cæsar, in order to secure the remainder of his fortunes to the unhappy Atilla. Gallio did not survive his two brothers; he took his own life.

"Such was the tragic end of these charming and cultured men. I have made two of them, Gallio and Mela, speak in Corinth. Mela was a great traveller. His son Lucan, while yet a child, was on a visit to Athens, at the time Gallio was proconsul of Achaia. There is therefore some show of reason for saying that Mela was then with his brother in Corinth. I have supposed that two young Romans of illustrious birth, and a philosopher of the Areopagus, accompanied the proconsul. In so doing, I have not taken too great a liberty, since the intendants, the procurators, the proprætors, and the proconsuls whom the Emperor and the Senate respectively sent to govern the provinces, always had about themselves the sons of great families, who came to instruct themselves in the management of public affairs under their guidance, and that of men of keen intellect like my Apollodorus, more frequently freedmen acting as their secretaries. Lastly, I conceived the idea that at the moment St. Paul was being brought before a Roman tribunal, the proconsul and his friends were conversing freely about the most varied subjects, art, philosophy, religion, and politics, and that there pierced the various topics absorbing their interest a deep anxiety as to the future. There is indeed some likelihood that on that very day, just as well as on any other, they may have sought to discover the future destiny of Rome and the world. Gallio and Mela stood among the most elevated and open intellects of the day. Minds of such a calibre are at all times inclined to delve into the present and the past for the conditions of the future. I have noticed in the most learned and well-informed men whom I have known, to name but Renan and Berthelot, a pronounced tendency to interject at haphazard into a conversation outlines of rational utopias and scientific forecasts."

"Here then we have," said Joséphin Leclerc, "one of the best educated men of his day, a man versed in philosophic speculation, trained in the conduct of public affairs, and who was of as open and broad a mind as could be that of a Roman such as Gallio, the brother of Seneca, the ornament and light of his century. He is concerned about the future, he seeks to grasp the movement which is most affecting the world, and he tries to fathom the destiny of the Empire and the gods. Just then, by a unique stroke of fortune, he comes across St. Paul; the future he is in quest of passes by him, and he sees it not. What an example of the blindness which strikes, in the very presence of an unexpected revelation, the most enlightened minds and the keenest intellects!"

"I would have you observe, my dear friend," replied Nicole Langelier, "that it was not a very easy matter for Gallio to converse with St. Paul. It is not easy to conceive how they could possibly have exchanged ideas. St. Paul had trouble in expressing himself, and it was with great difficulty that he made himself intelligible to the folk who lived and thought like himself. He had never spoken word of mouth to any cultured man.

"He was nowise capable of indicating a train of thought and of following those of an interlocutor. He was ignorant of Greek science. Gallio, accustomed to the conversation of educated people, had long since trained his reason to debate. He knew not the maxims of the rabbis. What then could these two men have said to each other?

"Not that it was impossible for a Jew to converse with a Roman. The Herods enjoyed a mode of expression which was agreeable to Tiberius and Caligula. Flavius Josephus and Queen Berenice discoursed in terms pleasing to Titus, the destroyer of Jerusalem. We know that bejewelled Jews were at all times to be found in company of the antisemites. They were *meschoumets* (accursed unbelievers—anathema to Paul). Paul was a *něbi* (prophet). This fiery and haughty Syrian, disdainful of the worldly goods sought for by all men, thirsting after poverty, ambitious of insults and humiliations, rejoicing in suffering, was merely able to proclaim his sombre and inflamed visions, his hatred of life and of the beautiful, his absurd outbursts of anger, and his insane charity. Apart from this, he had nothing to say. In truth, I can discover one subject only on which he might have agreed with the proconsul of Achaia. 'Tis Nero.

"St. Paul, at that time, could hardly have heard any mention of the youthful son of Agrippina, but on learning that Nero was destined to Imperial power, he would immediately become a Neronian. He became so later on. He was still one at the time Nero poisoned Britannicus. Not that he was capable of approving of a brother's murder, but because he entertained a profound respect for all government. 'Let every soul be subject unto the higher powers,' he wrote to his churches. 'For rulers are not a terror to good works, but to the evil. Wilt thou then not be afraid of the power? Do that which is good, and thou shalt have praise of the same.' Gallio might perchance have found these maxims somewhat simple and commonplace, but he could not have disapproved of them as a whole. But if there is a subject which he would not have felt tempted to approach while speaking with a Jewish weaver, it is indeed the ruling of people and the authority of the Emperor. Once more, what could those two men well have said to each other?

"In our own day, when a European official in Africa, let us say the Governor-General of the Sudan for his Britannic Majesty, or our Governor of Algeria, comes across a fakeer or a marabout, their conversation is naturally confined within restricted limits. St. Paul was to a proconsul what a marabout is to our civil Governor of Algeria. A conversation between Gallio and St. Paul would have resembled only too much, I imagine, that held by General Desaix with his famous dervish. After the battle of the Pyramids, General Desaix, at the head of twelve hundred cavalry, pursued into Upper Egypt the Mamelukes of Murad Bey. On arriving at

301

Girgeh, he heard that an old dervish, who had acquired among the Arabs a wide reputation for learning and sanctity, was living near that city. Desaix was endowed with both philosophy and humanity. Desirous of making the acquaintance of a man esteemed of his fellows, he caused the dervish to be summoned to headquarters, received him with honour, and entered into conversation with him through an interpreter.

"'Venerable old man,' he said, 'the French have come to bring Egypt justice and liberty.'

"'I knew they would come,' replied the dervish.

"'How did you come to know it?'

"'Through an eclipse of the sun.'

"'How can an eclipse of the sun have informed you as to the movement of our armies?'

"'Eclipses are brought about by the angel Gabriel, who places himself before the sun in order to announce to the faithful the misfortunes which threaten them.'

"'Venerable old man, you are ignorant of the true cause of eclipses; I shall impart the knowledge of it to you.'

"Thereupon, taking a stump of pencil and a scrap of paper, he traced some figures:

"'Let A be the sun, B, the moon, C, the earth,' and so forth...

"And when he had come to the end of his demonstration,

"'Such,' he said, 'is the theory governing eclipses of the sun.'

"And as the dervish was mumbling a few words,

"'What does he say?' asked the General of the interpreter.

"'General, he says that it is the angel Gabriel who causes eclipses, by placing himself in front of the sun.'

"'The fellow is simply naught but a fanatic!' exclaimed Desaix.

"Whereupon he drove the dervish out with well-administered kicks.

"I imagine that had a conversation been entered into between St. Paul and Gallio, it would have ended somewhat as did the dialogue between the dervish and General Desaix."

"It must, however, be pointed out," said Joséphin Leclerc, joining issue, "that between the Apostle Paul and the dervish of General Desaix, there is at the very least this difference: the dervish did not impose his faith on Europe. And you will admit that his Britannic Majesty's honourable Governor of the Sudan has doubtless not come across the marabout who is to confer his name on the biggest church in London; you must likewise admit that our civil Governor of Algeria has never come face to face with the founder of a religion which the majority of the French nation will some day believe and profess. These functionaries have not seen the future arise before them under a human form. The proconsul of Achaia did."

"It was none the less impossible for Gallio," replied Langelier, "to carry on with St. Paul a steady conversation on some important subject regarding morals or philosophy. I am well aware, and you yourselves are not ignorant of the fact, that towards the fifth century of the Christian Era, it was believed that Seneca had known St. Paul in Rome, and had expressed admiration of the Apostle's doctrines. This fable owed its spread to the deplorable clouding of the human mind following so closely upon the age of Tacitus and of Trajan. In order to obtain credence for it, certain forgerers, who at that time swarmed in Christian ranks, fabricated a correspondence which is mentioned respectfully by St. Jerome and St. Augustine. If these letters are those which have come unto us ascribed to Paul and Seneca, it must be that those two Fathers did not read them, or that they greatly lacked discernment. It is the absurd work of a Christian utterly ignorant of everything connected with Nero's time, and one totally incapable of imitating Seneca's style. Is it necessary to say that the great divines of the Middle Ages firmly believed in the truth of the intercourse between the two men and in the genuineness of the letters? But the classical scholars of the Renaissance had no difficulty in demonstrating the unlikelihood and the falsity of these inventions. It matters little that Joseph de Maistre should have garnered by the way this antiquated rubbish together with much of the same kind. No one any longer heeds it, and henceforth it is only in pretty novels written for society by skilful and mystical authors that the apostles of the primitive Church converse freely with the philosophers and people of fashion of Imperial Rome and expound to the delight of Petronius the novel beauties of Christianity. The words of Gallio and his friends, which you have just heard, are endowed with less charm and more truth."

"I do not deny it," replied Joséphin Leclerc, "and I believe that the personages of the dialogue are made to think and speak as they must actually have thought and spoken, and that the ideas entertained by them are those of their day. Therein, it seems to me, lies the merit of the work, and therefore do I reason about it just as if I were basing my arguments on a historical text."

"You may safely do so," said Langelier. "I have not embodied in it anything for which I have not the authority of a reference."

"Very well then," resumed Joséphin Leclerc, "so we have been listening to a Greek philosopher and several Roman literati engaged in speculation as to the future destinies of their fatherland, of humanity, and of the earth, and seeking to discover the name of Jove's successor. The while they are absorbed in this perplexing quest, the apostle of the new god appears before them, and they treat him with contempt. I maintain that in so doing they plainly show a lack of penetration, and lose through their own fault a unique opportunity of becoming instructed concerning that which they felt so great a desire to know."

"It seems self-evident to you, my good friend," replied Nicole Langelier, "that Gallio, had he known how to set about it, would have gathered from St. Paul the secret of the future. Such is perhaps the first idea that springs to the mind, and it is one that many have become imbued with. Renan, after having recorded, according to the *Acts*, this singular interview between Gallio and St. Paul, is not averse from discovering evidence of a narrow and thoughtless mind in the contempt experienced by the proconsul for this Jew of Tarsus who appeared before his tribunal. He seizes the opportunity thus offered to lament the poor philosophy of the Romans. 'What a lack of foresight,' he exclaims, 'is sometimes exhibited by intellectual men! In later times, it was to be discovered that the squabble between those abject sectarians was the great event of the century.' Renan seems to believe that the proconsul of Achaia had merely to listen to that weaver in order to be there and then informed of the spiritual revolution in course of preparation throughout the universe, and to penetrate the secret of future humanity. And this is also no doubt what every one thinks at first sight. Nevertheless, ere settling the point, let us look more closely into the matter; let us examine what both men expected, and let us find out which of the two was, when all is said and done, the better prophet.

"In the first place, Gallio believed that the youthful Nero would be an emperor of philosophic mind, govern according to the maxims of the Portico, and be the delight of the human race. He was mistaken, and the reasons for his erroneous assumption are only too patent. His brother Seneca was the tutor of the son of Agrippina; his nephew, the boy Lucan, lived on terms of intimacy with the young prince. Both his family and his personal interests bound up the proconsul with the fortunes of Nero. He believed that Nero would make an excellent Emperor, for the wish was father to the thought. His mistake arose rather from weakness of character than from lack of intellect. Nero, moreover, was then a youth full of gentleness, and the early years of his principality were not to give the lie to the hopes of the philosophers. Secondly, Gallio believed that peace would reign over the world after the chastisement of the Parthians. He erred owing to a lack of knowledge of the actual dimensions of the earth. He erroneously believed that the *orbis Romanus* covered the whole of the globe; that the inhabitable world ended at the burning or frozen strands, rivers, mountains, sands, and deserts reached by the Roman eagles, and that the Germani and Parthians peopled the confines of the universe. We know how much weeping and blood this error, shared in common by all Romans, cost the Empire. Thirdly, Gallio, pinning his faith to the oracles, believed in the eternity of Rome. He was mistaken, if his prediction is to be taken in a narrow and literal sense. But he was not so, if one considers that Rome, the Rome of Cæsar and Trajan, has bequeathed us its customs and laws, and that modern civilisation proceeds from Roman civilisation. It is in the august square where we now stand that from the height of the rostral tribune and in the Curia was debated the fate of the universe, and the form of constitution which to the present day governs the nations. Our science is based on Greek science transmitted to us by Rome. The reawakening of ancient thought in the fifteenth century in Italy, in the sixteenth century in France and Germany, was the cause of Europe being born anew in science and in reason. The proconsul of Achaia did not deceive himself: Rome is not defunct, since she lives in us. Let us, in the fourth place, examine Gallio's philosophical ideas. No doubt he was not equipped with a very sound natural philosophy, and he did not always interpret natural phenomena with sufficient precision. He applied himself to metaphysics as a Roman, i.e., with a lack of acuteness. At heart, he valued philosophy merely because of its utility, and devoted himself mainly to moral questions. I have neither betrayed nor flattered him when placing his speeches on record. I have represented him as serious and mediocre, and a fairly good disciple of Cicero. You may have gathered that he reconciled, by dint of the poorest of reasoning, the doctrine of the Stoics to the national religion. One feels that whenever he indulges in speculation as to the nature of the gods, he is anxious to remain a good citizen and an honest official. But, after all, he thinks matters out, and reasons. The idea he conceives of the forces which govern the world is, in its principle, rational and scientific and, in this respect, it conforms to that which we have ourselves conceived of them. He does not reason as well as his friend the Greek Apollodorus. He does not argue any worse than the professors of our University who teach an independent philosophy and a Christian antimaterialism. By his open-mindedness and his strength of intelligence, he seems our contemporary. His thoughts turn naturally in the direction followed by the human mind at the present moment. Do not therefore let us say that he was unable to recognise the intellectual future of humanity.

"As to St. Paul, he announced the future; none doubt the fact. And yet he expected to see with his own eyes the world come to an end, and all things existing engulfed in flames. This conflagration of the universe, which Gallio and the Stoics foresaw in a future so remote that they none the less announced the eternity of the Empire, Paul believed to be quite close at hand, and was preparing for that great day. Herein he was mistaken, and you will admit that this misconception is in itself worse than all the united blunders of Gallio and his friends. Still more serious is it that Paul did not base this extraordinary belief on any observation or any reasoning whatever. He was ignorant of and despised science. He gave himself up to the lowest practices of thaumaturgy and glossology, and had no culture whatsoever.

"As a matter of fact, in regard to the future, as well as to the present and the past, there was nothing the proconsul could learn from the apostle, nothing but a mere name. Had he learnt that Paul was of Christ's religion, he would not have been any the better informed as to the future of Christianity, which was within a few years to disengage itself almost wholly from the ideas of Paul and of the first apostolic men. Thus it will be seen, if one does not pin one's opinion to liturgical texts, and to the strictly verbal interpretations of theologians, that St. Paul foresaw the future less accurately than Gallio, and one will be inclined to think that were the apostle to return to Rome nowadays, he would discover more cause for surprise than the proconsul.

"St. Paul, in modern Rome, would no more recognise himself on the column of Marcus Aurelius than he would recognise on the column of Trajan his old enemy Cephas. The dome of St. Peter's, the Stanze of the Vatican, the splendour of the churches, and the Papal pomp, all would offend his blinking eyes. In vain would he look for disciples in London, Paris, or Geneva. He would not understand either Catholics or Reformers who vie in quoting his real or supposed Epistles. Nor would he understand the minds freed from all dogma, who base their opinion on the two forces he hated and despised the most: science and reason. On discovering that the Son of Man has not come, he would rend his garments, and cover himself with ashes."

Hippolyte Dufresne interrupted, saying:

"Whether in Paris or in Rome, there is no doubt that St. Paul would be as an owl blinking in the sun. He would be no more fit than a Bedouin of the desert to communicate with cultured Europeans. He would not know himself when at a bishop's, nor would he obtain recognition from him. Were he to alight at the house of a Swiss pastor fed upon his writings, he would astound him with the primitive crudity of his Christianity. All this is true. Bear in mind, however, that he was a Semite, a foreigner to Latin thought, to the genius of the Germani and Saxons, to the races from which sprung those theologians who, by dint of erroneous conceptions, mistranslations, and absurdities, discovered a meaning in his counterfeit Epistles. You conceive him in a world which was not his own, which can in no wise become his, and this absurd conception at once gives birth to an agglomeration of incongruous presentments. We picture to ourselves, to illustrate what I say, this vagabond weaver sitting in a Cardinal's coach, and we make merry over the appearance presented by two human beings of so opposite a character. If you persist in resurrecting St. Paul, pray have the good taste to restore him to his race and country, among the Semites of the East, who have not greatly changed these twenty centuries, and for whom the Bible and the Talmud contain human science in its entirety. Drop him among the Jews of Damascus or of Jerusalem. Lead him to the Synagogue. There he will listen without astonishment to the teachings of his master, Gamaliel. He will enter into disputation with the rabbis, will weave goat-hair, live on dates and a little rice, observe the law faithfully, and of a sudden undertake to destroy it. He will in turn be persecutor and persecuted, executioner and martyr, all with equal keenness. The Jews of the Synagogue will proceed with his excommunication, by blowing into a ram's horn, and by spilling drop by drop the wax of black candles into a tub containing blood. He will endure without flinching this horrible ceremony, and will exercise, in the course of an arduous and continually menaced existence, the energy of a headstrong will. In such circumstances, he will probably be known to only a few ignorant and sordid Jews. But it will be Paul once more, and wholly Paul."

"That may be possible," said Joséphin Leclerc. "Yet you will grant me that St. Paul was one of the principal founders of Christianity, and that he might have imparted to Gallio valuable information concerning the great religious movement of which the proconsul was entirely ignorant."

"He who founds a religion," replied Langelier, "wots not what he does. I may say almost the same of those who found great human institutions, monastic orders, insurance companies, national guards, banks, trusts, trade unions, academies, schools of music and the drama, gymnastic societies, soup-kitchens, and lectures. Generally speaking, these establishments do not for any length of time carry out the intentions of their founders, and it sometimes happens that they become diametrically opposed to them. It is as much as one can do to trace after many long years a few vestiges of their founders' original intention. In the matter of religions, at any rate among nations whose existence is troublous and whose mind is fickle, they undergo so incessant and so complete a transformation, according to the feelings or interests of their faithful and their ministers, that in the course of a few years they preserve naught of the spirit which created them. Gods undergo more changes than men, for the reason that their form is less precise and that they endure longer. Some there are who improve as they grow older; others deteriorate with the years. It takes less than a century for a god to become unrecognisable. The god of the Christians has perhaps undergone a more complete transformation than any other. This is doubtless attributable to the fact that he has belonged in succession to the most varied civilisations and races, to the Latins, to the Greeks, to the Barbarians, and to all the nations sprung from the ruins of the Roman Empire. It is assuredly a far cry from the wooden Apollo of Dædalus to the classical Apollo Belvedere. Still greater a distance separates the youthful Christ of the Catacombs from the ascetic Christ of our cathedrals. This personage of the Christian mythology perplexes one by the number and variety of his metamorphoses. The flamboyant Christ of St. Paul is followed, as early as the second century, by the Christ of the Synoptic Gospels, a poor Jew, vaguely communistic, who becomes, with the Fourth Gospel, a sort of young Alexandrine, a milk-and-water disciple of the Gnostics. At a later period, if we only take into account the Roman Christs and tarry merely with the most famed of them, we have had the dominating Christ of Gregory VII., the bloodthirsty Christ of St. Dominic, the mob-leading Christ of Julius II., the atheistic and artistic Christ of Leo X., the indeterminate and insipid Christ of the Jesuits, Christ the protector of the factory, the defender of capital and the opponent of Socialism, who flourished under the pontificate of Leo XIII., and who still reigns. All those Christs, who have but the name in common, were not foreseen by Paul. In reality, he knew no more than Gallio about the future god."

"You exaggerate," remarked M. Goubin, who disliked exaggeration in whatever form.

Giacomo Boni, who venerates the sacred books of all nations, here pointed out that Gallio and the Roman philosophers and historians were to be blamed for not having a knowledge of the Jews' Sacred Scriptures.

"Had they been better informed," he said, "the Romans would not have harboured unjust prejudices against the religion of Israel; and, as your own Renan has said, a little goodwill and a better knowledge would perhaps have warded off fearful misunderstandings in regard to questions of interest to the whole of humanity. There lacked not educated Jews like Philo to explain the laws of Moses to the Romans, had the latter been more broad-minded and possessed a more correct presentiment of the future. The Romans experienced disgust and fear, when face to face with Asiatic thought. Even if they were right in fearing it, they were wrong in despising it. To despise a danger constitutes a great blunder. Gallio displayed want of foresight when stigmatising as criminal fancies and profanities of the vulgar the Syrian beliefs."

"How then could the Hellenist Jews have taught the Romans what they were themselves ignorant of?" inquired Langelier. "How could that honest Philo, so learned yet so shallow, have revealed to them the obscure, confused, and fecund thought of Israel, of which he knew nothing himself? What could he have imparted to Gallio concerning the faith of the Jews except literary absurdities? He would have explained to him that the doctrine of Moses harmonises with the philosophy of Plato. Then, as always, cultured men had no idea of what was passing through the minds of the multitudes. The ignorant mob is for ever creating gods unknown to the literati.

"One of the strangest and most notable facts of history is the conquest of the world by the god of a Syrian tribe, and the victory of Jehovah over all the gods of Rome, Greece, Asia, and Egypt. Upon the whole, Jesus was simply a *nĕbi*, and the last of the prophets of Israel. Nothing is known about him. We are in the dark as to his life and death, for the Evangelists are in nowise biographers. As to the moral ideas grouped under his name, they originate in truth with the crowd of visionaries who prophesied in the days of the Herods.

"What is called the triumph of Christianity is more accurately the triumph of Judaism, and to Israel fell the singular privilege of giving a god to the world. It must be admitted that Jehovah deserved his sudden elevation in many respects. He was, when he attained to empire, the best of the gods. He had made a very bad beginning. Of him it may be said what historians say of Augustus, his heart softened with the years. At the time when the Israelites settled in the Promised Land, Jehovah was stupid, ferocious, ignorant, cruel, coarse, foul-mouthed, indeed the most silly and most cruel of gods. But, under the influence of the prophets, there came about a complete transformation. He ceased being conservative and formal, and became converted to ideas of peace and to dreams of justice. His people were wretched. He began to feel a profound pity for all poor wretches. And although he remained at heart very much a Jew and very patriotic, he naturally became international when becoming revolutionary. He constituted himself the defender of the humble and oppressed. He conceived one of those simple ideas which captivate the world. He announced universal happiness, and the coming of a beneficent Messiah whose reign would be peace. His prophet Isaiah prompted him as to this admirable theme with words delightfully poetical and of unsurpassed softness:

"'The mountain of the Lord's house shall be established in the top of the mountains, and shall be exalted above the hills; and all nations shall flow unto it. And many people shall go and say, Come ye and let us go up to the mountain of the Lord, to the house of the God of Jacob; and he will teach us of his ways, and we will walk in his paths: for out of Zion shall go forth the law, and the word of the Lord from Jerusalem. And he shall judge among nations, and shall rebuke many people: and they shall beat their swords into plowshares, and their spears into pruning-hooks.

"'The wolf also shall dwell with the lamb and the leopard shall lie down with the kid; and the calf and the young lion and the fatling together; and a little child shall lead them.'

"In the Roman Empire, the god of the Jews set himself to capture the working classes and the social revolution. He addressed himself to the unfortunate. Now, in the days of Tiberius and Claudius, there existed within the Empire infinitely more unhappy than happy ones. There were hordes of slaves. One man alone owned as many as ten thousand. These slaves were for the most part sunk in wretchedness. Neither Jupiter, nor Juno, nor the Dioscuri troubled themselves about them. The Latin gods did not pity their condition. They were the gods of their masters. When came from Judæa a god who hearkened to the complaints of the humble, they worshipped him. So it is that the religion of Israel became the religion of the Roman world. This is what neither St. Paul nor Philo could explain to the proconsul of Achaia, for they themselves did not see it clearly. And this is what Gallio could not realise. He felt, however, that the reign of Jupiter was nearing its end, and he predicted the coming of a better god. From love of the national antiquities, he went for this god to the Græco-Latin Olympus, and selected him of the blood of Jupiter, through aristocratic feeling. Thus it is that he chose Hercules instead of Jehovah."

"For once," said Joséphin Leclerc, "you will admit that Gallio was mistaken."

"Less so than you think," replied Langelier with a smile. "Jehovah or Hercules, it mattered little. You may be sure of this: the son of Alcmene would not have governed the world otherwise than the father of Jesus. Olympian as he might be, he would have had to become the god of the slaves, and assume the religious spirit of the new times. The gods conform scrupulously to the sentiments of their worshippers: they have reasons for so doing. Pay attention to this. The spirit which favoured the accession in Rome of the god of Israel was not merely the spirit of the masses, but also that of the philosophers. At that time, they were nearly all Stoics, and believed in one god alone, one on whose behalf Plato had laboured and one unconnected by tie of family or friendship with the gods of human form of Greece and Rome. This god, through his infinity, resembled the god of the Jews. Seneca and Epictetus, who venerated him, would have been the first to have been surprised at the resemblance, had they been called upon to institute a comparison. Nevertheless, they had themselves greatly contributed towards rendering acceptable the austere monotheism of the Judæo-Christians. Doubtless a wide gulf separated Stoic haughtiness from Christian humility, but Seneca's morals, consequent upon his sadness and his contempt of nature, were paving the way for the Evangelical morals. The Stoics had joined issue with life and the beautiful; this rupture, attributed to Christianity, was initiated by the philosophers. A couple of centuries later, in the time of Constantine, both pagans and Christians will have, so to speak, the same morals and philosophy. The Emperor Julian, who restored to the Empire its old religion, which had been abolished by Constantine the Apostate, is justly regarded as an opponent of the Galilean. And, when perusing the petty treatises of Julian, one is struck with the number of ideas this enemy of the Christians held in common with them. He, like them, is a monotheist; with them, he believes in the merits of abstinence, fasting, and mortification of the flesh; with them, he despises carnal pleasures, and considers he will rise in favour with the gods by avoiding women; finally, he pushes Christian sentiment to the degree of rejoicing over his dirty beard and his black finger-nails. The Emperor Julian's morals were almost those of St. Gregory Nazianzen. There is nothing in this but what is natural and usual. The transformations undergone by morals and ideas are never sudden. The greatest changes in social life are wrought imperceptibly, and are only seen from afar. Christianity did not secure a foothold until such time as the condition of morals accommodated itself to it, and as Christianity itself had become adjusted to the condition of morals. It was unable to substitute itself for paganism until such time as paganism came to resemble it, and itself came to resemble paganism."

"Granted," said Joséphin Leclerc, "that neither St. Paul nor Gallio saw into the future. No one does. Has not one of your friends said: 'The future is concealed even from those who shape it'?"

"Our knowledge of what the future has in store," resumed Langelier, "is in proportion of our acquaintance with the present and the past. Science is prophetic. The more a science is accurate, the more can accurate prophesies be drawn from it. Mathematics, to which alone appertains entire accuracy, communicate a portion of their precision to the sciences proceeding from them. Thus it is that accurate predictions are made by means of mathematical astronomy and chemistry. One is able to calculate eclipses millions of years ahead, without fear of one's calculations being found erroneous, as long as the sun, the moon, and the earth shall preserve the same relations as to bulk and distance. It is even permitted to us to foresee that these relations will be modified in a far distant future. Indeed, it is prophesied, on the strength of the celestial mechanism, that the silver hornéd moon will not describe eternally the same circle round our globe, and that causes now in operation will, by dint of repetition, change its course. You may safely predict that the sun will become darkened, and will no longer appear except a shrunken globe over our icy seas, unless there should come to it in the interval some new alimentation, a thing quite within the possibilities, for the sun is capable of catching swarms of asteroids, just as a spider does flies. It is, however, safe to predict that it will become extinguished, and that the dislocated figures of the constellations will vanish star by star in the darkness of space. But what does the death of a star amount to? To the fading away of a spark. Let all the stars in the heavens die out just as the grasses of the field wither, what matters it to universal life, so long as the infinitely tiny elements composing them shall have retained within themselves the force which makes and unmakes worlds? It is safe to predict an even more complete end of the universe, the end of the atom, the dissociation of the last elements of matter, the times when protyle, when the amorphous fog will have reconquered its illimitable empire over the ruins of all things. And this will form but a breathing-spell in God's respiration. All will begin anew.

"The worlds will again be born to life. They will live again to die. Life and death will succeed each other for all eternity. All sorts of combinations will become facts in the infinity of space and time, and we shall find ourselves seated once more on the flank of the Forum in ruins. But as we shall not know that we are ourselves, it will not be us."

M. Goubin wiped his eye-glass.

"Such ideas are disheartening," he remarked.

"What then do you hope for, Monsieur Goubin," asked Nicole Langelier, "to gratify your wishes? Do you aspire to preserve of yourself and of the world an eternal consciousness? Why do you wish to remember for all time that you are Monsieur Goubin? I will not conceal it from you: the present universe, which is far from nearing its end, does not seem to possess the property of satisfying you in this respect. Do not place any more store in those which are to follow, for they will doubtless be of the same kind. Do not, however, abandon all hope. It is possible that after an indefinite succession of universes, you shall be born anew, Monsieur Goubin, with a recollection of your previous existences. Renan has said that it was a risk to be taken, and that at all events it would not be long in coming. The successions of universe will take place for us within less than a second. Time does not count for the dead."

"Are you cognisant," asked Hippolyte Dufresne, "of the astronomical dreams of Blanqui? The aged Blanqui, a prisoner in the Mont-Saint-Michel, could get but a glimpse of the sky through his stopped-up window, and had the stars for his only neighbours. This made of him an astronomer, and he based on the unity of matter and the laws ruling it a strange theory in regard to the identity of the worlds. I have read a sixty-page pamphlet of his wherein he sets forth that form and life are developed in exactly the same manner in a large number of worlds. According to him, a multitude of suns, all similar to our own, have, do, or will shed light upon planets in every respect similar to the planets of our own system. There is, was, and will be, *ad infinitum*, Venuses, Mars, Saturns, and Jupiters, quite the counterpart of our Saturn, Mars, and Venus, and worlds similar to our own. These worlds produce exactly what our world produces, and bear fruits, animals, and men resembling in all respects terrestrial plants, animals, and human beings. The evolution of life in them is the same as that on our globe. Consequently, thought the aged prisoner, there is, was and shall be throughout the infinite space myriads of Monts-Saint-Michel, each containing a Blanqui."

"We know but little of the worlds whose suns shine upon our nights," resumed Langelier. "We perceive, however, that subjected to the same mechanical and chemical laws, they differ from our own world and among themselves in extent and form, and that the substances burning in them are not distributed among all of them in the same proportions. These differences must produce an infinity of others which we do not suspect. A pebble is sufficient to change the fate of an Empire. Who knows? Perchance, Monsieur Goubin, many times multiplied and disseminated through myriads of worlds, has wiped, wipes, and shall eternally wipe clean his eye-glass."

Joséphin Leclerc did not suffer his friends to expatiate any further on astronomical dreams.

"I am," he said, "like Monsieur Goubin, of the opinion that all this would be heartrending were it not too far from us to affect us. What is of paramount interest for us, what we are curious to know is the fate of those who will come immediately after us in this world."

"There is no doubt," said Langelier, "that the succession of worlds only fills us with sad astonishment. We should welcome with a more fraternal and friendly eye the future of civilisation, and the immediate destiny of our fellow men. The closer at hand the future, the more we are concerned about it. Unfortunately, moral and political sciences are inaccurate, and full of uncertainty. They have but an imperfect knowledge of the so far accomplished developments of human evolution, and can therefore not instruct us concerning the developments which remain to be completed. Equipped with hardly any memory, they have little or no presentiment. This is why scientific minds feel an insurmountable repugnance to attempt investigations, the uselessness of which they know, and they dare not even confess to a curiosity which they entertain no hope of satisfying. Willingly would the task be undertaken to discover what would happen, were men to become wiser. Plato, Sir Thomas More, Campanella, Fénelon, Cabet, and Paul Adam have reconstructed their particular city in Atlantis, in the Island of Utopia, in the Sun, at Salentinum, in Icaria, in Malaya, and established there an abstract social administration. Others, like the philosopher Sébastien Mercier, and the socialist-poet William Morris, dived into a far-off future. But they took their system of morals with them. They discovered a new Atlantis, and it is a city of dreamland which they have harmoniously built there. Shall I also quote Maurice Spronck? He shows us the French Republic conquered by the Moors, in the 230th year of its foundation. He argues thus, in order to induce us to hand over the government to the Conservatives whom alone he considers capable of warding off so great a disaster. Meanwhile Camille Mauclair, trusting in humanity to come, reads in the future the victorious resistance, of Socialistic Europe against Mussulman Asia. Daniel Halévy dreads not the Moors, but, with greater show of reason, the Russians. He narrates, in his *Histoire de quatre ans*, the foundation, in 2001, of the United States of Europe. But he seeks to show us more especially that the moral equilibrium of nations is unstable, and that a facility suddenly introduced into the conditions of life may suffice to let loose on a multitude of men the worst scourges and the most cruel sufferings.

"Few are those who have sought to know the future, out of pure curiosity, and without moral intention or optimistic designs. I know no other than H. G. Wells who, journeying through future ages, has discovered for humanity a fate he did not, according to every indication, expect; for the institution of an anthropophagous proletariat and an edible aristocracy is a cruel solution of social questions. Yet such is the fate H. G. Wells assigns to posterity. All the other prophets of whom I have any knowledge content themselves with entrusting to future centuries the realisation of their dreams. They do not unveil the future, being satisfied with conjuring it up.

"The truth is that men do not look so far ahead without fright. Many consider that such an investigation is not only useless, but pernicious; while those most ready to believe that future events are discoverable are those who would most dread to discover them. This fear is doubtless based on profound reasons. All morals, all religions, embody a revelation of humanity's destiny.

The greater part of men, whether they admit it to, or conceal it from, themselves, would recoil from investigating these august revelations, to discover the emptiness of their anticipations. They are accustomed to endure the idea of manners totally different from their own, if once those manners are buried in the past. Thereupon they congratulate themselves on the progress made by morality. But, as their morality is in the main governed by their manners, or rather by what they allow one to see of them, they dare not confess to themselves that morality, which has continually changed with manners, up to their own day, will undergo a further change when they have passed out of this life, and that future men are liable to conceive an idea entirely at variance with their own as to what is permissible or not. It would go against the grain with them to admit that their virtues are merely transitory, and their gods decrepit. And, although the past is there to point out to them ever-changing and shifting rights and duties, they would look upon themselves as dupes were they to foresee that future humanity is to create for itself new rights, duties and gods. Finally, they fear disgracing themselves in the eyes of their contemporaries, in assuming the horrible immorality which future morality stands for. Such are the obstacles to a quest of the future. Look at Gallio and his friends; they would not have dared to foresee the equality of classes in the matter of marriage, the abolition of slavery, the rout of the legions, the fall of the Empire, the end of Rome, nor even the death of those very gods in whom they had all but ceased to believe."

"'Tis possible," said Joséphin Leclerc, "but it is time for us to dine."

And, leaving the Forum bathed in the calm light of the moon, they wended their way through the populous streets of the city towards a famed but cheap eating-house in the Via Condotti.

IV

THE room was small, and hung with a smoke-stained paper dating from the pontificate of Pio Nono. Ancient lithographs were dependent from the walls, representing Cavour with his tortoise-shell-framed spectacles and collar-like beard, the leonine visage of Garibaldi, the stupendous moustaches of Victor Emanuel, a classic placing side by side of the combined symbols of the revolution and of the supreme power, a popular testimony to the Italian spirit which excels in juxtapositions, and in whose midst, in our own day, in Rome, the fulminating Pope and the excommunicated King daily exchange assurances of good-neighbourship, with an exquisite grasp of politics, and not without a certain flavour of delicate comedy. The mahogany sideboard was laden with plated chafing-dishes and alabaster goblets. The establishment affected for new things a contempt appropriate to long-standing renown.

Seated around a table bedecked with roses, and with flasks of Chianti before them, the five continued their philosophic discourse.

"It is quite true," said Nicole Langelier, "that the heart fails in the case of many men, when gazing into the abyss of future events. It is moreover certain that our all too imperfect knowledge of facts past and gone does not supply us with the elements required to enable us to determine accurately what is to succeed them. However, since the past of human social organisations is in part known to us, the future of those societies, a continuation and consequence of their past, is not wholly beyond our ken. It is not impossible to observe certain social phenomena, and to define from the conditions under which they have already occurred, the conditions under which they will reappear. We are not barred, when witnessing the commencement of an order of facts, from comparing it with a past order of analogous facts, and from deducing from the completion of the second a like completion of the first. By way of example: when observing that the forms of labour are changeable, that serfdom has succeeded slavery, salaried labour, serfdom, new methods of production may be anticipated; when it is shown that industrial capital has for barely a century taken the place of the small artisans and peasant property, one is led to ponder over the form which is to succeed capital; when studying the manner in which was carried out the redemption of the feudal burdens and conditions of servitude, one is enabled to conceive how the redemption of the means of production nowadays constituting private ownership may some day be carried out. By studying the great Services of the State now in operation, it is possible to form a conception of future socialistic methods of production; and, after having thus investigated in several respects the present and the past of human industry, we shall, lacking certainties, determine by aid of probabilities whether collectivism is to be realised some day, not because it is just, for there is no reason for believing in the triumph of justice, but because it is the necessary sequel to the present state of things, and the fatal consequence of capitalistic evolution.

"Let us, if you like, take another example: we possess some experience of the life and death of religions. The end of Roman polytheism in particular, is familiar to us. Its lamentable end enables us to imagine that of Christianity, whose decline we are witnessing.

"We may similarly seek to find out whether future humanity will be bellicose or peaceful."

"I am curious to learn," said Joséphin Leclerc, "how to set about it."

M. Goubin shook his head, saying:

"Such a quest is useless. We know its result beforehand. War will last as long as the world."

"There is nothing to prove it," replied Langelier, "and a consideration of the past leads one to believe, on the contrary, that war is not one of the essential conditions of social life."

And Langelier, while waiting for the *minestra* (soup) which was long in making its appearance, developed the foregoing idea, without, however, departing from the moderation characterising his mind.

"Although the early periods of the human race," he said, "are lost to us in impenetrable darkness, it is certain that men were not always warlike. They were not so during the long ages of the pastoral life; the memory of which survives only in a small number of words common to all Indo-European languages, and which reveal innocent manners. And there are reasons for believing that these peaceful pastoral centuries had a far longer duration than the agricultural, industrial, and commercial periods which, following them in a necessary progress, brought about between tribes and nations a state of all but constant war.

"It was by force of arms that it was most frequently sought to acquire property, lands, women, slaves, and cattle. At first, wars were waged between village and village. Next, the vanquished, joining hands with the victors, formed a nation, and wars occurred between nation and nation. Each of these peoples, in order to retain possession of the acquired riches, or to make further acquisitions, contended with neighbouring peoples for the possession of strongholds securing the command of roads, mountain passes, river courses, and the seashore. In the end, nations formed confederations, and contracted alliances. Thus it came about that men banded together; as they increased in strength, instead of contending for the goods of the earth, formally bartered them. The community of sentiments and interests gradually became broadened. A day came when Rome imagined she had established it the world over. Augustus thought he had inaugurated the era of universal peace.

"We know how this illusion was gradually and savagely dissipated, and how the barbarian hordes overwhelmed the Roman peace. These barbarians, who had settled within the Empire, cut one another's throats on its ruins, for a space of fourteen centuries, and founded in carnage countries baptized in blood. Of such was the life of nations in the Middle Ages, and the constitution of the great European monarchies.

"In those days, a state of war was alone possible and conceivable. All the forces of the world were organised solely for the purpose of maintaining it.

"If the reawakening of thought, at the time of the Renaissance, permitted a few sparse minds to conceive better regulated relations between nations, at one and the same time, the burning desire to invent, and the thirst for knowledge supplied fresh food to the warrior instinct. The discovery of the West Indies, the exploration of Africa, the navigation of the Pacific Ocean, opened up vast territories to European avidity. The white kingdoms joined issue over the extermination of the red, yellow, and black races, and for the space of four centuries gave themselves up madly to the pillaging of three great divisions of the world. This is what is styled modern civilisation.

"During this uninterrupted succession of deeds of rapine and violence, Europeans acquired a knowledge of the extent and configuration of the earth. As they progressed in this knowledge, so did their work of destruction proceed apace. To the present day, the whites come in contact with the black or the yellow races but to enslave or massacre them. The peoples whom we call barbarians know us so far through our crimes only.

"For all that, those navigations, those explorations undertaken in a spirit of savage cupidity, these tracks by land and by sea opened up to conquerors, adventurers, hunters of and traders in men, these life-destroying colonisations, this brutal impulse which has led and still leads one-half of humanity to destroy the other, are the fatal conditions of a further progress of civilisation, and the terrible means which shall have prepared, for a still undetermined future, the peace of the world.

"This time, 'tis the whole world assimilated, in spite of enormous dissimilarities, to the state of the Roman Empire under Augustus. The Roman peace was the fruit of conquest. Universal peace will most assuredly not be brought about by the same means. No Empire is there to-day which can lay claim to the hegemony of the lands and seas covering the globe, known and surveyed at last. But, in spite of their being less apparent than those of political and military domination, the bonds which are beginning to unite the whole of humanity, and no longer merely a part of humanity, are none the less real; they are both more supple and more solid, more intimate and infinite in variety, since they are connected, athwart the fictions of public life, with the realities of social life.

"The increasing multiplicity of communications and exchanges, the compulsory solidarity of the financial markets of every capital, of commercial markets vainly striving to guarantee their independence by recourse to unfortunate expedients, the rapid growth of international socialism, seem likely to guarantee, sooner or later, the union of the peoples of every continent. If at the present moment the Imperialist spirit of the great States and the haughty ambitions of armed nations seem to give the lie to these previsions, and to damn these aspirations, it will be perceived that in reality modern nationalism amounts merely to a confused aspiration towards a more and more vast union of intellects and wills, and that the dream of a greater England, a greater Germany, a greater America, leads, will or do whatever you may, to the dream of a greater humanity, and to a partnership between nations for the common exploitation of the riches of the earth...."

313

The speech was interrupted by the appearance of the tavern-keeper bearing a steaming soup-tureen and grated cheese.

And, from amid the hot and aromatic vapour of the soup, Nicole Langelier concluded his argument with these words:

"There will doubtless be further wars. The savage instincts coupled with the natural desires, pride and hunger, which have embroiled the world for so many centuries, will again disturb it. The human masses have so far not found their equilibrium. The sagacity of nations is not yet sufficiently methodical to secure the common welfare, by means of the freedom and the facility of exchanges, man has so far not come to be looked up to with respect everywhere by man, the several portions of humanity are not yet about to associate harmoniously for the purpose of building the cells and organs of one and the same body. It will not be vouchsafed even unto the youngest of us to witness the close of the era of arms. But, we feel within us a presentiment of these better times which we are not to experience. If we extend into the future the present trend, we may even now determine the establishment of more perfect and frequent communications between all races and all nations, a more general and stronger feeling of human solidarity, the rational organisation of labour, and the coming of the United States of the World.

"Universal peace will become a fact some day, not because men will become better ('tis more than we may hope for), but because a new order of things, a new science, and new economic necessities will force on men the state of peace, just as formerly the very conditions of their existence placed and kept them in a state of war."

"Nicole Langelier, a rose has shed a leaf in your glass," said Giacomo Boni. "This has not taken place without the permission of the gods. Let us drink to the future peace of the world."

Raising his glass, Joséphin Leclerc remarked:

"This wine of Chianti has a tart savour, and a light sparkle. Let us drink to peace, the while Russians and Japanese are waging a bitter war in Manchuria and in Korea Bay."

"That war," resumed Langelier, "marks one of the great periods in the history of the world. And, in order to grasp its meaning, we must hark back two thousand years.

"The Romans, assuredly, did not suspect the vastness of the barbarian world, and had no conception of those immense human reservoirs which were to burst on them one fine day, and submerge them. They did not suspect that there existed in the world any other than the Roman peace. And yet, an older and vaster one there was, the Chinese peace.

"Not but what their merchants had business relations with the merchants of Serica. The latter were wont to bring raw silk to a spot situated to the north of the Pamir table-land, named the Tower of Stone. The merchants of the Empire went thither. Bolder Latin traders penetrated as far as the Gulf of Tong-King and the Chinese coasts up to Hang-chau-fu, or Hanoi. Nevertheless, the Romans did not conceive that Serica constituted an Empire more densely populated than their own one, richer, and more advanced in agriculture and political economy. The Chinese, on their part, knew the white men. Their annals mention the fact that the Emperor An-tung, under which name we recognise Marcus Aurelius Antoninus, despatched an embassy to them, which was perhaps merely an expedition of navigators and merchants. But they were ignorant of the fact that a civilisation more seething and violent than their own, as well as more prolific and infinitely more expansive, was spread over one of the faces of the globe of which they covered another face: the Chinese, agriculturists and gardeners full of experience, honest

314

and expert merchants, led a happy life, owing to their system of exchange and to their immense associations of credit. Contented with their subtle science, their exquisite politeness, their singularly human piety, and their immutable wisdom, they were doubtless not anxious to become acquainted with the ways of life and thought of the white men who had come from the land of Cæsar. Perchance the ambassadors of An-tung may have seemed somewhat gross and barbarian to them.

"The two great civilisations, the yellow and the white, continued ignorant of each other until the day when the Portuguese, having doubled the Cape of Good Hope, settled down to trade at Macao. Merchants and Christian missionaries established themselves in China, and indulged in every kind of violence and rapine. The Chinese tolerated them, in the manner of men accustomed to works of patience, and marvellously capable of endurance; nevertheless, they could on occasion take life with all the refinements of cruelty. For nearly three whole centuries the Jesuits were, in the Middle Kingdom, a source of endless disturbances. In our own times, the Christian acquired the habit of sending jointly or separately into that vast Empire, whenever order was disturbed, soldiers who restored it by means of theft, rape, pillage, murder, and incendiarism, and of proceeding at short intervals with the pacific penetration of the country with rifles and guns. The poorly armed Chinese either defend themselves badly or not at all, and so they are massacred with delightful facility. They are polite and ceremonious, but are reproached with cherishing feeble sentiments of affection for Europeans. The grievances we have against them are greatly of the order of those which Mr. Du Chaillu cherished towards his gorilla. Mr. Du Chaillu, while in a forest, brought down with his rifle the mother of a gorilla. In its death, the brute was still pressing its young to its bosom. He tore it from this embrace, and dragged it with him in a cage across Africa, for the purpose of selling it in Europe. Now, the young animal gave him just cause for complaint. It was unsociable, and actually starved itself to death. 'I was powerless,' says Mr. Du Chaillu, 'to correct its evil nature.' We complain of the Chinese with as great a show of reason as Mr. Du Chaillu of his gorilla.

"In 1901, order having been disturbed at Peking, the troops of the five Great Powers, under the command of a German Field-Marshal, restored it by the customary means. Having in this fashion covered themselves with military glory, the five Powers signed one of the innumerable treaties by which they guarantee the integrity of the very China whose provinces they divide among themselves.

"Russia's share was Manchuria, and she closed Korea to Japanese trade. Japan, which in 1894 had beaten the Chinese on land and on sea, and had taken a part, in 1901, in the pacifying action of the Powers, saw with concentrated fury the advance of the voracious and slow-footed she-bear. And, while the huge brute indolently stretched out its muzzle towards the Japanese beehive, the yellow bees, arming their wings and stings together, riddled it with burning punctures.

"'It is a colonial war,' was the expression used by a high-placed Russian official to my friend Georges Bourdon.[D] Now, the fundamental principal of every colonial war is that the European should be more powerful than the peoples whom he is fighting; this is as clear as noonday. It is understood that in these kinds of wars the European is to attack with artillery, while the Asiatic or African is of course to defend himself with arrows, clubs, assegais and tomahawks. It is tolerated that he should procure a few antiquated flint-locks and cartridge-pouches; this aids in rendering colonisation more glorious. But in no case is it permissible that he should be armed and instructed in European fashion. His fleet must consist of junks, canoes and 'dug-outs.' Should he perchance purchase ships from European ship-owners, such ships shall naturally be unfit for use. The Chinese who fill their arsenals with porcelain shells conform to the rules of colonial warfare.

315

D M. Georges Bourdon, journalist, on the staff of *Le Figaro*.

"The Japanese have departed from these rules. They wage war in accordance with the principles taught in France by General Bonnal. They greatly outweighed their adversaries in knowledge and intelligence. While fighting better than Europeans, they show no respect for consecrated usages, and act to a certain degree in a fashion contrary to the law of nations.

"'Tis in vain that serious individuals like Monsieur Edmond Théry demonstrated to them that they were bound to be beaten, in the superior interest of the European market and in conformity with the most firmly established economic laws. Vainly did the proconsul of Indo-China, Monsieur Doumer himself, call upon them to suffer, and at short notice, decisive defeats on sea and on land. 'What a financial sadness would bow down our hearts,' exclaimed this great man, 'were Bezobrazoff and Alexeieff not to extract another million out of the Korean forests. They are kings. Like them, I was a king: our cause is a common one. Oh ye Japanese! Imitate in their gentleness the copper-coloured folk over whom I reigned so gloriously under Méline.' In vain did Dr. Charles Richet, skeleton in hand, represent to them that being prognathous, and not having the muscles of their calves sufficiently developed, they were under the obligation of seeking flight in the trees when face to face with the Russians, who are brachycephalous and as such eminently civilising, as was demonstrated when they drowned five thousand Chinese in the Amur. 'Bear in mind that you are links between monkey and man,' obligingly said to them my Lord Professor Richet, 'as a consequence of which, if you should defeat the Russians or Finno-Letto-Ugro-Slavs, it would be exactly as if monkeys were to beat you. Is it not plain to you?' They heeded him not.

"At the present moment, the Russians are paying the penalty, in the waters of Japan and in the gorges of Manchuria, not only of their grasping and brutal policy in the East, but of the colonial policy of all Europe. They are now expiating, not merely their own crimes, but those of the whole of military and commercial Christianity. When saying this, I do not mean to say that there is a justice in the world. But we witness a strange whirligig of things, and brute force, up to now the sole judge of human actions, indulges occasionally in unexpected pranks. Its sudden starts aside destroy an equilibrium thought to be stable. And its pranks, which are ever the work of some hidden rule, bring about interesting results. The Japanese cross the Yalu and defeat the Russians in good form. Their sailors annihilate artistically a European fleet. Immediately do we discern that a danger threatens us. If it indeed exists, who created it? It was not the Japanese who sought out the Russians. It was not the yellow men who hunted up the whites. We there and then make the discovery of a Yellow Peril. For many long years have Asiatics been familiar with the White Peril. The looting of the Summer Palace, the massacres of Pekin, the drownings of Blagovestchenk, the dismemberment of China, were these not enough to alarm the Chinese? As to the Japanese, could they feel secure under the guns of Port Arthur? We created the White Peril. The White Peril has engendered the Yellow Peril. We have here concatenations giving to the ancient Necessity which rules the world an appearance of divine Justice, and must perforce admire the astonishing behaviour of that blind queen of men and gods, when seeing Japan, formerly so cruel to the Chinese and Koreans, and the unpaid accessory to the crimes of Europeans in China, become the avenger of China, and the hope of the yellow race.

"It does not, however, appear at first sight that the Yellow Peril at which European economists are terrified is to be compared to the White Peril suspended over Asia. The Chinese do not send to Paris, Berlin, and St. Petersburg missionaries to teach Christians the Fung-chui, and sow disorder in European affairs. A Chinese expeditionary force did not land in Quiberon Bay to demand of the Government of the Republic *extra-territoriality*, i.e., the right of trying by a tribunal of mandarins cases pending between Chinese and Europeans. Admiral Togo did not come and bombard Brest roads with a dozen battleships, for the purpose of improving Japanese trade in France. The flower of French nationalism, the *élite* of our Trublions, did not besiege in their mansions in the Avenues Hoche and Marceau the Legations of China and of Japan, and Marshal Oyama did not, for the same reason, lead the combined armies of the Far East to the Boulevard de la Madeleine to demand the punishment of the foreigner-hating Trublions. He did not burn Versailles in the name of a higher civilisation. The armies of the Great Asiatic Powers did not carry away to Tokio and Peking the Louvre paintings and the silver service of the Elysée.

"No indeed! Monsieur Edmond Théry himself admits that the yellow men are not sufficiently civilised to imitate the whites so faithfully. Nor does he foresee that they will ever rise to so high a moral culture. How could it be possible for them to possess our virtues? They are not Christians. But men entitled to speak consider that the Yellow Peril is none the less to be dreaded for all that it is economic. Japan, and China organised by Japan, threaten us, in all the markets of Europe, with a competition frightful, monstrous, enormous, and deformed, the mere idea of which causes the hair of the economists to stand on end. That is why Japanese and Chinese must be exterminated. There can be no doubt about the matter. But war must also be declared against the United States to prevent it from selling iron and steel at a lower price than our manufacturers less well equipped in machinery.

"Let us for once admit the truth, and for a moment cease flattering ourselves. Old Europe and new Europe—for that is America's true name—have inaugurated economic war. Each and every nation is waging an industrial struggle against the others. Everywhere does production arm itself furiously against production. We are displaying bad grace when we complain that we are witnessing fresh competing and disturbing products invade the market of the world thus thrown into confusion. Of what use are our lamentations? That might is right is our god. If Tokio is the weaker, it shall be in the wrong and it shall be made to feel it; if it is the stronger, right will be on its side, and we shall have no reproach to cast at it. Where is the nation in the world entitled to speak in the name of justice?

"We have taught the Japanese both the capitalistic *régime* and war. They are a cause of alarm because they are becoming like ourselves. In truth, it is awful. They dare to defend themselves with European weapons against Europeans. Their generals, their naval officers, who have studied in England, in Germany, and in France, reflect honour on their instructors. Several of them have followed the classes of our special military schools. The Russian Grand Dukes, who feared that no good could come out of military institutions too democratic to their taste, must feel reassured.

"I am unable to foretell the issue of the war. The Russian Empire opposes to the methodical energy of the Japanese its irresolute forces which the savage imbecility of its government restrains, the dishonesty of a voracious administration robs, and military incapacity leads to disaster. The stupendousness of its impotence and the depths of its disorganisation stand revealed. Withal, its golden reservoirs, kept filled by its rich creditors, are all but inexhaustible. On the other hand, its enemy has no other resources than onerous loans obtained with difficulty, of which victory itself may perchance deprive them. For while English and Americans are one in assisting it to weaken Russia, they do not intend that it shall become powerful and to be feared. It is hard to predict the final victory of one combatant over the other. But if Japan makes the yellow men respected by the white men, it will have greatly served the cause of humanity, and paved the way unawares and doubtless against its own wish for the pacific organisation of the world."

"What do you mean," said M. Goubin, raising his eyes from his plate filled with a savoury *fritto*.

"It is feared," continued Nicole Langelier, "that Japan grown to manhood will educate China, teach it to defend itself and to exploit its wealth itself, and that Japan will create a strong China. No need to look upon such a contingency with alarm; it should, on the contrary, be hoped for in the universal interest. Strong nations co-operate to the harmony and wealth of the world. Weak nations, like China and Turkey, are a perpetual cause of disturbances and perils. But we are ever in too great a haste in our fearsand hopes. Should victorious Japan undertake to organise the old yellow Empire, it will not succeed in its task that quickly. It will require time to teach China that a China exists. For she knows it not, and as long as she is unaware of it, there will not be any China. A people exists only in the knowledge possessed by it of its existence. There are 350,000,000 Chinese, but they are not aware of the fact. As long as they have not counted themselves, they will not count for anything. They will not even exist by dint of numbers. 'Number off!' is the first word of command spoken by the drill-sergeant to his men. He is there and then teaching them the principle of societies. But it takes a long time for 350,000,000 men to number themselves. Nevertheless, Ular, who is a European out of the common, since he believes that one should be humane and just towards the Chinese, informs us that a great national movement is simmering in all the provinces of the huge empire."

"And even should it happen," said Joséphin Leclerc, "that victorious Japan came to infuse into Mongols, Chinese, and Tibetans a consciousness of themselves, and caused them to be respected by the white races, in what way would the peace of the world be better assured, and the conquering mania of nations be kept within stricter bounds? Would not negro humanity still remain to be exterminated? Where is the black nation which will insure the respecting of negroes by the white and yellow races?"

"But," interposed Nicole Langelier, "who can define how far one of the great human races may go? The blacks are not, like the red man, dying out through contact with the Europeans. Where is the prophet who will venture to tell the 200,000,000 African blacks that their posterity will never enjoy wealth and peace on the lakes and great rivers? The white men passed through the ages of caves and lacustrine villages. They were at that time wild and naked. They dried rude potteries in the sun. Their chiefs led barbarian dances at which they shouted. They knew no other sciences than those of their sorcerers. Since those days they have built the Parthenon, conceived geometry, subjected the expression of their thought and the motions of their body to the laws of harmony.

"Are you then going to say to the African negroes: 'You shall for ever carry on an internecine war between tribe and tribe, and you shall inflict upon one another atrocities and absurd tortures; King Gléglé, permeated with a religious idea, shall for all time have prisoners tied up in a basket and thrown from the roof of his royal hut; you shall for ever devour with enjoyment the strips of flesh torn from the decomposed cadavers of your aged relations; for ever shall explorers unload their rifles on you, and smoke you out in your kraals; the wonderful Christian soldier will enjoy in his bravery the amusement of hacking your women to pieces; the gay and festive sailor from the befogged seas shall for all time kick in the bellies of your little children, just to take the stiffness out of his knee-joints? Can you safely prophesy to one-third of humanity a state of perpetual ignominy?

"I am unable to say whether one day, as Mrs. Beecher Stowe predicted in 1840, a life will awaken in Africa full of a splendour and magnificence unknown to the cold-blooded races of the West, and whether art will blossom forth in new and dazzling forms. The blacks possess a keen appreciation of music. It may happen that a delightful negro art of dance and song shall see the light of day. In the meanwhile, the coloured folk of the Southern States are making rapid strides in capitalistic civilisation. Monsieur Jean Finot has recently supplied us with information on the subject.

"Fifty years ago they did not, as a whole, own two hundred and fifty acres of land. Nowadays their property is valued at over £160,000,000. They were illiterate. To-day fifty per cent. of them can read and write. There are black novelists, poets, economists, and philanthropists.

"The half-breeds, the issue of master and slave, are singularly intelligent and vigorous. The coloured men, both cunning and ferocious, instinctive and calculating, will gradually (so one of them has confided to me) reap the advantage of number, and one day lord it over the effeminate creole race which exercises so lightly over the blacks its fitful cruelty. It may be that the mulatto of genius, who will make the children of the whites pay dearly the blood of the negroes lynched by their fathers, is already born."

M. Goubin primed himself with his powerful eye-glass, and remarked:

"Were the Japanese to be victorious, they would take Indo-China from us."

"Thereby rendering us a great service," answered Langelier. "Colonies are the curse of nations."

M. Goubin's indignant silence was his sole reply.

"I cannot listen to such statements," exclaimed Joséphin Leclerc. "We require outlets for our products, and territories for our industrial and commercial expansion. What are you thinking of, Langelier? One policy alone governs Europe, America, and the world to-day—colonial policy."

Nicole Langelier, unruffled, replied:

"Colonial policy is the most recent form of barbarism, or, if you prefer, the term of civilisation. I make no distinction between these two expressions; they are identical. What men call civilisation is the present condition of manners, while what they style barbarism are anterior conditions. The manners of to-day will be styled barbarian when they shall be of the past. It is patent to me that our manners and morals embody the idea that strong nations shall destroy the weaker ones. Of such is the principle of the law of nations.

"It remains to be seen, however, whether conquests abroad always constitute a good stroke of business for nations. It would not seem so. What have Mexico and Peru done for Spain? Brazil for Portugal? Batavia for Holland? There are various kinds of colonies. There are colonies which afford to unfortunate Europeans desert and uncultivated lands. These, loyal as long as they remain poor, separate from the mother country as soon as they become prosperous. Some there are which are inhabitable; these supply raw material, and import manufactured goods. Now it is plain that these colonies enrich, not those who govern them, but whoever trades with them. The greater part of the time they are not worth what they cost. Moreover, they may at any moment expose the mother country to military disasters."

"How about England?" interrupted M. Goubin.

"England is less a nation than a race. The Anglo-Saxons know no fatherland but the sea. England, looked upon as wealthy in her vast domains, owes her fortune and her power to her commerce. It is not her colonies which should be envied her, but her merchants, the authors of her wealth. Do you imagine, by way of illustration, that the Transvaal represents so very good a stroke of business for her? For all that, it is conceivable that in the present state of the world nations who bring forth many children and manufacture products in large quantities should seek

319

territories and markets in far-off lands, and secure possession of them by stratagem and violence. How different it is in our own case! Our thrifty nation, careful not to have more children than the natal soil can feed without difficulty, and producing in a moderate degree, does not willingly embark on distant adventures; our France, who hardly goes beyond her garden wall, great heavens, what need has she of colonies? Of what use are they to her? What do they bring her? She has spent men and money in profusion, in order that the Congo, Cochin-China, Annam, Tonking, Guiana, and Madagascar shall purchase calicoes from Manchester, guns from Birmingham and Liége, brandies from Dantzig, and cases of wine all the way from Bordeaux to Hamburg. She has, for seventy years, despoiled, hunted, and shot down Arabs, and in the end she has peopled Algeria with Italians and Spaniards!

"The irony of these results is cruel enough, and it is hard to realise that this empire, ten or eleven times as big as France herself, has been formed to our detriment. But, it must be taken into consideration that whereas the French nation derives no advantage whatsoever from the possession of territories in Africa and Asia, the heads of its Government, on the other hand, find it to their great advantage to acquire them. They thereby secure the affection of the navy and army, which on the occasion of colonial expeditions reap a harvest of promotions, pensions, and crosses, to say nothing of the glory won in defeating the enemy. They conciliate the clergy by opening new paths to the Propaganda, and by allocating territories to Catholic missions. They make joyous the ship-owners, builders, and army contractors, whom they load with orders. They secure for themselves in the country itself a numerous following by the granting of concessions of immense forests and plantations without end. And, what is still more precious to them, they attach to their majority every parliamentary jobber and kerbstone-broker. Lastly, they cajole the multitude, proud in its possession of a yellow and black empire, which makes Germany and England turn green with envy. They are lookedupon as good citizens, patriots, and great statesmen. And if, like Ferry, they incur the risk of going under, as the result of some military disaster, they willingly run the risk fully convinced that the most harmful of distant expeditions will cost them fewer difficulties, and will inveigle them into fewer perils than the most useful of social reforms.

"You can now realise why we have occasionally had imperialist ministers, jealous of aggrandising our colonial domain. We must congratulate ourselves, however, and praise the moderation of our rulers, who might have burdened us with still more colonies.

"But all danger has not been averted, and we are threatened with an eighty years' warfare in Morocco. Is there never to be an end to the colonial mania?

"I am fully aware that nations are not sensible. How can it be expected of them, if one considers what they are made of? Still, a certain instinct oftentimes warns them of what is harmful. They are occasionally endowed with the power of observing. In the long run they undergo the painful experience of their errors and blunders. The day will come when it will dawn upon them that colonies are a source of perils and ruinous results. Commercial barbarism will be followed by commercial civilisation, and forcible, by pacific penetration. These ideas have to-day found an echo even in the bosom of parliaments. They will prevail, not because men will be more disinterested, but because they will know their own interests better.

"The great human asset is man himself. In order to rate the terrestrial globe, it is necessary to begin by rating men. To exploit the soil, the mines, the waters, all the substances and all the forces of our planet, it needs man, the whole of man; humanity, the whole of humanity. The complete exploitation of the terrestrial globe demands the united labour of white, yellow, and black men. By reducing, diminishing, and weakening, or, to sum it up in one word, by colonising a portion of humanity, we are working against ourselves. It is to our advantage that yellow and black men should be powerful, free, and wealthy. Our prosperity and our wealth depend on theirs. The more is produced, the more will there be consumed. The greater the profit they derive from us, the greater the profit we shall derive from them. If they reap the benefit of our labours, so shall we fully reap theirs.

"If we study the movements which govern the destinies of societies, we may perhaps discover signs that the era of violent deeds is coming to an end. War, which was formerly a standing institution among nations, is now intermittent, and the periods of peace have become of longer duration than those of war. Our country affords the observations of a fact full of interest, for the French nation presents an original characteristic in the military history of nations. Whereas other nations never waged war except from interest or necessity, alone the French have fought for the pleasure of fighting. Now it is remarkable that the taste of our compatriots has undergone a change. Thirty years ago Renan wrote: 'Whoever knows France as a whole and in her provincial varieties will not hesitate to recognise the fact that the movement swaying this country for the past fifty years is essentially pacific.' It is a fact attested by a large number of observers that in 1870 France had no desire to have recourse to the arbitrament of war, and that the declaration of war was greeted with consternation. It is an assured fact that few Frenchmen dream of taking the field, and that everybody readily accepts the idea that the army exists in order to avoid a war. Let me quote one example out of a thousand in confirmation of this state of mind. Monsieur Ribot, a representative of the people and a former Cabinet Minister, having been invited to some patriotic celebration, replied with an eloquent letter, begging to be excused. The same Monsieur Ribot knits his brows superciliously at the mere mention of the word disarmament. He has towards standards and cannon the leaning proper to a former Minister of Foreign Affairs. In his letter he denounces as a national peril the pacific ideas disseminated by the Socialist. He sees in them a spirit of renunciation he cannot endure. Not that he is of a bellicose turn of mind. He, too, sighs for peace, but a peace full of pomp, magnificent, and flashing with the same pride as war. Between Monsieur Ribot and Jaurès, the matter is merely one of form. Both of them are for peace. Jaurès, simply; Monsieur Ribot, superbly. That is all. Better still and more surely than the Socialist democracy which contents itself with a bloused or coated peace does the sentiment of the bourgeois, who demand a peace gleaming with military insignia and bedecked with emblems of glory, testify to the inevitable decline of all idea of revenge and conquests, since one discerns in it the military instinct, at the very time when it is losing its nature and is becoming pacific.

"France is acquiring by degrees the sentiment of her true strength, consisting in intellectual strength; she is becoming conscious of her mission, which is the sowing of ideas and the exercise of a sway over thought. She will within measurable time perceive that her only stable power has lain in her speakers, her writers, and her men of science. Hence she will some day fain have to recognise that the force of numbers, after having so often betrayed her, is finally escaping from her, and that the time has come for her to resign herself to the glory which the exercise of the mind and the use of reason assure her of."

Jean Boilly, shaking his head, said:

"You ask that France should teach other nations concord and peace. Are you so sure that she will be listened to and her example followed? Is her own tranquillity so assured? Has she not to fear threats from outside, to foresee dangers, to watch over her safety, and to provide for her defence? One swallow does not make a summer; one nation does not make the peace of the world. Is it so sure that Germany keeps up an army with the sole object of not waging war? Her Social-Democrats desire peace. But they are not the masters, and their deputies do not enjoy in the Parliament the authority which the number of their electors should give them. And Russia, who has hardly entered upon the industrial period, do you believe that she will soon be entering upon the pacific period? Is it not to be feared that after having disturbed Asia she will disturb Europe?

"Supposing even that Europe should become pacific, can you not see that America would become warlike? Following upon Cuba, reduced to the state of a vassal republic, Hawaii, Porto Rico, and the annexation of the Philippines, it is impossible to say that the American Union is not a conquering nation. A publicist of Yankee proclivities, Stead, has said amid the plaudits of the whole of the United States: 'The Americanisation of the world is on the march.' And then there is Mr. Roosevelt, whose dream is to plant the Stars and Stripes in South Africa, Australia, and the West Indies. Mr. Roosevelt is Imperialist and he sighs for an America mistress of the world. Between ourselves, he is planning the Empire of Augustus. He has unfortunately perused Livy. The conquests of the Romans banish sleep from him. Have you read his speeches? They breathe a bellicose spirit. 'Fight, my friends,' says Mr. Roosevelt, 'and fight hard. There is nothing like blows. We are upon earth only to exterminate one another. Those who tell you the contrary are men without morality. Mistrust men who think. Thought enervates. 'Tis a French failing. The Romans conquered the world. They lost it. We are the modern Romans.' Words full of eloquence, backed up with a navy which will soon be the second in the world, and with a military Budget of 40,500,000 francs!

"The Yankees declare that in four years' time they will fight Germany. If we are to believe this, they should first tell us where they expect to come into contact with the enemy. That a Russia, the serf of her Czar, that a still feudal Germany, should entertain armies for fighting purposes, this one is tempted to lay to the door of ancient habits and the survival of a strenuous past. But that a young democracy, the United States of America, an aggregation of business men, a mass of emigrants from all countries, lacking community, traditions, and memories, madly cast into the scramble for the mighty dollar, should of a sudden be swept with the desire of firing torpedoes at the flanks of battleships, and of exploding mines under the enemy's columns, affords a proof that the inordinate struggle for the production and exploitation of riches keeps alive the employment of and taste for brutal force, that industrial violence engenders military violence, and that mercantile rivalries kindle between nations hatreds that bloodshed can alone extinguish. The colonial mania of which you were speaking a while ago is but one of the thousand forms of the much-vaunted competition of our economists. The capitalistic state is just as much a warlike one as the feudal. The era has dawned of great wars for the industrial sovereignty. Under the present *régime* of national production it is the cannon which fixes tariffs, establishes customs, opens and closes markets. There exists no other regulator of commerce and industry. Extermination is the fatal result of the economic conditions in which the civilised world finds itself to-day...."

The perfume of Gorgonzola and Stracchino was pervading the table. The waiter was bringing in wax-candles to each of which was attached the *abbrustolatoio* wherewith to light the long cigars with straws, so dear to Italians.

Hippolyte Dufresne, who for some time past seemed to have remained indifferent to the conversation, here remarked in a low tone tinged with an ostentatious modesty:

"Gentlemen, our friend Langelier was asserting just now that many men are afraid of disgracing themselves in the eyes of their contemporaries by assuming the horrible immorality which is to be the morality of the future. I do not entertain a like fear, and I have written a little tale, which has perhaps no other merit than the one of revealing my calmness of mind when considering the future. I shall one day crave permission to read it to you."

"Read it right away," said Boni, lighting his cigar.

322

"You will be giving us pleasure," added Joséphin Leclerc, Nicole Langelier, and M. Goubin.

"I am not sure whether I have the manuscript with me," replied Hippolyte Dufresne.

With these words, he drew out of his pocket a roll of paper, and began to read what follows.

V

THROUGH THE HORN OR THE IVORY GATE

IT was about one o'clock in the morning. Before retiring for the night, I opened the window and lit a cigarette. The hum of a motor-car scudding along the Avenue du Bois de Boulogne broke the reigning silence. The trees were freshening the atmosphere by the swaying of their darkened tops. No buzzing insect, no living sound arose from the sterile soil of the city. The night was resplendent with stars. Their fires seemed, in the clearness of the air, more so than on other nights, of varied lines. The greater number blazed at white heat. Some there were, however, yellow and orange-tinted, similar to the flames of dying lamps. Several were blue, and I saw one of so pale a blue, so limpid, and so soft, that I could not avert my gaze from it. I regret being ignorant of its name, but I console myself with the thought that men do not give the stars their true names.

"When I reflect that each one of these drops of light enlightens worlds, I ask myself whether, like our own sun, they do not shed their rays on sufferings without end, and whether pain does not penetrate the utmost recesses of heaven. We can only judge the other worlds by our own. We know of life only the forms which it assumes upon the earth, and if we suppose that our planet is one of the least good, we have no reason for believing that all goes rightly in the others, nor that fortunate is he who is born under the rays of Altair, Betelgeux, or the fiery Sirius, when we know what a grievous affair it is to open our eyes on earth to the light of our old Sun. It is not that I find mine an unhappy fate, when compared with that of other men. I am not troubled with either wife or child. Love and sickness have left me unscathed. I am not very rich, and I do not go into society. I am thus to be numbered with the happy ones. Little joy, however, falls to their lot. What, then, can be the fate of the others? Men are really to be pitied. I impute no blame to nature for this; to hold a conversation with her is an impossibility; she is not intelligent. Nor will I lay the blame on society. There is no sense in opposing society to nature. It is as absurd to oppose the nature of men to the society of men, as to oppose the nature of ants to the society of ants, or the nature of herrings to the society of herrings. Animal societies are the necessary outcome of animal nature. The earth is the planet where one eats; 'tis the planet of hunger. The animals peopling it are naturally gluttonous and ferocious. Man, the most intelligent of them all, is alone avaricious. Avarice has so far been the fundamental virtue of human societies, and the moral masterpiece of nature. Were I a writer, I should indite the praise of avarice. It is true that my book would not reveal anything strikingly new. The subject has been dealt with a hundred times over by moralists and economists. Human societies have avarice and cruelty as their august basis.

"It is thus in the other universes, in the numberless ethereal worlds? Do all the stars I see shed their light on men? Do people eat and inter-devour one another beyond the infinite. This doubt troubles me, and I am unable to contemplate without fright the fiery dew suspended in the heavens.

"My thoughts imperceptibly become more lucid and gentle, and the idea of life, in its sensuality, violent and suave in turn, once more assumes a pleasurable aspect to my mind. I sometimes say to myself that life is beautiful. For, without such beauty, how could we discern its ugly features, and how believe that nature is bad, if at the same time we do not believe that it is good?

"For a few minutes past, the phrases of a sonata of Mozart have hovered in the air, with their white columns and their garlands of roses. My neighbour is a pianist, who at nights plays Mozart and Gluck. I close the window, and while undressing, I am pondering over the doubtful pleasures which I may give myself the next day, when of a sudden I remember that for a week past I have been invited to lunch in the Bois de Boulogne; I have a vague idea that the invitation is for the coming day. To make sure of it, I look up the letter of invitation, which lies open on my table. Its contents are:

"'16th September 1903.

"'My dear old Dufresne,—

"'Do me the pleasure of coming to luncheon with ... etc. etc., next Saturday, the 23rd of September, 1903, etc. etc.'

"'It is for to-morrow.

"'I ring for my valet.

"'Jean, wake me to-morrow at nine o'clock.'

"It happens precisely that to-morrow, the 23rd of September 1903, I shall enter upon my fortieth year. From what I have already seen in this world I can almost conceive what still remains for me to be seen. I can safely foretell the topics of to-morrow's conversation at the restaurant in the Bois: 'My automobile goes sixty kilomètres an hour.'—'Blanche has a nasty disposition; but she is true to me; of that I feel sure.'—'The Cabinet takes its pass-word from the Socialists.'—'In the long run, the *petits-chevaux* are a bore. However, there remains *baccara*.'—'The workmen would be fools not to do as they please: the government always gives in to them.'—'I will bet you that Epingle-d'Or will beat Ranavalo.'—'What I personally cannot make out is why there is not some General to sweep away all those blackguards.'—'What can you expect? France has been sold to England and Germany by the Jews.' This is what I shall hear to-morrow. Here you have the social and political ideas of my friends, the great-grandsons of the bourgeois of July, princes of the factory and foundry, kings of the mine, who knew the way of mastering and enslaving the forces of the Revolution. My friends do not seem to me capable of preserving for any lengthy period the industrial empire and the political power bequeathed to them by their ancestors. My friends do not shine by their intelligence. They have not indulged in too much brainwork. No more have I. So far, I have not done much in this life. Like them, I am both idle and ignorant. I do not feel myself capable of achieving anything, and if I do not possess their vanity, if my brain is not stored with all the foolish ideas encumbering theirs; if, like them, I do not feel a hatred for and a fear of ideas, it is due to a peculiar circumstance of my life. My father, a big manufacturer and Conservative deputy, gave me, when I was seventeen, a young and timid "coach," who spoke little, and who looked like a girl. While preparing me for my bachelorship, he was organising the social revolution in Europe. His gentleness was something refreshing. He has often been put in prison, and is now a deputy. I used to copy his addresses to the international proletariat. He made me read the whole Socialistic library. He taught me things all of which were not to be credited, but he opened my eyes to what was going on about me; he demonstrated to me that everything our society honours is contemptible, and that all that it despises is worthy of esteem. He led me into the paths of rebellion. In spite of his demonstrations, I came to the conclusion that falsehood should be respected and hypocrisy venerated as the two surest supports of the public order. I remained a Conservative, but my soul became saturated with disgust.

324

"As I am falling asleep, a few almost imperceptible phrases of Mozart still reach my ears now and then, and make me dream of temples of marble standing amid a blue foliage.

"It was broad daylight when I awoke. I dressed myself much more quickly than it is my wont. Unconscious of the cause for this haste, I found myself in the street without knowing how I had got there. What I now saw about me was to me the cause of a surprise which suspended all my faculties of reflection; and it is owing to this impossibility to reflect that my surprise did not increase, but remained stationary and calm. It would doubtless soon have become immoderate, and would have changed to stupor and terror, had I retained the use of my mind, so greatly was the scene which I was witnessing different from what it should be. Everything about me was to me new, unknown, and foreign. The trees and the lawns which I was in the habit of seeing daily had vanished. Where, on the day before, the tall grey buildings of the avenue stood out against the sky, there now stretched a fanciful line of brick cottages surrounded by gardens. I dared not look round to ascertain whether my own house still existed, and so I went straight towards the Porte Dauphine. I found it not. I took a street which was, so it seemed to me, the old road to Suresnes. The houses flanking it, of strange style and new form, too small to be occupied by rich people, were nevertheless embellished with pictures, sculptures, and brilliant potteries. A covered terrace surmounted them. I followed this rural road, whose curves produced enchanting perspectives. It was crossed obliquely by other sinuous ways. Neither trains, nor automobiles, nor vehicles of any kind went by. Shadows flitted over the soil. I looked upwards and saw masses of huge birds and enormous fishes glide rapidly through the upper atmosphere, which seemed to be a combination of heaven and ocean. Near the Seine, the course of which was altered, I came across a crowd of men clad in short blouses knotted at the waist, and wearing long gaiters. To all appearance they were in their working clothes. But their gait was lighter and more elegant than that of our workmen. I noticed women among them. What had heretofore prevented my recognising them as such was that they were dressed like the men, that they had long and straight legs, and, so it seemed to me, the narrow hips of American women. Although these folk did not present a savage appearance, I looked at them with fright. They presented to my gaze a more foreign appearance than any of the numerous strangers I had so far met upon the earth. In order to avoid seeing another human face, I turned down a deserted lane. Very soon I came to a circus planted with masts from which flew crimson oriflammes bearing in letters of gold the words: EUROPEAN FEDERATION. Placards in large frames ornamented with emblems of peace hung at the foot of the masts. They embodied announcements regarding popular festivals, legal injunctions, and works of public interest. In addition to balloon time-tables was a chart of the atmospheric currents drawn on the 28th of June of the year 220 of the Federation of Nations. All these texts were printed in characters new to me, and in a language of which I did not understand all the words. The while I was attempting to decipher them, the shadows of the countless machines cleaving the air flitted across my vision. Once more did I gaze upwards, and in this sky altered beyond recognition, more densely populated than the earth, cloven by rudders and threshed by screws, towards which a circle of smoke rose from the horizon, I perceived the sun. I felt like crying on seeing it. It was the only familiar figure which I had come across since morning. From its altitude I judged that it was about ten o'clock of the forenoon. Of a sudden I was surrounded by a second crowd of men and women, similar in appearance and in costume to the first. I was confirmed in the impression that the women, although some of them were very plump, others very skinny, and many beggared description, were on the whole androgynous in appearance. The crowd went its way. The open space once more was desert, just as our suburban quarters, which only come to life on the exodus from the workshops. I remained behind in front of the placards and read once more the date—the 28th of June of the year 220 of the European Federation. What did it mean! A proclamation by the Federal Committee, on the occasion of the festival of the Earth, furnished me with timely and useful data for comprehension of that date. This is what I read: 'Comrades, you are aware how, in the last year of the twentieth century, the old order

325

collapsed in a fearful cataclysm, and how, after fifty years of anarchy, the federation of the peoples of Europe was organised...." The year 220 of the federation of peoples was therefore the year 2270 of the Christian Era; this was certainly a fact which remained to be explained. How came it that of a sudden I found myself transported to the year 2270?

"I mused over the circumstance as I strolled at haphazard.

"'I have not, as far as I know,' I said to myself, 'been preserved for so many years in the mummy state, like Colonel Fougas. I have not driven the machine with which Mr. H. G. Wells explores time. And if, following the example of William Morris, I have, while asleep, skipped three and a half centuries, I am unaware of the fact, since, when dreaming, one does not know that one is doing so. I am utterly convinced that I am not asleep.'

"While indulging in these musings and others not worth recording, I was following a long street bordered with railings behind which pink-hued houses of various styles, but all equally small, smilingly peeped through the foliage. At times I perceived huge circuses of steel standing out in the landscape, and crowned with flames and smoke. Terror planed over these regions to which no name can be given, while the vibrating rush of air caused by the rapid flight of the machines resounded painfully through my brain. The street led to a meadow studded with clumps of trees and intersected by rivulets. Cows were pasturing in it. Just as my eyes were feasting upon the freshness of the scene I fancied I saw in front of me shadows flitting along a smooth and straight road. The whirlwind engendered by them, as they passed me, fanned my cheeks. I saw that they were trams and automobiles, real transparencies in their rapidity.

"I crossed the road by a foot-bridge, and for a long time I sauntered through small meadows and woodlands. I thought I was in the open country, when I discovered an extensive frontage of resplendent houses bordering on the park. Soon, I found myself opposite a palace of an airy style of architecture. A sculptured and painted frieze, representing a largely attended feast, stretched across the vast façade. I perceived, through the panes of the bay-windows, men and women seated in a large and bright room around long marble tables, laden with prettily painted potteries. I entered, under the impression that this was a restaurant. I was not hungry, but weary, and the coolness of the room, artistically hung with garlands of fruit, appeared to me delicious. A man who stood by the door asked me for my voucher, and, as I showed embarrassment, he remarked:

"'I see, comrade, that you are not of these parts. How is it that you are travelling without vouchers! Very sorry, but it is impossible for me to admit you. Go and seek the delegate who hires journeymen; or, if you are too weak to work, address yourself to the delegate who attends to those who need succour.'

"I informed him that I was nowise unfit for work, and drew away. A stout fellow, who was picking his teeth, said to me obligingly:

"'Comrade, you need not go to the delegate who engages journeymen. I am the delegate attached to the bakery of the section. We are one comrade short. Come along with me. You shall be put to work at once.'

"I thanked the corpulent comrade, assured him of my willingness, pointing out, however, that I was not a baker.

"He looked at me with some surprise, and told me that he could see I enjoyed a joke.

"I followed him. We stopped in front of an immense cast-iron building having a monumental gateway, on the pediment of which a couple of bronze giants were resting on their elbows—the Sower and the Reaper. Their bodies expressed strength unstrained. A calm pride irradiated their faces, and they carried high their heads; in this, greatly dissimilar to the fierce-looking workers of the Flemish Constantin Meunier. We entered a room forty mètres in height, wherein, amid clouds of a light whitish dust, machinery was working with a sonorous and calm hum. Under the metallic dome, bags tendered themselves spontaneously to the knife which disembowelled them; the flour which escaped from them dropped into troughs where powerful hands of steel kneaded it into dough which flowed into moulds, which when full hastened to put themselves of their own accord into an oven as capacious and deep as a tunnel. Five or six men at most, motionless amid all this motion, supervised the labour of the machinery.

"''Tis an old bakery,' said my companion. 'It hardly produces more than eighty thousand loaves a day, and its too weak machines employ too many hands. It matters little. Come up to the place where the goods arrive.'

"I did not have the time to ask for a more explicit command. A lift had deposited me on the platform. Hardly had I reached it, when a kind of flying whale alighted close to me and unloaded a number of sacks. No human being was aboard this machine. Other flying whales brought more sacks which they unloaded, and which offered themselves up in succession to the knife which ripped them open. The screws revolved, and the rudder did its work. There was no one at the helm, nobody aboard the machine. I could hear in the distance the slight hum of a wasp flying, and then the thing grew with astounding rapidity. It seemed quite sure of itself, but my ignorance as to what would happen, should it perchance go wrong, caused me to shudder. I was several times tempted to ask to be allowed to go down again. A false shame prevented me. I stood my ground. The sun was disappearing on the horizon, and it was about five o'clock when the lift came up for me. The day's work was over. I was given a voucher for board and lodging.

"The rotund comrade remarked to me:

"'You must be hungry. You may, if you wish, take your evening meal at the public table. If you prefer eating by yourself in your own room, you may likewise do so. If you prefer supping at my place, together with a few comrades, say so at once. I am going to telephone to the culinary workshop that your rations be sent to you. I am telling you all this in order to set you at ease, for you seem like a fish out of water. You have no doubt come from afar. You do not look as if you could take care of yourself. To-day, your task has been an easy one. Do not, however, imagine that one's livelihood is earned every day as cheaply as that. If the Z-rays which directed the balloons had worked badly, as will sometimes happen, your task would not have been so easy. What is your particular line, and where do you come from?'

"These questions embarrassed me greatly. I could not tell him the truth. I could not inform him that I was a bourgeois, and that I had come from the twentieth century. He would have thought me crazy. I replied in a vague and embarrassed manner that I had no trade, and that I came from far, from very far.

"He smiled, and said:

"'I understand. You dare not admit it. You come from the United States of Africa. You are not the only European who has thus given us the slip. But nearly all these deserters end by coming back to us.'

"I answered not a word, and my silence led him to believe that he had guessed aright. He renewed his invitation to supper, and asked me my name. I informed him that I was known as Hippolyte Dufresne. He seemed surprised at my having two names.

"'My name is Michel,' he said.

"Then, after a minute inspection of my straw hat, my jacket, my shoes, and the rest of my costume, which was no doubt somewhat dusty, but of a good cut, for after all I do not have my clothes made by a tailor who acts as hall-porter in the Rue des Acacias, he continued:

"'Hippolyte, I see whence you have come. You have lived in the black provinces. Nowadays there are only Zulus and Basutos to weave cloth so badly, to give so grotesque a shape to a suit, to make such ill-shapen footgear, and to stiffen linen with starch. It is only among them that you can have learnt to shave off your beard, while preserving on your face a moustache, and two little whiskers. This custom of scissoring the hair of the face, so as to form figures and ornaments, is the last word of tattooing, nowadays in vogue only among the Basutos and Zulus. These black provinces of the United States of Africa are wallowing in a state of barbarism resembling in many aspects the state of France three or four hundred years ago.'

"I accepted Michel's invitation.

"'I live quite close to here, in Sologne,' he said. 'My aeroplane scuds along fairly well. We shall soon be there.'

"He made me take a seat under the belly of a huge mechanical bird, and we were soon cleaving the air so rapidly that I lost breath. The aspect of the countryside was vastly different from the one known to me. All the roads were bordered with houses; countless canals intersected the fields with their silvery lines. As I sat wrapt in admiration, Michel remarked to me:

"'The land is fairly well exploited, and cultivation is "intense," as they say, since chemists are themselves agriculturists. One has tried one's best, and one has worked hard for the past three hundred years. The fact is that to make collectivism a reality it has been necessary to compel the soil to return four or five times more than it returned in the days of capitalistic anarchy. You, who have lived among the Zulus and Basutos, are aware that the necessaries of life are so scarce with them that were they to be divided among all it would amount to sharing poverty and not wealth. The super-abundant production which we have attained to is more especially due to the progress made by science. The almost total suppression of the urban classes has also been of great advantage to agriculture. The shopkeepers and the clerks have gone, some to the factory, others to the field.'

"'What!' I exclaimed. 'You have suppressed the cities! What has become of Paris?'

"'Hardly any one lives there now,' replied Michel. 'The greater part of those hideous and insanitary five-storied houses, wherein dwelt the citizens of the closed era, have fallen in ruins, and have been suffered to remain in that condition. House-building was very poor in the twentieth century of that unhappy era. We have preserved some of the older and better constructed buildings and converted them into museums. We possess a large number of museums and libraries: it is there we seek instruction. We have also kept a portion of the remains of the Hôtel de Ville. It was an ugly and fragile building, but great things were carried out within its precincts. As we no longer have tribunals, commerce, and armies, we no longer have cities, so to speak. Nevertheless, the density of the population is much greater on certain points than on others, and in spite of the rapidity of means of communication, the mining and metallurgic centres are densely peopled.'

"'What is that you say?' I asked him. 'You have done away with the courts of law? Have you then suppressed crime and misdemeanour?'

"'Crime will last as long as old and gloomy humanity. But, the number of criminals has diminished with the number of the wretched. The suburbs of the great cities were the feeding-grounds of crime; we no longer have big cities. The wireless telephone makes the highways safe day and night. We are all provided with electric means of defence. As to misdemeanours, they were rather the result of the scruples of the judges than of the perversity of the accused. Now that we no longer possess lawyers and judges, and that justice is administered by citizens summoned in rotation, many misdemeanours have disappeared, doubtless because it is impossible to recognise them as such.'

"In this fashion did Michel discourse while steering his aeroplane. I am recording the meaning of his words as exactly as I can. I regret my inability, owing to a lack of memory, and also from fear of not making myself understood, to reproduce his language in all its expressiveness and its movement. The baker and his contemporaries spoke a language astonishing me at first by the novelty of its vocabulary and syntax, and especially by its pithy and flowing construction.

"Michel came to ground on the terrace of a modest but pleasing dwelling.

"'We have arrived,' he said; ''tis here that I live. You will sup with comrades who, like myself, take an interest in statistics.'

"'What! You a statistician! I thought you were a baker.

"'I am a baker, six hours of the day. This is the duration of the day's work as determined for nearly a century by the Federal Committee. The rest of the time I give up to statistical labours. It is the science which has stepped into history's shoes. The historians of old related the brilliant deeds of the few. Ours register all that is produced and consumed.'

"After having conducted me to a hydrotherapic closet established on the roof, Michel led me down-stairs to the dining-room lit up by electricity, entirely white, and ornamented only with a sculptured frieze of strawberry plants in bloom. A table in painted pottery was covered with dishes with a metallic glaze. Three persons sat at it. Michel named them to me.

"'Morin, Perceval, Chéron.'

"These three individuals were all clad alike in rough-spun jackets, velvet breeches, and grey stockings. Morin wore a long white beard; Chéron's and Perceval's faces were callow. Their short hair and more especially the frankness of their looks gave them the appearance of young lads. Yet I felt sure that they were women. Perceval seemed to me rather pretty, although she was no longer very young. I thought Chéron altogether charming. Michel introduced me:

"'I have brought comrade Hippolyte, who also calls himself Dufresne, to meet you; he has lived among the half-breeds, in the black provinces of the United States of Africa. He could not get any dinner at eleven o'clock, and so he must have an appetite.'

"I was indeed hungry. They helped me to tiny bits of food cut into squares, which were not unpleasant to the taste, however new to me. A variety of cheeses were on the table. Morin poured me out a glass of light beer, and informed me that I could drink to my heart's content, as it did not contain any alcohol.

"'That's right,' I said. 'I am glad to see that you pay attention to the evils of alcohol.'

"'They have almost ceased to exist,' answered Morin. 'We succeeded in suppressing alcoholism before the end of the closed era. It would have otherwise been impossible to establish the new *régime*. An alcoholic proletariat is incapable of emancipation.'

"'Have you not also,' I inquired, while tasting a strangely carved bit of food—'have you not also perfected food?'

"'Comrade,' replied Perceval, 'you doubtless refer to chemical alimentation. So far, it has not made any great strides. 'Tis in vain that we send our chemists as delegates into the kitchen.... Their tabloids are of no good. With the exception that we know how to compound properly caloric and nutritious foods, we feed almost as coarsely as the men of the closed era, and we enjoy it just as much.'

"'Our scientists,' remarked Michel, 'are seeking to establish a rational system of food.'

"'That's childishness,' said the young female Chéron. 'No good result will be reached, as long as the big intestine, a useless and harmful organ, and the seat of microbian infection, has not been removed.... This will come in time.'

"'In what way?' I asked.

"'Simply by ablation. And this suppression, the result, in the first place, of an operation upon a sufficient number of individuals, will tend to establish itself by heredity, and will later on be common to the whole race.'

"These people treated me humanely and conversed obligingly with me. But it was difficult for me to chime in with their manners and their ideas, while I noticed that I nowise interested them, and that they felt an absolute indifference towards my modes of thought. The more I showed them courtesies, the more I alienated their sympathies. Following upon my addressing a few compliments, albeit discreet and sincere, to Chéron, she no longer even deigned to look at me.

"The meal over, addressing myself to Morin, who seemed to me intelligent and gentle, I said to him with a sincerity which indeed stirred me deeply:

"'Monsieur Morin, I am ignorant of all things, and I am suffering cruelly because of my lack of knowledge. I repeat to you that I come from far, from very far. Tell me, I entreat you, how the European Federation came into existence, and explain to me the present social system.'

"Old Morin protested:

"'You are asking me for the history of three centuries. It would take me weeks, nay months. Moreover, there are many things I could not teach you, as I do not know them myself.'

"I thereupon entreated him to lay before me a very concise summary, as is done in the case of school children.

"Morin, flinging himself back in his arm-chair, began:

"'To ascertain how the present society was constituted, it is necessary to go back far into the past.

"'The crowning achievement of the twentieth century was the extinction of war.

"'The arbitration Congress of The Hague, instituted in the middle of barbarism, did not to any degree contribute towards the maintenance of peace. But another more efficacious institution came into existence at that time. Groups of deputies were formed in the various Parliaments, who entered into communication with one another, and who in course of time came to deliberate in common on international questions. Giving expression as they did to the peaceful aspirations of a growing crowd of electors, their resolutions carried great weight, and supplied food for reflection to the governments, the most absolute of which, if one sets aside Russia, had at that time learnt to reckon with popular sentiment. What surprises us nowadays is that no one discerned in those meetings of deputies come together from all countries the first attempt at an international parliament.

"'But then the party of violence was still powerful in the several empires, and even in the French Republic. And if the danger of the old-time dynastic and diplomatic wars determined upon at a green-baized table for the purpose of maintaining what was known as the European equilibrium was averted for all time, it was still to be dreaded, considering the unsatisfactory industrial condition affecting Europe, that the conflicting industrial interests might bring about some terrible conflagration.

"'The imperfectly organised proletariat, as yet without the consciousness of its strength, did not put an end to armed struggles between nations, but it limited their frequency and duration.

"'The last wars were the outcome of that mad fury of the old world known as the colonial policy. English, Russians, Germans, French, and Americans joined in rabid competition, in Asia and Africa, for the possession of zones of influence, as they said, wherein they could, on the basis of pillage and massacres, establish economic relations with the aborigines. They destroyed everything they could destroy in those two countries. Then followed the inevitable. The impoverished colonies which were expensive were retained and the prosperous ones lost. But mankind had to reckon, in Asia, with a small heroic nation, taught by Europe, which made itself respected by her. By so doing, Japan, in barbarous times, rendered a great service to humanity.

"'When at last that detestable period of colonisation came to an end, no further was there any war. Still the States continued keeping up armies.

"'Having so far explained matters, I shall proceed to lay before you, pursuant to your request, the origins of present-day society. It issued from the one preceding it. In moral just as in individual life forms generate one another. Capitalistic naturally enough produced collectivist society. At the commencement of the twentieth century of the closed era, a memorable industrial evolution took place. The slender production of small artisans whose all were their tools was followed by a great production financially supported by a new agent of marvellous power—capital. Here was a great social progress.'

"'What was a great social step in advance?' I asked.

"'The capitalistic *régime*,' replied Morin. 'It brought humanity an untold source of wealth. By grouping the workers in considerable masses and multiplying their numbers it created the proletariat. By making the workers an immense State within the State it paved the way for their emancipation, and furnished them with the means of conquering power.

"'This *régime*, however, which was to be productive of such happy results in the future, was execrated by the workers, in whose ranks it made countless victims.

"'There exists no social benefit which has not been purchased at the cost of blood and tears. Moreover, this *régime* which had enriched the whole world came within an ace of ruining it. After having increased production to a considerable extent, it failed in its endeavours to regulate it, and struggled hopelessly in the toils of inextricable difficulties.

"'You are not totally ignorant, comrade, of the economic disturbances which filled the twentieth century. During the last hundred years of the capitalistic domination, the disorder of production and the delirium of competition piled up disasters high. The capitalists and the masters vainly attempted, by means of gigantic combinations, to regulate production and to annihilate competition. Their ill-conceived undertakings were engulfed in an abyss of gigantic catastrophes. During those anarchical days, the fight between classes was blind and terrible. The proletariat, overwhelmed in the same ratio by its victories and its defeats, overwhelmed by the ruins of the edifice which it was pulling down on its own head, torn by fearful internal struggles, casting aside in its blind violence its best leaders and most trustworthy friends, fought on without system and in the dark. It was, however, continually winning some advantage: an increase of wages, shorter hours of work, a growing freedom of organisation and of propaganda, the conquest of public power, and making progress in the dumfounded public mind. It was looked upon as wrecked through its divisions and mistakes. But all great parties are at odds, and all commit blunders. The proletariat had on its side the force of events. Towards the end of the century it attained the degree of well-being which opens the way to better things. Comrade, a party must have within itself a certain strength in order to accomplish a revolution favourable to its interests. Towards the end of the twentieth century of the closed era the general situation had become most favourable to the developments of socialism. The standing armies, more and more reduced during the course of the century, were abolished, following upon a desperate opposition of the powers that were, and of the bourgeoisie owning all things, by Chambers born of universal suffrage under the fiery pressure of the people of the cities and of the country. For a long time past already, the chiefs of State had retained their armies, less in view of a war which they no longer dreaded or could hope for, than to hold in check the multitude of proletaries at home. In the end, they yielded. Militias imbued with socialistic ideas supplanted regular armies. It was not without good cause that the governments showed opposition. No longer defended by guns and rifles, the monarchical systems succumbed in succession, and Republican Government stepped into their places. Alone, England, who had previously established a *régime* considered endurable by the workers, and Russia, who had remained Imperialist and theocratic, stood outside the pale of this great movement. It was feared that the Czar, who felt towards republican Europe the sentiments which the French Revolution had inspired the great Catherine with, might raise armies to combat it. But his government had reached a degree of weakness and imbecility which only an absolute monarchy can attain. The Russian proletariat, joining hands with the intellectuals, rose in revolt, and after an awful succession of outrages and massacres, power passed into the hands of the revolutionaries, who established the representative system.

"'Telegraphy and wireless telephony were then in use from one end of Europe to the other, and so easy of use that the poorest of individuals could speak, whenever he wished, and give utterance to whatever he saw fit to a fellow creature living in any corner of the globe.

Collectivist ideas rained down on Moscow. The Russian peasants could listen in their beds to the speeches of their comrades of Marseilles and Berlin. Simultaneously, the approximate steering of balloons and the exact course of flying-machines came into practical use. The result was the abolition of frontiers. This was the most critical moment of all. The patriotic instinct took a fresh life in the hearts of the nations so near uniting and fusing into one boundless humanity. In all countries, and at one and the same time, the nationalist faith, rekindled, emitted flashes of light. As there were no longer any kings, armies, or aristocracy, this great movement assumed a tumultuous and popular character. The French Republic, the German Republic, the Hungarian Republic, the Roman Republic, the Italian Republic, and even the Swiss and Belgian Republics, each expressed by a unanimous vote of their respective Parliaments, and at largely attended meetings, the solemn resolve to defend against all foreign aggression national territory and industry. Stringent laws were promulgated repressing the smuggling by flying-machines, and regulating severely the use of wireless telegraphy. The militia was everywhere reorganised and brought back to the old type of standing armies. Once more did the former uniforms, boots, dolmans, and generals' plumes make their appearance. Fur busbies were anew welcomed with the applause of Paris. All the shopkeepers and a portion of the workmen donned the tricolour cockade. In all foundry districts, cannon and armour-plates were once more forged. Terrible wars were anticipated. This mad spurt lasted three years, without matters coming to a clash, and then it slackened imperceptibly. The militias gradually recovered the bourgeois aspect and feeling. The union of nations, which had seemed postponed to a fabled remoteness, was near at hand. Pacific efforts were developing day by day; collectivists were gradually achieving the conquest of society. The day came at last when the defeated capitalists abandoned the field to them.'

"'What a change!' I exclaimed. 'History cannot show another example of such a revolution.'

"'You may well imagine, comrade,' resumed Morin, 'that collectivism did not make its appearance till the appointed hour. The Socialists could not have suppressed capital and individual property had not those two forms of wealth been already all but destroyed *de facto* by the efforts of the proletariat, and still more so by the fresh developments of science and industry.

"'It had indeed been thought that Germany would be the first collectivist State; the Labour Party had there been organised for about one hundred years, and it was everywhere said: 'Socialism is a thing German?' Still, France, less well prepared, got the start of her. The social revolution broke out in the first place at Lyons, Lille, and Marseilles, to the strains of *l'Internationale*. Paris held aloof for a fortnight, and then hoisted the red flag. It was only on the following day that Berlin proclaimed the collectivist state. The triumph of socialism had as a result the union of nations.

"'The delegates of all the European Republics, sitting in Brussels, proclaimed the Constitution of the United States of Europe.

"'England refused to form part of it, but she declared herself its ally. While having become socialistic, she had retained her king, her lords, and even the wigs of her judges. Socialism was at that time supreme ruler in Oceania, China, Japan, and in a portion of the vast Russian Republic. Black Africa, which had entered upon the capitalistic phase, formed a confederation of little homogeneity. The American Union had a while ago renounced mercantile militarism. The condition of the world was consequently favourable, upon the whole, to the free development of the United States of Europe. Nevertheless, this union, welcomed with delirious joy, was followed for the space of half a century by economic disturbances and social miseries. There were no longer any armies, and hardly any militias; in consequence of not being constricted, popular movements did not take the form of violent outbreaks. But the inexperience or the ill-will of the local governments was fostering a ruinous state of disorder.

"'Fifty years after the constitution of the States, the disappointments were so cruel, and the difficulties seemed to such a degree insurmountable, that the most optimistic spirits were beginning to despair. Smothered crackings foretold in all directions the dismemberment of the Union. It was then that the dictatorship of a committee composed of fourteen workmen put an end to anarchy, and organised the Federation of European nations as it exists to-day. There are those who say that the Fourteen displayed unparalleled genius and relentless energy; others claim that they were mediocrities terrified and influenced by the stress of necessity, and that they presided as if in spite of themselves over the spontaneous organisation of the new social forces. It is at all events certain that they did not go against the tide of events. The organisation which they established, or witnessed the establishment of, still subsists almost in its entirety. The production and consumption of goods are nowadays carried out, to all purposes, according to the rules laid down in those days. The new era justly dates from that time.'

"Morin then expounded to me most succinctly the principles of modern society.

"'It rests,' said he, 'on the total suppression of individual property.'

"'Is not this intolerable to you?' I asked.

"'Why should we find it unendurable, Hippolyte? In Europe, formerly, the State collected the taxes. It disposed of resources proper to it. Nowadays it can be said with an equal degree of truth that it possesses everything, while possessing nothing. It is still more exact to say that it is we who own all things, since the State is not a thing apart from us, and is merely the expression of collectiveness.'

"'But,' I asked, 'do you not possess anything proper to yourself? Not even the plates out of which you eat, nor your bed, your bed-sheets, your clothes?'

"Morin smiled at my question.

"'You are a deal more simple than I dreamt, Hippolyte. What! You imagine that we are not the owners of our personal property. What can well be your idea of our tastes, our instincts, our needs, and our mode of living? Do you take us for monks, as was said in the olden days, for men destitute of all individual character and incapable of affixing a personal impress on our surroundings? You are mistaken, my friend, altogether mistaken. We hold as our own the objects destined to our use and comfort, and we feel more attached to them than were the bourgeois of the closed era to their knick-knacks, for our taste is keener, and we possess a livelier sentiment of form. All our comrades of some refinement own works of art, and take great pride in them. Chéron has in her home paintings which are her delight, and she would take it amiss were the Federal Committee to contest with her the possession of them. Personally, I preserve in that closet some ancient drawings, the almost complete work of Steinlen, one of the most highly prized artists of the closed era. Neither silver nor gold would tempt me to part with them.

"'Whence have you come, Hippolyte? You are told that our society is based on the total suppression of individual property, and you get into your head that such suppression covers goods and chattels, and articles in daily use. But, you simple-minded fellow, the individual property totally suppressed by us is the ownership of the means of production, soil, canals, roads, mines, material, plant, &c. It does not affect lamps and arm-chairs. What we have done away with is the possibility of diverting to the benefit of an individual or of a group of individuals the fruits of labour; 'tis not the natural and harmless possession of the beloved chattels about us.'

"Morin next enlightened me as to the distribution of intellectual and manual labours among all the members of the community, in conformity with their aptitudes.

"'Collectivist society,' he went on to say, 'differs not only from capitalistic society in the fact that in the former everybody works. During the closed era, the people who toiled not were in great numbers; still, they constituted the minority. Our society differs more especially from the former in that labour was not properly classified, and that many useless tasks were performed. The workers produced without systematic order, method, and concerted action. The cities were full of officials, magistrates, merchants, and clerks, who worked without producing. There were also the soldiers. The fruits of labour were not properly distributed. The customs and tariffs established for the purpose of remedying the evil merely aggravated matters. All were suffering. Production and consumption are now minutely regulated. Lastly, our society differs from the old one in that we enjoy all the benefits derived from machinery, the use of which, in the capitalistic age, was so frequently disastrous for the workers.'

"I asked him how it had been possible to constitute a society composed wholly of workmen.

"Morin pointed out to me that man's aptitude for work is general, and that it constitutes one of the essential characteristics of the race.

"'In barbarian times,' he said, 'and right until the end of the closed era, the aristocratic and wealthy classes always showed a preference for manual labour. They put their intellectual faculties to an infinitesimal use, and in exceptional instances at that. Their tastes always inclined towards such occupations as the chase and war, wherein the body plays a greater part than the mind. They rode, drove, fenced, and practised pistol-shooting. It may therefore be said of them that they worked with their hands. Their work was either sterile or harmful, for the reason that a certain prejudice forbade them to engage in any useful or beneficent work, and also, because in their day, useful work was most often carried out under ignoble and disgusting conditions. It did not prove so very difficult to impart a taste for work to every one by reinstating it in a position of honour. The men of the barbaric ages took pride in carrying a gun or wearing a sword. The men of to-day are proud of handling a spade or a hammer. Humanity rests on a foundation which undergoes but little change.'

"Morin having told me that the very memory of all monetary circulation had become lost, I asked him:

"'How then do you carry on business without cash payments?'

"'We exchange products by means of vouchers similar to those just given you, comrade, and they correspond to the hours of labour performed by us. The value of the products is computed by the length of time their production has taken. Bread, meat, beer, clothes, an aeroplane, represent x hours, x days of labour. From each of these vouchers, collectivism, or, as it was styled formerly, the State, deducts a certain number of minutes for the purpose of allocating them to unproductive works, metallurgic and alimentary reserves, refuges and private asylums, and so forth.'

"'These minutes,' interjected Michel, 'are continually increasing apace. The Federal Committee orders far too many great works, the burden of which is thus on our shoulders. The reserve stocks are far too considerable. The public warehouses are crowded to overflowing with riches of all sorts. 'Tis our minutes of labour which are entombed there. Many abuses are still in existence.'

"'No doubt,' replied Morin, 'there is room for improvement. The wealth of Europe, which has accrued through general methodical labour, is untold.'

"I was curious to learn whether these folk had no other measurement of labour than the time required for its accomplishment, and whether in their case the day's work of the navvy or of the journeyman tempering plaster ranked with that of the chemist or the surgeon. I put the question frankly.

"'What a silly question,' exclaimed Perceval.

"Nevertheless old Morin vouchsafed to enlighten me.

"'All works of study, of research, in fact all works contributing to render life better and more beautiful are encouraged in our workshops and laboratories. The collectivist State fosters the higher studies. To study is akin to producing, since nothing is produced without study. Study, just as much as work, entitles one to existence. Those who devote themselves to long and arduous research secure unto themselves a peaceful and respected existence. It takes a sculptor a fortnight to make the *maquette* of a figure, but he has worked five years to learn modelling. Now the State has paid him for his *maquette* during those five years. A chemist discovers in a few hours the particular properties of a body. But he has spent months in isolating this body, and years in fitting himself to become capable of such an undertaking. During the whole of that time he has lived at the expense of the State. A surgeon removes a tumour in ten minutes. This is the result of fifteen years of study and practice. He has, as a consequence, received vouchers from the State for fifteen years past. Every man who gives in a month, in an hour, in a few minutes, the product of his whole life, is merely repaying in a lump sum what collectivism has given him day by day.'

"'Without reckoning,' said Perceval, 'that our great intellectuals, our surgeons, our lady doctors, our chemists, know full well how to derive profit from their works and discoveries, and to add beyond measure to their enjoyments. They cause to be allotted to themselves aerial machines of 60 h.p., palaces, gardens, and immense parks. They are, for the greater part, individuals keenly alive to laying hold of the world's goods, and lead a more splendid and more copious existence than the bourgeois of the closed era. The worst of it is that the majority of them are stupid fools who should be recruited for work at the flour-mills, like Hippolyte.'

"I bowed my thanks. Michel approved Perceval, and bitterly lamented the accommodating mind of the State in its system of fattening chemists at the expense of the other workers.

"I asked whether the negotiation of the vouchers did not bring about a rise and fall.

"'Speculation in vouchers,' replied Morin, 'is prohibited. As a matter of fact, it cannot be prevented altogether. There are among us, just as formerly, avaricious and prodigal, laborious and idle, rich and poor, happy and miserable, contented and discontented men. Yet all manage to exist, and that is already something.'

"I fell a-musing for a while; then I remarked:

"'Monsieur Morin, if one is to believe you, it seems to me that you have realised equality and fraternity, as much as possible. But, I fear that it is at the expense of liberty, which I have learnt to cherish as the best of things.'

"Morin shrugged his shoulders, saying:

"'We have not established equality. We know what it means. We have secured a livelihood for all. We have placed labour on a pedestal of honour. After that, if the bricklayer thinks himself superior to the poet, and the poet to the bricklayer, 'tis their business. Every one of our workers imagines that his form of labour is the grandest in the world. The advantages of this idea are greater than the disadvantages.

"'Comrade Hippolyte, you seem to have delved deeply into the books of the nineteenth century of the closed era; their leaves are hardly turned nowadays: you speak their language, to us a foreign tongue. It is hard for us to realise nowadays that the bygone friends of the people should have adopted as their motto: *Liberty, Equality, Fraternity*. Liberty has no place in society, since it does not exist in nature. There is no free animal. It was said formerly that a man who obeyed the laws was free. This was childish. Moreover, so strange a use was made of the word liberty in the last days of the capitalistic anarchy that the word has ended in merely expressing the setting claim to privileges. The idea of equality is still less reasonable, and it is an unfortunate idea in that it presupposes a false ideal. We have not to seek whether men are equal among themselves. What we must see to is that each one shall supply his best and receive all necessaries of life. As to fraternity, we know only too well how brothers have acted towards brothers during the course of centuries. We do not pretend to say that men are bad. We do not say that they are good. They are what they are, but they live in peace, when there are no longer any reasons for them to fight one another. We have but a single word to express our social system. We say that we live in harmony. Now it is an assured fact that all human forces act in concert nowadays.'

"'In the centuries,' I said to him, 'of what you style the closed era, one preferred the possession of things to their enjoyment. I can conceive that, reversing the order of things, you prefer enjoyment to possession. But is it not distressing to you not to have any property to leave to your children?'

"'In capitalistic times,' replied Morin with animation, 'how many were there who left inheritances? One in a thousand; nay, one in ten thousand. Nor must it be forgotten that many generations did not enjoy the faculty of bequeathing. Be this as it may, the transmission of fortune through the medium of inheritances was perfectly conceivable when the family was in existence. But now....'

"'What!' I exclaimed, 'you have no family ties?'

"My surprise, which I had not been able to conceal, seemed comical to the woman-comrade Chéron.

"'We are quite aware,' she said to me, 'that marriage exists among the Kaffirs. We European women do not bind ourselves by promises; or, if we make them, the law does not take cognisance of them. We are of opinion that the whole destiny of a human being should not hang on a word. Nevertheless, there survives a relic of the customs of the closed era. When a woman gives herself, she swears fidelity on the horns of the moon. In reality, neither the man nor the woman takes any binding engagement. Yet it is not of rare occurrence that their union endures as long as life. Neither of them would wish to be the object of a fidelity secured by means of an

337

oath, instead of by physical and moral expediency. We owe nothing to anybody. Formerly, a man convinced a woman that she belonged to him. We are less simple-minded. We believe that a human being belongs to itself alone. We give ourselves when we please, and to whom we see fit.

"'Moreover, we feel no shame in yielding to desire. We are no hypocrites. Only four hundred years ago, physiology was a sealed book to men, and their ignorance was the cause of dire illusions and cruel deceptions. Hippolyte, whatever the Kaffirs may say, society must be subordinate to nature, and not, as too long has been the case, nature to society?'

"Perceval, endorsing the speech of her comrade, added:

"'To show you how the sex question is regulated in our society, I must tell you, Hippolyte, that in many factories the recruiting delegate does not even inquire about one's sex. The sex of an individual does not interest collectivism.'

"'But the children?'

"'Well? The children?'

"'Not having any family ideal, are they not neglected?'

"'Whence did you get such an idea? Maternal love is a most powerful instinct in woman. In the hideous society of the past, mothers were to be seen courting misery and shame, in order to bring up illegitimate offspring. Why should ours, exempt as they are from shame and misery, forsake their little ones? There are among us many good partners, and many good mothers. But there is a very large number, which increases apace, of women who dispense with men.'

"Chéron made in this connection a somewhat strange remark.

"'We have in regard to sexual characteristics,' she said, 'notions undreamt of in the barbaric simplicity of the men of the closed era. False conclusions were for a long time drawn from the fact that there are two sexes, and two only. It was therefrom concluded that a woman is absolutely female, and a man absolutely male. In reality, it is not thus; there are women who are very much women, while others are very little so. These differences, formerly concealed by the costume and the mode of life, and disguised by prejudice, make themselves clearly manifest in our society. More than that, they become accentuated and more marked with each succeeding generation. Ever since women have worked like men, and acted and thought like them, many are to be found who resemble men. We may some day reach the point of creating neutrals, and produce female workers, as in the case of bees. It will prove a great benefit, for it will become possible to increase the quantity of work without increasing the population in a degree out of proportion to the necessaries of life. We entertain the same dread of a deficit in and a surplus of births.'

"I thanked Perceval and Chéron for having kindly supplied me with information on so interesting a subject, and I inquired whether education was not neglected in collectivist society, and whether speculative science and the liberal arts still flourished.

"The following is old Morin's reply to my question:

"'Education, in all its degrees, is highly developed. The comrades all know something; they do not know the same things, nor have they learnt anything useless. No longer is any time lost in the study of law and theology. Each one selects from the arts and sciences what suits him. We still possess many ancient works, although the greater part of the works printed before the new era have perished. Books are still printed in greater quantity than ever. And yet typography is on the point of disappearing. Phonography will take its place. Poets and novelists are already being published phonographically, while in connection with theatrical plays, a most ingenious combination of the phono and the cinemato rendering both the voice and the play of the actors has been devised.'

"'You have then poets and playwrights?'

"'We not only have poets, but a poetry of our own. We are the first who have delimitated the domain of poetry. Previous to our time, many ideas which could have been better expressed in prose were expressed in verse. Narratives were unfolded in rhyme. This was a survival of the days when legislative enactments and recipes of rural economy were drawn up in measured terms. Nowadays poets merely sing delicate subjects which have no meaning, while their grammar and language are as proper to them as their rhythm and assonance. As to our stage, it is almost exclusively lyric. A precise knowledge of reality and a life void of violence have rendered us almost indifferent to drama and tragedy. The uniformity of the classes and the equality of the sexes have deprived the old comedy of nearly all its subject-matter. But never has music been so beautiful and so beloved. We especially admire the sonata and the symphony.

"'Our society is greatly predisposed in favour of the arts of design. Many prejudices harmful to painting have vanished. Our life is more limpid and more beautiful than the bourgeois life, and we have a vivid appreciation of form. Sculpture is in a still more flourishing condition than painting, ever since it has taken an intelligent part in the ornamentation of public buildings and private dwellings. Never was so much done towards the teaching of art. If you will but steer your aeroplane above one of our streets, you will be surprised at the number of schools and museums.'

"'To sum matters up, are you happy?' I inquired.

"Morin shook his head and replied:

"'It is not in human nature to enjoy perfect happiness. Happiness is not attainable without effort, and every effort brings with it fatigue and suffering. We have made life endurable to all. That is something. Our descendants will do better still. Our organisation is not immutable. Not fifty years ago, it was different from what it is to-day. Men endowed with subtile powers of observation believe that we are on the road to great changes. That may be. However, the forward steps in human civilisation will henceforth be harmonious and pacific.'

"'Do you not fear, on the contrary,' I asked him, 'that the civilisation with which you appear to be satisfied may be destroyed by an invasion of barbarians? There still remain in Asia and Africa, so you have told me, large black or yellow populations which have not entered into your concert. They have armies, while you have none. Were they to attack you...'

"'Our defence is assured. The Americans and the Australians alone could enter upon a struggle with us, for they are as learned as ourselves. But the ocean separates us and a community of interests makes us sure of their amity. As to the capitalistic negroes, they have not got any further than the steel cannon, fire-arms and all the old scrap-iron of the twentieth century. What could these ancient engines of war do against a discharge of Y-rays? Our frontiers are protected by electricity. A zone of lightning encircles the Federation. A little

339

spectacled fellow is sitting I know not where, in front of a keyboard. He is our one and only soldier. He has but to touch a key in order to reduce to dust an army of 500,000 men.'

"Morin ceased speaking for a moment; then he continued, speaking more deliberately:

"'Were our civilisation threatened, it would not be by any outside enemy. It would be by the enemies from within.'

"'There are such enemies, then?'

"'We have the anarchists. They are many, fiery, and intelligent. Our chemists and our professors of sciences and letters are almost to a man anarchists. They attribute to the regulation of labour and production the majority of the evils which still afflict society. They argue that humanity will not be happy except in the spontaneous harmony to be born of the total destruction of civilisation. They are dangerous. They would be still more so were we to repress them. To do this, however, we have neither the means nor the desire. We do not possess any power of coercion or repression, and we get along very well without it. In the barbaric ages, men nurtured great illusions in regard to the efficacy of penalties. Our fathers suppressed the judiciary system entirely. They no longer required it. With the suppression of private property, they simultaneously suppressed theft and swindling. Ever since we have carried electric protectors, assaults are no longer to be feared. Man has come to be respected by man. Crimes of passion are still and will ever be committed. However, such crimes as these, if left unpunished, become rarer. Our entire judiciary body is composed of elected arbitrators who try gratuitously all offences and disputes.'

"'I rose, and thanking my comrades for their kindness, I begged Morin the favour of putting one more question to him.

"'You no longer have any religion?'

"'Quite the contrary; we have a large number of religions, some of them somewhat novel. To mention France only, we have the religion of humanity, positivism, Christianity, and spiritualism. In some countries there are still some Catholics, but they are few and split up into sects, as the result of schisms which occurred in the twentieth century, when Church and State drifted apart. For a long time now there has not been any Pope.'

"'You are mistaken,' said Michel. 'There is still a Pope. It is by a mere chance that I know of him. He is Pius XXV., dyer, Via dell' Orso, in Rome.'

"'What!' I exclaimed, 'the Pope is a dyer!'"

"'What is there surprising about that! He must perforce have a trade, just as everybody else.'

"'But his Church?'

"'He is recognised by a few thousands, in Europe.'

"With these words, we parted. Michel informed me that I should find a lodging in the neighbourhood, and that Chéron would conduct me to it on her way home.

"The night was illuminated with an opalescent light both powerful and soft. It gave the foliage the sheen of enamel. I walked by the side of Chéron.

"I looked her over. Her flat-soled shoes gave firmness to her gait and balance to her body; although her male habiliments made her seem smaller than she was, and in spite of her having one hand in her pocket, her perfectly simple carriage did not lack dignity. She gazed freely to the right and left of her. She was the first woman in whom I had noticed the air of a curious and amused lounger. Her features, seen from under her tam-o'-shanter, were refined and strongly defined. She both irritated and charmed me. I was in dread that she might consider me stupid and ridiculous. It was, to say the least, plain that my personality inspired her with supreme indifference. Nevertheless, of a sudden she asked me what my trade might be. I answered at haphazard that I was an electrician.

"'So am I,' she said.

"I prudently put an end to the conversation.

"Unheard-of sounds were filling the night air with their calm rhythmic noise, and I listened in affright to the respiration of the monstrous genius of this new world.

"The more I looked at the female electrician, the more did I feel a desire for her, a desire fanned by a dash of antipathy.

"'So of course,' I said to her of a sudden, 'you have regulated love scientifically, and 'tis a matter which no longer causes any one uneasiness.'

"'You are mistaken,' she replied. 'We have naturally got beyond the mad imbecility of the closed era, and the whole domain of human physiology is henceforth freed from legal barbarisms and theological terrors. We are no longer the prey to an erroneous and cruel conception of duty. But the laws governing the attraction between body and body are still a mystery to us. The spirit of the species is what it ever was and ever shall be, violent and capricious. Now, just as formerly, instinct remains stronger than reason. Our superiority over the ancients lies less in the knowledge of it than in proclaiming it. We have within us a force capable of creating worlds, to wit, desire, and you would have us regulate it. 'Tis asking too much of us. We are no longer barbarians. We have not yet become wise. Collectivism altogether ignores all that appertains to sexual relations. These relations are what they may be, most often tolerable, rarely delicious, and at times horrible. But, comrade, do not imagine that love no longer troubles any one.'

"I could not discuss such extraordinary ideas. I diverted the conversation to the temperament of women. Chéron informed me that there were three kinds, those who were amorously disposed, those prompted by curiosity, and the third, indifferent. I thereupon asked her to which class she belonged.

"She looked at me somewhat haughtily and said:

"'There are also various kinds of men. First and foremost are the impertinent ones....'

"Her reply caused her to appear far more contemporaneous than I had until then believed her to be. For that reason I began to speak to her the language used by me on similar occasions. After a few trifling and frivolous words I said to her:

"'Will you grant me a favour and tell me your first name?'

"'I have none?'

"She perceived that this seemed to vex me, for she resumed with some show of pique:

"'Do you think that a woman must, in order to be pleasing to you, possess a first name, like the ladies of former days, a baptismal name such as Marguerite, Thérèse, or Jeanne?'

"'You are a living proof to the contrary.'

"I sought her gaze, but it did not respond to mine. She seemed not to have heard. I could no longer entertain doubts: she was a coquette. I was delighted. I told her that I found her charming, that I loved her, and I told her so over and over again. She suffered me to go on with my speeches, and finally asked:

"'What do you mean by all this!'

"I became more pressing.

"'She reproached me for taking liberties with her, exclaiming:

"'Your ways are those of a savage.'

"'I do not find acceptance with you?'

"'I do not say so.'

"'Chéron, Chéron, would it cost you any great effort to...'

"We sat down together on a bench over which an elm cast its shade. I took her hand, and carried it to my lips ... of a sudden, I no longer felt, no longer saw anything, and I found myself lying in bed at home. I rubbed my eyes, smarting with the morning light, and I saw my valet who, standing before me with a stupid look, was saying to me:

"It is nine o'clock, sir. You told me to wake you at nine o'clock, sir. I have come to tell you, sir, that it is nine o'clock?"

VI

HIPPOLYTE Dufresne was warmly congratulated by his friends on his finishing the reading of his story.

Nicole Langelier, applying to him the words of Critias to Triephon, said:

"You seem to have dreamt on the white stone, in the midst of the people of dreams, since you dreamt so long a dream in the course of so short a night."

"It is not likely," remarked Joséphin Leclerc, "that the future will be such as you have seen it. I do not wish for the coming of socialism, but I dread it not. Collectivism at the helm would be quite another thing than is imagined. Who was it who said, carrying back his thoughts to the time of Constantine and of the Church's early triumphs: 'Christianity is triumphant, but its triumph is subject to the conditions imposed by life on all political and religious parties. All of them, whatever they may be, undergo so complete a transformation in the struggle that after victory there remains of themselves but the name and a few symbols of the last idea'?"

"Must we then give up the idea of knowing the future?" asked M. Goubin.

But Giacomo Boni, who when delving down into a few feet of soil had descended from the present period to the stone age, remarked:

"Upon the whole, humanity changes little. What has been shall be."

"No doubt," replied Jean Boilly, "man, or that which we call man, changes little. We belong to a definite species. The evolution of the species is of necessity included in the definition of the species. It is impossible to conceive humanity subsequent to its transformation. A transformed species is a lost species. But what reason is there for us to believe that man is the end of the evolution of life upon the earth? Why suppose that his birth has exhausted the creative forces of nature, and that the universal mother of the flora and fauna should, after having shaped him, become for ever barren. A natural philosopher, who does not stand in fear of his own ideas, H. G. Wells, has said: 'Man is not final.' No indeed, man is neither the beginning nor the end of terrestrial life. Long before him, all over the globe, animated forces were multiplying in the depths of the sea, in the mud of the strand, in the forests, lakes, prairies, and tree-topped mountains. After him, new forms will go on taking shape. A future race, born perhaps of our own, but having perchance no bond of origin with us, will succeed us in the empire of the planet. These new spirits of the earth will ignore or despise us. The monuments of our arts, should they discover vestiges of them, will have no meaning for them. Rulers of the future, whose mind we can no more divine than the palæopithekos of the Siwalik Mountains was able to forecast the trains of thought of Aristotle, Newton, and Poincaré."

CPSIA information can be obtained
at www.ICGtesting.com
Printed in the USA
FSHW021028030121
77368FS